PENNY VINCENZI

A PERFECT HERITAGE

headline
review

First published in 2014
by HEADLINE REVIEW
An imprint of HEADLINE PUBLISHING GROUP

First published in paperback in 2014
by HEADLINE REVIEW

1

Cataloguing in Publication Data is available from the British Library

ISBN 978 0 7553 7760 2 (A-format)
ISBN 978 0 7553 7759 6 (B-format)

Typeset in New Caledonia by Avon DataSet Ltd,
Bidford-on-Avon, Warwickshire

Printed and bound in Great Britain by Clays Ltd, St Ives plc

MIX
Paper from
responsible sources
FSC® C104740
www.fsc.org

Headline's policy is to use papers that are natural, renewable and
recyclable products and made from wood grown in well-managed forests and
other controlled sources. The logging and manufacturing processes are
expected to conform to the environmental regulations of the country of origin.

HEADLINE PUBLISHING GROUP
An Hachette UK Company
338 Euston Road
London NW1 3BH

www.headline.co.uk
www.hachette.co.uk

For my four darling daughters.
Who are all the world to me.

Acknowledgements

This has been a lovely book to write; I always enjoy doing the acknowledgements because they take me back on the journey through it.

I certainly couldn't have managed this on my own; a lot of very disparate knowledge has gone into it, gleaned from a huge range of people, all of whom gave me, with the utmost generosity, their time and attention in large measure. Most of them didn't just tell me things, they threw themselves into their task and made suggestions about possible plot twists in their particular areas.

A lot of people from the cosmetic industry were extraordinarily helpful: Robin Vincent, long-time boss of Clarins UK, breathed life into the House of Farrell for me; Charlotte Alexander gave me a most useful teach-in on the world of beauty PR today – very different from when I was a beauty editor – and introduced me to the world of the beauty blogger; Emily Warburton gave me a magnificent overview of the past fifteen years she has spent in the cosmetic industry; Beverley Bayne told me more amazing things about perfume and its formulation than I could ever have imagined; Ella Bradley, magical make-up artist, took me into her glamorous world, showed me the magic she works on a daily basis, and offered me an insight into such heady stuff as doing the make-up for London Fashion Week, and Julia Cruttenden, who very sadly died last December, allowed me to attend classes at Greasepaint, her completely wonderful make-up school.

Over in the City of London, Matt Frenchman, by way of a

brilliant teach-in, made the almost incomprehensible business of the hedge fund just about comprehensible, and huge thanks to Ben Noakes, who provided me with a most valuable insight into the world of the currency trader, and even allowed me to sit at his desk for one astonishing (and very noisy) afternoon.

Edward Harris, a wonderfully brilliant and creative solicitor, and his wife, the lovely Mrs Harris, provided me with the utterly ingenious idea of the tontine, without which the plot might not have reached maturity.

Ed Chilcott, advertising whizz-man, not only explained advertising today but also worked with me, via many a long and torturous phone call, on the advertising campaign that was to bring the House of Farrell into a most dazzling limelight.

Anthony Beerbohm guided me tirelessly around first Paris and then Grasse, with huge knowledge and skill, and thence into some wonderful restaurants and bars.

My granddaughter Honor Cornish imparted some much-needed knowledge of the clothes, shopping habits, customs and language of her particular age group.

Another granddaughter, Jemima Harding, generously agreed to lend me her (very nice) name for one of my (very nice) characters.

Peter Mayer, long-term friend and publisher extraordinaire, showed me the wonders of SoHo one sunny lunchtime and afternoon in New York and helped me to find the perfect location for the Farrell shop there. Jemima Barton did the same search for me in Singapore and Polly Harding in Sydney.

Moving nearer home, it has been the greatest pleasure to work with Imogen Taylor for the first time as my editor. She is not only supportive, creative and fun, but also has an extraordinary knack for getting the extra five per cent out of not just me, but also my plots. And her assistant Emma Holtz is not only brilliantly efficient, she's also talked me patiently through my interminable crises of a computer-y nature.

And thank you so, so much Yeti Lambregts, for what must be one of my most beautiful covers ever!

Thank you Jo Liddiard for some brilliant marketing thinking. And much gratitude to the incomparable Georgina Moore, who has worked her magic with the publicity campaign with a click of her high heels and a brisk wave of her wand.

I owe a huge amount, and for the umpteenth time, to Kati Nicholls (never give up on me, Kati!), most brilliant of copy editors, who manages to cut swathes of superfluous words from my books in a way that even I can't spot when they've gone, and checks and re-checks everything in a totally reassuring manner.

Life would be quite unimaginable without Clare Alexander, wonderful agent and friend, who has soothed, advised and reassured me through many books now, invited me to her dazzling dinner parties and, possibly most importantly of all, made me laugh. A lot.

And finally, of course, my long-suffering family, daughters, sons-in-law and grandchildren, who keep me sane in their various ways, provide answers to my questions about whatever their area of expertise might be – from wine to designer watches, cars to cameras – tell me I'm wrong when I say the book will never, ever be finished and have supported me most wonderfully through a long, tough year.

Character List

Athina Farrell, *a matriarch*
Cornelius Farrell, *her husband*
Bertram Farrell, *her son*
Caroline Johnson, *her daughter*
Priscilla Farrell, *Bertie's wife*
Lucy and Rob, *Bertie and Priscilla's children*

Hugh Bradford and Mike Russell, *venture capitalists*

Bianca Bailey, *a tycoon*
Patrick Bailey, *her husband*
Emily (Milly), Fergie and Ruby, *their children*
Guy Bailey, *Patrick's father*
Sonia, *their housekeeper*
Karen, *their nanny*

Florence Hamilton, *a director of the House of Farrell*
Duncan, *her deceased husband*

Lawrence Ford, *marketing manager at Farrell's*
Annie Ford, *his wife*

Lara Clements, *marketing director at Farrell's*
Mark Rawlins, *financial director at Farrell's*
Susie Harding, *a publicist at Farrell's*

Jemima Pendleton, *Bianca's secretary*
Peter Warren, *a non-executive chairman at Farrell's*
Francine la Croix, *a beautician at Farrell's*

Marjorie Dawson, *a beauty consultant at Farrell's*
Terry, *her invalid husband*

Jonjo Bartlett, *a City trader*
Pippa, *his sister*

Walter Pemberton, *the Farrell's lawyer*
John Ripley, *a trainee solicitor at Pemberton and Rushworth*

Saul Finlayson, *who runs a hedge fund*
Janey, *his ex-wife*
Dickon, *his son*

Fenella, *a student friend of Lucy's*

Guinevere Bloch, *a sculptress*

Carey Mapleton, *a new friend of Milly's*
Gillian Sutherland, *their form mistress*
Mrs Wharton, *their music teacher*
Mrs Blackman, *their headmistress*
Sarajane, Annabel and Grace, *Milly's friends*

Tod Marchant and Jack Flynn, *an advertising duo*
Paddy Logan, *an assistant at Flynn Marchant*

Hattie Richards, *a cosmetic chemist*

Elise Jordan, *a beauty editor*
Sadie Bishop, *her assistant*
Flo Brown, *a journalist*
Thea Grantly, *a journalist*

Jacqueline Wentworth, *a gynaecologist*

Leonard Trentham, *an artist*
Jasper Stuart, *an art dealer*
Joseph Saunders, *an art critic*

Jayce, *Milly's new friend*
Stash, Zak, Cherice and Paris, *her siblings*

Joanna Richards, *mother of one of Ruby's friends*

Tamsin Brownley, *a creative designer*
Lord and Lady Brownley, *her parents*

Henk Martin, *a photographer, Susie's boyfriend*

Jess Cochrane, *an actress*
Freddie Alexander, *a theatrical agent*

Lou Clarke, *a New York businesswoman*

Simon Smythe, *a solicitor*

Chris Williams, *Lara's new boyfriend*

Bernard French, *Janey's boyfriend*

Doug Douglas, *an Australian businessman*

Vicki Philips, *an assistant to Susie Harding*

Prologue

So – this was it.

Goodbye, really, in a way. However it was dressed up, the Farrell's that had been her life's work, her life's love really, was no longer to be.

The brilliant, colourful, joyous thing that had been born that coronation year, that she and Cornelius had created together, was to change irrevocably, move out of her control. No longer her treasure, her comfort, her sanity. Most of all, her sanity; in the first months after Cornelius died, she had turned to it for occupation, distraction, support in her awful, empty grief. How wonderful she is, people had said, still working all the hours God sends, refusing to give in or give up, how amazing to carry on like this. But they were wrong, so wrong. It would have been amazing, indeed, not to have worked, to have given in, for then the grief and the loneliness would have engulfed her, and she would have had nothing in her life at all. She might no longer have Cornelius to temper her excesses, but she had his legacy, the House of Farrell, its creation and its success a bright, brilliant memorial to everything she and he had done together.

Wonderful that you have your children so close to you, people said, and she would smile politely and say yes, indeed, but what they could give her was as nothing compared to her work. What they felt for her could hardly be described as love; she had been a distracted, neglectful mother, over-critical of the dull little girl that had been Caroline and the timid little boy that had been Bertie. And besides,

1

like all children of a successful marriage, they remained outsiders, intruders even, on two people who would have been just as happy without them, however much they might deny it. Whereas the House of Farrell, *that* was worthy of the brilliant pair of them; it did not fail them, it was their pride and their joy.

They had been stars in the social scene at the beginning, she and Cornelius, acknowledged as clever, daring, inventive, their creative instincts rewarded by financial success; they had had money, style, grace. Their circle, embracing both the establishment and the new, creative aristocracy of the late fifties and early sixties, was fun, colourful, interesting. They had a house in Knightsbridge, a week-end flat in one of the Regency terraces in Hove; they moved from one to the other, and to Paris and New York, in pursuit of further inspiration and success, leaving their children with nannies and boarding schools.

It had been an absurdly early marriage – Cornelius twenty-three, she twenty-one, but from the outset, a success; and creating the House of Farrell had been a natural, almost inevitable result of that.

It had been Cornelius's idea in the first place. Fascinated by the new sciences of marketing and advertising and with a fortune inherited from his banker godfather and an undemanding job in the same bank, he was an entrepreneur in need of a project. Fate provided it, in the form of an eccentric ex-actress mother who mixed her own face creams because she didn't like those on the market, and spent an hour every morning and another every night transforming a nondescript face into a thing of great beauty, and he had suggested to the lovely girl he had married, also well versed in the wonders make-up could work, that they might invest the legacy into a cosmetic business they could run together.

'You can develop it, my darling, and I will stay at the bank until it can support both of us.' Neither of them had ever doubted that the House of Farrell could do that, and indeed they were right.

They had bought the basic formula for her creams from the now ex-Mrs Farrell, who had run away from her academic husband, and set up production in a small laboratory where they employed a brilliant chemist who had trained with M. Coty in Paris, and had re-created not only The Cream, as it was christened, which was (as the early advertising said) 'the only thing skin really needs', but some colour products, too, lipsticks and nail varnishes; adding face powder and a foundation product, The Foundation, a few months after.

Recognising that they couldn't hope to beat the big boys at their own games, the Revlons and the Cotys and the Yardleys, and that they had to launch their business on a very different basis, they had transformed the Berkeley Arcade shop from a rather plain bespoke stationers into one of the prettiest shops in the row, installed the tiny salon on the first floor, and literally opened its doors to the world. They were lucky; they caught the eye and the imagination of the press, and the praise heaped upon it exceeded their wildest dreams. *Tatler* pronounced it 'THE place to find true individual beauty', *Vogue* as the 'first stop for charm and beauty care', and *Harper's Bazaar* proclaimed it 'the place to find your new face'. Cornelius, who had a genius for publicity, and after flattering the latter's beauty editor over a very expensive lunch at Le Caprice, converted that into their advertising slogan. He also sold the shop to the public on posters and, more controversially, sent sandwich men to stand all over the West End proclaiming the shop as 'The Beautiful Jewel in London's crown' and people flocked to it. It caught part of the great wave of optimism and creativity that was just breaking that summer, born of the coronation, the beautiful young queen, and the end, finally, of war-time economy. DeLuscious Lipstick, as their first great colour promotion was called, literally became part of the vernacular for a few dizzy months, and the rest swiftly became Farrell history.

It had faltered in the eighties, overwhelmed by the dazzling colour cosmetics and scientifically based skincare financed by the vast fortunes of large houses, had revived briefly in the nineties, and in the year of Cornelius's death, in 2006, had very nearly disappeared altogether, saved only by her tenacity.

Now, falling behind helplessly in the money-fuelled marathon that was the beauty business, even she could see that they desperately needed help – financial to be sure, but creative also. For although she would have joined Cornelius in his grave rather than admit it, her own vision was no longer flawless. She disliked the pseudo science spawned by the huge laboratories of the cosmetics giants that were, as one journalist had remarked, the size of General Motors, and nor did she understand it. She felt out of step, just a little bewildered; and while deeply hostile to her new colleagues – she refused to think of them as masters – she felt also a grudging sense of relief at their arrival.

But – it was going to be a painful process. She would have to sit, she knew, listening to different voices, new languages, speaking what would have once been heresies.

The owners of those voices would have no links with the House of Farrell; they would care nothing for what had made it great, for what it had stood for. What would matter to them were the grey columns of profit and loss, the harsh facts of commercial life. And she would have to yield to them – to a degree.

But she would fight on at the same time, she would hold true to Farrell's, she would not give in. It had done everything for her – she would not fail it more than she had to now.

Chapter 1

Love at first sight, that's what it was; heady, life-changing, heart-stopping stuff. It had happened to her only twice before, this sense of recognition, of something so absolutely right for her and what she was and what she wanted to do and be. She hadn't hesitated, hadn't played any silly games, hadn't said maybe, or I'll think about it, or I'll let you know, just yes, of course, of course she'd like to do it very much, and then looked at her watch and seen she was already late for her board meeting and, after the briefest farewell, had left the restaurant.

The first thing she did now, in the taxi, was call her husband; she always did that, he needed to know, and she needed him to know. He was so very much part of it all, his life hugely affected as well as hers; and he had been pleased as she had known he would be, said he would look forward to discussing it over dinner. Only of course she was going to be late for dinner, which she reminded him of, and he had only sighed very lightly before saying, well, he'd look forward to seeing her whenever it was.

He really was a truly accommodating man, she thought. She was very lucky.

'Well, that was very satisfactory.' Hugh Bradford sat back in his chair and ordered a brandy; he never drank at lunchtime normally, had gone through the whole lunch on water and one modest glass of champagne to seal the deal. He'd have liked to, had thought more than once that the superb beef Wellington he was eating really did deserve better than Evian to wash it down. But he'd resisted, and it was impossible to imagine Bianca Bailey allowing even the smallest sip of alcohol – well, she had a very few sips of the champagne, but he could feel her reluctance – to blur the clear-blue-sky clarity of her brain.

He wondered – briefly and inevitably, perhaps, for she was very attractive – if she ever surrendered control, whether, *in flagrante* at least, she might lose herself – and then returned to reality. Such meanderings had no place in his relationship or those of his colleagues with Bianca.

'Yes, it's excellent. I thought she would, but you never quite know . . . yes, thanks . . .' Mike Russell, colleague of many years, nodded assent to the brandy bottle. 'Now all we've got to do is sell her to the family.'

'The family don't have any choice,' said Bradford, 'but I think they'll like her. Or at least the *idea* of her. Better than some man – or so they'll think. Best fix a meeting for early next week?'

'Or later this? There really is very little time.'

'I'll get Anna to sort it.'

'So, I'm going to meet the family and board of Farrell's on Friday,' said Bianca to her husband that night. 'Friday afternoon. I can't wait. It's a fantastic set-up, Patrick, straight out of fiction. Or even Hollywood.'

'Really?'

'Yes. There's a matriarch, of course – there's almost always a matriarch in the cosmetic business—'

'Really?' said Patrick again.

'Well, yes. Just think. Elizabeth Arden, Estée Lauder, Helena Rubinstein . . .'

'I'm not sure that any reflection on the cosmetic industry on my part would be very rewarding,' said Patrick. 'It's not a business I know a lot about, at the moment. But I suspect I'm about to.'

'You could be. It's an industry you have to live and breathe, just to understand it. Anyway, she – the matriarch, Lady Farrell – founded it in 1953 with her husband who died five years ago – so sad, apparently it was a great love match, lasted nearly sixty years – and then there's a daughter and a son on the board, neither up to much as far as we can make out, and another old biddy called Florence Hamilton, who's been with them from the beginning and is also on the board, I presume for old times' sake.'

'My word. A completely family affair.'

'Anyway, they hold all the shares at the moment and she's not giving in without a fight, but she's got to because the bank is about to pull the plug, so hideously in debt are they – anyway, I – well *we*, Hugh, Mike and I – think there is some magic there. I can't wait to get to work on it. Going to be a long meeting, that's for sure. That OK?'

'Of course. I'm taking the children to see the Tintin film. You said you didn't want to go . . .'

'I don't,' said Bianca, 'can't think of anything worse.'

'That's all right then,' said Patrick Bailey lightly.

Bianca Bailey was, in business parlance, a rock star. The stage on which she performed was not the O2 Arena, or even Wembley, but the platform of high finance, its success measured in balance sheets and company flotations. A high-flying, high-profile figure, a female Midas, with a dazzling record in turning businesses around, she was, at thirty-eight, a gift to whatever publicity people she was working with, being extremely attractive. She was tall (five foot ten in her stockinged feet), slim, stylish and, if not quite beautiful, very photogenic and telegenic, with her mass of dark hair, and large grey eyes. She was highly articulate – an automatic go-to when anyone wanted a quote on some deal or buyout – and charming. She was also happily married, had three delightful children, lived in a stunning house in Hampstead and also, almost inevitably, in a very pretty country house in Oxfordshire which she persisted in labelling, rather inaccurately, a cottage. As more than one of the Baileys' friends had remarked, if they weren't so nice, the Baileys would be hugely dislikeable.

Bianca had been wondering what to do next, having been a crucial part of the very successful sale of the company of which she was currently CEO – a hitherto low visibility, almost down-market toiletry brand – when Mike Russell of Porter Bingham, a private equity firm, had called her to say would she like to come in for a coffee and a chat. They had teamed up before so she knew what that meant – they had a challenge for her in the form of another unsuccessful company that needed her considerable powers.

The prospect they had laid before her was daunting – and Bianca liked daunting. Indeed, she found it irresistible.

'They came to us,' Mike Russell had said. 'Well, the son did, Bertram. Looks like a Bertram too, but nice enough. They're currently losing five million a year and don't know what they're doing financially at all. But there's a load of potential, especially with you on board, probably with a view to selling the company in five to eight years. Have a look at it and see what you think.'

And Bianca had looked, shuddered at the figures and the state of the brand, saw what they meant about the potential, and the result had been the lunch at Le Caprice and the agreement between her and Porter Bingham to take things further towards an investment in Farrell's.

'I think what's possible is a turnaround from that five million pound loss into a ten million pound annual profit in five years,' she said. 'But I'd say you'll have to make an overall investment of around thirteen million, say ten upfront and another tranche of two or three million to complete later development work, but yes, I think it can be done.'

She smiled at them: her wide, Julia Roberts-style smile. She liked them both, which was important; they were straightforward, decisive and could be great fun. And Hugh was extremely good-looking, in a conventional, establishment-style way. She often thought it was as well he wasn't her type, or she might occasionally make some less than completely professional decisions. Knowing, however, that in her successful life she had never been swayed for an instant by personal considerations. It was one of the many reasons for her success.

о о о

'I'm really excited about this,' she had said to Patrick when she got home after that first meeting, 'but I'd like your agreement. It's going to be tougher even than PDN. What would you say to that?'

And Patrick said that if she really wanted to do it, then of course she must, resisting the temptation to ask her what she would do if he withheld his agreement. Bianca did what she wanted, always; anything else was just so much window dressing.

He knew what lay ahead of him; as with any new project of Bianca's there would be a lot of lonely evenings, a commitment from her to the new company that amounted almost to an obsession, and a feeling, quite often, that the company under her command was situated, if not actually in the marital bed, then certainly at the family table. He put up with it for two reasons: he found it quite interesting himself, observing it as he did from as dispassionate a vantage point as he could manage, and he loved Bianca as much as he admired her and he wanted her to do what made her happy. It required some unselfishness on his part, but on the other hand it allowed him to do whatever he wanted – like buying paintings – without too much interference from anyone.

He was not greatly given to tortured introspection – he was an only child, with all the self-confidence that condition trailed in its wake. 'We're not like other people,' Patrick often said and it was true.

Bianca had no siblings either and they often, in the early days of their relationship, discussed this and the bond it created between them. Indeed, she produced some statistic – she was very fond of statistics – that onlies were drawn to other onlies – 'or eldests, much the same really'. She went on to say that only children were statistically highly successful and driven; Patrick was not sure that this could possibly apply to him, but he was flattered by the observation. The last thing he wanted was for the dynamic Ms Wood to regard him as some kind of amiable low achiever. Or indeed her father, the distinguished and highly esteemed historian, Gerald Wood. He sometimes wondered if Gerald knew any of them existed, so immersed was he in medieval constitution and literature, always far more immediate to him than the twenty-first century and more so than ever since Pattie, his beloved wife, had died when Bianca was only nineteen.

'Hello, Mr Bailey. Good day?'

'Yes, not bad, thanks, Sonia. You?' He wasn't going to tell the housekeeper that he'd been so bored he'd actually dropped off in his office after lunch.

'Very good, thank you. I've done the menu for the dinner party for tomorrow week if you'd like to look at it – so you can order the wine.'

'Oh, thanks. I'll take it up to my study.'

'And I've made a bolognese sauce for tonight – Mrs Bailey won't be home you said?'

'No, she's got a big meeting tomorrow so she'll be working very late. I'll eat with the children in about – oh, half an hour? But I'll cook the spaghetti, don't worry about that.'

'Right. Well, I'll just make a salad and then I'll be on my way. Ruby's in bed – Karen's reading to her now and then she's off.'

Karen was the nanny; Ruby was still only eight and some one-on-one care was still necessary and outside Sonia's brief. Karen came in after school until Ruby was in bed and full-time in the holidays; a job, as she often remarked to fellow nannies on her social circuit, of unbelievable cushiness.

'Fine. Thank you, Sonia – oh, hi, Milly, how was your day?'

'Cool.'

'That's all right then.'

'And how was yours?'

'Oh, pretty hot.'

She reached up to kiss him.

'You're so funny,' she said kindly.

'I try. Done your homework?'

'Of course!'

'Sure?'

'Daddy! Don't be horrid.'

'She has done it, Mr Bailey,' said Sonia, smiling at Milly. 'She started as soon as she got in from school.'

'See! Thank you, Sonia.'

'What about your clarinet practice?'

'Done that too.'

'You're too good to be true, aren't you? Where's Fergie?'

'Playing on the Wii.'

'Tut-tut. Not allowed before seven.'

'Daddy! You sound like Mummy. See you later.'

She wandered off, her attention entirely on her phone. Patrick smiled indulgently at her back. Emily, nicknamed Milly at birth, was, at almost thirteen, tall and slender with long, straight dark hair and large brown eyes; sweetly bright and charming, not yet tarnished by adolescence, still affectionate, still chatty, and extremely popular – one of the girls everyone wanted at their parties and sleepovers. She was in the second year at St Catherine's, Chelsea, a new and fiercely academic girls' day school, that was giving both St Paul's and Godolphin a run for their money. A talented musician as well – Grade 6 Distinction on the clarinet – her only failure was games at which she was hopeless.

Fergus, at eleven, had the family charm and good looks, was as good at games as Milly was bad, was in every first team at his prep school, and, being clever, managed to hang on to his place in the scholarship class by the skin of his teeth.

Patrick went up to his study on the first floor of the house, a large, detached Victorian, and looked over the equally large garden. He loved the house, had spent his early childhood in a similar one only two streets away. The extremely large deposit had been a wedding present from his father; people always said that simple fact told you almost everything you needed to know about the Bailey family: that it was rich, happy, close, and generous.

Guy Bailey had been a stockbroker in the golden age of the City, made a fortune, retired early in 1985, 'just before the Big Bang, thank God,' he often said, and moved to a large country house with a considerable amount of land and some stables where he indulged in the life of a country gentleman, became a very good shot, and turned his lifelong hobby of antique dealing into a 'half-day job', as he put it.

* * *

11

Patrick had left Oxford with a respectable Upper Second in PPE and joined his uncles' chartered accountancy firm, based in the Strand. Here he was given a very nice office, earned an excellent salary, and was greatly liked by the staff and his clients alike; he did well, being charming and equable as well as clever. He would probably have left after a couple of years, finding the work at best uninspiring and at worst boring, but he had met and fallen in love with Bianca Wood, and in Patrick's world you didn't propose to a girl unless you could offer her a proper set-up, which translated as a nice house in a good area, and a handsome salary to support her should she wish not to work, or when she had children. He wasn't miserable at Bailey Cotton and Bailey; indeed he was very happy, he was just not very excited by the work. Which was not sufficient reason to keep him from proposing to Ms Wood in 1995 and marrying her in 1996.

He had met her at a dinner in the City and been immediately enchanted by her; she was sparkly and articulate, and clearly found him interesting too. She was, she said, a marketing manager at a toiletries company.

'Toothpaste and deodorant might not sound very exciting,' she said, 'but last year it was washing powders, so a big improvement. And of course it's exciting because it's not the product, it's what you can do with it. Sending the sales graph in the right direction is hard to beat!'

He asked her out to dinner that weekend and they talked for so long the waiters were piling chairs on to tables before they realised how late it was, and she invited him out the next Friday.

'My treat this time. No, that's how I operate, sorry, don't like spongers.'

Patrick found her signing the credit card slip extremely painful and said so; she replied that he was clearly very old-fashioned. 'Most of the men I know would be thrilled.' In the event, any discomfiture on Patrick's part didn't last very long because in three months they had moved in together.

By the time they were married in 1996, Bianca had moved jobs twice and become marketing manager of an interior design company. She continued to work until the week before Milly was born and was back at her desk in four months; when Fergie joined them two years later, she only stayed at home for twelve weeks. There was the nanny, she said, and she got very bored rocking cradles. Which did not mean she was a bad mother – she was intensely loving and passionately involved with her children. She just operated better maternally if she had something else to do and when Ruby made her embryonic presence felt, unplanned and the result of a bout of bronchitis, a strong antibiotic and a resultant decrease in the effectiveness of the pill, she did not, as some women in her position might have done, opt for a termination, just welcomed Ruby determinedly and said she liked to keep busy. Which she did.

Her career trajectory had been impressive; Patrick, while being immensely proud of her, couldn't help wishing she would take more time off when she had the children; but they certainly didn't seem to have suffered, they were all bright and charming and self-confident. He sometimes felt also that Bianca might take a little more interest in him and his work; but then, as he so frequently said, there wasn't anything much to take an interest in. He was a partner now, extremely well-paid, his hours were civilised – more than could be said for Bianca's – and on the whole he didn't mind being the ballast in their household, as he put it. He was exceptionally good-natured. Then, when Milly was five, Bianca was made sales and marketing director of a fabric company. That was when her salary overtook Patrick's and Patrick did mind that – quite a lot. Bianca teased him about it.

'Darling! It's our money, just as yours is; it pays for our family, our life, what do the proportions matter?'

He once asked her, when he had a great deal to drink, if she would give up her job if he really wanted her to; she leaned across the table and said, 'Darling, of course, if you really wanted it, but you wouldn't, would you? You're not like that – and that's why I love you.'

And she did: very much. As Patrick loved her. And when life was a little less than perfect, he would remind himself that a little

13

boredom at the office and an occasional sense of resentment was more than made up for by having a clever and beautiful wife who loved him, three enchanting children, a wide circle of friends and a lifestyle most people would envy.

Chapter 2

Bianca Bailey was often quoted as saying that meetings, like life, were not rehearsals. However small, they mattered; they needed proper attention and careful planning. No one, not the most junior secretary, not the least regarded maintenance manager, had ever left a meeting with the formidable Ms Bailey feeling they had not had a proper hearing and that their concerns were not being addressed.

The one in prospect that afternoon, when she, Hugh Bradford, and Mike Russell would try to persuade the Farrell family to come on board, mattered very much indeed; consequently, they had devoted several days and a great deal of work to planning its conduct.

'They've reached the point, I think,' said Hugh, 'where they know they need us, so that's good, but it's crucial they feel we like the company, that we're not just in it for a fast buck. In other words, that we want to make it work. They must also feel we understand it, and the whole industry. Your department, Bianca, obviously.'

'Of course. Hopefully, my background should convince them of my understanding of the industry. I've a lot to learn about cosmetics though, and they know it, and I'll use that fact to help get them on side: the brand itself – well there's quite a lot not to like. I've had a cursory look at it, products, outlets, image – pretty non-existent really – but there are a couple of areas I can talk about very enthusiastically. The hero product, for instance, The Cream it's called – great name, isn't it? – that's the sort of thing they should be building on, skincare and quality, and I'm going to say that. There is a wonderful Englishness about them, brand launched in 1953, coronation year, and I don't need to tell you how much we can capitalise on that in the immediate future, with things like royal weddings and next year's jubilee. I won't really know anything, of course,' she added, 'until I've done a deep dive – and I can't do that until I'm there.' Bianca's Deep Dives – a minute scrutiny of not just the finances and the products, but the infrastructure of a company – went very deep indeed. 'Let's hope we can talk them into that being sooner rather than later.'

'Indeed.'

'That's all from me – for now. Except I do feel so excited about it.'

'Excellent,' said Mike, smiling at her. He found her endless enthusiasm for new projects extremely endearing. It was, of course, one of the prime reasons for her success.

She had dressed cleverly for the occasion, in a dress with a cardigan over it, rather than the jacket and trousers that was her usual style, her hair swinging loose on her shoulders, not pulled sharply back, and just a little more make-up than she usually wore. The Farrells would see a woman who enjoyed clothes and cosmetics, who would be in sympathy with their world, not some brisk androgyne whose only concern was numbers and the crunching thereof. It would be important to them – and the fact that Bianca recognised it was what made her special, revealing that she cared about and understood a company and its products as much as its economics. In her own words, she *got* it. She could see the magic of a brand while absolutely recognising that it had to be made to work for its living. They were lucky, Hugh thought, to have her.

Athina Farrell had also dressed carefully. She might be eighty-five, but she was still absolutely in charge of Farrell's and she felt that needed to be spelled out in every possible way, starting with her appearance. She was wearing a calf-length Jean Muir dress in navy jersey, and red suede shoes, both emphasising her still extremely good legs; her silver bob was immaculate, her make-up minimal but skilful, the jewellery she was wearing carefully chosen: the pearl choker that Cornelius had given her on their thirtieth wedding anniversary, the Chanel pearl earrings, the Tiffany watch, a twenty-first birthday present from her parents, and her twin diamond rings – one for their engagement, the other identical, made up at Cornelius's request, for their golden wedding. 'These people' as she thought of them, more than a little disparagingly, would see a woman of considerable substance and style, not some foolish old has-been. She had run the House of Farrell for almost sixty years and yielding any part of it had been, until very recently, simply unthinkable, akin to giving away her children. Indeed, it was said by those who knew her best that she would probably have handed the children over with less anguish.

However, she had been made to face the fact that the company was approaching bankruptcy and needed help. And such help did not come free; there would be a price tag. Her main concern now was that the price tag should be as high as possible, to alleviate the intense pain of the yielding.

She had, therefore, been persuaded to the meeting that cold Friday afternoon in January with the people from Porter Bingham, Venture Capitalists, and was in a mindset that was brave, obstructive – and totally unconciliatory.

She had summoned her two children and Florence Hamilton for a briefing, as she put it, which actually meant telling them what they should say and do, before the meeting. They were all board directors: Bertram, known as Bertie, was managing and finance director, Caroline, known to close associates as Caro and everyone else as Mrs Johnson, was company secretary and personnel director and Florence, known simply as Florence, was board director with an overall responsibility for property.

Athina wasn't at all sure any of them should be on the board at all; were they not her children – or in the case of Florence, almost as much part of Farrell's as she and Cornelius – they probably wouldn't have been. Their lack of substance worried her. Bertie and Caro were both clever enough, but they lacked the instinct and the flair to carry on what she and Cornelius had created, and

Florence, who had the instinct and the flair, lacked drive. In truth, she had never been in favour of Florence's appointment to the board; the idea had come from Cornelius and she had been ill at the time and unable to argue with her usual force.

The highest Bertie would have risen, she felt, had he been working for a firm where there was no automatic assumption of privilege, was higher middle management.

However, the best had to be made of the situation, and so she had summoned them to her flat in Knightsbridge and, as she put it over a sandwich lunch, 'We need to present a united front, absolutely crucial, no dividing and ruling on offer to them. Of course, our lawyers, Walter Pemberton and Bob Rushworth, will be there—'

'You don't think they might be just slightly out of their league?' said Caro.

Athina said that she was perfectly confident in them.

'I've had several conversations with them and Bob has already made a couple of very shrewd observations. After all, they've been with us from the beginning; Cornelius appointed them, and he knew a good lawyer when he saw one.'

'Ye-es,' said Caro, 'but with every respect, Mother, that was sixty years ago.'

'Caro,' said Athina, and there was clearly to be no more discussion on the subject, 'Pemberton and Rushworth are not going to be a pushover.'

'Good,' said Caro. 'Well, I just thought I should mention it.'

'As you have,' said Athina. 'And now to this girl, Bianca Bailey. I have no idea what she will be like on closer acquaintance, but she clearly has a track record of sorts, and she knows the industry, I suppose – what she did with PDN was clever, although they'd better not think they can sell Farrell's. And we have to retain our majority share. That's non-negotiable.'

'And neither can they mess about with it,' Caro said sharply, 'turn it into some cheapskate thing. And of course they mustn't even think of selling The Shop. That's the sort of thing they're bound to want to economise on.'

The Shop, as it was known throughout the company, was Farrell's exclusive outlet in the nineteenth-century Berkeley Arcade just off Piccadilly. The arcade was a magnet for tourists, the shops exclusive purveyors (as they were still named) of jewellery, leather goods, bespoke shirts and other such delights. The Farrell shop was small and enchanting, with a glass-paned door and windows. It not only sold the Farrell range, but offered facials and was where Florence had her office. The lease had passed to Cornelius from his father and it was generally regarded as the company's treasure. It did not make any money whatsoever.

'They might begin to wonder,' said Bertie mildly, picking up his fourth sandwich, 'what they can do with Farrell's. Surely we have to allow them some freedom? They're here to sort the company out, not just pour money into it.'

Athina and Caro stared at him.

'Bertie, we are quite aware of that,' said Athina, 'but we have to set out our stall clearly from the outset. That's the whole point. Otherwise they'll be destroying everything that makes the House of Farrell what it is. And Bertie, I thought your doctor said you had to lose some weight?'

'I do rather agree with Bertie,' said Florence, reaching for a third sandwich of her own, as much to display support for Bertie as to satisfy her appetite which was greatly out of proportion to her tiny frame.

'Well, I don't,' said Caro. 'This is a huge opportunity for them. They wouldn't be coming on board if they didn't see that. They're going to make a lot of money out of the Farrell brand. We own something very precious. We must not forget that.'

'So precious the bank wants to pull the plug,' said Bertie. 'Porter Bingham are saving us from that. All I'm saying is, that's the bottom line.'

'It is,' said Florence, 'and Bertie is right. Which is not to say we shouldn't put up a modest fight.'

It was Bertie who had responded to Porter Bingham in the first place. He had received a letter addressed to him as the finance director. After introducing himself as a partner at Porter Bingham Private Equity, the writer, one Mike Russell, informed him that Farrell's had caught his eye recently while doing some research on a similar business, and that he wondered if Mr Farrell might be interested in a meeting: Porter Bingham was currently investing a £367 million fund and was looking for high-growth investment opportunities where they could support management to accelerate the growth of their business.

Since Farrell's had no growth to accelerate, Bertie didn't think Porter Bingham would be very interested in them as a proposition, but he mentioned it to his mother, who was dismissive.

'I know all about these people. They come in, take over, and before you know where you are, the company isn't yours any more. Don't even think about it, Bertie, as your daughter would say.'

'But Mother, something has to be done. I don't think you quite realise the – the mess we're in.'

Athina looked at him sharply. 'I prefer to regard it as a temporary difficulty, Bertie. And we should certainly not be rushed into some extremely unwise liaison of this sort.'

'I don't think it is temporary,' said Bertie, his voice firmer now. 'I think—'

'Bertie,' said Athina, 'no.'

But two days later the bank wrote to Lady Farrell and said they would like to remind her that Farrell's were in breach of bank covenant and that they could call in the overdraft at any time. Perhaps she would like to make an appointment to discuss the situation?

The meeting was unpleasant, culminating in a suggestion that the bank would put in a firm of accountants to do what they called an Independent Business Review and it was clear that they could end up with the company being declared insolvent. Athina, apparently cool, told them they would consider their position, but travelling back to the offices, Bertie could see, for the first time, a flash of panic in her eyes. His suggestion that they should, after all, perhaps meet with the people from Porter Bingham was met with a rather grudging nod.

'Yes, all right, Bertie, if you really think it might do any good. May I say I very much doubt it?'

The initial meeting at Porter Bingham's gleaming head office in the City had done nothing to reassure Athina and she had, in fact, told them there could be no possibility of a collaboration as far as she could see and left mid-agenda, trailing a highly embarrassed Bertie. However, a fruitless journey round her own connections in the banking firmament had resulted in a further approach to Mike, via the unfortunate Bertie.

'Mr Farrell,' Mike said, 'I greatly enjoyed meeting your mother and it only confirmed my opinion that she – all of you – have a considerable asset in your possession. She knows what she wants and where she is going, and believe me, that is a quality we value. Why don't we come to your offices for a further meeting with the three of you, and talk some more?'

Granted the confidence of being on her own territory, Athina became more malleable, and at a second meeting they had agreed to meet Bianca over lunch in the Porter Bingham boardroom; Bianca had been charming, displaying an almost equal blend of confidence and diffidence about the project, which had gained her, if not approval from Lady Farrell, a slight lessening of hostility. And so they had continued along the difficult, winding road towards today's meeting – the purpose of which was to reach Heads of Terms.

It was a long afternoon; progress was slow, patience stretched. Tea was brought in and cleared again, arguments came and went, concessions were offered and withdrawn, Pemberton and Rushworth raised endless points of order, argued every tiny detail, referred frequently to the past and generally held things up considerably.

Hugh and Mike remained admirably patient.

Six o'clock brought sherry, which everyone refused; another long hour passed.

Mike cleared his throat.

'I think it is time,' he said, 'to discuss the allocation of shares; that, after all, is the crucial issue as far as we are concerned. Your position is unaltered, I believe, Lady Farrell: you still insist on a majority share?'

'Absolutely,' said Athina. Her gaze was steely.

Hugh and Mike looked at one another; Bianca knew this moment well. She had witnessed it before. In a game of chess it would be check, if not checkmate.

'Lady Farrell,' Mike said, looking at her with an extraordinary blank face, 'the House of Farrell needs a very large investment to save it from extinction. At least ten million pounds to put it back on a sound footing, with a further injection of up to three million to fund the sort of development that Bianca might envisage. Are you really suggesting that we should do all that and still leave you with a controlling interest?'

'Yes,' said Athina, 'I am. Without us there will be no House of Farrell for Mrs Bailey to, er, develop.'

Walter Pemberton cleared his throat; it was clear this was the moment he had been waiting for. 'Our position on majority shareholding is non-negotiable. Absolutely non-negotiable.'

Bianca sat in silence as the negotiations went on, enjoying the rhythm, the exchanges of power, realising which victories were important, which window dressing, waiting for the kill. It was half past eight now and she marvelled at Lady Farrell, who appeared as fresh and as razor-brained as she had been seven hours earlier. Caro too had stayed the course, although she had contributed little; Florence had remained alert, but said even less. Bertie was clearly, within the family, the least important member: never consulted, his mildest opinion brusquely swept away by Lady Farrell. But she noticed something else too; a couple of arguments, one on the location of the factory, another on the advisability or otherwise of relocating the offices, were shrewd. He was undervalued, she realised, not to be written off lightly.

'Right,' said Mike Russell, after a lengthy discussion and a part-victory over company reconstruction, 'I think we're getting somewhere. But we do still have to solve this problem of the shareholdings. Lady Farrell – you're still adamant?'

'Absolutely. This is our company, and our company it will remain.'

'Perhaps you would excuse us for a moment,' said Mike. 'Hugh . . .'

They left the room and Bianca, left with the Farrells, smiled at them.

'Lovely room,' she said, looking round at the tall windows, the shutters, the fine Edwardian fireplace, the polished floor. 'I wish all boardrooms were as pleasant.'

'We pride ourselves on our buildings,' said Athina. 'My husband set up the House of Farrell in this very room. I don't suppose you've been to our shop in the Berkeley Arcade. That too is very special.'

'I have indeed been,' said Bianca, 'but only to look in from the outside. It's lovely. Quite charming.'

'And it has a value to the brand that is inestimable,' said Athina, 'in terms of image, and customer loyalty. A journalist once wrote in *Vogue* that it was the heartbeat of Farrell's. I wonder if you would agree with that?' Her tone was defensive.

'Lady Farrell, it would be impertinent of me either to agree or disagree,' said Bianca, smiling at her. 'I simply don't know enough of Farrell's at this stage to comment in any detail on anything. But I thought it was a delightful place.' She smiled at Florence. 'I believe it is your headquarters. How nice that must be for you.'

'It is indeed.'

Mike and Hugh returned.

'Right,' said Mike, 'this is what we propose in broad outline and by way of a compromise. You will keep your fifty-one per cent of the shares, we will take forty per cent and Bianca and the new finance director we will be appointing will have nine per cent between them.'

'Mrs Bailey will have shares in the company?' Lady Farrell's tone implied this was tantamount to handing over the entire control of the British government to the Monster Raving Loony party. 'Why on earth should she be given shares? I understood she was to be an employee.'

'Lady Farrell, I do assure you there would be no question of Bianca coming on board at all without her having shares. That is always one of the bases of these deals.'

'But – why?'

'Because she is ultimately the person who will be responsible for making the company profitable once more. Saving it, indeed. I do not use that word lightly. No salary could reflect the contribution she will be making, nor indeed the risk involved.'

'Well, I'm not sure that we could agree to that. Allowing you a share is reasonable, of course. And I suppose the finance director, who I presume would be part of your team. A reflection of the investment you are making. But . . .' her green eyes flashed briefly in Bianca's direction '. . . how can that apply to – to *her*?'

If Bianca had never been so utterly disparaged in her entire professional life, no one observing her would have suspected it. She leaned forward, smiled briefly at Athina, and said, her voice sweetly earnest, 'Lady Farrell, if we can reach a position today where I am to be appointed the chief executive of this company, my investment in it will be one hundred per cent, in terms of time, commitment, passion, and every skill I possess. My reputation will be on the line every bit as much as Farrell's own. I believe in the company absolutely and I know it has a future, or I wouldn't be here, I do assure you. I think that together we can take it forward and make it very successful once more. But – it has to be together. I need your commitment to me as much as you need mine to you. So – I need to be a part of the company, not just an employee. Does that help at all?'

There was a short, intense silence, then,

'Very well,' Lady Farrell said, 'we will agree to that. Providing the rest of what you offer is satisfactory, of course.'

Mike nodded. 'Let's hope it is. In return we will put the money in by way of a loan note, and shares, and if the company under-performs the loan note gets repaid first and the remaining value is for the shareholders. We would charge interest on that loan note, at fifteen per cent, but it means you keep your share and if you believe in the House of Farrell and its ability to survive, you will be prepared

24

to take that risk. Release a bigger share, and you get a lower loan rate. Simple as that.'

There was a silence.

'Clearly,' Athina said finally, 'we must discuss it further, particularly with our lawyers, but I think perhaps we have something to build on. Meanwhile it's late and we're all tired. We will get back to you on Monday. Thank you. I will have your coats brought in.'

And she rose and swept out, followed by her entourage, Walter Pemberton smiling graciously at Mike as they passed.

'Well done everyone,' said Mike with a weary grin as the door closed behind them. 'Nearly there. I was a little nervous that their lawyers might put a spanner in the works at the last minute.'

'I don't think Pemberton and Rushworth know about anything as useful as spanners,' said Hugh.

'It's a very clever deal,' said Bianca. 'Well done us.'

'I think so too,' said Mike modestly.

'And we gained some very good ground. That salary thing, they swallowed that.'

'Yes, I thought the lawyers might spot the flaw there, but—'

'Nah,' said Hugh, 'too busy admiring their own negotiating skills.'

'Fascinating, isn't it,' said Bianca, 'how vanity obscures common sense? They have no idea even now what a mess they're in. Just so busy hanging on to the past and its successes. The only one who seemed to have the slightest grasp of reality was Bertie. Funny, he seemed such an idiot at first.'

Chapter 3

Bianca burst into noisy tears.

This always happened. Patrick smiled at her tenderly, pushed her tangled hair back, and held her close. Soon she would stop and move into the absolute calm and sweetness that sex led her to, hunger satisfied, desire stilled, pleasure absolutely achieved.

She felt it now, the calm, reached for it, settled into it with a soft, appreciative sigh.

'Thank you,' she said as she always did. And, 'My pleasure,' he said as he always did.

She was quiet for a while, enjoying the warmth, the smell, the feel of him, contemplating what they had just shared and discovered and achieved. It surprised her, every time, the height, the intensity of it; that after so many years and such complete familiarity and knowledge of one another, it should be so fierce and so different. It was a source of great joy to her that it was so; of course, there had been times, after babies, during crises both domestic and professional, that it had been just a little less of a delight, indeed not a delight at all; but the crises had passed, the babies had grown and slept, and they had been able to return to this extraordinary thing, so vital and so precious to their marriage.

It surprised her when it happened, often at times when she would least have expected it, when she was exhausted or stressed, or even, indeed, after a day of quite mundane domesticity. She would look at Patrick and he at her, and they would acknowledge without a word what lay ahead, sometimes in minutes, sometimes many hours later, but they would know it was there, waiting for them, and enjoy the contemplation as much as the reality.

People – well, many people – thought Bianca must be the dominant one in their relationship, given her position in the world, her glossy public success, but it was not so, and Patrick was not dominant either: they were rather wonderfully equal. They discussed, they argued, they compromised; moreover, they respected and enjoyed one another and their entirely complementary roles within the family. It was, she knew, or might sound so to the cynical, rather too good to be true.

She raised her head a little now, looked at him, smiled.

'Want to talk?'

After sex they were both energised rather than tranquillised and moved into a state of emotional and intellectual closeness, discussing problems, sharing dilemmas, debating issues in a way that their standard days did not allow.

Bianca knew this was unusual; indeed, as far as she could gather, almost unheard of. She only knew that of all the unexpected blessings in their marriage, it was perhaps the greatest.

'Well actually,' said Patrick, 'yes, I rather do . . .'

Bianca now found herself seriously frustrated. PDN had decided she should go on gardening leave with immediate effect, while the Farrells, or rather Athina and Caro, had refused to agree to her joining the company until the deal was signed and sealed. They were not prepared to have her installed as CEO under, as Athina put it, false pretences.

'They're so bloody arrogant,' she said, storming into Mike Russell's office one morning after a fruitless attempt to persuade Caro to at least let her look at the consultants' sales figures. 'What do they think I'm going to do, sell their secrets to Lauder?'

'Probably,' said Mike. 'I'm sorry, Bianca, but hang on; won't be long now.'

'Let's go on that half-term skiing holiday after all,' Bianca said to Patrick that night. 'I've got nothing to do until the wretched Farrells deign to play ball, and it would be a distraction as well as fun.'

'Oh . . . right.' Patrick looked at her, almost sharply. 'You do realise I said we wouldn't be going? I'm pretty busy myself now, cancelled the time off, and the Rentons have probably filled our space in the chalet?'

'Darling, don't be awkward. You know you can always get time off,' said Bianca, 'you only have to tell them. It's only a week, and if the children are kicking their heels at home over half-term and I'm kicking mine with them, we'll all go mad. I'll have a word with Patsy, see if there's still room for us.'

Patsy Renton, who knew it would do her school gate cred no end of good if she announced the Baileys were going to join them in the chalet in Verbier, said she would see what she could do, while mentally already moving three sets of children into two rooms, and rang Bianca later that day to say that would be fine and they'd love to have them. 'Just the flight to sort,' she said.

'I'll get Patrick on to it,' said Bianca. 'Wonderful, Patsy, I'm thrilled.'

And settled as contentedly as she could into some extra sessions with her personal trainer preparing herself physically for the trip – there was no way she was going to find herself anything but as good as the other female skiers in the party – and spent a dizzily expensive morning at Snow and Rock, equipping them all with new skiwear. She was a lucky woman, she thought, able as she was to bestride the best of both her worlds, her family and her career.

'Cool,' said Milly, surveying her loot later.

'Really cool,' said Fergie.

'I hope I'll be better this time,' said Ruby, her voice showing just a slight lack of conviction. She had spent much of the previous skiing holiday falling over.

'Of course you will be,' said Milly. 'It was only because that instructor was such rubbish last time. I'll help you lots, promise.'

'I'm just going to do snowboarding,' said Fergie. 'Skiing's no fun. Can you get me a board, Mum?'

'I already did,' said Bianca.

'You're the *best*!' said Fergie.

'I know,' said Bianca modestly.

Patrick had actually had some trouble persuading the other two partners that the huge audit he was supposed to complete within the next seven days could wait until the week after that. And it had meant postponing his meeting with his friend Jonjo Bartlett which he'd been rather looking forward to. But Bianca did holidays like she did everything else – one hundred per cent. She was the best companion, joyfully energetic, full of ideas, up early, urging them all out of bed to go and see or do something before the day proper began, bringing an extra dimension to everywhere they went. And it would be great to have a real family holiday. The last one, sailing off the Turkish coast the previous summer, had been interrupted when Bianca had to fly home halfway through.

It was Bertie who first heard the bad news: Bertie, white with apprehension, who was forced into being the messenger, therefore, and thus placing himself in the firing line – being too decent to insist on that role going to the people actually responsible, Bernard Whittle and Sons, the firm of accountants employed by Farrell's ever since Cornelius and Athina had founded the firm.

It turned out that someone had totally failed to declare the income from The Shop for the last three years – and with interest and VAT a million and a half was owed.

'Well, of course it's absolutely ridiculous,' said Athina. 'But it's not our fault, except possibly yours, Bertie.'

'Why me?' asked Bertie, quite mildly. 'I don't do the accounts.'

'As financial director,' said Athina, 'it's the sort of thing that surely comes under your watch? Although I'm surprised at Bernard Whittle, I have to say. We shall have to tell those people, I suppose,' – she continued to refer to Porter Bingham as those people – 'because it's not the sort of money we can get out of petty cash, and another million won't mean anything to them, surely? You'd better get on to them today. Just ring them up and tell them – I'm sure they won't mind.'

'I think it would be better, Mother, if you did it,' said Bertie, 'or at least we should see them together. This isn't petty cash. It's quite major. I think we owe them the courtesy of a formal representation.'

'I see,' said Mike Russell, struggling to remain calm in the face of Lady Farrell's blithe assumption that a demand for a further one and a half million was a minor matter set against the overall sum they were investing in Farrell's, as she put it.

'Lady Farrell, we're talking quite serious money here. And a considerable incompetency on the part of your accountants. Frankly, I'm appalled. We shall have to go back to our board. Every deal has to be approved and I had trouble getting this one past them. I might have to ask you to find the extra money yourselves.'

'Well, that's ridiculous! *We* can't lay our hands on that sort of sum.'

'Perhaps one of you could sell your own property? You're all living in very expensive places, and—'

'I don't think so,' said Athina, looking slightly unnerved. 'Although, Bertie, your house is far too large for you and Priscilla's been talking about moving back into London for years. We might consider that.'

Bertie was silent.

'Well . . .' Mike stood up, walked over to the window, looked out, 'this has rather rocked my faith in the accuracy of any information you can provide. We are struggling to do our financial due diligence, and this sort of thing makes a bit of a mockery of it. As you know we are going to appoint our own accountants to work with Farrell's in future, and they are commencing their audit next week – I dread to think what else they might find. And I'm still not sure this isn't the sticking point on this deal. So it might be that we have to take a charge on the family properties, just as a gesture of good faith on your part. Mrs Johnson, I know, has a house in Hampstead. Mr Farrell, where is your property?'

'In – in Surrey,' said Bertie, 'in, er, Esher.'

'Very nice. And I presume there's no mortgage on it?'

'No.'

Bertie looked at his hands, clenched as they so often were, Mike had observed.

'Well, we might go down that route,' he said, 'or – and I would frankly prefer this, I want Bianca to have access to any information she might need with immediate effect. It is clearly crucial. She needs to draw up her own plans for the company and time is of the essence.'

'I don't see why there is such a rush,' said Athina.

'Well, I'm very surprised at that, Lady Farrell,' said Mike. 'We can't meander along, losing millions a year, hoping for the best. So if we are to continue with this, I want Bianca given your full cooperation from Monday. Otherwise, as I say, I begin to doubt if we can continue. One more disaster like this one and we certainly can't.'

'I really can't see any problem with that,' said Bertie. 'In fact, it seems very reasonable to me.'

'Well, it doesn't to me,' said Athina. 'But I suppose we should discuss it.'

Bianca was packing the children's cases when Mike rang her.

'Bianca, you're on. Or rather, in.'

'What?'

'Yes, from Monday. The old girl has graciously agreed you can have access to any information you require. She's told Lawrence Ford, that excuse for a marketing manager, that he's to cooperate fully with you, and that you can go round all the stores as well, talking to the consultants. Frankly, it's a huge relief to me. I've never seen goalposts shifted so swiftly and on an almost daily basis. OK?'

'Well,' said Bianca, looking rather wildly at the mountains of jackets, helmets and goggles on her bed. 'I was going to take a week's skiing—'

'Oh, what?' Mike's voice, normally so easy, sounded suddenly harsher. 'Bianca, I need you there; time is absolutely crucial, you know that. You can take a holiday later in the year, when it's all up and running. Don't let me down.'

'I – won't,' said Bianca and even as she stood there, listening to Fergie telling Patrick, who had just come in from the office, that he'd beaten every other boy in the group at the dry ski slope that morning, she felt the familiar thud of excitement at the prospect of actually getting to grips with the reality of Farrell and its complexities, and yes, being herself rather than some slightly unsatisfactory impostor.

'I'll be there,' she said, 'of course. Monday morning. Don't worry. Thanks, Mike.'

And walked out of the room, and into her study, calling to Patrick to follow her.

Chapter 4

This was so awful. She was going to have to chuck it in. It was getting worse every day. It wasn't just the job, and never feeling she was getting anywhere, it was what it was doing to her and her professional reputation. You couldn't afford to be associated with failure. She wished she'd never taken it in the first place – but it had sounded so enticing.

'I know we don't seem the most exciting outfit in the business,' Lawrence Ford, the marketing manager, had said, 'that's why we want you. To make us exciting. We've got a lot of plans, going to make big waves – with your help. And if you do it, well, Ms Harding,' he looked at her rather intensely, 'the sky will be your limit.'

Hmm. Pretty dark sky, Susie was thinking. She really should have known better. She hadn't even liked him very much, he was so smarmy, but he had also been talking, in some ways, a language she appreciated. Like offering her twenty-five per cent more than her current salary. Like health insurance, very generous expenses, company credit card. The Lot, in fact.

And lovely as it had been, working for Brandon's, the newest, wildest, colour cosmetic kid on the block, with people fighting to get near the counters at their space in Selfridges at lunch-time, she felt she had been there, done that, and was ready for a challenge. Her reputation was sky-high, she was the default PR girl all the journalists called when they wanted anything, from a story to the latest product. She had spent a couple of days studying Farrell's, googled its range and company history (plenty of PR

33

opportunities there, and old Lady Farrell sounded amazing) and decided she'd go for it. She could see where it had gone wrong; and she had lots of ideas of how it could be put right. Lawrence Ford had assured her he would welcome any such input so it had all sounded good.

She talked to Henk about it; Henk was her new boyfriend, a so far unsuccessful photographer. He'd urged her to go for it.

'It's more money, babe, and you'll be more your own boss.'

A small voice told her the appeal of that for him was that she'd be able to carry on paying for everything, and use him professionally, but she crushed it. And the biggest attraction was the challenge. She'd called Lawrence Ford and told him that.

Well, it *had* been a challenge. She had worked all hours, called in favours, thought laterally, created stories – all to absolutely no avail. An email or call from Susie Harding to the beauty editors and bloggers slowly, but obviously, became something to avoid. Make-up artists declined the invitation to stock their palettes with the full range, and the bait of a personal interview, so irresistible when it had been with Kris Brandon, carried no weight at all if it was to be with one of the Farrells – except of course Lady Farrell: everyone still wanted her. And she flatly refused to consider anything of the sort unless she was allowed to vet every word of the copy. As if!

And when she did manage the impossible and got The Cream listed on *A Model Recommends*, one of the top ten blogs, for God's sake, as 'absolutely yummy', they didn't even thank her. In fact, the old bat came in and complained that all she had managed was 'a blog'.

'It's *Vogue* we want here, Susie, *Vogue* and *Tatler*; I would like you to try to remember that.'

She closed her computer with a sigh, pulled on her coat, dropped her mobile into her bag and set off for the lift, her high heels (Louboutin, but honestly, these days who cared? She might as well wear sandals!) clacking across the wooden floor. She was meeting Henk at Soho House in half an hour; he'd approve; he'd been telling her she was wasting her time ever since she'd finished her first week at Farrell's. Not that he knew anything about it; he just missed being able to hang around while she entertained her mates in the press. He was getting rather worryingly stroppy about it. He was very possessive and getting more so. Which might have been all right if he was offering anything in return, but he wasn't. Sometimes, Susie thought, just sometimes, it would be nice to have a proper relationship that was supportive and ongoing, not just for laughs and sex. It had eluded her so far.

And at least she had someone. Someone cool and sexy. That was what mattered: being on your own didn't do your image any good, quite apart from its otherwise obvious drawback.

Anyway, she had to get away from Farrell's. She was getting depressed, and nobody could do publicity if they were depressed. It was a job that demanded absolute, upbeat self-confidence.

'Patrick, hello. Jonjo here. How are you, you old sod? Hope you enjoyed the skiing you cancelled me for! Anyway, I might have a proposition for you and I wondered if you'd got a minute in the next couple of days and we could meet, have a chat?'

'Of course. Love to.' And how did it feel, Patrick wondered, not to have a minute: to be properly busy and, even more, to be overstretched, stressed, exhausted, desperate for a break – all the things he was unable to imagine, as he made his calm, thoughtful, pleasant progress from client to client, meeting to meeting, lunch to lunch. It was what Bianca knew very well and although most of the time he was thankful not to operate like that, there were times when he envied her. For they could seem long, those calm, thoughtful, pleasant days and he knew very well that his presence in them was far from imperative.

'Great! Well, how about a drink, Thursday, L'Anima, just off Broadgate West. Six-ish suit you?'

'Bit early,' said Patrick in a desperate bid to sound busy. 'Six thirty'd be better.'

'Six thirty it is. How's Bianca?'

'Oh, fine. Probably about to start a new very, very high-powered job. As opposed to just a very high-powered one.'

'Why am I not surprised?' said Jonjo, laughing. 'She's amazing. But we all know that. See you Thursday.'

Patrick wondered what proposition Jonjo could possibly have for him. Jonjo Bartlett, coolest of the City boys, sharp, funny, clever, who made and lost and always made again millions at the drop of a computer key, Jonjo whose job as a City trader was almost incomprehensible to Patrick, with its vocabulary of options and income rate swaps and futures, whose friends were all sharp, funny and clever too, working-class boys made very, very good for the most part; Jonjo who lived in immense style in an apartment in Canary Wharf, spent a fortune on clothes and cars and an endless succession of flashily gorgeous girls, and professed on the occasions he visited Patrick at home to be jealous of him. He'd been married once and divorced two years later and since then claimed to have been looking for the next wife. As, along with being sex on legs personified with a perfect face and flawless figure, she would be required to have the patience and tolerance of Mrs Job, this seemed to Patrick a somewhat fruitless quest.

Unlike most of his colleagues, Jonjo came from old money, had gone to public school with Patrick, and a close, if odd, friendship had formed.

At the end of his time at Charterhouse, while all his contemporaries went off to university, Jonjo, tired of the academic, went straight into a job in the City and within two years was making large waves. At least once a year he and Patrick met for dinner and Jonjo plied Patrick with vintage Bollinger and, more recently, sushi, and towards the end of the evening, told him, his voice slurring increasingly, what a lucky chap he was and how he would give his new Ferrari to be in his shoes. And Patrick, who knew very well Jonjo would last for roughly a week in his shoes, would nod sympathetically and pat at first his hand, then his shoulder and finally Jonjo's head, slumped over his arms on the table, and tell him he was sure all would be well one day.

But it would be good to see him, Patrick thought; he'd had such a filthy time recently, what with work being increasingly unrewarding and that nightmare of a skiing holiday, with the children all crying, actually crying, when they were told their mother wasn't coming, and then trying to look after them when they were in Verbier, as they veered between feeling the lack of their mother rather acutely and running a bit wild and showing off their independence as a result.

He had never been so glad to get home from a holiday in his life.

'Hello! I do hope you don't mind me just dropping in like this. Lady Farrell said I could come in and talk to you, Miss Hamilton.'

Florence Hamilton smiled politely at her visitor, over the counter of the Berkeley Arcade shop.

'How very nice.'

Florence's voice lacked enthusiasm. There was no doubt in her mind that Bianca would want to close The Shop.

Bianca beamed. 'What a showcase this is for the House of Farrell. I think it's enchanting. And you've run it since – what? 1953?'

'Yes,' said Florence. 'Lady Farrell – Mrs Farrell then, of course – took me on in the March and we opened in May, just in time to get all the tourists who'd come to London for the coronation. They just flocked down the arcade, and the American ladies in particular loved it. It was a *very* exciting time.'

'It must have been,' said Bianca. She looked more interested than people usually were over such reminiscences. She picked up a sample jar of The Cream that was lying on the counter. 'May I?'

'Yes, of course,' said Florence.

Bianca opened the box, smiling like a child unwrapping a Christmas present, and rubbed a little of the cream into her wrist. 'I love this stuff.'

'You must take a jar for yourself.'

'Well, that's kind, but of course I have some already. I bought it, wanted to experience the product that made Farrell's famous.'

'And?' said Florence.

37

'Well, as I said, I love it And of course I look at least ten years younger than I did.' She smiled. 'I do love those boxes too. Now – body lotions and so on – where are they? Oh, yes, I see. And eye make up and so on are . . . ?'

'Here, under the glass counter,' said Florence.

'Oh how clever. This is just a lovely old-fashioned shop, isn't it? I imagine the trade here is a bit seasonal – more in the summer and so on?'

'Of course. But it's never very quiet,' said Florence firmly. 'Now, can I offer you a cup of tea? I have a small sitting room upstairs – I call it my parlour. Of course I work up there,' she added hastily, lest Bianca might think it was a piece of self-indulgence. 'It's where I do all the paperwork, the sales figures and so on.'

'I'd love that,' said Bianca, 'how kind. And you can tell me more about your long, long time here. It's such a wonderful story that I'm surprised it hasn't been featured in all the magazines. I mean, this is the heart of the brand, it seems to me.'

'Oh, Miss Harding – the PR, you know? She was pressing me to do exactly that. But Lady Farrell didn't consider it appropriate.'

'Why not? It seems very appropriate to me!'

'Well – we have never really courted that sort of publicity at the House of Farrell. What she was talking about sounded much too . . . personal. In the old days, *Vogue* and *Tatler* would do photographs here, have a model leaning on to the counter, applying one of the new lipsticks, that sort of thing. Which was wonderful. But Miss Harding wanted this to focus on me and my story here. Lady Farrell didn't approve of it at all.'

'Oh really?' said Bianca.

'Or my talking about past famous customers and clients. Well, many of them are still alive and we have always prided ourselves on our discretion.'

'I see,' said Bianca. 'Which magazines did she want to approach with this idea?'

'Well, the newer ones. Which I do rather admire. *Glamour* I enjoy, and *Red*. That's intelligent, as well as glossy. And even more recently, one of these blogs. Which I believe are very important now, almost as much as the magazines.'

'That's absolutely true,' said Bianca, impressed by Florence's appreciation of the modern media.

'But Lady Farrell was very opposed to the idea. She feels Miss Harding is not quite our style.'

'And how do you feel about her? Purely professionally, of course?'

'Well, I think she's rather fun,' said Florence, 'but of course Lady Farrell understands the brand and what it needs far better than I.'

Her expression was carefully innocent, Bianca thought. Interesting.

'Well, look, let's go up to your parlour and have that cup of tea and we can chat some more. About your work here, and how you see the House of Farrell, all that sort of thing.'

After Bianca had gone, Florence sat down rather heavily and thought about the small kingdom where she had spent so much of her life. A tiny, shabby place it had been the first time she saw it, transformed by Athina Farrell's vision – 'I want it to be like a little jewel box, filled with treasure.'

It had been the first exclusive outlet for Farrell's, the shop on the ground floor, with its curvy window and paned glass door with its brass handle and knocker, its old-fashioned glass showcases and gleaming mahogany counter, the salon on the first floor where women – only one a time, so utterly exclusive it was and wonderfully private – could have their faces cleansed and massaged and then anointed with The Cream, and then on the top floor, the parlour, with its pretty small desk where she did the accounts each day – by hand, of course, in a perfectly kept ledger – a small chaise longue where she read the glossy magazines, not as a self-indulgence but to acquaint herself with what mattered in the world of fashion and beauty, and the tiny kitchen to the side of it, where she could make tea, sometimes just for herself, sometimes for important visitors, as she had for Bianca today: always in fine china cups, sugar lumps in a matching bowl complete with silver tongs, and silver spoons with which to stir the tea. And of course, biscuits from Fortnum's just along the road.

It was home to Florence just as much as her small house in Pimlico, bought with a legacy from her father; it had been the setting against which she had lived out her life, the professional life that had replaced the personal one for the most part denied to her. Her young husband had been killed almost at the end of the war in a wonderfully successful Allied attack called Operation Varsity, which was agonising enough in itself, but had been made even more so by the way military historians had since questioned its necessity, meaning that perhaps Duncan had died for nothing. She had failed to find anyone else, had never really wished to. Once she recovered from her grief she had decided a single life suited her. Being a wife and mother seemed to her restrictive and exhausting while she was free to pursue her career, to travel where and when she wished, and to spend such money as she had entirely on herself. And indeed to conduct her entire life as she chose. Many people told her these days that she had been born considerably ahead of her time.

Florence felt anxious suddenly. For all Bianca's charming appreciation of The Shop, she had clearly been appraising it very carefully. And Florence was a realist; she could see quite clearly that, defend it as she might as an important jewel in the Farrell crown, the economics really did not add up. And then what would she do?

Chapter 5

It caused excitement in some of their employees, trepidation in most, the news – or rather rumour – that Farrell's was about to be taken over, or bought. Nothing had been confirmed, but neither had it been denied. The Farrells were utterly tight-lipped about it, so everyone was edgy, unable to concentrate, and both those who were excited and those who were trepidatious discussed the prospect endlessly, at water coolers, in wine bars and even in the lift and the lavatories.

The rumours that Bianca Bailey might be joining the company had sent Susie Harding googling her frantically; she was clearly a star, had relaunched the toiletries company PDN with great success and before that had done the same for an interior design company. It would be great to work with her; it would certainly make it worth hanging on.

Marjorie Dawson was one of the more anxious staff members waiting for news; in the world in which she lived, that of the beauty departments in the big stores, gossip moved with great speed. She didn't really have any good friends at Rolfe's of Guildford, where she was based these days – once she had been the Farrell queen bee at Selfridges – but she still pricked up her ears as she walked into the staff dining room.

Marjorie was fifty-five and had worked for the House of Farrell since her twenty-second birthday when it had still been a very respectable member, if not one of the stars of the cosmetic firmament. She had done well from the beginning, her weekly figures always among the top five accounts; Lady Farrell had picked her out quickly, appreciating the irresistible combination of sweet-voiced prettiness and a steely determination to reach the top. At the age of thirty-five, she had been put in charge of consultant training, visiting all the stores on a regular basis, often dropping in unexpectedly. The occasional young consultant, caught gossiping while a customer struggled to attract her attention, never repeated the offence again after a few to-the-point words from Marjorie.

She was also an invaluable source of information about the brand and its customers, reporting as she did to the Farrells on a twice-monthly basis; Marjorie could tell them not only which colours were selling best, and which promotions had worked, but how the customers actually felt about the latest advertising campaign or counter card.

But that was the peak of her career; as the eighties drew to a close and brash colours and intense, chemically based perfumes took over the market, one by one the Farrell consultants found themselves sidelined, smiling brightly and hopefully by their endlessly tidied counters while women walked past them unseeingly, lured by the hard, sexy sell of what was forever to be known as the shoulder-pad era.

Gradually the accounts in the big stores were closed down; the successful, clever girls, like Marjorie were moved on to smaller, less glamorous establishments, the less fortunate dismissed. Countrywide there were now only twenty-eight department stores with Farrell counters – and only a handful of them, Marjorie knew, justified their space. She was no fool; she had spent her life in the cosmetic business, and she knew that in spite of its fluffy image, its heart was as hard as nails. It was big business; and big business had to pay. As one of the gay make-up artists – there seemed to be more and more of them, these days – who did events at Rolfe's said to her over several very jolly glasses of wine, 'Marjorie, darling, it don't mean a thing if it don't go ker-ching!' Ker-ching being, of course, the music of the till.

Rolfe's did not do badly; she had a loyal clientele who had always used Farrell products, but sometimes she read of the millions of pounds annually turned over in the top stores and felt quite sick and anxious because she was the family breadwinner. When Marjorie walked out of the house in the morning she left behind her a husband who hadn't worked for fifteen years; he had been a scaffolder in his youth, a handsome young man called Terry, who had won Marjorie's heart, and for a time they had been a rather dashing young pair, with what looked like a very promising life before them. Then a horrible fall had crushed his spine and left him in a wheelchair. His disability allowance was smaller than ever thanks to 'the cuts', and they were fairly strapped for cash, as Terry put it. Marjorie's income was essential: without it, she had absolutely no idea what they would do.

Patrick looked round the incredibly cool bar Jonjo had brought him to, all glass and mirrors and black and white. He'd ordered a gin and tonic, which Jonjo had clearly found quite amusing, and was listening to Jonjo telling him about his new job. As usual, he didn't really understand much of what he was saying. He'd googled the company Jonjo now worked for which was called MPR, and learned that it provided brokerage services, trade execution trading platforms and other software products, and that its revenue in 2010 had been 702 million dollars – which he more or less understood. Jonjo was a foreign exchange trader.

'We've got some very blue chip companies,' Jonjo said now. 'It's high pressure, of course, but it's a genius set-up, all the guys on the desks are really cool, so good to work with. I'm having a great time. How about you?'

'Oh – you know,' said Patrick, deliberately vague, 'more of the same, really.'

'Yeah?' Jonjo looked at Patrick rather intently. 'You still enjoying it?'

'Absolutely,' said Patrick, trying to sound convincing. 'I mean, it's nothing to get really excited about, but I have a lot of good clients, my colleagues are great, and I more or less write my own job spec.' He wished it sounded just slightly more exciting.

'Yeah, well I suppose you would. It'll be yours one day.'

'Possibly,' said Patrick primly.

'Oh, P, come on, you know it will – it's a family firm and you're the only one of your generation. Anyway, that kind of brings me round to what I want to talk to you about.' He hesitated, looking mildly embarrassed; Patrick was intrigued.

'Well, come on, spit it out. You don't want me to cover up for some woman do you?'

'Patrick! Would I?'

'Yes,' said Patrick and grinned at him. 'Wouldn't be the first time.'

'I know, but I'm not married any more. God, which reminds me. I can't be much longer. I've got a hot date with a sculptor.'

'A sculptor?' Patrick struggled not to sound astonished.

'Yeah. Thinking of buying one of her – er – what are they called?'

'I could make any amount of suggestions,' said Patrick, with a grin, 'but the word I think you're looking for is pieces. What are her . . . pieces like, then?'

'Oh lord, no idea. Bronze, I think she said. A good investment anyway. Want to come along? It's the private view. Quite fun. Cork Street.'

'I'd love to,' said Patrick, and it was true: he rather liked private views with their heady blend of attractive people and pretentious chatter, 'but I can't. I've got a hot date with a history project.'

'Yeah?' Jonjo's expression veered between boredom and – what? Sympathy? It depressed Patrick.

'Come on, then,' he said, 'you'd better tell me what this proposition is. I don't want to keep you from your sculptor's pieces.'

'Right,' said Jonjo. 'Now, I don't know if you'd ever even consider it. But, well, it goes like this . . .'

'Bertie, I think we should move.' Priscilla Farrell's deceptively good-natured face wore its most determined expression. 'This house is too big for us now, with the children both away most of the time, and I never wanted to live out here, it was purely for their benefit.'

She made it sound as if Esher was the Outer Hebrides.

'And mine,' said Bertie carefully. 'I like it here, very much. And *I* have to do the commute, after all.'

'But look at the performance every time we want to go to the theatre or a concert, for instance. Do we take the car, where shall we park? When I look at people like Margaret and Dick, just walking into the Barbican – so much easier. And I've just taken on this new charity, it's London based and I shall be forever on the train—'

'Priscilla, I really don't want to move,' said Bertie, trying to sound decisive. 'There's enough upheaval in our lives at the moment, with Farrell's being taken over, and God knows what will happen – I could be out of a job for starters.'

'You're the financial director! Of course you won't be out of a job. I talked to Athina about it and she said all your positions would be absolutely unchanged, that you'd still got your majority share—'

'I don't think *anything* will remain unchanged,' said Bertie. 'These deals don't allow for it.'

'Well, I'd back your mother against a venture capitalist any day of the week,' said Priscilla. 'And anyway, if you're right and you might be in a less certain position, all the more reason to move now, into something smaller and cheaper, rather than later on in a panic. I really think a flat at the Barbican would suit us very well and I thought you'd like the idea.'

'Did you really? I can't think why. And what about the children, where are they supposed to live in the holidays?'

'Oh – we can get one with two or three bedrooms.'

'Which will cost as much as this house. Priscilla, I love it here. And I love the garden – you know what it means to me. What would I have at the Barbican? A window box at best.'

'You can grow herbs in window boxes,' said Priscilla, swinging as always into a well-informed attack. 'I was reading about it in the *Sunday Times* only last weekend. Or flowers, of course; whatever you like. Anyway, I've asked some of the local agents to come and do a valuation, but as a rough guide we should get at least three million for this house. Which, if you are going to be out of a job, will come in pretty useful. Bertie, I really want you to give it some serious consideration.'

'I will consider it,' said Bertie. 'Of course. Now I'm going to go outside and have my gin and tonic on the terrace. Such a lovely evening.'

Bertie fixed himself a very strong gin and tonic and went out into the March dusk. It had been an incredible spring, with temperatures at a record level, and the garden was thick with birdsong, the great clumps of daffodils he had planted years ago seeming to shine through the half-light. The magnolia tree was heavy with its hundreds of pink candles, the camellia studded with white stars, and he felt, as he always did on such occasions, the garden enfolding him, soothing his ever-present sense of anxiety. Esher might be laughably suburban to the metropolitan dwellers; to him it meant peace, the place where all was right with the world.

Priscilla's desire to move was intensely worrying. She was so very good at getting her own way.

As was his mother. For the two of them, negotiations could only mean one thing: winning.

'Mr Russell, no.' Athina's voice was icy. 'It's unthinkable. We cannot run the House of Farrell from an office in some squalid area in South London. I can't believe you're even suggesting it. It would seem to indicate a complete lack of grasp of the cosmetic industry. We *need* to be in the West End. Revlon are in Brook Street, Lauder in Grosvenor Street. Are you really suggesting the House of Farrell has an address in *Putney*?'

'Lady Farrell, Putney is not squalid. It's extremely pleasant. Boots are there, in—'

'Boots!' Athina's voice would have withered a row of vines. 'Well, there you are. That makes my point.'

'In magnificent offices on the river,' Mike continued, without drawing breath, 'probably at a fraction of the cost we are paying in Cavendish Street. I'm sorry, Lady Farrell, but you have to think about it. You can't afford not to. Looking at alternative office sites was agreed in the Head of Terms – and I intend to put into the contract that when your lease expires, in January 2014, there will be no question of renewing because the rent will probably quadruple then. As will the rates. You've been very fortunate to have it for so long at the level you do. Now, I would also like to propose we dispense with your personal chauffeur—'

'Out of the question! Colin Peterson has driven us for thirty years. There is no way I am going to tell him he is out of a job.'

'Well, that is your prerogative, Lady Farrell, but I'm afraid you will have to pay him yourself.'

'But Mr Russell, not only has Colin Peterson worked for us all his life, his father did so before him. What do you suggest I say to him? That he has to go on the dole?'

'*You* won't have to say anything, Lady Farrell: we will of course negotiate with Mr Peterson. It may be that he can come up with some proposal himself. But the current situation is financially untenable. I'm sorry.'

'And do I understand that I am now to pay rent on my flat? A property owned by the company?'

'I'm afraid so, Lady Farrell.'

'I think that is probably the most outrageous of all your proposals.'

'Well, I'm sorry. But you see, what is happening now is against current tax laws. It's forming a tax-free component of your income. And that is simply wrong.'

'But Bernard Whittle has always said it was perfectly ethical.'

'Lady Farrell, this is not the first time that I have found Mr Whittle to be under some very erroneous impressions. Now, either you must pay rent for the apartment, or it must be set as a taxable benefit against your income. One or the other. I'm sorry.'

Athina was perfectly sure that he was not sorry at all. She drew herself up as she asked her next question.

'And what is this about a new chairman? I've spoken to Walter Pemberton and the rest of the family and none of us recollect any such suggestion being mooted. I am the chair of this company and intend to remain so.'

'Lady Farrell, the chairman will be a non-executive position. That is to say, he will not have shares in the company, he will only be in attendance two days a month, let us say, and he will certainly have experience of the cosmetic industry, so he'll know what he's talking about—'

'Are you suggesting I don't?'

'No, no of course not. No one understands the industry better than you. But we need someone to run the board.'

'I don't understand you. Run the board in what way?'

'Primarily at board meetings. Which, as you will remember, will be held monthly. He will control the agenda, the debate at the table and so on. The official jargon is that he will force structure, compliance and good governance on the board.'

She looked at him witheringly. 'It sounds to me rather insulting to suggest that we need such – such discipline.'

And so it went on, day after painful day, with what seemed to Athina endless concessions; she was exhausted by it, not just the actual discussions but the emotional strain, as she felt the control of Farrell's slip irreversibly away from her.

They were painful and desolate, those days; and more than once she considered sending them on their way, her tormentors, choosing death rather than dishonour for her life's work. On those occasions, surprisingly, it was Bertie, rather than Caro, who helped her stand firm, who told her it was what Cornelius would have wanted, that it was worth anything, anything at all as long as the House of Farrell lived on.

'But Bertie, it won't *be* the House of Farrell,' she said. 'It will be some other bastard brand, not the thing that Cornelius and I created.'

'No,' he said. 'I know it's hard, I know there is much change, but we shall still have ultimate control and I think, too, we can trust Bianca. She will see us and Farrell through.'

'Well, I can only say I do hope you are right.'

'I hope so too,' he said.

Chapter 6

'So – yes. I am interested. Of course.' Patrick smiled at Saul Finlayson. 'It sounds like a fascinating opportunity.'

That was, he knew, a rather understated response to Finlayson's proposition, conveyed via Jonjo, that Finlayson, one of the biggest movers and shakers in the City of London, and runner of a very successful, fairly new hedge fund, was looking for someone with Patrick's qualifications and experience to work for him personally as a research analyst. And that was a dizzying prospect, of possibly finding himself in the heady uplands of a market that he hardly understood, let alone where he might have something to offer.

Jonjo had arranged for them to meet in the Blue Bar at the Berkeley Hotel, near Finlayson's office, so that he might meet the man and hear his proposition first hand. 'I think you'll like him, extraordinary fellow,' Jonjo had said, 'but you must make your own mind up about that.'

Finlayson smiled back at him now; but so briefly that a blink would have obscured it. It was one of his trademarks, Patrick discovered, that brief smile, unnerving to anyone who didn't know him. He had other unnerving habits; he spent a lot of time during a conversation with his fingertips together, staring up at the ceiling, and he ate and drank with extraordinary speed. His plate was often empty before his companions had so much as picked up their knives and forks and he was leaning forward again firing questions, demanding answers, generally making a mealtime as uncomfortable

49

as it could be. Fortunately for Patrick they were not having a meal, merely an early evening post-work drink; Finlayson had ordered a tonic on the rocks and downed it in one, while Patrick and Jonjo were taking preliminary sips of their martinis.

'Well,' said Finlayson, 'I don't know about the fascinating, but it's important. Now, you are a chartered accountant, and one of the things you do, or are trained to do at any rate, is look at the accounts of a company in huge detail. That sound right to you?'

'Yes, it does. But—'

'OK. So you can be given an annual report that's two hundred pages long, look at it for two days, and then come back with stuff most people couldn't possibly find out or know in a month of Sundays. You are someone who can look into what I call the weeds of the company, who knows how and where to look for possible problems, someone who has a sort of instinct about something that doesn't seem to quite add up. Because to my mind – *our* minds – that's where genuine ideas can come from. About what might happen to that company and what it's actually up to. All right?'

'Yes, I . . . think so,' said Patrick. He felt increasingly edgy. 'I don't know that I'm your man, not if you want ideas.'

'No, no,' said Finlayson impatiently, 'the ideas would come from your reports and observations, not you. Most people don't have time to do that sort of in-depth stuff, and don't employ anyone who does, either. But to me it's essential. Jonjo suggested you, so do you think you have that sort of ability? To trawl endlessly through stuff and spot anything that – well, asks a question. I've always maintained,' he added, 'a really good accountant would have spotted that Enron was fudging their accounts.'

'Really?' said Patrick. 'Good God. Well, you really should know that the stuff I'm involved with at the moment is pretty tame by anyone's standards. I really don't know that I'm high-powered enough for that sort of thing.'

'That's for me to judge,' said Finlayson. 'Look, it boils down to this: if I feel you're the right man for the job, then you probably are – and I'd like to take it on to the next stage.'

Patrick felt a mild sensation of panic.

'Well . . .' he said. 'Well, I'm deeply flattered but I'd like to think about it a bit more, talk to my wife about it, that sort of thing . . .'

'Yes, yes, OK,' said Finlayson. He seemed to find this understandable but irritating. 'And on that tack, you should therefore point out to her that even though you'd be doing familiar work, it would be a much more demanding environment than you're probably used to and you'd work pretty long hours. Think she'd be up for that? You'd probably have a few uneaten dinners, that sort of thing.'

'My wife's very realistic about all that,' said Patrick, hoping this was true. 'She works pretty long hours herself.'

'Of course. I googled her. Clever girl. Well, have a think, and so will I. The package should be pretty attractive but we can discuss that when you've made up your mind. I get the feeling we'd work OK together and Jonjo thinks so too. Want another of those?'

'No, no, thank you,' said Patrick.

'OK. Well I've got to go – dining with a client, God help me.'

And he was gone. Jonjo sat back in his seat and said, 'I think he liked you. Up to you now, I'd say.'

'Really?'

'Yeah. Whether you think it's your bag, whether you can work with him.'

'Bit hard to say,' said Patrick, 'after . . .' he looked at his watch . . . 'twenty-five minutes.'

'That's a long time in his day, believe me. I think you'd enjoy it, you know. Only thing is, it would be pretty stressful. You'll be working longer hours and you won't get home to see the children nearly so much. Better spell that out to Bianca. She might get a bit of a shock.'

Patrick was so used to his orderly existence, it was hard to imagine getting home late from time to time, and not being able to play his role of semi house-husband quite so devotedly. He could see he might even be unable to attend some crucial parents' meeting while Bianca sat in all-night financial sessions or jetted off to New York at little more than a moment's notice. For some reason – and he was shocked at himself as he realised it – it was a rather intriguing notion.

Lucy Farrell was leaving university. She was leaving, however, not in a cloud of glory, with a First, but in the middle of her course. With no degree of any size whatsoever.

She was hating the course. English literature – or certainly the way it was being presented to her – was a load of crap. Like the last essay, 'the Marxist view of Jane Austen', indeed. What could be less relevant to Jane's work than that, for God's sake? There'd been loads of others, just as hideously stupid, and almost two more years stretched ahead of her. She just couldn't face it, wanted out. And she'd taken a deep breath and said so to her tutor. And he'd said she should take time to think about it and she said she didn't want time, she was quite sure. And he'd been really very nice about it and said well, if that was how she really felt, then perhaps it would be better, and asked her politely, clearly not really wanting to know the answer, if she had any other ideas about her future.

She'd said no, and it wasn't true, but she knew that if she'd told him, he wouldn't even begin to understand. He would have certainly thought it wasn't a proper job, think she was only doing it because, given that her family was in the cosmetic business, she could just walk into a job, no problem at all.

She wanted to be a make-up artist. She had read lots of articles about it, had watched a programme on the fashion shows, showing the make-up artists working in the chaos of the Paris collections. It looked like hard work, but huge fun. And she would be good at it, she knew that. She loved doing her own face, painting it all kinds of wonderful ways for parties, and had a bit of a reputation for doing her mates' as well. And, while she didn't think she'd ever want to work at Farrell's, and had always resisted any idea of going into the business on a managerial level, there were lots of people there who'd be able to advise her how to go about this plan at least. She'd read in the article that you had to do a course somewhere, but that'd be fun, and if her father wouldn't pay for her, she could fund it working at bars and stuff like that.

She was a bit worried about her father; he might not like her new plans. But he could hardly argue about them, when the cosmetic business was his whole life. Not that he particularly liked it being his whole life; in fact, he never seemed to enjoy it very much.

Hopefully Grandy would be pleased. Lucy was very fond of her grandmother. She found her more fun – and in many ways she seemed years younger – than her mother. Grandy was still quite incredibly glamorous, took her to lunch at The Ritz every year on her birthday, and quite often they went (mostly window) shopping in Bond Street. Lucy had tried to persuade her to go to Westfield, but Grandy said she hated shopping malls.

And then they'd go and have tea in the Berkeley Arcade with Florence – she was allowed to call her Florence once she was sixteen, before that it had been Miss Hamilton – Grandy was very strict about things like that – up in the little room at the top of The Shop.

She'd loved Grandpa too, and she'd been terribly upset when he died; but the good part of it was that it meant she could see a bit more of Grandy because she was suddenly alone a lot at the weekends. Well, she would see lots of her now; that would be fun.

But first she had to break the news to her father that she was leaving uni . . .

John Ripley, who was working for Pemberton and Rushworth on a vacation placement, had been given the draft contract between the House of Farrell and Porter Bingham, Venture Capitalists to read.

'Interesting one, this, John,' Walter Pemberton said, 'we've worked very hard on it. You could learn a few things from it.'

Ripley did indeed study it very carefully, and when he had finished wondered why nobody had raised the question of voting rights. The more he thought about it, the more he wondered. He thought perhaps he ought to raise the subject with Mr Rushworth, but the question seemed to him to represent something of a criticism of Mr Rushworth's legal skills and he didn't want to alienate him in any way. He was hoping to get a training contract with the firm, and they were pretty thin on the ground these days.

He decided finally that it was impossible they could have failed to discuss it, and let the matter rest.

Chapter 7

Athina called them all into the boardroom before the final formal signing: the family, of course, all the key people who worked in the offices, and some extraneous ones as well, such as senior consultants and sales reps, and talked to them about what was going to happen. She explained that the deal had not been reached without considerable heart-searching, that they had struggled to find a different, independent solution, but that had, in the end, proved impossible. The arrangement with Porter Bingham had been essential for the House of Farrell, for the family . . .

'And for you. I am aware that without the help we have now secured, some of you would have lost your jobs. These are hard times; many companies more stable than this one are failing every day. I am deeply grateful to the people at Porter Bingham for providing a chance for us but I cannot pretend to you that things will be the same. I fear, and I use the word advisedly, they will not. In spite of absolutely retaining for ourselves a majority share of the company, my family and I will have to make concessions and accept change, and I know we shall have to ask the same of you. But at least the House of Farrell will live on; I think and hope that is what we would all most wish for it. Certainly I know my husband would have done.

'Thank you for your loyalty, for your hard work over the years, and for sharing our vision of the company; I assure you I have never, and will never, take any of it for granted.'

She stopped then. Susie Harding, watching her intently, felt her heart lurch as the clear, precise voice suddenly trembled, and the brilliant green eyes shone with tears. The House of Farrell would be no longer hers, and that would be hard, so hard for her, for the company was part of her, as she was part of it, and now the two must be wrenched apart . . .

Bertie Farrell thought he had never admired his mother more.

And Florence Hamilton, standing close to Susie, thought what a great loss to the stage Athina had been.

And there it was, next morning, on the front page of the *Financial Times*, lest anyone might not realise how important it was, and also, Susie thought, how important the part Porter Bingham would play. They had ensured it would be there, she and the PR guy at Porter Bingham, who she had actually found rather sexy in spite of his rather condescending attitude, and it was he who had managed to coerce Lady Farrell into what was actually a very generous quote. There was no doubt about it, Athina Farrell much preferred the opposite sex to her own.

The Prufrock column in the *Sunday Times* also had a lead item on the story.

Bianca Bailey, ex-CEO of toiletries firm PDN, which was sold under her aegis for £40 million, is seen here arriving at the Berkeley Arcade shop that is the showcase for the cosmetic company House of Farrell. Bailey, 38, who has just been appointed CEO of Farrell, following a deal signed this week between the Farrell family and Porter Bingham, Venture Capitalists, said she was 'excited and daunted in equal measure' by her new job. 'The House of Farrell is such a marvellous brand and I am so fortunate that Lady Farrell, who founded it with her husband in 1953 – coronation year – still plays such an incredibly active role in it. She is truly a living legend, and it will be wonderful to work with her – particularly in the next twelve months, with all the excitement in London created by the Queen's Diamond Jubilee and, of course, the Olympics.'

Bailey went on to say that several members of the royal family had visited the shop over the years – 'although not, alas, the Queen herself but maybe we can tempt her now!'

'Living legend indeed!' said Athina, hurling the *Sunday Times* across the room. 'Why not just say very, very old and be done with it. And she's looking forward to working with me, is she? I find that a little condescending. And there's another piece in the *Telegraph* about the Porter Bingham people, saying how marvellous they are and how successful they've been over the past ten years. If this is an indication of how things are going to be in the future, I feel even more depressed.'

'Oh, come on,' said Bertie, mildly, 'you know what they say about all publicity being good—'

'Bertie, this isn't publicity for Farrell's,' said Caro, 'it's for them, Bianca Bailey and the venture capitalists. They could at least have got a picture of Florence at The Shop . . .'

Had Susie Harding been there, she would have told them that both she and Bianca had tried to persuade Florence to pose outside The Shop with Bianca, and that Florence had said she couldn't, not without Lady Farrell there as well, and that endless requests for interviews with Lady Farrell had come in from the diary pages – all of which she had refused, saying she had no wish to court what she called irrelevant publicity.

It had all been rather agonising.

Patrick had seen the papers heaped up on the kitchen table of the Oxfordshire house, clearly intended for Bianca to read when they were back in London that night. He never failed to be impressed by her ability to compartmentalise her life; the weekends were, as much as humanly possible, for the family, they had both agreed that and she never did anything for the media at the weekends, not even Radio 4 who were always asking for her. And while she periodically checked her emails and her messages, she only acted on them if they were truly urgent; the rest waited till they got home on Sunday evening, when she did disappear into her study. Supper, and getting the children ready for school, was Patrick's job – those were the house rules, drawn up long ago.

Just the same, he couldn't help flicking through the top two papers while Fergie sank into his Nintendo and Milly her phone and clocked very nice pictures of Bianca on the front of *Mail on Sunday Money* and at the top of Prufrock. As usual, the captions made her sound like a single, or, rather, a divorced woman, unless it was a woman-focused piece which went overboard about the children and the houses and her 'wonderful, life-support accountant husband', but he'd got used to that. He hadn't had much choice.

Which brought him back to the one matter that he *did* wish to discuss with her, and fairly urgently. So far she had eluded him three times, pleading meetings, the children, or her own exhaustion; tonight – no, tomorrow night, when she would definitely be home early – he intended to insist on at least broaching the subject. It was too important to be postponed indefinitely, bringing changes as it would, into both their lives, of considerable proportions.

Patrick felt a little nervous about her reaction, to say the least.

Chapter 8

The image was so hopelessly wrong. About Day One.

The image of some kind of dynamo rushing in, righting wrongs, firing people, hiring more, slashing budgets, cancelling campaigns, closing departments – all practically before lunch on Day One. What actually happened was you moved in quietly and slowly, finding out who was really there and what they actually did; talking to people, asking for things; studying reports and checking on status; getting a feel for and an understanding of the most important areas; gaining people's confidence, grasping how they saw things. You had to find your core people, the ones with some insight, a few ideas; you had to find who was driving each department, and who was putting the brakes on it; you had to get your own handle on the politics and to take nothing at face value; you had to be respectful, patient, and extremely brave.

What Bianca found, on Day One, was a demoralised staff, and a slack work ethic. She found disinterest and self-interest. She found lethargy and cynicism. She found hostility and suspicion.

She sat in her new office, bland and beige as they always were, with a temporary PA, and an odd, dull silence outside it. Nobody was talking or laughing or shouting or arguing; they sat in a kind of siege condition, waiting for they knew not what. And for the time being they must go on waiting, for nothing very visible would happen at all. And certainly not on Day One.

The only thing that she always did on Day One was go home early.

Athina was perhaps the only person in the company not to expect huge change and dramatic action on Day One; mainly because she would not have allowed it, nor on Day One Hundred and One either. She had gone into the deal, recognising at last its inevitability, but determined to make things as difficult for her new colleagues – she refused to admit the word masters – as she possibly could. If they wanted changes, they must fight for them. Apart from anything else, she argued to herself, that would ensure those changes were truly necessary. Nevertheless, once the deal had become inevitable, she had forced herself to take a hard look at the House of Farrell, and she could see that the brand was indeed in a mess.

She more or less knew why: in a swiftly changing market, there was a loss within the House of Farrell of a sense of direction, and an ageing clientele – but there any certainty ended.

One of her major uncertainties was caused by, she knew, the fact that she didn't really like much of what she saw of the new market and its prime customer: both seemed to her either rather tacky, or indulging in a mystique of pseudo-scientific jargon that she found rather irritating. When they had founded the House of Farrell, in a glory of fantastic colour promotions, posters lining all the main roads into London and other big cities, and adorning the sides of double-decker buses, a good quality, high-image skincare range – The Cream its star product – was the perfect counterpart. It hadn't needed the added benefit of hyper-high, double-depth, super-charged ingredients developed in a laboratory; but then, nor had any of the others.

That was the difference. Skincare had been skincare then, vital but straightforward, as laid down in the immortal concept and routine of Elizabeth Arden: you cleansed, you toned, you nourished, and after that your well-fed skin would take its make-up and look as good as it could. Now science had been smoothed on to the beauty counters in a big way, with talk of cellular levels, free radicals, ultra-hydration. Half the stuff the beauty editors wrote sounded like A Level biology papers. Did women really want that? Athina wondered, and if so, why?

Finding no satisfactory answer to that one, she faced down again her fears for the future of Farrell; too late now, she knew, but still she wondered – was it really going to be safe with its new masters? Would the new management team, led by the dangerously powerful and glossy Bianca Bailey, really understand what treasures there undoubtedly still were, lying within its admittedly old-fashioned packaging and clearly out-of-date marketing and advertising?

She half-liked Bianca – she represented too much that was disagreeable to her life to go further than that – but she did respect her. Moreover, she knew both those emotions were returned. And Bianca certainly seemed to understand the importance of charm; and charm went a very long way in cosmetics. The most dazzling colours, the most earth-moving perfumes counted for nothing without it. A cosmetic brand must, at the end of the day, have an aura of pleasure about it. Bianca, she felt, would bring that to the brand at least, and she must encourage her. But it wasn't going to be easy. And she knew, moreover, that she couldn't afford for one second of one day to lose one millimetre of whatever ground she had left.

'I really would like to talk about this job,' said Patrick. 'Can we . . . ?'

He had his heavy expression on, a sort of brooding reproach. It was unusual, but Bianca had learned to respect it. Patrick's breaking point was seldom reached; the last time had been when Fergie had broken his arm playing rugby and she had refused, initially, to cancel an overnight trip she was on to Edinburgh.

'Darling, it's a huge sales conference and my speech is top of the bill – I *have* to be here.'

A few well chosen words had her on the next plane.

'Darling, of course we can,' she said now, ladling pasta on to his plate. 'I am totally at your disposal. So – are you more worried than excited by it? That's how you felt at first. Excited, I mean. And if so – well, tell me why.'

'Yes, well I did feel excited at first. But I've been thinking about it a lot more and actually it could be too exciting by half.'

Bianca reached for the Parmesan. 'The thing is—'

'Hi, Mum!'

'Oh – hello, Fergie. I thought you were supposed to be getting ready for bed?'

'I am, but I remembered I had to ask Dad something. Dad, can you play in the Parents' Day cricket match?'

'I expect so. But why on earth are you asking me now? It's not even this term.'

'I know, but I was meant to take the note back last week.'

'What note?'

'The one I didn't give you. And Mr Squires gave me a bollocking and—'

'Fergie, that's not a nice word!'

'Oh, Mu-um! Dad uses it.'

'Well . . . anyway, Fergie, yes,' said Patrick quickly, 'of course I'll play in the cricket match. Tell Mr Squires. Now off you go.'

Bianca looked rather helplessly at Patrick.

'Now what were we talking about?'

'My new job?'

'Of course. I'm sorry. Oh, God, Milly darling, what is it?'

'Mummy or Daddy, I need you to sign off my homework.'

'Milly, I asked you about that hours ago,' said Patrick.

'I know, but I hadn't done it then. And Mummy, I really need a new denim jacket.'

'Milly,' said Patrick, 'I'm sorry to be a boring old fart, but when exactly did you buy your last denim jacket?'

'Last term.'

'So it's not too small?'

'No, of course not. But it's, like, the wrong sort of denim.'

'Milly darling, that is not needing, that's *wanting*. We've talked about this before.'

Milly raised her large brown eyes briefly to the ceiling, folded her arms and waited in silence.

'I think,' Patrick said firmly, 'that since you now have about three denim jackets it should come out of your own allowance, not the clothes we buy for you. We're not a bottomless money pit – and oddly, we do have other things to spend our money on.'

'Well,' said Milly, 'it said in one of those articles about Mummy that she could command any fee she wanted. So—'

'Milly,' said Bianca sharply, 'I've told you before, most things you read in the papers are total rubbish. That's a silly remark put in by a silly journalist. And anyway, the sort of fee they're talking about is what I might need for a company.'

This wasn't quite true, but it seemed to deal with the situation.

'No! It said your personal fortune was considerable.'

'Well, I wish, is all I can say! Now, give me your homework and I'll sign it and then you must go to bed. It's late.'

'But—'

'Milly, I said bed!' said Bianca.

Milly looked at her, half snatched the book and walked out, closing the door rather firmly behind her. Bianca looked at Patrick.

'Do you think our little glow-worm is about to turn?'

'It would seem so.'

'Well, it was nice while it lasted. Oh, God, I'm sorry darling—'

'It's quite all right,' said Patrick, 'but I do want to talk to you some more now. I know it's not as important as your job, but . . .'

Bianca looked at him sharply. He didn't often resort to such tactics. When it happened it was a shock.

'Darling Patrick, don't be silly. You know perfectly well our jobs are equally important.'

'Are they?' His tone was mild, but it had an edge to it.

'Well, of course they are. It's just that right now mine is being extra-demanding. But – I'm sorry, and I should have listened before. Let's do it now. I meant it. I'm all yours. I'll go and say goodnight to the children and you make us some coffee.'

Patrick was just pouring the water on to the coffee grounds when the gentle ripple of notes that has become the trumpet call of the twenty-first century, the text message signal, came from Bianca's phone. He sighed. She was bound to check it when she came back; and looking at it, he saw it had come from Mike Russell.

'It can wait,' she said firmly when she saw it. 'Mike knows not to contact me at this time. Let's get back to your job. Tell me what you'll actually be doing.'

'Researching companies, looking into their accounts in huge detail, analysing things like – well, this is the example Finlayson gave me – let's say it's an international company: where they put their factories, what they pay for them, whether that really makes economic sense, or might it be a cover-up for some other expenditure, or does the wages bill seem a bit high—'

'But Patrick, what you do now is pore over company accounts. This would be the same, surely?'

'Yes, but suppose I missed it?' said Patrick.

'Missed what?'

'Well, some vital bit of information. I'd be letting them down totally.'

'But I just don't think you would,' said Bianca. 'You've got a mind like an electric drill. You just go on and on till you're satisfied every tiny thing is right. So you wouldn't miss whatever it was, the high wages or whatever.'

'Maybe, but—'

'Well, it's a huge move, I can see that. But it could be a terrific opportunity for you. You're so understimulated at BCB. *And* under-utilised, in my opinion. How do you feel about it? Do you want to do it?'

'Well, in some ways,' said Patrick. 'But it's just a bit daunting. And you know how I can't bear to let people down. You're right about the understimulation, though. I sometimes think if I died at my desk, it would be some time before anyone noticed.'

'Patrick!' Bianca felt remorseful. Spending most of her working life as she did, in a state of overstimulation, she realised she took the pleasure of that entirely for granted. 'Is it really that bad?'

'Not all the time,' said Patrick more cheerfully. 'I still quite enjoy it. But – if you think I should pursue this a bit further, I will. Only it does mean such changes in our lives. Like – well, like knowing the firm'll be mine one day. That's a pretty big thing to give up. We have huge commitments. Children, two properties, school fees—'

'Darling, I know all that. I just think you being so understimulated is as dangerous in its own way. Tell me more about Saul Finlayson.'

'Well, he's been working for one of the big banks based in

Switzerland. And he's not exactly setting up on his own, he's doing it with several others. Apparently a hedge fund isn't just run by one guy, it can be ten different people running the funds in ten different ways.'

'Yes, I think I knew that,' said Bianca and then added, carefully tactful, as she tried to be when her knowledge and experience outstripped Patrick's, 'but it's all a bit of a mystery, that stuff. What's he like? As I person I mean.'

'Odd. Awkward. Very direct. Apparently he's famous for never telling a lie. Which can be awkward personally, and Jonjo says has caused some tricky situations but I guess makes people more likely to trust him in business. I did like him, I have to say.'

'Well, that's important.'

'Indeed. The only thing I really grasped was that hedge funds need to make money every year and are judged on how often they do – not just do better than the market, which is what the pension funds do, for instance; and as we all know, that means they can end up not making money if it's a bad year. Hedge funds actually have to make money all the time, day on day, no matter what. They just cannot lose. That's a pretty scary proposition – incredibly stressful, apparently.'

'And how do you think you'd cope with that?' said Bianca. Patrick's stress threshold was notoriously low. He started worrying about traffic jams the night before a journey and they had never arrived at a wedding or a flight less than an hour before they needed to. 'And would that actually apply to what you'd be doing?'

'Not sure. I should think so. And stress is pretty contagious, wouldn't you say?'

'Can be. Well, I think you should see him again at the very least, tell him your worries and concerns. He won't expect you just to accept this job without exploring what it means pretty fully. If he does, you most assuredly don't want to work for him.'

'Yes,' said Patrick.

'And – hours, that sort of thing?'

She tried to keep the question casual, knowing how important it would be to her if the job made him unavailable to the family and its demands, hating herself for even glancing at, let alone probing into that facet of it.

'Well, obviously it would be rather different. I couldn't call my own shots, in that way, no doubt about it.'

'Yes, well we can get round that I'm sure,' she said briskly, knowing that sometimes they wouldn't. 'Away much?'

'I – didn't ask that.'

'Maybe you should, just so we could put that into the equation. I think you still need to know a bit more before you make your decision.'

'*We* make it, I hope,' he said.

'Patrick, it's your job, your life.'

'No,' he said, his eyes on her, thoughtful. 'It's ours.'

'Well, that's very nice of you. And I'd like to meet Saul Finlayson, please.'

'Of course. But only if you really think it's a good idea.'

'Let's say I really think it might be,' said Bianca. 'How is Jonjo? I'd like to see him again. Ask him to dinner soon, will you?'

'Yes, all right. He's got a new girlfriend, some sculptor.'

'A sculptor! God, he covers all the professions, doesn't he?'

'Literally,' said Patrick and grinned at his own joke.

'Maybe he and Mr Finlayson could come together. Is he married?'

'Divorced. I should imagine, though, he spends weekends on his yacht or jetting somewhere in his private plane rather than attending suburban supper parties.'

'Our supper parties are not suburban,' said Bianca briskly. 'Our life was described in the *Standard* last week as high-metropolitan, Patrick Bailey. I mean, how important is *that*?'

'Terribly. And I'll be sure to mention that when I meet Mr Finlayson,' said Patrick. He leaned forward and gave her a kiss. 'Thanks, darling.'

'What for?'

'Not underestimating me.'

'I never do that,' said Bianca. And it was true: she didn't.

* * *

Just the same, alone in her study later, she thought further about Patrick's possible career change. She would love him to have some glorious opportunity which would offer his excellent brain something to challenge him. Most of the time working at Bailey Cotton and Bailey seemed to her rather like a ramble in the park: comfortable, pleasant enough, but all on the flat with limited views.

If there was one thing more dangerous than an underutilised brain, it was an awareness of it. It rotted the soul and she could sense that he was beginning to acknowledge it and compare it with her own absorption. And she genuinely and deeply loved him and wanted him to be happy.

On the other hand – the present situation meant he was home at the same time every night and could give the children the sort of attention they needed. Which she really couldn't. And working long, late, stressful hours, neither would he. At a stroke her life as well as his would be altogether different and more difficult.

She was also genuinely concerned that he might find himself out of his depth; he was unused to stress, to harsh decision-making; he would be very much out of his comfort zone. And his was a gentle soul; he would know much anguish if he felt he had failed.

She wished she knew more about the job and, indeed, more about Saul Finlayson. She googled him.

Saul Murray Finlayson, Wikipedia informed her, had been born in Glasgow, but his parents moved to Lancashire while he was still very small and he had attended Manchester Grammar School, one of the great launch pads for successful male careers, from the age of seven onwards. He then went to Durham, where he got a First in history while still making time to deal, with modest success, in antique coins. After a few years with UBS he went to New York and worked for Chase Manhattan and then moved to Zurich where he ran the trading division of a large investment bank. He was now joining with four others setting up a hedge fund.

He was divorced with one small son, aged eight, and had homes in London and Berkshire; his hobby was flat racing.

A 'Twenty Questions' interview in the *FT* elicited some further facts: his three best features he said were patience, attention to detail and decisiveness; his three worst a bad temper, intolerance and a tendency to over-acquisitiveness. The two lists seemed slightly incompatible. He said he never switched off his phone, his guilty pleasure was chocolate – 'I know that's usually one for the girls' – and had he not been a banker, he would have liked to be a brain surgeon.

He sounded, depressingly, a cliché, apart from the chocolate; a photograph of him, presumably taken a few years ago, showed a shock of blond hair, a slightly gaunt face and a distinctly reluctant smile.

She wondered if the real thing might be a little more interesting or even engaging.

Florence was sitting at home, looking out some papers – her solicitor had told her to check something on her pension fund – and found herself drawn irresistibly to her stash of cuttings books on the House of Farrell. They went right back to 1953, when the company had just launched, before she had really known Athina, and when she was still working as a beauty consultant in Marshall and Snelgrove for Coty. She had met the already legendary Mrs Farrell when she presided over the counter of the new brand, coming in every week, sometimes to stand behind the counter, sometimes just to talk to the consultants. So elegant she had been, always perfectly groomed, in wonderfully tailored suits, and high-heeled court shoes with matching handbag, her nails long and varnished, her make-up impeccable. The girls on the Farrell counter were totally in awe of her.

Florence was not so easily intimidated, but then she didn't work for her. After a few weeks, Mrs Farrell would come over to her counter every time she came in, telling her how lovely it looked and admiring the products; she quite often bought something and would carry it away in the lovely flowery Marshall and Snelgrove bag. Florence knew perfectly well why she had done so (Coty's were not the only products she bought); it was to compare them with the Farrell offering, to study the packaging and the leaflets, and possibly to find something she could imitate.

And then one day Mrs Farrell had come over to her counter and asked her if she would telephone her when she had finished work and gave her a card with her address and number on it. Intrigued, Florence had done so, and found herself invited to join Mrs Farrell for tea, 'or a cocktail if that would be easier with your hours. We could meet at the Savoy, or the Dorchester; my husband would like to meet you, I know, and I might have a proposition for you, but we need to have a proper conversation and to get to know one another.'

Flattered but wary, Florence had said that would be delightful and agreed to meet the Farrells in the cocktail bar at the Dorchester the following Thursday. She spent a lot of time working out what to wear – her wardrobe was rather limited, as decreed by her modest income, but she felt this was so important she actually bought a Frank Usher dress and jacket in navy, trimmed with white, for the occasion. She wondered what exactly the glamorous Farrells might want to discuss with her – she could only hope it was employment, but it could be that they were simply trying to do some more espionage work. Whatever it was, cocktails at the Dorchester were not to be missed.

During the week, she did some research on the Farrells, and particularly Cornelius who was an unknown quantity. She was friendly with the press officer at Marshall's who kept all the articles about the store in her office; having heard why Florence wanted to know about them, she sorted out a manila folder of cuttings for her.

'He's quite a dish, Mr Farrell,' she said. 'I wish *I* was having cocktails with him.'

Florence reminded her briskly that Mrs Farrell would be there too, and took the folder home to study it.

Mr Farrell, photographed at Mrs Farrell's side at several functions and even with the two salesgirls in the store, was indeed quite a dish: tall and dark, with slicked-back hair and burning dark blue eyes, and wearing what were clearly very well-tailored suits.

It was hard to get much of an idea of what he was like, but he clearly laughed a lot, and he had given one interview to a paper on the brand: 'We think we are giving our customers something a little bit special, very skilled advice at the counter.' Cheeky, thought

Florence, as if none of the other brands did that. 'And we listen to them carefully and try to turn their ideas and what they want into products and colours for the next season.'

The interviewer had asked him how he had become involved with the rather feminine world of cosmetics and he had replied that his mother had been an actress and he used to watch her making up for her performances when he was quite a small boy and was allowed to go to her dressing room – 'a very big treat' – before a matinee. 'It was wonderful to watch her eyes growing bigger, her lips fuller as I sat there. I've been fascinated by what make-up could do for women ever since.'

Asked if he had ever thought of being an actor himself he had said, with what the journalist described as charming modesty, that he wasn't nearly talented enough. 'I thought I could succeed with cosmetics rather than on the stage. With my wife's help, of course. No, a great deal more than help: she is the prime mover behind the House of Farrell. I want us to be regarded as a team.'

Florence liked that; it showed modesty and some rather up-to-date thinking. Her view of men was coloured by the distinctly bombastic ones who ran the store and treated the women who worked there with a condescension that came close to rudeness. She much preferred the rather flamboyant chaps who did the make-up for special promotions, clearly homosexuals, although that was only hinted at, with reference to fairies and amidst much giggling in the ladies'. They were fun and gossipy and treated the girls as equals, admiring their hairstyles and their clothes and discussing films and music with them.

Cornelius Farrell clearly belonged to neither camp; he was a red-blooded man who not only admired women but liked them and valued them. Florence sat looking at his picture and rereading the article and thought how very fortunate Mrs Farrell was to have captured such an unusual example.

'Daddy! Hello, it's me!'

'Hello, my darling.' Bertie's heart always lifted when he heard Lucy's voice.

'I'm – well, can I come home this weekend?'

'Darling, of course you can. Want me to come and collect you?'

'Um – that might be nice. If you really don't mind.'

'Sweetheart, of course I don't mind. What time will you be ready?'

'Well, actually . . .'

'Yes?'

'I'm ready now.'

'But it's only Thursday. Lectures been cancelled?'

'Um, sort of . . .'

'Now what does that mean? You're not cutting them, are you, Lucy? You know that's not a good idea.'

'Well, you see, Daddy, I'm not going to any more. I'm leaving uni. Now.'

'Lucy, you can't take that sort of decision on your own, there's far too much at stake.'

'Like – like what?'

'Like your future.'

'Dad, have you read the statistics lately? Half the graduates in the country can't get decent jobs. They're working in coffee shops. And that's the lucky ones. I honestly don't think a degree's going to do me any good at all. Unless I wanted to be a teacher and I don't. It's different for Rob, he's doing medicine and there's a cast-iron job at the end of it. Not for me there isn't. Honestly, I've thought about it really hard, and I know I don't want to stay here. Some days I feel so bored and – and disillusioned I could cry. Oh, Daddy, I'd like to come home and explain properly. Try and make you understand.'

'Well, of course I – we – will listen very carefully to what you have to say. But Lucy, it's not even the end of term. Surely it would be better to see that out at the very least?'

'Daddy, what would be the point?'

'The point,' said Bertie, 'is that it might look just a little better on your CV. You have to think of these things, Lucinda. You're not a child any more.'

71

He hardly ever called her Lucinda. It meant he was serious. If not actually cross.

'Well, all right. I'll – think about it. But – well, when can you come? I so want to see you.'

'I'll come on Saturday morning. As early as I can.'

Bertie put the phone down. He had a sense of frustration at the thought of what she was so wantonly throwing away, but she was touchingly interested in him. It was soothing, set against Priscilla's uber-involvement in her charities and her slightly disdainful disinterest in him.

And Lucy would provide a most useful tool in the battle over the house – the valuation of it at two and a half million had sent Priscilla into overdrive. For a time at least Lucy would need her room, and besides she loved the house, would be horrified at her mother's plan. And it would be lovely to have her at home, very lovely indeed. Apart from adoring and admiring his children, Bertie loved their company, they interested him and made him laugh and, perhaps most important of all, restored his faith in himself.

They were his greatest accomplishment, without a doubt: and actually, as he thought increasingly these days, his only one.

Chapter 9

'Could I have a word?'

Bianca looked up; the person she most liked to see in the office – one of the very few people she *ever* wanted to see in the office – Susie Harding, stood in the doorway. So pretty, with her long blond hair, her rather remarkable grey eyes, so well-dressed, mostly in wrap dresses or shifts, her long, tanned legs – God, these girls must spend a lot on tanning products – her wonderful collection of high, high heels; so cheerful always, smiling that amazing smile of hers. She was a life enhancer of the very highest degree. Only right now she wasn't smiling.

'Susie, of course. Sit down. Glass of juice, water?'

'No, no I'm fine. Sorry to barge in but your secretary wasn't there—'

'She wasn't there because I've returned her to the agency,' said Bianca. 'She was depressing me. You don't have a friend do you who'd like a very nice job as PA?'

'I'll put my mind to it, if you're serious.'

'Utterly. I want someone bright and calm and, above all, cheerful. And who doesn't mind working late sometimes. And who finds the same things funny as I do. I mean, you'd do perfectly, but you're overqualified and anyway, you're already taken.' She smiled at Susie.

'Well – thanks. But it's actually my job I've come about. I'm sure you're going to brief me in due course and I know you're terribly busy and—'

'Don't let's worry about that.'

'It's just that I'm completely kicking my heels at the moment. The press aren't interested in us at all, the way we are, and – well, it would be great to get some idea if there was anything I could do now. Instead of irritating all the journos and bloggers trying to interest them in – well, diddly squat.'

Bianca laughed. 'I love that expression.'

'You see, I just can't wait to get to work. Relaunches are the toughest things of all, of course, but they're also a huge challenge.'

'You're right,' said Bianca, with a sigh. 'We're talking about taking something old and stale and difficult and untidy and making it vibrant and desirable and accessible all at the same time. On a fairly tight budget, I might add. Walking on water, easy by comparison.'

'I know. And then there's risking losing all the old customers, and finding enough new ones to make that worthwhile. But – goodness, you can do it if anyone can. And it would be huge fun.'

'Tell me, Susie, if you were me, what would be your first line of attack? The first thing you did?'

'The products. They're ghastly, most of them. Too many bad, not enough good. Have you been down to the lab yet?'

'No, I'm going on Thursday.'

'Honestly, everyone is at least fifty. All hired by the Farrells decades ago, mostly briefed by Lady Farrell. Ghastly. No use repackaging, or re-advertising anything *they* make. Might as well try and tell people baked beans are strawberries. That's not a very good analogy,' she added. 'Sorry.'

'Oh, I don't know. What products *do* seem right to you?'

'The Cream,' said Susie without hesitation.

'Really? Even to someone as young as you?'

'Yes. It's just the best skincare product in the world.'

'But it's not very scientifically based. Surely in these days of free radicals and superdepth vitamin balance . . .' She made a face at Susie.

Susie laughed. 'No. But I think it just might be time for a bit less of all that stuff. The Cream is just a yummy, incredibly absorbent night cream. You can wear it to bed with your boyfriend without smelling like an old lady.'

Bianca grinned. 'Oh, I wish we could say that! What wouldn't that do for the brand!'

'Well, you could sort of imply it I suppose,' said Susie. 'You couldn't actually say it, because all the ladies who love it would be shocked, stop buying it and buy Estée Lauder or Clarins instead.'

'They might not,' said Bianca, 'if it was done cleverly enough. But you'll have to tread water a bit longer, I'm afraid, Susie. I'm still so much thinking, getting the feel of everything – but any ideas you have, let me have them. I need all the help I can get.'

'OK, thanks. I just didn't want you to think I was a complete waste of space.'

'I certainly didn't.' Susie would make a brilliant member of a new team, Bianca thought. Also a key one. PR and the social networks were so clearly the way to tell people about the new House of Farrell. The advertising budget she had agreed with Mike was tiny, a guttering candle set against the huge arc lights of Lauder and Chanel. She was going to have to box clever; use brains rather than brawn. Well, that was what she was about. That was what the whole thing was about. Meanwhile, she had an appointment with Caro; a rather less promising team member . . .

Caro was clearly highly intelligent and hugely confident, but as far as Bianca could see, had entirely failed to make any kind of proper career for herself. Unless you counted being personnel director of Farrell's, at which she was spectacularly bad. Of course she did have a very successful, high-flying husband, but they had no children. She could have been anything, Bianca thought, a lawyer, a banker, gone into commercial life . . . why settle for a job in a business with which she seemed to have no sympathy? Well, the obvious answer was that she was Athina Farrell's daughter and did what was expected of her.

Bianca wondered, as she waited for Caro, what Cornelius had been like; obviously charming and good-looking to judge by the various photographs of him that still adorned the boardroom, and everyone seemed to have loved him, but there any real sense of him ended. Intriguing.

'Ah, Caro,' she said, standing up as her door opened. 'Do come in. How are you? Coffee, tea?'

'I am well, thank you. These are difficult times of course, everyone is in a state of slight anxiety—'

'Really? I'm sorry. I can understand it, of course. Is there anyone in particular I should know about? Talk to them, perhaps?'

'No, no,' said Caro, looking rather edgy. 'I can deal with it perfectly well. Thank you.' In other words, I don't need you to tell me what to do.

'OK. Well, if anything changes let me know. Now, what I really need your help with is getting a handle on the report lines and I thought you, as personnel director, could help me.'

'Report lines?'

'Yes,' said Bianca, smiling at her sweetly. 'You know, who reports to whom. I'm finding it a bit baffling. The consultants, for instance, seem to be part of marketing. I don't quite get that. Why not sales? Particularly as we don't have a marketing director to report to.'

'Well,' said Caro, 'we did. Until last year.'

'And?'

'Well, he clashed increasingly with my mother.'

'I – I see.'

'Perhaps you don't,' said Caro, her tone growing cool. 'Marketing, in the sense we have always understood it here, product development, promotion, advertising, image, always came under the aegis of my mother. And my father, of course, when he was alive. They moulded Farrell's, after all. And my mother has always felt the consultants, the face of Farrell, as we call them, should be her complete responsibility when my father died. Then, in the nineties, we decided that a marketing specialist in the field should be hired. The person we had, a woman, was extremely good and worked very happily and successfully, was responsible for many innovations and developments, but shortly after my father died she left. After that we had two more, both men, but my mother found them impossible

76

to work with, whereas Lawrence Ford, the marketing manager, works well with her.'

'And that's why the consultants come under marketing?'

'Yes.'

'I see,' said Bianca again. 'Now, how about IT?'

'Well, each department has its own IT manager. So we have one for marketing, one for sales, one for the finance and admin.'

'You've never envisaged having an IT department as such?'

'Well, no. The support we have is perfectly adequate. It's not as if we have a serious online presence.' She felt rather proud of that phrase.

'Not at the moment,' said Bianca.

'You surely wouldn't contemplate selling Farrell online?' said Caro, shocked. 'My mother would never agree to such a thing.'

'Caro, right now I'm contemplating everything and anything. And all the other houses have an online presence, as you call it. It's an invaluable promotional tool, apart from anything else. Have you looked at the websites recently?'

'Not . . . too recently,' said Caro.

'You really should. They're impressive.'

'I'll try and find the time,' said Caro. She clearly saw studying rival websites akin to reading glossy magazines. Which of course it was, in a way . . .

God, this place is a nightmare, Bianca thought, sinking into her chair. The financial meltdown, the falling sales, the disastrous marketing, the frankly lousy products, the incompetent management, the complete lack of morale – they were familiar demons, she had fought them before and won. But the infiltration of this family into every corner of the company, the power it wielded, this was new. She had realised, of course, that they must be taken on and that Lady Farrell was a powerful and difficult force, resistant to her very presence; but she had not reckoned with the breadth and depth of that force, and the unquestioning faith in its tenets. Everybody, at every level in every department, saw Lady Farrell as the unarguable authority on everything and believed that the failure of the company was simply an unfortunate fact that had been forced upon her and thus on them. And anyone who did not share that view must clearly be wrong.

In order to change the company, and make it work, Bianca was coming to realise, she had to overcome not only Athina Farrell but the faith of her followers and convert them to her.

Creating world peace looked rather simple by comparison.

'You want to be *what*?'

'Oh, darling! Waste all that very expensive education!'

'Waste what's a very good brain, anyway!'

'. . . completely pointless existence . . .'

'. . . find it terribly boring . . .'

'. . . ghastly models . . .'

'. . . training costs what???!!! . . .'

'. . . you can just forget all about it, Lucy . . .'

'. . . really quite worried about money at the moment . . .'

Lucy faced them down, her green eyes, her grandmother's eyes, steady in the face of their horror. It was pathetic; anyone would think she'd announced she wanted to go on the streets.

'You know what,' she said, 'you're being ridiculous. It's a great job, one of the most sought after there is these days, fun, and according to one lovely girl I talked to, being a make-up artist is more than fifty per cent psychiatrist, so whatever brain I do have would actually be used quite a bit. I think you're dishing out some very old-fashioned prejudice and actually, seeing as the beauty industry is what's supported all of us, and paid for the very expensive education you're banging on about, I think you're being a bit hypocritical. You should be grateful I've left uni – it was going to get a lot more expensive by the time I'd got my degree. And I'm sorry you think a course costing nine thousand pounds a year is out of the question. It seemed pretty reasonable to me.'

'Well, if it's so reasonable why don't you find the money yourself?' snapped Priscilla. 'The London College of Fashion, indeed! It sounds little better than a finishing school to me.'

'Oh stop it!' said Lucy, her voice growing tearful. 'You're being so – so blind. And unkind. Dismissing what I really want to do, making it sound pathetic.'

'Lucy,' said Bertie, sounding nervous, 'darling, don't get upset.'

'I *am* upset. I think you just showed how little you understand me. Well, I'm going to do it anyway, I'll find a way, just you see. I'll talk to Grandy. *She* won't think it's a – a – what did you say? A pointless boring existence She might even think it's a bit odd you thinking it would be.'

'Lucy –' said Bertie nervously. His mother would accept anything Lucy told her, however distorted or far from the truth. 'Lucy, don't be silly—'

'It's you who's being silly,' said Lucy witheringly, and walked out of the room.

That was a lie, Bianca thought, watching and listening. Told with much conviction and an earnest smile.

'This is a very lovely product, madam, and in some new shades for summer . . .' The consultant's voice, as she attempted to make a sale, trailed off. The product did have some lovely shades, to be sure, but the product – a new foundation, in colours that were old-fashioned and a texture that belonged twenty years back – was appalling. She had tried them, tried all the products, day after day, growing increasingly dispirited. These products were years out of date, not just months. The consultant was talking again. 'Let me put it on the back of your hand – there! How does that look? Too heavy? Ah, well we do have a lighter one, let me just see . . .'

She rummaged in a drawer under the counter and while she was doing it, the customer walked rather self-consciously off, drawn to a rival display across the hall. Bianca had been there for almost an hour now, occasionally moving to a different part of the department, observing the ebb and flow of customers to the Farrell counter. Not that flow exactly described it; in that hour, only three women had stopped for long enough for the consultant to approach them, the rest hurrying past with an apologetic 'not now thank you'. Of those three, one had bought The Cream, of which she was clearly an aficionado – the consultant had seemed to know her. The other two had bought minor items – lipsticks and eyeshadows, and now this one was being pressed into trying the new summer foundation. Actually more suited to an Arctic winter . . .

But at least they were potential customers; and that was what Bianca was doing here, standing in a rather quiet corner of this hugely busy department in White & Co Chemists in Birmingham, studying them, doing her own personal survey. Like most of its sisters, the concession in Birmingham was haemorrhaging money.

The customers, to whom Bianca had just devoted her time – customer knowledge and the harnessing of it being the key to success – were middle-aged, middle-income, middle-class, and definitely not fashionable. Bianca had deduced this rather unscientifically by hanging around cosmetic counters and talking to the consultants – but there was precious little of a more scientific nature available. And as far as she could see, the typical Farrell customer was, for the most part, wedded to the brand by The Cream, moving to the other counters for make-up and, more dangerously, in terms of potential desertion, sometimes to other skincare products as well. There was no way the nice, kindly, old-fashioned Farrell ladies serving them were paying their way. Bianca was moving swiftly to the conclusion the consultants would all have to go . . .

Chapter 10

Dinner, which Jonjo insisted was to be on him, had been arranged for the following Saturday. The sculptress would be there – it was getting serious, Jonjo had told Patrick, which meant he'd now seen her more than three times – and Saul Finlayson would join them for a drink beforehand.

'He just doesn't do dinner at the weekends,' Jonjo explained on the phone to Bianca, 'insists on spending the time with his son. Who's with the ex during the week, so weekends are pretty sacred.'

'I approve of that,' said Bianca.

'You're lucky they're in London this weekend because the little chap—'

'What's his name?'

'Dickon.'

'Nice name!'

'Yeah. Anyway, he's got some birthday party he really wanted to go to. Then Saul's picking him up, so he'll only have half an hour. But at least you'll be able to get some sort of handle on him. Can't wait to see what you make of him, lot of women find him very sexy.'

'Oh really?' said Bianca. 'Jonjo, my only interest in him is whether he's going to be nice to Patrick.'

'I don't know that he's into being nice,' said Jonjo. 'If he pays the old boy well and doesn't throw too much shit at him, that'll be doing pretty well.'

'Yes, well there are ways and ways of throwing shit,' said Bianca, 'and I should know.'

81

'You should, darling. How's the new muck heap?'

'Pretty mucky. Tough one, this one. I'm at the stage of wondering what I'm doing there. Now tell me quickly about your sculptor lady. Then I must dash.'

'She's – well, she's fantastic,' said Jonjo. 'Very sexy, amazing legs—'

'Jonjo, I'm not interested in her physical attributes! How old is she, what's her name, what's her work about?'

'She does bronzes,' said Jonjo, 'sort of abstract. Which sell for shedloads. Can't see quite why, to be honest, but anyway . . . name's Guinevere. Guinevere Bloch. Very, very clever lady, successful too.'

'Goodness, yes, I've heard of her,' said Bianca. 'She's very A-list. There was a piece in the *Standard* last week about the new faces in the art scene. She was in that. No pictures, though. How old is she – sort of?'

'Oh – mid-thirties. I'll send you a picture of her. Coming over now . . . Got to go, darling, see you Saturday, Fino, just off Charlotte Street, it's really cool – Spanish food, all tapas, Guinevere's mad about it.'

'Well, in that case I'm sure I'll like it too,' said Bianca. 'Bye, Jonjo, really looking forward to it.'

Sixty seconds later a picture of Guinevere Bloch arrived by email. She was sitting against the incredible backdrop of Canary Wharf at night, clearly taken in Jonjo's apartment, pouting at the camera, Posh-style. She had a great mane of rather artfully curled blond hair, was wearing a very low-cut black top with an extremely impressive cleavage tipping out of it, and a great deal of gold jewellery. Bianca thought she would put quite a lot of money on her being at the upper end of mid-thirties, and then settled down to the daily horror of trying to round up the sales figures.

There was a tap on the door.

'Sorry. Only me . . .' She felt inordinately pleased to see Bertie. He might not be the most dynamic person on the staff and was probably the worst financial director she had ever known, but he was one of the very few people she actually liked at Farrell's.

More importantly, everyone else seemed to like him too – and he was certainly trying hard to do what she wanted.

'Hi, Bertie. Come on in. I'm just trying to sort out the KPIs, get them off to Mike.'

He looked at her anxiously, then said, 'KPIs?'

'Key Performance Indicators.' How had this company survived at all? 'Basically sales figures. I have to get them in every day. They don't make very cheerful reading, but – anyway, glad to stop for a bit. What can I do for you, Bertie?'

'Er – Susie said you might be looking for a PA.'

'Oh, yes.' It seemed very unlikely he would know anybody remotely suitable.

'Friend of my son – well, older sister of said friend. Charming. Came to supper last night. She's between jobs, very impressive, very tall – not that that's got anything to do with it – got her CV here if you'd like to look at it, married to a very steady chap.'

Bianca half smiled at this observation, so like Bertie, and so apparently irrelevant, and then she reflected that a PA married to an unsteady chap could well cause her problems.

'She sounds good so far,' she said carefully.

'Yes, I just felt you and she would get along really well. And she's extremely calm, which I imagine would be a good thing.'

'It certainly would. Thank you so much,' she said, smiling politely and taking the CV. It seemed highly unlikely that this tall girl, whoever she was, would be remotely suitable, but she didn't want to discourage him. 'Thank you, Bertie, very thoughtful of you.'

She glanced at the CV – then sat back and read it intently. And looked up at Bertie.

'When do you think she could come in and see me?' she said.

Jemima Pendleton moved into Bianca's office three days later. She was indeed very tall, six foot of breathtaking calm and efficiency, rather beautiful in a quiet sort of way, with long brown hair and large brown eyes, a voice that would have stilled a hurricane, low and gentle, and a smile that made Bianca feel better just looking at it.

She was just thirty, had worked for the Foreign Office, a

barristers' chambers and an IT company where she'd been secretary to the managing director. She could type at eighty words a minute, and do shorthand at 140 if required, plus her technical skills were awesome. She could, as she said to Bianca with a quiet smile, tame a spreadsheet, a set of sales figures (she had taken over the KPIs by the end of the week), absorb information as if by osmosis, and had a near-photographic memory. Caught without her phone or her iPad and therefore Bianca's diary, she could still recall every engagement for several weeks to come. She didn't mind dealing with domestic crises, liaising in her very first week with Sonia with cool competence when Fergie got hit on the head by a cricket ball and was taken to hospital with suspected concussion and neither Bianca nor Patrick could be reached for at least an hour, and on another occasion, when Bianca had a formal dinner and brought odd shoes to the office and Sonia was out collecting Milly from a party, called a cab, fetched the missing shoes and brought them back to the office while continuing to answer emails on her iPad almost without a break.

In spite of her steady husband she worked as early or as late as Bianca; the only thing wrong with her, as far as Bianca could see, was that she could quite clearly be running the company herself in a matter of months, and being a PA was not going to satisfy her for long. However, she explained to Bianca with her lovely, gentle smile that actually she loved being a PA and she didn't want to do anything any more ambitious. When Bianca asked her why not, she said she had a project she was very involved in that absorbed her evenings and weekends, and she liked to keep some energy in reserve for that. She didn't elaborate any further and Bianca didn't press her, much as she wanted to. She just thanked God almost hourly for her – and Bertie too whenever she saw him.

'Lady Farrell?'

'Yes, this is she.'

'Lady Farrell, it's Marjorie, Marjorie Dawson. Do forgive me for telephoning you like this, but I am rather – rather worried and I wonder if you could find the time for a – a conversation.'

'Marjorie, of course.' Athina's voice dripped graciousness. She was very fond of Marjorie Dawson. 'But this is not it. Come in and see me, why don't you?'

'Oh – well – that would be very nice, but I'm working full-time at Rolfe's, as you know, and evenings are out of the question, with Terry – my husband – to look after.'

'Ah, yes, poor man.' Athina's voice did not exactly vibrate with sympathy. 'How is he?'

'Not – not very well. And we've just heard that due to the cuts his care will almost undoubtedly be less good.'

'I'm sorry. But of course deeply necessary for the country, these cuts; no one seems to quite understand that there's no alternative, that there's simply no money in the kitty . . .' Had Bianca heard this conversation, she might have found it puzzling that Lady Farrell was not able to extend this piece of financial savvy to her own position and that of Farrell's. 'But of course it's difficult for everybody. We're all in it together, as Mr Cameron says. Anyway, Marjorie, take a morning off. How about Friday?'

'Well, if you're sure . . .'

'I'm quite sure. Shall we say eleven? Here in my office?'

'Thank you, Lady Farrell, so much. Er – there is one other thing. It is rather – confidential, what I want to talk to you about. It concerns the – some new regulations.'

'Marjorie,' said Athina, 'you can rest assured I will mention your visit and its cause to no one. Especially to the new management. We are still in charge, you know. Everything they do has to be with our approval. So if something is seriously worrying you, then I need to know about it first.'

'Thank you, Lady Farrell. Till Friday, then.'

'Jemima – '

'Yes, Bianca?'

'I'd like to do a couple of store checks on Friday morning. I thought Kingston, and then perhaps Rolfe's in Guildford.'

'Fine. I'll sort out a car.'

* * *

'My darling, I think that's a lovely idea. Your grandfather would have been thrilled! So much more sensible than the other idea, far too many graduates about these days.'

Lucy smiled at her.

'I know. And I'm so excited about it. The thing is, Mummy and Daddy aren't keen . . .'

'Why not?'

'Oh, they wanted me to stay at uni and aren't prepared to pay for any course I might need to do.'

'Very stupid of them, in my view.'

'Well, I've found a really good short course, much cheaper than the big famous ones, run by a school called FaceIt. It only takes three months and then, when you've graduated, they become your agent.'

'That sounds wonderful, darling. And I can't help feeling three months is quite enough.'

'Well, I'm glad you approve. I thought you would.'

There was a silence; then, 'So, Lucy, how much does this course cost?'

'Oh – two thousand pounds.'

'Good gracious! Quite a lot, Lucy, for three months. You could learn most of it from one of our own consultants so I think you might consider that.'

'Well, that's a wonderful idea as far as it goes,' said Lucy, swiftly tactful, 'but this course does things like theatre make-up – I want to work in films you see, one day – and hairstyling and things like that, which would mean more job opportunities for me.'

'Yes, I see. Even so, one of our girls could give you a grounding. One of our top consultants, Marjorie Dawson, is coming in to see me on Friday as a matter of fact; I'll have a word with her.'

'That'd be great.' She could hardly refuse; and she might learn a bit. 'But I also wondered if—' Their eyes met in perfect under-standing.

'If I'd pay for the course?' said Athina briskly.

'Well, not pay for it, but maybe lend me the money. I'd pay you back, set up a standing order and everything.'

A long silence; then 'Yes, Lucy. And I'm glad you didn't ask for me to pay for it.'

'I wouldn't dream of it! Thank you, Grandy. Very much.'

'That's all right. One other thing you might consider, which would provide you with a bit of pocket money, is working on one of the Farrell counters on Saturdays. You'd learn a lot. How would you feel about that?'

'Oh, it would be brilliant!' said Lucy, carefully enthusiastic.

'Good. Well, I'll organise that then. It will be good to have one of the younger generation involved in the firm. All helps with coping with these people.'

'Yes, I suppose so. Um – what are they like?'

'Oh, the chief woman, Bianca Bailey, is impressive and not unlikeable, but I've yet to see proof that she's going to do any good. Now darling, how would you like to come out to tea with your old granny one day soon? I'm told the Wolseley is rather splendid.'

'I'd love to.' How many grannies knew about the Wolseley, coolest place in town for tea at the moment?

'Good. Then it's a date. One day next week? And then you can show me a prospectus of this place and tell me more about it. Can they take you?'

'Yes, next term. They had a cancellation and it's quite important they have an even number of people on each course.'

'Why?'

'Well, you work in pairs, you see, making each other up. It does make sense. I'm so excited Grandy, thank you so, so much.'

'That's all right, darling, I'm glad you felt you could ask me. Now, how about next Thursday?'

'Can I help you, madam?'

Bianca looked gloomily at the Farrell's display in Rolfe's of Guildford. It was neat, dull and uninviting. Not that that was the fault of the consultant: the promotional material was sent from head office. And the stand itself, horribly dated looking, was down to Farrell's as well, of course. The cost of building it and maintaining it and then the cost of the space in the store – it all consumed a lot of money.

Moreover, there was no one apparently in charge. She asked to see the manager, who told her Marjorie had been summoned to head office for a meeting . . . 'By Lady Farrell herself – she's still in charge of the whole firm, you know. The young lady on the opposite counter is keeping an eye on things but is there anything I can help you with?'

'No, no, that's fine. Thank you very much.'

'Marjorie, dear, do sit down. Would you like tea or coffee? And how are things at Rolfe's? Such a nice store, one of my favourites.'

'Oh – a bit quiet. Of course, no one's having an easy time, it's the recession . . .'

Marjorie's voice tailed off as she tried to crush the picture of the heaving mass that had been the Brandon counter the evening before during late-night shopping.

'Yes, of course. Well, it can't go on for ever, I remember the one in the seventies – sugar, Marjorie? – it was far worse, although no one will admit it now. Anyway, tell me what you're worried about.'

'Well, recession or not, our weekly takings are quite – quite seriously down.'

'How seriously?'

'Oh, over the past twelve months, about forty per cent.'

'I see. Well, that *is* serious. I haven't seen your figures for the past two weeks—'

'Oh, but now we have to submit them daily.'

'On whose instructions?'

'Well, we have to send them in to Mr Ford.'

'I have never heard anything more absurd. Complete waste of your time. I shall stop it at once. Christine . . .'

'Yes, Lady Farrell?'

'Ask Mr Ford to come up here right away, would you?'

Lawrence Ford came in looking in equal parts anxious and unctuous.

'Lady Farrell?'

'Mr Ford, what is all this nonsense about the consultants having to submit daily sales figures?'

'Oh – well yes, they do. And other sales figures as well. From the reps and the warehouse.'

'By whose instructions?'

'Mrs Bailey's, Lady Farrell.'

'Such an absurd waste of time and effort. Are they sent by post? Or telephone?'

'No, no, by email. It is rather tedious because I have to collate them all and, of course, there is very little change from one day to the next. But I believe that when the new IT system is installed it will be very simple, because they'll come in automatically.'

'The new IT system? Oh, yes, I see. Well, thank you, Mr Ford. I think until then this ridiculous new system should be cancelled. I'll have a word with Mrs Bailey. You remember Marjorie Dawson of course?'

'Yes, of course. Good morning, Marjorie. Everything all right down at Rolfe's?'

'Yes, thank you, Mr Ford.'

He left after making something akin to a bow.

'He's very good, you see,' said Athina, her voice tinged with complacency, 'he knows exactly where you all work. Anyway, Marjorie, those figures aren't good, I agree.'

'No indeed. And I do know that there is a minimum margin that makes the concession viable in a store. I – I fear very much that in Rolfe's I am not meeting that margin.'

'Marjorie, you can leave me to worry about that, I think.'

'But I can't, Lady Farrell. I hear there are big changes in the pipeline, and I just wondered if – if – well, you see, many of the smaller houses don't have consultants any more . . .'

'Never listen to gossip, Marjorie. I do assure you that if there is anything to worry about you will hear it from me.'

'Yes, but if I were to lose my job – well I don't know what would happen. Terry can't work as you know, and – well, of course I could get another job, but in this climate I think that might take time and so the sooner I know the better . . .' She was very pale and her lip trembled slightly.

Athina looked at her, her expression at its most indomitable. 'Marjorie, listen to me. The consultants are absolutely essential to us, for information about the range and the customer for a start. I cannot envisage a situation where Farrell's would cease to employ you. I am having a meeting with Mrs Bailey today, and I shall of course speak to her and get her confirmation that this is right; meanwhile I want you to stop worrying and concentrate on your job, which is selling the House of Farrell.'

'Yes, Lady Farrell.'

'I want to hear how the spring lipstick colours went in a minute, but first I have a favour to ask you. My granddaughter Lucy would very much like to come and work on the counter on Saturdays. She is interested in joining the company but first she wants to work as a make-up artist; nothing like first-hand practical experience. And I think you can be very helpful to her. And she to you, of course. She is attending some college or other, but I thought she could help you with the ladies on Saturdays. Would that be all right?'

Bianca went into the boardroom early for lunch with the Farrells. She wanted to give herself every possible advantage and had her laptop open and was studying the screen when they came in. All together as they always did.

'Hello,' she said, smiling at them, standing up. 'Can I get you anything, juice, elderflower water? Sandwiches will be in in a minute. Er – Lady Farrell, before we begin, can I just ask you if a consultant called Marjorie Dawson came in this morning?'

'Yes, she did,' said Athina, 'at my invitation.'

'I see. Might I ask why?'

'She was worried about something. I felt I could reassure her. And I was right.'

'I see. Was it a personal matter?'

'Not entirely. Although her circumstances made it more so.'

'And – you arranged this with the manager at Rolfe's – that she should not be there this morning?'

90

'I did.'

'And – who did you think might do her work while she wasn't there?'

'A colleague. Mrs Bailey, I really don't—'

'Because I went there this morning, to Rolfe's, to do a store check. The Farrell counter was quite obviously not being looked after. It wasn't very impressive. I would have liked to have known about it.'

'Mrs Bailey,' said Athina, 'if I want to call in a member of staff I shall do so. Mrs Dawson was personally hired by my husband, as were most of the consultants, and if one of them is worried about anything, I think I should make it my business to reassure them. It's called personnel management,' she added. The words 'in case you didn't know' hung in the air.

'Well, I'm afraid it is not for you any longer to call a girl away from her work, without a word to anyone. And if that girl has a professional problem, then it is *my* concern.'

'I would have thought your concerns were greater than that at the moment,' said Athina.

'Lady Farrell, *everything* is my concern. Until I am satisfied that reporting lines are in place and—'

'Reporting lines? Ah, yes. Perhaps you could tell me what this nonsense is about everyone reporting their figures daily.'

'Not nonsense, Lady Farrell. Those daily figures are absolutely key in helping me to assess how the business is doing. Every modern company – every retail modern company, certainly smaller ones – requires such information. You've never heard of Key Performance Indicators?'

'I have not. I only know that their collation is causing considerable extra workload in several departments.'

'Well, when we have a new director of IT – Information Technology – he or she will install a system of sales reporting, among other things. And that will make the collation of information very much quicker and simpler.'

'I see. And – why have we not been informed of this?'

'It is on the agenda today. I propose to brief an agency to look for one.'

'Why an agency?' asked Caro. 'I am in charge of the appointment of staff.'

'Caro, with the greatest respect, I don't think you would quite know the sort of person we are looking for, or even where to look. I don't know myself. Meanwhile, Lady Farrell, I would like to express my disappointment that you feel you can remove people from their places of work at will without recourse to anyone—'

'Mrs Bailey, I repeat, Mrs Dawson is a friend. She has an invalid husband, feared the new regime here might be putting her job at risk and needed to know if that was likely. So I told her her job was absolutely safe, that there was nothing for her to worry about. She seemed very grateful.'

Bianca's expression changed. 'Lady Farrell, you have no authority to give that kind of assurance.'

'I beg your pardon?'

'No one can give Mrs Dawson that assurance. Not you, not I, not anybody. Like everything else at the moment, the consultants, and their costs and effectiveness are being assessed. They are an extremely expensive department and they must pay their way. At this moment, they don't seem to be. That's all I have to say.'

'So do I understand you to say that there is a serious likelihood that all these extremely nice women loyal to Farrell's over many years, will be thrown on the scrap heap?'

'You're over-anticipating what I might be going to do. What I refuse to say is that any of their jobs are guaranteed. They can't be. The company isn't paying its way and I am here to find ways to make it do so.'

'At an appalling cost,' said Athina, 'of personal happiness and security.'

'Unfortunately, personal security has to be paid for.'

'That,' said Athina, 'is one of the harshest things I have ever heard in all my years in this business.'

'Well, I'm sorry, Lady Farrell. Unfortunately, operating in the real world requires commercial reality.'

'So what am I to tell poor Marjorie Dawson?'

'Nothing at the moment. Hopefully we can continue to employ

her, possibly in another capacity. When will you be speaking to her again?'

Athina hesitated, then said, 'As a matter of fact, next Saturday. I have arranged for my granddaughter to work on the counter with Mrs Dawson, to gain some work experience. I'm taking her down there personally, to introduce her to the manager and so on.'

'I'm sorry, Mother, what was that?'

Bertie had been listening to the exchange with an expression of devout misery on his face.

'Lucy has been to see me, told me about her plans to be a make-up artist. I think it's a splendid idea, I've encouraged her—'

'Mother, you shouldn't have done that! Priscilla and I are very opposed to this plan of hers to leave university. We'd told her we can't possibly encourage it.'

'She told me. A great mistake if I might say so. Far better in this economic climate to have some practical experience than a fairly useless degree. I've agreed to loan her the money for the fees of this course she wants to do.'

'Mother!' Caro, unusually, came on to her brother's side. 'I think that's a little unfair to Bertie and Priscilla. Lucy is their daughter.'

'And she's my granddaughter and I like to help her. She can earn a bit of money and gain a great deal in other ways.'

'And who will pay her this money?' asked Bianca, who had been listening patiently.

'Farrell's can pay her. She will be working, after all; she's not just going to sit there all day.'

'No, Lady Farrell, Farrell's will *not* pay her. There is an absolute freeze on any extra staff, as you very well know,' Bianca said evenly.

'But she's part of the family!'

'Then I suggest the family pay her. Ah, look, sandwiches! How very welcome. I have here the agenda for the rest of this meeting, so may I ask you to look at it while we begin our lunch?'

Athina stood up. 'I'm sorry. I really don't feel I can stay for the meeting. I have been extremely upset and, I might add, humiliated. I am shocked at you, Mrs Bailey, I had thought you had more humanity. Clearly I was mistaken. Bertie, Caro, you can stay if you wish. I am leaving.'

'So – she left,' said Bianca, recounting this to Patrick over supper. 'And Caro and Bertie stayed. I think they felt they had to, or it would have looked as if they were totally under her thumb, which of course they are. She – Caro – is completely useless, but I do like him more and more. I wish I could find something I thought he could do but so far . . . oh God, Patrick, this is a tough one! And I still don't know what I'm doing: the more I dig, the less there seems to be there. No good people, no systems, nothing to build on. It's a classic.'

'There must be *some* good people.'

'There's Susie and Jemima, of course, but I brought her in. Lady Farrell is an asset, I suppose, or could be, but she's a complete nightmare and warfare's now open between us, so it will be even more difficult than it was . . .'

'There must be something right with the company,' said Patrick. 'You said yourself they had the magic.'

'I did, didn't I? I suppose it was with the potential, the name, the legend. Certainly not the products which are simply awful, apart from The Cream. That's a little nugget of gold, that and the Berkeley Arcade shop, but I can't work out how they're going to work together. I've mined the data until I'm blue in the face, can't find anything. I'm beginning to feel as if a huge millstone is settling round my neck.'

'You always say that, when it comes to your data mining, it can be something bad as well as something good,' said Patrick, 'a major cock-up just sitting there, something you can remove, and then a lot of things go right because of that.'

'I know – darling, you're so wonderful, the way you listen to me and remember things, it must be so boring! But I can't find anything, not even a cock-up. Now that's serious! Grrr! Oh, I'm sorry, let's stop. I'm looking forward to dinner tomorrow, that'll distract me . . .'

Chapter 11

She would resign. It was the only thing to do. She was hating it now, looking so stupid at meeting after meeting and that was not a situation she enjoyed. Well, who would? She knew that she wasn't up to the job any more – if she resigned she could do so with dignity and it would appear her choice. If she hung on, there would be no dignity whatsoever.

And her mother's behaviour was – well, not ideal. Caro didn't like Bianca Bailey and she hated the way she operated, but they had signed up to it out of necessity, and they had to go along with it. She wondered if she might point that out as forcibly as she could to her mother? No. Athina didn't take kindly to criticism.

Of course, Bertie would be let go. He was so hopeless, so timid. God knows what would happen to him. He was only fifty-seven, far too young to retire, and had no discernible business talents – no talents whatsoever, in fact.

Well, Bertie was not her problem. She wrote a note to Bianca asking if she could see her first thing on Monday morning to discuss the future.

Caro had spent most of her life in a state of frustration. She had read law at university, and dreamed of a career at the Bar but her mother had crushed this ambition and told her her future lay with Farrell's.

'Frankly, Caro, Bertie isn't up to much; you could find yourself in my position one day, running the company. And I find it hurtful, that you should wish to reject your heritage.'

Partly for the sake of peace, and partly because the promise of inheriting Farrell's was undeniably attractive, Caro gave in. And hated every day of her new life.

She met and married Martin Johnson a year later; he was attractive in a rather dry way, successful and rich. She was not in love with him, but she saw in him a chance to escape from Farrell's, certainly for five or ten years, raising his children and being a good corporate wife. But the children did not materialise; after several wretched years, as she miscarried eleven times, and was then told she had no chance of conception, she went back to Farrell's more by way of an escape than inclination. A serious depression had ensued a few years later, born of the awareness that her fine brain was rotting quietly and a sense of absolute humiliation that she could not fulfil even her most basic function, that of motherhood. And her husband, aware that she had never loved him, embarked on a series of affairs which he scarcely tried to conceal.

She recovered from the depression, but it was replaced by an ongoing bitterness, which had never left her.

'This is nice!' Bianca smiled at Jonjo. 'Great choice.'

'Glad you think so.' He seemed less at his ease than usual. 'Let's get some drinks and shall we go to the table or stay at the bar till the others come?'

'Oh, the bar.'

'Right. Well, shall we get some champagne?'

He shunned the house champagne, insisted on Roederer. Bianca exchanged a brief smile with Patrick; they were both familiar with Jonjo's excesses, found them amusing, but endearing.

He didn't sit down, kept a watch on the door. His phone jangled; he looked at it, seemed to relax a little.

'Ah. Nearly here. Five minutes.'

'Who, Saul Finlayson?'

'No, no, Guinevere. She's stuck in traffic.' The waiter appeared with the champagne and glasses.

Jonjo looked slightly anxious. 'Should we open it yet, do you think?'

96

'Of course,' said Bianca.

'Only thing is – don't want it to go flat before she gets here . . .'

'Jonjo, it won't go flat in five minutes. Now sit down, please,' said Bianca, taking a sip and wondering if it was really worth the extra fifty pounds. 'You're making me feel dreadful.'

'Sorry. It's just that – ah, here we are!' He rushed outside to greet a large black Mercedes which had just pulled up.

'He must be in love,' said Patrick.

'Hmm. You know what? I'm not getting good vibes about Ms Bloch. I think he's exhibiting terror rather than love. Anyway, time will tell. Oh, my God! Patrick look.'

A dazzling vision had come through the door ushered by Jonjo. Guinevere's photographs did not do her justice. She was over six foot on her Louboutin heels at least, with hair falling in great golden ringlets over her shoulders, a small face, perfectly made up, with blue eyes almost too big for it, a small straight nose and a pouting mouth, very full, very sexy. She was wearing a white bandage dress (Victoria Beckham, thought Bianca), only just long enough, and her arms were perfect, slender but toned, and her incredible golden legs moved her smoothly and very slowly over to the bar. Everyone had stopped talking and she acknowledged the fact with a dazzling smile. Patrick, clearly as impressed as all the other men, stood up and held out his hand to her.

'Hello, I'm Patrick Bailey.'

'Hello, Patrick.' Her voice was low and throaty, with an American-European accent: German, Bianca supposed, given the name.

'And this is Bianca, Patrick's wife,' said Jonjo, chipping in a little late. 'Old, old friends of mine.'

'Really?' Her gaze settled on Patrick. 'You look too young to be an "old, old friend".'

Patrick, thought Bianca, don't fall for that, don't, I shall be so ashamed . . . Patrick fell for it.

'Oh, afraid I am,' he said. He was actually blushing.

'Guinevere, glass of champagne . . .' Jonjo urged her into a seat, sat down beside her, poured her a glass.

'Thank you; I'm exhausted, I've been working all day in the studio.'

'Have you?' said Bianca. She had googled Ms Bloch and didn't like what she had seen of her very abstract bronzes, most of them rather phallic, some extremely so. The prices seemed to her absurd, starting at £20,000, rising to £50,000. A clear case of the emperor's clothes, in her (admittedly uninformed) view. 'Very commendable, working on a Saturday.'

'Well, I felt – you know – inspired. One has to catch those moments, I find. Don't you?'

'Well, I wouldn't know,' said Bianca. 'My work is a great deal more prosaic than yours, I'm afraid. But it must be marvellous, what you do.'

'It is, of course. I feel very fortunate. What line is your work in?'

'Oh, management,' said Bianca vaguely.

'Really? I would love to hear all about it.' The blue eyes flicked at Bianca briefly, then settled on Patrick. 'And you?'

'Oh, I'm in finance.'

'Finance? With Jonjo? Thrilling, that world. Excuse me . . .' she whipped out an iPhone, 'I'm just tweeting where I am and who with. It's such a pressure, isn't it, keeping up, on Twitter? Oh my God, Joan is in town. I'd forgotten.'

'Joan?'

'Collins. Very amusing tweet here about the airport queues. She came to my exhibition in St Tropez, she's a complete sweetheart.' A long pause. 'Oh, God, Stephen is just *so* funny!'

She was lost in a twittering universe.

'Jonjo! I'm sorry. Had an argument with some traffic.'

'Saul, hello mate.' A cockney accent always appeared, Bianca had noticed, when Jonjo was with anyone in the financial world. 'You know Patrick, of course, this is Bianca, his wife, and this is Guinevere Bloch. You've probably heard of her.'

Saul Finlayson looked rather vaguely round the table.

'Don't think so. Hello, Guinevere, hi, Patrick. Nice to meet you, Bianca. I'll sit next to you, if I may – I hear you want to vet me. Or that's what Jonjo said. Hope I'll do.'

He said this rather seriously; then flashed a sudden smile at her, gone almost before she had seen it. No photograph could have prepared her for the reality of him: not good-looking but absolutely arresting, with the startling green eyes with dark brows and lashes at odds with the blond hair, the wide face and high forehead; none of it seeming to fit together somehow. He was very thin, quite tall and strangely restless, shifting from one foot to another even as he stood there, greeting them. He was wearing jeans, a white, rather crumpled shirt, and a pair of very kicked-about Timberlands. He certainly didn't spend any of his millions on his clothes, she thought.

'No thanks, Jonjo.' He turned his head as a glass of champagne was proffered. 'I'd rather have a beer.'

'Saul, I've just been tweeting that we're all here.' Guinevere tossed her golden ringlets back, leaned an imposing golden cleavage towards Saul. 'Can I add you?'

'If you do,' said Saul, looking at her, and there was only a glimmer of a smile, 'that thing goes down the toilet.'

He means that, thought Bianca. It seemed unnecessarily aggressive, however much she sympathised with him.

He turned back to Bianca.

'I read you'd got a new project.'

'Yes.' She felt flattered that he should know.

'How's it going?'

'Too early to say.' She could do economy of words too.

'Of course. Dumb question.'

Silence.

'I think I'd like a sherry,' said Guinevere suddenly, throwing back her golden ringlets. 'This place is all about Spain, so why are we drinking French champagne? Jonjo, can we have sherry? And – oh my God! There's Leon and Mardy, they must join us!' She jumped up and glided towards the door; her bottom, Bianca noticed with a touch of pleasure, was just a little too rounded for the dress.

'That is a terrible creature,' said Saul in Bianca's ear. 'Thank God I'm not staying.'

She turned, intending to look cool, and found his face six inches from hers, intent gaze probing, and felt a rush of – what? Hard to say. Irritation and confusion in equal measures. If he was trying to charm her, he wasn't doing much of a job.

'She's – she's all right,' she said.

'Really? I'm surprised you should say that. Friend of yours?'

'No, but Jonjo is our host, and she's . . .'

There was a silence.

'You're right,' he said then, surprising her, 'I'm being rude. Right then, since I haven't got long, how do you feel about your husband coming to work for me?'

'I don't know,' she said, smiling at him for the first time. 'And of course he hasn't made up his mind yet.'

'I'm banking on it being yes. Look . . .' He glanced at his watch, not the Tag Heuer she might have expected but a very unshowy Swatch. Which was probably as much of a pose as the other way round, she thought. Like Bill Gates flying Economy. 'Look, I've only got about ten more minutes. I like your husband – I think he'd be an asset and I know I could work with him. Any more questions? Of your own, I mean.'

She hesitated.

'It's difficult. I know so little about what's involved.'

'I presume you mean in so far as how it affects his life. I can see that's important to you. I'd pay him well. And – I believe he's a family man. So am I.' (Yes, and I'm Angelina, thought Bianca.) 'Don't think he'll be working crazy hours. He won't. He'll be working at his own pace. That's what I want. Jonjo may have to be on call, 24/7. I certainly do. Patrick doesn't. You don't have to worry.'

'Saul,' she said, anxious that he should not think Patrick was pussy-whipped, 'there isn't a problem with that. It's the least of my concerns, I do assure you.'

'Good. Well, that's dealt with, then. So what's the greatest?' The green eyes were at once thoughtful and impatient.

'I suppose – that he'll enjoy it. He's extremely clever but he's led a sheltered life professionally. It's a very harsh world, yours, wouldn't you say?'

'Yes, extremely so, but it won't affect him. Don't worry about that. Well, look, I'll talk to him again next week. Oh God!'

'Saul . . .' Guinevere was weaving towards him, holding a glass of sherry in one hand, pulling a short, balding man behind her with the other, 'here's your drink, it's their very finest oloroso – El Maestro Sierra Oloroso Wine Extra Viejo. I insisted.'

'I'm sure it's very nice, but unfortunately I have to leave now; domestic pressures – I was just discussing them with Bianca.' And he turned one of his nanosecond smiles on her.

'What a shame. Well, can I have your email, I want to invite you to my next show, it's in six weeks' time in Paris. It'll be a great party.'

She has the hide of a rhinoceros, thought Bianca; and what on earth might he say now?

'I'm a complete philistine I'm afraid,' said Finlayson. 'I'd be a waste of a valuable invitation. But – thank you.' This was clearly an effort. 'So goodnight, Patrick, we'll talk. Jonjo, see you on Monday. We need to discuss that European problem first thing and—'

'European problem? Oh, you must mean Greece and the Euro,' said Guinevere, her large eyes fixed on Saul again. 'Saul, I know some very important German financiers, quite close to the Chancellor, I could help . . .'

God, she was a nightmare, Bianca thought. What was Jonjo doing with her?

'Thank you. Very kind. Jonjo will let you know if we need them. Well – goodnight, Bianca.' He turned, and the smile lived just a fraction longer this time. 'It was – very nice to meet you.'

'You too,' she said, giving a half-smile back, and held up her hand to shake his. He looked at it, her hand, as if it was the last thing he might have expected, then took it and enfolded it rather than shook it, and his grasp was very warm, very strong. She felt odd, disconcerted, as if she was alone in a completely unfamiliar situation, not in the bar of a London restaurant with her husband and some friends.

He was gone then, out into the street. She found it hard to stop contemplating him and then shook herself mentally, smiled at Patrick, so wonderfully charming and reassuringly normal, and looking rather handsome, she thought absent-mindedly. And took a rather large gulp of Roederer to try and find normality.

'God,' said Bianca, when she and Patrick finally fell into a cab, 'it feels like we've been there for ever. What a nightmare evening. She was grotesque.'

'Well,' said Patrick, as always anxious to be fair, 'not altogether.'

'Patrick! She was totally terrible. You must get Jonjo to see the light about her.'

'Don't think I can do that. Anyway, any light that surrounds her is coming right out of her rather beautiful bottom.'

Bianca stared at him. Then she laughed. 'Oh, Patrick, that's why I love you so much. You do see everything properly straight.'

'Nice of you to say so. And what did you think of Saul? He seemed to be having quite a chat with you.'

'Saul Finlayson doesn't do chatting,' said Bianca, 'but I thought he was . . . all right.'

'That's not much of a testimonial,' said Patrick, looking anxious.

'Actually,' she said, thoughtfully, 'given what he could be like, I think all right is pretty flattering.'

'Really?' He looked more anxious still.

'Yes. To say Saul Finlayson is ruthless is the understatement of the millennium.'

'Oh, dear. So you think it could be a mistake, taking the job?'

'I think it could be. I also think it could be absolutely fascinating. Patrick, you need to talk to him some more, get a bit more of a feel for it, what doing it would be like.'

'But I can't really tell that, can I? He's not going to give me an hour-by-hour rundown of my day.'

'I don't see why not.'

'Oh darling, don't be ridiculous. And I think it might be irritating for him.'

'Patrick, if you're worried about irritating him at this stage,' said Bianca, 'you certainly shouldn't be going to work for him.'

She spoke lightly, but she meant it. She was beginning to worry about the inroads Saul Finlayson might make into their life.

Florence was having supper with Athina in her flat; they did that occasionally on Saturday, if neither of them was otherwise occupied. Which Florence was more often than Athina; she was on the committee of a small local theatre and tried to see everything they put on. She had, of course, invited Athina many times, who always refused. 'So kind of you, dear, and of course it's marvellous what you do for them, but I really don't admire suburban theatre.'

The talk this evening revolved round the theatre; Athina had seen *Noises Off*, the much-acclaimed new version of the Michael Frayn play.

'It was excellent, dear, you would enjoy it. Very funny. I do enjoy comedy. Cornelius taught me that, of course, that great theatre doesn't have to be all drama and tragedy. Would you agree? More champagne?'

'Absolutely I would,' said Florence, 'and yes, please.'

'Of course the theatre was one of the first bonds between you and Cornelius. I always remember you discussing it the first time we met, you'd both seen some Rattigan thing, and him saying afterwards that we really must employ you, you were so intelligent.'

'Indeed,' said Florence. 'I don't mean indeed I'm intelligent, although I suppose I am, but I do remember the conversation, of course. And how you interrupted it, Athina, because you said we had to talk business.'

'Well, it was what we were there for,' said Athina, 'and we'd have been there all night if I hadn't stopped you.'

'It's possible,' said Florence. 'Or at least until the bar closed.'

'I – oh, excuse me,' said Athina, as the phone rang, 'I must get that. I'm sure it's Margaret Potterton, calling about a dinner she's giving next week, fundraising for the Friends. I'll take it in the other room, so help yourself to champagne, dear.'

She was a Friend of Covent Garden, and very active; it was another comparison she made frequently with Florence's aptly named Little Theatre.

And Florence poured herself a very full glass of champagne, and sat sipping it, allowing her mind to wander back to that first meeting with Cornelius in the cocktail bar at the Dorchester.

Very tall he had been, that was the first thing she noticed about him, well over six foot, and incredibly, if slightly showily, well dressed in a Prince of Wales suit and a Garrick tie. He had taken her small hand in his and shaken it very gently, as if he was afraid he might crush it, but it wasn't a feeble handshake even so, it was firm and very steady and his eyes, smiling into hers, were steady too, not wandering round the bar, looking for more interesting or important people.

He ushered her to a seat, and then asked her what she would like to drink: 'Sherry? G and T?' His voice was quite light and actor-y, Florence noticed. She smiled at him and said could she have a Gin Fizz.

'Of course. How very adventurous of you. Darling, what about you?'

'Oh, I'll just have a sherry,' said Athina, clearly slightly surprised by Florence's order (good, Florence had thought, point to me), 'but very dry and on the rocks.'

'And I'll have a Gin Fizz, keep Miss Hamilton company. It's a lovely drink and I haven't had it for a while.'

Florence smiled at him and waited in silence while he waved the waiter over, gave the order.

'Right,' said Athina, 'now, if we might get down to business—'

'Oh, there's no hurry, darling,' said Cornelius. 'And anyway, I think we should get to know Miss Hamilton a little first. I like to mix business with pleasure.' He smiled at Florence again. 'Tell us about yourself, what are you interested in, what you enjoy?'

'Oh, I have many interests,' said Florence, taking a cigarette from the silver case he was offering. 'Music, tennis, the theatre—'

'The theatre! We love it too. Do you like serious theatre, musicals, what?'

'I like classic drama best,' said Florence, 'Shakespeare, Shaw, Oscar Wilde – if I can have some humour built in so much the better.'

'Well, I'm with you there,' said Cornelius Farrell. 'I think *The*

Importance of Being Earnest is the most perfect play that's ever been written.'

'Oh really, Cornelius!' said Athina. 'Better than *Hamlet*, or *Romeo and Juliet*?'

'Well – let's just say I'd enjoy it more,' said Cornelius. 'What would your perfect play be, Miss Hamilton?'

'I think,' said Florence, '*She Stoops to Conquer*. The plot is just perfection in my view.'

'Good choice! Well done. Ah, our drinks. Goodness me, that was a good choice of yours.' He raised his glass to her and smiled. 'Cheers. Wonderful to meet you. What a good idea of yours, Athina. Is your sherry all right, my darling?'

'Yes, it's very nice, thank you,' said Athina.

'Good. Now – books, Miss Hamilton. Tell me, who are your favourite authors?'

'Oh – Galsworthy. Trollope. I do like those family sagas so very much. And just now, Somerset Maugham.'

'Isn't he marvellous? I read one of his short stories every Sunday.'

'Rather than the Bible?' said Florence.

'Oh, rather!'

'Although there are some very good stories in the Bible. Cain and Abel, Lot and his wife, Adam and Eve . . .'

'You're right. David and Goliath, Samson and his unfortunate haircut . . .'

Florence laughed.

'I think, perhaps, Cornelius,' Athina's voice was just a little cool, 'we should discuss our proposition with Miss Hamilton. I'm sure she hasn't got all evening and we certainly haven't.'

'I suppose you're right. This is rather fun, though. Well, darling, you take over the talking now.'

'Very well. Miss Hamilton, I've been observing you in the store and I've been very impressed with you.'

'Thank you,' said Florence quietly. This is a clever woman, she thought. My husband may be flirting with you, Athina had actually said in those brief sentences, but I am actually in control here, of you as much as him.

105

'And I hear very good reports of you from the management. You seem to be more – how shall I put it? – more intelligent than most of the girls.'

'Don't suppose many of them watch Goldsmith,' said Cornelius.

'We don't know that,' said Athina, somewhat perversely Florence thought, 'but – no, I agree it is unlikely. Anyway, what we were thinking about – and it is only an idea at the moment – was a little shop we've been lucky enough to have inherited the lease of in the Berkeley Arcade. You'll know the arcade, of course?'

'Of course,' said Florence.

'We see it as a sort of flagship for the Farrell brand, a perfect setting where women can go to browse the new colours and products and have a facial at the same time.'

'I don't think I could do that,' said Florence, 'not facials.'

'Oh, my dear, of course not. There would be a beautician. What we are looking for is a manager, someone who can run it with style as well as efficiency, someone the customers feel they can communicate with. Someone more of their own class,' she added with an emphasis on the 'more'.

Florence stared at her, too excited to be distressed by the mild insult.

'You mean – you'd consider me for such a position?'

'Absolutely,' said Cornelius.

'*Consider*, certainly,' said Athina.

'I am honoured,' said Florence. She smiled at Athina expectantly. Instinct told her not to smile at Cornelius.

'Well, that is excellent,' said Athina, 'but now I think we should learn a little more about your personal life. You wear no ring. And I'm sure you would understand that we couldn't employ anyone about to get married and have children.'

'I was married,' said Florence simply, 'but he was killed in the war.'

'Oh, how sad,' said Athina. She spoke rather as if Florence had told her a pet dog had had to be put down.

'Thank you,' said Florence, 'but it was eight years ago. Time heals the deepest wounds and I find myself enjoying the single life.

I certainly have no intention of marrying. I have never, in any case, met anyone who could hold a candle to my husband.'

'Excellent,' said Athina, and then realising that this was not an entirely appropriate response, said hastily, 'I mean that the man you chose was so absolutely first-rate.'

'He was,' said Florence. 'Absolutely. But now my career is of prime importance to me. And I would be very proud to work for the House of Farrell – by far the most exciting brand there is at the moment, in my opinion. The colours – quite wonderful.'

'Thank you,' said Cornelius, 'that's exactly what we want to hear. Isn't it, darling?'

'Indeed,' said Athina. 'Well, clearly, Miss Hamilton, we need now to discuss this between ourselves, consider one or two other candidates. But—'

'But,' said Cornelius, and his dark eyes on Florence were very thoughtful, almost probing, 'but please, whatever you do, don't take another position in the next few days. Wouldn't you echo that, darling?'

'I – think so,' said Athina. 'Yes, please don't, Miss Hamilton. And now Cornelius, we mustn't delay Miss Hamilton. I'm sure she is busy and we have a dinner party to attend.'

'Yes, I should go,' said Florence. 'I'm going to the cinema. With friends.' This was quite untrue, but she didn't want the Farrells to see her as going home alone to a spinster-ish dwelling somewhere.

'Are you indeed? What are you going to see?' asked Cornelius.

'Roman Holiday,' said Florence firmly, pulling the title out of the air. 'Have you seen it?'

'Oh, it's marvellous. Marvellous,' said Cornelius. 'That new girl, Audrey Hepburn – so very good. And simply beautiful. Well, enjoy it, Miss Hamilton. And we'll be in touch.' They all stood up, walked to the front door of the Dorchester. A line of Rolls-Royces stood in the small crescent outside, in between the taxis. A chauffeur leapt out of one of them and opened the rear door.

'Well, goodbye,' said Athina, moving towards the car. 'Thank you so much for coming.'

'Thank you indeed,' said Cornelius. 'What a pleasure it was to meet you. I do hope we can work together.'

And he shook her hand again, with that same warm, gentle grasp. Florence looked up at him, and smiled.

'I hope so too,' she said.

Chapter 12

'Yes! YES! Oh, my God! Yes, yes, YES!'

Mike put his head round the door and smiled at her.

'All right, Bianca? You sound like Meg Ryan in that film.'

Bianca giggled. 'Did I? Sorry. Yes, sooo all right! Mike, there is a God. Caro Johnson has just resigned. In writing. How amazing is that?'

'Pretty amazing. How wonderful for you.'

'I know. I had a bit of a showdown with her mother on Friday and it didn't reflect well on Caro and – well, obviously she's got more sense than I imagined. Fantastic.'

'Fan-bloody-tastic indeed. Now – about these sales figures. They really are abysmal. How is your interim plan working out?'

Lucy felt absurdly nervous as she walked into the reception area of FaceIt. The eleven other girls had all arrived earlier and were standing in a group, looking rather alarmingly sophisticated with full, elaborate make-up and carefully styled clothes. She had come as if for lectures at uni with scrubbed face, T-shirt and jeans.

She smiled at them and said 'Hi' before walking up to the desk and introducing herself.

'Ah, Lucy, yes. Welcome. You're the last.'

'Sorry,' said Lucy.

'No, no, you're not late. Everyone else was early. I won't introduce you – our first lecture takes care of that. Follow me, girls, we'll go over to the studio.'

They walked into a large, light room with long benches down three sides, carved into separate work areas. Each had its own dressing-room style mirror, surrounded with light bulbs, a large chair rather like a dentist's and a towelling mat beneath each mirror, laid out neatly with a palette of lip and eye colours, a pouch of brushes of varying sizes, a range of foundations and powders and a set of electric hair rollers. In a corner stood a cluster of hairdryers on wheels.

A tall, dark woman who had been sorting out the make-up on the big central desk smiled at them.

'Hello, all of you, and welcome to FaceIt. Now, adopt a work station each, put your things down there and then I'd like you to introduce yourselves one by one – no need to be nervous, it's the one thing a make-up artist can't afford to be. When you're doing the make-up for London Fashion Week or a Paris show, you'll have about two minutes to find yourself somewhere to work, sort out which model you're working with, get a relationship going with her – *very* important – and start work. OK then, here we go. I'm Dinah Lawson, the chief tutor here, and this is Shona Parkin who'll be at most of your lectures and demos, especially the ones that relate to hair. We have a lot to get through and not much time; this course is only seven weeks, as you know, with an extra two for the theatrical sessions. Which of you is doing that?'

Lucy and one other girl put up their hands. Dinah Lawson nodded.

'Right. Well, we might as well start with you two. You are . . . ?' she said, looking at Lucy. 'Tell us just a couple of sentences about yourself, how old you are, why you're doing the course, what you've been doing up till now.'

The only constant was their ages, all of them except one being very early twenties. Two were married, one had a young child, two came from abroad; there were two more dropouts from university, several had been beauty consultants in big stores, another had worked in an office and been bored out of her head.

'It's not wall-to-wall glamorous and fun in this business either,' said Dinah. 'It's not all fashion shows and models, it can be making up some frankly very plain girls for a set of studio shots with a local photographer, or doing a bride's make-up, scary and very stressful, and you don't get a second chance. Now then, we're going to start today with absolute basics, cleansing the skin, getting it ready for make-up, absolutely crucial. Right, now who's going to be my model for the day? Not you, Lucy, because you've come sensibly barefaced – interesting name yours, incidentally, one of the make-up houses as I'm sure you know. I presume you're not related to the family?'

'Oh no,' said Lucy hastily. 'Just – just coincidence.'

'Right, what about you – Fenella, was it? You've got lots of make-up on – let's have it all off and start again . . .'

Lucy liked the look of Fenella; she was one of the other uni dropouts, tall and thin with a mass of shining conker brown hair.

It was a very different world from that of Jane Austen and its possible Marxist connotations. But one Lucy felt already more at home in.

Lawrence Ford had enjoyed his eighteen years as marketing manager of Farrell's. Athina still held him in high regard, he had a very reasonable expense account, a moderately good car, he dined and wined the trade and attended department store events conscientiously, and whatever his failings in other areas, he was very clever at spotting important new developments by other brands and talking about them rather as if they had been his own idea. His shortcomings were considerable, but he was gloriously unaware of them: he had a total lack of grasp of the advertising industry, his briefings on point-of-sale materials were very derivative and indeed retrospective, and his entire persona suggested someone from two decades earlier, with his formal suits, over-polished laced-up shoes, and insistence on being called Mr Ford by everybody in the company.

His wife, Annie, was a perfect corporate wife, loyal, admiring, always beautifully turned out and coiffed, and always over-wearing Farrell products. She had not worked since her son was born – she said it was a wife's duty to support her husband in every way, and a career in itself.

The Fords lived in a four-bedroom house in a new development in Kent; it was immaculate as was the garden, and Lawrence Ford, unlike most of the company, had been completely unconcerned by the takeover; he knew his value was considerable and he had nothing to fear.

Athina didn't know quite what to do with herself. This was a new sensation and one she found disturbing and even frightening. All her life, every moment had been busy; her presence required constantly. She moved from office to boardroom to conference to department store to work-based social engagement, and very occasionally home – always appearing calm and in control. At even their worst crises – an entire batch of lipsticks wrongly formulated and growing something akin to mould, a national poster campaign cancelled because some absurd new regulatory body refused to pass its claim (that The Cream made skin grow younger every day) – she had gone resolutely on, minimising damage where possible, accepting inevitable defeat graciously, restoring faltering morale by sheer determination and courage. Now, suddenly, she felt close to redundant; her traditions rejected, her power reduced, her talents unused.

For the first few weeks, she had continued to call meetings, discuss products, approve advertising and publicity campaigns; slowly, then with gathering speed, these functions were all taken from her.

First it was: 'Lady Farrell, may I join your meeting?' then: 'Lady Farrell, I think I would rather we called a halt to developing new products just for a few weeks' and finally: 'Lady Farrell, I think while the budgets are all under review, we cannot commission an advertising campaign.'

It was all done very courteously, always by Bianca Bailey personally, but the end result was that she found herself with almost nothing to do and at the end of each day she would arrive back at her flat knowing that she had accomplished nothing since she left it that morning. She had few friends and no hobbies, which she saw as rather silly work replacements. Now she was bored, lonely,

112

and – though she would have died rather than admit it – experiencing the entirely unfamiliar situation of being unsure of herself. And, far worse, unsure what to do about it.

She decided to go and visit Florence in the arcade.

Florence was rather disconcertingly busy; Athina waited at first impatiently and then irritably as she dealt with a small but demanding queue of customers, and finally went upstairs and made herself some tea.

'Athina, dear, I'm so sorry, everyone turned up at once. I've locked the shop for half an hour, so we can talk.' Florence appeared at the top of the stairs, slightly out of breath.

'I don't know that that's a very good idea,' said Athina. 'We can't afford to turn away clients.'

'They'll come back,' said Florence, 'they always do. I used the sign of course.'

'Mrs Bailey won't like that,' said Athina.

Bianca Bailey had already been confronted with this sign which said, rather quirkily, '*Closed for thirty minutes for private consultation*', and had complained that the thirty minutes was open-ended, having no apparent start time, but Florence had argued that she knew her customers very well and they responded to it without complaint; when Bianca said mildly that new customers might not be so obliging, Florence had replied that new clients found it intriguing and had often told her so. At which, rather than point out that there might be a number of new clients who did not return, Bianca had apparently given in, which both Florence and Athina were learning meant nothing of the sort.

'Well, never mind,' Florence said mildly, 'she's either going to close us down or she's not and a little respite now for half an hour will make no difference. What can I do for you, Athina?'

'Oh Florence I don't know,' said Athina fretfully, 'I just feel so – so impotent. Bianca Bailey clearly thinks I have nothing to offer and Caro's resigned, says she feels totally disregarded. As do I, of course, but I don't have that luxury. Someone has to keep a watchful eye on everything.'

'Does her resignation affect our shareholding?'

'No, no, not at all. But it does mean we have a less visible presence, which doesn't help. I suppose Bertie will be gone soon – he has nothing to offer, far less than Caro – but I'm certainly not going to allow him the luxury of resigning and I've told him so. Anyway, I thought perhaps I might have a facial. I always enjoy talking to Francine, she knows more about our customers than anybody.'

'I'm sorry, Athina,' said Florence, 'but Francine is fully booked this afternoon. Tomorrow perhaps?'

'Quite out of the question, I'm far too busy. Talking to the consultants,' she added hastily, lest Florence might find this statement too much at odds with her earlier one.

'Well, might you go and have a facial with one of the other brands?' said Florence. 'The Clarins treatments are quite wonderful, I hear.'

'Well, perhaps . . .' said Athina. 'We always used to do that, didn't we? Pick up ideas, check out the competition. I could go round several over the next few days.'

'Absolutely,' said Florence. 'Ah, that's the shop bell, so that will be Francine. Stay as long as you like, Athina, but she and I have things to discuss.'

'I wouldn't dream of holding you up,' said Athina icily.

She left then, and soon Francine la Croix, who had been born Pauline Crossman, disappeared to her salon and her first customer, and Florence was left alone with her memories of another afternoon, forty years earlier, when she had closed the shop and put the sign on the door and the parlour had been filled with first sighs and then cries of pleasure as skilful hands had worked on her breasts – so wonderfully responsive – and moved down to her stomach, so strangely a source of pleasure also, and thus into the places beneath it, and the great tangle of pleasure that lay therein, sweet and lush and utterly engaging of every sense that she possessed, of sight and sound and smell and feel; and as the long bright afternoon passed, and the sunshine that filled the little room slowly faded, and the thirty minutes spoken of on the door were multiplied three, four,

114

five times, she lay finally sated, smiling with pleasure, her hair fanned across the chaise longue that had served as a bed, her legs entwined with her lover's, their eyes exploring one another and what the time had meant and done for them.

And then, 'I'm sorry,' he said. 'I'm sorry, Little Flo. Not to be able to be more . . .' And she had said she didn't want more, that what he gave her was exactly what she needed; and then finally he was gone, and she was left only with the memory of the day, and for the time being, such had been her pleasure, her unutterable pleasure, that it was indeed happiness enough.

Patrick followed Jonjo along the corridor towards the trading room. He had never been in it before because Jonjo discouraged visits; but today, because he was almost part of it and Jonjo was in the vicinity, he was to be allowed in. It was exciting.

'Right,' said Jonjo, 'follow me.' And they walked into what seemed to Patrick a parallel universe. The sound was the first great shock, a wall of it, thuggish in its violence; he felt it physically, like a blow. And then the light, harsh, brilliant, coming from screens on the desks as well as huge banks on the ceilings, illuminating the large room filled with rows of desks facing each other, where people shouted and gestured, often obscenely, or stared fixated at screens, not just one to a person either, but stacks of six or eight to a desk. Phones were banged on those desks, fists were punched in the air, shouts of exaltation and, at times, loud obscenities.

Every so often a roar would fill the floor; Patrick, imagining at first that it was because of some new multi-billion deal, suddenly realised that the vast TV screens, set at regular intervals along the wall, were showing not the latest trade figures or currency values, but a football match, and the roars and subsequent obscenities were greeting goals or some less satisfactory event.

'When important investors come along we put Bloomberg TV on,' said Jonjo, 'but something vital like this match? Well, obviously it takes priority.'

The camaraderie was almost tangible; the relationships forged within this world were clearly close, generous and unquestioning, the bedrock of the whole apparently chaotic structure.

'OK,' said Jonjo, 'come and sit here. Desk next to me. This is Ali,' he said, gesturing towards the next chair. Ali nodded briefly, then returned to shouting unpleasantries at the person working opposite him.

'How on earth do you concentrate?' said Patrick in wonder.

'We don't,' said Jonjo and Ali in unison.

'OK,' said Jonjo, gesturing at the screens on his desk, 'this is how it works. We have our trading screens and our phone boards, and on the phone boards we have squawk boxes that we and the clients can shout into. It's like an open line. On the left is information – what's worth what – on the right, what's happening. And here, emails coming through, and these keys, look, these put us through to clients. You just press the relevant key and you're through and you shout. You don't get an answer till you've shouted several times, louder and louder, and then they shout back. Hang on, Patrick, someone coming through . . .' He leaned forward, spoke into a mike on his desk, said, 'Got one week to go at 6.5 . . . I'm 6.0 bid for you, Matt, keep showing it round.' He waited a moment, staring into the noise, sat down again, then flicked the switch and turned back to Patrick. 'OK?'

Patrick smiled at him weakly.

The floor was peopled ninety-five per cent by males, with a smattering of extremely pretty girls.

'They're called screen girls,' said Jonjo. 'They go round the clients making sure they're getting all the information they need and it's coming through all right on their screens. Obviously, they're not ill-looking,' he added. 'All our customers are extremely hairy blokes, so it's nicer for them, the girls don't mind at all, possibly need to be a bit thick-skinned.'

Patrick tried to crush any thoughts of what some of Bianca's more feminist associates and friends might make of this statement.

And all the time the money, the lead role in the cast of this absurd theatre, hung over it. 'Four trillion dollars done in a day,' Ali said, 'cash that is, the trades are done in a microsecond.' Trillions of dollars, up for grabs, there for the taking – if you could only translate the script.

And thank God I don't have to, Patrick thought, feeling himself quail in the face of it all; for he knew he was to be taken from here, to a quiet place, safe from this sound and fury but somehow, and God knew how, what he did there, if he took the job, would have a bearing, and possibly an important one, on what they did here.

He felt excitement and fear in almost equal proportions.

'Right,' said Jonjo, 'let's go and find Saul.'

Mrs Blackman, the First Mistress (as she was called, in an attempt to emphasise St Catherine's bid for equality with St Paul's and their High Mistress) did not like taking girls in the middle of the academic year; but Carey Mapleton was the daughter of a knighted, Oscar-winning actor father and an ex-supermodel mother, and the report from her former school – The International Academy in Paris – would have set any headmistress salivating: five-star academic prowess plus considerable achievement on the sports field, the gymnastics class, and the flute. All this, plus an offer of input into the school's drama department from Sir Andrew, and Carey was clearly a pupil not to be lost.

It was agreed that she should join the school after the Easter holidays, and should join Form 3X; this would put her, as it happened, into the same class as Milly Bailey.

'They are a particularly gifted group,' said Mrs Blackman. 'I think Carey will fit in extremely well there.'

Sir Andrew and Lady Mapleton murmured their thanks and thought, not for the first time, that it was as well that they had bestowed upon The Academy sufficient funding to build the foundations of a new theatre and a drama scholarship, thus removing any fear of Carey's slight – very slight – behaviour irregularities being mentioned in her report . . .

'Mrs Bailey—'

'Bianca, Bertie, please.'

'Sorry! Bianca, could I have a word?'

'Of course.' Increasingly she enjoyed words with Bertie; he was so calming, so sensible, so nice. 'Come in, sit down. Jemima, could we have some – what, Bertie? Coffee? Tea?'

'Oh, coffee, please.'

Jemima disappeared in the direction of the kitchen and Bianca smiled at Bertie. 'Now – what can I do for you?'

'Well, just something I heard. I was at a drinks do last night – Nip's annual knees-up.'

Nip, as it was affectionately known, was a professional body – National and International Perfumiers.

'Oh yes, I couldn't make it. Thank you for going, Bertie.'

'Oh, nice to be of service. Yes, well, it was all the usual, of course. But I did hear something that I thought might be helpful. The marketing director of Persephone is looking to move on – frustrated by the present management. Nice woman, not sure if you've met her?'

'Very briefly. What's her name, Lara something?'

'Lara Clements. Now, forgive me, but I imagine you would be looking for a marketing person?'

'Yes,' said Bianca. 'A marketing person is absolutely key. Lawrence Ford is – not quite up to snuff, as my grandfather used to say. So it would be good to talk to Lara Clements. In strict confidence, of course.'

'Of course. So what I could do—' Jemima had come into the room with the coffee and Bertie stopped abruptly, looked at her anxiously. Bianca smiled

'Jemima *is* confidence. She knows more about the company and the people here and even me than I do. Goodness, Bertie, I don't know what I'd do if you hadn't produced her. I say that nearly every day, don't I, Jemima?'

Jemima smiled modestly, poured the coffee and disappeared again.

'Right, back to Mrs Clements?'

'I was impressed by her, just felt instinctively she'd suit you. She's divorced,' he added, 'about – oh, late thirties, early forties? I liked her . . . not that that's important.'

'I think it could be *very* important,' said Bianca, smiling at him. 'Thank you Bertie. I'll get on to her. I don't suppose you've got any details . . . ?'

'She said she was going to see Meredith Cole over the next few days, the headhunters, you know – sorry, of course you do – anyway, if you want to avoid a big management fee, you might like to strike first. I – well, I took the liberty of taking her email. I hope that's all right.'

'Bertie, it's very much all right. Thank you so much. Could you email her, please, better if it comes from you as you've been talking to her, ask her if she'd like to come in for a chat with me?'

'Yes, of course. If that's how you'd like to play it.'

'It is,' said Bianca, 'absolutely how I'd like to.'

Lara Clements came in for a chat the next evening; she was small, blonde and dynamic, with a slight, but unmistakable, Birmingham accent. Her credentials were superb: Business Studies degree at Manchester, going on to do a Masters (Distinction), marketing manager with two of the big food companies, and thence to Persephone, once a lyrically successful perfume house, now tumbling swiftly into oblivion, kicked on its way by a hopeless management team who appointed her as marketing director and then ignored everything she said.

'I'd love to work for you of course,' she said. 'Your reputation goes before you. And I'd have a few ideas about Farrell's which I'm not going to voice now, it would be cheeky—'

'Be as cheeky as you like,' said Bianca.

'Oh, OK. Well, I'd minimalise the brand, only thing to do really. I mean, it's very messy – lots of dated stuff, half buried, not getting decent displays, but still some great products. Now The Cream, that is a bit of gold dust.'

'It is indeed.'

'I'm glad you agree. Anyway, I imagine you don't have unlimited funds to compete with the really big boys. So – cutting back, only thing to do really. And I'd love to get my hands on it, frankly. But I'll be honest with you, I'd be afraid of the same thing happening to me here, of being not listened to. I mean, the Farrell family – still here, still with controlling interest . . .'

'Believe me,' said Bianca briskly, 'the same thing would not happen here. I don't do not listening. Waste of money and even more of time. Well, thank you for coming. And please don't sign up with anyone else for a day or two. I have to talk to my board and of course there are a lot of other things to be sorted out.'

'Of course. Your HR person couldn't be here, I presume?'

'No,' said Bianca, 'pity, just one of those things. Well, I'll get back to you in twenty-four hours.'

After Lara Clements' small and impressive presence had left her office, she sat staring out of the window, thinking about her HR person. It would be ridiculous of course – and yet so sensible. It fitted in with her philosophy of seeking out existing potential, however unexpected. It would deal with one set of problems, while undoubtedly creating at least one more serious one. God, it was complicated!

Well, that had been awful, Lucy thought. Terribly awful. The longest four hours she could ever remember. Nothing to do except smile and try to look interested. And rearrange some already rearranged lipsticks. If this was the future of Farrell's it didn't look very bright – and Marjorie Dawson had told her that Rolfe's one of the prime consultant sites.

There'd been a much jollier counter over the other side of the department and she wished she'd been with them, especially around midday when they'd practically disappeared they were so surrounded with people and her corner remained hopelessly empty.

It had been quite embarrassing, at the end of it, as she said goodbye to Marjorie, who had looked really awkward and said, 'I'm sorry it's been so quiet, dear, it's usually busier than that. Perhaps best not mention it to your grandmother, it might worry her . . .'

And Lucy, understanding immediately, had smiled at her and said of course she wouldn't mention it, and indeed she wouldn't, but it must be quite worrying for the poor lady . . .

Anyway, if enduring the Saturdays was the price she must pay for her grandmother's encouragement and interest, then it was worth it. Meanwhile she'd got a job working in a pub in Surbiton, three nights a week.

But it was awful living at home; her mother was so totally horrible to her father, and he tried so hard to do what her mother wanted; he'd even gone on her wretched diet and Lucy actually did think he was beginning to look a bit thinner; he'd been quite handsome when he was young, rather like his own father indeed, only not quite so good-looking. Grandfather Cornelius had looked a bit like a film star, and she'd been terribly upset when he died. She'd never forgotten his memorial service; the church had been completely packed, not just with family and friends and people Lucy recognised from the company, but countless distinguished-looking old people. A famous actor person read one of the lessons and her mother had been in her element, barging up to people and introducing herself. Her father had stayed quietly at her side, talking to Florence who had been a study in silent dignity, very pale and subdued. Grandy was flitting about, drinking glass after glass of champagne, looking extremely glamorous, sparkling away at everyone.

It had been the first time Lucy had been properly aware of belonging to something rather more famous and important than most families. Remembering it now, she felt sad that clearly it was that no longer and was probably going to disappear into nothingness.

All for getting things wrong and being hopelessly out of date, when once clearly it had got everything right and was bang on the money. She wondered if she could, in some way, help reverse that. Silly she supposed, but she did rather like the idea.

Chapter 13

This was, without doubt, the presentation of her life, the toughest she had ever done. It was only just within the time frame that had been allotted, perhaps a little over – no, not perhaps, Bianca, actually, and by nearly two weeks.

It would take all morning, this meeting; there was a lot to present, her overview of the company, what was wrong with it and what would be right and she had her own clear vision now of the House of Farrell, of what she must do, where she could take it, her vision for it.

What she was doing today was selling them all, with their complex and differing demands and expectations, her plan; and she had to take them with her, persuade them it was right and workable, and for that the numbers had to add up. She was under no illusions; the most brilliant marketing strategy in the world would mean nothing whatsoever to her audience unless the financial bottom line was convincing; that was all the Porter Bingham people would be interested in.

It would get quite brutal, at times, she knew; she would, having outlined the changes she felt necessary, present her organogram, who was in charge of what, what needed doing, what was going to be put on the scrap heap, and then her plans for the staff for the next stage: which jobs would be put in place, which reorganised, which would disappear; and the line of reporting would be defined. If you cut out confusion, you cut out a lot of objection.

She woke up at five, slithered out of bed, kissing Patrick goodbye, went for a run and then drove straight to the office to bathe and dress – one of the more valuable legacies bequeathed her by Lady Farrell was an old-fashioned but perfectly functioning bathroom adjacent to her office. She had planned her outfit thoughtfully: sleek cream Joseph dress, red LK Bennett shoes, red Reiss cardigan – the air conditioning could go crazy and the last thing she wanted was to be distracted by feeling cold.

The meeting was timed for nine and that meant an hour with Jemima for the run through of the technical part of the presentation, so that there was no chance of any kind of a fuck-up, or even a faltering.

She stood quietly composed in the boardroom while Jemima set out copies of the agenda. And then Liz in reception announced the arrival first of Hugh and Mike, then Peter Warren, the non-executive chairman, with his air of charm and calm, then Caro and Bertie, and Florence, looking rather determinedly composed, and finally, almost fifteen minutes late, the temptation to phone her almost beyond endurance, Lady Farrell at her most imperious, dressed all in black – dress, jacket, shoes, bag, even her hat, a vast saucer of a thing, swathed in black ostrich feathers – the only relief her triple string of pearls and a large gold and emerald brooch on one lapel. Let no one mistake how I feel about today, those clothes were saying: that a tragedy is about to befall the House of Farrell . . .

'So very sorry,' she said, smiling sweetly, removing the hat, holding it out to Jemima to hang up, 'traffic too awful. I'm sure I'm not the only one held up.'

'Oddly yes,' said Bianca, returning the smile, 'but of course we knew you were coming. And we could hardly start without you.'

Bianca presented her overview of the brand as it was now, a 'once high-end brand founded on colour products, with a sound footing in skincare', had moved down into the mastige market – that is, mass market trying to be prestige – 'but you'll all know that' swamped by the competition and not up-to-the minute on trend, which a colour brand must be. 'Skincare, The Cream apart, has seriously lost its way, formulations and concepts are out of date, no presence in the major stores, doing all right in the self-selection areas of upmarket chemists', summed up in a sentence as 'respectable, quite good, even, but yesterday's . . .

'But we do have strengths,' she went on. 'We have a wonderful history, which we have totally failed to capitalise on, sixty years – and I don't need to tell you how relevant that is in next year's Diamond Jubilee year – of amazing stories and proud connections. We have traditions of quality also uncapitalised. We have some magnificent products, our hero – or if you would prefer it, heroine product – being, as I have said, The Cream.

'We have an archive that our more modern competitors would kill for, photographs of the classiest of society ladies in the Berkeley Arcade shop, written testimonials from models and actresses as well as those ladies, a founder who is still most wonderfully working for and with us, with superb connections and many honours, including an MBE, The Shop itself, and I believe, indeed I *know*, we can use all that and much much more to restore the House of Farrell to where it belongs.'

She smiled round the table. The family were looking complacent and quite benign; she had them with her for the time being. However . . .

'Time for the less good news,' Bianca said and launched into the figures, the falling sales, the rising costs, the wastage, a shortage of relevant staff, an embarrassment of irrelevant.

'I would now like to present to the board the organisation of the new company.' This was the kind of occasion when she felt it most: the total dependence on her and her talents to deliver. The buck stopped with her and she was very, very alone. She felt a rush of fear at the sheer enormity of her task, followed by one of adrenalin. This was it. This was what she was about.

'Mrs Bailey . . .'

'Yes, Lady Farrell?'

'This is *not* a new company. The House of Farrell, as you have already told us, is sixty years old. I would be grateful for further recognition of that fact. We, the family, do not wish to be told we are on the board of a new company. And indeed I am most thankful that my husband is not here to hear it.'

'Lady Farrell, forgive me. Perhaps I should have said the newly *structured* company.'

'Perhaps you should.'

'I'm sorry. I would now like to present the organisation of the . . . newly structured company . . . and the report lines for any business and any vision starts with having the best people, in particular the senior management team and the reporting.'

'Reporting? What is a reporting?' Having found her voice, Athina was reluctant to lose it again.

'Put simply, it is who reports to whom.'

'I see. Do go on.'

'Thank you, Lady Farrell.'

She talked on: the need for new people and departments: 'All the people who will work along with me to deliver the vision I am about to share with you. We need a new marketing director – I have a candidate, an excellent one, who I hope you will approve; a sales director, in association with the marketing director, both reporting to me – I would like to consider as a matter of urgency a change of advertising agency—'

'Mrs Bailey?'

'Yes, Lady Farrell?'

'Langland Dennis and Colborne have worked extremely effectively and loyally for the House of Farrell from its birth. Why should you want to change them for another, untried, agency?'

'Lady Farrell, they have done some excellent work in the past, but the brand has to change dramatically and the advertising agency has to understand that. I am also, having talked to them, not at all confident that they are up to speed on present-day media, but obviously I would ask them to present along with any other agencies we are considering. Now, if I might move on?'

'Essentially we need an HR director since Caroline Johnson has resigned, and I am formulating that appointment and will present my ideas to the board on another occasion – and of course, an IT director. I am also giving serious consideration to outsourcing product development; the lab can possibly be dispensed with, once a product development manager has been appointed.'

There was a rustling of papers from Lady Farrell before she spoke of the problems of supervision from a distance, and confidentiality; Bianca dismissed her objections swiftly and smoothly and Lady Farrell rummaged in her bag, pulled out a notebook and gold propelling pencil, and made a lengthy note, passing it across the table to Bertie when she had finished: it was a masterclass in attention-seeking. Bianca waited until it was done, then smiled at her and cleared her throat.

'I also propose giving the position of publicity manager greater seniority, and that Susie Harding is made publicity director.'

'Oh, I'm sorry but no. I simply cannot agree to that.' Athina stood up. 'Miss Harding's work has been extremely poor, she has no concept of class, or quality, she consorts professionally with the most extraordinary people, these – these *bloggers* – and she has no respect for our traditions.'

'Lady Farrell, when I move on to how I see the House of Farrell, my vision for it indeed, it will, I hope, become clear that Susie is remarkably *au fait* with a very high-class, prestigious indeed, House of Farrell, that her ambitions for it are as great as yours.'

Caro raised her hand, her normally rather pale face flushed. 'I would just like to say at this juncture that I fully support my mother in opposing this appointment.'

'I will make a note of that, Caro,' said Bianca with a sweet smile. 'Now, I have other personnel considerations and observations which I would like to present for your approval, but they are in broad outline and need detailed discussion. They include the future of the consultant force.'

'Well,' said Athina, 'I'm sure we can hardly wait for them. In the light of your other extraordinary ideas.'

This was so rude that even Bianca flinched; Peter Warren cleared his throat, and said, firmly charming, 'Lady Farrell, I would suggest that we give Bianca the courtesy of hearing her out,

126

without further interruption. I can imagine you find some of her views unsympathetic, difficult even, but she has the progress of the company absolutely at heart and I'm sure I speak for the whole board when I say that.'

He smiled round the room, and then at Athina, his handsome face clearly settling her. Here was a man, her frosty smile at him and curt nod to Bianca said, who knew what was what, and how to behave. Bianca took a deep breath, and continued.

This was where her presentation had to sing, had to mean enough to the family to at least reach them. This was the part that they would be most concerned about, would have strongest objections to; she had to take them with her now, or she would lose them for ever and, therefore, any hope of enjoying their cooperation.

'There is so much that is good about the House of Farrell,' she began, 'and my hopes and plans and indeed, my vision for it, are all based on that fact.

'First I would like to outline what I know we cannot do. We cannot compete with the big colour brands, Mac, Brandon, Bobbi Brown. We don't have the budget, or even the capacity. Colour launches now are much more complex. There has to be an added benefit: lip colours have to plump up mouths, eye colours care for delicate tissue – you all know the sort of thing. In skincare I believe we still have an edge, and a story to tell, largely thanks to The Cream, and I believe we should build on that. I have ideas for a new concept—'

'Mrs Bailey,' said Athina, standing up, 'The Cream is our greatest product. I do warn you, to tamper with that would be an act of considerable folly.'

'Lady Farrell, I have no intention of tampering with The Cream, I mean merely to extend its range. Of course that won't be easy, and we don't have research facilities in any way comparable with those of say, L'Oréal and Lauder—'

'And your response to that is to close down our own lab altogether?' said Athina, her voice shaking. 'I really find much of what you say complete madness.'

'Lady Farrell, I'm sorry. Please hear me out. And of course we will still have a laboratory, even more creative than the present one.'

They faced one another, Athina brilliant-eyed, flushed, Bianca, coolly patient, waiting to resume. Finally Athina sat down.

'Thank you,' Bianca said. 'So, what is left to – or rather *for* – us?'

Lady Farrell was heard to murmur 'what indeed?', Caroline Johnson to sigh and raise her eyebrows at her mother, Bertie Farrell to look uncomfortable on their behalf and to smile at Bianca, whereupon his mother gave him a murderous look.

Hugh Bradford and Mike Russell sat impassively, benignly poker-faced. Earlier colleagues who had been in similar situations with them would have said, however, that neither of them was evincing any real sign of enthusiasm. It was not a receptive environment.

Bianca Bailey took a long drink of water, walked to the other end of the table, and without either props or electronic aids, began to speak with more passion than she had displayed before.

Because there was the overall plan, the detailed plan, the financial plan – and then there was the real plan. The key, the idea that made sense of it all, brought it alive, gave it identity. She always feared it would not come, while knowing it would, because it had to. And once more she had found her alchemy, as a journalist had once called it. Such a whimsical name for so crucially pragmatic a skill as she possessed. It had a lot to do, her alchemy: it had to inspire imagination, earn trust and respect, unite staff, attract investment – and above all, make money.

'So,' she said, taking a deep breath, 'this brings me to what I know we should do and I'm extremely excited about it.'

She drew a picture for them: of a brand transformed from within itself – of a small, exclusive range, with a face that was younger, and more fashionable but still in possession of the same class and quality and grace that had long been its greatest strength.

'This range will sit beside the original one, on the counters; it will feature in the advertising, it will be an ambassador, if you like, for the rest. New people will see it, try it, people who would not have come to Farrell's before, or perhaps have ceased to come. The packaging will echo the present style, but it will look cleaner, more modern, more luxurious. I had hoped to have something to show you today, but I'm not satisfied I have the answer. When I am, you shall all see it.

'But there is more, much more. We are fortunate that at this time, while fashion has never moved faster, the higher end still looks backward and draws with great success from the past. Nostalgia was never so valued a currency, delivering as it does a sense of security and quality in so uncertain a world. And among the Diors and the Chanels, and the Ralph Laurens, consider the great classic English names who have brought themselves into today, while still harvesting from their past glories: the fashion houses – Burberry, Mulberry, Pringle; the stores – Selfridges, Harvey Nichols; the hotels – the Savoy, Claridge's, The Ritz. I intend that we shall do the same for the House of Farrell; it will be a brand for today and tomorrow, but its strength and its legacy will come from its past.

'Hugely expensive advertising campaigns are out of reach, but the new weapons at our disposal, the social media, can work with incredible power. Providing we have enough that is interesting and original to say – and we will – I believe that the ripples we create at our launch will spread with a speed and efficiency unimaginable before now.

'And now I would like to talk about The Shop . . .' She paused and looked at Florence, whose face was impassive, who was clearly preparing herself for some mortal blow, and smiled at her. 'The Shop is perhaps the most exciting thing of all, to me. I think we have an absolute treasure there in the Berkeley Arcade, in the heart of expensive, exclusive London, a stone's throw from Bond Street. So,' she looked round the room and smiled, 'so I have decided that, in time, we should have more of these treasures of ours. Not in London, of course, but in other great shopping centres of the world, replicas of the Berkeley Arcade. We would have to start slowly – they will not be cheap – but in Paris, for a start, possibly Milan. There they will be tiny little jewels of places, telling the world that this is what we're about. Exclusive, beautiful, luxurious – and unique. They'll be our equivalent of the Elizabeth Arden red door salons. They can be small, in fact they should be, the opposite of Selfridges' cosmetic hall, something intimate and luxurious and personal, the places to buy not only the products, but incredibly luxurious and exclusive treatments. And they will give us our branding. They'll set a style, a tone. I want the packaging, the advertising, *everything*, to echo them, and vice versa.'

She looked at Florence again, who was flushed now, her eyes brilliant, and the smile she gave Bianca, swift, almost imperceptible, was one of excitement as well as relief.

'And finally,' Bianca said, returning the smile as swiftly, 'we have two great national events on our side too, next year: the Olympics, of course, which will focus the eyes of the world on this country, and, still more relevantly, the Diamond Jubilee. The House of Farrell was founded in coronation year: how wonderfully serendipitous that it can be relaunched at the Queen's Diamond Jubilee, in the same spirit of pride and delight in our country and its heritage. We will be the envy of the cosmetic world.' She paused for a long moment, then, 'And that, for now, is all I have to say.'

There was a complete silence. But she had done it, she knew. She had carried them with her, albeit briefly, had shown them her vision and persuaded them to share it. Even Athina's face was on hers, intent, intrigued. And Mike and Hugh had the slightly complacent expressions that she had seen before when she had presented well: we chose her, their expression said, we found her, she would not be here without us.

The Shop idea was, she knew, brilliant. She'd been so excited she'd practically choked on her bedtime hot chocolate. And unable to sleep then, had lain, envisaging them, a chain of shops, a bejewelled girdle around the world, encircling the big cities, shaping the image of the brand, presenting it in all its unique, upper crust high quality, changing how people thought about the House of Farrell . . .

Mike spoke finally, cutting into the silence.

'Thank you, Bianca. You've given us a great deal to think about. And to plan. We will all obviously have observations but, personally, I would like to take this away with me –' he patted his folder – 'and digest it further. Then we can reconvene.'

'Of course. Thank you for listening.'

'It was a pleasure.'

Chapter 14

'Oh my God,' said Susie Harding on Monday morning, hearing Bianca's plans for the future Farrell brand, 'that sounds just amazing. I can pick this up and run with it. It's a brilliant concept, Bianca, it really is. The press will totally love it! That whole thing of Englishness and heritage and the brand within a brand: not just a predictable relaunch of the lot. It's so exciting! And the shops, and next year of all years—'

'Yes, well that was a bit of a gift,' said Bianca, with a grin. 'I didn't personally arrange that. But I'm glad you think it will work. With the press at least.'

'Totally. We need to get cracking quite soon, though: there's only fifteen months to go to the Jubilee.'

'Yes, and it's a major problem,' said Bianca, 'I have to find a totally brilliant chemist, an utterly brilliant packaging designer, a cracking marketing and advertising campaign and a sales director who could sell not just fridges to Eskimos but freezers as well!'

'And maybe a range of sunscreen stuff?' said Susie. 'Oh, I can't wait to get started.'

'Good,' said Bianca, 'and in that case I'll tell you the other bit of news I have for you . . .'

OMG! read Susie's text to Henk, *she's only made me f***ing publicity director!*

* * *

Having formulated her strategy and got the go-ahead from the board, Bianca was on an almost impossibly tight schedule. Therefore by mid-morning on the Monday Lara Clements had received an email offering her the job of marketing director of the House of Farrell; Lawrence Ford had been summoned to Bianca's office for a chat; Florence Hamilton had been asked if it would be convenient for Mrs Bailey to come to the arcade at four that afternoon; Lady Farrell had left Mrs Bailey's office in a state of impotent fury on hearing that there could be no question of Marjorie Dawson being kept on; Langland Dennis & Colborne had been warned they would not be the only agency pitching with a new campaign; Mike Russell had suggested a couple of recruitment agencies who might find the financial director that Farrell's so urgently needed; and now Bertie was being ushered into Bianca's office by a worryingly solicitous Jemima . . .

'Now girls, as I told you at the end of last term, we have a new member of the form – Carey Mapleton.' Gillian Sutherland's earnest, unmade-up face smiled briefly, as she ushered her slightly resistant charge forwards. 'I know you're going to make a great effort to welcome Carey – it's not easy starting at a new school in the middle of the year, and she hasn't even been at school in this country, she's been at the International Academy in Paris. Carey, you're not going to remember everyone's name immediately, so we'll start you off gently; I'm putting you in the care of Emily Bailey and Grace Donaldson. They'll look after you and show you where everything is, and introduce you to everyone else in the class in due course. Now Emily and Grace, will you escort Carey into Assembly please?'

Milly smiled at Carey and walked forward with Grace to lead her and the class into Assembly. Carey smiled back. She was very pretty indeed, small but nicely curvy, with very dark auburn hair and huge brown eyes; she seemed nervous, and indeed as they took their places in the Great Hall, Milly could feel her trembling. Poor thing, she thought, smiling at her again reassuringly, she was obviously very shy. Milly decided she must take her duties very seriously seeing Carey settled in, and that she might ask her to tea one day very soon.

'Bertie, hello. Please sit down. Coffee?'

'Yes, that would be very nice thank you,' said Bertie, wondering how he was to swallow anything at all.

'Right,' said Bianca, smiling across the desk at him. 'Let's get straight to the point. I think we're probably agreed that financial director is not a position you're very comfortable with. Or that you've been entirely successful at.'

'I – I suppose we should. Or rather, I should. Agree, that is.'

'I'm already briefing a couple of headhunters.'

So – this was it. He was about to lose the job he had done for the past twenty years; the job that he struggled so hard to do effectively and efficiently and was forced to realise at every board meeting he had performed ineffectively and inefficiently.

He looked at Bianca, feeling rather sick.

'But what I don't want is to lose you.'

What had she just said? Surely he must have misheard?

'I'm sorry?'

'I said we don't want to lose you. I think you have a great deal to offer this company so, I wonder if, Bertie, you would consider what some might see as a demotion.'

Oh God. She was going to give him some awful token job. Could he cope with that? With everyone being kind and careful about what they said to him, and pretending he was doing something really useful and important.

'It would – depend what it was,' he said. 'I mean obviously I would try to – to see the positives in it.'

'What I have in mind would be a very big challenge for you,' said Bianca. 'Bertie, I wonder if you'd consider being human resources director? It's a board appointment, although of course you're on the board already, and I could match your present salary.'

Bertie sat staring at her, trying to imagine being capable of such a job, wondering if she was banking on him turning it down simply so that she could claim she had tried to find him something to do.

Finally he said, 'But Bianca, I don't know anything about HR. Personnel we always called it here, of course. It's very kind of you, but—'

'Bertie,' said Bianca, 'I'm not being kind. I can't afford to be kind. I know you don't know anything about the *theory* of HR but you have what I'd call a deep grasp of who could do what job. Of course that's not all of it, but it's the hub.'

'Yes, but—'

'Who is responsible for Jemima being here, the one person above all who makes my life possible and moreover who knew she would be? Who headhunted Lara Clements, knew she'd fit in, knew she'd be right for the job, knew we'd get on? *You* did, Bertie. I think you have a very sure instinct for people. I've watched how everyone is always pleased to see you, how they like to tell you things, how even the secretaries and the marketing assistants tend to come to you with problems – I just know it's worth a try.'

'Yes, I see,' said Bertie. He wondered why Bianca's face had suddenly become rather blurred and realised with horror his eyes had filled with tears at this tribute. Appreciation was an almost unknown quantity to him. He pulled out a handkerchief, blew his nose.

Bianca, reading his embarrassment, started flicking through a document on her desk.

'Now,' she said, 'we have some very tricky situations personnel-wise in the offing; for instance, Marjorie Dawson, to whom your mother has given a rather rash reassurance about her future and who has an invalid husband. I mean, what on earth am I to do about her? I couldn't be more sorry for her but we don't need the consultants in their present guise and frankly, I can't see that many of them will be a loss.'

'No, I agree with you, but Marjorie is a cut above the rest and I do have one idea—'

'Which is?'

'Well, frankly, Francine la Croix, our beautician at the arcade, is a little past her sell-by date . . .'

'So – were you thinking Marjorie might replace Francine?'

'In due course. Francine is only part-time, anyway.'

'I'm sorry, Bertie, but the person replacing Francine will be our prime ambassadress. Young, classy, sophisticated – everything that Marjorie is not, nice as she undoubtedly is.'

'Yes, I see. And – and what about Florence?'

'Florence is a gift from heaven. She is our link from the past to the future, and though not young it is difficult to think of her as old, and she is certainly very classy and extremely sophisticated. As is your mother, of course, the two of them have so much to offer, invaluable sources of knowledge, experience, instinct, and, of course, glamour. I only hope that—' She stopped.

Bertie met her eyes.

'There is no knowing how my mother will react to anything,' he said. 'Anything at all. May I speak frankly?'

'Bertie, there's no time for anyone to speak otherwise. Go ahead.'

'Well, I wonder about the wisdom of there being so few consultants – they are a valuable source of information about our customers, apart from anything else.'

'I know, but we simply can't afford them. We shall have to find a clever solution. Perhaps you'll be able to help us with that as well. Meanwhile, please Bertie, would you put me out of my misery? Would you accept this job, please? We can put it on a three months' trial basis and you need to get on to a course asap, learn the science of it. I'll ask Jemima to source some. So – what's your answer?'

'Mrs Bailey,' said Bertie, smiling at her and standing up, holding out his hand, 'I accept with pleasure. I shall do my very best to justify your somewhat unfounded faith in me.'

'Good,' said Bianca. 'I'm so very pleased.'

It wasn't until he was back in his own office that Bertie realised he would be doing Caro's erstwhile job, and began to think about the true repercussions of that.

'Florence, hello. May I come in?'

'Please do,' said Florence, smiling at Bianca over the counter. 'How very nice to see you. Can I offer you a cup of tea, perhaps? We aren't too terribly busy and Francine is here and has only a few clients so she will come down if necessary. I cannot tell you how excited I am about your plans for The Shop.' She paused. Athina was not the only person to wonder if she might be replaced; it seemed not only possible but probable; heritage was after all not only about the past but the future. And the wildest optimism could not regard someone of her age as that.

She was resolved to remain calm; if she lost her job that would be very dreadful, the end not only of an era, but a lifetime. But she had lived out that lifetime according to her own strict standards and rules; one of which was not to make a fuss about things.

'Do sit down,' she said to Bianca, ushering her into her parlour. 'And what would you like? China tea, Indian, something herbal.'

'I like Indian tea,' said Bianca, smiling at her, 'good and strong, with just a dash of milk. Thank you, Florence.'

'Very well. And I have some excellent shortbread from Fortnum's, or some small teacakes . . . ?'

'Oh, no thank you. Just the tea.'

Florence made the tea, poured it into the fine china cups that Cornelius had insisted on buying when the kitchen was stocked, and sat bolt upright in her chair.

'Now,' she said, looking very directly at Bianca, 'I imagine you have not come here to discuss the weather . . .'

'I've seen Saul Finlayson again,' said Patrick.

Bianca closed down her iPad. This was a conversation which required her absolute attention.

'And?'

'He was very – very patient with all my queries and reservations. I – think I'd like to accept the job.'

Her heart lurched; she hadn't realised until that moment how extremely anxious she was about the entire Finlayson scenario. Not merely how it would affect her life, but how it affected Patrick. The awe in which he held Saul worried her intensely.

'In – what way did he reassure you?'

'Well, first in that I won't be working out of my depth. He seems convinced that I have all the skills he's looking for.'

'Well, I expect he is. He's wouldn't have asked you if he hadn't thought you could do it.'

'But being a friend of Jonjo's, that sort of thing—'

'Patrick Bailey, get a grip. Do you really think a man as successful as Saul Finlayson would give anyone a job to oblige a friend?'

'Darling, don't be impatient with me. This is a huge decision.'

She felt remorseful. 'I'm sorry. I know it is.'

'He is also adamant that I needn't work the absurd hours he does, weekends and so on. I can work at my own pace, on my own, and only report to him when I'm ready.'

'Fine.' And thought: did pigs fly? Or water flow uphill?

'And he's such a nice chap, Bianca, in spite of his success. You've only met him for a few minutes but I know you'd get to like him.'

'Darling, I don't *dis*like him. I just want you to be quite sure you know what you're getting into.'

'Well, I think I do. And it's not a chance I'm going to get again.'

'No, I know.'

'So – if I have your blessing, I'd like to accept it.'

She was still uneasy, but she could see it would be pointless, as well as unwise, to discourage him. He wanted to do it badly enough to experience serious discontent if he didn't. Nevertheless – it was a huge risk. For him, his self-esteem, his very future. And – well, she wouldn't even look at the 'and'. They would work such things out together.

Nevertheless, even as she smiled at Patrick and said that of course he must do it, that she was extremely happy for him, as she watched him so clearly relieved to have her blessing, opening a bottle of champagne, as she raised her glass to him and kissed him, she was filled with a sense of foreboding such as she seldom knew.

'You what?'

'I've – I've accepted it.'

'That job?'

'Yes.'

'Well, really. I thought you had at least a little common sense

138

left. I've never heard anything more ridiculous. What makes you think you can do it?'

'I don't know. But I don't think it's my decision. It's hers.'

'Well, I suppose so. Have you told Caro?'

'No. I thought I would tell you first. And she did resign. It's not as if Bianca fired her in my favour.'

Athina considered this. 'I suppose not. Well, Bertie, I really don't know what is happening to this company. It seems to be in the hands of a madwoman.'

'Thank you for that, Mother,' said Bertie, in a rare surge of defiance, 'thank you for the vote of confidence.'

He walked out of the room.

Priscilla's attitude had been not a lot more encouraging; he had told her and Lucy at dinner the evening before. She had stared at him for a clearly baffled moment and then said, 'Well, I hope it's a success, but I have to say I doubt it.'

'Mummy!' Lucy had jumped up from her chair, put her arms round her father's neck and kissed his cheek. 'That just so isn't fair. Congratulations, Daddy, I'm really pleased. It just shows Bianca Bailey is aware of how versatile Daddy can be, and I think it's wonderful.'

Bertie took the coward's way out and called Caro. He couldn't face another session of face-to-face disbelief. There was the predictable silence, then she said in a stiff voice, 'Well, congratulations Bertie. That's – that's very good. Of course it's the most ghastly job. That's why I resigned. I wish you well in it, but I don't think you're going to enjoy it in the least and it will be virtually impossible to function under Bianca Bailey. She has to have her own way in everything.'

'I wouldn't say that's been my experience,' said Bertie.

'Because you haven't worked under her. But it's a very good move for you. Who will be in your erstwhile job? Someone more *au fait* with modern accounting methods and so on, I imagine. That's what Martin said was needed.'

'I imagine so, yes,' said Bertie.

He decided he needed some fresh air, and walked out of his office and down the stairs; someone was running up them.

It was Lara Clements.

'Bertie, hello. I've been meaning to call you and say thank you. I'm sure you had quite a lot to do with me getting this job. Now I can do it in person. I'm thrilled, I really am.'

'Oh – well, you know. All in the day's work,' said Bertie. He could feel himself blushing. 'Very glad you're joining us.'

'Me too. You must let me buy you a drink one night. I'll email you with some dates.'

She smiled at Bertie and continued on her upward journey; he had two thoughts. One was that she really was a very attractive woman, with her small neat figure and rather amazingly coloured hair – strawberry-blond someone had described it; the other was to wonder how anybody could possibly run in those incredibly high spiky heels. He looked after her, smiling, and then continued downwards, thinking how really his life seemed to be improving day by day.

'Saul Finlayson's asked me if I'd like to go up to his yard near Newbury one Saturday morning and see some of his horses,' said Patrick. They were sitting at the kitchen table, she with her iPad switched on, trying to work out some of the newly complex report lines at Farrell's. 'He said if you wanted to, you could come too.'

'Oh, I don't think . . .' said Bianca and saw a fleeting look of disappointment on Patrick's face. 'I mean, horses really aren't my thing, and—'

'I think I'd like you to come,' said Patrick. 'It was a friendly gesture and he is about to be my boss.'

'Of course. Sorry. No darling, of course I'll come and be a good corporate wife.'

'Well, it would be nice,' said Patrick, and there was an edge to his voice. 'I haven't made many demands of that sort on you over the years.'

'No,' she said, and felt a flash of remorse, leaning forward to kiss him on the cheek. 'No, I know you haven't. Sorry. When will you leave BCB?'

'Not for three months,' said Patrick.

'Three months! Darling, that's a lifetime in your new business.'

'Can't help that, I'm afraid. It will take that long for them to sort out a replacement for me, juggle with the team, all that sort of thing.'

'And how did Mr Finlayson react to that?'

'Well, he seemed to think as you do,' said Patrick, 'and then asked if I could do some work for him on the q.t. and I said I didn't think I could. Just not fair to the chaps at BCB, it'd be bound to get out and – well, I'm not prepared to do it.'

'I see,' said Bianca, and the wild hope came to her that Saul Finlayson would find this unacceptable, find someone else. But she crushed it. 'Well, darling, you know best of course. Oh, Milly tells me she's asked the new girl to tea tomorrow. She seems a bit smitten, bit of a girl crush brewing, I'd say. Have you heard much about her? Carey somebody?'

'Mapleton,' said Patrick. 'Yes, a bit. Father's the actor, Sir Andrew, and she sounds perfectly nice.'

'Bit of a difficult background from the sound of it. Always changing countries and schools, poor little thing. Apparently she spent a year at Hollywood High, with "oh. my. God!", some really famous people's children but Milly couldn't actually name any names.'

'Maybe Carey couldn't either,' said Patrick. 'Would the really famous people's children go to Hollywood High? I wonder . . .'

Bianca stared at him. 'Do you know, I hadn't thought of that. You're a sharp chap, Patrick Bailey, and no mistake.'

'I hope I'm sharp enough,' said Patrick, sounding anxious again.

'Darling, of course you are. Don't be silly. Mr Finlayson knows quality when he sees it.'

Chapter 15

Milly stood staring and staring at it, unable to believe her eyes. It had come in the post, a really grand invitation, stiff white card with a little gold crown on it, and black and white curvy writing, saying, *You are invited to the marriage of Prince William of Wales and Miss Catherine Middleton on 29th April, 2011* and then she moved down a line and saw the slightly smaller writing *On the personal screen of Miss Carey Mapleton, The Boltons, London, SW3 at 10.30 a.m. A wedding luncheon will be served after the ceremony, followed by a viewing of the highlights and then a disco. Dress: Formal. RSVP.*

She got to school lit up with excitement, and found half the class in the same state, chattering endlessly about what they might wear and whether their mothers might agree to get them something new and how mean if they didn't; the other half were subdued, pretending they were really busy with other things.

Even while she felt proud to be in the right half, a small part of Milly did think that if she'd been a new girl in Carey's situation she'd have asked the whole class or just two or three of the ones she was properly friends with. It was a bit, well, random.

Susie had intended to look really glamorous and behave uber-coolly that day. Bianca had told her – and she had been hugely flattered – that she wanted her involvement in appointing a new advertising agency.

'It always seems to me quite crazy for PR and advertising

campaigns not to be at least conceived in tandem, and Lara Clements will be coming too.'

Which had spurred Susie on to further ambitions on the personal presentation front; Lara wasn't working at Farrell's full time for another fortnight, but she'd been in and out of the offices quite a bit, and although she wasn't majorly glamorous, not into designer, she was chic, and carried with her a confident gloss that was extremely attractive so it was important to impress her as well.

This was the first meeting with any of the agencies on Bianca's shortlist and it was a bit of a wild card: Flynn Marchant was a young group, employing only twenty people, but they had done a very clever one-off campaign for a range of hair products that Bianca had admired and they had clearly been delighted with her email, saying they would like to come and see her, and adding with rather charming candour that their portfolio was a bit limited and their showreel more so, but they were certain nonetheless that she would like what they had to show her. Their offices were what they described as 'Marylebone border country, actually more Paddington', which Bianca had liked.

'I so disapprove of wasting money on huge rent, when it could go on better things, like staff, for instance,' she said, when Tod Marchant had apologised for the slightly unsmart address. 'We're moving ourselves as soon as we can find something clever.'

Tod Marchant felt immediately more positive about the outcome of what he described as a chemistry meeting – 'the most important thing is that we all feel we can work together, that the chemistry's right, otherwise we'll never get off the starting blocks.'

Bianca was very taken with the idea of a chemistry meeting.

Susie got up very early on the day of the meeting, partly so she had plenty of time for things like her hair and make-up but also to listen to the radio while she did it – Bianca was very hot on current affairs, particularly politics, said it was as important as fashion when it came to selling things. Susie really didn't think the girls who flocked to the Mac counters gave more than a moment's thought to the effectiveness of the coalition, but so far Bianca had been right about pretty well everything.

She was easing out of bed as quietly as she could when Henk put out a hand and tried to pull her back in.

'Babe! What are you doing? It's fucking six o'clock.'

'No, it's six thirty,' said Susie, 'and I've got an early meeting.'

'Fuck that. Come here, I don't want you leaving me. I hate being alone in bed. And you know what, I could get to feel a bit horny, if I really tried . . .'

'Henk, I'm glad to hear that,' said Susie briskly, 'but it'll have to wait.'

'That's what you said last night.' His tone was plaintive.

'Well, I'm sorry about that too. But there are other things in life and it's a work day.'

'So I'm relegated right down below the work, is that right?'

'Actually, yes,' said Susie. 'Henk, I have a job to do, money to earn, that sort of thing, OK?'

'Oh, and don't I just know it. You never stop reminding me that you're the breadwinner, that I'm just a hanger on, doing nothing.'

'And maybe I could do a little more reminding? Like you turned down at least three jobs over the last month because you said they were crap, or you didn't do weddings, or you couldn't work for the guy who wanted you as his assistant, you had no respect for him. I'm surprised your agent keeps you on, I really am. Do you think I enjoy every single thing I have to do?'

'Oh for God's sake, Susie. I've had just about enough of your critical attitude.'

'Well, in that case, maybe you should consider your options. I don't have time for this. Just go back to sleep, or get up yourself, but leave me alone. OK?'

But he had sat up in bed and was glaring at her.

'Does it ever enter that narrow little mind of yours that I slave my guts out most days, trying to find the perfect shot, to catch the right moment, just improving my skills and my portfolio? And how much encouragement do I get about that? Fucking none, just a load of nagging about couldn't I have done some shopping or made the bed. Could I just remind you that it's a tough world I'm trying to get into, it takes time and a whole lot of effort—'

'Henk, I said I don't have time for this!'

But an over-familiar panic was beginning to leach into her. It was always like this; she would be angry with Henk, resentful of his behaviour, and then, confronted with the danger of losing him, go into a state of terror, she wasn't sure why. She certainly wasn't in love with him, she wasn't even sure she *liked* him half the time. Probably it was because she'd lived the single life one time too often and knew what it meant in its bleak joylessness. Just being sexy and successful and cool and having a great job, and even a great social life, wasn't enough. She just didn't seem to have the strength to fight it. But why, why?

It was ridiculous to allow herself to be bullied like this. And it was bullying, no doubt about it. It was pathetic; she owed herself a lot better than this.

'I'm sorry, Henk,' she said, shaking off the hand that had reached out to her, slipping inside her bathrobe, caressing her breasts, 'I absolutely don't have time for this. I'll see you tonight.'

'You frigid bitch,' he said, staring at her with such dislike that she felt literally shaken. 'What the fuck am I doing with you? I really don't think I can go on with this. It's not what I call a relationship, Susie, it really isn't.'

'Henk, please! Please understand—'

'No,' he said. 'No I don't understand. Sorry. And I don't like it either. I think it's time you got your priorities—'

'Henk, if you'd only . . .'

She tried again, very half-heartedly, to pull away; but he had sensed her hesitation by then, seen the doubt in her eyes.

'That's better,' he said and suddenly smiled, pushed her on to her knees by the bed, forcing her to take him in her mouth. 'That's more like it. Go on, baby, go go go . . .'

Jemima was alone in her office when Susie rushed in, pale and breathless, her hair tousled, her eye make up smudged from doing it on the bus.

'I'm sorry, so sorry, Jemima, I—'

'Don't worry, they've only just gone in. Lara's in there too. I'll just let Bianca know you're here.' She got up, put her head into Bianca's office, turned and said, 'Yes, she says you're to go in.'

Bianca nodded at her coolly. 'Susie, hello. Sorry, we didn't wait. This is Susie Harding, our publicity director,' she said to the two men sitting at the coffee table. 'Susie – Tod Marchant, Jack Flynn. They were just explaining how they work. You'll have to pick it up from there.'

'Yes, of course, sorry Bianca, sorry, I—'

Bianca turned from her, clearly with no wish to reassure her.

'Tod, do go on.'

Tod Marchant was very cool in black leather jacket and black trousers, Jack Flynn less sexy, almost old-fashioned-looking in Levi 501s and a plain white shirt; they both smiled at Susie, almost embarrassed by the situation, and then Tod started talking again.

'Yeah, like I was saying, Susie, Jack and I worked together for ten years, met in quite a large agency and went solo – no, duetted – five years ago.'

He was a charmer; funny, easy, deceptively relaxed. Jack Flynn was quieter, more serious, with an engaging way of listening very intently and then coming in every so often with an observation of considerable shrewdness.

'We find clients really appreciate being involved in the thinking and the development of ideas, discussing things together. It makes a much more productive relationship, but it does mean the chemistry has to be right, hence this meeting. We call them chemistry meetings.'

'Sounds marvellous,' said Lara, clearly anxious to make a contribution. And scribbled something on the notebook she had brought with her. Susie had no notebook; she pulled out her phone and used that instead.

'Good. So, it's an ongoing conversation. Right, Jack?'

'Yes. We aim for a sort of alchemy with clients, an ability on both sides to know our limitations.'

Bianca smiled.

'I like alchemy,' she said. 'Alchemy is exactly what we need. So, suppose – and this is a *very* preliminary meeting – just suppose we did decide to work with you, what kind of process would we all go through?'

'Right,' said Tod, 'the first thing we'd want to do is learn everything about Farrell's. We'd go into the outlets, get to know the products—'

'Even though,' said Bianca, 'they'd be pretty unlike the ones we'd be advertising?'

'I realise that, but we have to start somewhere. There'd be a lot of meetings where we'd come down to your offices, the factory, the lab, just get immersed in the brand.'

'Yes,' said Jack, 'it's understanding not just what you do, or plan to do with the new brand but where you are right now.'

'Exactly,' said Tod. 'And we'd then go away and do some insight work – that's advertising jargon for understanding what would make people want to buy into your brand. And that would form the basis for a creative brief. Which we would work on with you. And then we give that brief to the creative team, and after that – well, we'd come back to you with what we think would work. And we'd have some more conversations.'

'Lot of conversations then,' said Bianca, smiling at him.

For goodness' sake, Susie, think of something to say . . .

'And . . . media?' she managed. Hardly brilliant, but it was better than nothing.

'Obviously,' said Jack, 'we'd look at everything.'

Obviously. Well, that had gone down like a lead balloon.

'We don't have a TV-sized budget, of course,' said Bianca.

'I appreciate that. But there are ways of squeezing money out of a campaign. What there'd undoubtedly be is a lot of online stuff because digital is the heart of everything we do these days. And it could be that the advertising would be part of the PR story, more than the other way round.'

'That sounds absolutely fantastic,' said Susie, and promptly felt inane again. Shit. She had really not been impressive. Bloody, bloody Henk.

There was a silence.

'Well,' said Bianca, 'we'll get back to you. Unless, Lara, you've got anything to ask?'

'Oh, not really,' said Lara. 'Thank you. It's been great to meet you.'

'And you,' said Tod, standing up, holding out his hand to each of them in turn; Jack followed suit.

'Susie, maybe you could show them out?' said Bianca. 'Lara, do you have five minutes? Just want to run something past you . . .'

Susie had never felt so clearly dismissed in her life.

Athina was getting ready, rather reluctantly, to have lunch with Bianca Bailey. A table had been booked, Jemima Pendleton had told her the day before, at Claridge's – 'in the Gordon Ramsay restaurant'.

'I'm afraid I don't like Gordon Ramsay,' said Athina. 'I don't admire his language and the little I have experienced of his food I like still less. Perhaps it might have been wise to check with me before booking.'

'Well, I will pass that on to Bianca,' said Jemima, her voice courteous as always, 'and come back to you.'

Half an hour later, she phoned again. 'Bianca wonders if the Dorchester Grill room would suit you better?'

'Far better,' said Athina graciously. 'Thank you.'

Bianca was waiting for her at the table. 'I was out all this morning, or we could have shared a cab. You're quite right, it's lovely here.'

'It is,' said Athina. 'Of course it's not quite what it was, it used to be more elegant years ago, more stress on the surroundings, less on the food.'

'I'm surprised, I'd have thought the food was always terribly important.'

'Yes, but one took that for granted, there wasn't this need for the chefs to put their ridiculous names on all the menus. And of course it was all less overdone. The décor, that is. Everywhere now seems to have had a rather vulgar refit.'

Bianca laughed. 'Well, I hope the food will meet with your approval at least. Was your husband a great bon viveur?'

'Of course,' said Athina, 'all well-bred people were. They enjoyed their food and their wine, and were knowledgeable about it. But it wasn't an obsession as it seems to be now. All the chefs at the great restaurants knew Cornelius and he them, but he wouldn't have expected half the world to know them as well. Still, one must try to keep up with the times, I suppose. The alternative is being written off completely.'

'I hope you don't feel that,' said Bianca.

'Of course not,' said Athina.

'Good. Are you ready to order? And would you like some wine? Or perhaps something else to start with, a gin and tonic, for instance? I'm so sorry, I should have asked you before. I can't drink at lunchtime, but you must if you want.'

'Some wine,' said Athina, 'and perhaps a dry sherry?'

'Of course.'

Athina sat quietly while Bianca ordered the food and the wine and, to her intense amusement, the water. Of all the modern trends she found the custom of spending money on bottled water one of the most baffling. Caro had told her that in New York several of the top restaurants had water sommeliers, to advise on which brand of water would go best with which course.

'Right,' said Bianca, raising her glass of San Pellegrino to Athina, 'I do, of course, have a reason for wanting to talk to you over lunch where we can be private. So – first question – how do you feel about Bertie's appointment?'

'Well, since you ask, I think it's a mistake. A great mistake. It seems odd to put him in a position of which he knows so little.'

'But my job is to utilise talent where I see it,' said Bianca, 'and I think Bertie has a great talent for people and for spotting their potential. And a very sure instinct for who will work best with whom, and how.'

'Well, of course you have a right to your opinion,' said Athina.

'Indeed. Now, I hope you agree with the relaunch plans so far.'

'Some of them,' said Athina.

'Good. Where are your reservations?'

'Well, I don't approve of your suggestion that we pull out of the stores.'

'Lady Farrell, I'm simply proposing that we get rid of the less-productive consultants, for the time being at any rate. We simply can't afford them, as things are.'

'Yes, well, that is a matter of opinion. Incidentally, I have told Bertie that some employment must be found for Marjorie Dawson. I imagine that is the sort of thing that will fall within his aegis.'

'It is,' said Bianca, 'although he will be concerned with rather weightier matters. Anyway, I am aware of the importance of finding employment for Marjorie Dawson and of her difficult personal circumstances and I do assure you I will do my best. But—'

'Mrs Bailey, Marjorie needs *certainties* and I wish to assure her of them.'

'Lady Farrell, I've just told you that I'll do all I can. We will, if necessary, put this to the vote at the next board meeting. Along with other new appointments. How would that be?'

'I think that is an acceptable solution,' said Athina graciously. She felt pleased; the family after all still held the majority share, and therefore the casting vote, and so Marjorie's future was absolutely assured. She would tell her this afternoon. The lunch moved slowly on.

'Now,' Bianca said, as they reached consideration of dessert, 'timing is crucial and difficult, but because of the importance of the heritage of the brand, and the story is so wonderful – your first launch in coronation summer, this one in the Diamond Jubilee – I'm determined we shall manage it. Well, we have to. And I do really want to work with you – and closely – in certain areas.'

'I'm very surprised,' said Athina, 'since you're changing everything we've ever done.'

'Lady Farrell, we're not changing everything. We're updating, we're relaunching, but we're building on the past glories of Farrell in a big way, on its connotations of quality and glamour – and the Britishness, of course, and sheer imaginativeness. The House of Farrell still has a magic; we just need to bring it up to date, without destroying all the things that are good about it.'

'Yes, I see. Well, that's – that's good to hear.' Athina heard her voice quaver and cleared her throat, took a sip of the Chablis Bianca had ordered.

'Is that a yes? You will work with me – us?'

'I will, of course. I can't guarantee I will always agree with what you are doing . . .'

'No, I don't suppose you will,' said Bianca. 'Anyway, disagreement is healthy as I'm sure you'd agree.' She smiled at Athina.

'So, I assume you mean I am to be involved in product development? That was always my forte. And the colour promotions, of course.'

'Well,' Bianca took an near-imperceptible breath, 'well, Lady Farrell, perhaps not directly on the products, no.'

Athina's green eyes became diamond hard.

'Perhaps you would like to tell me why not?'

'Because . . .' Bianca took a deep breath, 'because product development is something I prefer to handle myself, together with the marketing department. So that product concepts, campaigns, promotions are all rationalised. Working with the lab, of course.'

'I find that a rather extraordinary idea,' said Athina. 'You have no experience of cosmetics. None whatever.'

'I would have to argue with that.'

There was a silence; finally, Athina said, 'So what would you like me to work on?'

'Publicity,' said Bianca.

'Publicity? But you've just promoted the Harding girl to do that.'

'Bear with me. Of course we can't start talking about the new range to the press for many months, or our plans for the new shops, but we do want to keep Farrell's name very much alive, and so what Susie Harding has suggested, and I think it's an excellent idea, is that we do some personal publicity.'

'And what precisely do you mean by that?' said Athina. 'Not, I trust, a spread in a gossip magazine saying how happy we are, or all that Twittering nonsense.'

'Well, not exactly,' said Bianca, 'although Twitter might come into it . . . No, I would very much like to see some stories in the other magazines – *Vogue*, for instance, and *The Times* magazine, any of the glossy newspaper supplements, actually – about the history of Farrell's, how you and your husband started it, the early struggles and successes, the Berkeley Arcade and the part it's played in the story, perhaps some famous customers there.'

'But what would be the point?' said Athina. 'We want to publicise the products, not the people behind it. That sort of thing is so vulgar. We've had royalty in the Berkeley Arcade, as you know.'

'Perhaps we could do a story about that.'

'Oh, I don't think so! That would be a serious betrayal.'

'I see. Well, we could hint at it. High society, that sort of thing.'

'I would prefer not.'

'In that case, can you imagine any publicity about the family, its history, possibly even your husband, that you *would* be happy with? That you would be prepared to talk to a journalist about?'

'Not really, no.' Athina gave her a brief, cool smile.

'Oh, dear. That *is* a shame. Susie is tremendously keen, thinks it would bridge the gap between now and the launch. Perhaps we could come back to it a little further along the road.'

'You could,' said Athina with an emphasis on the 'could', and then aware that this might sound a little rude, 'but yes, we could discuss it again. I really see little prospect however of changing my mind.'

'Very well. Maybe Florence could help. She's been with you from the beginning, after all.'

'No, that's not correct. The brand was extremely successful before she joined us. And her views on publicity are totally in accord with my own.'

'Really? I had got a slightly different impression. Well, we shall see. Now, there's something else I'd like your opinion on and that I would like your involvement in. I'm thinking of including a perfume to go with the new range. I know it will be expensive, but it will raise our profile and if it's clever enough and classy enough, will justify the cost. What do you think?'

'Oh, my dear, don't even think about it,' said Athina, 'it's the equivalent of pouring your money straight down the drain. You cannot launch a perfume on a shoestring. We did consider it once and decided we couldn't do it. And that was when we were at the very top of our game. Buyers and store managers and so on all advised against it, said the investment would be huge. Cornelius decided it would be a waste of our time and resources, and he was right.'

'I see. You didn't start work on any formulations, I suppose?'

'Mrs Bailey, a successful perfume launch is ninety-nine per cent about money. Please believe me. I know.'

As if, Athina thought, sitting and raging in the car on her way home, as if she was going to share anything with Bianca Bailey that would help her. Especially as she had been so firmly dismissed from the area of product development.

Back in her office, Bianca called Lara.

'Lara, do you know – yes, of course you do – people who develop perfumes, and might do one for us? What? Well, let's just say I'm thinking about it. Absolutely top secret of course. But if you could draw me up a little list . . .'

Chapter 16

'Be who God meant you to be and you will set the world on fire.'

Really? Bianca thought. Was it really that simple? No, not really. God might have meant you to be someone very very humble and self-sacrificing. Would that set the world on fire? And if you were pushy and driven, which possibly would set the world on fire, God probably wouldn't like it at all.

'How clever!' said Gerald Wood.

'What, Daddy?' She hauled herself back to the present and the television coverage of the Royal Wedding. Her father had been invited to watch it, had come reluctantly, and was now, as she had known he would be, enjoying the whole thing.

'Of the Bishop of London. To use a quotation from another Catherine. That quotation was by St Catherine of Siena, and it's her festival today. He must have worked pretty hard to find that. My word, *she* looks jolly nice. Who is she?'

'Carole Middleton, mother of the bride.'

Patrick came into the room, bearing champagne. 'Champagne, Gerald?'

'Oh, how very nice, thank you.'

Bianca returned her attention to the screen and wondered if Kate had really done her own make-up that morning, as the PR story went. If she had, she could have a great future as a make-up artist . . .

Lucy was also studying Kate's make-up. She'd have made Kate's eyes a bit softer and smudgier and given her a bit less blusher. Otherwise, it was pretty well perfect.

She looked across at her father; he was watching, as instructed by her mother, who took royalty very seriously indeed. Her main ambition was to be involved in a charity that had a strong royal connection. Her father was clearly not concentrating, though.

Her brother, Rob, who'd come home from uni for a few days, was totally absorbed in making arrangements for the evening on his phone.

It was lovely to have him home. They'd been discussing their father the night before in the pub and agreed he seemed much happier these days and how great it was he had this new job.

'And he's looking much better,' Lucy had said. 'Better, as in thinner, all his clothes are hanging off him.'

'Well, we have to thank Mum for that, I guess,' said Rob. 'She's been very strict with the diet.'

'Yes, but she's tried before and failed. He obviously suddenly feels it's worth it. Want another?'

Lawrence Ford was watching the wedding with his wife and nine-year-old son, Nicholas, who was texting his friends about how boring it was.

Later they had to go and join some neighbours for a wedding party; and the next day, someone else was having a barbecue. He wasn't looking forward to either. Every social occasion was a hideous challenge suddenly; indeed, every day was a hideous challenge. And he just didn't know what to do about it.

He should have told Annie immediately; told her he had been made redundant, told her everything had to change, but somehow he hadn't been able to. It had been such a shock when Bianca Bailey and Bertie Farrell told him, such an awful, dreadful blow, physical in its violence. He'd never imagined he'd be out on his ear, even if it was with two years' salary, tax-free and the company car his to keep.

'We shall miss you,' Bianca said, 'and your department will miss you too. But hopefully, with your track record, you will find another job quite quickly and I do assure you that we will give you very good references.'

Lawrence thought that if he could have very good references he might well still have the job.

It had been agreed that he should leave almost at once.

'This coming weekend being the royal wedding, with the extra day's holiday, will give you time to adjust, talk to your family and so on.'

After which he'd left the meeting and the building and gone and sat in the pub and wondered what on earth he would do; he knew he should tell Annie straight away, but until he had sorted out his story, it seemed quite impossible; he simply wanted to go home and go to bed and take a sleeping pill and not talk to anyone. It was a nightmare, a bloody awful, unjust nightmare. And he really didn't feel he could go on sitting here, pretending to care about this absurd carry-on any longer.

He turned to Nicholas, who was kicking the coffee table, albeit with his socked feet, and said, 'Tell you what, old chap, I'm not really enjoying this much either. Let's go out on our bikes, shall we? I'm sure Mummy won't mind, will you darling?'

'No,' said Annie, smiling at him. 'Not really boys' stuff this, is it? And you do look very tired, darling. You work so hard and they rely on you too much, they really do. Yes, go on, and I'll see you later. Oh, this music is lovely . . .'

She turned back to the television and Lawrence went upstairs to put his tracksuit on and wondered if perhaps he could possibly tell her before the barbecue tomorrow at least . . .

Florence had agreed to watch the wedding with Athina and now she was regretting it. In the first place, Athina's television had a rather small screen – she said large ones were vulgar – and, in the second, she was finding Athina's constant sniping at Bianca increasingly irritating.

Florence liked Bianca; she found her straightforward and courteous and she did admire her ideas for the House of Farrell. She had been deeply touched that Bianca had taken the time to come and talk through her plans for The Shop; she had laughed when Florence had asked rather tremulously if she really wanted her to stay on.

'Florence, of course I do! You're a vital member of the team and part of our history, it's *vital* you're involved. I don't want some young manager who doesn't understand the legacy and the history of the place; I want *you* there – if you're willing, of course. I might change the treatment set-up, indeed I know I want to, and I'm sure Francine's facials are perfectly lovely, but they are very old-fashioned. And she did hint to me that she was finding it all rather tiring. I'd love your ideas about new treatments and which ones would suit us. I mean, do you think we could extend beyond facials, and do massages and so on?'

When Florence had said she did and she had thought so for some time, but Lady Farrell had been very opposed to the idea, Bianca had simply said, 'Well, we must try to persuade her,' and asked her to make a list of which treatments Florence thought would be suitable.

Florence had said she would email her with some ideas and Bianca had clearly been a little surprised to hear Florence talk about emailing, although she had simply thanked her and said she would look forward to hearing them. Florence had sent her a short list, which included Hot Stone Massage, Personalised Aromatherapy ('It would be wonderful if we could formulate some essential oils of our own, we could call them Farrell Bespoke or something like that') and Head and Neck Massage.

Bianca had emailed back immediately and said she liked all those ideas, especially the bespoke oils, and that she would get back to her with more ideas.

Florence had even become slightly less opposed to personalised publicity. 'I suppose, after all, many of our early clients are long dead, so we're not giving away any secrets, and we had some very big names – the Duchess of Wiltshire, Lady Aberconway, the Countess of Jedburgh – and they all signed our visitors' book.'

Bianca had been very excited about the visitors' book and asked if she might see it and she and Florence had spent a marvellous hour poring over the legendary names, some from the aristocracy, many showbiz. 'And no one's going to tell me those sorts of people would mind,' Florence said, 'if they're still alive – which is quite unlikely I'd say. Those musical comedy actresses, Dulcie Fleming, look, and Aurora Chanelle, she was one of Ivor Novello's favourites, you know . . .'

Bianca had asked her to draw up a shortlist and asked her if she would mind if Susie Harding came in to discuss it; Florence said of course not, she was increasingly impressed by Susie.

On the whole, Florence felt her life to be considerably improved by the arrival of Bianca Bailey.

So sitting and listening to Athina criticising her constantly wasn't really very agreeable; especially as it had drowned out first the commentary on the arrival at the Abbey, which was always so interesting, and now it was the service and she wanted to be able to listen to the couple making their vows, not a long diatribe against Bianca Bailey's publicity proposals.

When Florence said that she thought the stories about clients and customers over the years, confining it to those who had long since shuffled off their mortal coils, was a good idea, Athina looked at her witheringly and said had she not thought of the descendants of those clients and how they might feel about it.

'They might even sue. I really would not advise it.'

Florence said she thought it was very unlikely anyone would sue for reading about their beautiful grandmother and that it could do Farrell's nothing but good.

'Well, of course they could sue, Florence,' Athina said. 'You never have thought things through properly.'

Florence decided she had had enough.

She stood up; Athina was still talking loudly over the Archbishop.

'I'm sorry, Athina dear, but I thought we were here to watch the wedding? If you don't want to do that, I shall get a taxi home. Which would mean my missing the rest of the ceremony live and that would be a pity, but I've set my TV to record and I think I should enjoy that rather more.'

At which Athina looked very startled and said she was extremely sorry in a voice that made it plain she wasn't at all, but she did stop talking and went to fetch a bottle of champagne which she opened and poured a glass for them both in a rather tense, but very welcome, silence and they made it up over an extremely nice lunch.

Susie was watching the wedding alone. Henk was out working. He had said that of course it wasn't what *she* would consider work, as he wouldn't be earning any money, but he wanted to catch the mood of the day on camera, and in order to do that he needed to be on his own.

She had gone home the day of the meeting, determined to tell him it was over and that she wanted him out, but as she opened the door, delicious cooking smells wafted towards her and he appeared, bearing two glasses of champagne, a rueful smile on his face.

'Decided you were right and I should work a bit harder for my keep,' he said, kissing her on the cheek. 'How was the meeting? Did you shine?'

'Not exactly,' she said, determinedly cool. 'I was almost late.'

'Oh no! Well, I'm sure you did brilliantly just the same. Come on in and recover. I've cooked a tagine, your favourite.'

He'd been on his best behaviour for a few days, but gradually he was slithering back into his old self, awkward, lazy, touchy . . . And had left quite early, without so much as a farewell kiss. Well, good. It was great having him out of the flat – for a bit.

He had come into her life via a thirtieth birthday party for one of her oldest friends – God, she hated they were all that old! – all brooding good looks and cool clothes. He'd told her she was gorgeous, made her laugh, and they'd left the party as soon as decently possible and went home to bed. He hadn't been in London long, had grown up in Yorkshire but talked Estuary English – she'd never quite known why. He'd christened himself Henk, although his real name was John, and was struggling to make his name as a photographer. He was a good photographer but he didn't have the spark to make it really big. Still, she enjoyed being with someone who spoke her language.

Henk made her laugh – although that didn't happen very often now, she reflected as she made herself a bacon butty and a cup of coffee – and he was also an extremely good cook, another skill that didn't get much of an airing. He was also very good in bed, so they had been fine for about three months, then the novelty had worn off. Henk's income had remained at zero and she couldn't help, just occasionally, referring to the fact that he wasn't paying her any rent, or even buying any food; whereupon a rather nasty temper had manifested itself and the rows had begun.

Marjorie poured herself a second glass of cava and settled back on the sofa; what a wonderful day. She was a great royalist. And Kate, although she was a commoner, was really very lovely and William was charming, just like his mother, and they were both deeply in love. And she felt so much happier now that she knew her future with Farrell's was guaranteed; clearly Bianca Bailey had been no better at overruling Lady Farrell than anyone else.

Chapter 17

'Oh yes! How cool is that? Sounds great. I'll just ask – hold on. Or shall I call you back? Yeah, OK. No, no, of course, really soon. What? Oh, I'll tell her. Thank you so much!

'That was Carey,' said Milly, switching off her phone, her great eyes shining, 'she says can I go to Paris with her next weekend?'

'Paris!' said Bianca.

'Yes. With her and her parents.'

'Well – I don't know,' said Bianca. 'I mean . . .'

She felt mildly worried without knowing quite why. Except Milly was rather dazzled by Carey and had come back from the wedding party goggle-eyed at the size of Carey's house, and her personal sitting room and walk-in clothes cupboard; but she seemed a very nice child, had been for a sleepover with Milly since and behaved very nicely, had charming manners . . .

'Oh, Mummy! You're not going to say no, are you?'

'Um, well, I'd like to know a bit more about it.'

'There isn't any more,' said Milly, her voice heavy with exagger-ated patience, 'she's going to Paris with her parents, they've got to see about letting their flat, and Carey wants to have a friend with her. She says we can go shopping!'

'I see. Er – Patrick, did you take that in?'

Patrick looked up from the *Financial Times*. 'Sort of. Carey wants to take Milly to Paris. Very smart. How long for, Milly?'

'Oh – just the weekend. Please don't say no, *please*.'

'Well, I think perhaps we'd like to know a bit more about it.'

'But why?'

'Darling, we've hardly met Carey's parents. It seems a bit – I don't know, extreme.'

'Oh, what! What's extreme about it? We're not going to the moon on our own. We're going on Eurostar with her parents. It's no big deal.'

'No, of course not. But—'

'Oh, you're both so pathetic! You just don't want me to have a good time. Well, I'm going anyway, and that's *that*!'

The last word was accompanied by a slammed door; and then another from the floor above. Bianca and Patrick looked at one another.

'What did we do?' said Patrick.

Ten minutes later Milly reappeared, swollen-eyed.

'You are so horrible,' she said. 'Carey says if I don't reply straight away she'll take someone else.'

'Milly,' said Bianca, gently, 'tell Carey to go and speak to her mother.'

'Why?'

'Because I have just had a conversation with her and she said of course she was going to ring us and Carey wasn't supposed to invite you until she had, OK?'

'Oh. So can I go?'

'Yes, darling, you can. But another time, just wait for a few minutes before you go into the attack, will you? Good lesson for life altogether.'

'Oh. Oh, I see. Yes, all right.' A sheepish smile had appeared on her face and she moved forward and hugged first her mother then her father. 'Sorry.'

'It's OK,' said Patrick, 'just don't go asking us for extra spending money.'

'But Dad! Dad, it's Paris!'

He grinned at her.

'Just joking. Of course you can have some. You'll have to earn it though.'

'How?' She looked half surprised.

'You can start with cleaning your room.'

'But the cleaner does that . . . I mean, yes all right. Course. Thank you.'

She kissed them both and skipped out of the room.

'I think we should watch that friendship a little bit carefully,' said Bianca. 'A manipulative little person, is Carey Mapleton.'

'Bertie, I need to talk to you about Marjorie. It was agreed we should discuss what might happen to her at the next board meeting, that she was a special case—'

'I think that was what Mother wanted. I'm not sure that it was actually agreed, Caro, and I'm also not sure it's a matter for the board. But—'

'It hasn't taken you long to join the enemy, has it, Bertie? Bianca's blue-eyed boy. Yes Bianca, no Bianca. Just because she's given you a job. *My* job. Now could you please see that Marjorie's situation is put on the agenda for next Thursday, because it's not there at the moment – if it's not beyond your extremely limited remit . . .'

'Goodbye, Caro.' Bertie put the phone down and sat staring at it. His entire family, with the exception of his children, seemed hell-bent on putting him down. It was – well, it was totally humiliating. Suddenly more than anything in the world he wanted a bar of chocolate. Just a small one. He'd go and get one and it would make him feel better. It was nearly lunchtime anyway.

He walked into the corridor and towards the stairs.

'Bertie! Hello.' It was Lara Clements. 'Look, would this be a good time to buy you that drink? Or are you on your way somewhere important?'

'Er – no, no,' said Bertie. 'No, I was just – just popping out.'

'Right. Well, we can't be very long because we've got those interviews to do this afternoon, but it might be nice to have a quick chat about them out of the office.'

She smiled at him, and she had a very nice smile. It had a sort of engaging, conspiratorial quality, as if she was saying, 'Wouldn't you agree life is really rather nice?'

He smiled back at her. 'Well, that would be . . . would be . . .'

'Good. Where would you like to go?'

'Oh, there's a very nice pub just along the road. Or don't you like pubs?'

'I love pubs. Much prefer them to swanky bars, as a matter of fact. Yes, let's go there. Lead the way.'

The pub was still quiet and it was a lovely day.

'Let's sit outside, shall we? Now, what can I get you, Bertie? What's your poison?'

'Chocolate,' he said and laughed. 'As a matter of fact, I was about to weaken and buy a bar just now. My wife's got me on this very strict diet and—'

'Well, I don't think they serve that here. How about a nice red wine instead? Or a spritzer, even better. Nothing I don't know about dieting.'

'Really? You could have fooled me. You're so slim.'

'Only because I never stop counting calories. And have the statutory fat picture of myself at university on my fridge. Now – red or white, which is it to be?'

'I do confess to hating those spritzer things.'

'I'll get two glasses of red, shall I?'

'That'd be lovely,' said Bertie. 'Thank you.'

She reappeared with the drinks, sat down opposite him and raised her glass. 'Cheers, Bertie. Thanks so much for putting me forward for this job.'

'Honestly I hardly did anything,' he said. 'Feel like a bit of a fraud actually, taking this off you.'

'Well, you shouldn't. Feel a fraud, I mean. Bianca would never have heard of me without your help.'

'I think she would, but anyway – how's it going?'

'Oh, I love it. Bianca is so great to work for, so good about just leaving you to it once she's satisfied you're going in the right direction, and so inspiring. If anyone can turn Farrell's round, she can. I love her ideas.'

'They're great,' said Bertie. 'My mother would never let us so much as think about any of them, of course. Like being on the internet. She said it would be disastrous for our image.' He sighed. 'And of course, that's one of the many reasons we got into the pickle we're in.'

'Yes, well I'm sure there were many, many strengths that she brought to the brand as well,' said Lara carefully. 'It must be very difficult for you. Divided loyalties and all that.'

'A bit,' said Bertie carefully.

There was a silence; then, 'So – you have a wife, I know that, because you told me of her dietary disciplining. Children?'

'Two. Daughter, Lucy, who lights up her old dad's life, and son Rob. He's at medical school.'

'And what does Lucy do?'

'Oh. Well, she was at uni, reading Engish Literature. Now she's – well, she's learning to be a make-up artist.'

'Good for her. And why the hushed voice?'

'I'm sorry?'

'Bertie! You looked as if you were confessing to her being on the game. What's wrong with being a make-up artist? Damn sight better than being an unemployed graduate.'

'That's what she says.'

'Well, she's very smart.'

'I'd just rather she'd finished her course.'

'I think you should get with the programme as they say,' said Lara briskly. 'It sounds to me like your daughter's got her head screwed on. And you know, make-up artists are big stars these days, earning big money. Not all of them, but the best. And it's a great life zooming round from fashion show to photographic studio, London to New York.'

'Yes, I'm sure,' said Bertie, 'but—'

'Bertie! Come on. What does your mother think?'

'Oh she thinks it's quite a good idea,' said Bertie.

'I bet she does. Now there's a lady who knew where she was going, all those years ago. No, I think you should be very proud of your Lucy. She sounds great. And when she's finished, who knows? She might be able to work for us. Now, we ought to just review the candidates.'

'Of course,' said Bertie. He raised his glass to her. 'And thank you, Lara, for this.'

'My pleasure. I – whoops! Oh God, Bertie, I'm so sorry.'

A man had walked past them and jolted her arm, sending her red wine all over Bertie's linen jacket. The man said, 'Sorry mate!' and disappeared into the pub.

Lara dabbed rather ineffectually at the jacket. 'Oh, God, and it's such a nice jacket. Shit!'

'Wasn't your fault,' said Bertie.

'I know but – and God, it's gone over your shirt too. Oh, I feel terrible. And we've got those interviews . . .'

'Oh that doesn't matter,' said Bertie. 'Who's going to look at me? As my nanny used to say.'

'Nanny was wrong. Lots of people are going to look at you. Six to be precise. Oh, bloody hell! Look – come on. We can just make it.' She raised her arm, hailed a taxi.

'M&S Oxford Circus, please. Pronto!'

'But,' said Bertie, 'but we can't—'

'Yes, we can. We've got to. I'm not interviewing some of London's brightest with you smelling like a bar at closing time. Unless you've got a spare shirt in the office?'

Bertie shook his head.

'We'll start with a shirt,' Lara said. 'Blue stripe? Or check?'

'I'm not sure—'

'Right, we'll get both. Or – oh look, that's lovely, the pale blue linen. That's the one. OK, size?'

'Seventeen,' said Bertie miserably.

'Bertie, you are not a seventeen. You might have been once, but all your shirts gape at the neck. I'd say sixteen. OK, jackets – there, the very fine check linen. See, in blue and beige? Here, hold it up . . . yes, great. And it'd look fantastic with the shirt. Right, that's it. Let's go!'

And thus it was that at precisely two forty, the first young (female) graduate from Manchester was shown into Lara Clements' office and was interviewed with great skill and insight. Not only by the woman she immediately longed to be her boss, bright and sassy and tough, but the HR director, a charming, gentle and clearly very clever middle-aged man, who asked her what were definitely the more difficult questions. She noticed that they seemed to have quite a rapport going between them, and that, oddly, he was wearing a rather stylish shirt and jacket, but his trousers were baggy and far too big for him.

'Florence, dear, I'm so sorry, but I'm not well.' Athina's voice sounded genuinely weak. She was no stranger to the diplomatic illness, as Florence knew, but . . .

'I'm sorry, Athina, what is it?'

'Oh, migraine, I suppose. You remember how I used to suffer from them? Anyway, it's quite appalling. So I won't be able to join you this evening. I'm so sorry.'

'That's perfectly all right. I'm sorry too, but there will be another evening. Let me know if I can do anything, won't you?'

'Yes, yes.'

Athina put the phone down and walked over to her cocktail cabinet, mixed herself a gin and Dubonnet, still one of her favourite drinks. She couldn't face another session with Florence telling her how busy she was and how she was enjoying working with Bianca – it was so very disagreeable when she herself had nothing to do.

And Florence, mildly relieved, was left to remember all those evenings, all those migraines . . .

The first time had surprised her; Athina had seemed the opposite of fragile.

But the voice was faint, clearly pain-filled.

'Florence, dear, I wonder if you'd like to take my place tonight? We were going to a concert at the Wigmore Hall, with friends, but I simply cannot face it. I would have thought Cornelius could go on his own, but he says he'd be miserable and suggested we asked you. Well, to be frank, dear, it's such short notice, it would seem rude to ask most people, and we thought you'd be free and would enjoy a treat.'

'Well, that would be lovely,' said Florence, swallowing the insult. 'And, yes, I am free.'

'As we thought. I told Cornelius he should ask you himself, but he said he was too shy. Ridiculous of course, but we have to humour him.'

A little surprised at being considered suitable – the acutely sociable Farrells must surely have countless far grander friends – Florence said she would be delighted to attend the concert and went to review her puny wardrobe. She thought, as she rifled through, it was time the Farrells began to pay her a little more money. The Berkeley Arcade shop was doing extremely well.

She picked a black cocktail dress, a copy of the one worn by Audrey Hepburn in *Sabrina Fair*, the year before. It was still extremely fashionable: black taffeta, full skirted, very waisted and fastened on the shoulders with indisputably daring bows.

It suited her, she knew; black emphasised her white skin, and the shape accentuated her tiny waist. She put her hair up in a French pleat, made up her eyes in the rather bold manner of the season – which the House of Farrell was featuring strongly – sprayed herself liberally with *Diorling*, which her friend at Marshall & Snelgrove had provided at cost price, and went out to the waiting car when summoned by her doorbell with a black mohair stole draped round her shoulders and the highest heels she possessed.

Cornelius had been waiting by her front door; he clearly, and flatteringly, did a double take before ushering her into the back seat beside him.

'You look wonderful,' he said, taking her hand and kissing it, 'really quite marvellous.'

'Thank you, Cornelius. It's very kind of you to take me.'

'No, no, kind of you to come. I'm sure you had much better things to do.'

'Not really,' she said and laughed, 'unless of course you count listening to a Paul Temple mystery on the wireless?' She took the

168

cigarette he offered from his silver case. 'Tell me about your friends. I don't want to arrive unbriefed.'

'Ah yes. Jennifer and Geoffrey Millard. Geoffrey and I were at Malvern together. Became friends over a shared dislike of rugger. He went into the City, runs a big stockbroking firm. He's been very successful. I think you'll like him.'

'I'm sure I will. And Mrs Millard?'

'Jennifer's very nice indeed. Salt of the earth. Does a lot of charity work.'

Florence could already imagine Mrs Millard. She thought she was probably overweight . . .

As it turned out both the Millards were overweight. They were pleasantly polite – and very dull.

The concert, Handel, was lovely, and mercifully short. They were outside again by eight forty-five. It transpired that a supper had been planned afterwards, but Jennifer disappeared into a telephone box in the foyer and came back, asking if they might be excused.

'Sylvia, you know, our youngest, has chickenpox, not at all well. I think, Geoffrey, we should go back. If Cornelius and – er – Florence don't mind.' Her hesitation over Florence's name clearly emphasised her below stairs status.

'Of course, of course. I do hope she'll be all right, poor little thing.'

'She's just very fretful, apparently. Nanny says she's been asking for us.'

Florence would not have wished illness on any child, but given that poor Sylvia was already suffering, she sent up a silent prayer of gratitude.

They parted from the Millards and Cornelius looked at his watch.

'I say, it's jolly early. Do you know, there's something else I'd like to do this evening, if you didn't mind?'

Florence said she was sure she wouldn't mind.

'Friend of mine, Leonard Trentham, he's a painter, got a private view tonight. I said I couldn't go because of the concert, but I bet it's still going. Would you mind if we popped down to Cork Street?'

Florence said again she wouldn't mind. She hoped Leonard Trentham would be more interesting than the Millards. She asked what sort of paintings he did.

'Oh, pretty conventional, landscapes, seascapes, things like that. But he sells pretty well. This exhibition is paintings he's done in France. Quite a few of Paris apparently.'

'How lovely,' said Florence.

'Indeed. Have you been to Paris?'

'No,' she said, 'but I would so love to.'

'Now that is a small tragedy. If not a large one. Everyone should go to Paris. It should be compulsory.'

'Sadly, not everyone can,' said Florence briskly. 'Money and even time will not allow.'

He looked at her rather directly, and said, 'Of course. Stupid remark. I'm sorry. What I meant was that it should somehow be part of everyone's education. A school trip.'

'The sort of school I went to didn't go on trips,' said Florence.

'What sort of school was it?'

'A convent.'

'Ah. So you're a convent girl? Quite a reputation you all have.'

'I know,' said Florence, 'but undeserved for the most part. Most of my friends were too frightened of hellfire to do more than hold hands with a boy. And all were very innocent when they married.'

'I'm pleased to hear it,' said Cornelius easily.

Florence said, 'But of course you're right and I would love to go to Paris. Perhaps one day.'

'I hope so, for your sake. Well, perhaps we can find a small painting at the exhibition which will serve in lieu for now. Until you can go for real of course.'

'Perhaps,' she said thinking that it would be most unlikely that she would be able to afford so much as the corner of a frame of one of Mr Trentham's pictures.

'It's at the Medici – in Cork Street,' said Cornelius, as the car wove its way down Bond Street. 'Very nice gallery. Athina and I go there quite a lot. Do you know it?'

'Not well,' said Florence carefully. She was beginning to feel increasingly unsuited to the role she had been called upon to play this evening.

'Ah. Anyway, you'll like Leonard, he's a very good egg. And he'll like you, I can assure you of that. He's got an eye for a pretty woman. I don't know why he doesn't paint them. I would if I were a painter.'

'Well, I suppose you do in a way,' said Florence. 'You enable us to paint our own faces.'

He smiled. 'I like that thought, Florence. Thank you. In fact, it's given me an idea.'

The party was still in very full swing, and was occupying a large part of the pavement as well as the gallery itself. Florence had been afraid that Cornelius would be caught up in a crowd of friends when they arrived, leaving her to fend for herself, but to her surprise he was most solicitous, steering her towards a waiter bearing a tray of drinks. She took a glass of champagne and sipped it cautiously.

'Isn't this nice?' he whispered in her ear.

'It's lovely, yes. But I have a weak head for alcohol. I have to drink it with great caution.'

She expected him to laugh, but he looked at her rather seriously and said, 'How self-aware you are, Florence. It's a very charming characteristic. Between you and me, it is not one that Athina possesses.'

She didn't know how to respond to this; it seemed a little disloyal to her.

'There's Leonard. Leonard, congratulations old chap. Fantastic show, incredible turnout. Critics here?'

'Oh, a few,' said Leonard Trentham. 'Thanks for coming, Cornelius.'

He was tall and very thin, and looked a caricature of an artist, wearing a linen suit with a floppy cravat.

He took Florence's hand in his and smiled at her. 'And you are?'

'Ah yes, let me introduce you,' said Cornelius. 'Florence, Leonard Trentham, artist. Leonard, Florence Hamilton. Florence works with us, in the company.'

'Well, how fortunate for the company. And you,' said Leonard Trentham. He smiled at her, a wide, childlike smile. His eyelashes were very long and looked suspiciously as if they had mascara on them. She supposed he must be queer.

'I'm so glad you could come Miss Hamilton,' he said. 'You grace our gathering. And where is the fair goddess this evening?'

'Oh, not well. That's Leonard's nickname for Athina,' he said to Florence, 'after Pallas Athena, of course. The goddess of wisdom.'

'Yes, I did know,' said Florence, slightly cool, 'and the patron goddess of Athens. But of course she spelt her name differently, didn't she?'

'Clever as well as beautiful, I see,' said Leonard Trentham. 'And you have replaced Athina with an "i"?'

'Only for the evening,' said Florence.

'Well, you're a lucky man, Cornelius,' said Leonard, 'one lovely woman after another. Poor Athina. Well, now go and have a look at the pictures. I hope you like them.'

'I know we will,' said Cornelius, 'Florence is specially interested in any you've done of Paris. Come along, Florence, let's see what we can find for you.'

They wandered round the gallery; the pictures were lovely, representational but with a dash of impressionism. Trentham had a supreme talent for capturing light: you could tell at a glance, Florence thought, what time of day each one had been painted.

'They're lovely,' she said, 'really beautiful.'

'Aren't they? Now here is your Paris.'

Florence stood smiling at the collection, a view of the Sacré Coeur, painted from below, shining in the dawn; a streak of gold that was the Seine at dusk; a group of clearly chattering tables at midday on the pavement outside La Closerie des Lilas, her catalogue told her; and then some smaller ones, tiny streets, a flower market, a doorway half-open, leading into a paved courtyard, filled with trees and flowers at late afternoon.

'Oh,' she said, 'that is so, so lovely.'

'Which? Let me see. Oh, yes, I agree. Perfect. That's in – ah, off the rue de Buci, St Germain, my very favourite area of all.'

'I feel I could open that door,' said Florence, smiling, 'and walk in.'

'Indeed. So – is that your favourite?'

'Yes,' said Florence. 'It makes me feel warm, with that sunshine, and really really happy.' And then, seeing him examining the catalogue for prices, said anxiously, 'Oh Cornelius, I couldn't possibly possibly afford to buy it.'

'I didn't think you could,' said Cornelius. And then, smiling, 'If you could we would clearly be paying you far too much. But it is very lovely. And not sold. No red dot.'

'No indeed.'

He looked at the picture and then at her, very intently, his dark blue eyes moving from one to the other and then back again.

'Yes,' he said finally, 'you suit one another very well, you and the picture. You should be together.'

'I . . .' She found her gaze, caught up in his, hard to pull away. He was standing quite close to her and she was very aware of him suddenly, as a man, an attractive, amusing, charming man, not a colleague, not the husband of her boss. She felt the moment freeze in time, as if the camera had clicked, holding them there together, staring at one another – a long, oddly dangerous moment. She stepped back, collided with someone, said, 'Oh, I'm so sorry.' It was Leonard Trentham.

'Perfectly all right,' he said, 'I just wanted to make sure you had found the Paris collection.'

'We have, thank you. They're wonderful.'

She smiled at him, and then up at Cornelius, hoping he would approve of this; he was staring at her as if he had hardly seen her before.

'Florence particularly likes the courtyard. In St Germain,' he said into the odd silence that had formed. He seemed tense suddenly, his usual easy charm briefly deserting him.

'She does?'

'Yes,' she said, equally tense, flustered. 'Yes, it's perfectly beautiful. It – it transports you.'

'Yes, you both look a little transported,' said Leonard Trentham.

'Another painting, in fact. If I painted figures I would paint you looking at my painting.'

'Why don't you?' asked Florence. 'Paint portraits, I mean.'

'Mostly because, you know, if you paint someone, you are alone with them for many, many hours, and you have to talk to them. I am dreadfully shy, I couldn't possibly cope with that.'

Cornelius burst into laughter and moved further back into the room, lighting a cigarette.

'Shy! Leonard, you don't know the meaning of the word.'

'That's what you think,' said Leonard Trentham. 'Now – how about supper? A crowd are coming back to my place.'

Cornelius looked at Florence. 'Florence, what do you think? Do you need to get home?'

There was a long silence; she stared at him, and felt suddenly that she was nearing some dangerous place . . .

'I think I should go home,' she said finally, reluctantly. 'Cornelius, you stay.'

'Oh, no, no,' he said and she could hear the disappointment in his voice. 'No, I should be going home. Duty calls. Poor Athina will be wondering where I am.'

'*Quel dommage*,' said Leonard. 'How glad I am duty never calls me. But I understand.'

He took Florence's hand and kissed it.

'It has been a great pleasure to have you grace my gallery,' he said, 'I hope I shall see you here again.'

Cornelius drove Florence home in silence. She felt a little anxious, that he might think she was spoiling his evening, but every time she looked at him, he seemed to sense it and glanced at her, smiling.

'I liked Leonard very much,' she said finally.

'Yes, he's a wonderful chap. Queer as a nine bob note, of course, but I'm very fond of him.'

'Yes, I thought he might be.'

'You don't mind that sort of thing?' he said.

'No,' she said, 'no of course not. Why should I?'

174

'Unfortunately, many people do. Which is why, of course, it's against the law.'

'I know. So stupid.'

'Well, it's very good to know you think as you do. What a perfect person you are, Florence Hamilton.'

She said nothing, just smiled out of the window.

'It's been such fun,' he said, when they reached her flat. 'Thank you so much for coming.' He jumped out of the car, opened the door for her, bent to kiss her on the cheek. It lasted just a fraction of a moment too long.

'It was entirely my pleasure,' she said, and smiled up at him. 'Thank you, Cornelius. I won't – won't ask you in,' she added, and the words, for all their innocence, sounded faintly provocative to her.

'No, indeed,' he said, 'you mustn't.'

And then he was gone.

Ten days later, early in the morning, there was a knock at the door; a young man was holding a large flat brown paper parcel.

'Miss Hamilton?'

'Yes?'

'This is for you. Personal delivery.'

It was the painting. With a note attached. From Leonard Trentham.

'I am bidden to send you this,' it said, 'a gift from a secret admirer. Who wishes to remain so. Please enjoy it. I am glad it is to be yours.'

And then a flamboyant signature.

She was sure, of course, who it was from. But she could not say so, could not thank him, for fear of compromising him. And, indeed, herself.

Chapter 18

'It was amazing!' Milly's great dark eyes glowed with excitement. 'Their apartment was just so cool. You went into, like a courtyard, and then into the building and up in a lift and there it was, right on the top, with a sort of garden outside and a lovely view over the rooftops. Sooo nice.'

'Where was it, exactly?' asked Bianca.

'In St Germain,' said Milly. 'In one of the streets off the Boulevard. I can't remember the name.'

'Oh, lovely! My favourite area of Paris. So you went to the Café de Flore I would guess?'

'Yes, we did. For breakfast every day. And Les Deux Magots. And we had dinner at the Brasserie Lipp on Saturday night.'

'Did you, indeed?' said Bianca. 'You can't get a table for love nor money there usually, unless you're a regular.'

Milly looked rather complacent. She had come back just a little superior, slightly know-it-all. God, children were dangerous little creatures, Bianca thought. If three days with Carey had done that to her, what would a longer period do?

'Well, jolly nice. And where else did you go? Up the Eiffel Tower?'

'Nooo.' The expression became more superior still. 'Carey says that is so not cool, just what the tourists do.'

'Right, I see. Silly me.'

'But we went on that wheel, a bit like the Eye, only smaller, and that was fun; and we had cocktails at the Crillon.' Her pronunciation,

176

the French 'r', was perfect. 'Carey says it's one of the things you *must* do in Paris.'

'I see. And they allowed you to drink them in the bar?'

'No, but we went out into the garden, and Andrew brought them out to us.'

'Andrew? Not *Sir* Andrew? You *are* well in.' Patrick spoke for the first time.

'Daddy, don't be silly. I couldn't have spent the whole time calling him Sir Andrew!'

'Anyway, he brought you your cocktail. What was it?'

'A Bellini.'

'Milly!' Bianca couldn't help it. 'Andrew Mapleton brought you a Bellini?'

'Yes.'

'Well, he shouldn't have done.'

'Mu-um! Don't be so old-fashioned.'

'Milly, you're a child. You're not allowed alcohol. How on earth did it make you feel?'

'Fine. A bit dizzy. But it was only a tiny drop of champagne, he said. Nearly all peach juice. That's what a Bellini is,' she explained to her mother with a touch of condescension, 'peach juice and champagne.'

'Yes, I did know that, thank you.' She was going to have to speak to Nicky Mapleton about this; it was too important to let go. 'And what else did you do on this wonderful weekend?'

'Oh, lots of shopping. We went to Galeries Lafayette which was really cool. And then we went over to the Marais, where there are lots of little shops. And on Sunday we went to the flea market and it was so cool. Nicola said she wanted to look at pictures and fabrics, so Carey and I went to an amazing part, called the Marché Malik, all retro stuff, and I got this denim jacket, it's just gorgeous, got all flowers embroidered on it, so much cooler than some mass-produced thing from Hollister. I'll go and get it.'

'And there we were spending squillions on one from Hollister,' said Bianca, 'so uncool. Silly us not to know. I'm not sure about this friendship, Patrick.'

Patrick grinned at her.

'It won't last. They'll probably fall out next term.'

'And I really don't like this thing of giving her cocktails. So irresponsible.'

'. . . she had such a lovely time. She is writing to you properly—'

'Oh, she doesn't have to do that!' Nicky Mapleton's voice was amused. 'I'm impressed she even knows about writing. Carey thinks writing means texting.'

'Oh, well I'm a bit old-fashioned like that,' said Bianca briskly. 'Anyway, it was obviously a gorgeous weekend and she's still talking about it. It was just so kind of you to take her.'

'I'm glad she enjoyed it. She's very sweet, Bianca, lovely manners.'

'Well, we try,' said Bianca. 'Doesn't always work.'

'Oh my God, I know,' said Nicky.

'I'm sure you do.' She paused, then said, almost casually, 'but Nicky, and I hope you won't mind my mentioning this, it just worried me a bit: Milly tells me she had a cocktail at the Crillon, a Bellini . . . I assumed it was non-alcoholic but she said it made her feel dizzy . . .'

Her voice tailed away and she felt absurdly as if it was her in the wrong.

'Oh, my dear Bianca, I'm so sorry. We've been giving them to Carey for a couple of years now. We think it's important for her to learn about alcohol, not regard it as something dangerous and forbidden. It was only the tiniest dash of champagne, of course, not a full blown Bellini.'

'Yes, I see,' said Bianca, 'and of course I do agree about the alcoholic education. But – I feel Milly is just a little young . . .'

'Then we'll never do it again,' said Nicola. 'Anyway, we love having Milly here, and Carey just adores her. She's been a great help to her at school, you know, got her over the new girl hump.'

'Good,' said Bianca, 'I'm so glad. And Carey must come for a weekend with us soon. We have a house in Oxfordshire . . .'

'Wonderful,' said Nicky Mapleton, 'she'd love that. Well, bye Bianca, and so sorry you were worried.'

'No it's fine,' said Bianca. 'And thank you again.'

She put the phone down and sat staring at it, wondering if Nicky Mapleton would tell Carey about the conversation. She hoped she wouldn't.

'Bye then, darling. Have a good day. Don't forget drinks with the Cussons tonight. Will you be late?'

'Oh – no. Don't think so.'

'Good. See you around seven then?'

'Yes. Around seven. Bye darling.'

Lawrence Ford shut the door behind him, got into his car, drove to the station and got on to the train. He felt rather sick. Another night when he couldn't tell Annie. He'd sort of thought he could, tonight. But not after drinks with the ghastly Cussons.

And as if he'd be late; the days were endless as it was, moving from public library to coffee shop, choosing areas where he was unlikely to meet anyone he knew, places like downtown Hammersmith and Chiswick, whiling away the hours . . . He'd always thought he'd do something useful if he lost his job, a degree, or a course in carpentry, but that had looked so easy then, wrapped in the cosy self-confidence of a well-paid job that seemed utterly secure – where would the motivation for that be now? When he lacked the courage even to tell his wife he'd been fired?

God, how long could it go on? How stupid he would look when finally he was forced to confess and what would Nicky think of him – his bright, charming little boy who thought he was so wonderful – when he found out? He'd regard his father with something like pity, and that would be unbearable. OK then. Tomorrow. He'd do drinks with the Cussons tonight and tell Annie tomorrow night. Pretend it had only just happened. That would be – well, not all right, but better. And it would be over. Sort of.

She had hardly ever seen him other than cheerful, she realised. His courage had kept them both going over the years. It was certainly greater than her own. But . . .

'What is it?' she said, sitting down on the bed, taking his hand.

'It's got to come off,' Terry said. The words, the ugly raw words made no sense to her.

'What has?' she asked, fear making her stupid.

'My leg,' he said. 'My fucking leg! What do you think?'

He never swore either; it frightened her.

And he lay down, turned his face away from her; and unable to find any words at all that could even begin to make sense, she just sat there, silent, terrified at what lay ahead of them.

Trina Foster had only been working for the Human Resources department for a week; she had previously been a junior member of the IT team, which was currently being reconstructed, but she was bright and ambitious and considered worth holding on to; Bertram Farrell needed a secretary and she was given a month's trial. She determined to prove herself and win the job permanently.

One of her tasks to be completed before the weekend was to get the letters out to all the Farrell consultants, giving them their redundancy notices. Mr Farrell had told her that it was a top priority. Unfortunately, it had been a very hectic week and she hadn't managed to do the letters and Mr Farrell had told her on the Thursday evening that he would be out of the office the following day on a course, and wouldn't be able to sign the letters personally so they would have to wait.

'It would look very harsh and discourteous to them – some of them have been with us a long time – they'll have to wait till Monday.'

Well, at least she could get them ready. Trina spent part of the morning printing them and they were sitting on her desk in a neat pile when Bianca Bailey came into her office in the middle of the afternoon.

'Mr Farrell not here?'

'No, Mrs Bailey, he's on a course. He said he'd try to get back, but he wasn't too hopeful.'

'Yes, I see.' She looked at the letters. 'Were you hoping he'd sign those?'

'Yes, I was. He did say they were urgent, but he wanted to sign them himself. They're going out with the redundancy notices to the consultants.'

'Oh, I see. Well, look, I'll sign them myself. I'm sure that would be all right. Presumably he's approved them?'

'Oh yes. It took him a long time to get them to his satisfaction. But they're good to go now. Apart from the signatures.'

'Fine. Well, give them to me, and I'll sign them and Jemima will get them in the post. Don't worry, I'll explain to Mr Farrell on Monday. He said you'd coped very well this week. Keep it up.'

And she smiled her dazzling smile – she was so lovely, Trina thought, so friendly – and left the room, taking the letters with her.

Trina spent the rest of the afternoon catching up on emails and filing and it was only when she decided to give Mr Farrell's desk a bit of a tidy that she saw the postcard, half buried under a pile of notes, in Bertie's scrawling hand, and with a Post-it note stuck on it saying 'to be included in Marjorie Dawson's letter'.

Panicking slightly, Trina pulled off the Post-it and read the card.

My dear Marjorie,

I am so very sorry that we have to say goodbye to you. I hope you will understand the reasons, and I would like to thank you for all the years of loyal service you have given us. I do hope your husband is doing well, and I know you will continue to look after him in your inimitable and courageous way. I would also like to assure you that if a suitable vacancy does occur in the near future, you will be one of the very first in line. If you would like to discuss your situation with me personally, please don't hesitate to call, or make an appointment with my secretary.

'Oh my goodness!' said Trina, grabbing the card and running along the corridor with it, bursting into Jemima's office.

But Jemima had gone, as had Bianca, and so, clearly, had the post.

And indeed, when she went back to her office there was an email

181

from Jemima saying *Don't worry about the letters, I'm posting them personally when I leave – a little early as I have to go to the dentist. Have a lovely weekend.*

The only thing she could do, Trina thought, was post the card herself. Even though the Friday post had gone, Marjorie would get it on Monday, and surely that would be all right? She wondered what the matter with Mrs Dawson's husband was; clearly he was some kind of an invalid. Very sad. Goodness, it was a hard world, Trina thought, and switched off her computer and went to meet her boyfriend, dropping the card into a letter box on her way.

Lucy arrived for her Saturday stint at Rolfe's to find the counter unattended. She was a little surprised; Marjorie was always there long before the store opened, dusting, rearranging, doing anything that might entice the customers. Lucy had grown quite fond of Marjorie because she was always cheerful and helpful, went to a lot of trouble to explain anything Lucy didn't understand, and she was very popular with the other consultants. Lucy whisked off the dust sheets and had just started doing her own bit of rearranging when the manager came over.

'You'll have to cope on your own today, Lucy. Marjorie's just phoned, won't be coming in. Said she was ill.'

'Oh, OK,' said Lucy. She smiled at him. She was sorry poor Marjorie wasn't well, but it would be fun managing without her; actually give her something to do.

Next week was her last but one week at FaceIt: an exciting one. The big local hotel was putting on a catwalk show and the students were all going along as make-up artists. As a sort of graduation piece, they had to create what FaceIt called their final look, based on a mood board, an individual compilation of photographs of models, colour swatches – pieces of ribbon, lace, even buttons, building up the colour family they were using, plus fashion photographs, beauty and hairstyle shots – all resonating their own final creation, a make-up and hairstyle on a model. A photographer would then come in, take photographs – and that would be the start of their portfolios.

Marjorie had been sitting at the kitchen table, staring with incredulity at the letter that had come that morning. A courteous, if short, note informed her that she was to be made redundant with effect from the end of August.

> That will give you a little more than the statutory notice period. We would like to thank you for your loyalty and hard work for the House of Farrell over the years and we hope you will be able to find alternative employment in the near future. Please sign the enclosed form and return it in the stamped addressed envelope.
>   Yours sincerely,
>   Bianca Bailey
>   pp – Bertram Farrell, Director of Human Resources

Human Resources! When did it get to be called that? Marjorie thought savagely. *In*human more like it. How could they do it to her, just sling her out like a discarded tissue? Where was Lady Farrell now, with all her fine words and promises? Not exactly standing at her side.

Marjorie decided to call her but the phone rang for a long time without an answer. Well, she would try again and keep on trying. She wasn't going to let her hide behind a cloak of company formality. Meanwhile she had to go to the hospital – where she sat by Terry's bed, her eyes fixed on him, willing all the drips that were going into what seemed like a great many veins to do their work and destroy the hideous infection that was threatening his life now, as well as his leg.

'Hello, Looby Loo,' said Bertie, looking up from his *Times* crossword as Lucy walked in. That was his nickname for her; she didn't particularly mind, but Priscilla hated it and he knew it, which encouraged him to use it more than he would have done. 'How many millions of ladies did you serve today?'

'No millions,' said Lucy. 'No tens even, and hardly any units.'

'Oh dear.'

'Yes, and Marjorie wasn't there: she's not well, the manager said.'

'Oh dear, poor Marjorie. So what plans do you have for the rest of the day?'

'Working at the pub tonight. Really looking forward to it. Not.'

'You're a good girl,' said Bertie. 'Well, I'm off to cultivate my garden. Know about Candide?'

'Of course I do,' said Lucy, slightly impatiently. Honestly, just because she'd left uni everyone seemed to think she was a complete airhead. 'Really, Dad!'

'Sorry, sorry! Oh, there's the phone. Damn. I hope it's not Mummy wanting reinforcements for her jumble sale.'

'I'll get it,' said Lucy, 'and tell her you're not here.'

She came back into the room, smiling.

'It was Grandy. She wanted to speak to you. I said I'd see if you were here and she said don't be ridiculous, of course he's there. Sorry, Daddy.'

'It's all right,' said Bertie with a sigh. 'God knows what she wants but it can't be worse than the jumble sale.'

Chapter 19

'I am absolutely appalled. And disappointed. I have to say I actually find it hard to believe and I'd like to hear your defence – if you have one.'

None was forthcoming.

A long silence, then,

'I'm horrified at both of you but more particularly you, Emily. Carey has at least the excuse of perhaps being not quite familiar with the school's extremely high standards. You on the other hand,' the ice blue eyes seemed to bore into Milly's, 'have had the very great privilege of having been here for almost two years. I would have expected far better of you. I shall have to tell your parents, of course. And devise a suitable punishment for the pair of you. Now go back to your classroom and apologise to Miss Sutherland for your absence.'

Outside in the corridor, Milly blinked back her tears; she was very upset and terrified of what her parents would say to her. Carey looked at her and smiled, not entirely kindly.

'Mills, it's not the end of the world. Just a bit of, like, bunking off. We did it all the time in Paris.'

'Well, we're not in Paris, are we?' said Milly. 'We're in London. And St Catherine's is very tough about that sort of thing.'

'Oh, for God's sake, why did you do it then? One of the others would have come with me. You were well excited when I first suggested it.'

'I know, but . . .' Milly bit her lip, Hard to explain that an idea mooted in the giggly darkness of a sleepover hadn't seemed so cool or such fun when she was sneaking out of lunch break and following Carey at the three-minute interval they had agreed – no, Carey had *instructed* – out of the gate of St Catherine's, half hoping someone would ask her where she was going. On the bus, of course, bound for Westfield, adrenalin kicked in and she felt hugely excited and clever and then Carey grinned, removed her tie and undid several of her shirt buttons, and started applying make-up.

'Well, we did it,' she said.

'We did,' said Milly, grinning back. They exchanged a high five.

It was the perfect afternoon to choose – half the class did painting, the other half sculpture, followed by choir practice, which was not compulsory; girls not choosing it moving to the library for private study.

Milly had been a little sorry about missing choir practice because she loved singing and was a leading member of the middle school choir, but Carey had told her witheringly if she thought warbling away under the baton of Mrs Wharton could be even compared with doing Westfield she'd better go and warble. And of course, she did surrender entirely to Westfield's vaulted splendours, and with two tops from TK Maxx, a new pair of Converse trainers, and some fake eyelashes, all hidden under her geography file, she walked into the house a little late, having first called Sonia to say she'd missed her bus, feeling very cool indeed. It was the first time she'd done anything seriously naughty and it was, she discovered, quite a heady drug.

Unfortunately, she was not to know that Mrs Wharton had decided to audition the more promising girls for solos at the end-of-term concert and finding, to her surprise, that Milly was not at choir practice, had sent someone to fetch her from the library . . .

Bianca, arriving back in her office from a not entirely happy meeting with the Porter Bingham people, was informed by Jemima that Lady Farrell was expecting her in her office.

'She was very agitated about something.'

'Happily agitated?'

'I would say quite *un*happily,' said Jemima.

'Have you any idea what you've done?'

'I'm sorry, Lady Farrell, you'll have to tell me. Obviously if it's something unfortunate—'

'Unfortunate! I would say a great deal more than that. I feel thoroughly ashamed, on behalf of the company, and indeed of my family, since Bertie is also involved. I cannot believe you can have acted in so high-handed a way but then, I suppose it's only to be expected, balance sheets being the only thing you care about, rather than people and their lives, however difficult.'

'Lady Farrell, please tell me what your concerns are.'

'My concerns, or rather my *concern*, is about Marjorie Dawson. Marjorie's husband is at this very moment facing life-threatening surgery. She was informed of this on Saturday morning – just as your letter arrived.'

'Oh. Oh, I see.' This was quite serious. She could see that. On the other hand, she could hardly have known. 'Well, I am so so sorry, but—'

'The shock of receiving the letter might have been ameliorated had it been accompanied, as my son intended, by a personal note he had written. At least he still understands the importance of human relations. Rather than human resources, which is the ridiculous term extended to the new department you have set up. He was as appalled as I was that the note was not included in his letter.'

'I see.' Jemima had told her that Bertie had also wanted to see her that morning, but she was already in the taxi on her way to Porter Bingham. 'Well, I am very sorry, but please tell me, what surgery is Marjorie's husband undergoing? Do we have any news?'

'Not yet. He is having a leg amputated.'

'Oh, no!' Bianca was genuinely shocked. 'I'm so sorry.'

'A little late for such regret. In addition, he has a very serious general infection and is quite possibly unlikely to survive the shock of the surgery. A terrible situation for any wife, but to have received this brutal dismissal from her employers of many years in the same morning – unbearable. I hope now you can see what harm you have done.'

'I – I can only apologise for what is clearly a very unfortunate coincidence,' said Bianca, 'but—'

'An unfortunate coincidence! Is that all you have to say?'

'Well, yes. I am extremely sympathetic – it must be dreadful for Mrs Dawson – but I had no idea this extra letter existed, from Ber— Mr Farrell; how could I have done?'

'In that case,' said Athina, 'I have nothing more to say to you. The secretary must be dismissed. Shocking carelessness. I've told my son that already.'

'Of course she can't be dismissed! It was a genuine mistake, Lady Farrell. And I do accept responsibility for telling her to send out the letters. For which, again, I apologise.'

'Mrs Bailey . . .' Athina rose to her feet. 'Please leave me. I have things to do. And I plan to drive down and see poor Marjorie this afternoon. I do assure you that in future you will have a great deal of trouble enlisting my help with anything whatsoever you may wish to do with this company. Your methods appal me. I would far rather the House of Farrell had not survived than come under your control.'

Bianca turned and walked out of the room.

Mr Stevenson had told her it would be at least three hours, possibly longer, before he could give her any significant news; she knew what significant meant, even though her mind turned away from it. She did indeed go for a walk as he suggested, although where she could not afterwards have told you; and then returned to the hospital, and went up to the ward. Terry wasn't there, of course, and they suggested she went to the coffee shop and had a nice drink. She wondered why all such conversations had to be so banal; she supposed it was an attempt to lessen the horror.

She was on her third cup of vile coffee when she heard an imperious female voice calling her name across the café. It was Athina Farrell.

'You look terrible.' Lara's slightly husky voice cut into Bertie's silent self-flagellation. He had had forty-eight hours of complete hell, taking in two attacks by his mother, a dressing down from his wife: 'Well, I knew it was a mistake, that job, just not the sort of thing you should be doing . . .' and this morning the news that Terry Dawson was undergoing surgery. Bertie had tried to work, but lunchtime had found him unable even to decide whether he wanted to see the prospective candidates for a marketing assistant vacancy in his office or in Lara's that afternoon.

It was for this reason that Lara had come to find him; she was sorry to bother him, she said, but she needed to know. 'Just so I can sort out a few things before they arrive.'

He tried to smile at her, said he thought her office would be better.

'It's tidier for a start.'

'Fine. Well, I'll tell reception.' She looked at him, her intense blue eyes thoughtful. 'Do we need to discuss anything first?'

'What? Oh – no, no, I don't think so. Sorry.'

That was when she suggested they went out and had a sandwich together.

'You clearly need to get out of the office.'

She was looking particularly dazzling in a coral linen jacket and white skirt and her eyes on him seemed even more fiercely blue than usual. Bertie, surprised to be able to absorb such information, said perhaps it would but . . .

'There aren't any buts,' said Lara, 'and I don't want you sitting in our meeting with your stomach rumbling. Come on, we'll go to Pret.'

But seated obediently at a table in Pret A Manger he said he didn't really think he could eat anything, just a coffee. He'd hardly swallowed anything since Saturday afternoon.

'Course you can,' she said, and went and brought a tray bearing mineral water, a carton of green salad which she said they could share, and sandwiches, and it did look rather appetising. He fumbled for his wallet; she waved it away.

'Don't be silly. Now, want to tell me what the matter is?'

Her directness was one of the things Bertie most liked about her.

'Come on, Bertie,' said Lara, 'spit it out.'

Bertie managed to spit it.

'I think I will go up to the ward.' Athina's voice was at its most unarguable. 'They'll give me the information, I'm sure. You have to be firm with these people, otherwise they treat you like complete idiots.'

Marjorie felt a new panic, overriding the agony she was already experiencing. She was fond of Lady Farrell and deeply touched that she had driven all the way to Guildford to see her, but she was finding her presence almost unbearable, with its determination both to distract her and to persuade her that the letter she had received from Bertie had nothing whatsoever to do with her. However, since no power on God's earth could hold Lady Farrell from a course she had set herself on, there was clearly no point in arguing with her.

'Now listen, Bertie,' Lara had finished her lunch and was looking at Bertie with a mixture of exasperation and concern, 'you really cannot blame yourself for what's happened. It was an unfortunate coincidence, and of all the people involved, you are the least guilty.'

'Really?' said Bertie, his tone slightly hopeful.

'Well yes. You'd taken the trouble to write the card; you'd put the note to Trina on it. Trina should have checked your desk when you'd gone, to make sure that there wasn't anything important – but then, finding a needle in a haystack would be a doddle, given the state of your desk. It was a little high-handed of Bianca to offer to pp the letters but again, she was acting for the best. Perhaps Trina shouldn't have agreed to it, but if the CEO makes a suggestion, you don't usually argue with it. The one person who comes out of this completely blameless is you.

'You're feeling bad, of course you are, and poor Mrs Dawson

is having a hideous time, but you know what? If my husband was having a leg amputated, redundancy would come way down my list of priorities. The thought of facing anything so hideous, and a life sentence of dealing with it, and knowing the poor chap was going to be feeling totally emasculated as well as ill and in pain – God, what's a little thing like redundancy? She can get another job. He can't get another leg. Please, Bertie, believe me. I know what I'm talking about. Well, not exactly, but well . . .' She hesitated, then went briskly on, 'I found out my husband was cheating on me the same week as I got a new, rather good job. Which do you think took priority in my emotions?'

'I – I – well, I suppose the – the cheating,' said Bertie.

'Of course it did. Bertie, you're only so upset because you are such an over-conscientious, kind person. Most HR directors in your position would have shrugged, possibly sent Mrs Dawson some flowers—'

'Oh, God! Do you think I should have done that?' said Bertie, his voice rising in anguish. 'I didn't think of it.'

'Of course you didn't. It would be sort of saying "sorry about that, but here are some flowers to make you feel better". Crass. I'm just saying it's what they'd probably do. Nothing on earth can help that poor woman at the moment, certainly not an overpriced offering from a florist. So please, *please* stop the self-flagellation. You're doing this job really well but you've got to grow a bit of a tough skin. To protect yourself from your mother, just for starters. She is something else. Oh! Sorry, Bertie, I shouldn't have said that. Sorry.'

'No,' said Bertie, and he actually smiled now, for the first time, 'no, you should. All of it. You have made me feel better. Put it into perspective a bit. Maybe it wasn't entirely my fault.'

Lara smiled. 'Now – I've got another idea. It's still only half past one, first applicant not arriving till half past two. I think a quick visit to the pub, drop of Dutch courage. Don't look like that, Bertie! I'm talking about half of lager, not two double Scotches. Come on. And stay away from anyone holding a glass of red wine!'

* * *

191

'Don't cry, please. That isn't going to do any good, is it? Now come on, sit down and let's talk. It's so unlike you and I want to know why – and how – did it happen? Was it your idea?'

'No!'

'Carey's?'

She hesitated; then, 'Yes. But I did agree,' she added, clearly anxious not to be seen as a sneak.

'Why?'

'Because – because—'

'What Carey says goes?'

'No! No, really.' She sounded defensive.

'All right. Why then? Because it seemed exciting?' Patrick's eyes on her were thoughtful.

'Yes. Yes, I s'pose so. It was exciting.'

'What, wandering round Westfield? You do it often enough.'

'Yes, but not when it's not allowed. You don't understand, I'm always so good! I mean—'

'I do understand, Milly. I was only teasing you. And you are always so good, you're right. You do your homework, you get good marks, you pass all your exams, practise your music. Too good to be true, aren't you?'

'Well . . .'

'I was like you,' Patrick said, after a pause. 'Always top of the class or near it, picked for all the teams, captain of cricket, never did anything wrong. The worst was smoking a quick fag behind the art block.'

'Daddy!'

'Oh, I know. Then a new boy arrived, rather glamorous – his dad was a maharajah or something like that, and everyone thought he was wonderful. Bit like your Carey I suspect. Anyway, he had access to some whacky baccy. I think you'd call it weed. Hash. Marijuana, anyway. He used to sell it, and if you didn't buy it and smoke it with him, God help you. He was a vicious little so and so.'

'He sounds awful. Carey's not like that,' she added quickly.

'Well, not exactly. I tried it of course, the hash, but it had an awful effect on me, made me sick and gave me awful headaches.

And I said I wouldn't do it any more; he wasn't very pleased, and his little gang were pretty nasty to me. And then he got caught. Someone – not me – sneaked, and he was expelled. And it all settled down again. But I felt really bad about it. Crazy, isn't it? As if I'd missed some kind of opportunity. For not joining in, being part of the bad gang.'

'Really?'

'Yes. So you see, I do understand how these things happen. But it doesn't make it right, Milly. More importantly, it isn't sensible. You're such a lucky girl, and you have such a head start in life. If you go further down that route, get a bad reputation, it could all go horribly wrong. Mrs Blackman's pretty tough about these things. And you don't want that, do you?'

'No.' Milly's eyes met her father's. 'No. But – but I really like Carey. She's fun. More than my other friends. It's not just going to Paris, just the things she says and knows about – her dad is just so cool, and the people they know—'

'And you don't?'

'Well, you and Mum, no offence, but you, *our* lives, are not exactly exciting.'

'Well, I'm sorry we're so boring—'

'Daddy, you're not boring,' said Milly, her large dark eyes anxious. 'I just meant your jobs were.'

'I know. But anyway, the important thing about all this, Milly, is that I wanted you to know that we, Mummy and I, are always there for you. Whatever happens you can come to us to help sort things out. But that doesn't mean we're going to think everything you do is OK. And if this sort of thing happens again, which I hope it won't, you might find us all a bit less tolerant. Do you understand?'

'Yes.' The voice was subdued again. 'Yes, I do. What about Mummy, what does she think?'

'I – I haven't had time to talk to her about it properly yet, she's away till tomorrow night.'

That sounded lame, he thought, putting Milly's behaviour into a different perspective, something that didn't qualify for immediate attention. But it was true. 'And then she'll want to discuss it with you too.'

'But is she – is she very cross?'

'More disappointed, I'd say.'

This was an overstatement; Bianca's reaction to the news, in a quick break between sessions at a conference, had been distracted.

'Milly? Bunking off from school? Heavens! But it doesn't sound too serious. We'll have to watch it, though. It's that Carey, of course, she's trouble. Patrick, I've got to go now, sorry, I'll call you later tonight, discuss it properly.'

Only later that night there'd been a dinner and she'd been exhausted and said could it wait till she'd got home.

After Milly had left him, with a kiss and a 'Thank you, Daddy, I promise I won't do it again' he went for a walk and thought about his own life: his own indisputable dullness, as he saw it, his dutiful career path – and the chance he had with this new job to seize some excitement, success. Saul Finlayson was his own Carey Mapleton, offering him some brilliance, some danger even; and he wanted to do it more than he could remember wanting anything. Except Bianca, of course, and she had seemed pretty exciting.

Well, not much longer. Fortunate that this little hiccup with Milly had happened while he was still with BCB.

Terry had survived the surgery.

'His heart stood up to it,' Mr Stevenson said, 'and his vital signs are good. Early days, of course, and we won't be able to relax for forty-eight hours, but I'm very hopeful.'

'So he's still alive?' she said, stupid with relief. 'He's all right?' And burst into tears.

Mr Stevenson put his arm round Marjorie's shoulders and proffered her a handkerchief with his other hand.

She took it and wiped her eyes and then smiled at him.

'Thank you very much. You've been so kind and I'm grateful to you. Thank you.'

'That's what we're here for,' he said.

* * *

Florence felt quite anguished for Marjorie. She was very fond of her, and indeed of Terry, who she had got to know over the years; he reminded her of her own long-dead husband, with his cheerful courage and sexy flirtiness. Of course, Duncan had been a rather different social class, but . . .

One of the worst things, of course, had been not knowing for a long time how Duncan had died; only that it had happened right at the end of the war, in Operation Varsity, meant to secure three bridges over the River Issel. It still haunted her, the thought that he might have lain in agony for hours, with no one to comfort him, let alone relieve his pain, for something that perhaps hadn't made any difference at all. She would wake in the night crying out, not just from grief but from what were truly terrible dreams. And she had been hugely comforted when a fellow officer came to see her and told her what had actually happened.

'He was so brave, Miss Hamilton, so brave, gathering his men after the drop, making sure they knew what to do, where to go. There were dead men everywhere and the Germans kept on firing. Duncan was – was lucky for a long time, and then a shell hit him. I know it's army policy to tell you that people died instantly, but he really did. Just like that. I saw it. He couldn't have known a thing.'

'Oh,' said Florence, and it was almost as if he had told her Duncan hadn't actually died at all, so sweet and refreshing was the relief. 'Oh, thank you so much. That is so good to know.'

'Yes, well I wanted to tell you. And I think he managed to see what we were doing as an adventure. Well, you know what he was like.'

'Yes,' said Florence, 'I do.'

Three months later she had a letter from the war office, commending Duncan's courage and saying he had been posthumously awarded the military cross . . .

Now she wrote Marjorie a note, saying how sorry she was about Terry, and how she would love to visit them both when he was a little better . . . 'and I was so sorry too to hear that you had been made redundant. These are very difficult times for all of us but to have it coinciding with your husband's illness must seem so hard. I shall miss you and if ever you feel like a free facial at The Shop, then you have only to ask.'

She didn't make any optimistic remarks about Marjorie's future; she felt Athina was doing quite enough of that – and possibly hindering, rather than helping, Marjorie's cause.

Chapter 20

Susie looked as surreptitiously as she could at the text that had just arrived: *Where r u?*

Not surreptitiously enough; Bianca had noticed. Her forehead contracted very slightly and Susie was still on probation, she knew, had been ever since being late for the advertising presentation. She switched her phone right off and turned her attention one hundred and one per cent back to the discussion.

They were in a meeting with Bianca, she, Lara, the perfumier who had yet to arrive and, rather surprisingly, Florence. Susie might have been less surprised had she known that while Lady Farrell had been extremely opposed to the idea of the perfume launch, Florence was extremely in favour. She had voiced this view to Bianca on one of her visits to The Shop, and did so again now.

'As I told you, Mrs Bailey, many of our customers, for as long as I can remember, have asked if we do a perfume. And more recently, scented candles, that sort of thing. I think it's a wonderful idea – but very expensive of course. Perfume launches cannot be done on the cheap.'

'Of course not. But I'm glad you like the idea, Florence. Now, I have a perfumier coming in to see me next week; just to talk concepts. I wonder if you would have the time to join us? I really would like you there and to have your input. Oh, and Florence, do please call me Bianca.' She smiled at her quickly and walked out of the door and into the arcade; thereby making the suggestion an order rather than a suggestion. Florence felt flattered, if a little unnerved. It had been many years before she had been able – or rather permitted, by way of a gracious conversation with Lady Farrell – to address her employers as Cornelius and Athina. Out of the office, of course, things were sometimes rather different . . .

She arrived a little early; she had walked, unlike the other attendees.

'What an example you set us, Florence,' said Bianca, smiling. 'Nobody else coming to this meeting would walk that far, I'm quite sure.'

'I love walking in London,' said Florence briskly. 'You get an absolutely different view of everything, the shops, the people, the clothes, even things like the posters – of course one has to change one's shoes on arrival, but that is not such a hardship.'

Bianca glanced down at Florence's feet, clad in low-heeled but extremely elegant pumps. So unlike the trainers people forty years her junior seemed to consider essential to walk even half a mile. She was looking extremely elegant altogether, in a navy calf-length crêpe dress which bore Jean Muir's unmistakable signature, under a softly swathed cream jacket which Bianca would have loved to own herself, a small straw hat with the brim turned down on one side, and she carried a small cloth bag which presumably contained her other shoes.

'Of course,' she said. 'Jemima, do show Florence into my bath-room – she can change her shoes there. And do leave your jacket and hat there, too, Florence. I love the jacket! Well, I love everything you're wearing, of course.'

'Thank you. The jacket is from Zara,' said Florence, 'several seasons ago now, I'm afraid. One does have to look rather hard in there – well, I do – but I'm very fond of it as a store.'

Bianca had a rather challenging vision of Florence advancing through the teeming halls of Zara, and rifling through the rails, picking out a jacket that would have looked as well on someone a quarter of her age.

The perfumier, Ralph Goodwin, had been suggested to Bianca by Maurice Foulds, the chief chemist at the lab. She didn't like

Maurice, but though Lara had come up with a couple of people, one of whom she liked very much, he didn't have the capacity and Maurice Foulds assured her that Ralph Goodwin would be ideal: he worked at a big set-up out in the wilds of Sussex, and did work not just for the cosmetic trade, but for everything which needs perfuming – washing powder, cleaners, and of course toiletries.

He didn't look much like a perfumier: early fifties, smooth to the point of smarmy, Susie thought, dressed in a pinstripe suit, with neatly cut hair, highly polished loafers and a BBC accent. But then, she was probably over-romanticising the whole thing. Perfumiers, especially these days, were probably just technicians.

He shook hands with them all and sat down beside Susie.

'This is a great pleasure,' he said. 'Thank you so much for inviting me – us – to help. As you know, we are quite a large firm and I am only one of three perfumiers. Where shall we begin?'

'I think we begin by deciding if we can work together,' said Bianca, 'so we would very much like to hear what you would require from us, for instance, how long you think development might take. Suppose we decided you would go ahead – what would you need to take away with you today?'

'Ah,' said Goodwin, 'well, above all, a story.'

'A story?'

'Yes. I need a vision, a story from you of what this perfume is about, what it will say and do. We can start with a picture of your ideal consumer. The sort of clothes she'll wear, the sort of food she eats, the job she does, the furniture she buys, the flowers she likes. And then, narrowing it down, colour swatches, fabrics, tear sheets from magazines – anything visual that interprets your idea of her and what she aspires to.'

'Music?' put in Susie. 'I always think music and perfume are a bit the same.'

Goodwin smiled at her. 'Music, yes, very good. What music does your perfume sound like?'

'Oh – goodness,' said Lara, 'that could be quite a fun game. Let's see – *Eternity* has to be Mahler.'

'*N°5*, Gershwin. I think anyway,' said Susie.

'No, too heavy,' said Bianca. 'Mozart, I think. *Diorling* – Rachmaninov . . .'

'Jean Paul Gaultier's *Classique* – Cole Porter,' said Florence rather unexpectedly.

'Wonderful,' said Goodwin, who had been scribbling in a note-book. 'I can see we could all work together very well. I don't often find so imaginative a client. Then I want mood: is she eccentric, your consumer, is she hugely intelligent, happy, unhappy?'

'We certainly don't want perfume for an unhappy person,' said Florence firmly. 'I think perhaps Mrs – that is, Bianca – how would you feel about a slightly rebellious woman? A little wild? Below the surface at least.'

'I'd feel good about that,' said Bianca.

'And – tell me, Mr Goodwin,' said Florence, 'do you still sit at an organ? In my day that is what perfumiers used to do, sit at this high sort of desk, with dozens of tiny bottles ranged on its shelves, florals, musks, woods, and literally mixed them together.'

'Sadly not. That was when perfume was a romantic art. Now we do a formulation from a computer – although I would bring to our first meeting several phials of scent, which we could literally play with, using spills and sticks, mixing the fruity, the vanilla, the patchouli which is woody, the rose perhaps, which is powdery and sweet – so that I can begin to understand what I call your odour language.'

'It doesn't sound very attractive,' said Bianca, laughing.

'I know. But it is. And the more complex the better. And then I would bring three or four fragrances, based on that original briefing.'

'Goodness,' said Lara, 'it does all sound very exciting.'

'Mrs Clements – Lara, if I may – perfume is the most exciting thing in the world. It can be anarchic, it can be submissive – you simply need to choose, and I am confident I can discover it for you.'

'And you do really feel you can develop it in time? We shall need finished samples by next January when we have our first big conference.'

'Definitely. Of course we're not talking huge business here, your numbers are rather . . . small.'

'Well, I don't know,' said Susie. 'Look at Jo Malone, just a few perfumes made in her tiny factory, but thanks to a clever story and her brilliant sampling campaign – I'm sure you know about that, a tiny phial of a new one enclosed with whatever the customer was buying? – she went global, as they say. We can do something like that. The same but different.'

'If you say so, Miss Harding, I'm sure you can. I like the project very much, I must say, and I would like to work with you.'

'Yes, well, I'll get back to you, Mr Goodwin,' said Bianca. 'And do I take it I can come and visit your headquarters, see all these wonderful things for myself? I hear you have mock-ups of bathrooms, kitchens, wonderful things like smelling booths.'

'Indeed. And we have a very strong reputation for landing appeal.'

'Landing appeal?'

'Yes. The smell wafting out from the bathroom, urging people into the bath.'

'Good heavens! What a lot we've all learned today.'

'I'm glad. And we can arrange a date for your visit before I leave today.'

'Excellent,' said Bianca.

Francine was working on a client when Florence got back to The Shop but she was not alone. Athina was there, looking mutinous.

'As well I was here to deal with things,' she said, as if a queue was snaking down to Piccadilly. 'Where were you?'

'In a meeting,' said Florence, taking off her hat and releasing her hair into its wild curls. Once dark, those curls were now kept, at some expense, a kind of variegated gold and brown colour – tortoiseshell, was how she described it to a new colourist.

Athina, who had kept her sleek bob snow-white for over a decade, was always very disparaging about Florence's hair, saying without ever relating it directly to her, that she considered hair colouring rather pathetic after a certain age. 'Everyone knows, after all, that it can't be genuine. Such a waste of time!'

But the white hair suited her and her porcelain skin, as Florence always said in reply, while it did not Florence's darker, olive colouring.

'What sort of meeting? And with whom?'

'With Bianca Bailey. And Lara Clements and Susie Harding,' said Florence, her voice as honey-sweet as her smile.

'What about?'

'Perfume.'

'Perfume? You don't mean she's going ahead with it? How extraordinary. I told her not to. Why?'

'I imagine because she disagrees with you,' said Florence. 'Would you like some tea, Athina?'

'No, thank you. I don't have that sort of time. I'm going to Farrell House. I have a great deal to do there.'

Half an hour later, as she sat in her office raging with boredom, she began to think about perfume. Another perfume, dreamed of four decades earlier . . . How excited she had been by it, and how disappointed when it proved impossible to further its development . . .

Back in her office, Susie switched her phone on: it announced she had three text messages and two answerphone messages. They were all monosyllabically hostile. Shit! Bloody Henk. He must not do this to her when she was trying to work – and she mustn't let him rattle her so badly either.

Stay cool, Susie, she thought, you actually hold all the cards. You do, you do.

He did look really angry. Angry and – what? Contemptuous, she supposed. It was so unlike him; he usually understood such problems.

'Look,' she said, quite shaken, 'look, I can't help it. I just can't be there.'

'Of course you can help it. It's a meeting, cancel it.'

'I can't.'

'Oh, for fuck's sake!' He never swore either. 'I don't know what your meeting's about—'

'Product concepts. I told you.'

'Yes, and this one is about our daughter's future. I find it hard to believe you can't see that's more important.'

'Patrick, you're exaggerating. It's a parents' evening. You've done it before, gone for both of us, I just don't see why—'

'Mrs Blackman has specifically asked us to see her afterwards.'

'I didn't know that!'

'Bianca, I sent you an email about it, the minute she emailed me. Forwarding hers. Don't tell me you didn't get it.'

'I . . .' she hesitated. She remembered now. She had seen the email, headed Parents' Evening, St Catherine's, and because she'd been already late for a meeting, she'd not even opened it, promising herself she'd look at it later. Only then there had been two dozen more and . . .

'I'm sorry,' she said. 'I – well I had to go to a meeting and then it got buried. I never opened it. Sorry, Patrick.'

'That's OK,' he said, easily mollified by her apologies as always, 'but now you know . . .'

'No, Patrick, I'm sorry, I really can't.'

'*What?*'

'It is so, so important this meeting, it's with Lara, and the lab.'

'Bianca,' he said, and his expression was anxious now, 'I do think you have to come.'

'But Patrick, she's only going to talk about this bunking off nonsense, but we've spoken to Milly about it—'

'*I've* spoken to Milly. I don't think you ever quite got round to it.'

'That's not right. I had quite a long chat with her—'

'Over the phone! What kind of message do you think that gives her? That really, it can't matter too much because your job outweighs its importance. This is a potentially dangerous situation and she needs our full attention.'

She knew he was right. As always when cornered, where she might have been expected to go into the attack, she became more conciliatory.

'Well, I am truly sorry. But she seemed very clear about what

203

she'd done and why it was wrong. And she said you'd talked about it for a long time. We don't want to labour the point, Patrick. She's approaching it in a very adult way. And I'm sure you can make Mrs Blackman see we're treating it seriously.'

'So, you're not prepared to come and see her?'

'Patrick, please.' She could feel her temper slipping. 'Mrs Blackman is playing games to an extent, making a point. And you can handle that. Anyway, she much prefers you to me,' she added with a brief smile. 'And you know the deal, it's always been understood that except for *really* important things, it has to be you.'

'Bianca, this *is* really important. All right, if that's your final decision. But I have to say I'm quite – shocked. Now, if you'll excuse me, I've got a lot to do.'

He walked out of the room, leaving Bianca feeling rather unsure of herself suddenly. It was an unfamiliar sensation.

'Bertie, I need to talk to you.'

Bertie was enjoying a quiet glass of claret in the garden after dinner; the air was full of birdsong and the problems with Marjorie Dawson and, indeed, everything to do with the office seemed just for the moment far away; he looked warily at Priscilla, advancing towards him down the path with two mugs containing what he knew to be herb tea on a tray.

She sat down beside him, took the glass of claret from his hand, and passed him one of the mugs. 'Green tea. Very good for you. You really must cut down on the wine, Bertie, it's bad for you and it isn't helping your diet.'

'Actually,' said Bertie, 'I've now lost well over a stone.'

'Well, maybe, but you need to lose a lot more. Anyway, it's very bad for your liver. At your age, it's just stupid. Now, I want to talk to you about the house. We've had an offer I think we really can't refuse – the American couple I told you about who loved the house and the garden, said it was by far the most beautiful they'd seen.'

'Which is possibly why I don't want to leave it,' said Bertie.

Priscilla ignored this. 'They've made a very good offer, the agent rang me this afternoon. And—'

'Priscilla,' said Bertie, 'I don't want to sell the house. I like it here, I don't want to leave it. I don't see how I can make things any clearer.'

'Well, I can only say I hope you won't regret it,' said Priscilla, standing up and snatching her mug off the table.

'I'm sure I won't,' said Bertie, and returned to his contemplation of his flowerbeds and the small victory behind him with some satisfaction. A month ago, he would never have stood up to Priscilla like that; clearly his new career suited him. Of course it was difficult and challenging, and he still felt terrible about the Dawsons, and his mother was making life completely impossible, and tomorrow evening he had to go and have dinner with her and Caro as she said she wanted to plan strategy for the next board meeting – and yet he seemed to be able to cope with it all.

'Susie, I don't mean to interfere and ignore me if you like, but you look terrible.' Jemima's large brown eyes overflowed with concern. Susie was so touched that she felt the tears rising again. The treacherous tears that she had tried so hard to hide from Henk, as he shouted at her, accusing her of ignoring his calls, and of trying to belittle him.

She had failed, of course, and was immediately at a disadvantage; he saw them, recognised her weakness, changed tack, went into wounded mode and said he thought she loved him, and before she knew what was happening was pushing her down on to the kitchen floor and wrenching off her pants.

'Henk, please, no, not here!' she said.

'Oh what? Don't be so fucking prissy. You liked doing it here once.'

'I – I know.' But it hurts, she was going to say, but he was already stabbing into her, his mouth crushing hers, his hands hard and claw-like, holding her buttocks, lifting her up, pushing her round him. She wasn't ready and it did hurt, and it hurt her emotionally too that he could subject her to this violence. And she lay there beneath him, as he ground and thrust her into the hard floor, faking for all she was worth, just to get it over.

Only she did too well, and when it was over, he rolled off her, and turned his face to hers, smiling in a sort of triumph, and said, 'That was more like it, babe, more like my Susie. Shall we continue in bed?'

Finally, after what seemed like hours of pain and misery, she felt him grow heavy beside her and fall into the deep, undisturbable sleep that sex always brought him. She crawled carefully out of bed and went into the bathroom and lay in a hot bath for a long time, sore and aching all over, her breasts literally bruised where he had bitten and sucked at her, and her thighs too, from his heavy, almost vicious, hands; and when finally she got out and looked into the mirror, she saw that her neck bore several bruises too, dark and unmistakable legacies of his violence that would take days to fade, and even her mouth was swollen and red.

She wrapped herself in a bathrobe, and, weeping again, went into the sitting room and curled tightly up on the sofa, wondering for the hundredth, the thousandth time why she submitted to it, and failing to find an answer. Finally, after several Nurofen and a cup of warm, sweet tea, she began to feel better, physically at least, and rather feverishly slept.

'I – I'm all right,' she said feebly now, longing more than anything to tell Jemima, and knowing she could not, and indeed that added to her misery, the impossibility of confessing to this ugly cycle of brutality and submission: 'Just – just got my period. Slept really really badly. But thank you. I'll be fine.'

'Poor you,' said Jemima. 'Well, nice cup of tea then? And I have some really strong pills in my bag.' And Susie loved her for that, for not pressing her inquiries when it was so clear that she believed not a word of Susie's explanation, but respecting her reasons for giving it. And, 'Yes, please,' she said. 'That'd be lovely, thank you.'

'Bianca did want to see you,' Jemima said, 'to talk about the perfume a bit more, but I'm sure it could wait a while. Till the pills work at least.'

'Oh – yes. Yes, OK,' said Susie. 'Yes, that'd be lovely, if it could be a bit later. But I don't want to upset her plans, she's always so busy.'

'She actually has a fairly clear morning,' said Jemima. 'I'll see if she could see you around twelve thirty, OK?'

'Yes, that'd be wonderful,' said Susie, 'but Jemima, don't tell her I'm feeling rough will you? It's such a bad excuse.'

'I'll tell her you're talking to Anna Wintour about an exclusive in American *Vogue*,' said Jemima, with a grin, and then, seeing Susie's expression, 'Don't worry, Susie, I'll fix it.'

What she actually did was tell Bianca that she was worried about Susie, and that she clearly had some kind of problem, but the only thing to do was respect that and try to give her an easy time for a bit. When Jemima added that there were a couple of nasty bruises on Susie's neck, too high to be covered even by the ruffled white shirt she was wearing, clearly not acquired by way of an altogether happy experience, she had said, 'Fine, OK.' And then added, 'Keep an eye on her, Jemima, would you? She clearly needs some sort of help.'

Given Bianca's absolute impatience with any form of weakness in her staff, and indeed herself, Jemima saw this as the huge concession it was and was able to tell Susie that twelve thirty would be absolutely fine.

Chapter 21

Hattie Richards did not look too much like anyone's idea of a cosmetic chemist. She was tall and plain with a make-up-free face, mousey of hair, and wore a light brown trouser suit that did nothing for her colouring or her figure. The profession that she would seem most likely to represent was that of an old-fashioned nanny. Bianca smiled at her determinedly and signalled to her and Lara to sit down.

'Thanks very much,' Hattie Richards said, her voice the first surprise, being light and rather pretty. 'So – tell me what you're looking for,' she said.

'Well,' said Bianca, slightly thrown by being cast as interviewee, 'a chemist obviously. And Lara tells me—'

'No, no,' said Hattie. 'I mean in the way of a range.'

'Ah, well – well, it's not exactly a range. Rather an offshoot of one.'

'I'd call that a range,' said Hattie Richards.

'Yes, possibly,' said Bianca, 'but anyway, a range within a range, to be sold alongside the present one, spearheading our relaunch next summer. This is naturally very confidential,' she added.

'Yes, of course,' said Hattie Richards. 'And still in the mastige market, which is where you are at the moment, or further towards the prestige end?'

'Oh, definitely more prestige. I'm looking for a product advantage that I can add to The Cream. Well, what I want to do is develop a new version of it. To go with the new range.'

'I really don't think you should do that,' said Hattie Richards, 'it would be madness. Your hero product? Madness.'

She didn't lack self-confidence, that was for sure. Bianca didn't know whether to be pleased or irritated by this.

'Well, you may be right,' she said, managing to sound polite, 'but it is, as you say, our strongest product, something we can build on. I feel new ones should be built around it.'

'Well yes,' said Hattie, 'around it. But not on it, OK? The Cream is a *wonderful* product. So . . . I would imagine five or so products initially? Something like day cream, toner, cleanser, mask or some such, and, of course, The Cream itself. Quite enough to start with, I'd say. Unless you did an additional version of The Cream, but I think that would denigrate the original, imply it was missing something.'

'Well – yes.' This was hugely irritating. Who was hiring who?

'What you could do,' said Hattie Richards thoughtfully, 'is perhaps launch a SuperCream. To use for exceptional situations – you know, icy winter weather, flying, hotel living—'

'What on earth is wrong with hotel living? When it comes to your skin?' said Bianca.

'Oh, Mrs Bailey, central heating, closed windows, air-conditioning – anyway, even that might not be the answer. I could think about it if you like.'

'Well – maybe.' Bianca wasn't sure if she could work with Hattie Richards, but she was certainly extremely clever. 'And then I think we need to do a few colour products.'

'But the trouble is you can't do a few colour products, can you? It's all or nothing, twenty of everything. I'd advise against that.'

'Well, it's interesting to hear your views, as an outsider,' said Bianca, struggling to retain control of the situation, 'but I am of the opinion we need it.'

'What I'd probably do,' Hattie said, 'is something you could call a lip treatment: basically a moisturiser for lips, and then five glosses, and a mascara. There's something about mascara that makes it like skincare. Don't you agree?' she said, addressing herself to Lara, clearly assuming Bianca would be of the same mind.

'Well – yes, actually, I do,' said Lara. 'I hadn't thought of it before, had you Bianca?'

'I don't know that I agree, but—'

'Well, the point is,' said Hattie Richards, 'you wouldn't entrust your eyes to rubbish mascara, would you? You need to protect them. In fact, you could call it protective mascara. If the legals let you. Don't see why not. I hadn't thought of that before. Looking after your eyes for you . . . good product plus.'

'Right,' said Bianca, recognising the near-brilliance of this as a cosmetic concept, 'well, could certainly look at that. But the thing is, Hattie, much as I like your ideas, there are certain problems. I'm building a team from scratch—'

'Why?' said Hattie.

'Because – well, because I feel we need a completely fresh start.'

'Why?' said Hattie again.

'I think,' said Lara, cutting in, 'and again this is very confidential, Hattie, because the chemists we have aren't quite in the league we need.'

'But why?' said Hattie. 'They manage The Cream after all. And I know it's been updated slightly in the last five years. Lighter, but just as rich.'

'Yes, I know, but it's basically a very old formulation.'

'OK, but they still do it. Clever, that. Anyway, there's no such thing as a bad chemist. Not really. It's the briefing that's bad. The briefing and the standards.'

'You mean, you could work with our funny old team?' said Lara, genuinely fascinated.

'Of course – if they were willing, and that would be up to you. I'd provide the ideas, I'd brief them, I'd set the standards. How many people have you got, by the way?'

'Er – three altogether. But soon to be down to two,' said Bianca.

'Well, that sounds about right. Anyway, what I was going to say is, as long as they're reasonably competent, I could almost guarantee I could work with them. There's a couple of good colour products in your range, like the Smudgeys – they're gorgeous.

The actual colours are just slightly off-key, in a couple of cases, but the concept and the formulation are great: they must have done those.'

'Well – yes. Yes, they did.'

'And the lab is here? What about the factory?'

'Islington.'

'Yes, well, that sounds fine.'

'It is fine, but it's expensive,' said Bianca. 'That's why—'

'You could move everything, offices, studio, the lot, lock, stock and barrel, maybe. Be good if the whole operation was in the same place—'

'Look, Hattie,' said Lara, seeing that Bianca was getting increasingly irritated by this reorganisation of her entire company, 'would you just give us five minutes? We need to discuss something rather urgently, nothing to do with you. I just got a text from Sales. Then we'll be back.'

'That's fine,' said Hattie. 'My husband's picking up the children from nursery today. I've got all the time in the world.'

'You've got children?' asked Bianca. She struggled to sound interested, rather than astonished.

'Yes, twins. Girls, three in a couple of months. I presume that's not a problem?'

'No,' said Bianca. 'Absolutely not. I have three children myself, and the sales team are a positive production line.'

'That's all right, then.' Hattie smiled approvingly; she rummaged in her bag. She's going to produce a photograph, thought Bianca, and if she does . . . but only a large linen handkerchief appeared, on which Hattie blew her nose rather loudly. 'Well, I'll wait here shall I?' she said.

'Yes, if you wouldn't mind. A drink? Jemima . . .'

A week later Hattie Richards was interviewed with Bertie in attendance, and the next day her appointment was confirmed. Maurice Foulds was told he might, if he wished, take early retirement and that he would be given a very large payoff. He was on the north side of fifty and had, unfortunately for him, complained vociferously for years about his health and the strain of the journey to and from Harpenden every day.

He accepted rather grudgingly, and the other two chemists were told they would be working with their new boss as from the following Monday.

Bertie had also discovered in Hattie a passion for gardening, and as he saw her off the premises said he would be very interested to hear any ideas she had for treating honey fungus which was plaguing his privet hedge, and on which she revealed she had written a paper after leaving Oxford.

'Oxford?' said Bianca when Hattie was safely out of earshot, her own voice rising rather unattractively. 'I don't believe it!'

'Bianca Bailey,' said Lara, laughing, 'you are such a snob.'

It was the last day of the course and Lucy felt sad. She'd enjoyed it so much, learned a lot, made some good friends – and now it was Final Looks day, the girls' own creations after two months of tuition. Most of them, she thought secretly, were either boring, or self-consciously wild and dramatic, but she had done something she'd called Creamy Dreams, a look that was literally all shades of cream and beige and brown – eyeshadows, liners, blusher, lips – and somehow it wasn't the pallid nothing that it could have been, but dramatically interesting, vibrant and gentle at the same time. She had found a girl to model for her – they were allowed to do that, if it didn't cost anything, and Lucy had found a junior in H&M with wonderful wavy chestnut brown hair which she'd made very big indeed, and was thinking, not for the first or even the hundredth time, what an incredible thing make-up was. The girl had actually looked quite ordinary when she came in, but by the time Lucy had finished she was stunning. Make-up and hair – they really did have some sort of sorcery to them, making the plainest face pretty, the pretty beautiful, and the beautiful quite extraordinary.

Over lunch that day they all talked about their futures – suddenly so real and so scary.

Fenella, who could have been a model herself, had just got a place at Central St Martins to study photography, but in the meantime had made friends with a local photographer who had offered her some steady work doing the make-up for girls coming in for portraits; one of the other girls had got a job as an assistant at a local beauty salon, and Lucy had found a girl who was getting married and she was going to do her make-up and had been asked to do all the bridesmaids too. That was her only assignment so far, but she'd been told that such jobs often led to many more.

Her job, if you could call it that, at Rolfe's was going to last a little longer; Marjorie had been retained for another two months, while a scheme of her father's was put in place, what he called 'Roving Consultants' – girls, newly hired, to move from store to store, working on promotions, doing demos, safeguarding the Farrell counter spaces, and keeping the lines of communication with the customers open. When the relaunch happened, there would be a further investment in new girls, but for the time being this met many of the problems caused by losing the girls altogether.

'Florence! That is just such a brilliant idea!'

Florence smiled down the phone at Bianca. She liked her very much, especially when she responded to one of her ideas. Which seemed to be coming rather fast these days. And it was rather wonderful to be appreciated. 'Yes, well, I thought it might work.'

'Might! Florence it will. I'm sure. You're a genius. Thank you.'

He had said that: exactly. She knew, as he said it, that she would always remember: and she had. Fifty years later. 'You're a genius. Thank you.'

He had insisted then that they should go to tea at The Ritz: 'Just to talk it over a bit more.'

And there, among the palms, as the harpist played all the tunes from *Oklahoma!*, and they had champagne at Cornelius's insistence, as well as Earl Grey tea – they went oddly well together – and smoked salmon sandwiches and scones and cream and tiny delicacies of cakes, they talked for a long, long time, first about her idea – that with every major new promotion, loyal customers at least should be rewarded with a small gift, in the form of a sample size of a product

– and then of other things, how the company was growing, how well it was regarded, how it was written about endlessly in magazines and the women's pages in newspapers; and then they moved on, to how Cornelius hoped that Florence was as happy as she could be, how wonderful it was to have her on board, how much he and Athina valued her. At which point the maitre d' tactfully came over and said teatime was actually over and they realised everyone had gone, and laughing, apologised, and he said, no, no, it was an honour to see them enjoying themselves so much but if they would now like to move into the bar . . . ?

Whereupon Cornelius said how would that be? And she said she really shouldn't, and he said why not? And suddenly she thought why not indeed, why not one last glass of champagne?

'Or would you rather have a cocktail?' Cornelius asked, and she said well, perhaps a champagne cocktail would be nice, and it had been ordered and she was sipping it, and actually, now, was really rather tipsy, but pleasurably so, and Cornelius was telling her what fun she was to talk to, she was so well informed about everything, both flippant and serious, and what did she feel about the much-discussed affair between Princess Margaret and Group Captain Peter Townsend.

Florence said she really thought that if Princess Margaret wanted to have an affair with a divorced man she should have one, but perhaps rather more discreetly than she had hitherto done; 'picking that bit of fluff off his jacket at the coronation, so very blatant – she was inviting the world to notice and to guess. Whether she should actually marry him, as all the women's magazines keep hinting she will, is another matter altogether. I'm not sure that would be very good for the country. Or her sister,' she added, 'since she is the head of the Church.'

'I see,' said Cornelius. 'So you are an advocate for the extra-marital affair are you, Florence? How very emancipated of you.'

'I would hope I'm emancipated,' Florence said. 'It would hardly become any working woman with career ambitions to be otherwise, would it?'

'Ah, so you do have career ambitions?' said Cornelius.

'Of course.'

'And what form do they take? I mean, if it was a seat on the board you had in mind – and I have to tell you I would not oppose that, in the fullness of time – well, that would change the balance of power in the House of Farrell, just a little. Or perhaps you have your eye on another company, another board.'

'I suppose – ultimately – I do. Yes.'

'Why?'

'For the reason you just gave: if I reached some lofty position in the House of Farrell, I would inevitably find myself pitted against you and Athina from time to time. Which wouldn't do at all. Whereas, were I to go to Yardley, or Coty, for example, it wouldn't matter. And I also think it would be hard for you to take me seriously enough.'

'Oh, now that's not fair. I think we take you very seriously – and may I say, I could hardly bear to contemplate your leaving us?'

'Oh, really?' She had had enough champagne now to become flirtatious. Something that so far she had resisted. 'Why?'

'Why? Well, because your ideas, your vision of The Shop, your whole philosophy of the company are so totally in line with our own.'

'I see.' She felt foolishly disappointed; but not for long.

'And,' he added in his musical voice, leaning forward and looking into her eyes. 'I would miss you on a personal level. Very much. I – well, I have grown rather fond of you, Florence. I might even say, very fond. Very fond indeed.'

And he leaned forward and put out his hand, and started to stroke, very gently, one of hers.

This, she knew, was the infinitely important, crucial moment: when she could have refused what she recognised as an invitation, turning it lightly, easily into a piece of foolish flirtation. Or accepted it, welcomed it and shown that she would like to pursue whatever might come next.

It was a long moment that she sat there, her great dark eyes fixed on his brilliant blue ones, leaving her hand where it was, beneath his.

A casual observer, seated also in the bar, would have seen and been charmed by this tableau of a lovely woman, dressed with a certain chic, being propositioned, however mildly, by an extraordinarily handsome man, and might have wondered as to their circumstances and, indeed, what was the outcome to be.

What the observer could not have seen was the almost imperceptible tightening and mingling of the fingers of their two hands, before the woman sat back and picked up her cocktail once more and sipped it, only the hint of a smile on her lovely mouth. Nor could he have seen, after they had left – quite soon after that – a really rather hasty entry into a taxi, and a brief moment as they sat in opposite corners, still smiling at one another quite calmly, before literally falling forward into one another's arms, and exchanging hungry, greedy, almost desperate kisses.

Chapter 22

Well, this was it, Patrick thought. His leaving party from Bailey Cotton and Bailey. It felt quite extraordinary, as if he was walking out on his family. Which of course he was, in a way.

His father had come up from Wiltshire to attend; his two uncles had booked the superb, leathery, woody Bank of England Room, at Green's in the City, and an incredible feast was being served round the huge oval table.

'Pity it's not the oyster season,' one of his uncles said, 'but never mind, we can still do you proud, young Patrick.'

He ate rather mechanically and suddenly a spoon tapped on a glass. A stillness in the roistering, bantering room. And then his senior uncle got to his feet: 'Gentlemen – and Patrick (much laughter). Accustomed as I am to public speaking, I still intend to keep this short. Mostly because there's not a lot to say.

'Simply: good luck, Patrick. We'll all miss you. We wish you weren't going, but you probably need a challenge. You're too young and too bright to be in a rut, however comfortable. It's brave what you're doing. So you've clearly got courage as well as your other virtues. I won't list your vices (more laughter).

'Of course Bianca and the family are behind you – I just wanted you to know that we are too.

'And – goes without saying, really – if it doesn't work out don't come running to us (huge laughter).

'Now. You're too young for a gold watch but since you are venturing into the unknown, here's a different variety. It'll take you

217

full fathom five, or rather, to be precise, thirty foot in depth, although I wouldn't like to test it out personally!

'It comes with our love and best wishes. Enjoy wearing it, enjoy your new life – and come and see us occasionally. Gentlemen – Patrick!'

'Patrick!' roared the room.

Don't, Patrick, don't don't cry. Don't even let on you might be worrying about crying.

'Thank you. So much. So generous, all of it. I'm not only gutted to be leaving I'm pretty fucking terrified.' Laughter. 'But – a man's got to do what a man's got to do. Unfortunately, perhaps. Anyway, this has been a great evening, and the one certainty in my future is that I'll be back. Often. Hopefully not begging for my job back –' More laughter – 'but to see you all. Can't imagine life without you. Right. That's quite enough of that. Carry on drinking, gentlemen. I believe there's sticky toffee pudding coming up, and again, thank you.'

Applause. Slaps on the back. Cheers as he put the watch on. It was a superb thing, an IWC Aquatimer, with the famously exclusive blue face and one blue, one yellow hand.

Even louder cheers for the sticky toffee pudding.

Later, coming out of the lavatory, he bumped into his father.

'Oh – hi, Dad. Fancy meeting you here!'

'Indeed. Patrick, just wanted to say I agreed with every word Ian said. Admire what you're doing very much. Wish I'd had the guts myself.'

Shit. Now he was going to cry. Well, he had tears in his eyes. Bloody hell. His father would think he was some kind of wuss. And what had he meant by the last bit? He asked him.

'Oh, not to be anything different in the City. A friend offered me a job in his advertising agency. Thought I could make a copywriter. Really wanted to do it.'

'So?'

'I thought it would endanger all our futures. Not so much money, lot more risk. You don't have that sort of problem, of course, you've got Bianca. Anyway, you'll make it work, I know you will. And – if you don't like it – well. You can always come back, you know. You mustn't feel you can't. Now excuse me, old chap, need to go and water the roses. Old waterworks not quite as well built as they were.'

Patrick stood aside, smiling; and then noticed that his father's blue eyes as he looked at him were undoubtedly moist. 'I'm sorry, Dad,' was all he said. But he felt better about what he was doing.

It wasn't until he was almost home that what his father had said sank in. 'You don't have that sort of problem . . . you've got Bianca.'

He had Bianca: more successful than he and with so much money she could support him and the family for ever if needs be. If this new life didn't work out, and even if he didn't feel he could go back to BCB, no one would suffer for it. Not materially, anyway. And that wasn't entirely comfortable. Was that how everyone saw him? As the lesser weight in the partnership? A potentially kept man?

It had never properly worried him before, although of course he had been aware of it. Now it did. So he *had* to succeed.

'That's a very good idea. Thank you.'

Bianca smiled rather uncertainly at Saul Finlayson across the lunch table. He induced uncertainty in her and she wondered if he did it to everyone, wondered indeed if it was something he had developed in order to conduct his extraordinarily successful life more easily. She had never known anyone so completely self-confident. He had brought Dickon for Sunday lunch in the country at Patrick's rather tentative suggestion, had accepted with surprising alacrity.

'Very good' was high praise, his mode of expression being so extremely economical. But – he was actually smiling at her. Or had been. It had been the usual fleeting affair.

'Yes, very good idea,' he said again.

'Well – I'm glad you think so.' It seemed to her that it hadn't really been a very clever idea at all, rather simple indeed: that Dickon might enjoy the judo classes Fergie went to on Monday after school. Saul had been complaining that he didn't do enough after school.

'Just goes home and mucks about as far as I can make out.'

'I think there's quite a lot to be said for that,' said Patrick. 'They have too much direction these days, not enough time to get bored.'

'Really?' said Saul, looking at him in astonishment. 'You think it's OK to be bored?'

'Yes, I do. You need to be bored to develop inner resources. I was bored a lot as a child, and that was when I discovered how much I liked reading.'

'Oh, I don't want Dickon spending his evenings with his nose in a book,' said Saul. 'Bad as being hunched over some game on his computer.'

'Saul! That's a terrible thing to say,' said Bianca, laughing.

'Why? He needs something physical. He's got too much energy.'

'So, what did you have in mind?' asked Patrick. 'Something like swimming?'

'No, he hates swimming,' said Saul, ignoring the shouts of joy that were coming from the pool area. 'And anyway, he does it at school.'

Which was when Bianca made the suggestion, because Fergie's judo classes were in Hampstead and Dickon's mother, Janey Finlayson, with whom he lived during the week, was in Highgate.

'Good. I'll tell her to organise it.'

Bianca wondered if she shouldn't feel rather sorry for Janey.

'Right,' said Patrick, 'I think I might have a swim myself. Want to join me, Saul?'

'No thanks. But you go ahead, Patrick, I'll read the papers. Lot to catch up on.'

'Oh – OK. Bianca, what are you going to do? Fancy a swim?'

'No, I might go for a walk. I haven't moved all weekend.'

'I'll join you,' said Saul, and then, like a child told to mind its manners, 'if that's OK?'

'Of course,' said Bianca. The prospect was not entirely pleasing, but she managed to smile at him.

'Right, well enjoy,' said Patrick. 'I'll see you at teatime.'

'Keep an eye on the kids, won't you?' said Bianca.

'Of course,' he said and then, 'Don't I always?' His tone was unmistakable and she looked at him sharply.

'Yes, you do. Of course. Thank you.'

She led Saul Finlayson to the edge of their land and through the five-bar gate that went into the wood. It was cool in there, and dark: a lovely contrast to the brilliant day.

'This is nice,' he said. 'I don't really like the sun.'

'I suppose you burn? You're very fair.'

'Yes, I do, but I just don't like being hot. I keep trying, but it doesn't work.'

She laughed. 'No need to try, surely. You're over twenty-one. As they say.'

'True.' He pondered this and then said, 'You're right. Trouble is, a lot of the things I do like take place in the sunshine.'

'Like what? I'd put you down as an English climate man. Racing – not ideal in the heat. Working – likewise. And I don't know any of your other pursuits.'

'There aren't many. I spend most of my life working. I presume that's what you meant. Like you, I imagine,' he added, in a clear attempt to make polite conversation.

'Yes, it is. And then my children take up a lot of what you'd call hobby time. I love being with them, doing things with them.'

'I can see. I'm surprised.'

'Why?' She felt defensive. 'I hope I don't seem like one of those awful, power-crazed workaholics?'

'No,' he said, looking at her very seriously. 'But I don't know how you accomplish what you do, without being one of them.'

'I'm a very good delegator,' she said.

'Says?'

'Me. Oh, and everyone who works for me. Every journalist who interviews me.' She smiled. 'Who am I to argue?'

'I'm lousy at it,' he said. 'Absolutely hopeless. Of course, it's very hard, delegating what I do. If a client rings me at three in the morning, I have to be there. Not physically, obviously, but mentally – absolutely. I enjoy it, though. Wouldn't have it differently.'

'It's not about the money then?' she said, suddenly bold.

'Of course not. It's about what I do, knowing I can. That's what it's about, isn't it? You must know that.'

'I – well, yes.'

'You make money on your wits and your skill and your knowledge in my business,' he said after one of his silences. 'It's a war of nerves. If you run a hedge fund, you're taking on the world. No text book tells you how to do it, there are no guarantees. It doesn't matter what anyone else is doing, it only matters if you're doing it right.' He stopped. 'Sorry, I don't usually talk this much.'

'No,' she said, with a smile at him, 'I had noticed.'

'But – you invite confidences,' he said, suddenly. And the swift smile flashed at her, and was gone. 'I suspect that is one of the reasons for your success. I like you,' he said unexpectedly, 'I like being with you, talking to you. I don't often talk.'

She smiled at him, unable to think of a response.

'And your children are nice. A credit to you. I worry about Dickon,' he added after a long silence.

'Of course you do. But he's a dear little boy. Not spoiled at all, as far as I can see.'

'Of course he's spoiled!' he said and he sounded irritable. 'How could he not be?'

'Saul, I don't mean he doesn't have a lot of life's goodies. But he's not a brat. He's really grounded.'

'I hate that expression,' he said. 'Grounded. What does it mean?'

'I'm sorry.' She withdrew from the conversation; walked on in silence. He looked at her.

'No, I'm sorry,' he said after a long pause. 'That was rude. What did you mean?'

'I meant he had his feet on the ground, he's happy and self-confident. And nicely mannered.'

'Well, we have his mother to thank for that. The manners, I mean. Although I do try. I've tried very hard today.'

'And you've done very well,' she said and laughed. 'So – in what way do you think Dickon is spoiled?'

'Bianca! He has two warring parents fighting for his favours. He's not stupid. Of course he's spoiled. And it's going to get worse. As he grows up. He'll use that, he'll get manipulative—'

'Not necessarily.'

'Oh, he will. His mother's very fair though, she doesn't do that "Daddy's mean to Mummy" stuff. She's a very nice person. I often wish I was still with her,' he added.

In the face of all this revelation, she felt brave enough to go on.

'So – why?'

'Oh, it was all my fault. I'm impossible to live with. Impossible. Anyway, let's change the subject. I'm glad you like Dickon.'

'I do. Very much.'

'And your husband joins the firm next week. How do you feel about that?'

'Oh – delighted, of course.'

'No, really, how do you feel?'

'I'm delighted,' she said firmly again. 'He needed a change, a challenge. Of course I'm anxious. Not that he won't be able to do it, he's terribly clever. But that he won't like it. He's very gregarious and I think it sounds rather solitary, what he'll be doing for you.'

'So – did you encourage him?'

'Yes,' she said, unsure if she was speaking the truth. 'I thought it would be . . . good for him.'

He laughed suddenly, a rather childlike, spontaneous laugh.

'And I hope for me.'

'I hope so too.'

They had reached a lake, a flat, calm lake. Saul bent down, picked up a few pebbles, threw one. It skimmed across the water five times. She smiled at him.

'You're very good.'

'Yes, I am,' he said. 'I've practised. When I was a little boy,

223

endlessly. Making bets with myself. If I get it to hop three times, I'll get picked for the cricket team, five times and I'll get into Oxford, six times and—' He stopped.

'Six times?' she said. 'What did six times do for you?'

'Oh, I'd moved on to girls by then.'

'I see. So, seven times and you got the girl?'

'Sort of.' He looked slightly embarrassed.

She laughed. 'What's your highest score? Eight? What would that do for you?'

'I've never managed eight,' he said. And he looked down at her, very intently.

She felt awkward, almost flustered, bent down and picked up a pebble herself. 'I'm going to try,' she said. 'I know the theory, my father tried to teach me. He could do about three. But I never could.'

'OK, try. It's not that hard.'

She couldn't do it – every stone sank immediately.

'Your father was obviously a bad teacher.'

'No, he wasn't,' she said, stung. 'He was wonderful.'

'OK, what else did he tell you?'

'Don't take no for an answer, don't follow the pack. The most important thing of all he said was to only do what I was good at, not to struggle with the rest.'

'That's very good advice. Is he still alive?'

'Yes, he is. My mother died when I was nineteen, so she didn't see me married, or her grandchildren.'

'Or your success?'

'She wouldn't have cared about that. She was very non-materialistic So was – is – my dad. He's an academic, lectures in medieval history, lives in another world. Which is good in a way, of course, he doesn't miss Mummy as much as he might, but he can't make me out at all. Sometimes it quite hurts.'

She stopped, feeling absurdly emotional. She bent down, picked up another pebble.

'Let me try again . . .'

'No, don't. Take your father's advice. Leave it to those who can.

224

Here I go.' He threw. The stone bounced obediently. 'Perfect six. One more.'

A five.

'It's been nice,' he said. 'As I told you, I don't often talk. Do you think,' he said suddenly, 'talking to women is important? Making them happy, I mean? Do you and Patrick talk a lot?'

'Oh yes,' she said, 'to both questions.'

'Yes, I see. And – have you enjoyed talking to me?'

The question was so childlike she laughed.

'Yes, of course. And I'm flattered that you have. Talked, I mean.'

'Yes, well . . .' He stopped, was completely silent for a long moment, then, 'Yes, well, it's time we got back.'

'OK,' she said, surprised by the change of mood.

But he didn't move, just stood there staring at her, in silence. Finally he said, 'You're very attractive, Bianca. Patrick's a lucky man.'

And then he was ahead of her, striding back to the house, silent the entire way.

'So, are you coming or not? I'd like to know.'

'Well, I – I'm not sure yet.'

'Oh for God's sake! Why not? I want to get it settled.'

Milly looked at Carey and tried not to feel panicked. It wasn't that she still hadn't dared ask her parents; nor that she was terrified they'd say no; more that she was half scared they'd say yes.

Of course she wanted to go, anyone would. It had sounded wonderful – at first. Two weeks on a yacht, sailing round the Greek islands. But then Carey had told her about the other people coming. Somehow she'd thought it'd be just the two of them and Carey's parents. 'Two other adults, best friends of my parents, and their two sons. Boys, Mills, boys! Really cool, and one of them is a serious *god*. Sixteen, I sooo fancy him.'

'Oh – oh, how exciting.' Milly struggled to sound enthusiastic. She really didn't like that idea; Carey would spend the whole time pursuing the god, and she would be left with . . . 'And the other one?' she said.

'Oh, he's a baby. Thirteen. Quite fun, but . . .'

'Cool,' she said.

She had seen Carey in action pursuing boys a couple of times now; she was obsessed. And a weekend in Paris was one thing, a fortnight on a boat quite another. She almost wanted an excuse to say no.

'I'll make sure to get an answer tonight,' she said. 'But they've got some family holiday planned as well. I – I think the dates might clash.'

'You didn't say that before.'

She hadn't, because it wasn't true. Nothing had been planned. Her parents just kept saying they must sort something out, but they were both so engrossed in their jobs it never seemed to happen.

But her father was working late every night that week and her mother was distracted, said she hadn't had time to plan a holiday. 'But we will, darling, we will, promise. I thought maybe a villa somewhere, just the five of us, be nice wouldn't it?'

Sort of nice, Milly thought, sort of boring too. Not like sailing round the Greek islands. But – not scary. No god to worry about.

'Well?' Carey said next day.

'Sorry, Carey, they were both out. My mum's going to be home tonight, she promised, so I can tell you in the morning.'

'Well, mind you do. Otherwise I'll have to ask someone else.'

That did it for Milly. The thought of someone else taking her place on this magical, privileged holiday was far worse than worrying about going on it.

'Look,' she said, 'I'm sure it'll be all right. I mean, they haven't got anything booked yet, I was wrong about that, so . . .'

'I don't want you letting me down,' Carey said. 'Your parents are a bit controlling, aren't they? Look at all that fuss about you and the cocktail. Your mum ringing mine. I mean, how old are you? Ten?'

Milly felt torn between embarrassment and defending her parents.

'Well, tomorrow's the deadline, OK?' said Carey. 'I know Bea would love it.'

'Yes, OK.'

But her mother didn't come home until after eight and she looked tired and distracted.

'Oh, darling, I'm sorry. You've been on your own all this time? I'm sorry. I forgot about Daddy being late and I need to do a bit more work, I'm afraid.'

'Mummy, Carey's asked me to go on holiday with them. For two weeks.'

'Oh, really? Where?'

'A yacht in Greece. They're hiring one.'

'Sounds fun. Do you want to go?'

'Course,' she said, crushing the doubt.

'I'll call her mother. Talk about it.'

'When? Carey really wants to know.'

'I'll call her now.'

The Mapletons were out, the Filipino housekeeper informed her.

'Oh, Mummy! That's awful. What am I going to say to Carey?'

'That I'll talk to her mother. Milly, I need to know a bit more, before I agree.'

'Yes, of course. But – you do think it'll be all right?'

'Oh, Milly, yes. I just said I did.'

So: 'It's cool,' she said in the morning to Carey. 'My mum was fine about it. She's going to call yours.'

'Cool,' said Carey. 'God, I can't wait till you see Ad. He's primo.'

'Cool,' said Milly dutifully.

She hoped it was going to be all right.

'Patrick, hi. How's it going?'

Patrick was really pleased to see Jonjo.

'Jonjo, I was wondering when you might appear. Really good to see you.'

'You too. Wondered if you'd like to come for a drink?'

'Well . . .' Patrick hesitated. 'I've not really finished here.'

'Let me tell you, old chap, you never will. It's not that sort of job. How's it shaping up, so far?'

'Oh, good,' said Patrick. 'Yes. I'm enjoying it. Really fascinating. I wouldn't have believed quite how fascinating, actually.'

'Great. Well look, I think you should leave it for a bit and come for a drink. All work and no play and all that. And contacts – very important in your game, I'd have thought.'

'Possibly,' said Patrick, grinning. 'Yeah, OK, why not?'

He felt rather good suddenly; able to converse with Jonjo on equal terms – as someone who was doing something fascinating and living on his wits rather than just marking time until the partner above him retired.

The first day Saul Finlayson had come in to say hello and that he was sorry, he was flying out to Geneva in half an hour, but it was really good to have him on board and he hoped he'd enjoy it.

'I'd like you to get stuck into this,' he said, handing Patrick a slender file. 'It's a fertiliser company, offices mostly in Africa, but one in the Middle East as well, profits look good, but I want to know why they're paying so much for their factories when their wages bill is so low. See what you think. I'll be back tomorrow morning. Cheers!'

It was enthralling work, he could see that, and that he could become very good at it; the only thing was it was rather solitary. But during those first few weeks he had not once felt bored; his brain felt as if it had been put to work in the gym, stretched, honed, tautened. He felt, for the first time since he had left Oxford, that he was not just in the right place at the right time, but in the very best place he could possibly be. It was extremely nice.

'OK. Let's go.' Jonjo looked at him and grinned. 'Corney and Barrow round the corner, good as anywhere, I think. See much of Saul?'

'No, not much,' said Patrick, 'although he came to lunch in the country the Sunday a week before I joined.'

'You're kidding!'

'No. Why?'

'Because he never does anything social, like that. Good God. But workwise?'

'He just throws files at me and then vanishes again. And so far hasn't complained about anything. He seems quite happy.'

'You'd know if he wasn't,' said Jonjo. 'He doesn't mince his words. And you know what? You look about five years younger already. Clearly suits you.'

'Yes,' said Patrick, hearing the pleasure in his own voice. 'Yes, I really think it does.'

Chapter 23

'This is great, Hattie! So much along the right lines. I'm really, really pleased.'

'Good,' said Hattie Richards, 'I'm glad you like it. I don't think we can improve on it much.'

Just as well she did like it then, Bianca thought; it was hard to imagine arguing with Hattie. She looked at her, at her plain face, her mousey hair, clearly uncombed since she had left the house that morning, her distinctly unflattering clothes – and marvelled at what Hattie had set down before her: a skin tonic, so pretty to look at, palest swimming-pool blue, so fresh smelling, so cooling on the skin.

'What I really wanted to ask you was, do you think we could instruct them to keep it in the fridge? That way it would always be cool and make it feel so much more refreshing . . . even if it wasn't.'

'Well, we could. I don't suppose they'd do it, but that would be their problem. It's a nice touch.'

'I thought so,' said Hattie. 'The other thing I wondered was, could the bottle look like a little tonic water bottle? Although, of course, that could mean tooling up specially . . .'

'Hattie,' said Bianca rather feebly, 'I think you should be doing my job.'

'Oh, I don't think so,' said Hattie. 'I really wouldn't enjoy it.'

She was distinctly lacking in a sense of humour.

◦ ◦ ◦

Bertie looked at the email that had just sprung on to his screen. It was from Lara.

'Call me if you're still there.'

He called her. 'Hello, it's me,' he said cautiously.

He wasn't sure he wanted to talk to anyone. He'd been engrossed in what he called his legal homework on employment law – it was complicated and he preferred to do it in the office, particularly as Priscilla refused to leave him in peace, but interrupted him constantly with questions about the house and if he had changed his mind yet. And she and Lucy had declared more or less total war, and squabbled constantly.

'Look, I've had one hell of a day, and so I suspect have you, and it's quite late. I fancy a bite to eat and we could just whizz over those contracts for the two new marketing people. What do you think?'

Bertie hesitated. 'I shouldn't really. I'm totally embroiled in—'

'In what?'

'In my legal studies.'

Lara went into a peal of laughter.

'Bertie, it's after nine and any normal person would be desperate for an excuse to get away! Come on. I'll pick you up in five. I want to try that new place in Marylebone High Street – it's not much more than a wine bar, really, but the food looked pretty good last time I was there. See you.'

Bertie closed his files. It would be fun, having supper with Lara, and there was no arguing with her. She was like a Force Nine gale when she got an idea into her head. Added to which, it would be very pleasant to be with someone who didn't treat him with total contempt . . .

And it was a very nice evening; she was such good company. Funny and friendly and so – well, so encouraging. She told him she thought he was doing brilliantly, that the company already felt a different place from the one she had joined, that the new marketing team – she and her two assistants – were working together like a dream. 'You were right about that funny little chap, and I was wrong, he's a minefield of ideas. Bottle of white, shall we have? Or

231

do you want red? And let's see . . . I fancy the monkfish, what about you?'

Bertie said he would have the puttanesca. 'Or tart's spaghetti, as I believe it's called.'

'Bertie, that's the most risqué remark I've ever heard from you!' She grinned at him. 'You know, you really are doing very well with your diet. Your face has completely changed shape since I arrived.'

'For the better?' asked Bertie anxiously.

'Well, of course for the better. I wouldn't have said anything otherwise.'

'Well, that's a relief,' he said and was so not angling for compliments that she laughed aloud.

'You really are amazing, Bertie. Where does it come from, this rather low opinion of yourself?'

'I suppose because there's never been much reason for a high one. Parents like mine – lot to live up to. And my mother isn't exactly easy in her judgments.'

'How about your dad?'

'Well, he was a bit gentler. But he was so perfect, so handsome and charming and clever, and my mother was always drawing unfavourable comparisons. I suppose that was it.'

'Well, I'd say you're beginning to look more like the portrait of your dad every day. The one your mother insists on keeping in the boardroom.'

Bertie was torn between astonishment and defensiveness on his mother's behalf.

'It's important to her,' he said, 'that picture. And as she always says, the company wouldn't have happened without him.'

'Yes, sorry. I'd no business saying that.'

'It's OK. Anyway, I really don't think I look remotely like him.'

'You do. My dad was a bank manager, very good-looking and charming, and the ladies of Edgbaston all adored him. But the difference was, we got on really well, and he'd tell me how lucky I was to be young and how the world was my oyster. He was very proud of me. And he encouraged me to go to uni, told me he'd always regretted not going himself.'

'Well, you're very lucky,' said Bertie.

'I know,' said Lara, sitting back, starting on her wine with great enthusiasm, 'very lucky.'

'And what about your husband?' Bertie didn't usually ask personal questions, it seemed to him to border on rudeness, but he was intrigued by this background of love and supportiveness, so different from his own.

'My husband? Oh, he was just an out-and-out bastard. Cheated on me, went out of his way to diminish me whenever he could. He told me I lacked class – that was his favourite. He'd been to boarding school and I was a comp girl and he teased me about my accent. But he was very sexy.'

'Oh, I see,' said Bertie. Of course. That would matter to her. He took a large gulp of the wine.

'And he had a bit of money.'

Bertie felt slightly depressed by this account of Lara's husband.

'He used to do all the right things in the early days, send me flowers, bought me champagne, took me on amazing trips – Paris for the weekend, South of France for my birthday, Maldives for our honeymoon. That was amazing.'

She looked at her wine contemplatively. 'And then, once he was married, he didn't have to bother any more. Always going out drinking with his mates, and we were both working for the same company, and he'd be making up to all the girls in the pub and at sales conferences, and when I said I didn't like it, he told me I was just a little suburban girl and he wasn't going to be a suburban husband. He liked to show me off, but he behaved as if we'd only just met and I was just one of his girls for the evening.'

'He sounds dreadful,' said Bertie. He felt hugely indignant on Lara's behalf.

'Then when I began to do better than him in my career, he didn't like it, he was jealous. He got this idea we should have children, and I knew why, he wanted me at home, with nothing to do but look after him. I refused, and that was when the cheating began. But – oh, I'm sorry Bertie, you don't want to hear all this!'

'Yes, I do,' said Bertie. He wasn't sure that he did, but it was telling him a lot about Lara.

'Of course he was very remorseful, and I decided to go along with the baby thing, and actually got pregnant, but then I lost it. Yeah, it was awful,' she said, seeing Bertie's agonised half-embarrassed sympathy, 'but, you know, life's tough. Just get on with it, that's my motto. I began to recover, got a new job and he was angry and – well, it all started again. Big time. So I left him. I was doing very well in my career, and then I had a really nice fella and I was very happy with him. We were going to get married, and then he was diagnosed with prostate cancer, just like that. Dead in six months.'

'Oh, Lara!' said Bertie. 'That is the most dreadful story.' Fate seemed to have been quite kind to him by comparison.

'Oh, it's OK. Honestly. I survived. As you see.'

His phone rang. 'Sorry,' he said looking at it. 'It's my wife, better take it.'

He turned away from the table.

'Priscilla, hello. Any problems? Oh, I see. Well, I'm sorry, but I had to work late this evening, thought I'd told you? I'm having a bite to eat with a colleague. What? Oh, I see. Well, perhaps tomorrow . . . no don't wait up for me, we're going over some contracts here – yes, all right. Yes, I am sorry. I said so, several times. Bye Priscilla.'

He ended the call and looked at Lara rather shamefaced.

'Sorry. And now I'm well in the doghouse. She'd kept supper for me.'

'Oh, dear,' said Lara. 'Well, should we just whizz over these contracts before we're both properly drunk and then we can turn our minds to other things? Like . . . your marriage.' She looked at him, her big blue eyes dancing.

'Oh, don't think there's anything to be said about that,' said Bertie. 'It's a perfectly normal, happy marriage. Few ups and downs, but nothing to talk about, really.'

'Oh really?' said Lara. 'Well, that's good.'

◦ ◦ ◦

It was late when they left. They had drunk at least half of a second bottle of wine and Bertie was feeling a little confused. He was helping her into her coat at the door when she turned and smiled at him and said, 'I've had such a nice evening. Thank you, Bertie. And you really do look like your dad.'

And somehow – and the old Bertie, even the sober Bertie, would never have done such a thing – he felt suddenly completely happy, and he smiled back at her and then bent down and kissed her – very gently – on the mouth.

'I've loved it too,' he said. 'Thank you. It was your idea.'

And she looked at him, slightly startled, then gave him a hug and it was all completely and perfectly innocent. Of course.

And so very very enjoyable.

It was heady stuff this. A love affair it could be called. First-thought-in-the-morning-last-thought-at-night stuff. Missing meals, too excited to sleep, unable to concentrate except on the beloved; he could hardly recognise himself.

And all because of a job. Ridiculous really. But – undeniable. And making him very happy.

'Hi, mate! Coming for a drink?'

It was Jonjo.

'Can't. Too much to do. Have work to finish tonight.'

'Blimey! You really are hooked.'

'Yes, I am,' said Patrick, very seriously. 'It is totally fascinating. I only have to see the words "exceptional profits" and I'm off. And I've spotted a few things.'

'Great. I've clearly unleashed a great new talent into the financial world. Not feeling lonely?'

'No. I get so absorbed, I hardly know if it's morning or night.'

'Excellent. And what about your parental duties?'

'You know what?' said Patrick and the smile was not apologetic at all now, 'I've handed them over for a while. It's not my turn.'

'I never thought to hear you say anything like that,' said Jonjo. 'Well, cheers mate. See you tomorrow.'

'Yes, great,' said Patrick. He had never thought to hear himself say anything like that either.

He had had several – well, not rows, disagreements – with Bianca about it. The most recent had been a talk at Milly's school, marked 'High Priority' in the email; Bianca had said she simply couldn't go, and he'd have to; Patrick said he simply couldn't go either so what was to be done? They'd had a straightforward, adult conversation about it, affirming that they must agree on priorities which hadn't got them anywhere, followed by a rather brisk discussion disagreeing on priorities which hadn't got them anywhere either, and finally a tense talk agreeing on priorities but disagreeing on which of them should meet them and when, Patrick making the point that he had been meeting them for the past thirteen years and maybe it was Bianca's turn, and Bianca the point that she was signed up to a new project that was non-negotiable in terms of commitment, and Patrick pointing out that the same could be said of his.

The event went unattended, followed shortly by another – a swimming gala of Fergie's. This had never happened through their entire parenthood. Milly was shocked, and even Ruby was upset by proxy and cried all through her bedtime story. Fergie had arrived home with a medal for winning the Under Twelves' freestyle, which he threw into the bin and retired to his room, most unusually, in tears. When Bianca arrived home, she went up to see him and he refused to talk to her. She went downstairs, upset, started clearing up the children's supper things and was confronted by Milly, who had retrieved the medal. 'You should have been there for him!' she said and flounced out of the kitchen and upstairs, slamming her door behind her. Patrick, arriving home a little later, found Bianca – also most unusually – in tears.

'It's just – just wrong,' she said, wiping her eyes on the back of her hand, smudging her mascara. 'It's not their fault, they need better than this.'

'I totally agree,' said Patrick.

'Well, what are we going to do about it?'

'By that, I suspect you mean what am *I* going to do about it.'

'No,' she said, 'I don't.' But there was a note of bravado in her voice.

'Bianca, I'm sorry, but I've done it for at least twelve years. Been there, whenever *we* were needed.'

'That's not fair. I've done my share, whenever I could.'

'Yes, and when you couldn't, you didn't have to give it a moment's thought. Patrick can go, you thought, that'll be fine, and off you went, to New York or Edinburgh or Manchester. It was very very easy for you.'

'That is so unfair! We *agreed* that was how we'd play it. You know we did. It's not my fault you had a totally flexible job and I didn't.'

'Indeed not. But it suited you very well.'

'Patrick, this is a ridiculous conversation. Our whole family structure was based on that.'

'But – don't you think, sometimes, there has to be flexibility in these things? I was quite happy at work in those days. I became very unhappy—'

'Oh, don't give me that! You were not *very* unhappy.'

'And how do you know that? Did you ever think to inquire? As you rushed from one terribly important job to another, did you think "maybe I'd better make sure this is all right with Patrick first"?'

'Actually, I did,' she said, stung. 'Before I went to Farrell's, I asked you, I said it would be worse than PDN, I said I'd like your agreement, and you said if I really wanted to do it, then I should.'

'My God, you don't take any prisoners, do you, Bianca? I'm glad I don't work for you.'

'Oh, don't be so ridiculous!' she said.

'You know,' he said and his eyes meeting hers were more hostile than she could ever remember, 'sometimes it just feels like that. Being part of your team.'

'Fuck you, Patrick Bailey,' she said, 'that is a monstrous thing to say.'

'Is it? When everything I do has to be cleared with you, just in case?'

'Oh, what!'

'Yes. Yes it does. Moreover, I do remember having roughly the same conversation with you when I went to Finlaysons. And you said – unfortunately I don't have your gift for total recall – I should go ahead.'

'That was because of what you said about being miserable, about dying at your desk and nobody noticing. Not about how you might not be able to do so much with the children.'

Patrick was silent. That was unarguable. That was the trouble with all of it; it was all unarguable. There was absolute justice on both sides: he was reneging on the deal with Bianca, and she took advantage of him to the most appalling degree, often staying at the office and working through when really she could perfectly well have made a school or doctor's appointment, and then carried on at home.

'Well, something clearly has to be done,' he said now, 'we can't go on like this. We'll both have to make concessions, you'll simply have to be a little more—'

'More what?' she said, her voice heavy with suspicion.

'More flexible,' he said, 'and I will do my best to bring work home whenever possible, rather than staying on in the office. Saul said that would be fine by him. But Bianca, I've just started that job. I desperately need to make a good start. You of all people should see that.'

'I do,' she said suddenly, becoming visibly more conciliatory, and he wondered how much of it was genuine and how much was her taking advantage of a weakness in his argument. 'Of course I do. Patrick I'm – well, I am sorry. I know I've been very lucky. And I do really appreciate it. And now I'm just beginning to see the wood for the trees, I will try very hard to do better.' She smiled at him, a rueful, almost shamefaced smile.

'Good,' said Patrick, taking this olive branch slightly coolly, 'I'm delighted to hear it. Well, we seem to have a semi-solution, in theory at least.'

'Yes, we do.'

She smiled at him, wishing she believed even in the semi-solution. Theory was so easy; it was practice that was hard.

Chapter 24

She knew what had done it; what had made the thing thinkable when the moment presented itself – it was Athina saying, 'Look, take Florence, she'll be of some use to you, I expect. She speaks French for a start, don't you, Florence? And I really am far too busy to go myself.'

It wasn't the dismissal of her professional abilities; it was the clear assumption that there could be no possible danger in sending her husband off to Paris – Paris, of all places – in Florence's company, no fear that he might find her even remotely desirable, or their situation in any way compromising, or even beguiling.

However, she steered herself away from such reflections, merely thought that three days in Paris, a city she had never visited, would be a glorious treat, despite the fact that they would be largely devoted to work, and even managed not to show her further irritation when Athina said that Cornelius must find Florence somewhere to stay near his hotel. Indeed, when Cornelius said that perhaps Florence should stay at the same hotel, she felt a flash of danger along with the pleasure and was almost relieved when Athina said, 'I hardly think that would be appropriate, Cornelius, some nice little *pension* nearby will do perfectly well.'

The trip – to investigate the possibility of the House of Farrell having a presence in Paris, had been planned for some time; appointments had been made and hotels booked. But at the very last minute, Athina had been asked to work on an exclusive promotion for Harrods and it was simply too good an opportunity to miss. On the other hand, rescheduling Paris had proved impossible; and thus it was that, in the last week of May, 1957, Cornelius and Florence boarded the Golden Arrow at Victoria station, bound for the Gare du Nord and Paris, by way of Folkestone and the Channel ferry.

The crossing was rough and took longer than its allotted span; Florence stood on deck, enjoying the rise and fall of the boat, and the wind in her hair, one of very few people to do so.

'How brave you are, Florence,' Cornelius said. 'I was afraid you might have been overcome with *mal de mer.*'

'Of course not,' said Florence, 'I love it. My godfather had a yacht, a small one, and he used to take me sailing in the Solent, and the rougher the better. It comes close to flying, at times, especially if you look up at the sky. He had a sort of canvas seat, fixed to the deck that swung right out over the water, a cradle it was called, and I used to sit in it, pretending I was one of the seagulls screaming overhead. "Hold tight, Little Flo!" he used to shout, "I'm not coming in after you!"'

'How full of surprises you are,' said Cornelius, 'and I like the nickname, Little Flo.'

'Yes, well it was a very private one,' she said, 'and I only allow very special people to use it.'

'I see. I presume that doesn't include me?'

'No, Cornelius, it does not.'

They reached the Gare du Nord at five that evening, and took a cab to the rue Jacob, where the Hotel d'Angleterre was situated; Florence's *pension*, which was modestly charming, was on the rue de Seine, a minute's walk away.

'Can you be ready in an hour?' Cornelius asked, having seen her safely in. 'For an aperitif before dinner?'

'Of course. But nowhere too smart, I hope. I don't have anything very grand to wear.'

'Not too grand at all, a café indeed, but with a certain chic. You will like it, I'm sure. And we will go somewhere similar for dinner. I will be here at six.'

Which he was, wearing a dark suit, his pink and green Garrick tie, a raincoat slung over his shoulders.

'You look perfect,' he said, studying her black woollen dress, with its slash neckline, swirling skirt and wide red belt. 'Quite perfect. And we are going to the extremely famous Café de Flore, which is so fortuitously near.'

'I know that, and I also know it's extremely famous,' said Florence briskly.

'Oh, darling Florence, forgive me. Of course you do. I should have known that.'

The darling made her forgive him; forgive him for thinking she was just a foolish little girl from London, who he employed to run a shop for him, and could not possibly be expected to know about the smart cafés of Paris.

'Now. What will you have?' he said when they were seated.

'Oh – I don't know. What would you recommend?'

'I think . . . a kir. Made not with champagne but white burgundy. Which is, of course, as it should be. And I will have the same.'

He lit a cigarette, offered her one; she hesitated, then took one, and they sat back and watched the world go by, down the Boulevard St Germain, couples strolling, talking, laughing, arm in arm, some with small dogs in tow, the younger ones pausing sometimes to kiss, the older ones to call their children to them, some very old and touchingly hand in hand, and all so stylishly, so beautifully dressed, so at ease with themselves and the place where they were.

'You realise, of course,' he said, 'that we are in Leonard Trentham's Paris. This is the area he loved, where our courtyard was. Where we had our first tryst.'

'Yes, so it is,' she said, 'and I hadn't realised.'

And she was silent, careful not to look at him, remembering that evening at the gallery and the sudden dangerous intimacy between them, and in a way it was as if they had been there before and this felt like a return to somewhere well-known and loved. Which was of course both fanciful and absurd.

'Tomorrow we will go and find our door, our courtyard. Would you like that?'

'I would very much,' she said determinedly brisk, 'but we're here to work, Cornelius, in search of business, not courtyards. What would Athina say if she knew we were wandering the streets, indulging ourselves?'

'I dread to think,' he said, laughing, 'but she will not know for neither of us will tell her. And of course we will work, but one cannot visit Paris and not have fun as well. Now have your drink and we will consider a venue for dinner. There is no work to be done now.'

And she gave herself up to enjoying herself. She had been avoiding him lately in London, determined that the disgraceful, if delectable, event that had taken place in the taxi should remain what it was, a piece of reckless, irresistible foolishness, never to be repeated, for it had been conducted not only between herself and a married man, but a married man who just happened to be the husband of her employer. But – here she was, in Paris, with the married man, at the suggestion of his wife; surely therefore she could allow herself to enjoy it?

'So, I think we will dine just down the street there, a small bistro, very, very French. We will find no English there, and very simple food, but oh, so delicious. Now will you have another of those or . . .'

'No, I think I have to limit myself. I'm not used to all this good living.'

'Then you should be. And I intend to rectify that, over the next few days. But tonight we will take things quietly.'

Which they did; dinner was indeed simple, onion soup followed by chicken, and then some amazing cheese, all so very delicious, so infused with the quality of Paris; they parted at ten with the briefest kiss on the doorstep of her *pension*.

They breakfasted – if a croissant and a café au lait could be described thus – at Les Deux Magots, adjacent to the Flore and as deservedly famous, and planned their day.

'We will begin just over there,' Cornelius said, gesturing across the street, 'at the Bon Marché – we have an appointment at ten.

Now, my French is not of the highest standard, but I shall employ the well-known English method of shouting increasingly loudly, in my mother tongue if needs be. How is your French?'

'Oh, passable.'

'*Bon*. And my plan is for us to alternate business with pleasure. All through the day.'

'Cornelius—'

'No, no, I insist. There is too much for you to see for us to leave it until the last few hours. This is, without doubt, the most beautiful city in the world but we clearly have to be sparing. Of course you must visit the Louvre and Notre Dame, and we must stroll the rue de Rivoli. The Champs-Élysées is essential; you will never see a more beautiful street as long as you live, so I think we will go there for lunch to Fouquet's, a legend in itself, then cocktails at the Ritz, of course.'

'The Ritz! Cornelius I have no clothes for the Ritz.'

'Nonsense. You have natural style, Florence, you don't need to worry about such things. The Ritz here in Paris is the most famous hotel in the world, although I prefer the Crillon myself, and you must visit it. It is as iconic as the Eiffel Tower. To which I think we may give a miss – there are other more beautiful places and things to see. Now, have you finished your coffee?'

'Oh – yes, thank you,' said Florence, 'and Fouquet's sounds wonderful, but rather expensive and—'

'Florence, dear Florence, this is all on company expenses, so neither of us need worry about it for one moment. Now – to work. We have to go to Galeries Lafayette and to Printemps, one of the sights of Paris in itself, as well as Bon Marché, and then to Fouquet's. After that, Sacré Cœur.'

She shook her head.

And so the day went on; now a little work, now rather more pleasure. Florence marvelled at the chic of the women who stood at the Bon Marché counters, trying and testing colours, asking for advice on their skincare, wondering what was it about French women that gave them that astonishing edge, that could only be described in their own language – chic. They looked younger than their English counterparts, but more sophisticated, their hair simpler, their outfits less elaborate, their colours more muted. There was something else too, which she couldn't define, but pressed by Cornelius when she remarked upon it, she realised they had a self-confidence and a self-awareness that was very – well, very sexy. English women, she thought, were not often sexy. Not obviously so.

She considered her light grey woollen dress, with its nipped-in waist and swirling skirt, her carefully chosen low-heeled court shoes, half-hat set on her unruly hair, and compared it with the clothes of her nearest neighbour. She wore a narrow black suit with the new longline jacket that reached almost to her knees; her hair was swept back into a flawless chignon, and her hat was a small, neat affair, in dark red, little more than a beret, set firmly on the middle of her head. Her shoes were also dark red as was her bag; she looked – well, she looked chic.

Florence sighed.

They visited the cosmetic buyer at Printemps on the Boulevard Haussmann, with some success: she loved Athina's paintboxes, agreed to order them along with The Cream and some lipsticks, and when Cornelius went to the accounting department he dispatched Florence to the fashion floor, and she wandered through it, pausing every five minutes or so to gaze upwards at the dazzling stained-glass cupola that arched over the entire store. She found a pair of shoes, lizardskin courts with the new narrow heel and pointed toe, and was trying them on when Cornelius found her.

'Very nice, Florence.' He gave her name the French pronunciation. '*Très chic*! Are you going to buy them?'

'I am not,' said Florence firmly. 'They are far too expensive for me. Really, Cornelius, I'm just a poor little shop girl, I can't afford this sort of thing.'

'But you should have them. They flatter your ankles so beautifully. And you have such very pretty ankles. No, you must buy them. I insist.'

'Well,' said Florence, 'you will have to give me a rise.' She said it lightly, not imagining that he would take any notice, but he was pulling out his wallet and peeling off a fifty-franc note, handing it to the sales girl before she could stop him.

'Cornelius, stop it! I don't want charity.'

'This is not charity, and you are buying them yourself. With an advance on your new, higher wages.'

'Cornelius, no!'

'Florence, yes. Now come along, and I want you to wear them to our lunch at Fouquet's. Where they will feel very much at home.'

'Here we are,' he said as their taxi drew up in front of Fouquet's. 'I think you might remember this from another painting . . .'

She did; remembered the wide, curved frontage, its so-distinctive red canopy, miniature trees lining its entrance, remembered it and smiled at him; he smiled back.

'I like it so much that we have already enjoyed Paris together,' he said. And she felt she had taken another step, another dangerous step back – or was it forward? – into the intimacy of that evening. 'Now, we could have lunch in the restaurant, but the *terrasse* is more fun. See, just through there, the long room, and the line of tables by the window, looking on to the street. How would you like that?'

'Very much indeed,' said Florence, 'but—'

'Florence, do stop saying but. There's nothing to but about.'

'Cornelius,' she said, 'there is something to but about. It's Athina, as you very well know. What would she think, if she knew you were buying me cocktails and shoes and lunches?'

'The very worst I imagine,' said Cornelius cheerfully, 'but she doesn't know, and she won't know, and the worst isn't going to happen anyway – is it, Florence?'

'No,' she said quickly. Very quickly. Sensing that his presenting it to her as a possibility, however slight, was a provocative thing to do.

'Of course not. So, she would be misjudging us terribly. Now come along . . .' He held out his hand, and she knew as she took it that, in spite of his words, there was a great deal to worry about and that really she should insist they left the restaurant now, at once, and return to their work. But . . . 'Right,' he said as they settled by the window, 'there are lots of wonderful things to eat here but I can recommend the *moules marinières*, they are simply magnificent. Do you like *moules*?'

'I've never had them,' said Florence.

'Then it's time you did. *Moules* – mussels in plain English, sounds so much less attractive – are completely delicious served with *frites* and a nice dry white wine, a Muscadet, I think. The perfect lunch. A martini while we order?'

'No thank you,' said Florence faintly.

They left at three; she felt happy and slightly dizzy, but otherwise totally and dangerously relaxed. Somehow, and by some strange alchemy of the wine and the surroundings, and the view of the sun shining through the chestnut trees, and Cornelius's dark blue eyes fixed on her, her conscience, so active two hours ago, had been settled. Or was taking at least a siesta, she thought.

She went to the ladies', and looked at herself in the mirror, and saw a woman a little flushed, her dark eyes brilliant, and smiled at her.

'*Bonne chance*,' she said aloud, as she sprayed herself rather liberally with her scent.

'Right,' said Cornelius when she had finished her coffee, 'Galeries Lafayette, and then Sacré Coeur. Come along. No time to waste.'

They did not waste it, and every moment, every step took them nearer to the heart of the Paris that Cornelius knew and she was discovering, the dangerous, sexually beguiling city that Leonard Trentham had so rightly said would suit them both so well.

He was right, Florence decided; Sacré Cœur was astonishing and as lovely as the painting had promised. Standing high above Montmartre, white, dazzling, shining in the evening sun, it was like some heavenly vision in itself.

'Oh,' she said, gazing at it in awe, 'how beautiful it is. I can't believe it. Thank you so so much, Cornelius, for bringing me here.'

'Entirely my pleasure,' he said, and his eyes on her were very thoughtful. And he suddenly reached out and pushed one of her wild curls behind her ear and then pulled her hat off, and stood back looking at her.

'Much, much better. It's a very nice hat, but the hair beneath it is so much more beautiful. You should leave it uncovered whenever you can. Especially when you're with me.'

Florence said briskly that she really didn't imagine she would be with him very often and that her hair got very untidy without a hat.

'Of course. Which is why you should leave it be. All those wonderful curls and tendrils, asking to be set free. Why try to shut them away?'

'Oh, all right,' said Florence, laughing. 'But perhaps in the church I should wear my hat?'

'Perhaps in the church. Now, you will be glad you have had such a good lunch because it's quite a climb. Or would you prefer to take the *funiculaire*, it takes us a little of the way?'

'No,' she said, 'I want to walk. I feel very energetic suddenly.'

'Good,' he said, 'but save some of it for later, that energy, won't you?'

She tried and failed not to think of what he might mean.

'Now,' he said as, sated with the beauties of Sacré Coeur, they returned to their own neighbourhood, 'I think we should leave finding our courtyard until tomorrow because we are both a little weary. So this evening we will have cocktails at the Lutetia, which is just up the street – indeed, we can walk there on this lovely evening – and you need to wear your new shoes.'

'And – anything else?' she asked. 'Or will they be enough?'

'For me they would be quite enough,' he said, 'but for the Lutetia, perhaps a little more.'

And he suddenly leaned down and kissed her cheek, very lightly, and said, 'Oh Florence, what wonderful company you are . . .' Then drawing back immediately, and she was aware of the effort that cost

247

him, and that was oddly exciting too, he said, 'Now, one hour. Wear your finest.'

'Is it very grand?' she asked, nervous again.

'Quite grand. But it is a carnal place, very, very sexy. So . . . it will suit you.'

'Cornelius?'

'Yes, Florence . . . ?'

His voice was innocent; but his expression was not.

'Only two more weeks, Mills. Sooo exciting. Have you got your clothes yet?'

'Um, no, not yet,' said Milly. 'We're – we're going shopping on Saturday. So what have you got?'

'Oh – some ace bikinis of course. Lots of ripped shorts, white ones, so cool, and some gorgeous dresses.'

'Will we need many dresses?'

'Of course! Mummy says we can eat dinner with them at night and if they go ashore, they'll take us if they can.'

'Oh, I see.'

'I can't wait. Think of all the pictures we'll have to put on Facebook.'

'Yes . . .'

Carey's brown eyes seemed to pierce Milly's in a way she had begun to dread.

'You don't sound that excited, Mills. You sure you want to come still? Because Bea is just sooo envious. She said she'd give, like, anything, to be coming. I mean if you want to change your mind—'

'No,' said Milly, 'no of course not. I'm terribly excited.'

Her half hope that her mother would say she couldn't go had not materialised. Bianca had called Nicky as promised and seemed to have no reservations about it.

'It sounds lovely, darling, and we've found a villa for the following two weeks, so it's all working out beautifully. Lucky girl.'

'Yes, I know. Did she – did she tell you about the others going?'

'Oh yes, including two more children, two boys she said. There'll be snorkelling, water skiing, and swimming and it sounds lovely. Oh, and darling, she did assure me there'd be no champagne cocktails! So I'm very happy about it, darling, really very happy indeed. And so is Daddy.'

'Cool,' said Milly. She felt comforted that her father had agreed to it. He was always even more fussy than her mother. Which was saying something.

Chapter 25

She must not do this; she must not give in, and at precisely the same time, knew that she would; it was as if she had become two people, the one wise, the other foolish, the one sweetly cautious, the other joyfully abandoned, the one a little ladylike, the other sexily self-confident. They were waiting on the steps of her *pension*, the two Florences, when Cornelius walked up the street, smiling, to collect her. And one Florence stayed behind, in the small pretty room, and the other took his arm and walked down the street and into the Lutetia.

Which did indeed look very grand, with its superb carved and stuccoed frontage, curving round the Boulevard Raspail, the huge deco letters spelling out its name shining golden in the evening sun.

'Isn't it lovely? And you look very worthy of it.'

She hoped so; her finest was the black taffeta cocktail dress she had worn on the night of the exhibition; perhaps he would not remember it.

But, 'I love that dress,' he said. 'It reminds me of our wonderful evening together. Come along.'

'Oh my goodness,' said Florence, following him into the bar, 'oh my goodness!'

The bar was absurdly exotic, occupied with life-size nude figures in bronze, elaborately fringed hanging lights, mirrors set square on every inch of wall; Cornelius ushered her into a deep, low, curved backed chair that somehow seemed too big for her and ordered two Grand Royales.

'Cornelius, what is a Grand Royale? And how do you know I'll like it?'

'I just do. It's champagne, and Grand Marnier. Quite exotic. Really the only cocktail for this place.'

She looked around her in silence, unable to think of anything to say that might be clever enough for such surroundings.

He smiled.

'You're very quiet.'

'I feel very quiet. Sorry.'

'No need to apologise. It's marvellous, isn't it? It makes no concession to the passing of time, it is as it was, a simple statement of its era.'

'Which was?'

'Oh, it was built in 1910. The end of the *belle époque*. It was considered awfully daring. *Le tout Paris* gathered here, not just the social set, but artists, dancers, writers, and they drank champagne, ate wonderful food, danced, and, I am quite sure, took lots of drugs. Then it was requisitioned during the war and was used to house and entertain the officers in command of the occupation. Afterwards it became a hospital for refugees from the camps and prisoners of war. And it is now restored to its incredible splendour as you see. It is, of course, all about sex.'

'Is it?'

'Yes, it is. Don't you feel it? It's a very sensuous place. Or am I talking nonsense?'

'Whether it's nonsense or not, Cornelius, it's exactly the sort of conversation we agreed we should not be having.'

'No, Florence, that is not what we agreed. It is impossible to be in Paris and not talk about sex. The agreement was that there should be no impropriety between us. That is very different.' He sighed. 'Unfortunately.'

'Well . . .' she said, her voice tailing away.

'Oh, Florence,' he said, his tone different suddenly, solemn, oddly gentle, 'this has been so very special. Such a very special day.'

'It has indeed,' she said. 'Very special. Thank you. Thank you so much.'

'It has been entirely my pleasure. Now, I have decided we should eat dinner at the Brasserie Lipp. It's very near, on the Boulevard St Germain, and I am hoping very much we shall be allowed a table.'

And the two Florences once again took his arm and walked into the rest of the evening.

The Brasserie Lipp was indeed just a walk away: more painted ceilings, lamps, *belle époque* flowers, and decorated mirrors (artfully tilted, Cornelius told Florence, so that every part of the main room could be seen from every other part of it) and *le tout Paris* were slowly filing in. Not the dazzling, show-offy Paris of the Ritz, or the Crillon, but chic, intelligent Paris, writers, artists, musicians, the *vrai beau monde*, for all of whom Lipp approval was required before admission to a table. It was impossible to book; you had to stake your claim and were either told to wait twenty minutes, in which case you had a drink on the *terrasse*, or to wait an hour '*au moins*', in which case the only thing to do was dine elsewhere. But a smile was bestowed on Cornelius and a table on the terrace and Florence sat entranced, watching people come and go. She saw an elderly lady carrying a small dog admitted; she saw people overdressed and people seriously underdressed; she saw men on their own and women together; she saw . . . 'Oh my goodness Cornelius, is that – yes it *is*, Yves Montand! And I can't believe this, Simone Signoret, and—'

'Hush,' said Cornelius laughing, 'you will have us banned. This is a place for discretion. But yes, it is Montand and Signoret. We are lucky to be here. And I am very lucky to be here with you. I hope you feel the same way.'

Then it was that the one Florence withdrew, and the other stepped forward: she felt outside time, outside reality, outside conscience, that this was an evening of pure class and style, and that it would be a crime against Paris to primly refuse, albeit for several very good reasons, a sexual adventure.

And so they were launched on this sweetly promising journey; for Cornelius read her answer as she suddenly, and with an unmistakable sexuality, pulled out the pins that held back her wild hair, and shook it out, her eyes fixed on his the while.

'Give me your hands,' he said, and he took them, her small pretty hands, in both of his and turned her palms upwards and bent his head over them and kissed them, one at a time; and she felt a reckless excitement that completely overcame any sense of guilt or even fear, and kissed both his hands in return.

'Good,' was all he said, his eyes probing hers very fiercely, very hard, and she felt that too, felt it as a physical thing, a promise of what was to come.

They deliberately postponed then, with an agonising pleasure, the joys that they knew lay before them, as they drank and ate and talked and laughed.

'Now,' he said, as they finally went outside into the night, she holding his arm, her head resting against him, 'now we must find a safe harbour, Little Flo.' And she agreed, laughing now, with excitement and recklessness, that they could go neither to Cornelius's hotel nor hers, for his would be too risky, and hers too undeserving of what was to follow.

And he led her through the narrow, maze-like streets of St Germain, and they paused outside one small restaurant where a crowd of people sat on the pavement, drinking and smoking, enjoying the Parisian air, full as it was of laughter and camaraderie and music, drifting from street musicians and cafés; they waved to them and called them over, offering them cigarettes and wine, but they could wait no longer, by mutual consent, simply smiled back and shook their heads and Cornelius, his arm around Florence's shoulders, now bent and kissed her on the mouth, making their intentions very clear. Which delighted the group who raised their glasses to them as one man and called 'bonne chance'. To which Cornelius tipped his hat and Florence made a small mock curtsey.

They went to a small hotel, little more than a *pension*, where Cornelius seemed to know the proprietor. Shown to a small but charming room, with a large, brass bed, quite unafraid or even anxious, she lay down on the bed with Cornelius beside her and asked to be kissed.

'I wonder,' he said, leaning over her and slowly, very slowly, playing with her hair, stroking her face, kissing her neck, 'my dearest Little Flo, if there was pleasure with your husband?'

'Cornelius, of course there was. Wonderful pleasure. I loved every moment of every time, even the first.'

'I see,' he said, 'a challenge then.'

'Yes. But I think it will be all right.'

And it was: wonderfully, brilliantly, shakingly, explosively all right. She lay there, hungry for pleasure, aching for release, laughing as he professed surprise at her lack of inhibition.

'Really, Cornelius, what do you take me for?'

'I take you,' he said, kissing first one breast, then the other, 'for what you are, the most sexually intriguing woman I have ever known.'

'I can't believe that,' she said, pushing her hands through his hair, arching her back, half shouting already, throbbing, aching with pleasure, and: 'Oh be quiet,' he said, 'and let me have you.'

He did have her; and more than once, the first time swift, almost desperate; and again and then again, each time sweeter, more intense, more ferocious than the last. She had not forgotten the pleasure, but time had softened the memory, and she was surprised, almost startled, by the fierce, probing hunger, the desperation as her body neared release, and then the sweet, bright freedom as she broke through, found it, found the unfolding pleasure, over and over, wave upon wave, found herself.

'Oh, Miss Hamilton,' said Cornelius finally, as the early dawn of midsummer was just breaking over Paris, 'you have exhausted me.'

'And you me,' she said, lying back on the lace-edged pillows, smiling at him.

'But not for long I suspect,' he said.

'Oh, a while. You may have a little sleep now. And then I think you should return to the Hotel d'Angleterre and I to the *pension*, and we should become ourselves again, and remember who we are.'

'Must we?'

'We must.'

And of course, he knew she was right.

They had two more days, and they spent as little time as possible working.

'I think that might be the thing that Athina might mind most,' said Cornelius with a grin when she pointed it out.

He showed her the real Paris, the Seine with its bridges and walks, the twisting and turning of the huddled narrow streets of the Marais, the winding criss-cross lanes of Montmartre, the boulevard of Montparnasse and its wonderful cemetery, with its writers' graves and its romantic embellishments – a couple sitting in bed on one grave, a version of Brancusi's *The Kiss* on another.

'How can a cemetery be sexy?' Florence asked, smiling. 'But it is.'

And on and on it went, until she was confused, almost wanting to be weary of it, so that leaving would not be so hard.

And on their last evening, in the still bright light, they went to find their courtyard, wandering up and down the streets, peering into alleys and pushing open half-open doors, and after many false starts:

'Look!' cried Florence, 'there it is, look Cornelius, there, see.'

And they stood there on the edge of it, peering inside at their courtyard, small and green and filled with light even then. 'Stay there,' said Cornelius, and he took his camera and photographed her standing there, laughing, and a second one as she blew him a kiss; and then she took one of him, blowing a kiss back, and then a passing stranger, as would only happen in Paris, asked if they would like him to photograph them together and they thanked him and posed together, smiling, he with his arm round her shoulders.

'You'd better take good care of those,' said Florence, suddenly sober, when the stranger had moved on. 'Here, give the film to me and I'll have it developed. Safer that way.'

And on their last evening, they dined at the Café de Flore. 'Only I shall think of it as the Café de Flo for ever more,' Cornelius said, and they looked at one another in a sort of wonder that they had travelled so far in so short a time.

'I don't know how to go back,' he said, 'how to be Mr Farrell again, husband to the famous Mrs Farrell.'

'You are quite famous yourself,' said Florence briskly, 'and you have to go back, and so do I, to our other lives. They are real, they are what matters and—'

'No,' he said. 'This has been real too, and this matters too, and we must not lose it, it is too precious. And, with your agreement, I see no reason why not.'

'I see many reasons,' said Florence, 'but I am prepared to let you try and persuade me.'

'I shall try and I shall succeed,' said Cornelius. 'And I should warn you, I am not accustomed to failure.' And he smiled at her with great self-confidence.

Chapter 26

'Lawrence, hello. What on earth are you doing here?'

Lawrence started; anyone suspecting him of a crime would have immediately assumed his guilt.

He looked up, closed his laptop quickly. It was Isobel Baines, one of their neighbours.

'Oh,' he said, 'Isobel. How lovely to see you. How are you?'

'I'm fine. Up in town looking for a dress for Teresa's engagement party.'

Teresa was their daughter; their pride and satisfaction at her engagement to a rich young banker was immeasurable. The fact that bankers were now considered the scourge of the earth seemed to have passed them entirely by.

'Anyway, it's very nice to see you. May I join you?'

Lawrence cursed the recklessness that had led him to a Starbucks in Knightsbridge; but he had had an interview – his first – and he'd been desperate for a coffee afterwards. 'Oh, I'm just leaving,' he said. 'I'm just – just between appointments, killing a bit of time.'

'Oh, I see. Nice to see you, anyway. We're all meeting on Saturday, aren't we? At the Davies'?'

Oh God, this got worse and worse. She would be bound to mention it, and then . . .

'Yes. Well, bye Isobel. Have a good shop.'

It was no good, he thought, he'd have to tell Annie now. Maybe he'd just wait until he heard about the job this morning; that would soften the situation and the interview had gone quite well, he thought.

Two hours later he got an email: *Dear Lawrence, thanks for coming in this morning. Good to meet you, but frankly, you're overqualified for the job. Good luck in your search.*

That was it then. God, he was a failure. He'd go straight home and tell Annie now. Get it over. Anything would be better than this. He was beginning to feel like a hunted man.

He was coming out of Tunbridge Wells station, his entire being focused on how he was going to tell Annie, just as a large white van pulled into the courtyard. It was raining and Lawrence was fumbling for his umbrella, not looking at what was in front of him as he stepped into the forecourt. As a lady standing in the taxi queue said, it was an accident waiting to happen; the van tried to stop as Lawrence walked straight into its path, skidded, hit him on the head and knocked him twenty yards down the road.

He was taken to the nearest hospital where he was put in Intensive Care but he never recovered consciousness and when Annie, who had sat by him through his long, last hours, phoned the company in the morning to say that he wouldn't be in, a hugely embarrassed and distressed secretary, too shocked even to realise what she was saying, told her that she was terribly sorry, but Mr Ford had left the company a month earlier.

Bianca sat in the crematorium at Lawrence Ford's funeral service and thought she had never been so miserable. Or ashamed.

She knew that in theory such an emotion was absurd, that it was not her fault that Lawrence had been unable to confess his failure to his wife, or indeed that he was a failure in the first place, and certainly not that he had not seen the white van careering across his path, nor it him. But she did feel some responsibility – had she not fired him he would be alive and well today and his nice-looking wife and enchanting little boy, not much older than Ruby, would not be standing hand in hand at the front of the crematorium dressed in black and weeping as they stared at the flower-covered coffin. Lawrence Ford had been a nice, kind, if pompous man who had worked hard, loved and looked after his family, paid his taxes, and whose worst crime was probably being self-opinionated. And now he was dead because of her: because she had come into the company where he had worked and cut a swathe through it and told him, among many others, to leave it, taking with him his dignity, and his self-respect.

Patrick had told her not to go to the funeral, saying that she had hardly known Lawrence and had no real business there, and Mike and Hugh had counselled the same, but she knew they were wrong, that such an absence would have implied a lack of concern. She had discussed it with Bertie, amongst others, and he, finding it hard to meet her eyes, said he thought it would be nice if she came and that had clinched it; she asked if she could sit with him in the crematorium, and he had said, flushed and anguished, that he would be with his mother and sister and perhaps it might be better for her to come with someone else. There was no one: Patrick had never met Lawrence and it seemed absurd to bring him, although he did offer.

She knew there were many people in the company, all the old guard, who did hold her responsible, however illogically. Christine Weston, Athina's secretary, was particularly hostile, and Athina went out of her way to avoid her; when she went into Athina's office to tell her she was going to the funeral, Athina looked at her with intense distaste and said, 'I don't know what good you think that can possibly do.'

'I didn't think it would do any good, Lady Farrell, I just thought it was the right thing to do,' she said, managing with great effort to keep her voice steady.

'Personally, I would imagine it might be quite the wrong one,' Athina said.

In the end it was Susie who came to see her and asked her if she would like her to accompany her.

'I worked with him, if you could call it that, so I ought to go anyway. I think it's awfully brave of you, Bianca, I really do.'

Bianca stared at her, then got up from her desk, walked round and gave her a hug.

'You just made my day. No, my week. Thank you, Susie, so much.'

'It's OK,' said Susie, 'and if you're beating yourself up about it, try not to. He was useless. I know that's harsh, but he was, and honestly, how could you possibly have known he was so incapable of coping with it? Of course if it was me, I'd feel exactly the same. As it is, I'm thinking I should have been nicer to him – I never laughed at his awful jokes or anything. But I wasn't. And Bianca, you must try to remember you're here to make the company work. That's what your brief is. Not make life beautiful for everybody.'

'And what sort of person does that make me?' said Bianca. 'I mean, why don't I do a job that doesn't damage people? Why can't I be happy not doing a job at all? Just looking after my children and Patrick. Oh dear . . .'

She felt near to tears suddenly; heard her own voice shake. She looked at Susie who was clearly slightly embarrassed.

'I'm sorry, Susie,' she said. 'Not fair. Now I'm wallowing in it. You're right, of course. I do what I do and we are where we are, and – oh, let's have a drink.'

'Good idea,' said Susie.

Sitting there beside Bianca in the packed building, Susie started worrying about Henk. He was getting worse, angry almost all the time, and once he'd had a drink . . . Oh God . . . why did she have to be so pathetic, why couldn't she deal with him in the way she dealt with everything else in her life, in a positive, sensible, clear-sighted way?

She wrenched her mind away from him and tried to concentrate on the service.

A young organist was playing 'Jesu, Joy of Man's Desiring'. She risked a look at Annie, at Lawrence's wife. No, widow. She was a widow and probably in her early forties at the very most. It was awful, awful. But it wasn't as if he had deliberately done it . . .

She glanced behind her. There was quite a contingent from Farrell's. The family of course, Lady Farrell dressed up to the nines, black from head to toe, literally, and very grandly too, as if for a funeral at St Paul's Cathedral, in an ankle-length dress and a large black silk hat. Her expression was tragically aloof and occasionally she dabbed her eyes with a handkerchief. For heaven's sake, Susie thought, give it a rest, you often weren't very nice to him yourself when he was alive. Caro and someone who was presumably her husband stood on one side of her and Bertie and his wife – Priscilla, was it? – on the other.

Bertie looked shattered; he would be going through the torments of the damned, Susie thought, with his tender heart and his overdeveloped sense of guilt. He had always been nice to Lawrence, because he was nice to everyone. Poor Bertie – he was such a victim. Priscilla looked nice enough – her plump face, under its black beret, was carefully concerned. But why on earth had they brought their poor daughter? What had Lawrence been to her? People were very odd.

And then there was a whole range of Farrell staff, Christine of course, the sales people, half a dozen women standing in a row – who were they? Oh God, there was Marjorie among them, must be the consultants.

And standing alone, not with the family as she would have expected, was Florence; Susie was getting to really like Florence. She was so sharp, removed from Lady Farrell's icy influence, and good fun; and full of ideas these days, and so, so beautiful. God, she must have been glorious when she was young. How sad that she'd never married again – just the one great love affair with her husband and then a lifetime alone. How had she stood that?

Susie wrenched her mind away from the prospect of life alone and tried to concentrate on what the vicar or whoever he was was saying. He was calling up a lifelong friend of Lawrence's to speak. He wasn't too bad, actually, seemed to be speaking with real affection. She looked again at Annie; she was managing to smile at some of the funny incidents on the golf course that were being described. Poor woman.

◦ ◦ ◦

It was too ghastly, Athina thought; that poor soul, clearly completely devastated. What a life lay ahead of her; or rather half a life. At least Cornelius had been quite old when he died.

She felt genuinely grieved, her own loss resurfacing; nothing more final than a funeral. All very well if you had faith. But if not – she remembered the horror as Cornelius's coffin was brought in, hearing the dreadful words, ashes to ashes, dust to dust – and then the priest spouting all the nonsense about how he had gone to the next world, and how they would all be reunited there in God's love. She had felt enraged at the idiocy of it, had wanted to stand up and argue with the priest, ask him how he could be so sure, tell him it was she who was sure, and that she and Cornelius would never be together again, she would never see him again . . . But of course she did not. One had to behave. And she'd agreed to it, after all, and the alternative was some ghastly humanist ceremony, and she wasn't having that. At least Cornelius was leaving as he had lived, in style.

Not that this was very stylish, this service. That awful tinny organ, and the thin, reedy singing of 'God Be in my Head'. She had had a choir for Cornelius, a wonderful choir, and a thunderous organ; it had been a comfort to her to do things well, to add some musical class to the occasion. If there was a God, she often thought, He would be in some way a musical presence; nothing could consume and lift the spirit as music could.

But that poor poor girl. What must she be feeling? What must she feel about Bianca? She had made a point of ringing Annie herself the day after she heard the news; making it very plain that it would never have happened if she had been running the company. And she had ordered a huge wreath of white roses, with a message that read 'With every sympathy and in deep admiration of a fine man, Athina, Caroline and Bertram Farrell'.

Outside at last, Bertie stood a little away from his mother and sister as they walked through the flowers, reading the messages as everyone did. He felt deeply embarrassed by their wreath and message, considering both horribly over the top; even Caro, he knew, felt it was a little much. It was as large as the wreath that had lain on the coffin.

'Hello, Bertie.' It was Florence, dear Florence, smiling at him. He was so pleased to see her, he bent and kissed her.

'Hello, Florence. How are you? So good of you to come.'

'Oh, not at all. The House of Farrell needed to be well represented – although your mother has certainly seen to that!'

There was a slight, mischievous sparkle in her brown eyes; Bertie allowed himself to smile back, very briefly.

'Indeed. Poor Mrs Ford, I feel so sorry for her.'

'I too. Such a pretty woman. And that dear little boy. Er, are you going to the reception afterwards?'

'I'm afraid so. Mother insists. I think it is rather intrusive personally, but . . . how about you?'

'No, I'm not; I agree with you, they want to be with their family and friends. Oh, look, here she comes now.'

Annie Ford, pale but composed, walked over to Athina, holding out her hand; Athina covered it with her own.

'It's so very kind of you to come, Lady Farrell. I appreciate it so much.'

'Oh, my dear, it was the least we could do. Such a dreadful day for you. I'm so very sorry. My husband would have been also. He admired your husband greatly.'

'Did he really?'

'Well of course. Cornelius would have been horrified at what has happened.'

He would never have fired him, this would never have happened, that's what she means, Florence thought, but possibly it's what the poor woman wants to hear.

It was also quite untrue. Cornelius, to her certain knowledge, had considered employing Lawrence a mistake, and had told Athina so; she, however, had been rather bowled over by his slightly sycophantic charm, and by the following he had among the consultants and even the store buyers.

She stepped forward herself. 'I'm so sorry, Mrs Ford. I'm Florence Hamilton, I run the Berkeley Arcade shop and your husband was a frequent visitor. I was always pleased to see him.'

'Yes, he often mentioned The Shop, said how lovely it was,' said Annie. 'Thank you for coming.'

And then she stiffened as Bianca came over to her, followed by Susie.

'Mrs Ford, how do you do. I'm Bianca Bailey. I'm so sorry about your husband.'

'Yes,' said Annie Ford, suddenly a stronger, more forceful person. 'Yes, I expect you are.' Her expression, as she looked at Bianca, was hostile, her eyes very hard.

Bianca met them steadily. 'I wanted to come,' she said, 'to tell you that myself.'

'But there was no need. You must excuse me now.'

'I'm sorry . . .' Bianca said again; but Annie had turned away. It was a display of hostility, combined with considerable dignity.

Bianca flinched physically. Susie stepped forward, took her arm. 'Come on,' she said, 'let's go.'

She walked with her to the waiting car and they both got in. Watching them intently, Bertie saw Bianca slump in the back seat and bury her face in her hands. Susie put her arm round her.

'Poor woman,' said Florence; and he wasn't sure if she meant Annie Ford or Bianca Bailey.

Chapter 27

'This is just so amazing, isn't it? I mean, perfect or what?'

'Perfect.'

'And, like how many kids have a holiday like this one?'

Milly suddenly realised Carey was looking rather beadily at her. She hated it when she did that; it scared her. She smiled at Carey, said, 'Hardly any. Lucky us!'

'We-ell – lucky you. I mean, I'd be here anyway.'

There was a certain lack of logic in this; but Milly knew better than to argue.

'Yeah. Lucky me.'

'Seen Ad this morning?'

'No.'

She so didn't like Ad. He was a brat. A sexist, spoiled brat. What-ever he asked for he got. From his parents. From his little brother. And from Carey.

'Do my back, Carey,' he'd say and she'd take the sunscreen and with great care start rubbing it in.

'Get me a drink, Carey.' And when she'd brought it, if it wasn't quite right, 'Get some ice,' and she'd get him some ice.

Occasionally his father, Rick, who was equally gross, would say, 'Now, Adam, Carey is not your slave.'

And Ad would shrug and say something like, 'She's a girl, isn't she?' and laugh and make out he was joking, but he wasn't.

He didn't like Milly; she didn't mind, because she was quite happy to stay on the yacht and play cards with Toby, who was cute, although interestingly scared of his big brother. Adam teased him, told him he was a wimp because he wouldn't dive off the deck and had trouble getting back into his water skis when they came off halfway round a ride.

Milly had trouble with that too, and preferred to lie in the huge rubber ring and be towed round on that; she suggested Toby did the same, and he loved it. Carey laughed and called them a pair of babies. She was horribly good at water skiing, better even than Adam, which he didn't like, so after a bit she had to pretend she wasn't and kept falling over on purpose.

They were halfway through the holiday and Milly was looking forward to it being over. Carey was increasingly difficult with her, mooned about after Adam, and took it out on Milly if he didn't seem very keen. Which was often.

Of course it had been lovely in lots of ways. It was so beautiful sailing round the islands, the endless swimming and sunbathing was gorgeous, and so were the long lunchtime beach picnics when they went ashore. The Mapletons were lovely to her and she liked the evenings on deck after supper, when it was cooler, and they played things like Scrabble and consequences, which Andrew and Nicky Mapleton liked, and even charades sometimes. Milly was rather good at charades, which annoyed Carey, who was hopeless. Adam put his head in his hands when she was trying to act, and groaned in mock agony.

There was no doubt he was really good-looking, tall and dark and not skinny like most boys of his age; he was at Eton and was clever and very self-confident. He spent a lot of time texting his friends on his phone and getting in a rage whenever they lost a signal, which was often.

That night the adults were going to join some friends from another yacht on shore and it was decided the children should all stay on board, under the rather unwatchful eye of Daisy, who was the sailing equivalent of a chalet girl; she had to do the cooking and clean the cabins, but a lot of the time she just sunbathed and flirted with Antoine, the water sports guy.

'Now look,' hissed Carey after Nicky Mapleton had outlined the plans for the day, and then dived into the water for a swim, 'once supper's over and Daisy's disappeared, you disappear as well, OK? And take Toby with you. Ad and I want a bit of peace to listen to some music together, maybe have a smoke.'

'A smoke?' said Milly.

'Yeah, a smoke. Weed, hash, a spliff, you know. Ad has some amazing stuff and he says it's time I discovered how good it is.'

'OK, cool,' said Milly. She had learned not to remonstrate with Carey, whatever she said she was going to do, but she couldn't stop herself when, later that afternoon, Carey suddenly removed her bikini top.

'Carey!' said Milly.

'Now what?'

'Ad might see. Or Antoine.'

'Oh, don't be such a dork. This is two thousand and eleven, Mills, not the nineteenth century. I'm not going to have white boobs.'

'OK,' said Milly and shrugged.

'Oh God, here comes Mummy! Mills, take your top off as well. Back me up, OK?'

'No, Carey, I don't want—'

'Mills! God, I wish I hadn't brought you. You are such a *baby*. Come on, take it off!'

She reached out and grabbed Milly's top hard which gave way and fell off. Milly, mortified, turned over on her tummy as Nicky Mapleton walked up to them.

'Getting rid of your strap marks, girls? Good idea. Make sure Ad isn't around though. Listen, we're off now. Have a great time, see you tomorrow. Oh, and Milly, I had a text from your mum. About meeting you next week. We've sorted out a flight from Athens for you. She sends her love, says she hopes you won't find a family holiday too dull after this!'

'Thank you,' said Milly. The villa holiday with her parents and Fergie and Ruby suddenly looked rather wonderful.

Nicky was gone; Carey looked thoughtfully at Milly, then said, 'Take a picture of me will you?' She passed Milly her phone.

'What, without your top?'

267

'Without my top, Miss Modesty. Go on!'

'OK,' said Milly reluctantly. She took a few pictures of Carey, then handed her the phone back.

'Right, now let's have some of you.'

'Carey, no!'

'Mills, yes. Come on, don't be boring. I'll do one of us together too, if you like.'

'We-ell . . .' She knew she'd have to give in. Carey would just nag and nag if she didn't. 'OK.'

She sat there, hating every minute, horribly aware that her breasts were only half the size of Carey's and very white. Carey had obviously been working with the fake tan. Carey pouted at the camera, pushing her tits about like a porn star.

'Cool,' she said, studying the pictures, 'really cool. Right, I'd better put lots of stuff on or they'll burn. Red tits, not a good look. God, I can't wait for tonight.'

'So, what happened?'

'Oh . . . nothing.'

'Darling, yes it did. I can tell.'

'Mummy, nothing happened.'

'All right,' Bianca sighed. 'Well, if you change your mind—'

'I won't! I mean, there's nothing to change it about. Hey, Ruby, want another diving lesson? Come on, Fergie, don't you dare start bombing her. Just don't!'

'She seems all right,' said Patrick, watching Milly disappear into the pool very neatly, head first, long legs pointed behind her, followed by a rather untidy plunge from Ruby, rather shorter plump legs wide apart.

'She's not all right. I told you, she was crying last night, and when I asked her why, she said she'd tell me today, so there *was* something. She's – Patrick, *please*.'

'Sorry. Won't be a minute.'

He grabbed his phone, walked away quickly into the pool house, listening intently. Saul. Bloody Saul. He was hanging over this holiday, calling endlessly, quite late at night sometimes. She was quite shocked at Patrick; when she was on holiday she would check her phone three times a day and then switch it off. It was an unbreakable rule. Well, almost unbreakable.

'What this time?' she asked Patrick, as he came back looking sheepish.

'Oh – just questions. Will I look at this, did I look at that. I – don't mind though,' he added in an attempt at bravado.

'Well, you should.'

'I don't think you understand. Saul's not like anyone. Or hardly anyone. He's absolutely obsessed. That's how he does what he does. He's a bit – well, I hesitate to say it, but a bit unhinged. In a way. Maybe that's rather harsh, but he is distinctly odd, sort of random. As a person, that is.'

'Really?' She was reluctantly intrigued.

'Yes. You couldn't get to where he is unless you were. You need to have no emotions, basically.'

'Oh, really?' That hadn't been quite how she'd read Saul. 'He's quite emotional about Dickon, I'd have said.'

'He is, but it's obsessive emotion, lacks judgment. Dickon is the most important, indeed the *only*, person in his life. He doesn't see him as part of a whole, part of a family.'

'He doesn't have a family, poor little boy.'

'Well, he has a mother. Although Saul does treat her like some sort of staff member. She only exists in so far as what she does for Dickon.'

'No wonder they're divorced.'

'Jonjo says she really struggled to be a good wife to Saul.'

'And?'

'Well, no one could be. He just wants people who do what he thinks they should. Thing is, he only really cares about the money he makes. Not so that he can have it, but as some kind of abstract thing. It's so hard to explain. He doesn't care about anything else, doesn't think, am I offending this person, am I going to upset that one? Ninety per cent of the time that's how he is.'

'Goodness. Well, don't you get like that, darling. And do remind him you're on holiday. Otherwise I might.'

'Bianca . . .' Suddenly Patrick's voice was very serious, his expression intense. 'Please don't. This is my job, remember, and he's my boss. I'll deal with it as I think best.'

'I was only joking,' she said, half startled.

It wasn't quite true; but she suddenly saw what Saul represented to Patrick: not just success, but self-respect and a chance to achieve on his own account, rather than by the endowment of his father. She would intrude on that at her peril.

'So good of you to come.' Henk's voice was at its most dangerous. Susie spun round. Against the background of the crowded bar, the noise, the heat, his face, white and taut, was the only thing in focus, frightening her.

'Oh, I'm sorry. I thought you'd still be at home. Was – was everything all right? Happy birthday,' she added belatedly, reaching up to kiss him; he pulled away.

'I suppose so. A load of crap food and not enough booze; it was a pretty poor attempt at a birthday party.'

'Henk, I'm sorry.' She had to shout above the din, aware that even now there was a row building. 'I – I did tell you I'd be late.'

'Did you? You tell me so often I suppose I didn't notice.'

'And . . . did you find the present I left?'

As if he couldn't have: placed on the kitchen table as she crept out, tied up with a huge red bow, the new, vastly expensive lens he had been longing for.

'Yeah, I did.'

'And was it OK? The right one?'

'Yeah, it was. The presentation lacked the personal touch, but yeah. Yeah, thanks.'

'Well . . . good.' Even now, she'd have expected something a bit more fulsome; maybe he was embarrassed to show his gratitude in front of these strangers.

'Aren't you going to buy me a drink?'

'There's a tab at the bar.' He turned away, started talking to someone; stung to tears she made for the loo. And then came back, smiling, apparently ready for anything.

Which was rather more than even she had expected: inside the flat, several hours later, he turned as she followed him in, pushed the door behind her and raised his hand and hit her, straight across the face. He was very, very drunk.

'You're such a bitch,' he said, 'such a selfish, up yourself cow. All you care about is that fucking job, even on my birthday you put it first.'

She didn't dare antagonise him, or stand up for herself.

'Henk, I'm sorry, so sorry, I told you, I couldn't help it, that's why I organised the food and everything—'

'Yeah, well, this is what I think of the food,' he said and he picked up a half-empty plate of canapés and hurled it at the wall. It smashed, the contents splattering everywhere. A bowl of fruit salad followed, trickling down the wall, the glass smashing as it caught the fireplace.

'Henk, stop it, stop it! You're mad!' And then, as he turned to look at her again, his eyes glittering, she said, terrified of what he would do, 'I'm sorry, so sorry you're so upset, I should have been here—'

'Yes, you fucking should,' he said and hit her again, on the other side of her face; she staggered, almost fell, managed to make the bathroom, slammed the door and locked it. After a bit she heard the front door open and then slam shut; and she went out nervously, afraid he was tricking her, but he had gone, and she locked the door and put the chain across it and started, for it seemed the only thing to do, to clear up the mess. Thinking that any amount of loneliness would be better than what she had been enduring over the past few weeks.

She woke, exhausted, aching all over, and looked at her phone; she hadn't set the alarm and it was after nine. Thank God she didn't have any meetings. She could be in by ten, could spend the day quietly— Her phone rang; it was Henk. She ignored it. Then the landline rang, the machine picking it up and she heard his voice: 'Babe, babe, I am so, so sorry. Forgive me, please please forgive me. I love you, I love you so much. I can't live without you. It will

271

never ever happen again, I swear. Please, please say I can come home.'

She went into the bathroom, switched on the shower. And then caught sight of herself in the mirror. One black eye, one hideously swollen cheekbone, a bruise at the side of her mouth, a cut lip. She couldn't go into work like that, she absolutely couldn't! She'd call Jemima, tell her she was ill – thank God Bianca was away. She stood in the shower for a long time, trying to wash off the misery and the shame and the pain, forcing herself to confront the truth; and then she came out and wrapped herself in her bathrobe and sat on the sofa, her mobile switched off now, drinking coffee, ignoring Henk's endless calls on the landline, telling her how much he loved her, how it was only because he was so hurt, because it was his birthday, thinking maybe if she persuaded him to stop drinking, guilt creeping into her now, guilt and shame. It had been his birthday, his thirtieth birthday, pretty important . . . No, Susie! You mustn't give in, don't do this, you mustn't! He's dangerous, awful . . .

'I need you,' Henk's voice said, 'I need you so much . . .'

'Is she here?' Athina's voice was irritable.

'Er, no,' said Jemima, 'I'm afraid not, Lady Farrell. But she will be – you're a little early. Can I get you a cup of tea, or a cold drink perhaps, while you wait?'

'I find the taste of the tea out of that machine most unpleasant. Perhaps a glass of water, that at least can't be ruined.'

'Of course, Lady Farrell,' said Jemima, standing up as Athina swept past her into Bianca's office.

Bianca was sitting in a traffic jam in Piccadilly in a fury of impotence, thinking that the state of affairs at Farrell's was rather similar. Everything at a standstill, an expensive engine ticking over relentlessly, using up fuel and doing little else, and Lady Farrell, the equivalent of the white van man, constantly raising two notional fingers at her and endeavouring to cut across her path whenever she made to move forward. The most recent manifestation of this was to have taken against Hattie and criticise every sample that came out of the lab, demanding it go back and be completely reformulated. Which Bianca then had to countermand – it was time-wasting and expensive.

Mark Rawlins, the new financial director, had just completed a very thorough financial survey, up to and including the launch, and his own take on the financial health of the company as he found it. He was nice, sharp, and funny, but he did not mince his words and had already told Bianca that she had no hope of hitting her targets for the following year, even with an incredibly successful launch. 'And if it isn't incredibly successful, just modestly so, which is rather more likely, you're looking at results a lot worse than these. And if it doesn't work at all—'

'Mark, can we not go there please? That just isn't an option.'

'Pleased to hear it,' was all he said.

Mark had sent her an email that morning summarising the whole situation; Jemima had printed it out and put it into a folder on Bianca's desk, with other equally important matters, like a report from Hattie on the staff in the lab – *Marge pretty good, Jackie frankly disappointing and extremely stroppy, she should be let go* – and a reminder from Lara that she had promised to discuss the form and exact timing of the all-important pre-launch sales conference. *It needs to be a humdinger Bianca, raise the morale of the troops, pretty low right now as you know.*

Jemima, mindful that Lady Farrell might not be entirely honourable in her behaviour given the run of Bianca's office, had hurried in after her, suggested she sat in one of the low chairs by the coffee table and asked her if she would like to look at a magazine while she was waiting.

'Not particularly,' said Athina, 'I find most magazines these days deeply depressing. But I would like my water. With some ice, if it isn't too much trouble.'

'Of course,' said Jemima. 'I'll just . . .' She let her voice drift off and had turned to the desk, ostensibly to tidy it, but actually to scoop up any files that Bianca might not wish Lady Farrell to see, when Lara popped her head in and said she really needed to see Bianca soonest and was there a window in the diary?

'Sorry to rush you, Jemima, but I've got the Debenhams buyer on the phone.'

'Of course,' said Jemima, 'let's have a look at the diary, I think she might have a couple of hours in the afternoon. Excuse me, Lady Farrell, I'll be back in a moment.'

Athina, a masterly reader of body language, who had been watching Jemima closely, closed the door and made her own survey of the files on the desk. When Jemima came back, Athina was sitting by the coffee table as she had suggested, leafing through the latest *Vogue*.

'I dread to think,' she said, 'what Diana Vreeland would have made of this.'

Jemima smiled at her sweetly, picked up the files on the desk, and withdrew, then ten minutes later Bianca called to say she would be at least another quarter of an hour; this was relayed to Lady Farrell by a sweetly apologetic Jemima. She stood up and dropped the magazine on the coffee table.

'I'm sorry, but I really can't afford any more time. I'm surprised that Mrs Bailey cannot organise herself better.'

Back in her own office, she asked Christine to check when the next board meeting had been arranged; and when she got home that night, having made herself a rather stronger gin and tonic than usual, called Caro.

Chapter 28

'I've got to go to Germany for a few days next week. I'm going to visit a company over there.'

'What sort of company?'

'Does it matter?'

'Patrick,' said Bianca, mildly exasperated, 'I'm only taking a friendly interest.'

'Oh, we're a bit intrigued by a company over there and I need to go and meet some of the people.'

'Oh, all right. You know I'm going to Paris the following week?'

'Yes, of course.'

He didn't ask her why.

'We won't clash? Both being away I mean?'

'No, of course not. Oh, excuse me . . .'

He pulled his phone out of his pocket and Bianca glared at him. She could remember a time when his phone was often mislaid, frequently switched off; it had simply not played a very important part in his life. Now he had it with him constantly. He went out of the room, came back fifteen minutes later.

'Don't tell me. Saul.'

'Yes.'

'Patrick, it's nearly eleven o'clock. What's he doing, ringing you at this time?'

'He wanted to discuss this German company.'

'Why can't he discuss it in the office?'

'Because usually in the office he's absorbed in the markets.

He only has time to think in the evenings. And weekends, of course.'

'So he wrecks the evenings and weekends for everyone else.'

'He doesn't wreck them. For heaven's sake, Bianca, I don't mind. Why should you?'

'Oh,' she said, her voice unusually sarcastic, 'oh, I can't imagine. I mean, why should I want to sit and talk to you at the end of the day? Or play with you and the children for more than ten uninterrupted minutes at a time while we're on our only holiday?'

'Bianca,' said Patrick, his voice rather quiet, 'might I remind you about another holiday? A skiing holiday earlier this year. Which you pulled out of altogether.'

'That was – different.'

'Oh, really?'

'Yes. Time was against us, I *had* to do that.'

'And time isn't against me, I suppose?'

'Patrick, please. It was exceptional, a one-off thing. You work for Saul and I know it's all very demanding and everything, but there are lots of other people who work for him. It's not all down to you and—' She stopped, aware that she was on dangerous ground.

'So you're saying that you're indispensable and I'm not? That I can't cancel holidays, but you can? Well, just possibly you're wrong there. I do happen to be the only research analyst working for Saul and he relies on me heavily. And I don't want to let him down. Correction. I'm not going to let him down.'

'All right, all right,' said Bianca, 'no one's asking you to. Just to keep a sense of proportion.'

'Which you always do?'

'At least I try,' she said, and got up and left the room.

She went upstairs slowly, and as she passed Milly's door, she heard her talking.

She was worried about Milly; weeks after the holiday with the Mapletons, she was still subdued, slightly hostile, resistant to questioning about it. She knocked, and then, without waiting for an answer, went in.

The room was lit only by Milly's bedside lamp. She was on the phone and switched off with 'got to go', then met her mother's eyes defiantly.

'Darling, what are you doing? It's eleven o' clock. You should be asleep and whoever you're talking to should be asleep too. Was it Carey?'

'No!' said Milly, her voice fierce and defensive. 'No it wasn't.'

'Well, there's nothing – nothing wrong, is there?'

'No!' The same defiant tone. 'Course not.'

'All right. Good. Night-night darling, sleep well.'

She bent to kiss her and Milly offered a hostile cheek, then turned to face the wall. But not before Bianca had seen two things. A heap of tissues lay on the duvet, wet tissues. And Milly's hairline was wet too, where the tears had clearly trickled down as she had lain on her pillows.

'I can't do that,' said Bertie.

'Why not?'

'Because I totally don't agree with you.'

'Bertie, I do wish you wouldn't try to talk like your children. It sounds so pathetic. Now look. We have to stand united otherwise there will be nothing left of the House of Farrell. I hope you are not going to betray everything the company that your father and I spent our lives creating stands for. Now listen to me . . .'

Bertie listened.

'Marjorie, how are you dear? Oh, I'm so sorry. And of course you're finding it hard. Now, there's a board meeting later this month and your future is very much on the agenda. What? Yes, of course. And I shall come down and visit you again soon. Perhaps that will cheer you up a little. And I would like to see Terry, of course. Do give him my best wishes.'

'Mrs Ford? This is Lady Farrell. Yes. Good morning. I just rang to see how you were getting on, it must be so very difficult for you – oh, my dear, I cannot tell you how much I sympathise with you, and of course having been widowed myself I do understand. I feel a great burden of guilt about your husband – no, no, my dear, I do. Although of course everything is out of my hands and has been for some time. He was such a loyal and really very clever man. So sad. So very sad . . .'

'Ah, Jackie. Do come in and sit down, my dear. What a very pretty dress that is. Of course I usually only see you in the lab, in your white coat. I just wondered how you were finding the new regime. It must be rather different, I imagine. You must miss Maurice, being used to his way of working. You can speak quite freely to me, Jackie, this is a confidential discussion. I just like to keep in touch with our employees, see how they're getting along in what must be rather difficult circumstances.'

'Milly's been crying,' said Ruby, 'ever since she got home.' Her small round face was concerned. 'You must go and sort her out, Mummy.'

'Oh darling, that's awful. Where is she?'

'In her room. She won't come out. Not even for tea. And it was meatballs,' she added, as if to dispel any lingering doubt Bianca might have that things were serious.

'I'll go up straight away. Daddy's not home, I suppose?'

'No, he's going to be late, he rang and told Sonia.'

'OK.' Bianca took a deep breath. Patrick had promised to be home by seven, so that she could get herself organised for the board meeting the next day and it was already half past.

'Is Karen still here?'

'No. She left ages ago. I was watching *Shrek* with Sonia so can I go back to it now, please? Now you can sort Milly out?'

'Yes – well actually, I might have a word with Sonia first.'

Sonia was clearly anxious.

'She's very upset, Bianca. Just walked in and ran straight up to her room. I tried, of course, but she told me to go away and I thought – well – better to wait till you came in.'

'Yes, of course. Where's Fergie?'

'He's in his room, doing his homework. He's fine.'

'OK. Well, can you hang on a bit longer, Sonia? Till I've talked to Milly? Or Patrick gets home. Which he should any minute. Ruby's a bit worried and I don't want her left on her own.'

'Well, only about another quarter of an hour.'

'OK, fine. Won't be long.'

She ran upstairs, listened a moment outside Milly's room; it was very quiet. She knocked.

'Who is it?'

'It's Mummy. Can I come in?'

'Oh – all right.'

Bianca went in; Milly was lying on the bed, her face flushed, her eyes swollen. He mobile was clutched to her as if it was the teddy who had once comforted her in earlier griefs. If only it was still that simple.

Bianca sat down on the bed, stroked her hair back.

'Darling, what is it? Please tell me.'

'I – don't want to.'

'But how can I help, if you don't?'

'No one can help. You don't understand!'

'Well . . .' Bianca hesitated. She remembered this situation from her own childhood, the absolute certainty that no one could understand or help with her problems. 'Maybe I can't. But sometimes just talking helps. I find that a lot. At work.'

'Really?' Milly looked at her doubtfully.

'Yes, really.'

There was a long silence; then Milly said, as if taking an irrevocable decision, 'No, I can't. I really can't.'

'Milly . . .' Bianca hesitated. 'You haven't been happy since you got back from holiday with the Mapletons. Is it anything to do with Carey? Something she's doing?'

Milly shook her head listlessly.

'No.'

'Darling, I think it is. Did you fall out with her on holiday? Milly, please tell me. *Please*. I promise I won't do anything you're not happy with, but let me at least understand.'

'I told you, I can't.' Then her small face crumpled and she said, desperation in her tone, 'I *can't.*' And she started crying again.

'Well – I have to respect that. But will you at least come down and have something to eat? With me? We can have an omelette together and watch telly in the snug. Ruby's about to go to bed. And it's *Waterloo Road* tonight, isn't it?'

'Oh . . . yes, all right. Thanks, Mummy.'

The thanks were clearly as much for not pressing her questions, as the offer of the grown-up supper.

'Come down in fifteen minutes, OK? I'll just sort out Ruby.'

As she went past Fergie's room she heard him call her name and went in.

'Hi.'

'Mum,' he said, 'I don't know what's going on, but that girl's evil.'

'Carey?'

'Yup. I heard Milly on her phone, and she was saying "I didn't, Carey" over and over again. And then Carey obviously cut her off, because she kept saying her name and then she realised I was there and came over and slammed the door.'

'Hmm,' said Bianca. 'Well, thank you for telling me, Fergie. I don't know how to help her. Milly, I mean.'

'Nor me. Maybe Dad'll have some ideas.'

In Fergie's eyes, world peace could have been accomplished by his father any day before breakfast, no trouble at all.

Bianca looked at her watch; it was already after eight. Where *was* Patrick? Damn. He'd promised and they needed to talk about this; it was looking serious.

But nine came and then ten and still there was no sign of him apart from a couple of texts saying he'd been delayed. What was happening to them? Her family seemed to be falling apart before her eyes.

'Mrs Bailey . . .'

Athina's voice was treacherously sweet.

'Yes, Lady Farrell?'

So far the board meeting had gone pretty well; they'd rattled through the agenda and she'd managed to put a fairly good optimistic spin on the figures, some new premises in Hammersmith looked promising and would save a lot of money, she'd been able to talk enthusiastically about the new range and its development so if the old witch tried to throw a spanner in the works now, not a lot she could do.

'I wonder if I might ask you to leave the room?'

'What?' She was stunned. She looked at Athina whose expression was as sweet as her voice.

'I'm so sorry, I obviously didn't make myself clear. I wonder if you would leave the room?'

'Oh. Yes. Very well.'

'Thank you.'

She stood in the corridor for a few minutes, expecting to be called back in, then when that didn't happen, went to her office.

'Just having a break,' she said in response to Jemima's raised eyebrows. 'Won't be long.'

'Oh, fine. Well, maybe you could just look at these letters, let me know if there's a problem with any of them, and if not sign them. Oh, and your husband phoned, said he'd call from Munich.'

Bianca remembered her rage and frustration the night before, when Patrick had finally come in at midnight, too tired, he said, to talk about anything. He said he was sorry, but maybe the morning, first thing?

'I have to be in very early, Patrick, I've got a crucial board meeting to prepare for. Couldn't you—'

'No, I really can't. I need to sleep, I'm dropping.'

'Patrick, it's important. It's about Milly.'

'But not so important that you can't delay your meeting?'

'Of course I can't!'

'Then Milly and your concerns will have to wait. And may I suggest that they can't be that pressing?'

'That is so not fair! She's very upset about something and—'

'If she's very upset, then isn't that quite a pressing reason for you to delay your meeting?'

'Or for you to stay awake for half an hour now?'

'Darling,' and never had the endearment sounded less genuine, 'I'm sorry, I can hardly focus.'

'Fine. We'll leave it,' said Bianca and walked out of the room.

'I would like to put a vote of no confidence in Bianca Bailey,' said Athina.

Hugh's secretary, who was taking the minutes, looked round the room. The reaction was interestingly varied.

Mike and Hugh both looked completely astonished; Peter Warren's face wore the bland, unsurprised expression that it could take on with the speed of light; Florence was looking startled; Caro was looking admiringly up at her mother – and Bertie was staring at his hands which were knotted together on the table, clearly relentlessly miserable.

'May I ask why?' said Hugh finally.

'You may. There has been a complete loss of morale in the company since Mrs Bailey took over. Complete. We all know about the appalling tragedy of Lawrence Ford, a life lost, a family ruined, all for the want of a little patience.'

'What does patience have to do with it? Acknowledging the tragedy of his case, he died as the result of a terrible accident—'

'An accident that would never have happened had he still had his job.'

'Lady Farrell, he was not up to his job.'

'Oh, nonsense. He was loyal, clever and charming, everyone in the trade liked him, and all that was needed was perhaps a little training in the new ways of the company. No effort was made to do this. There are several other casualties: poor Marjorie Dawson, so cruelly and wrongly dismissed on the very day her husband was told he would need terrible surgery, the company driver, Peterson, most unhappy and struggling at his age to rebuild his life, and then there is Jackie Pearson in the lab who finds working under Mrs Richards extremely difficult: she is overbearing and critical, apparently, and has allowed no time for the existing staff to learn her methods. My own secretary, who has worked for me for over twenty years, reports a serious lack of morale among most of the original staff. They feel ignored and their skills disregarded. All these things may seem of little importance to you, Mr Bradford and Mr Russell, but believe me, a successful company needs a happy workforce. I find Mrs Bailey arrogant, unwilling to take advice or even to listen to the opinions of others who might well be able to arrange things more happily.'

'Lady Farrell—'

'Moreover, I have seen certain documentation that makes it very clear that the financial situation is not improved, rather the reverse; and I have therefore come to the conclusion that, far from saving the House of Farrell, Mrs Bailey is destroying it. That is why I move the vote of no confidence. Mrs Johnson seconds the motion and, obviously, Mr Farrell supports me as well.'

Here Bertie lifted his head and took a breath, seemingly about to speak. A look from his mother silenced him.

'Well,' said Hugh Bradford, 'that is all most interesting.'

'I thought you would find it so,' said Athina. 'The vote is only a formality of course; the Farrell family do hold the majority share.'

'Lady Farrell,' Mike's face was as carefully courteous as always, 'your input is much appreciated. However, there can be no question of our agreeing to Mrs Bailey leaving us. We think she is doing an excellent job.'

'Well, you are in something of a minority,' said Athina. 'However, your views are of little import, since I insist it goes to the vote. And we have three votes to your two—'

'May I speak?' said Bertie.

'Not now, Bertie, no. We will hear your views later.'

Hugh Bradford cleared his throat. 'If I might make a point, Lady Farrell. I'm afraid what you say is incorrect.'

'What do you mean?'

'There are three votes on either side in this debate.'

'I hope you're not suggesting Mrs Bailey has a vote? That would display a serious lack of awareness of company law.'

'No, no, of course not.' He met her eyes. 'But Mr Warren has a vote.'

'Mr Warren? Has a vote?' Athina's expression relegated Peter

Warren to the level occupied in her mind by the cleaners and the much-lamented typing pool.

'I do, yes. And he is of the same mind as we are about Mrs Bailey; he would vote with us.'

'But you assured me his was a non-executive chairmanship!'

'Which is quite true. But he does have a vote.'

There was a long silence. Then Athina rallied.

'I can only say this was never made clear to me. I regard it as extremely duplicitous behaviour.'

Warren smiled a charmingly regretful smile.

'I'm extremely sorry. Your lawyers were obviously remiss in not taking you through the structure of the company at the time of signature. But it is rather easy to miss these things, I'm afraid.'

'Mr Warren, Pemberton and Rushworth are lawyers of the highest distinction, and have looked after this company since its inception in 1953.'

'I'm sure. But the fact does remain that I do have a vote.'

'And you would vote against *me*. Us?'

'I would, Lady Farrell, I'm afraid. Yes.'

The secretary, looking again around the room, saw a most interesting expression on Bertie's face: one of a slowly dawning relief.

Athina rose to her feet once more, swept them all with a look of acute derision, and said, 'Well, none of this really matters very much, however disgraceful this last deception. This is a shareholders' vote and clearly we will win. We own a fifty-one per cent share of this company, and that is something you cannot ignore. That is enshrined in law.'

Milly was sitting in one of the lavatory cubicles, leaning against the wall; her head ached and she felt sore all over. She could hear girls coming and going, and waited, longing for the silence that meant lessons had begun and which would release her. She wasn't sure what she would do next; she had actually been sick and she supposed she could go to Nurse Winter, who would probably organise for her to be collected and returned home; but she knew Sonia was out until lunchtime having some complex dental work done, and the rule for girls who had been in the sickroom was that they must be escorted. So the only answer was to say she'd been sick and didn't feel up to lessons; she emerged cautiously from the cubicle and looked at herself in the mirror. She did look awful, sort of white-ish green, her eyes all sort of black-ringed, so they were bound to believe her; she took a deep breath and opened the cloakroom door.

Carey was standing there, smiling.

'Oh for God's sake!' Bianca half shouted at the street below. 'What the fuck is going on in there?'

The street did not reply; however Jemima, hearing her voice and the extremely rare expletive, hurried in.

'Is everything all right, Bianca?'

Bianca hesitated, then, 'No. Not really. I was asked to leave the board meeting, and I have no idea why and that was nearly forty-five minutes ago. The old witch is up to no good, I know it. And – oh, hello, Mike. Are you inviting me back in?'

Mike's face was at its most bland and pleasant.

'No, Bianca, I'm afraid I'm not.'

Chapter 29

This was a nightmare. Walter Pemberton was still awake, fully dressed at midnight, having spent the entire evening poring over the contract he had had so large a part in drawing up between the House of Farrell and Porter Bingham only a few months ago. It was true. He had missed this dreadful, dangerous point about voting rights, thus delivering Lady Farrell and the whole family into an unarguable loss of control of the company.

And there was no way out, no way at all; it was his fault. How could he have been so careless; how, how? It was unthinkable.

Which had been the very word he had uttered when Lady Farrell, her voice terrifying in its suppressed rage, asked him whether it was possible that the family did not, after all, have control of the company.

'My dear Lady Farrell,' he had said, mildly amused, 'that is absolutely absurd. Quite unthinkable. You own fifty-one per cent of the company; your control of it is enshrined in English law. Of course I will go through the contract again, but I am perfectly confident about it.'

And then she had started talking voting rights, and for the first time a rustle of anxiety stirred in Pemberton's brain. Voting rights, and their relevance, were not something he could recall discussing in any detail.

Bianca sat in her study, playing *La Bohème* – she always turned to opera in times of crisis – assuaging the feelings of betrayal, rage and hurt. And the acute loneliness that was inevitably part of her job. People lower down the organisational scale could turn to one another, say isn't it awful, you'll never believe this or that or the other; and receive sympathy, empathy and advice. She, alone at the top of the mountain, had no such resource available to her. Every judgment had to be her own, each course of action settled upon personally, every criticism absorbed entirely without support. It was the price of success, of her professional satisfaction, her salary, her fame.

It required huge self-confidence to cope with it and Athina was robbing her of that, slowly and relentlessly. It was, quite literally, frightening. And she couldn't see quite what she should do about it.

Mike and Hugh had taken her out for lunch and tried to give her a sanitised version of what had happened, saying that Lady Farrell had said she was unhappy with much of what Bianca was doing and that she would like to express that formally.

'Cut the crap,' Bianca said briskly, 'I suppose it was a vote of no confidence?'

'Well – yes. It was.'

'On what grounds?'

'Well, that company morale was low, that there was little progress being made in spite of some extremely drastic action, and in some cases deeply regrettable results.'

'Lawrence Ford?'

'Yup. 'Fraid so. And also that she happened to know that the sales figures were appalling and getting worse.'

'How did she find that out?'

'God knows. Anyway, Bianca, it's perfectly all right. Because she can't win, she has no grasp whatsoever of the structure of the board and the voting rights, thanks to that pathetic cave of dinosaurs she calls her lawyers. We told her we're very happy with you, backing you all the way, as indeed we are, and she left in high dudgeon. We're reconvening tomorrow morning. By which time, I imagine, Messrs Pemberton and Rushworth will have admitted negligence and taken a long walk off a tall cliff.

Peter Warren's been marvellous, tried to smooth her ruffled feathers, although I'm afraid she now sees even him as tarred with the same brush as the rest of us, since he told her he had a vote!'

'Oh God,' said Bianca, 'what a filthy mess.'

'No,' said Hugh. 'It's fine.'

'Hugh, the fact is, there's a lot in what she says and it's going to get a whole lot tougher now. I'm beginning to wonder what I'm doing here . . .'

'Bianca! Pull yourself together.'

Hugh smiled at her; but she could tell from his expression that there was an irritation behind his bonhomie. It was enough; she stopped. This was bad. She couldn't afford to display so much as a touch of self-doubt and frailty.

She stood up, smiled back at Hugh, and said, 'OK. Let's put the whole bloody thing behind us. You're quite right. We can't let her rock the boat, just as we've got it almost floating again.'

'Indeed not,' said Mike. 'That's better. Well done, Bianca. And you know, we're totally behind you as always. As I said.'

'I do know,' she said. 'And thank you.'

But now, quite, quite alone, Patrick away, the children asleep, she wasn't entirely sure.

Patrick was waiting for his flight out of Munich when Bianca called him.

'Hello, darling, how are you?'

'Oh,' she said, 'you know. Fine. I was hoping you might ring last night.'

'I'm sorry, it was back-to-back meetings all day and then a lot of notes to write up when I returned to the hotel. Then Saul called with some other thoughts, and – well, suddenly it was midnight. And I knew you wouldn't want me ringing you then. Are you all right?'

'Oh – yes, I'm fine, thank you.'

'Everything all right there?'

'Well, Milly had to be collected from school yesterday, she'd been sick, and Ruby's probably got chickenpox, but I think that's about it. Oh, and I'm just about to go into a board meeting, which was adjourned yesterday after Lady Farrell proposed a vote of no confidence in me.'

'Really? Silly old trout. Well, she won't get that through – they've got swamping rights, haven't they, the VCs?'

'Yes, Patrick,' said Bianca, keeping her temper, 'yes, they have. So it doesn't matter at all.'

'All right, darling, rotten I know, but I'll be back tonight. And I haven't forgotten about Milly, of course.' His tone was carefully solicitous; he was obviously feeling guilty. 'And don't get chickenpox – that won't go down well in Paris.

'Oh, by the way, Saul's going to be in Paris next week too, one of his horses is running at Longchamp. Maybe the two of you could have dinner together; be nice for him since he spends so much time alone and it'd be nice for you too, I expect.'

'Patrick,' said Bianca, keeping her voice level with a huge effort, 'I'm taking Florence with me so it would be very rude to leave her alone for an evening. And I don't think Saul would be too delighted with being lumbered with two of us.'

'Well, just an idea. I'll mention it to him anyway. And if he, well . . .'

'Yes, all right, Patrick. If he turns up under my hotel window and serenades me, I'll have dinner with him.'

'Don't be silly, Bianca. I'm just asking you to – to be courteous to my boss. That's all. Oh, my flight's been called, better go. See you later, darling.'

Bianca put the phone down with unnecessary force and stuck her tongue out at it. Then she laughed. This was absurd! Patrick pushing her into the arms of another man, urging her to spend time with him in Paris, of all places. Suppose, just suppose, she did fancy him? How would that look in a divorce court?

'But your honour, I was just doing what my husband told me, trying to be a good corporate wife.'

Well, there was no way he was going to want to have dinner with her; pigs flying down Montmartre was infinitely more likely.

* * *

'Oh, hello!'

'Hello. I hope this is a good time. How are you?'

'I'm – I'm fine.'

'Good flight?'

'We came on the train.'

'Good idea. Much more civilised.'

'I think so. And you?'

'I drove, with George Barnes, my trainer. As did my horses, although in a different vehicle. Got two of them running tomorrow at Longchamp. You could come and watch.'

'Saul, I can't. I'm here to work. Much as I'd love to,' she added quickly. She didn't want to appear too rude.

'You should take a day off occasionally. Very good for you. I do.'

'You could have fooled me,' she said briskly.

'Oh, really. How do you know that?'

'Well, there could be a clue in the fact that you call my husband at least three times every evening, more at the weekends.'

'Oh, I don't count phone calls. I just do that. You don't mind, do you?' he added, sounding interested, rather than concerned.

'No, of course not. Although I must give you a note of our mealtimes. Best avoided, if it's all the same to you.'

'All right.' He sounded serious.

'Saul,' said Bianca, half amused, half incredulous. 'It was a joke.'

'Oh. Oh, I see. Well anyway, your husband told me you were here and he seemed to think we should have dinner together.'

Romantic proposal or what? How was she meant to respond to that?

'You don't have to. It was his idea.'

'Yes, I see. Well . . .'

It was obviously the last thing Saul wanted to do. And she really didn't want to have dinner with him. It would almost certainly be boring. A lot of silences. And she and Florence had already agreed to have an early dinner at the hotel.

'Saul,' she began again, 'if you don't mind, I am quite tired . . .'

'Oh, fine,' he said. 'I understand.'

A very long silence while she wondered if she could just say goodbye and hang up.

'I realise it's short notice,' he said finally. 'It just seemed worth asking you.'

What did that mean? That he liked the idea? Possibly. He certainly didn't have to, he wasn't into pleasing Patrick. And she had said she'd do it if he turned up. And Patrick was at home now, dealing with a very fractious, chickenpoxy Ruby and she had warned Florence . . .

'Well, as long as it's – we're – not too late, I'd love to,' she said, struggling to sound as if she meant it.

'Good. Yes. Well look, where is the Hotel d'Angleterre? I've never heard of it.'

He wouldn't have, she thought. Not his sort of place.

'In St Germain. It's lovely. Small, used to be a house, very peaceful, very pretty. No public bar, no one's allowed in if they're not staying here.'

'Very nice. I think I might move in.'

'It's full,' she said, panicked, and there was a silence.

Then, 'Bianca,' he said, 'it was a joke.'

'Oh!'

'I'm staying at the Crillon. The service is good.'

It seemed an odd reason to stay at a hotel so famous for its five-star, flamboyant luxury. But then he was – odd. 'Anyway, we could eat there . . .'

She put the phone down and called Florence in her room.

'I'm sorry. It's just that he's Patrick's boss and—'

'It's all right, Bianca.' Florence's voice was amused. 'I understand. Bosses have to be looked after. I shall be quite happy, take a little walk – I love this area – and then perhaps have an omelette in my room. Where are you going?'

'Don't know. He said the Crillon, but I loathe those sorts of places.'

'May I suggest Le Petit Zinc, just round the corner from here? Charming, and wonderful food.'

'You may indeed, and thank you. I shall tell him. Of course you could join us – it would be nice . . .'

'I don't think so,' said Florence. 'And your Mr Finlayson would be appalled to be forced into a threesome by an old woman.'

'Florence, I don't think so,' said Bianca, laughing, 'but if you're sure . . .'

She looked at Florence as she sat in the enchanting green garden courtyard, sipping the kir she had asked the waiter, in fluent French, to make with white burgundy, rather than champagne. 'That is the only way, really,' she explained to Bianca, who was drinking pastis. Bianca was impressed and intrigued; how had Florence, who had always worked for very modest pay, achieved such sophistication? Perhaps her family had been well-to-do? It would be rude to pry, but possible, perhaps, to find out over the next two days. Damn Saul Finlayson! How much nicer to dine with this charming, interesting woman, dressed with a chic that easily matched Parisian standards, a simple navy jersey suit (Jean Muir – or was it – could it be? Chanel?). It made her own white shift dress feel somehow a bit . . . obvious.

'Please don't worry about me, Bianca. And enjoy your dinner.'

'I'll try,' she said. She was still feeling wounded and insecure after the vote of no confidence. The board meeting, reconvened, had ended comparatively amicably. Peter Warren had taken Athina aside beforehand and said he presumed she had now consulted her lawyers – a gracious inclination of her head – and that he imagined she would not want a confrontation in the boardroom.

'So I propose, if it is acceptable to you, to say at the beginning of the meeting that we will forget the vote of no confidence, and ask Mrs Bailey to join us. We can then resume. I think there was very little business left on the agenda. Does that sound satisfactory?'

Athina, clearly realising that she was getting off very lightly, said it did sound as satisfactory as possible under the circumstances, and Peter Warren, grinning broadly, joined Mike and Hugh in the boardroom.

'She really is something else. She managed to make me feel she was entirely in the right and it was very good of her to agree to drop the motion, so let's crack on before she thinks of something else she can do to scupper things.'

And for the time being at least, Lady Farrell came quietly.

But it had been a very shocking experience; and Bianca had not fully recovered.

She smiled across the table at Saul. He had agreed to Florence's suggestion and they were sitting in Le Petit Zinc, which was totally enchanting, an art nouveau treasure trove, all exquisite lamps and mirrors and bronze carvings and etched and stained glass, and waiters in the Paris uniform of long white aprons and black jackets. She waited for Saul to admire it, but he simply looked round, nodded briefly, then said, 'Fine. Do you want a drink?'

'Actually,' she said, 'I really won't. Some mineral water would be lovely.'

'Fine. I'll join you in that.'

'We're going to be a bit of a disappointment to the sommelier then.'

He looked at her blankly, then said, very seriously, 'Does that matter? I wouldn't have thought so.'

'No, Saul,' she said. 'No it doesn't. Of course. It was—'

'A joke?'

'Well, yes. Sort of.'

'Sorry. I don't have much of a sense of humour,' he added, with one of his swift smiles.

'Well, you have other qualities, I'm sure.'

'I hope so. Look, let's order, shall we? What do you like?' He was clearly not into lingering over the meal.

'I like fish,' she said quickly. 'And one of their most famous dishes is sea bass baked in clay. Which I would like, please. Florence told me all this.'

'She must know the area well,' he said.

'Yes, she does seem to. She knows the whole place well, that's why I brought her. Well, that and another reason which I won't bore you with.'

'I don't suppose you'd bore me,' he said. 'Now, would I like the sea bass?'

'Saul,' she said laughing, 'how am I supposed to know that? Do you like fish?'

'Not much.'

'What *do* you like?'

'I don't really take much interest in what I eat. It's something I have to do, really.'

'But you must like some things more than others.'

'Well, I like steak. On the raw side of rare. *Bleu* since we're in Paris.'

'So, order that, then. Are you going to have a starter?'

'No,' he said. 'I might have a pudding, though. I quite like puddings.'

'OK. They do the best profiteroles in the world here. You could have those.'

'Now how do you know,' he said, 'that they are the best in the world? That's very possibly an inaccurate statement.'

'Er, just possibly,' she said and then looked at him and saw he was actually grinning.

'Joke?' she said.

'Sort of. Let's order then, shall we?'

He launched into a stream of perfect French to the waiter. She looked at him, slightly surprised.

'Ah,' he said, 'you thought I would just speak loudly in English, didn't you? I was sent to Geneva briefly, by Chase, and decided I was going to get more out of it if I spoke all the languages properly. So I went to a private tutor the bank employed. I did French on Mondays and Wednesdays, German on Tuesdays and Thursdays and Italian on Fridays.'

'Goodness! Didn't you ever mix the days up, launch into Italian on a Monday or whatever?'

'No, of course not. I just explained: different days were for different languages.'

Bianca gave up, then, as they waited for their food, his phone rang; he pulled it out, looked at it, said, 'Excuse me' and left the table to go out on to the street. He was gone for almost ten minutes; when he came back, he looked at her awkwardly.

'Sorry. It was Dickon. He rings me every night, to say goodnight, tell me about his day. I – well, I had to take it. I'm sorry.'

'Of course you did.' She was touched by this. 'I spoke to all mine before I came out.'

A long silence while she consumed her gazpacho; then, 'How's it going? The job?'

'Oh, fine. Yes – yes fine.'

'Really?' he said and she met his eyes and could see he was not deceived.

'A bit less than fine,' she said. 'Since you ask.'

'Tell me about it.'

'You don't want to hear about my work.'

'I do. And,' he added, reading her hesitation, 'I'm famous for my discretion. I have to be. And I would find it quite insulting if you didn't tell me about it.'

That really would make it all pointless, insulting him. She'd have done better to stay in the hotel with Florence.

'Bianca,' he said, 'go on. It might help.'

It might indeed, she thought. To be able to be honest about it; to discuss the situation, without putting a spin on everything – the only other person in the world she could do that with was Patrick. And he certainly wasn't listening to her very much at the moment.

She told Saul everything.

He listened intently and then, when she had finished, said, 'Right. Some observations. I like the shop idea. But I really don't see why you're looking for it yourself, wasting time away from the office. Someone else can surely do it for you?'

'No, they can't. These are hunch things, Saul, it's totally essential they're exactly, exactly right. Estée Lauder, with all her thousands of employees, still personally approved every piece of packaging, every lipstick colour.'

'Oh, all right. I suppose I don't understand your business. Anyway, back to the shops. But you must have enough. Not just one or two. They have to be everywhere that tourists shop seriously: Dubai, Sydney, Singapore, New York, LA – very important, LA.'

'Yes, but Saul, I can't afford all those places! My hope is that we can establish a small presence in France and—'

'Then it won't work. The shop device, I mean. You're playing the English heritage card here, right? Doing a Burberry?'

'Yes.'

'Right now, with the English thing flying, and more so next year with the Diamond Jubilee and the Olympics, you should go global with that. Might take a bit of time, but we're not talking a block of Fifth Avenue, or Rodeo Drive. It's the presence you need. To give you the publicity.'

'Well, yes. But the shops will all need staff, attention. And the tiniest rent is huge in those places.'

'It'll be worth the investment. Bianca, this is a very clever idea. Tell them, your VCs, that you need more money. Tell them that if they don't get it, they'll lose what they've given you and then some. They'll come round. I know these people, I spend a lot of time with them. You should have made sure they'd go with you all the way.'

'So it's my fault?'

'To a degree, yes. Anyway, you must keep going. Keep going and don't look down. And don't worry about all the other stuff, Lady whatshername and the dead marketing manager. Sounds like a bad detective story,' he added with a grin. 'None of that is your fault.'

'It – it feels like it.'

'Well, it isn't. And you mustn't let it distract you.'

'I know, I know. You're right. I've never felt like this before, uncertain and even—' she stopped.

'Even?'

'A bit scared.'

'Oh, now you can't be scared,' he said. 'You mustn't even *think* about being scared.'

'Don't you get scared?' she asked, curious.

'Sometimes. But I just fight it off. I decide what I've got to do and then do it.'

'And is that ever wrong?'

'It can be. Losing is bad, but I mostly win, so it's OK. So, what exactly are you planning to do tomorrow?'

'Find these shops. With Florence. She runs the Berkeley Arcade shop, has done from the day it was opened, way back in 1953.'

'Oh, I see,' he said, 'I hadn't realised. Then that was a good idea, to bring her. I wish you well. I wish you well altogether. And don't be scared, Bianca. Don't look down.'

He walked her back to her hotel, keeping a clear distance from her, and when they arrived he didn't even kiss her on the cheek, merely said, 'It's been a very nice evening.' And he turned and walked swiftly up the street. He was – odd. She kept trying to find another adjective for him and failing. He was just extremely – odd.

All the same, she felt much happier; it had, in its own, odd way, been a very nice evening. As he had said. She was very glad she had gone. And Patrick would be pleased.

Examining that thought she found that she didn't give a toss about whether Patrick would be pleased or not. The evening had been about her. Her and Saul.

Athina was also, at that moment, feeling a bit scared. Well, if she was honest, very scared. She had thought briefly – very briefly – of resigning, but that idea was gone before it had a chance to take hold. It would be cowardly, apart from anything else, and she still intended to win, to retain the House of Farrell as her own creation; she was not going to allow these people to take it over, change it beyond recognition, but she seemed to have increasingly few weapons at her disposal. She could create difficulties, she could cause delays and frustrations, but that was not enough. Indeed, it risked destroying Farrell's altogether. Bianca had the wherewithal to do what she wanted, she had money and power at her disposal, while Athina had neither. But it was not the first time she had had her back to the wall. She suddenly remembered one of Cornelius's doctrines. 'If you can't beat them, join them,' he used to say, 'and then beat them after that.'

It suddenly seemed the answer now. Maybe a charm offensive should replace the overt hostility; she could manage that, indeed she was very good at it.

Abandoning any idea of sleep, Athina made herself a pot of strong coffee and settled down to some very intensive thought.

Chapter 30

'Excuse me. Would you forgive me if I just checked my emails?'

'Of course. I can then read the newspaper without appearing rude. It is an excellent paper, *Le Figaro*. I enjoy it so much.'

'Your French is awfully good,' said Bianca, seeing her chance for a little prying.

'Thank you,' said Florence, 'I just – improved, over the years. I love Paris and I came here whenever I could. Just a week or so here or there, you know.'

Which didn't explain how she had been able to afford to do so, Bianca thought.

'Lucky you,' she said.

'Yes indeed. Lucky me.' She disappeared into the newspaper. She was looking even more chic this morning, Bianca noticed, in a simple navy jacket and skirt, in her preferred mid-calf length, with a white silk T-shirt, her slender feet clad in the ubiquitous pumps. Bianca, who had chosen jeans, a thin leather biker jacket and some red Prada trainers, felt suddenly a bit crass. She was wondering whether she might go and change, when her attention was hauled into a group email. From Athina Farrell. It was headed 'Confidential' and sent to what seemed like most of the company. Bianca felt sure that if she could have reasonably included the receptionist and the catering team, she would have done so.

I would like to propose a name for the new Farrell range it said. Very good, Lady Farrell, let everyone who might catch sight of this know what we're doing, so confidential that it even has a code name. (TC 2, as in The Cream 2 – she had been rather pleased with that.)

It is The Collection.

It seems to me to encapsulate all our ambitions for the range: it has fashion connotations, it echoes the product names, particularly The Cream, of course; it defines and describes it perfectly. I would be most grateful for comments, naturally, but I think it will be very hard to improve upon.

Old witch. Bianca looked at her watch; it was only seven in England. How had she done that? She would have no truck with emails, ever, sending out old-fashioned typed memos which had to be delivered by hand by Christine, painstakingly, office by office. Of course she could see why it was by email. It had had to be done this way, so that no one could possibly fail to know that the name had come from 'The Office of Lady Farrell' as all her stationery read.

Bianca felt outclassed and outflanked; she kept hearing Saul's voice saying 'Don't look down', but the precipice she was clinging to looked suddenly a lot steeper.

But it was a good name. *Such* a good name. She turned to Florence who was pulling apart her croissant, eating it plain, small piece by small piece.

'So sorry to interrupt your reading,' she said, 'but could I just ask you something?'

'Of course.'

'I – I just had an email from Lady Farrell. About the new range.'

'Oh really? I wonder if she's sent it to me.'

She pulled out the iPhone that had astonished Bianca on the train the day before. 'Well, one must keep up,' she had said then. 'Nothing more ageing than not being able to communicate properly.' She tapped at it, studied it intently.

'Well,' she said finally, 'it is a very good name. What do you think, Bianca?'

'I think it's excellent,' said Bianca and never had a remark cost her more. 'Really excellent. But I'm a bit surprised. Mostly because it's sent by email. I always thought Lady Farrell had no truck with emails.'

'Lady Farrell has truck with whatever suits her,' said Florence, smiling very sweetly at Bianca. 'And this must be annoying for you, because she should have told you about it first. That would have been more . . . professional.'

'It would,' said Bianca carefully, 'but I'm just delighted she's cracked it. Which I do think she has.'

'Christine will have done the email for her,' said Florence. 'Athina often gets her out of bed at seven, or even earlier, to do things. Or used to. Dictating endless memos over the phone. Poor old Christine, she works her very hard.'

'It would seem so. Goodness, a reply from Susie's just come in. And Lara. And . . . everyone likes it. And Mark Rawlins. Oh, and Jonathan Tucker.'

All these people, fawning around Lady Farrell, she thought, somewhat unfairly, and busy showing off how early they were attending to their emails. Jonathan Tucker, the new sales director, had only started that week.

'Good. Well, more coffee? Or shall we go?'

'I think we should go,' said Florence, 'we have a lot of ground to cover. Literally. How was your dinner?' she added. 'I'm sorry, I should have asked.'

'It was all wonderful. The place, the food, thank you!'

'And the company?'

'Even that was better than I hoped.'

'I'm so pleased.'

'Now, I've hired a car for the day,' Bianca said, 'but I think, this being the area we agree is the most likely to offer what we want, we should walk the streets here first. If you don't mind, that is.'

'Of course not! There's only one way to see Paris and that is on foot. Anything else is sort of second-hand, out of focus.'

'Good. And then we can head over to the Marais after that. Pity it's so misty.'

'Mist suits Paris,' said Florence.

'Oh Grandy, hello. How are you?'

'I'm very well, darling. We're going to be working together this

Saturday. At Rolfe's. I need to do a bit of research into our customers.'

'But Grandy, we don't have a proper counter there any more. Just a stand.'

'Yes, yes, I know. But this Saturday – and possibly the next – is an exception. I fixed it personally with the manager. He was delighted with the idea. We'll have fun. Anyway, darling, I'll be there well before nine and so must you. And I have a small favour to ask: I want to be introduced to the girls on the Brandon's counter.'

'Oh Grandy, I don't think you'd like them very much.'

'Nonsense. Why on earth not? Now no more objections, Lucy, please. I need your help.'

Bianca and Florence set off down the tiny, pretty streets of St Germain. 'It's lovely,' said Bianca, 'it really is. Perfect.'

They kept finding them, over and over again: tiny jewels of places, exactly right for their purpose, and then felt it had been too easy, agreed they must go on and on peering down alleyways, walking down narrow streets, glancing into windows. It was a paradise for their quest, the small, colourful galleries, the tiny bookshops, the minute antique sale rooms.

'This is perfect!' Bianca would cry and then, 'No, this is better!' Florence would call a moment later.

Miraculously there were even two for rent, one selling rather modern jewellery, another books and prints. The prices were high, but not impossibly so.

'I thought we'd find it here,' Florence said happily, as they made their way back to the car, parked at the bottom of the rue de Seine. 'Just felt it in my bones.'

Bianca heard Saul's voice suddenly, echoing from the night before, as they walked back to the hotel: 'Don't look down.'

If she could find the perfect shop, she thought now, make that work, it would make up for Athina christening the range. 'Now, you think the Marais next?' she asked Florence.

'Yes, indeed. Slightly less charming, but it's becoming very fashionable, and it's undoubtedly cheaper.'

The Marais – or the part of it that they were interested in – was charming, all cobbled streets, arcades, endless cafés and fashion boutiques, similar to St Germain, but more commercial-looking and touristy.

'It is lovely,' said Bianca, 'but I still think St Germain has it.'

'Me too. Oh, look,' said Florence, pointing up at a charming house, 'that is where the Marquise de Sévigné lived.'

'And she was?'

'Renowned for her letter writing. She was married to Henri de Sévigné, who was mortally wounded in a duel over his mistress. He died two days later and she moved back to Paris. Her daughter, to whom she was devoted, was married to the governor of Provence, and moved to live there. Mme de Sévigné wrote to her every day. And her descriptions of Parisian life in the letters were copied and circulated. She was, if you like, the blogger of her day.'

'How wonderful,' said Bianca.

'Indeed. The letters were published later, over a thousand of them, by her granddaughter.'

'Goodness. I must read them. How do you think I could get hold of a copy?'

'I have one,' said Florence. 'I will lend it to you.'

Hi Milly! What are you going to wear to Carey's Halloween party? Or aren't you going?

Milly sat staring at her phone. And the text. From Sarajane. Surely, surely she wouldn't be joining in? She was her friend. Had been her *best* friend. Only – well, she supposed she had dropped her, rather. Which hadn't been very nice of her. But that was what being Carey's friend entailed. She had to come first.

Talk – or rather whispers – about the Halloween party had been going on for a few days now. Elaborate invitations had been delivered by hand, on to people's desks. Not everybody's desks. Just the chosen, as with the royal wedding. But more, far more. Only three people weren't invited.

Rose, who was, well, pretty overweight. Lottie, who had terrible spots. And Milly.

Planned for the day before Halloween, Sunday, it was starting with a special ghost tour at Ham House, followed by a drive in two stretch limos to a 'spooky supper' and ghost hunt at the Mapletons' house in the Boltons and there would be a prize for the best costume.

Flic Barton, who had been heard to remark just a bit too loudly, 'Guess who'll win that? Not the party girl, surely?' was promptly told her invitation had been a mistake.

Well, at least she'd *had* an invitation, Milly thought, looking at the text through blurred eyes. There was no question of Carey sending one to her, even to cancel it.

She would never have believed how much her life could have changed in the space of three months. At the beginning of the holidays she had been popular, happy, successful, endlessly enjoying parties and sleepovers, a year of being form prefect behind her, a lovely summer ahead. Her report had been glowing, and she had won the music prize. The only worry had been the holiday with Carey and her Facebook page was full of selfies of her having fun; her phone was full of pictures of herself, giggling, her arm round one or other of the same friends. The huggy-kissy farewells to everybody as they broke up took for ever.

Now she hardly dared look at Facebook, or her phone; the ripple announcing a text was terrifying. She hadn't been to a sleepover or a party for weeks, and she had been reduced to going out on her own at weekends, telling her mother, if they were in London, she was meeting friends and then wandering about on her own for hours, killing time. The thing she most dreaded was meeting Carey and her friends somewhere; once she saw them all looking at her and giggling from the other side of a jewellery stall in Covent Garden, and fled to the public lavatory where she sat in a cubicle for ages in case they hadn't left, or worse, came to find her.

Recently Carey had taken to texting her late at night, so even if she was asleep it woke her up. The texts were apparently innocent, in case they fell into grown-up hands; saying things like *So sorry you can't come on Saturday* or *What a pity you won't be at Annabel's on Sunday*.

The most awful thing was the way everyone had joined in. That hurt most of all, the joining together in the sly texts, the whispers, the passed notes when they were sure she was looking.

How had Carey done that? Sometimes Milly thought she must have magic powers, something close to witchcraft. She was so horrible, and obviously always had been, but Sarajane and Annabel were nice, kind and generous. Now they were just all Carey clones.

What frightened her most, of course, was the photograph; the one of her topless on the boat, that Carey had on her phone. Quite early on in the term she said she was thinking of putting it on her Facebook page.

'Carey, you can't!' Milly had said, terror making her stomach turn over. 'You can't, everyone will see.'

'What? See your teeny-weeny, flat little tits? Wouldn't have thought you'd mind – they're like a ten year old's.'

'Well, I *would* mind,' said Milly, tears starting in her eyes, 'and it's so unfair of you. I didn't want you to take that picture!'

'And I think it was quite unfair of you, sneaking off with Ad like that. When he just so didn't want to.'

'I didn't sneak off with him! He – he made me. You *know* he did. He called me into his cabin and I—'

'No, I don't know. And he said you were all over him, he was quite embarrassed.'

'He's a liar!' said Milly. 'I tried to get out, I—'

'Mills, it's *you* that's the liar. And you tried to spoil things between me and Ad, on my parents' boat, on my holiday. And I'm going to make sure everyone knows it. And if you're not very careful, if you go running to those over-controlling parents of yours, this picture goes on Facebook, OK? And YouTube.'

'Carey! You couldn't!'

'Just watch me.'

And so it had begun, Milly's torment. And there was no way, no way at all, she could get out of it . . .

'She's cool, your gran. Really cool.' Jade Harper looked across the Rolfe Beauty Hall at the temporarily reinstated Farrell counter, where Athina was rather imperiously informing a woman that if she didn't start using The Cream shortly, she would regret it for the rest of her life.

'I know,' said Lucy.

'I mean, founding the whole range and still working on it, sixty years later. She said she was still involved in product development. I mean, well cool. And selling products to the royal family, in that shop. I must go and see it next time I'm in town. She says she works there sometimes as well.'

As far as Lucy knew her grandmother hadn't stood behind the counter at the Berkeley Arcade shop for decades, but it would clearly be unwise to tell Jade that.

It had been an extraordinary morning; she had arrived at eight thirty to find her grandmother laying out the newly reclaimed counter, smiling sweetly at the consultant beside her and telling her how much she appreciated her allowing Farrell's to share her space for the morning while encroaching considerably on her territory with the Farrell showcards and colour testers. An hour later, Athina had made three sales, more than poor Marjorie had sometimes managed in an entire morning, and had Lucy doing a makeover on a fourth customer.

'Very good, Lucy darling,' she would say from time to time, walking over and turning the woman's face gently with a heavily beringed hand. 'Perhaps a little more concealer, just here look. You've got lovely skin, my dear, but it's a little thirsty – I think you haven't been using The Cream, so you must start today. Lucy is my granddaughter,' she added, 'trained at a very well-known school. She used to play with my make-up for hours when she was just a tiny little girl, "I want to be a make-up lady, just like you, Grandy," she used to say, and here she is, her ambition fulfilled. Try the translucent powder, Lucy, that one you're using could be a little too heavy . . .'

Lucy, who had no recollection whatsoever of telling her grandmother, when a tiny little girl, that she wanted to be a make-up lady, reached meekly for the translucent powder.

She was dreading introducing Athina to the Brandon girls; she would probably consider them very common, and tell them their display material was vulgar, but she had them hanging on her words in minutes, admiring their skill at handling so many customers at a time, buying one of the colour palettes for herself and asking them how involved they were in product development.

'We're not,' said Jade, 'just told this is what we've got to sell. Be nice to be asked though,' she added. 'After all, we talk to the customers ourselves, we know what they want. Mind you, Mr Brandon doesn't make many mistakes.'

'He clearly has a feeling for what's in the air,' said Athina. 'My husband, Sir Cornelius Farrell, had that gift too. As did I, of course. But we always asked the consultants to give us a view. We felt, as you clearly do, that daily contact with the customers gave them a lot of insight. Now tell me, these lip crayons, they must sell awfully well . . . and do you have a perfume range of any kind?'

'And tomorrow we go to Grasse?' Florence said, leaning back in the car.

'You're not too tired? It's been a wonderful day, thank you so much.'

'Of course I'm not tired. I love Grasse. And the museum is quite inspiring.'

'Great. Now you know what? I would really like to have a little wander in the posh bit. The rue Cambon and so on. Well, specifically Chanel. I quite fancy a bag . . .'

'Oh! May I come with you?'

'Florence, I'd love it.'

She redirected the car to the rue Cambon and they swept along the river, over the vast Concorde bridge, into the Place de la Concorde, all drenched in the exquisite afternoon light.

'So lovely,' said Florence, sighing with pleasure. 'How wonderful to be here, Bianca, I'm so grateful to you for bringing me.'

'It would have been a lot less wonderful for me, without you,' said Bianca. She looked at the long frontage of the Crillon Hotel as they swerved past it, and wondered if Saul was there. No, of course he wasn't, he was at Longchamp. Pity, she would have liked

Florence to meet him. They could have had tea in the Crillon garden and – Bianca Bailey, why are you even thinking about Saul Finlayson and his meeting Florence?

'*Le voilà.*' The driver had pulled up outside Chanel.

'Oh, wonderful. *Merci*. Oh, my God, why do I want everything they ever do?' said Bianca. 'Come on Florence, in we go.'

Within the black and white mirrored space, the chicest of Frenchwomen, some of them very young, wandered silently, gazing about them as if in church, worshipping at the shrine.

'You know, I suppose, that she had an apartment here, on the third floor,' said Bianca. 'It's amazing. I've seen photographs of it and I'm sure you have.'

'I have, yes, of course.'

'But it has no bedroom – she lived at the Ritz across the road. She's my absolute heroine,' Bianca said. 'When I think of the new range – The Collection as we must now call it – I think of her.'

'A very good style guide,' said Florence. 'Of course, we can't do black and white packaging, too many already: Chanel's own, and Quant and Jo Malone, of course – although hers is cream – but I wonder, navy and white? How would that be?'

'Perfect, I think,' Bianca said, staring at her. 'What a wonderful idea. I shall brief the studio the minute we get back.'

She moved over to the handbags and Florence followed her, smiling. Bianca exclaimed, pointed, requested; bags were taken down, set reverently on the counter, examined, and finally, one was chosen, a large tote in cream.

'I know it's not really seriously Chanel style, not sure she would have liked it, but I adore it,' said Bianca.

'It's very nice,' said Florence, smiling. 'And I think you are wrong: Chanel *would* have liked it. She was all about fashion being practical, geared to real life, and this will suit you – and your life – very well.'

'Excuse me, madame . . .' The assistant was smiling at Florence now. 'But that is a vintage Chanel jacket, I think?'

'Oh . . .' Florence looked down at her navy jersey jacket, as if half surprised to see what she was wearing. 'Yes, yes it is.'

'Very, very lovely. It becomes you, madame. Might I guess at the date? Around 1970?'

'Around then,' Florence said, and for the first time, she appeared a little flustered, Bianca thought. 'I like – well, I like to bring it back to Paris sometimes.'

'Beautiful. Beautiful.' She returned to packing Bianca's bag. '*Le voici*, Madame. It is a very lovely bag, you have chosen well. Enjoy it.'

'Thank you,' said Bianca.

They returned to the car; and she smiled at Florence.

'A real Chanel jacket. Lucky you!'

'Yes, indeed,' said Florence. 'Well, you know. One of the vintage shops, a lucky find.'

Bianca didn't believe her for a moment, without knowing why.

Later, before they had dinner, Florence said she would like to take a walk. She set off down the street, surprisingly briskly for a lady in her eighties who had been walking most of the day. Bianca looked after her thoughtfully.

When she hadn't returned after half an hour she decided to go and look for her and found her within five minutes, just two streets away, standing in front of a large wooden gate opening on to a large, leafy, cobbled courtyard. She was looking into it with an odd expression on her face, an absolute blend of happiness and sadness; when she saw Bianca she smiled at her.

'I'm sorry. I got carried away. I wanted to walk down to le Pont des Arts, you know, the lovers' bridge, with the padlocks; the view from there is so dazzling.'

Bianca didn't believe that for a moment either.

Chapter 31

It had been so amazing in Grasse. Probably the best two days of all. Such a lovely town, built in layered terraces, like some exquisitely designed film set, its wonderful rich colours, all shades of cream and pink and terracotta, its walkways strung with roses and wisteria, its gorgeously ornate houses with their own ornate stucco, its tiny meandering streets and arches and steps, its ravishing cathedral.

It was also where he promised her she would be safe for ever and made arrangements in order to keep the promise.

They met at the airport in Nice, having travelled separately of course: Florence, who had spent at least half of her week's salary on her wardrobe for the trip, had changed in the ladies' lavatory at the airport, not wishing to appear crumpled when she walked through to meet him. She was wearing what was almost her favourite outfit: a simple cardigan and matching skirt in cream wool, daringly short, at least an inch above the knee – but then, she did have very good legs as she was well aware – over a black silk T-shirt. Her hair was cropped short, her curls forming a shining golden brown cap, and her make up was bold, her brown eyes made huge with dark shadow and eyeliner, her fake lashes multi-layered, her lips pale and ultra glossy.

'You look like an advertisement for make-up,' said Cornelius, shaking her hand formally as they met.

'Yes, it's from an awfully nice range called Farrell,' she said.

He had hired a car, a most dashing thing, the Mercedes 300SL with the famous gull wing doors. 'Goodness, Cornelius, this is amazing,' she said as the doors sank slowly downwards.

'Well, I thought it was a fairly special three days, and we had to have a car that deserved it.'

He was looking wonderful, as always, very casual in a white open-necked shirt and a denim suit, and the new Chelsea boots; his hair was longer, and he was wearing some very dark sunglasses which gave him a raffish air.

'Oh my goodness,' said Florence as they sped along the coast road, 'I feel as if I'm in a slightly bad film. Have you seen *Jules et Jim*, Cornelius? Not that that's bad, I simply adored it. I went last night, just to put me in the mood.'

'I have indeed. I shall endeavour, though, not to drive the car over a cliff.'

It was a shining May day, blue and golden and almost hot. 'See the sky,' said Cornelius, 'it has been polished for us by the Mistral.'

'How very poetic you are,' said Florence, smiling, and he admitted it was not an original observation but one which Lawrence Durrell had made. 'But I'm sure I would have come to it in due course.'

Florence was staying in a charming small *auberge* in the outlying village of Pont du Loup, booked by herself through a small travel agent in Ealing, while Cornelius was staying in one of the best hotels in Grasse, a fine chateau of a place, booked by his secretary. Athina had been irritated by the trip, claiming it was unnecessary.

'I fail to see why you're going. We are so busy at the moment, all the summer promotions and considerable competition, I might add. Revlon, Rubinstein, Arden – we have to work very hard to stay ahead. And now this Lauder woman is doing awfully well too. The stores are very impressed with her, and all her monstrously expensive creams.'

'If they're monstrously expensive,' said Cornelius mildly, 'why do you worry about her?'

'Cornelius, have you learned nothing over the past ten years? Every brand must have something special about it. A concept, a legend. Miss Arden has her red doors and her cleanse-tone-nourish programme, Revson has his colour promotions – who will ever forget Cherries in the Snow? Anyway, the whole point about Re-Nutriv cream is its price. "I would never spend thirty pounds on a pot of cream," people say. "How ridiculous!" – and then buy it.'

'And what do we have that's special? On that basis?'

Cornelius's face was innocent. His voice was not. Athina gave him a withering look.

'We are English, with a great heritage,' she said, 'and we understand the Englishwoman and the English skin. People know that. That is our unique claim. Of course we give them everything else besides, but we do have something very much our own. Although sometimes I feel we don't get that message across strongly enough. I never cease talking about it, of course, and the advertising helps, but I feel you could do more in that way. You could be the English Charles Revson if you wanted to be.'

'Good God, I hope not!' said Cornelius. 'The most unpleasant man, as I understand it, and a dreadful philanderer. I hope that's not how you see me.'

'Well, you are certainly not unpleasant and no one could ever dream you could be a philanderer. But you do have style and class.'

'Thank you, my darling.'

'I'm not trying to flatter you,' said Athina, 'merely stating a fact. And I think we should capitalise on it more.'

'In what way?' said Cornelius. He looked slightly alarmed.

'The cult of the personality is a very powerful tool. All this stuff, complete nonsense of course, about Miss Arden using her creams on her racehorses, but people remember it. Mrs Lauder has a genius for that sort of thing, I have to say. We should learn from her. I once managed to get into one of her sales conferences for her consultants. It was like a revivalist meeting. They all sat gazing up at her and she preached a sort of sermon about the products and ended with, "Now remember, you are the star on stage, the public are your audience and the cash register is your applause".'

'Rather good,' said Cornelius.

'But vulgar. Which is hardly surprising. She's American for a start and her roots are very humble.'

'I don't think my mother was exactly grand,' said Cornelius. 'She was a dressmaker before she became an actress.'

'Oh, dressmaker, couturier, who would know the difference? And she was a very successful actress until she married your father. I shall think about it. Mrs Lauder has done very well with claiming the Duchess of Windsor wears *Youth Dew*. Anyway, that's the sort of thing you should be doing, Cornelius, not wasting time on non-productive nonsense like trips to Grasse.'

'On the contrary, I think it would be an excellent story, were we to go down that particular road, that I had gone to the very heart of the world's perfume industry to develop Madame Farrell, or Farrell Dew or whatever you want to call this scent of ours.'

'I suppose you're right, it could make an interesting story . . .'

Florence and he walked for a long time around Grasse that first day and felt they had hardly seen the half of it. They stopped in the lovely old square at the top of the town, with its three-tiered fountain and incredible market where he bought her a great armful of flowers, and she protested, laughing, reluctant to return them to the car where they would wilt. The man took pity and offered to keep the flowers until the end of the day.

'As well he might,' Cornelius said, laughing. 'It's probably the largest sale he's made for weeks.'

Florence didn't visit the perfumiers with him – it would be far too indiscreet; instead she gazed in awe at the great Fragonard mansion that sat high on one of the terraces of the town, and wandered round all the tiny shops selling perfume, the very air seeming scented in the warm afternoon.

And then she went to the Fragonard parfumerie, where she joined a tour and listened earnestly to the details of how a perfume was made and bought a book about it, and studied the bottles; two particularly charmed her, a miniature silver cart, bearing four bottles, pulled by two silver horses, and an exquisitely cut glass bottle with a silver cupid aloft, as its stopper.

'Did you know,' she said to Cornelius later, as they dined in a tiny restaurant near her *auberge*, 'they have to pick the jasmine flowers at dawn, when the scent is at its most developed. Isn't that a lovely thing?'

'It is. And do you know that Grasse enjoys a micro-climate, very warm but sheltered from the sea air, which is ideal for the flowers, and that there is a great abundance of water in the area?'

'Well, yes, and I have some rather less charming information for you: civetone, which is one of the crucial ingredients in perfume, is extracted from a cat's anal glands, and ambergris from the intestines of a whale.'

'Lovely! We must make sure that's in the advertising.'

'Indeed. Now here, on my wrist, is a perfume I created myself today. Why you are employing an expensive perfumier I have no idea. Tell me what you think?'

He took her small wrist in his hand and raised it to his nose, sniffed at it and then kissed it tenderly.

'Not bad,' he said, 'but not nearly beautiful enough for you.'

Later, lying in bed in her room – small, but charming, with its lace curtains and cushions, fine glass wall lights, and the great jug of flowers on the scrubbed chest of drawers, he turned to her and sighed, and said, 'My darling, darling Little Flo, there is something I want to tell you.'

'You – want to finish it?' she said, very calm, for she had been anticipating it ever since the first time in Paris.

'Finish it? Dear God, no, never, never! As long as you will have me, I will want this to continue. It is worth every risk, every sadness. What I don't quite understand is why you put up with it. You could find a real lover, a full-time one, who would marry you and care for you—'

'And who I would never stop comparing with you,' she said. 'Cornelius, you may not be the best of prospects but I have never known such happiness as I know with you. Well, not since Duncan. I was happy with him. And had great – what shall we say – fulfilment.'

And she leaned over to kiss him.

'I have often wondered about that with him,' he said, 'the fulfilment, as you call it.'

'Well – it was there. I loved him and he taught me to, well, to enjoy it.'

'He did a very good job,' he said and smiled at her.

'He did. But we had so little time to learn and explore one another. So it was – different. With you, there is – more. In bed, that is,' she added, laughing.

'And out of it? How much then?'

'Well, when we are together, a great deal. I love being with you so much. You interest and intrigue me, you make me laugh . . .'

'And cry? Sometimes? When we have to part.'

'No,' she said very seriously, 'no. I have never cried over you. I wept so much for Duncan, because there couldn't be a future. With you there is one. Of sorts. I miss you, but there is always the next time to think about.'

'And yet you thought then I was going to end it?'

'Well, yes. I'm always prepared for that. And I promise not to make a scene if you do. Meanwhile, what we have now is enough, Cornelius, really it is. I love my job, and I love my freedom; I love my Sundays, roaming London and the galleries and museums, and spending time with my friends. I'm perfect mistress material, you see.'

'And – guilt? Does that trouble you?'

'Yes and no,' she said. 'I don't like to deceive Athina; on the other hand, she does treat me rather disgracefully and I take a certain comfort in the thought of our relationship. Which is probably very wicked of me.'

'Probably. I too,' he said, laughing, kissing her shoulder. 'She is not always very kind to me either.'

'But so long as she doesn't know, and isn't hurt – well, what harm are we doing? And then, I have never for a single moment wanted motherhood. I do like children, but I hate babies. I have two goddaughters who satisfy what maternal instincts I have. So you see, although I would like to spend more time with you, I have no desire to have you father my children. And I know how much you love Bertie and Caro, dear little things that they are. Especially Bertie. He is the sweetest little boy. So – what did you want to say to me?'

'Oh, not a great deal,' he said, and his expression was very tender now. 'And I think that this is not, after all, the right time. I suddenly have rather more urgent plans for us.'

'Oh really?' she said, lying back. 'I cannot imagine what they might be. Oh – oh, yes, I see . . . Oh, my God, Cornelius, please, please, don't stop doing that, it's so lovely, so very lovely . . . God, oh God . . .'

'I will stop just for a moment,' he said, laughing, 'and tell you that tomorrow I plan to take you somewhere special, and then I shall tell you what I am going to do for you. I think you will be pleased. But now – oh, God, I love you. I love you so much, Florence. I wish we could be together all the time. And I'm glad we have talked as we have, because it seems as if you wouldn't want to be married to me anyway.'

'Cornelius, I'm afraid I wouldn't,' said Florence, sweetly serious. 'I want what we have. But more of it. Oh, God!'

And she pulled him towards her; and downstairs *Madame la Proprietress*, who was turning out the lights, heard the bed begin to creak and then a little later, as she went upstairs, first moans and then cries of pleasure, and thought how very nice it was that the charming Mlle Hamilton, so beautiful and so really rather chicly dressed, should not, after all, be the lonely spinster she had imagined.

The special place next day to which Cornelius took her was the Colombe d'Or restaurant in Saint-Paul-de-Vence, which Florence had read of in her guide book, but had never thought to see, haunt as it was of the famous, the talented, the creative, of actors, singers, artists (most notably Picasso).

They ate an amazing meal. 'Oh, I love food,' said Florence happily as she devoured first bouillabaisse, then veal and finally crêpes suzette.

'You're so fortunate,' he said, 'not to put on weight. Athina has a constant battle with hers, and taking her out to dinner is no fun at all. Do you have a secret?'

'Yes, I do. It's my mother. She was like a bird, although my father always said she ate like a vulture. I must have inherited that from her.'

'Then let us drink to your mother.'

They were sitting outside in the sunshine; he was wearing a linen suit and his sunglasses were very dark.

'You look like Yves Montand,' said Florence.

'I do? Perhaps they will think I am him, with a glamorous new film star girl friend. I love that dress, Florence. It suits you so well.'

'Thank you.'

She had hesitated about its purchase from Jaeger; cream bouclé wool, sleeveless, gently shaped to her body, it had been terribly expensive, eight guineas, but she had decided it was an investment rather than an extravagance. She had acquired some sunglasses herself, wandering around Grasse the previous day; they were large, with tortoiseshell frames, Jackie Kennedy-style, and gave her a slightly exotic air. Several people had stared at them, as they sat, drinking aperitifs and smoking, making up their mind what to order.

After eating, they moved to the terrace to drink their coffee.

'People dance here in the evening, it's very chic,' he said.

'Could we come back? I do love dancing. And it's our last evening.'

'Of course. I have a meeting with the *parfumier* first though, so we should have to go back to Grasse.'

'Oh, well then don't let's waste time driving backwards and forwards.'

'Florence, with you beside me, driving is a rather erotic pleasure.'

'Good heavens. But still – I have another erotic pleasure in mind and I think we need to leave a lot of time for it.'

'I'll drink to that,' he said, raising his coffee cup. 'And now, listen to me very carefully, Little Flo. I have made some arrangements for you, which will keep you safe for ever, should I suddenly shuffle off this mortal coil. I love you and I worry about you, and I want to know you are assured of a secure and, I hope, happy old age. So this is what I have done . . .'

317

And when he had finished speaking, she sat staring at him, in awe of his generosity and his thoughtfulness.

'You can't do that, Cornelius,' she said.

'Oh, but I can,' he said. 'In fact, I already have.'

Chapter 32

She seemed to be on a downward spiral. It had begun with Athina's name for the new range, which everyone had loved, and now Athina seemed to be taking over the cosmetic departments of all the major stores in the country, with her absurd roadshow. The formulations of the new brand were lovely, but she still wasn't satisfied with the packaging, and she sensed an impatience in Hugh and Mike. She tried to talk to Patrick about it, but he was distracted and only kept telling her that she was always like this halfway through an assignment. Bianca knew this wasn't true. She'd had moments of doubt, but not weeks on end of the stuff. And Ralph Goodwin seemed to have stalled on the perfume, in spite of what she could only describe as florid phone calls, and said that his board had pronounced the Farrell numbers too low, which had been a blow; but then he had suggested, over a rather expensive lunch, that he had managed to talk them into a different arrangement, a fee upfront and then sharing the development costs.

'I want to work with you, I think we can do something quite wonderful together, so if you could see your way to doing something like that?'

Bianca, desperate for a success of her own, paid him an advance of three thousand pounds.

And she was increasingly anxious about Milly, who was clearly unhappy but stubbornly refused to tell her why.

Bianca tried to persuade herself that it was a phase and it would pass, but she couldn't convince herself and it was an awful thing to watch.

And Patrick – well, Patrick seemed to be in love with Saul Finlayson. They hadn't had sex for weeks; mostly owing to the fact that Patrick was either working terribly late, or ploughing through endless documents, even at the weekends, and had rejected her advances to him just once too often, wrecking her confidence still further; she wasn't going to risk that again.

She often thought of Saul, and his advice not to look down, and reflected miserably that she was falling now, rather than just looking, struggling to scramble up.

And in spite of her finding the shop in Paris, Mike and Hugh had refused even to consider any more outlets.

She was sitting at her desk, one dark December morning, trying to summon up some enthusiasm for the sales conference at the end of January and wondering what exactly she would be presenting, when her phone rang.

'Mrs Bailey? Lady Farrell here. Mrs Bailey, I would like to speak at the sales conference. Many of the people there will expect to hear from me, and the new people need to realise how deeply I am involved in the company still and, of course, the relaunch.'

'I'm sure they're very well aware of that, Lady Farrell,' said Bianca crisply, 'how could they not be, indeed?'

'I'm sorry?'

'Because you keep—' Telling them so, she had been about to say, then thought this would sound childish and changed it to, 'Doing your wonderful roadshow in the stores.'

'Oh. Well, that's very kind of you to say so.'

'I'll – I'll think about the conference.' And then, with a huge effort, 'And of course you're right, people will love to hear from you. What did you imagine you might want to talk about?'

'I just told you that,' said Athina, 'my involvement in the relaunch and—'

'Yes, well, that's the basis of my own presentation, and we don't want to overlap.'

'Indeed not,' said Athina, 'but I think I can avoid that. I shall have further-reaching things to say, the legacy of the Farrell past, that sort of thing.'

'Well, I do think that would be very interesting.'

'Of course. So very much more interesting, indeed, than simply talking about a lot of products.'

Bitch, thought Bianca, putting down the phone. Bitch bitch bitch.

And then . . .

'Susie?'

Susie looked up. Bianca was standing in her doorway.

'Yes, Bianca?'

'Have you seen the *News* today?'

'Not yet.'

'Then listen: "Athina Farrell, still one of the great doyennes of the cosmetic industry, talked to me today of her comeback from the golden days of the House of Farrell, in the 1950s".'

'What?' Susie reached for the paper but Bianca held on to it; her expression was not friendly.

'It gets worse. "Sitting in her stylish drawing room, with its art deco furnishings, she talked with huge enthusiasm about her work. 'I find I still have so much to offer,' she said, 'despite there being a number of new, young people at the company. Time and time again I sit in meetings, making suggestions, proposing campaigns, which are almost invariably accepted. I feel very fortunate that at my age, I can still be a vital part of the company'".'

'Oh what?'

'Exactly. When did she give this bloody interview, when was it arranged?'

'Bianca, I don't know.'

'Well, you should. You're in control of publicity here. We can't have this anarchic approach.'

'Yes but—'

'And listen to this. "'Of course, when my husband and I ran it together it was such fun and a huge success, but since he died, I have found it difficult to work and consequently the brand has suffered. Now, however, I feel revitalised. Only the other day I solved a problem which had been defeating even our dynamic new chairman, Bianca Bailey. For whom I have the greatest respect and

321

with whom I enjoy working very much. We will be relaunching the brand next year and it's wonderful to know I am at the heart of that.'" I mean, really Susie, what is going on? I simply don't understand why this journalist didn't check with you!'

'Bianca, Lord Fearon, the chairman of that group of papers, is an old friend of Lady Farrell's. She must have called in a favour. And you know, this sort of story, family dynasties, all that stuff, people do love it.'

'Yes, well clearly they do. And I know we're going to capitalise on it, but not yet. Oh, God!' Bianca looked very tired, Susie thought, her usual vibrancy muted. 'The old witch! I could kill her. A whole lot of stuff about the old days with Cornelius as well, exactly what we wanted her to do and she refused. And she has me totally painted into a corner. I can't deny any of it because it will look like sour grapes. God, she's buggered up everything, our timing, our story – I could *kill* her!'

'I'm – well, I'm sorry. I don't know what to say. I wish I could . . .'

Susie's voice faded into silence.

'Yes, well it's got to be stopped. I'm going to see her right now. Is there anything you can do to counteract this, Susie, get something out on Twitter or on our Facebook page?'

'Yes, of course I will. I'll get on to it straight away. Except—'

'Except what?'

'Well, short of saying she's a liar in that she's not responsible for it all, I don't think there's much we can do. We *are* going to relaunch, we *are*—'

'Susie,' said Bianca, 'something has to be done, OK?'

And she was gone, the door shut rather too firmly behind her.

Susie felt panicky. Just as she was redeeming herself, she had thought, in Bianca's eyes, working late and early, entirely focused, coming up with ideas for the launch, this had to happen. Making her look seriously incompetent. She'd lose her job if she didn't do something.

Maybe she could persuade a journalist to do a life in the day of the House of Farrell, something like that. That would show rather more clearly exactly how much influence Lady Farrell actually had. But would Bianca consider that weighty enough to counteract the dreadful *News* article? And if Athina knew a journalist was in the building she'd be bearing down on her, talking herself up.

Shit. Shit shit shit! Life was so bloody difficult. And she was getting emails from Henk, day after day, telling her how sorry he was and he missed her and—

Her phone rang. It was Sadie Bishop, assistant to Elise Jordan, the legendary beauty editor of *Tomorrow*, cooler-than-cool lifestyle magazine.

'Hi, Susie. How are you? Long time no speak.'

Yes and whose fault is that, thought Susie, recalling months of unanswered emails and unreturned calls.

'I'm good, thank you. Lovely to hear from you. How are you?'

'Fine, yes. Look, Elise saw the piece in the *News* this morning, about your boss.'

'My boss? Oh, you mean Lady Farrell. She's not really my boss, she's pretty remote from all the action, really. My boss is Bianca Bailey.'

'Doesn't sound that way, from the article. Lady F sounds pretty hands on. And seriously cool. Anyway, Elise would like to talk to her about an exclusive on the new range, wondered if she'd like to have lunch with her next week, at The Ritz.'

'Oh. Well, Sadie, I'm sure she'd absolutely love to, but it's a bit soon really, we're not ready to talk about the relaunch yet.'

'Never too soon to sign up for an exclusive, Susie. When I say exclusive, I mean preview, of course. And serious coverage, guaranteed. Double-page spread, that sort of thing . . .'

Susie's head spun. Now what did she do? A guaranteed product exclusive in *Tomorrow* magazine – incredible! The Holy Grail of PR. But – all the others would be hugely displeased. *Vogue*, *Tatler*, *Elle*, *Red*, *Style* magazine in the *Sunday Times*, *You* magazine – and the influential weekly magazines too, *Grazia*, *Stylist*; she needed them all. It was hideous. She hesitated for a moment, then said, 'It sounds wonderful, Sadie, but it really is too soon, there's not very much to talk about yet. Lady Farrell has just slightly—' She stopped.

'Just slightly what?'

'Well, jumped the gun.'

'Really? So are you saying no? You *don't* want Elise to meet Lady Farrell?'

'Not quite yet. I'll – I'll have to ask Bianca.'

'Bianca?'

'Bianca Bailey, my boss. The CEO of the company.'

'I see.' Sadie's voice was cooling. 'We very much had the impression here that Athina Farrell was in charge of the company overall. Elise will be very disappointed. She doesn't offer this sort of thing very often, as you know. I think you would be unwise to turn this down. The lunch, at least, with Lady Farrell to discuss it.'

'Yes, of course. Of course. And I'm terrifically excited about it, naturally, about Elise's interest. Sadie, let me get back to you. I promise I won't be long.'

Slowly, reluctantly, Susie walked down the corridor and asked Jemima if she could see Bianca.

'Bertie, hi. Got a moment?'

It was Lara with her efficient, determined face on. Not the 'shall we have a drink' one. Pity, it had been a few weeks now. And he had never felt confident enough to initiate anything himself.

He said he had a moment, of course, and indicated for her to sit down.

'I want to discuss the sales conference. It's only two months away now, and I'd like your opinion on a few things. And of course you'll have to do a presentation.'

'Me!' Bertie looked appalled. 'Lara, I couldn't possibly. I'd be hopeless. Especially with you lot of pros. Anyway, my mother wouldn't allow it.'

'Bertie,' said Lara, genuinely shocked, 'your mother is not going to dictate who speaks at the sales conference.'

'Want a bet?' said Bertie.

'Bertie, I'm sorry, but I want you to do this and I want you to start thinking about it now.'

He sat looking at the closed door when she had gone. She was so extremely attractive. Far too attractive for him, of course, even if he had been single; he knew his place. And anyway, he wasn't single, he was very much married. And he was at least fifteen years older than Lara; she must see him as an old man. Or certainly getting on a bit. She was very kind to him, of course, and she hadn't actually seemed to mind when he'd kissed her after their dinner. Bit rash that – he wasn't quite sure what had come over him. But she hadn't responded, and she would have done, he was sure, if he'd been more her type.

Lara, back in her office, sat staring out of the window and thinking about Bertie. He was so very sweet, and charming, and gentlemanly. She'd really liked it when he'd kissed her; she'd longed to respond properly, but then he'd have been frightened off. And he was probably just being friendly.

He wasn't exactly available either; long and dutifully married to the dreadful Priscilla – and anyway, she was sure Bertie hardly considered her as a sexual being. It was absurd, there was no way he regarded her in that way, found her attractive. Completely absurd.

It was the invitation that made her realise she couldn't go on, that it was worse than how things had been before – or certainly as bad.

Such horrible things, those invitations. That as good as said you were a loser, that you hadn't got your life together and, moreover, that everyone knew it. She sat there at her desk, staring at it, *Susie plus one* and burst into tears.

It wasn't true that it didn't matter, that there was more to life than men and having your own: it mattered horribly. She'd tried everything – and she was more ashamed of that, of the desperation – than of the trying. She'd done speed dating, internet dating, answered small ads. Nothing worked, everything was disappointing.

It really was the end of a perfect day; there'd been an advertising meeting she hadn't been invited to, and Sadie Bishop had emailed to say sorry, but Elise had decided that she really couldn't be expected to wait for several more weeks before planning her spring schedule and so was cancelling the lunch with Bianca Bailey. Susie had had to break that to Bianca, who had been unfairly hard on her – 'I thought you said it was a definite arrangement, Susie? I cancelled two other things for that. Could she make it brunch?'

'No, I already tried that,' said Susie. It was a lie, but she knew there was no way Elise was going to meet Bianca now. She was hugely offended by what she perceived as a snub: and nobody *ever* snubbed Elise Jordan.

'Susie, hi! You all right?' It was Jemima, smiling her lovely smile. Gosh, she was nice, Susie thought. How did people get to be like that? Even Jemima's private life was totally and sweetly perfect: she had a lovely husband called Jim who was a solicitor, they'd been married for five years and seemed to live in a state of perfect harmony. No doubt any minute she'd produce a perfect baby. 'I'm going now. Saw your light was still on. Don't work too late.'

'How – how did the advertising meeting go?'

'Oh, all right I think. Not fantastic. But they're getting there, Bianca said.'

'Good.' It seemed to Susie that it was getting a bit late, if they were going to do any press ads, which she presumed they were. Thank goodness that wasn't down to her.

'Well I'd better go,' said Jemima after a pause, 'we've got people coming to supper.'

She even managed that: working till – what? Half past seven. How were other people so – so together?

'Bye, Jemima. Have a nice evening.'

'I will.'

Susie started packing up her things; saw the invitation and started crying again. It was actually rather nice, just giving in to it, being miserable. She'd go home, have a bath, wallow away in it all;

and then – then what? It would still only be nine o'clock. Another DVD? Another early night . . .

Her phone rippled: text message. It was Henk.

Hi babe. How about a quick drink? Just one. I need to talk to you. Pleeez!

She wouldn't. She mustn't. She'd be letting herself down so badly. She'd come this far. She must stick to her resolve. And . . .

It was like looking at someone else's phone, reading the words that appeared on the screen.

She must be the most amazing actress. That she should be going through this and nobody thought there was anything wrong. Really, properly wrong. How could that happen?

Her mother was clearly worried, of course, always trying to get her to tell her what the matter was; but if she knew, her mother would go to the school, demand Milly's tormentors were brought to justice, and that would just make things ten times worse. Or a million times worse. When her mother had been at school and bullies were disciplined and expelled they were never heard from again. Now, they could still get at you online, through Facebook and Ask.fm, and Carey would put the photograph of her up, she really would. So she had to keep it to herself and pray that the attention would switch to someone else. She felt bad for wishing what she was going through on some other unfortunate girl, but she knew it was the only way it was going to stop.

If she could just get to the end of this term, she'd have a break from it all.

Carey was going skiing immediately after Christmas and taking Sarajane and Annabel with her. They talked about it all the time, really loudly. Well, at least the rest of the class was left out of that. Then, on the last day of term, Carey arrived with a mountain of invitations to the ice rink at Somerset House and then tea at the café afterwards.

'To make up for not taking you all skiing. Sorry! Wish I could.'

Only one person didn't get that invitation. Milly.

Then the class post box was opened; everyone got a huge pile of cards. Except Milly. She didn't get any. Not one.

She sat there, head bowed, her fists clenched, eyes wide open, staring at her desk, to stop the tears as everyone's piles grew, unable to believe it; how had Carey done that? But she had.

Later she got a lot of texts: they all said the same thing, more or less.

What a shame, no cards for you. So sorry. Never mind.

And then when they were exhausted, another lot: *So sorry you can't come to the skating party.*

She sat in her bedroom, staring at her phone, and now she did let herself cry. She could never remember feeling so alone. And once she started, she couldn't stop. The house was empty, she could let herself go. What could she do, what was there to do?

There was nothing. Absolutely nothing.

She decided she had to get out of the house. It seemed to be suffocating her. She walked down to the O2 Centre at Swiss Cottage and sat down in the public area and started crying again, the tears rolling down her face, silently.

'You OK?'

It was a girl, about her own age, not particularly nice-looking, in fact rather the reverse. She was quite – well, not thin (Milly had been carefully trained in non-references to people's weight), and she had very greasy hair and spots. But her face was concerned and her eyes were kind. Milly managed to smile at her.

'Yeah, fine thanks.'

'You don't look it.'

'Yes, well – I got a bad report,' she lied. 'My parents are really cross.'

'That's awful. You on your own?'

'Yes.' And freshly reminded of her predicament, of always being on her own, Milly started crying again.

'Oh, look, it can't be that bad. They'll get over it. Here, want a doughnut?'

She produced a box of six brilliantly coloured iced doughnuts. Of all the things she shouldn't be eating, this poor overweight spotty

328

girl, Milly thought, a doughnut was probably the worst. She shook her head.

'No thanks.'

'Oh, go on, they're really nice. I can't eat them all.'

'No, no really.'

'Anything you would like?'

'No. Well – yes. Maybe a cup of tea.'

'OK. Let's go to Maccy Ds. I'll come with yer – I haven't got anything to do.'

Inside the comforting familiarity of McDonald's, and at least not on her own, Milly felt better.

'This is really kind of you. Do you want one?'

'I'll have a Coke, please. And I might have some chips.'

'Fine. I'll get them. You go and bag us a table.'

She bought the drinks and the chips, went and joined the girl at the table.

'Thanks. Want some money?'

'No, no of course not. You've been so kind – what's your name?'

'Jacintha,' said the girl. Never did a name seem less suited to anyone. As if reading Milly's thoughts the girl added, 'But everyone calls me Jayce. What about you?'

'I'm Emily. But everyone calls me Milly.'

'Cheers,' said Jayce. She raised her drink to Milly. 'Want a chip?'

'No thanks.' But they did look awfully good. 'Maybe just one.'

'Where do you go to school, then?'

'Oh, nowhere near here. St Catherine's.'

'Where's that then? Private?'

'Yes,' said Milly reluctantly.

'Thought you was posh,' said Jayce with a certain amount of smugness. 'D'you like it there?'

'No. I *hate* it,' said Milly and was surprised at the violence in her voice.

'I hate mine and all. Lot of cat fights at yours?'

'Well . . .' Milly considered this. She'd heard of the playground fights between girls, spitting, scratching, kicking, hair pulling. But what she was enduring was surely as bad. If not worse.

And to her horror she started crying again. Jayce looked at her consideringly, her plump face soft with sympathy.

'You being bullied?'

'Yes,' said Milly simply, 'yes, I am.' And then added, blowing her nose on a McDonald's scratchy napkin, 'But not – not like that.'

'Oh, OK. On your phone and that?'

'Yes,' said Milly. 'Yes.'

'That's awful. I get that. Very bad it got last year, but then someone else with, like, really bad spots who talked a bit lah de dah – like you – she arrived and they started on her instead. She was fat and all,' she added. 'It's horrible, that. I'd hate to be fat.'

Milly realised that Jayce clearly didn't see herself as fat. She supposed she wasn't, not really. Just – big.

'Did you – did you tell anyone?' asked Milly. 'When it was going on, I mean?'

'No!' Jayce's expression was horrified. 'Course not. They just get back at you. In the end, she drank some bleach, this girl. Not enough to kill her, but she had to be, like, rushed to hospital.'

'And then what happened?'

'It got worse. She did tell, and the girls got a massive bollocking. Didn't do no good; one of them texted her and said *Next time have a bit more on us.*'

'Oh my God!' said Milly.

'Yeah. So then her dad saw it, and went to the school and the girls was all suspended for a week. And she went to another school.'

'I – hadn't thought of that,' said Milly.

'Yeah, well, you could try it. But they find yer just the same, and if they've got friends in the new school, they're like, there as well.'

Suddenly there was a loud cry of, 'Milly! Hello. Oh, you've got a new friend. Aren't you going to introduce us?'

It was Carey with Annabel and another girl Milly didn't recognise. They stood, looking at her, giggling, whispering to each other. Milly sat staring at them, like a rabbit in a trap. Then Carey produced her phone.

'I must take a picture of you. Smile for the camera, girls!' She snapped away. 'Lovely. Just one more, to be sure.' And then they were gone, still giggling.

'Nice!' said Jayce, her tone heavy with disdain. 'Them your friends?'

'Not,' said Milly. 'They are *so* not my friends.'

Later, shaking, she looked at Carey's Facebook page. Sure enough, there it was, a photograph of her and Jayce, Jayce looking enormous and very plain, and her looking petrified.

Milly's got a new friend, it said. *Nice! here they are, sharing some doughnuts. Not too many, Milly! Happy Christmas both of you.*

Milly lay down, pulled the duvet over her head, and started crying again.

Chapter 33

Wow! Now *he* was good-looking. And really, really cool, great clothes – black shirt, really well cut dark grey trousers, and fantastic two-tone brogues. Close-cropped dark hair, rather heavenly brown eyes, just exactly the right amount of five o'clock shadow. And he was actually walking toward her . . .

'Hi! I'm Jonjo Bartlett. And you are . . . ?'

'Susie Harding.' Pity, he was well and truly taken. No future there. Nice thought. 'I work for Bianca.'

'Oh, you're the publicity director. Great. It's so nice of you to come. Glass of champagne?' He plucked one from a tray.

'Thank you. It's not nice of me at all, the alternative was sitting in front of a boxed set of *Mad Men*.'

'Well, I hope this trumps it.'

Just about. A champagne-fuelled party, in a penthouse suite on the Chelsea stretch of river, and all she had to do, she'd been told, was smile a lot and look at some sculptures.

She'd been going through her emails when Bianca came into her office and asked her what she was doing that evening.

'Oh – nothing that can't be cancelled.'

'Well, how'd you like to come to a party? Or rather, an exhibition. Patrick has this old school friend, Jonjo he's called, Jonjo Bartlett. Cityboy, you know the sort of thing, bit flash, loads of dosh, you'd like him.' Susie wasn't sure how to take that. Was she really that shallow? She smiled carefully at Bianca. 'Anyway, Jonjo's girlfriend is a sculptor, and it's her exhibition. Most peculiar stuff, I think, but she's very successful and very A-list. Turns out some other artist is having an exhibition tonight and a lot of the critics and at least half the A-list and quite a lot of Bs are going to that. So she's thrown a hissy fit, says she's facing a public humiliation. And instructed Jonjo to find a few extras so at least the place isn't empty. He rang and asked if I could bring anyone suitable. And I thought of you.'

'Bianca, I'm not very A-list. More like D.'

'Well, me too – but you know lots of journos and stuff, you can talk yourself up. I asked Jonjo and he was very keen. I'm taking Jemima as well, partly because she's so beautiful and also her father's a well-known expert on Pre-Raphaelite painting, and she can talk about him, so I thought that might be impressive. Oh, and if the sculptress talks to you, just say how amazing they are and she'll do the rest. She's not exactly a shrinking violet. You don't have to come, but I'd be very grateful. And so would Patrick.'

'I'd love to,' said Susie, and now she sipped her champagne and cased the room. The incredible-looking creature with blond ringlets and a dress that looked as if she should have bought the next size must be Guinevere Bloch. She was standing next to an extremely phallic-looking object, at least four feet high, made of marble, with a stiff net ballet skirt fastened round where its waist might be, if it had one. The exhibition was called Where Worlds Collide and this was clearly the centrepiece. Guinevere was talking very fast and laughing manically, her enormous blue eyes constantly roving the room.

The dress code was varied; from the hyper chic – one woman had on a black tube of a dress, the collar snaking up into her hair where it turned into a gold coronet, another a white tuxedo suit, the long skirt dangling not from the wearer's waist but below her hips, revealing a good stretch of brown, toned flesh in between – to the near fancy dress. Her own pale pink tux suit seemed very dull.

Bianca arrived, looking wonderful in a long black silk dress, utterly simple, with sleeves just to the elbows and a wide red belt. Susie decided she should go to greet her, and was about to set out through the throng, but Jonjo had appeared at her side.

'Hi. Guinevere sent me to bring you over.'

She followed Jonjo, managing somehow not to knock into people's glasses and the sushi they were waving about.

'Guinevere, this is Susie. Who works with Bianca. Susie's a PR, so she knows everyone in the press, all the critics . . .'

'How marvellous,' said Guinevere, her eyes resting very briefly on Susie. 'I wonder if you could fix an interview this evening? It's such a good moment, and it would make fascinating reading, especially as this is my apartment. We could even do some pictures, or I have some ready of course, I – oh look, Jonjo, lovely tweet from Graham, said he'd love to come, but he had to get to the studio. Anyway, Susie, what do you think, good idea?'

'Um – really good idea,' said Susie, wondering if the Graham who had to get to the studio could be Graham Norton, and decided it was perfectly possible, 'but possibly not this evening. It would be so hard for you – and the journalist – to concentrate on what you were saying. All these people—'

'Oh, nonsense. I can talk about my work wherever I am. It's quite literally a part of me. Who do you actually know who's here?'

'Well . . .' Susie looked desperately round the room, '. . . no one just now. Maybe they haven't arrived yet. I do love your work though. It's marvellous.'

'Isn't it?' It was Bianca's voice. 'Hi, Susie. Hello, Guinevere, what a turnout you've got. So exciting. Patrick's on his way.'

'Oh good – yes. Jonjo, look, Those people look a bit lost, do go and see to them. Oh my God, Marcus! How amazing, how wonderful of you to come.'

Dismissed most thoroughly, Susie and Bianca smiled at one another and slithered across the room.

'Sorry,' said Bianca, 'should have warned you.'

'You did,' said Susie, 'and I'm enjoying myself. Truly. It's fascinating. Oh my goodness, there is someone I actually know! How exciting.'

'Who's that, then?'

'Caitlin Meredith. She's the beauty editor of *In Fashion*. She'd love to meet you and she's really nice.'

'Well, as long as she doesn't ask to interview Athina Farrell, that's fine,' said Bianca, laughing.

Caitlin did seem quite pleased to meet Bianca; she said that a relaunch was always such good copy, adding that she was addicted to The Cream. If Susie had rehearsed her, she could hardly have done better.

'I've got to try and talk to this sculptor lady,' she said, 'get a quote from her. I'm moonlighting for the *Sketch* gossip column. Don't tell anyone. And do either of you know her?'

Susie and Bianca's eyes met in a perfect understanding; then, 'Susie does,' said Bianca, 'she'll get you an intro.'

'That was amazing,' said Susie next day. 'Look Bianca, here it is. Main picture in the diary. And here's what Guinevere said about her centrepiece: "The phallus embracing *haute couture*. It's what life is all about, clothes and sex? And I adore both." It takes a certain talent to dream up a sentence like that.'

'It does indeed,' said Bianca, laughing. 'Anyway, she's very pleased, according to Jonjo. And speaking of the devil,' she said, looking at her phone, 'he's just sent a text: we've all just been invited to have a drink with them tomorrow evening at Shoreditch House, to say thank you. I can't go, and one evening of that lot is enough, thank you, but if you can face it . . .'

Susie thought of the dazzling Jonjo Bartlett, and the schmoozing she could do at Shoreditch House if she got there a bit early, and said she thought she could face it.

'You are coming to the conference, aren't you?' said Bianca. She was having a Christmas drink with Mike and Hugh. 'It's going to be quite something.'

'Try and stop us,' said Mike.

She hoped it would be quite something. It needed to be. But they were hardly up to speed and with Christmas eating into schedules it was going to be touch and go to get everything together. They would, of course, but the price would be high.

She wasn't looking forward to Christmas much. They were

breaking with tradition and staying in London. This was partly down to Patrick, who had been the one – astonishingly – to suggest it. He usually loved the whole country thing, the Boxing Day meet, the halfway hike as they called it, across the fields on Christmas Day in between main course and pudding, decorating the house. She became less astonished by his change of heart when he announced that he had invited Saul and Dickon for Boxing Day supper.

'You don't mind, do you, darling? Christmas is clearly grim for him because Dickon spends it with his mother and Saul's on his own. Boxing Day they go to Kempton Park, and you know I've always been sad missing that, and he suggested we should all go.'

'Patrick,' said Bianca, 'I am not going to spend Boxing Day at a race meeting, OK? Milly and Ruby would hate it!'

'They might not – Fergie's very excited about the idea and—'

'What? You've talked to Fergie about this before you talked to me?'

'He and Dickon chatted about it after judo, apparently. Dickon said it wasn't that much fun going alone with his dad and I just thought it would be great for him – and Saul, of course. Anyway, Milly said only last year that she'd like to spend Christmas in London sometimes, see her friends.'

'Milly doesn't seem to have any friends at the moment,' said Bianca rather sadly.

'Really?'

'Patrick, I keep telling you! Not one Christmas card from school. She pretended she'd left them behind but I know that wasn't true.'

'I don't remember you telling me that.'

'I expect you were thinking about your friend Saul at the time.'

'Oh, don't be so ridiculous,' said Patrick. 'I'd have heard you saying that. Unless you tacked it on to the end of a long diatribe about how the VCs wouldn't let you have any more money for your shops and how short-sighted that was. I do tend to drift off after half an hour or so of that . . .'

'Oh, shut the fuck up!' said Bianca.

Patrick left the room, closing the door very quietly. She looked at it, startled. She almost never swore, and certainly not at Patrick. What was happening to them all?

'I just called to say thank you for the invitation.' It was Saul. 'Dickon's over the moon.'

'You're very welcome.'

'I hope so.' Long silence.

'I probably won't be coming to the race meeting though,' she said, 'or the girls.'

'Oh really? That's a pity.'

He rang off as he always did, abruptly. Bianca sighed; he wasn't going to be exactly a fun addition to their table.

She went upstairs. Milly's door had a 'do not disturb' sign on it but she could hear her voice going on and on, and occasionally a giggle. Well, at least she wasn't lying there weeping.

She tried Ruby; her door was open, but she was completely engrossed in the last *Harry Potter* book.

'Mummy! Can't talk now.'

Fergie's door was shut; she knocked on that.

'Who is it?'

'It's Mum.'

'What do you want? I'm busy.'

So this was where it all led, all those years of exhaustion and caring and worrying and mess and a love that was as unconditional as love could be: to closed doors and an instruction to go away. She wanted to cry.

She went downstairs again, very slowly, reflecting upon herself, and the mess she was making of just about everything: her family, her marriage and the company she had taken on so blithely and hopefully and which was getting the better of her, it seemed, day by day. It seemed almost alive to her at that moment, the House of Farrell, not just a collection of products, of offices, laboratories; not merely marketing tactics, balance sheets, business plans; but another wilful child, draining and hideously dependent.

But it was all down to her; she alone had to save it, make it work again. If she failed, a great deal would be lost; not just millions of pounds, but professional reputations, personal pride, and indeed, people's very livelihoods. It was those people who mattered, above all, lured by her vision and her promises, all to be flung into the wilderness of unemployment if she failed.

And so – she couldn't. She had to hold on. And she had to win.

This was bad. People had definitely started to notice. There really was nothing worse, she thought, than being apparently stood up in a public place. Especially in a place where appearances of every sort were majorly important.

She'd been early, and settled into a deep sofa in the Square Bar at Shoreditch House. That was fine, it wasn't exactly full and the only other people there were also on their own and clearly waiting for friends. She pulled out her phone and started checking on her emails and then switched to Twitter. God, what did people do in this situation, before there were smartphones?

She ordered an Apple Cooler and sat sipping it as slowly as she could, sat back, trying to look relaxed. She'd dressed with huge care; chic but not showy – cream skirt (Zara) and brown knee high boots (Office) and a very pale pink silk shirt (Hugo Boss), with long full sleeves and a floppy collar, cut quite wide at the neckline. She'd gone out and bought it at lunchtime, not for tonight, obviously, just because it would be so useful over Christmas. Then she'd noticed the pale grey sweater she was wearing looked a bit worn, and she wanted to look – well, nice for this evening, so she decided to wear the shirt, which told the world its wearer knew exactly what was what, without trying too hard. Her hair was at the perfect stage too, a week out of being trimmed, highlights perfect; that was lucky.

All she needed now was someone sitting on the sofa with her . . .

The place began to fill up. Mostly newspaper journalists from Wapping; she recognised several people, including Jane Moore from the *Sun*. She'd met Jane once or twice; she was really nice. She waved at her slightly nervously; Jane waved back, said, 'Hi, lovely to see you. Just going upstairs.'

Susie hoped she'd thought someone was getting her a drink from the bar . . .

A text arrived from Jonjo; she'd taken the precaution of swapping numbers with him earlier. Just as well: *Sorry running bit l8 order a drink cu 6.30*. She texted back *Fine* and reached for an *Evening Standard* someone had abandoned.

'Susie, hi. Lovely to see you.' It was Flo Brown, the lovely woman's editor of the *News*; she was really friendly, sat down for five minutes, chatting, asking how things were. Susie could have kissed her. Actually, she did kiss her. Flo's actor boyfriend joined them, briefly, and then two more friends: please, Jonjo, arrive now while I'm looking cool and popular. He didn't. Then they left to go upstairs and eat. Please, please, Jonjo don't arrive now, while I'm looking such an obvious no-mates. He didn't.

It was almost seven. Bloody Guinevere. Had to be her fault. Had to. Although she was feeling quite irritated with Jonjo as well now.

Maybe she should go to the loo; that would pass five minutes. She slipped her phone into her bag, stood up: as she did so she heard a text arriving. No doubt to say they were going to be even *l8-er*. She was fumbling for it, when: 'Susie! I'm *so* sorry. Got stuck in hideous traffic and I ran the last quarter mile.' He did look quite flushed and was breathing heavily. 'Guinevere's given up, got to meet some critic, she sends her apologies. God, I'm sorry, really rude – what are you drinking?'

He looked even more amazing today in his City suit and white shirt, dark hair ruffled. He really was – well, something else. Lucky, lucky Guinevere.

'You needn't have worried,' she said, kissing him briefly on the cheek, wondering what kindly god had seen off Guinevere for her, even if just for an evening. 'Honestly I've been quite happy, chatting to people.'

'No, well, it was bad,' he said, 'specially as we invited you and after what you did for Guinevere. It's been tweeted round the world, that picture. What are you drinking?'

'It was an Apple Cooler, but I'm a bit tired of it.'

'How do you feel about champagne cocktails?'

'I feel great about champagne cocktails,' said Susie, laughing.

'Me too. They do good ones here. Look – you grab those two seats over there, I'll get the drinks.'

'So – how's it working for Bianca?' said Jonjo when they were settled. 'She and Patrick are my best friends – well, Patrick really, but she's been so kind to me too. I love her.'

'She is great. And she's wonderful to work for. Of course.'

She could hardly tell him how totally bloody it was.

'And were you there before her, or did she bring you in?'

'She kept me in,' said Susie, grinning. 'I was leaving and she persuaded me to stay.'

'Cool.'

'Yes, and it's all very exciting. Relaunch of the brand coming up, lots to do.'

'I don't know much about cosmetics,' said Jonjo, 'except the size of the market of course. Mega.'

'Yes, bigger than the car industry, I believe. Well people, women anyway, will pay anything for dreams. Dreams and promises.'

'Promises? Not the actual thing, eternal youth and all that.'

'I couldn't possibly comment,' said Susie, laughing.

'Oh, OK. Must be fun, though, your job.'

'Oh, it is. Huge fun.' Liar, liar! 'How about yours?'

'Well, I like it. It keeps me awake through the day.'

'And what exactly do you do? I mean, I know you're a trader, but . . .'

'I'm a foreign exchange trader. We speculate on the fluctuation values of currencies – it's all a big gamble, really. I love it. It's high pressure, very much non-stop, quite exciting at times. And we have a lot of fun during the day, lot of laughs, bit boy's own, all totally politically incorrect of course.'

'Yes.' Susie had heard about this. 'I imagine you don't have any girl traders?'

'A couple. Hired for their looks rather than their brains, though. Feminists keep out. You a feminist?'

'Um, yes, of course,' said Susie primly.

'You don't look like one,' said Jonjo.

'Is that a compliment?'

'Yeah, course.' He grinned again.

'Thank you.'

'Guinevere is a feminist. Or thinks she is. She talks the talk anyway. Not sure about walking the walk. Want another?'

Susie's glass was still half-full and her head was beginning to spin – the champagne cocktail had been extremely strong on top of the Apple Cooler, and she hadn't eaten anything since a Danish on her way to the office.

'No I'm fine,' she said, 'thank you. But could you grab some nibbles, nuts or something?'

'Sure. Oh God!' He looked at his phone. 'Guinevere. I'm probably meant to be somewhere – oh, no, hang on – oh, right – she says this critic is taking her out to dinner. I'm not allowed on those gigs.'

'Why not?'

'Because I'm a complete retard when it comes to art. Don't know anything about it. Don't know the words, don't know the people, don't know the galleries even. I got into awful trouble the other night because they all started talking about the Prado and I said I'd got some really cool trainers from them, went on about how special they were, the America Cup ones, you know, they're patent leather, and they all just stared at me.'

'Oh my God,' said Susie, giggling, 'you thought they meant Prada!' This struck her as quite extraordinarily funny.

'That's it. I mean, honestly you'd think I'd killed a puppy, the evils I got. None of them spoke to me the rest of the evening.'

'It's all so stupid, that snobbery,' said Susie. 'It goes on in my business as well, the girls from the glossies can hardly bring themselves to speak to the mass market weeklies and then there's the totally unbridgeable gap between the magazine journalists and the bloggers. I mean, none of them are exactly curing cancer, are they?'

'Unlikely. Well I'm glad you're not shocked. Guinevere was.'

'Really?'

'Yeah. I almost wasn't allowed to come to the party, forbidden to even mention anything that wasn't about champagne or where to put coats. I'm glad you think it was funny.'

'I think it was hilarious.'

'That's really nice,' he said. And then he just looked at her, smiling, his dark eyes crinkling at the corners the way George Clooney's did – he did look a little bit like George Clooney, actually, a young George Clooney . . . Get a grip, Susie, what are you like?

'You know what, I'm so hungry,' he said suddenly, 'and I know you are. Look, would you'd like to get a bite to eat? Seeing as I've made you so late.'

Oh my God. How amazing. She opened her mouth to say she'd love to, that it would be really nice, and then stopped – didn't it look a bit sad to have nothing on, to be totally available all evening, a week before Christmas?

'I'm all right for a bit,' she said cautiously. That was always a good one. Late dates looked excellent.

'That's fine. We could eat here. Or grab a cab, head up West. Where've you got to be later?'

'Oh – oh, sort of Chelsea way.'

'OK. Well maybe we'd better go there. Come on, I'll get them to call a cab.'

While they were waiting she went to the loo, checked her phone. *Still on for 8?* Well, she wasn't; it was almost that now. She texted back: *Sorry, thing's going on forever. Maybe 9.30–10.*

Then she could text again later – if necessary . . .

Alone in a bar, Henk went into the gents' and punched the door violently.

She came out, smiled at Jonjo; he was looking at his phone.

'This is fine; she's at the Bluebird with those creeps. Oh, did I *say* that?'

'You did.'

He looked stricken.

'OK, what I meant was those *critics*. Here we go, here's our cab, after you.'

She'd slung her coat over her shoulders and it slithered off as soon as she sat down. He tried to help her pull it up again, failed; somehow his arm remained over her shoulders. Just casually. She smiled at him. Just casually . . .

Susie, think what you're doing. He's not yours, he can't be yours, he's the property of a very important high-profile person and anyway, your boss's husband is his best friend.

He looked down at her suddenly, grinned, and kissed her cheek. Just her cheek.

'This is turning into a fun evening.'

'Yes,' she said. 'Yes it is.'

He studied her face, started at her mouth, moved up to her eyes, then her hair.

'You know,' he said, 'you are totally gorgeous. I—'

And then his phone rang; he rummaged in his pocket.

'Excuse me. Guinevere! Hi. Yes. Yes, I see. Oh, but – sorry? But – Guinny – sorry, sorry, Guinevere, you don't like me being with those people. I – what? But actually I'm sort of fixed up for the evening now – what? Oh, just – just . . .'

Just me, Susie thought, just me, the PR who was useful to his girlfriend, and who he was spending the evening with because his own plans had changed.

'It's fine,' she mouthed at him.

'Well, all right. But it could be a bit difficult. Well, it looks quite – rude. Yes, I know those people are important, but—'

Susie waved at him, mouthed, 'Go, go.'

'Yes, all right, Guinevere. Yeah, I'll come over right now. To the Bluebird. Could be a slow journey. Yes, of course I'll do my best. OK. OK. Bye.'

He switched his phone off, looked at her remorsefully.

'I'm sorry. But the original idea was we should spend the evening together. Her and me I mean, so . . .'

Which she then cancelled, Susie thought. Bitch. And now maybe the art critics weren't important enough, or were too dull.

'Honestly, Jonjo,' she said, 'it's fine. Fine. I have to meet these people later, anyway.'

'Yes, I know. But still, I was looking forward to our little supper.'

'You'll have a much nicer one at the Bluebird.'

'Not necessarily. And you won't be there. So where can I drop you? Where do you live?'

She looked out; they were already zooming across Holborn Viaduct. Damn. Too quick. 'I live in Fulham. But I don't want to get all the way out there. Listen, drop me in Sloane Square, presume you're going that way?'

'Sure.'

They sat in silence, the fun fractured, an odd sadness, disproportionate to the nature of their parting, between them. They reached Hyde Park Corner, the back streets of Belgravia absurdly easily – *where was the bloody traffic, come on, just a little jam somewhere, please!*

'OK,' said Jonjo, as they drove down Eaton Place. 'Well, sorry again. And thank you again. It's been really nice. I . . .' And then he did it. He leaned over and kissed her, hard, on the mouth. It was surprising. And lovely. And very, very sexy. And there was something else too, that wasn't just sex; something new to her, a sense of being close to where she had always wished to be, somewhere warm and calm and absolutely in accord with her, the real her, not the cool flirty person she pretended to be.

And then he pulled away and said, very quietly: 'I think it's just as well we're not going to have dinner together. It would have been quite – dangerous.' And then he kissed her again, only this time more thoughtfully, exploring her mouth, his hand in her hair, pushing through it, his tongue working on her – his other hand now moving up her leg, under her skirt, stroking her, pushing at her, and she felt herself filling up with sex. It was the only way she could describe it, leaping, lovely, yearning, sweeping sex. She felt she would have done anything at that moment, taken her clothes off, done it there and then in the taxi, in the middle of Sloane Square; she had never wanted anyone so badly in her life.

'You are very lovely,' he said. 'Very, very lovely. The best thing that's happened to me for a long time. I – oh God!'

'Sloane Square, mate,' said the taxi driver, sliding back his window with a sadistic flourish.

And Susie pulled down her skirt, hauled her coat from where it had fallen on the floor, shook her hair back, and then, getting out of the taxi rather slowly, said, 'Bye Jonjo, and thank you . . .'

'It was—' he said and then she leaned back in and kissed him, a cool, social kiss, and then slammed the door shut and walked very unsteadily towards the station.

Chapter 34

She had always kept a lot from him – it was an essential part of their relationship. Small, shadowy secrets, as well as bigger, darker ones. If he had known them, any of them, he would have felt sometimes pressured, occasionally irritated and this time, this once-in-a-lifetime, or so she hoped and prayed, heartbroken. If he knew or guessed this, their lives would become immeasurably complicated, dangerous, and changed for ever and so he must not.

She knew exactly when it had happened; firstly, because such occasions were obviously limited, and secondly because it had been so wonderful, so brilliantly, sweetly, astonishingly wonderful that she felt there was something inexorable about its completion. Only, of course, there could be no completion, she thought confusedly, hanging on to common sense determinedly in the hours after they told her that the test had been positive, that she was indeed pregnant, the one thing she had always dreaded so much and that now she was in danger of welcoming.

And it *was* a danger: for she felt, unbidden within her, growing alongside her baby, a small shoot of joy.

She allowed herself a day or two of that, of savouring the joy and the thought of what might be, and then crushed it, ruthlessly and savagely. For it would not be joy, if she allowed it, it would be hardship and unhappiness and a betrayal of everything she truly believed, everything that justified the relationship, and of Cornelius, who she loved and Athina to whom she owed so much and who she also loved – although who would believe that, she wondered, lying

346

awake through a long, long night, staring out at the dark sky.

No, there could be no baby, no child of this union; and she must deal with the situation in her own formidable, clear-sighted way.

She was forty-two. She had thought it would not happen now, which was why she had begun to be just a little careless, had failed to take her pills – the wonderful pills that modern girls took for granted and her generation regarded as near to magical – and therefore missed taking not just one, but two.

They had been in Paris, of course – where else was the sex so wonderful, where else was Cornelius so very much her own, where else did she feel not only physically but emotionally safe? The nights they spent in English places, beautiful to be sure, in small hidden hotels in the heart of the English countryside – never cities, for there were people who knew them, or rather, knew Cornelius and Athina, in every one of them – were often wonderful, but in Paris they owned the world, could contain themselves safely within it. Cornelius who was, by now, extremely rich, had bought a tiny apartment in Passy, just one bedroom and one *salon* on the top floor of a beautiful old building. An attic, really, but still most beautiful with its panelled doors and tall windows opening on to a minuscule balcony. There they would meet and talk and walk around Paris and eat and make love; sometimes only a twenty-four-hour visit for Cornelius, a longer one for Florence, for absences could not be allowed to coincide too precisely. That was when they had come to know Paris so well; every district of it explored and dissected and learned as if by heart.

And that was when Cornelius had bought her the occasional – for she would not allow it very often, being proud as well as cautious – beautiful dress or coat or pair of shoes. This was the time when almost every Englishwoman was dressed as a milkmaid, courtesy of Laura Ashley, or in the muted Biba-chic of dark skinny jersey dresses or long black coats, coloured suede boots laced to the knee, and wild, long hippy curls. But Parisian women were still classically stylish in slender dresses and cardigan suits.

Athina, at forty-seven, was at the peak of her beauty, her ice-blond hair slicked back from her lovely, sculptured face, and photographed by every famous photographer for *Vogue*, *Queen*, *Tatler*, dressed mostly by Saint Laurent or the ubiquitous Jean Muir and Ossie Clark, feted, admired, adored.

Cornelius would take her to Paris on shopping trips, albeit brief ones, for Athina would seldom allow them to be away together. Those were the times Florence hated; she could see the necessity, but knowing they were together, staying usually at the George V, in the city she and Cornelius had claimed as their own, made her physically ill with jealousy. Yet she never told Cornelius, never complained – for what right had she – and would work twelve-hour days at the arcade, refusing to go home to her little house until she was so absolutely exhausted that she was fit only for collapsing into bed.

The love-making that had left her with child had been one long, dark weekend in early November when she and Cornelius had scarcely ventured outside, so fog-ridden were the Parisian streets and so cold the air. The apartment was cold in spite of the small real fire and endless electric ones but Cornelius had acquired a very dashing long fur coat, Dr Zhivago style, which he spread across their bed and there they stayed for almost the entire two days.

'I shall never be able to wear this coat now without thinking of you, Little Flo,' he said, laying it tenderly over her as she rejoined him after fetching some champagne. 'I shall see you, and I shall feel you, and above all I shall hear you, those disgracefully loud noises that you make, the sound of love. Oh, Florence, how lovely you are.'

She was ignorant about pregnancy for she had had no occasion to discuss it as married women did throughout their lives, and certainly about anything to do with terminating it. Lurid visions of hot baths and gin and backstreet butchery were the nearest and she had no intention of submitting herself to either. She had an idea that abortion was now legal and she went to the library and looked it up; it seemed that a termination of pregnancy, as defined in the 1967 Abortion Act, could be legally conducted by a doctor in a hospital 'providing that continuing the pregnancy could be deemed necessary to prevent grave permanent injury' to her physical or mental health, and that two medical practitioners were required to sanction it. She read this in growing distress, could see there could be considerable barriers to achieving the swift and efficient removal of her baby. Weeks could pass as she saw doctors, attended clinics, waited for beds; weeks of unhappiness and fear and sickliness and indeed, danger, for her condition might manifest itself to others. Athina had the sharpest eyes and might spot an ongoing nausea, or even a thickening waistline and burgeoning bosom, for Florence was bird-thin.

No, it must be done swiftly and discreetly and her best hope, she decided, was a visit to the expensive gynaecologist she saw regularly, a glamorous and worldly woman, who cheerfully issued prescriptions for Florence's pill and even asked her from time to time how her sex life was and how her affair was going.

Everything went as she had hoped; Jacqueline Wentworth, sitting in her very grand rooms in Harley Street, confirmed her pregnancy, was most generous with her advice, and said she was absolutely sure Florence was doing the right thing.

'And no silly guilt – apart from all the other people who would be made unhappy by your having that baby, he or she would not have the best of lives.' Two thousand pounds would see her safely into a clinic in the wilds of rural Kent – 'It's really delightful there, lovely grounds and rooms and the most charming staff . . .' – the possession of the two signed letters, and a painless and extremely safe conclusion to her pregnancy.

Florence's initial relief was slightly tempered by the fact that she didn't have two thousand pounds or anything near it.

She wondered if she might mortgage her house, but that, it seemed, would take several weeks, and the largest bank loan she could obtain was five hundred pounds.

She was fretting over where she might turn when she found herself staring at Leonard Trentham's painting, the one of the Parisian courtyard, given to her, she was sure, by Cornelius – although it was one of his teases that he refused to admit it. She could sell that if it was sufficiently valuable, and she could get it copied, easily, although possibly not quite in time. But Cornelius seldom came to her little house, would never spot a good fake. She took it down from the wall, wrapped it carefully in brown paper, and set off in the morning for an art gallery in St James's where she often went to exhibitions; the owner, Jasper Stuart, was always welcoming and indeed friendly. She had once told him that she owned a Leonard Trentham and he had said that if she ever wanted to sell it, he would be waiting with his arms open.

'My dear Miss Hamilton, what an absolutely wonderful opportunity! Of course I will sell it for you, it would be an honour to have it on our modest walls, it's—'

'When?' said Florence, interrupting him. 'How quickly could you sell it?'

Jasper Stuart rallied from this rather unseemly haste and said he was having an exhibition of English watercolours in the next couple of months. Would that be soon enough for her?

'Not really,' said Florence. 'I need the money most urgently. I shall have to take my picture elsewhere. I really can't wait two months.'

'Oh dear . . .' Jasper Stuart hesitated. 'Oh, Miss Hamilton that would be such a pity. I could make some inquiries, and if there was any interest I could advance you a sum which would approximate to the value of the Trentham – minus my commission, of course.'

'Of course. And – and how much do you think . . .'

'Oh, I think it would be valued at around . . .' He paused theatrically, then, 'At around a thousand pounds, maybe fifteen hundred?'

'That's not enough,' said Florence briskly. 'My own research indicated that Trenthams were priced much more highly than that.'

'Well, perhaps the sources of your own research might be persuaded to take the picture on—'

'Not possible,' said Florence, and this was the first truthful thing she had said that morning. 'The person in question is an art critic, writing for one of the glossy magazines.'

'Which one?'

'*Rural Life*, the one with all the beautiful houses. Perhaps you know him? Joseph Saunders?'

She was safe there; Joseph Saunders, her friend, and indeed a highly esteemed art critic, had once described Jasper Stuart to her as a poisonous little poofter who he would not be willing to exchange the time of day with.

'Well, I know the name of course,' said Stuart, slightly tetchy now. 'And what value did he put on your Trentham?'

Joseph Saunders had actually said it was a very nice example of Trentham's work, that they were out of fashion at the moment, but if she was lucky, she could get up to fifteen hundred for it.

'Two thousand pounds,' said Florence, her lovely eyes meeting Jasper Stuart's slightly watery ones.

'Less commission, I imagine?'

'Absolutely. But I'll take it elsewhere, Mr Stuart, I really don't want to pressurise you.'

'No, no, Miss Hamilton, I'll make some inquiries and get back to you in – what shall we say? Three or four days?'

'That would be very kind,' said Florence. 'And there is something else. I am very fond of that painting and for reasons of sentiment I would like to have it really well copied. Can you recommend anyone?'

Jasper Stuart said he could; he looked after her small figure clutching the painting and on her way to the copyist and wondered what sort of difficulty she might be in; presumably she'd got into debt with one of those new-fangled credit cards. He reached for the phone and dialled the number of one of his clients, a very rich American, and they had a deal within ten minutes. The man said that three thousand sounded very fair if it was a genuine Trentham and Jasper Stuart said that of course it was, and a very charming one too.

The night before she had to go into the nursing home, Florence hardly slept. She was suddenly attacked by the thought of what she was keeping from Cornelius. The baby was his as well as hers; was

351

she really right to keep it from him, this tiny, enormously important thing they had created together?

She changed her mind hourly, feeling at one and the same time she would be causing him enormous grief by telling him about it, and sparing him a great deal of angst and guilt if she did not. Days might pass as he wondered what to do, if she told him, and time was crucial.

And then, even as she decided not to tell him, never to tell him, she was assailed by a most painful and difficult grief and remorse of her own: that she was removing most ruthlessly from her body a living, breathing creature, entrusted to her to nurture and protect. Would the baby be alive when it was taken from her? And if so, how long would it take to die? Would it suffer? And what would happen to it then?

She tried to recall the reassurance given her from Jacqueline Wentworth: 'Do remember, Miss Hamilton, we're talking something the size of perhaps a quail's egg. It doesn't have any feelings (how could she know? How could anyone know?) and if doubts should assail you, and they probably will, think of the sort of life you could give this child, bringing it up alone as an unmarried woman, with very few resources.'

It was her last words that helped Florence to feel she was doing the right thing by terminating the pregnancy. She was above all a pragmatist, and it was hard to contemplate with optimism the long-term future of this child of hers.

And so, as the day dawned and she rose and put the last few things into her case and took a taxi to Charing Cross, she settled into a rather soothing certainty that her decision was the right one, and embarked upon the necessary action with a heart that, if not light, was courageous and positive.

Nevertheless, as the anaesthetist's smiling, rather smug face came into her room to give her her pre-meds, she felt a hostility and a misery she would not have believed, and when she came round from the operation, to a smiling nurse assuring her that all was well, she felt not relief and happiness, but guilt and sorrow and a dreadful remorse that she had flown in the face of nature and not done for her baby what every instinct told her she should have done, that ripping it out of her body had been a wicked thing to do, and that she had deprived herself of perhaps some of the greatest joys, as well as difficulties, that she would ever be likely to know.

She felt better in the morning, having set her tough, determined mind to work, and telling herself that what was done was done, and that there was little point in doing it if she was now to waste emotion on grieving over it.

She returned to work after a week – she had pleaded flu – her charming, confident self, full of plans for the Christmas she was to spend with Duncan's family who adored her. But the first time she saw Cornelius after the termination, she had the strongest urge to attack him physically, to bite him, scratch him, generally inflict upon him any pain she could; no one would ever know, she thought, the cost of the sweet, fleeting smile she gave him as he walked into the shop with Athina and wished her Happy Christmas; and when she attended the Christmas crib service she broke down in spite of all her intentions and wept quietly into her handkerchief as the shepherds and the kings knelt before the Baby Jesus and offered him their gifts and their love.

He had called, after two long, hopeful, hopeless days, when she had known he wouldn't, of course he wouldn't, while thinking he might, just might, if only to say – don't be ridiculous Susie, what can he say? He's spoken for, taken, by a woman of unarguable achievement and considerable beauty. Just grow up and regard it as what it was, a fun evening, a little bit of happiness and get on with your life. And stop checking your phone, every five minutes . . .

And then it rang; or rather rippled. With a text. Which she had so determinedly assumed must be from Henk that she refused to look at it for at least thirty – well, all right, maybe twenty seconds, since she was really so extremely busy in writing her speech for the conference and absolutely wasn't going to interrupt her train of thought.

Only, it might be from Bianca; or dear old Bertie who had asked her for a kind of bio of herself, for his speech at the conference, and she hadn't done it yet; so she picked it up from where it lay face downward on her desk, and she was so sure it was from one of those people that she had to read it several times over. Because the name on it was Jonjo Bartlett.

And then it said *Are u free for a drink tonite?*

And feeling extremely light-headed she went to the loo, taking her phone with her, and sat staring at it for quite a long time. And after a bit she went for a walk down the corridor and bumped into Bertie, who said, 'Hello, Susie, I wondered if you'd got a minute?' And she said, 'Bertie, any number of minutes for you.' Because really, looking at his no doubt incredibly pedestrian speech would be pure, sheer joy at this moment, and he said, 'Maybe in thirty, then?' And then she passed Lara's office, and Lara saw her and called out that she would really love to discuss the running order of the conference again, if Susie had a minute, and Susie said, 'Whenever you like, Lara.' Because that too would be so, so wonderful, debating at great length whether Lara should come on before Jonathan Tucker or after, which was her current preoccupation, and Lara said, 'Maybe in fifteen, then.' And Susie said fine, but she was seeing Bertie in half an hour, so possibly after that might be better, and Lara said OK, and then she went and sat at her desk and felt another and even stronger great rush of happiness, and thought that perhaps a decent interval had now passed in between receiving the text and replying and settled down to the hugely important task.

She had reeled home that first evening, filled with the sense of him, thinking that it had been a lovely evening, a lovely happening in her life, a life rather drained of lovely happenings recently, and that he would now go back to Guinevere who had him so clearly and absolutely possessed.

And she must go back to Henk, who had abased himself, telling her how much he loved her, how desperately he missed her, how he was going to see a shrink, how he was determined to prove to her that he had changed, that he would not expect her to believe him without that proof, but if she would only give him the chance, he would. And struggled to tell herself that the heaviness in her heart, the doubt in her head, was merely the natural result of so much disappointment and disillusion and even fear. If only she had waited just a little bit longer . . .

So what, exactly, should she say now? How should she respond to this amazingly beautiful invitation? She started saying *Yes, cool* only that sounded a bit corny and then changed it to *Yes, great*, only that sounded a bit keen and changed that to *Yes, think so*, only that sounded a bit too unkeen and changed that to *Sounds good, when?* and was just going to change it again when Bertie walked in, looking nervous and said was it a good moment because she looked a bit distracted and she said, 'No, no, Bertie, it's fine.' And pinged the text off.

And while Bertie was still rustling pages Jonjo's text came back saying *Cool, 6.30, Ivy Club OK?* and she had to reply straight away with *Fine, see you there* and then devote herself to Bertie's speech, which, instead of being dreadfully dull as he had promised, was amusing and charming and warm and all about how he, too, was new to the company in a way, and certainly to the job, and enjoying it very much and he hoped everyone else was enjoying it too. And then moved on to introducing and welcoming each department and the new people therein, personally, one by one.

It was so good that Susie insisted on getting Lara in to listen to it, and when Lara had listened and admired the speech too, she said they might as well all look at the running order together with Bertie as well, if Susie didn't mind, and Susie, who wouldn't have minded at that moment being asked to scrub out the lavatories with a toothbrush, said what a good idea, so they did that, and then Lara said crikey, which was one of her favourite words, it was five thirty already and what about a drink at the wine bar, and Susie said no, she couldn't, she was meeting someone at the Ivy Club at six thirty and felt herself blushing, as if they could have known who that someone was, and fled to the loo to get ready, while noticing, albeit subliminally, that Lara said, 'Just you and me then, Bertie, that OK?' and that Bertie was smiling at her in a slightly goofy way and saying, 'Of course.' And noticing also that Bertie had most definitely lost a lot of weight and was wearing a very nice shirt and that Lara was smiling back at him, in a way that could only be described as enthusiastically, and that when she joined Susie in the ladies' she started spraying herself with perfume and applying lip gloss to her already quite shiny mouth, while clearly not wishing to engage in any kind of girly chat. But it was only subliminal and Susie's mind was far too occupied for anything to surface further.

She couldn't see Jonjo at first, and feared a repeat of the Shoreditch House fiasco, but he suddenly appeared behind her as she stood at the desk and made her jump and said, 'Hello . . .' in that voice of his that sounded like well-chambré'd red wine.

'Hi,' she said, smiling at him, and he leaned forward and kissed her, only socially, of course . . .

'Come on in. You look lovely. Great shoes.'

'Thank you.' God, she loved men who noticed shoes. It was really sexy . . .

He ushered her to a table, sat her down, asked her what she'd like to drink; she decided wine would be safer than cocktails, and he ordered a Pinot Grigio and a beer for him, and then sat smiling at her.

'You look lovely,' he said again.

'Thank you,' she said again.

'Busy day?'

'Oh – yes. Very. You?'

'No, not really. The markets close down, more or less, this time of year. Lot of drinking though, so a really heavy lunch. Your life must be one long party too, I suppose.'

'Well, I actually had lunch at my desk, today.'

'Oh no, that's a shame.'

'I don't mind. I'm not a great luncher. I'm just so pleased there's this new thing for brunches and breakfast and things. Then you get into the office and there's still a lot of day left.'

'So where do you go for these power meals? I presume they are powered.'

'Sometimes. Sometimes pretty powerless,' said Susie, laughing. 'Oh, the usual places like the Wolseley, Brown's Hotel, Cecconi's

– they do a mean breakfast there. My totally favourite place at the moment is the Delaunay, have you been there?'

'No, I haven't. Is that a mistake?'

'Huge. It's gorgeous – very much the grand cafés of Middle Europe with really good eggs benedict, and even kippers.'

'Kippers! Oh, my God, do I like kippers! How amazing. Well, I shall go there very soon in that case. Maybe even with you.'

'That would be nice.'

There was a silence. Then 'So – plans for Christmas?'

'Oh, not very exciting. Home to my parents. You?'

'Same. Well, with my mum.' Not Guinevere then. That was – well, it was good. No, it was – great. 'We do it every year,' he went on, 'and sometimes, if I'm lucky, my sister and her husband and kids join us, and they are this year. They're divorced,' he added, 'my parents, I mean.'

'And – is your mum married again?'

Was that too personal a question? She hoped not. It seemed relevant.

'No, she never did. My dad did, unfortunately. To someone I can't stand. But hey. That's life. And Mum's great.'

'What does she do? Or doesn't she?'

'She's in the home dec business.'

'Oh cool,' said Susie and promptly felt silly.

'Yeah, she's very good at it. She lives in Cheltenham, so a lot of nice houses to work on. My dad's in the property business, that's how they met. But it didn't last. She's too nice for him,' he added with a rather surprising candour. 'What about yours?'

'My dad's a solicitor. Not the sort that makes buckets of money out of divorces, just a family solicitor. They live in Bath, all rather cosy.'

'Lucky you. And your mum?'

'She teaches geography at a girls' school.'

'And you have sisters and brothers?'

'One of each. Both married, both live in London, my sister's about to have a baby.'

'So you're going to be an auntie. Cool.'

'Yes, I'm looking forward to it.'

'Guinevere's an auntie,' he said. It was the first time he had acknowledged her existence this evening. Susie braced herself. 'Complete brat,' he added. 'Its mother's a fashion designer, truly terrible clothes, and its dad's a sound engineer. It had three nannies at the last count. How's the wine? Want another?'

'Lovely. Yes please.'

'I was married,' he said suddenly.

'Oh. Really?' What else could you say to that? She felt nervous suddenly.

'Yeah. Terrible mistake. On her part, anyway.' He grinned at her, his brown eyes crinkling at the corners in their Clooney-like way. 'Lasted about a year. No kids, thank God.' He looked at her thoughtfully. 'And what about you? Is there a deeply significant other, Miss Harding?'

'That French bike company you were interested in . . .' Patrick's voice was at its most diffident.

Saul's was at its most impatient. 'What about it?'

'I've been looking at it for a bit now. I think it could be dodgy. Over and over again, they're declaring money's in the bank, when if you really look, and it's very well hidden, down in note ninety-two, I think it is, you can work out it's *owed* to them; they haven't got it yet. Only a few days over, but of course it adds up. Anyway, their share price is going up all the time and they look like they're flying, and bikes are huge. But . . .'

How could this be so fascinating, Patrick wondered, this apparently dry-as-dust information? But it was. That facet alone of his new job never ceased to amaze him.

'OK. Look, I've got to go. Keep it up, Patrick.'

'I will. See you at Kempton. George VI should be really good this year.'

'I reckon so. Sorry Bianca won't be there.'

'Won't she?'

'She said not.'

Patrick went back to his office, frowning.

Milly was finding it very difficult to feel remotely interested in Christmas. The thought of going in for the usual careful, excited shopping she did left her feeling totally sick. She could just about manage presents for Ruby and Fergie, she decided, both of whom had tried to be kind, but her parents deserved nothing. They hadn't recognised the depth of her misery, or the trouble she might be in – and she could be pregnant or doing drugs for all they knew; they hadn't gone to school – however deep her misgivings, it would have shown they really seriously cared – and demanded an explanation.

The only person she wanted to give a proper present to now was Jayce who, in the two weeks since she had met her, had been her greatest comfort, her linchpin, her confidante. And so she had bought her a beautiful friendship bracelet from Links, which Jayce would gaze at for hours every time they went shopping and say how gorgeous it was. It had cost her over a hundred pounds, more than two-thirds of the Christmas money her mother had put in her bank account, and every time she looked at it she felt, in some strange way, better.

She went to meet Jayce every day at the shopping centre and they would chat for hours, sitting in McDonald's (Jayce's favourite) or, if Milly could persuade her, which was difficult, for a walk outside and once, which had been very difficult indeed, but it was a lovely day, to catch the bus up to Primrose Hill and walk there.

Jayce puffed beside her as they walked to the top, then sank gratefully on to one of the benches, gazing at the view.

'It is nice, I'll say that,' she said. 'I've never been up here, but I can see on a nice day like this why people like it.'

'I love it,' said Milly. 'Or used to. We came here for picnics when Fergie and I were little, rode our bikes round, that sort of thing.'

'But you don't no more?'

'Well, no. Thing is, we've got the house in the country now—' She stopped, aware she had been less than tactful; Jayce stared at her.

'Thought you lived near here?'

'Yes, well I do. But we've got this other place. Honestly, it's really rubbish, sort of a cottage—'

'You've got two houses? Your family? No one else like sharing it or anything?'

'Well, not really. But honestly, Jayce, it's so not grand or anything. It's just – well, you know, for the – the—'

She stopped. Clearly to say 'just for the weekends' would sound worse. 'Just some weird idea of my parents,' she finally finished lamely. 'It's quite boring, after a bit. I mean, I'd never go there if I didn't have to.'

'I'd like to,' said Jayce. 'I really would. You're lucky, Milly, I'd say.'

She smiled at Milly; and Milly thought how nice she was, so devoid of envy or resentment. Yet her home sounded like an invention for reality TV: there were five children, of whom Jayce was the middle one. 'There's Stash, he's my mum's eldest, he's seventeen, he's quite nice to me, and then there's my other half-brother Zak, he's like totally vile, and then Paris, she's nine and Cherice is two.'

'And they're your real sisters?' asked Milly carefully.

'God no. I wish they was, but they're my mum's with her new boyfriend, he's a bit of a bully. He doesn't live with us all the time, thank God, but when he comes, we all have to watch it. Paris can deal with him, she's his favourite, but Cherice, she really gets up his nose. Mind you, she's properly annoying. She put Stash's iPod down the toilet last week. He thumped her well hard, she screamed for hours, anyway, then Ryan, that's Mum's boyfriend, he turned up and said he'd get Stash a new one if everyone would shut up and let him have a bit of peace.'

Milly listened, fascinated. It all sounded a lot more interesting than her own family.

Jayce pulled out a couple of Hobnobs from her pocket; she kept a supply permanently about her person, in case of emergencies.

'Want one?'

Milly shook her head.

'So how's it with them girls today? Had anything from them?'

'Not much,' said Milly.

Only a text saying *Do hope you're enjoying shopping with your lovely new friend. We all thought she looked just GREAT. Lovely skin.*

And a whole lot of stuff on Facebook about what a great time they'd all had skating at Somerset House the day before and so sorry she hadn't been there. Lots and lots of pictures of them and then one of a big group, all laughing and sticking out their tongues and then *You should take your new friend skating, Mills, wouldn't hurt her at all to fall down, lots of padding.*

They'd made Milly so angry she'd nearly replied. It was all very well them being mean to her, but to pick on Jayce, with whom they had no quarrel at all, that was just so horrible. Milly looked at Jayce, at her good-natured, plump face and thought she'd really be quite pretty if she wasn't so spotty. But they'd just come back even worse. Ignoring them was the only way.

'Milly! Hello!'

It was Ruby, Ruby and one of her friends, both on their scooters, and the friend's mother. Milly stared at them in horror.

'Hello, Milly,' said the mother, clearly wondering what on earth Milly was doing with Jayce. 'Lovely to see you. We're just off to see the new *Shrek* film. I'd ask you to join us but I expect it'd be much too babyish for you.'

'Oh, please Milly!' Ruby was always so proud of her big, cool sister, and her friends were so impressed. 'Please come!'

'No, no,' said Milly, horribly aware that the mother was looking worriedly at Jayce, in case she had to invite her too. She knew she should have introduced Jayce to them, but she couldn't face that. 'No, we're going to have lunch. Thanks though,' she added. 'Come on, Jayce.'

And she pulled Jayce up from the seat, and set off briskly down the hill.

'You could at least have let me tell Saul you weren't coming to Kempton on Boxing Day,' said Patrick. 'It's rude enough without him having to hear it from you.' He glared at Bianca over the

361

omelette she had made for their supper, before going out to Fergie's Christmas play.

'Oh, for God's sake,' said Bianca, 'what difference does it make? He needed to know, he mentioned it, I told him.'

'It just looks – bad. He issued the invitation to me, you hardly know him – I'd have liked to reply properly, for both of us.'

'Patrick Bailey, you are insane,' said Bianca, trying to turn it into a joke. 'Like I said, you act like you're in love with him, or something.'

'Don't be so absurd. When did you tell him anyway?'

'When he rang up to thank me for having him and Dickon on Boxing Day. It was a perfectly natural opportunity to tell him. He was saying how good it would be and—'

'And you just pour cold water on the whole idea. Without telling me you'd told him. He's my boss, Bianca, not just any old acquaintance.'

'I—'

There was a ring at the door and Bianca went to answer it. She was a while, talking in the hall, then came back frowning.

'Who was that?'

'Joanna Richards. She brought Ruby back. She – well, she just told me something. She was obviously embarrassed, but she said she felt she had to.'

'What?' said Patrick.

'She said she saw Milly on Primrose Hill today, with – with a girl. Apparently this girl was very working class. Overweight, that sort of thing.'

'Do remind me never to invite the Richards to this house again,' said Patrick, 'if that's the sort of thing they feel they should tell us.'

'Patrick, please. You know how odd Milly's been lately. Withdrawn, miserable, never sees her old friends. I just wondered – well, it's horribly easy at that age to get in with a bad lot. And she's never mentioned this girl to us.'

'And what would she say if she did? Oh, hello, Mummy and Daddy, I've got a new friend, she's a bit common and quite overweight, you'd really like her. Are you mad, Bianca? Milly's thirteen, this sort of thing is bound to happen, she'll want to make interesting new friends, not just the old gang.'

'She didn't sound very interesting,' said Bianca.

'Oh really? And how could the delightful Mrs Richards tell that? Did she try to engage with her in conversation about the political situation? Or maybe she suggested a new diet the girl might try—'

'Oh, just shut up,' said Bianca wearily, 'and don't blame me if it turns out Milly's getting into drugs or something.'

'Which of course all young working-class people, especially overweight ones, are. I'm disappointed in you, Bianca, I really am.'

'So you don't think we should even mention this girl to Milly? Ask her who she is?'

'You can. I'm certainly not going to. Anyway, we must go, we'll be late for the play. Is Milly coming?'

'She said she would, but she's still up in her room.'

As if on cue, Milly arrived. She was dressed to go out, wearing rather more eye make-up than usual.

'Shouldn't we go? We don't want to be late for Fergie.'

'Of course not. Um – had a nice day, darling?'

'Yes, thanks.'

'What did you do?'

'Oh, you know. Went shopping, and stuff.'

'On your own? With friends?'

'Mostly on my own, not that it matters. Look, come on, you know you can never park anywhere near that place. And Fergie'll be so upset if we're late. Not that you'd care,' she added under her breath.

'Milly, what did you say?'

'Nothing. Just come *on*!'

Chapter 35

So why had she said that? Why had she said that there wasn't a
significant other? Well, of course she knew why, because she didn't
want things to go in any but the best possible way. And, in a way it
was true. Only of course it wasn't. It was just that she could make it
true quite easily. Well . . .

So she had said it, had said no, there wasn't and he'd looked
seriously pleased. Of course, he didn't *live* with Guinevere, but
there was living together and living together and of course she and
Henk didn't either, not full-time, not any more. She hadn't allowed
that, had said they'd have to see, but most nights he did still stay,
and he was only dossing down on a friend's sofa when he wasn't at
Susie's, so it was a bit different. But what should she have said?
'Well, not exactly. In fact, I'd thrown him out because he knocked
me about but now I've sort of taken him back although we're not
actually living together any more, or sleeping together.' That was
the truthful answer, and she could see it would result in Jonjo
leaving The Ivy pretty swiftly and never calling her again. But
presumably he was sleeping with Guinevere, so . . .

'Oh God,' she said aloud, as she helped her mother clear the
lunch table.

'What was that, dear?'

'Oh, sorry. Nothing. I just – just remembered I hadn't called
someone. I'll do it later.'

'All right dear. Now, are you coming in for drinks with the
Raymonds this evening? I know they'd love to see you.'

364

And because she was feeling so bad about herself and the way she was behaving, Susie said yes, of course, because she knew it would please her parents and some sort of penance might help a bit. She heard her phone go from the sideboard where she had left it; she looked at it.

Happy Christmas! it said. *How's yours? Wish u were here. Jonjo.* And then a kiss. God. She could feel that kiss, just looking at it on the screen. He was an amazing kisser. He had given her another spectacular sample on the night of The Ivy, as she thought of it. They'd sat there for hours, getting drunker and drunker and then he'd suggested they had dinner: 'To make up for the one we didn't have.' So they did, and then he suddenly looked at his watch and said, 'Jesus, it's one o'clock! Look, I'm really sorry, but I'm going to have to take you home. I've got to be in the office by five, don't ask why.'

'Jonjo,' she said, 'you don't have to take me home, I'll just get a cab.'

'Sure? I'll call you one. I feel really bad, but—'

'No, no it's fine,' she said. And she meant it, although she couldn't help feeling just very slightly disappointed, but then when the cab came and she climbed into it after kissing him briefly on the lips, he said, 'Oh shit' and climbed into it beside her.

'I'm sorry,' he said, drawing her to him, his lips already in her hair, 'but I can't deny myself half an hour in a taxi with you.'

And the half hour was an amazing rollercoaster of kissing and stroking and longing and wanting and just sheer sexual excitement, so violent that when they finally reached her street she could hardly move for it.

'Jesus,' he said. 'Jesus. Susie, you are amazing. Extraordinary. I cannot tell you how much I want to – well, you probably worked that out for yourself. But I just have to go home.'

Which was just as well, she thought, as she gave him a last, comparatively brief kiss, as there were, without doubt, traces of Henk in the flat, like his dressing gown hanging beside hers on the bathroom door. It had annoyed her, that, and he promised every time to take it away again, but he hadn't yet.

'Next time, you must come to mine,' Jonjo said. 'I'm a terrible cook, but I have several very good takeaway arrangements. I'll call you. Goodnight. Thank you for a really lovely evening.'

And he banged on the window of the cab and it carried him away.

Only time ran out and it was Christmas and they both had to leave London, so it was down to a quick drink, and a brief snog, and he said, 'I'll see you soon. I'm kind of booked up for New Year and I'm sure you are too.' And she said, yes, she was, of course. Which she wasn't, except for Henk booking her without saying what for, and she could have cancelled that without a qualm – but maybe she could use the occasion to finish things with him . . .

'Coffee, darling?' said her mother.

'Dad! I just heard your phone. You've got a text. Oh, wow you're so cool.' Lucy leaned over in the middle of cracker-pulling and gave her father a kiss.

'A text?' said Priscilla. 'Who on earth would be sending you one of those things, in the middle of Christmas lunch?'

'No idea,' said Bertie, thankful that his phone was in his trouser pocket, rather than left on the hall table. 'I expect it's a charity or something. Or from Orange. They're always telling me I can look at my bill online or some such nonsense.'

'Well, aren't you going to look?'

'No, of course not. Why should I?'

'Well, most normal people would – it's such an odd time to do it.'

'Mum,' said Rob, 'leave him alone.'

Rob had arrived home late on Christmas Eve, after a heavy evening drinking with his mates, too late to go to Midnight Mass which was one of Priscilla's absolute traditions. Such was the degree of favouritism he enjoyed, he had already been forgiven and his interjection now saved Bertie. Priscilla sighed heavily, but then returned to dishing up the Christmas vegetable platter that was the *spécialité* of her *maison*: parsnips and sprouts were joined by carrots, tenderstem broccoli, baby courgettes and squash. In another bowl was red cabbage and in yet another, potatoes mashed with grain mustard. Then there were the pigs in blankets, the roasted potatoes, the— Bertie, who already had indigestion, asked to be excused, went into the loo, and looked at the text. It was from Lara.

Happy Christmas Bertie. Hope you're having fun. Love Lara and then a whole row of kisses. And although he knew she was probably drunk, and that everyone put 'love' on their texts, the row of kisses did seem a little bit special and he sat smiling at it, filled with a warmth that had nothing to do with the Christmas spirit and everything to do with something happy and filled with promise and far removed from Priscilla's indignant, red-faced Christmas exhaustion. Although promise of what he could not imagine.

Much against his will, he deleted the text, for Priscilla was bound to return to the subject, and went back to the table, to be reprimanded for not serving the cranberry sauce, which he had made and which was his particular job. But the warmth, and indeed the happiness, stayed with him for the rest of the day.

Christmas Day had been all right, Bianca thought. Better than she'd feared. She wondered if the heady, magical quality it had once had was gone for ever, and tried to be grown up about it.

Milly had managed to stay cool and sulky until she opened her main present, an iPad, whereupon she got very excited. Bianca was slightly shaken by the modest presents Milly gave her and Patrick, a DVD of *Downton Abbey* for her, and one of *The Killing* for Patrick; Milly usually put an enormous amount of thought into her gifts and these were a bit of a non-event. But she gave lovely things to the others, a new riding whip for Ruby, and two new computer games for Fergie.

Saul only called twice on Christmas Day, one of them to fix a meeting place for Kempton, and Patrick and she called a truce and actually had some very good sex late on Christmas night when the children had gone to bed, which was a long-time tradition of theirs. It was the first time for weeks and she thought of mentioning the fact, but decided not to, mostly because afterwards, when she had finished crying, Patrick told her how very much he loved her and gave her another present – also part of the tradition – a very beautiful silk scarf from Alexander McQueen in the most wonderful muted colours which would go with almost everything in her wardrobe.

Even Boxing Day was all right. Saul, Patrick, Fergie and Dickon arrived home soon after five, and Saul, clearly working very hard at being communicative, talked quite a lot over an early supper and revealed, in a rare piece of soul-baring, that he was completely gutted that his horse hadn't done better at Kempton that day.

'She's done so well recently, three firsts in a row. George, my trainer, decided a couple of months ago she'd do better held at the back of the field for longer, very successful until today and the going was perfect for her, but anyway . . . and I had such hopes for her at Cheltenham.'

Bianca thought it was the longest speech she had ever heard him make.

He brought a couple of bottles of superb claret for Patrick and some vintage Bollinger for her and Dickon was sweet, trailing round after Fergie who was not altogether displeased with the adoration, and they all played charades with the children in the evening. Saul was worse at charades than anyone Bianca had ever known, stiff, unimaginative, embarrassed, but then confounded them all in his third go when he suddenly took off and staggered in, falling over his own feet, the trilby hat he had worn to the races dangling rakishly over one eye, drinking straight from a bottle of whisky, and said he was the Christmas spirit.

As they left, he kissed her on the cheek, and said it had been the best Christmas he could ever remember, which she thought was a sad reflection on all others, and said he hadn't forgotten her shop problem and how was it going?

She said very well, and he asked if she'd persuaded the VCs to give her some more money for the shops; she said no, she hadn't, and he said more fool them.

Patrick asked her, when Saul had gone, why he was so well-informed about the Farrell relaunch and she said, slightly irritably, that she had discussed it with him over dinner in Paris. 'We had to talk about something, and he was very perceptive.'

Whereupon Patrick said Saul was one of the most perceptive men he had ever met, and then thanked her for giving him and Dickon such a nice evening, and he was extremely grateful to her. And they went and sat on the sofa and held hands and watched the *Downton Abbey* DVD. Fergie and Milly came in and saw them and Fergie said, 'Look at them, they're holding hands, yuk or what?' and Milly told them to budge up and sat down with them to watch as well, snuggled up to her father, her hand reaching across him for her mother's. Which was the best moment for Bianca of the whole two days.

Perhaps, she thought, perhaps everything was going to be all right.

Athina had spent Christmas with Caro and Martin at their house.

They exchanged stocking gifts in the morning, then went to church and for a walk and returned for a very nice meal which Martin had cooked – pheasant and then syllabub – and then exchanged proper gifts. Caro presented her mother with a piece of sheet music of 'Let's Fall in Love', actually signed by Cole Porter, and Martin did rather well, giving her a framed cover of *Vogue* dated June 1953, which of course was not only the year of the coronation, but the year Farrell's was launched and it contained a glowing review of the new brand. Athina found herself near to tears by the thoughtfulness of these gifts and Caro, noticing, put her arm round her mother's shoulders – an unheard of event – and said how very brave and wonderful she thought Athina had been over the takeover and that the brand would still be nothing without her mother's style and instinct. Martin then nodded off over his port and Caro and Athina got out some of the old press cuttings and spent a very happy two hours reminiscing and saying that really Bianca Bailey didn't have the slightest idea what she was doing.

There was a very charming photograph of Athina and Cornelius tying a huge red Christmas bow on the door of The Shop in the

Berkeley Arcade and another of Cornelius dressed as Father Christmas inside with Florence, of all people, perched on his knee, his arm round her, she planting a very perky kiss on his cheek.

'How sweet!' Caro said.

'Yes, well, I often thought she had a bit of a crush on him,' said Athina. 'He was always so good to her, of course, so courteous and considerate.'

'She was very pretty, wasn't she?' said Caro thoughtfully. 'Didn't you ever worry she might actually make a play for him?'

'Good heavens, no!' said Athina. 'And even if she had, she was so absolutely not his type. He saw Florence for what she was, which was just a little shop girl, when all was said and done. Poor Florence, what a sad, unfulfilled life she has led.'

She should never have allowed herself to think everything was going to be all right. It was fatal.

But she'd checked and re-checked everything, rehearsed herself, rehearsed everyone else, foreseen problems, worked round them and even Athina seemed rather sweetly agreeable. Bianca looked at her watch: forty-eight hours to go to the start of the conference, the meet and greet. Everything seemed in order. Except – well, except she still didn't have the perfume samples. But Ralph Goodwin had called her to reassure her that they would be with her in the morning. He was bringing them up himself, he said, and wanted to talk her through the fragrance. Bianca had said, slightly testily, that she wanted to smell the fragrance, not be talked through it, and he had said of course, of course, he just wasn't one hundred per cent happy with it yet, but they were very nearly there. She tried not to worry about it; it would be all right, of course it would.

The hotel, a flashily over-impressive pile (but that was what you wanted for a conference) converted from the original Victorian Gothic mansion, with amazing grounds, was ready for their arrival, the ballroom converted into a conference hall, its doorway (at considerable expense) mocked up as the entrance to the Berkeley Arcade shop. Jemima was there now supervising things together with Jonathan Tucker.

Dinner on the first night would be an informal buffet, attended by everyone from the highest to the lowest and absurdly, Bianca felt – but she had had no option but to agree – including the family's personal driver, Colin Peterson, who Athina now rather grudgingly paid herself, and his wife.

'Mrs Bailey, they are to drive me down; how can I possibly turn them away at the door? They can go home in the morning.' The entire Farrell family was to attend, again at Athina's insistence: 'This is still a family firm, and it's important that all the new people should see that for themselves.'

There were a lot of new people, sharp salespeople, newly hired, sassy young beauty consultants, bright young IT people, and this would be their first impression of the company en masse; they needed to be impressed. In rather different ways according to whether the viewpoint was Bailey or Farrell, but impressed nonetheless.

Caro's husband Martin, who rather enjoyed a good sales conference, said that would be very nice, but Priscilla said she was far too busy to give up two whole days and would simply arrive for the meet and greet and the buffet supper and leave after breakfast the following day.

Bianca was to open the conference briefly in the morning, then pass on to the various departments, via Bertie. It was felt that he, as a Farrell, would carry an important link with the past.

Susie was, of course, to do a spot. 'I'll have to blag it a bit,' she said, 'but PR's always so pie in the sky and people love hearing about the beauty editors and bloggers and we can flash endless covers and pages on to the screens while I'm talking.'

She smiled radiantly at Bianca – who thought what a different creature she was from only a few weeks ago. She glowed with sexy confidence, had gone blonder, bought a lot of new clothes, and would clearly, for the men at least, be one of the conference's highlights. Bianca wondered vaguely what had wrought this change and presumed there must be a new boyfriend. She wished, rather wearily, that she could resort to so simple a solution but at the moment she felt the opposite of either sexy or confident and didn't like it.

Tod Marchant and Jack Flynn were coming, of course, and would do a spot, talking about the campaign, with special reference to the perfume launch.

Lara was privately alarmed by Ralph Goodwin's failure to produce any perfume samples. There should have been several along the way for them to try and there had only been one, and it was way off the mark.

She knew Bianca was worried too, just not admitting it. But even if it wasn't perfect, she told herself, he'd do a great job. And the bottle, which they were basing on a fifties Arpège one, was being mocked up to something very close to the real thing.

Lara appeared in Bianca's office now, flushed and slightly breathless.

'The show cards have just arrived and they look wonderful! Have you got time to look at them?'

The showcards were indeed beautiful: glossy, classy, the model's lovely face reflected in a mirror with the products set in front of it. The mirror stood on a counter that just hinted at the Berkeley Arcade; it had been tricky to do, but the agency had masterminded the shot and their eye-watering bill was, Bianca felt, entirely justified.

'Lovely,' said Bianca, 'well done, Lara. You'll unveil them during your bit, I presume, and then I will talk about the perfume. And I thought the model could take it round to them, and that's the practical stuff done, perfume being the icing on the cake, the magic so to speak, and then lunch. In the afternoon I'll talk about the heritage stuff, and The Shop of course, then let Athina have her bloody go – she'll be wonderful, of course – and that'll get them all wound up. Add lots of music and stuff and they'll all be on their feet, cheering. Well, awake at least. Then tea, a few fun and games, and into dinner. It all seems pretty straightforward.' She stopped suddenly and Lara saw the fear in her eyes, put out a hand and touched her arm just briefly.

'It'll be fine,' she said, 'best conference I've ever done, that's for sure.'

'Oh God, I hope so. Everything's riding on it, Lara.'

'Of course. But you've done a fantastic job, Bianca—'

'I hope so. Now all I need is Ralph Goodwin here with his samples and I'll be a completely happy woman. The perfume is so sooo important.'

Goodwin finally arrived after lunch. He was flushed, nervous, and much of the over-smooth charm had gone.

'I'm so sorry, Bianca, to have let it get so late in the day. But at least we have it now.'

'I hope so,' said Bianca briskly.

'Bianca, we do. You'll love it. It's Billie Holiday in a bottle, smoky nightclub and all.'

He opened his briefcase, took out one of many small phials. 'Now remember, you have to let it mature a little before making a judgment.'

'Only a little I hope. If people don't like it straight away they're not going to hang around waiting. You said yourself that top notes were crucial.'

'Of course. But a perfume as rich as this does take a little time.'

'Just bring it on,' said Bianca, holding out her wrist. 'Or rather put it on.'

He opened one of the phials, dabbed the perfume on to her wrist. She sniffed. Sniffed again. And again. And felt sick. And hot. And cold. And panicky.

'Well? What do you think?' Goodwin was smiling a bright, empty smile.

'I think,' said Bianca, and it was difficult to get any words out at all, 'I think it's horrible. Really horrible. More like a hooker's lavatory than Billie Holiday in a nightclub. It's unbelievably ghastly!'

She sent him packing, unable to face his excuses, his rationales, his surprised disbelief, his insistence that she should give it time.

'I don't want to give it time! I want to wipe it off the face of the universe. Please leave. I am shocked that your firm could release something so tacky and – and horrible. I've never felt so let down.'

* * *

She was sitting with her head in her hands, trying to calm herself, trying to think what on earth she should do about this vast black hole created in her personal universe when Lara came in.

'You OK?'

'No. No, I'm not,' said Bianca and she could hear her own voice, struggling to sound calm. 'That perfume was just – just disgusting, Lara. Top notes of Woolworths finest, and an underlying hint of cat piss. Oh God, what am I going to do?'

'Can I smell it?'

Bianca thrust out her wrist.

'Oh God, Bianca, I'm so, so sorry.'

'Lara, unfortunately the pair of us feeling sorry – which of course I do – doesn't help. We are where we are. With no perfume to present tomorrow. Now, I think I'd like to be alone if you don't mind. I need to think.'

'Mrs Clements, I'd like to see Mrs Bailey. Do you know where she is?'

'I'm afraid I have no idea,' said Lara, struggling to smile at Athina. 'She's gone out. She's very busy with the conference, you know and—'

'Well, where is Mrs Pendleton?'

'Jemima is down at the conference hotel, Lady Farrell. Look, unless it's really urgent, I think tomorrow would be better. Bianca may not even come back tonight and—'

'Not come back? But it's only five. I can assure you, in the old days, when I was in charge of this company, I was always here until at least seven.'

Lara went into Bertie's office; he was looking rather wild-eyed, frantically rifling through some papers on his desk.

'Lost something?'

'Only my notes. And would you believe my sanity?'

'Oh Bertie, mine too.'

'What's happened?'

'I can't tell you – oh, what the fuck! Sorry, Bertie. We have a real

374

problem. The perfume is complete shit and it leaves a vast hole in Bianca's presentation tomorrow. I've never seen her so upset. She's gone out now, God knows where. She's as close to panic as I've ever seen her. And I couldn't come up with a perfumier who met our needs so she took Maurice Foulds' suggestion and I feel horribly responsible.'

'Well, you mustn't feel that,' said Bertie. 'She met them, made her own judgment. You cannot blame yourself. You really can't. Why are you smiling?'

'I was just thinking that this is a bit of a role reversal,' said Lara. 'Usually it's me telling you not to blame yourself. I feel better already!'

'How nice if it's done some good,' said Bertie. 'Now if you can only help me find my notes . . . '

'Aren't they on your computer?'

He looked at her and smiled, the quick, brilliant smile that she didn't often see.

'Of course! I'm going crazy. Thank you, Lara.'

'That's all right.' She looked at him, wondering how he could be quite so other-worldly, yet so extremely good at his job. He had even managed to find a replacement model for the next day, since the one they had booked had gone down with flu. The model agencies had had no one of similar calibre but a phone call to Lucy had produced a beautiful friend, Fenella, who had done the make-up course with her.

'I don't suppose you'd like a quick drink after work?' she said now.

'I'd love one, Lara, but I really can't.' His voice was genuinely regretful. 'I've got so much to do before tomorrow. And I mustn't be late home; Priscilla wants to discuss the wretched house before I go off to the conference.'

'I thought she was coming?'

'Only for the supper. She's leaving early the following morning.'

Lara, who had heard of Priscilla's attendance with something approaching horror, albeit of a rather fascinated variety, felt suddenly more cheerful.

'That's a shame,' she said carefully.

'Yes, well she's extremely busy. Now look, you don't know where Bianca is, do you?'

'No, I don't,' said Lara firmly.

'Only my mother wanted to talk to her.'

'Really? No, sorry, can't help. Night, Bertie, see you tomorrow.'

And he listened, smiling, to the clacking of her high heels going down the corridor, a sound he had grown rather addicted to.

Bianca was actually, at that very moment, weeping silently in a ladies' lavatory in the John Lewis department store in Oxford Street. Without having a very clear idea why, she had gone to its beauty department, newly designed, with its beautifully styled individual boutiques for each brand, sampling perfume – oh, so many beautiful perfumes – and listening to the consultants' polished presentations, desperately searching for a solution to her problem, and finding, of course, none.

She was shocked at herself, as much for the panicked state she was in as her situation. She never panicked. She remained steely calm, thought round a problem until she had found a solution and then put the necessary wheels in motion. She had never known anything like this hot, despairing state with her thoughts consuming one another, blundering backwards and forwards, shocked and, yes, frightened, by this blatant piece of stupidity.

She should have known not to trust Ralph Goodwin, should have insisted on more and more frequent sampling. But she had been in a hurry, desperate to make the perfume project her own, to win some accolades for that, at least, driven into dithering insecurity by Athina and her power games. And now she was left with nothing: no perfume to present tomorrow, no power games of her own to win, an incomplete brand, a damp squib of a relaunch. For however lovely the products in The Collection, however beautiful the packaging, however brilliant the publicity, they needed The Perfume to complete it. And now it simply didn't exist: and the blame for all that could only be laid at her door. She had blown it. One hundred per cent blown it. It was like putting on a ballet without dancers . . .

Athina was waiting for the lift when she heard Jemima's voice. And heard the word 'Bianca'. She walked very quietly back down the corridor, stood outside Jemima's half-open door.

'Hi, Bianca. Is that better? Can you hear me now? Good. I'm back in the office. You all right? What? What? The perfume? Oh no, Bianca, that is terrible. I'm so, so sorry. What a nightmare. Is there anything at all I can do? No, I don't suppose so. Bit of a gap in the proceedings, I can see that . . . And it all looked so promising. Well, look, we have the bottles, and the boxes, can't you just talk about the smell, describe it, say – no, OK. I can see that. What? The phials? They're in one of the cupboards, down in the lab. You must be so angry. They're perfumiers for God's sake, you'd think they'd come up with something half decent at least. Yes, of course I'll bring them. No, don't come back now, no point, everyone's gone. Yes, she's gone definitely. I just checked her office. Christine said she'd gone to the hairdresser. Mmm. OK, Bianca. We'll just have to find another perfumier. Fine. I'll see you at the hotel tomorrow. Around ten, ten thirty. Yes. Try not to worry too much.'

Jemima clicked her mobile off, shaking her head in sympathy, then she went out into the empty corridor and down the stairs to the lab. It was locked. Odd. Hattie had obviously got security conscious. That was awkward. But she was coming in first thing, she'd get the phials then. God alone knew what Bianca thought she was going to put into them. She texted Hattie, who didn't reply, and went back to her office.

In her car, Athina patted the large padded envelope of tiny phials that lay in her lap, and smiled out of the window.

Chapter 36

It was beautiful. So, so beautiful. She had forgotten the magic of it, the richness, the sexiness.

She looked at the bottle as it lay there, folded carefully into a cream lace bedjacket in her blue satin nightdress case. It was ten years since she had even unwrapped it.

Of course it was dangerous, what she had done: opening Pandora's box literally. It might have all been lost. And of course darling Daniel wasn't there to ask. She had asked his son though, had rung him that evening, and he had said, yes, it should be fine, just very quickly, a tiny bit, put it on your wrist and then put the stopper back.

Sealed and in a cool dark place, that had been Daniel's instructions for storage, all those years ago. Well, her bedroom was cool because she loathed warm bedrooms. And she had kept the other, equally carefully wrapped, in Caro's christening robe, in the drawer at the bottom of her wardrobe.

She had made that perfume, created it with Daniel, who looked like a poet, and talked like one too, about the emotion in a perfume and the sanctity. Such nonsense. But he said it so beautifully, gazing into her eyes as he did so. She was half in love with him, of course, their sessions together a physical as well as a romantic delight, as he stroked the latest versions, the precious oils, on to her skin, on her wrist, the back of her neck, just above the valley of her breasts. He said he agreed with Chanel that perfume should be worn wherever you wanted to be kissed. And then kissed those places to prove it.

Cornelius loathed him, said that whatever Daniel created,

however beautiful, he would never agree to market it.

'It's a dangerous place, the perfume industry, has lost people vast fortunes. Ours is not vast, and we can't afford to lose it.'

'But it will be,' she said, for these were the early years, when they could do no wrong, 'and then we will develop it, my perfume, and we will call it Athina, and it will be the one product I can claim as entirely my own.'

For it had been her idea to produce a perfume, seeing it as the passport to a higher quality image, a more prestige range. It was the late sixties and they had been a great success for almost fifteen years. Cornelius had humoured her, telling her to see what she could come up with, promising he would give it his serious consideration if it was wonderful enough. And it was, it had been wonderful, and she had never quite been able to forgive him for not going ahead and launching it on the world.

She had met Daniel at a Christmas trade fair, at a small stall where he had set up his perfumier's organ, with his name on a card at the top of it: Daniel Chagard, perfumier. The organ was set with rows of tiny bottles, and he was dipping spills into them and then wafting the spills around in the air, calling people over to come and sniff them.

She went over and sat down.

He was, she thought, one of the most good-looking men she had ever seen, tall and very slim, with burning dark eyes, wild, wavy dark blond hair and a very full, sexy mouth. He was French, but his English was perfect, albeit a little florid.

'I'd like to try your wares,' she said.

'Good, good, yes. Let me find something you would like. I would put you as a citrus girl. Try this . . .'

She tried. 'It's all right – but too sharp.'

'Ah. So – some woody notes, maybe even a little bergamot – that better?'

'A bit.'

'You're hard to please. Are you in the business?'

'I'd hardly be here if I wasn't,' said Athina briskly. 'Yes, of course, I'm Athina Farrell.'

'Ah, well you are legendary. I am honoured by your interest. And your husband? Is he here?'

'No,' said Athina.

'I see. So – you are interested in launching a fragrance, Mrs Farrell?'

'I am very interested,' said Athina.

'Very good. Then tell me more about your vision for it.'

'My vision! Isn't that a strange word for a fragrance?'

'Of course not. Fragrances have colour, shape, style. Not for nothing do we talk about *wearing* them. Now – is that more to your liking?'

Athina sniffed the spill. 'A little more,' she said.

She stayed at his stall until Florence, who had accompanied her, appeared.

'Ah, the perfumier's organ. Such wonderful romantic things.' She held out her hand to Daniel. 'I'm Florence Hamilton, I work with Mrs Farrell. I run The Shop in the Berkeley Arcade.'

Daniel bowed over her hand. 'I have heard of that shop,' he said. 'A perfect place to sell perfume.'

'Indeed,' said Florence. 'We often say that, don't we, Athina?'

'I really don't recall saying it very often,' said Athina, 'but yes, it would certainly be a good outlet. Florence, Mr Chagard and I are discussing formulations – perhaps you could come back in half an hour or so.'

'Of course. Lovely to have met you Monsieur Chagard.'

'Lovely indeed, Miss Hamilton.'

Florence turned away.

'Now,' said Athina, 'you were saying, I think, that jasmine can be very sensuous. May I try that?'

He invited her to his studio in Hampstead. He was modestly successful, had formulated perfumes for several of the smaller houses, certainly knew what he was doing.

An afternoon passed while he talked passionately of the different notes and blends: how the top note of a fragrance, the one that developed first, was usually citrus, the middle one, floral, which would develop after half an hour, and the base note could last up to eight hours. He talked of the heart note, of fragrances that possessed warmth and character; he taught her about musk and spice and vanilla and how they worked together. She left as darkness fell, half in love with him, with a brief for what she called a passionate perfume; he said she must come back in a few weeks and see what he had done.

The passionate perfume was sublime; she allowed him to test it on her skin and then took it home to Cornelius and begged him to market it. He agreed it was lovely, but refused to commit himself. He visited Daniel in the studio, and then invited him to the Farrell laboratory. He was not quite as enamoured of the perfume as Athina. *Passion*, she had christened it, but he agreed it was promising. He asked for more and more samples and Athina could see that he was making things as difficult as he could for Daniel so that he would weary of the project. But he didn't, of course, because Athina visited him again and again, flirting, playing games, coaxing the ultimate fragrance out of him. And then, there it was. Waiting for her, one dark afternoon in November.

'Here,' he said, 'here it is, your *Passion*. Try it on. And then wait, as I have told you. Here, my beautiful Athina, here, where it belongs.'

And he stroked it on to the nape of her neck, then bent and kissed her there, did the same with her breasts.

'It is engaged in foreplay, our perfume,' he said, smiling at her, 'but soon it will be making love and then, then we will have the – the *orgasme*. What is that in English?'

'It's orgasm,' said Athina primly.

He was a very different lover from Cornelius, swift, almost impatient, but skilful too; bringing her to orgasm that first afternoon with a confidence that surprised and delighted her. He was only her second lover; she had been a virgin when she met Cornelius.

She had actually always considered sex rather overrated, it was pleasant enough if she was in the mood, and of course one had to accommodate one's husband and his desires, for there was danger

381

of him straying if one did not, and occasionally, as Cornelius sent her soaring into the heights of pleasure, she thought how fortunate she was. But as the years went by, with the inevitable easing of her desire – and how grateful she was that Cornelius was increasingly less demanding in bed – she had simply thought not to know it again, the intensity, the sudden, sweeping invasion of longing, the flying physical joy, which Daniel created for and in her.

She was never in love with Daniel, but she was in love with the idea of him, and of having an affair. She enjoyed the relationship, the flattery, the tenderness, the fun; in a life that was dedicated to long, grinding hours of work, there was a delight to be found in the pursuit simply of pleasure, and particularly of the most carnal kind.

Cornelius seemed to suspect nothing, which surprised her, for he was the most worldly of men; he was undoubtedly jealous of Daniel, but that was of his professional persona, the image he so clearly worked on, of his romanticism, his looks, the nonsense he talked. But he seemed quite unaware that Daniel was seducing her. Well, his self-confidence had always tended towards complacency, and of course he knew, as she did, how much depended on their relationship, the ongoing success of the House of Farrell. Which mattered to her more than anything else.

Men, sex, passion with a small 'p': how could that compare with the dizzy heights of success, of triumph, of fame?

He pretended still to be working on the perfume, simply so that she could take new samples back to Cornelius, asking his advice, but they both knew that Daniel had found it, the holy grail, their *Passion*, and whenever she was going to meet him, which was necessarily seldom, she would wear it.

And then, one afternoon, Daniel complained of stomach ache. 'You eat too much foie gras,' Athina said, 'it is very bad for you.'

He always prepared a picnic for her: the nearest to French bread he could find, cheese, fruit, and foie gras.

'You should eat plain chicken, drink clear soup, tisanes rather than coffee.'

'It sounds very dull.'

'It's less dull than stomach ache!'

But the stomach ache did not go away; driven to seek medical aid, he found himself undergoing blood tests, x-rays, barium meals, began to need ever stronger painkillers.

Athina found herself caring for him more and more, traipsing up to Hampstead with flasks of soup – and the marijuana that was the only thing that eased his pain. Surprisingly, for she was the least caring of women, she half enjoyed it, feeling for the first time she had a mission in life; motherhood had not worked that miracle for her and she could be honest now with Cornelius, telling him that Daniel was sick and they were the only true friends he had in London: who could be jealous, could imagine a relationship with a desperately ill man?

Finally, exactly three months after the first stomach ache, he was told he must go into hospital for exploratory surgery and there was one last wonderful afternoon when she visited him and he gave her two bottles of the perfume he declared his masterpiece.

'Here it is, my darling one, our *Passion*. Take care of it, and wear it for me. Not your husband, I beg of you. Promise me, never that.'

She promised.

He didn't survive the surgery . . .

Thirty-five years later Athina had received a letter purporting to be from his son, one Claud Chagard. He had grown up in France, he said, in Paris; his mother had been a seamstress and his father had never married her, although he sent her money on a regular basis until he died. He had read of the House of Farrell and he knew from his father's records, painstakingly kept, it seemed, that he had worked for her. Could he come and see her?' He was a perfumier.

Athina said he could and found it very disturbing. He was eerily like his father, same wild hair, same dark eyes, same beguiling voice.

He gave her some of the formulations for the perfume, for *Passion*; she looked at it in awe. It was written in the old apothecaries' measures, minims, scruples, roman numerals.

'They're wonderful,' she said, 'amazing. Thank you. Could they be used as a modern formula, could we reinterpret them?'

'Possibly. They would need converting – and many of them I don't understand. And then there are far more natural ingredients than we would use now, much more expensive, and some of them, the animal ones, are banned: things like musk and civetone. But just to have such a thing is wonderful and I thought you would like it.'

'I do, I do. Thank you so much.'

She put them in the nightdress case with the bottle, and every so often would get it all out and gaze at it. The temptation to open the bottle, to sniff it, was huge. But she didn't, was too afraid of ruining her *Passion*, losing it altogether. One day, one day . . .

And now it seemed the day had come.

It was amazing how loved up she felt, and they hadn't even done it yet. But endless texts had come all over Christmas and then from bloody Megève where he was with bloody Guinevere – no doubt she was a brilliant skier. Susie could just about manage a blue run, on a good day. She wondered if that would matter to Jonjo, who would surely be permanently zooming down blacks. In the relentless year-round progress from Christmas to skiing to sailing to swimming to tennis to polo – and don't forget race meetings, Jonjo's boss was seriously into racing, so that would be compulsory, probably – anyway, all that, she wasn't really up to scratch, not the Guinevere Bloch sort of scratch. She was a bit – ordinary. He didn't know how ordinary yet. And maybe when he did . . .

She stuffed her phone into her bag and made for the dining room. She had more pressing things to worry about today, like her presentation being suddenly made longer by the absence of the perfume. It was such a shame about the perfume. No, it was a small tragedy. Jemima had told her about it and a lot of Bianca's credibility hung on it. Well, at least they had managed to keep it from Lady Farrell. It was quite scary to think of the capital she would make of the whole thing. After advising Bianca not to do it in the first place.

The hall looked amazing, Bertie thought. Only yesterday evening it had been chaos when he looked in, chairs piled up, huge buckets of flowers standing around, people up ladders, lying on the floor taping down wires and every so often a blast of sound would fill the room, only to be switched off again abruptly.

Today it was slick and glamorous, the mock-up of the Berkeley Arcade at the entrance intriguing. A vast screen behind the lectern and two smaller ones on either side of the platform showed photographs alternately of the Berkeley Arcade and the products in The Collection. Carly Simon was singing her heart out through the speakers.

'Doesn't this all look great?'

It was Lara, looking amazing in a red and white check suit, her heels even higher than usual. She came up to him, gave him a kiss on the cheek, looked round the conference hall approvingly.

'It really does. Bit of a change from yesterday. Your people have done a great job.'

'Yes, I'm really pleased. How are you feeling?'

'Oh, fine. Just feel I might throw up any minute. I've never had to do anything like this in my life.'

'Has your wife gone?'

'Oh, yes, She left early. Big day for her today.'

Lara nodded and smiled at him rather feebly.

'Pity she can't see you strutting your stuff.'

'Well – yes.'

In fact Priscilla had behaved quite appallingly and the only good news was that she had gone. Bertie had been deeply embarrassed by her; she had stood apart from everyone at the welcome drinks, talking into her phone and wearing an expression of some disdain. She had made no effort to dress up and wore a tweed suit that was very uncompromisingly daywear.

And later she had been very unfriendly to Bianca when she had told her how wonderful Bertie was.

'Yes, well I'm pleased to hear you've found him something that occupies him,' was all she said. 'He seemed very under-employed before.'

And she'd been just plain rude to Lara, looking her up and down disdainfully, her eyes lingering on her cleavage, and implying that her job as marketing director of Farrell's was of no comparison in terms of importance to her role in the charity world. Her main aim throughout the entire evening seemed to be belittling Bertie and his role in the company. Lucy had noticed, kept coming up to him and giving him a quick kiss and endeavouring to introduce her mother to other people, but she might as well have been working on the large pillars that stood round the bar for all the good it had done.

'Anyway it's all going to be fine,' said Lara now, 'even without the perfume. Oh, look, there's your mother. Doesn't she look amazing?'

Bertie looked and saw his mother coming into the hall, dressed all in white. She had always worn white for conferences, it was a strong tradition.

Well, so far so good, Bianca thought, putting on a last slick of lip gloss before leaving her room. The meet and greet drinks had gone fine, she'd made quite a nice little speech, and the buffet supper had been a very happy occasion. Athina had behaved really well, chatting to everyone, and she'd looked amazing, in a black dress and red sequinned jacket, very thirties, her silvery hair clipped back with two diamante barrettes. Florence, standing loyally at her side, had looked utterly lovely too, in the navy crêpe. The only person who had really let the side down – God, she was a cow! – was Priscilla. She had practically reeled at some of the things Priscilla had said, particularly about Bertie. What was the matter with her? Athina was a saint by comparison.

She thought of Bertie, whom she'd seen chatting and laughing with Lara; there was a chemistry between them, no doubt about it. Clearly the relationship was an innocent one so far; but maybe, under Conference Conditions, that well-known accelerator of bad behaviour, and with the departure of Priscilla, it might develop a little. If it did, Bianca thought, she for one would be cheering on the sidelines.

She looked at her watch: time to go down. Mike and Hugh were arriving any minute. God, she was scared. She couldn't remember ever feeling so bad about a conference before. It was the perfume thing of course. Her phone rang; probably Patrick wishing her luck. It was Saul.

'Hello,' he said, 'I just called to wish you luck.'

Bianca was so astonished she felt quite dizzy. Astonished that he should remember, astonished that he should care.

'That's really – really nice,' she said, rather helplessly.

'Well, I know how important it is to you. You said at Christmas you were worrying about it. How's it going?'

'Oh – incredibly well. Not.'

'I'm sorry. What's wrong?'

'You don't want to know.'

'Well, I do, but I haven't got much time. What's the worst thing?'

'The worst thing is that the perfume, about which much hype, and which was only delivered yesterday, was complete rubbish. Tart's boudoir would be classy by comparison No perfume, no hype. Me with mud on my face.'

'That does sound bad,' he said.

'Thanks.'

'Well, there's no point me saying it doesn't matter, is there?'

'No,' she said, and she smiled in spite of herself. 'No point at all.'

'But you'll manage.'

'Will I?'

'Of course you will. Good luck, Bianca. Don't look down.'

He was the most extraordinary person, she thought for the hundredth time, putting her phone away. She would have put a million pounds against the likelihood of him calling. So not entirely without feelings, it seemed. Or thoughtfulness at least. And it was more than Patrick had done.

Athina dressed for it, as she always had for conferences, in the white woollen Chanel suit, the gilt and pearl earrings to match and the chains of course, and Cornelius's twin diamond rings. She would show them what class was, what class would do. She looked round the room now, and didn't see much of it. That Clements woman, wearing red – so vulgar, with her cleavage on show, her too-high heels.

387

The sales director wasn't too bad, at least he was wearing a half-decent suit, and Bertie, she had to admit, looked very nice, Priscilla had done wonders getting the weight off him.

Just as well she'd gone home, though. She really was a very dull woman, no social graces, and no dress sense whatever. Bianca Bailey did look good however. She usually did. One had to admit it. A cream silk dress, none of that ghastly cleavage nonsense, blue belt, very good blue shoes . . . And she looked very calm, very much in control. She was too self-confident by far. Well, she was about to be given a lesson in the cosmetic industry – and in running a conference – that she'd never forget . . .

God, Lara thought, she loved doing presentations. She knew she was in a very small minority and supposed it was something to do with being self-confident, a bit of a loudmouth. But she loved standing up there, seizing their attention and then holding it, spinning a web of excitement and promise, feeling the hall increasingly with her, teasing them, drawing it out. Jonathan Tucker had gone first, and he'd been very good; bit flash, hamming it up, thumping the lectern, striding about the platform a bit, but then, a successful low-key sales director was a contradiction in terms. His own story, that he'd left Lauder to join Farrell's, was persuasive enough: who could doubt his faith in the new company?

'We won't just do it,' he finished now, 'we'll leave all the others behind. This is a great company with a great past and a fantastic future. And it's yours. Go for it!'

And now she had to lay out for them exactly what they would have to work with, this new, classy, imaginative package, with all her ideas for selling it in.

She described The Collection, the glamour it would give the whole Farrell brand, the high quality of the products, the classy packaging; and then called on Hattie to introduce them in detail – Hattie, who looked just sensational. No one could stop staring at her. That dress was a bit torch singer, slit up her thigh and with a plunging neckline, but it didn't matter, it suited her, the first thing Susie could remember ever seeing her in that did. And her make-up was brilliant, her eyes suddenly huge and smoky, her lips glossy and sexy. Sexy? Bossy, self-opinionated, nanny-style Hattie. It was amazing. And my God, she could talk products. You could feel the moisturiser going on, believe what the foundations could do for you, long to get to work with the palettes. She was genius. It had been genius to bring her in.

And now Tamsin Brownley, their creative designer. More torch singer clothes, but she was good too, in quite a different way, so wonderfully young, and excited, practically jumping in her Doc Marten boots as she talked about her designs, the colours, the style, the typeface she had created. They all loved her and she got the biggest applause so far; everyone was smiling as she left the platform.

OK, nearly there, Bianca thought. Just Susie and her frankly rather fluffy presentation, but it was brilliantly done, lots of glossy spreads from the magazines, names flashed about, a discussion of the new all-powerful bloggers and then – then it would be her. The damp squib at the end of the firework display. Don't, Bianca, don't think like that! She heard Saul Finlayson's voice suddenly, 'Don't look down' and literally straightened up on her chair, and thought, as the applause for Susie swept the room, come on Bertie, do it, introduce me, let's get it over. Fuck you, Ralph Goodwin, fuck you, putting me through this! OK, here we go. She could do it. She stood up, walked towards the platform . . .

The moment had arrived, totally electric, as she had known it would be. She had been savouring it all morning. Pure theatre. Showmanship. Well she'd always been good at that. She'd learned it from a most brilliant source – herself.

She smoothed her hair, checked her earrings, and stood up, quite still, waiting.

Something was wrong, Bianca thought. Well odd, anyway. Bertie was silent, his eyes weren't on her, they were somewhere else entirely, on another woman who was walking up the steps and on to the platform, a woman with her hand held up imperiously, a woman all in white, with silver hair, the eyes of everyone in the hall fixed upon her.

Athina Farrell, moving very determinedly towards the lectern, paused, looking out over the hall, clearly savouring the moment. And then she smiled and said, 'You must forgive me. I am an extra item. Not quite extracurricular – a compulsory subject indeed, in the world of cosmetics, and one that you could not have heard about today, if it were not for me . . .'

Shit, thought Bianca. Fuck! thought Lara, old witch is going to steal the show. Oh, no, no, thought Susie, she's taking over, making it her moment. Oh God, thought Bertie, what do I do, what *can* I do? How *amazing*, thought all the new people, the young slick salespeople, the sassy roving consultants, another of Bertie's brainwaves, that this beautiful, brilliant woman with sixty years of experience in the cosmetic industry behind her, with so many stories to tell – and they had heard some last night of course – who had met the Queen of England, who had run the House of Farrell for decades – what might she have to tell them now?

'What I am going to tell you is a true story, although it sounds at times too romantic to be true. It is the story of a fragrance, which we all hope,' she smiled graciously down at Bianca, 'will be not just part of the new range, The Collection, as I personally christened it, but the very heart of it.'

She held up a small, plain bottle.

'I have in here a perfume. It was created many years ago by my husband and me, when we were still in charge of the House of Farrell. It was to be the ultimate element in the Farrell range. It was masterminded by my husband, Sir Cornelius Farrell, who was a genius in the mould of Charles Revson, and Estée Lauder, who understood cosmetics in a way few people can, who had this rare instinct in his very bones for doing what was absolutely right for the House of Farrell.

'"We must create a perfume," he said to me one day, "and by we I mean you. Go and find a perfumier and explain to him what we want."'

'And I did indeed find a perfumier, another genius, a Frenchman, of course. Daniel Chagard was his name, and the three of us spent many hours and days and weeks together, bringing our vision to life.

'We knew what we wanted: a fragrance that would inspire and even create *Passion*. Indeed, that is the name we were going to give it. And finally Monsieur Chagard came to us, from his artist's studio – and he was an artist, make no mistake – with a small phial of perfume that was so rich, so special that we all just smiled at one another and knew we had found what we were looking for . . .'

You old witch, thought Florence, how can you stand up there and lie like that? How can you betray Cornelius again, and Daniel too, who adored you so much, how *can* you!

For of course Cornelius had known about Daniel. It had made him actually rather happy.

'It grants us greater freedom, wouldn't you say, Little Flo, to pursue our own passion,' he'd said, adding that the fellow was a complete charlatan and he could not imagine how Athina could not possibly see that.

The hall was silent; absolutely so.

'So – we planned to launch the perfume, our *Passion*, in the early seventies. But, as many of you will know, that was a disastrous time for this country, and for all the industries struggling to survive. The House of Farrell came close to bankruptcy more than once.

'Cornelius was as heartbroken as I. He knew what a treasure we had in our possession, but *Passion* had to wait. I kept it as instructed by Monsieur Chagard, in a sealed bottle in a dark place, waiting for the right moment to arrive, for prosperity to return.

'Only, when it did, the perfume market had changed; the fashion was for a different style of perfume altogether, for the strong fragrances like *Youth Dew* and *Eternity*, and we knew that once again we could not launch.

'Tragically, Monsieur Chagard died soon after finishing his creation; his last words to me were "take care of our perfume". And so it has waited for almost fifty years, kept as instructed in the dark, stoppered up. Safe, precious, a treasure indeed. And when Mrs Bailey talked to me about a perfume for the new range she was thinking of doing, I knew the moment had finally come.

'I smelled *Passion* for the first time for decades the other evening and it is truly breathtaking. I know you will agree and although I am unable to give you samples to keep, I have some phials here with a few precious drops in them. If you pass them amongst you, you will recognise its magic. Lucy darling . . .' she walked to the edge of the platform, handed a few phials down to Lucy who was waiting there as instructed, 'take them round, let people experience the magic. Lucy is my granddaughter,' she said, smiling first at her, and then again round the hall, 'working for Farrell's now, the next generation; I am very very proud of her.'

She is amazing, thought Lucy, while realising her grandmother was doing something quite wrong, stealing Bianca's moment, telling a story that might or might not be true; and she felt a stab of pride, despite this realisation, that the spirit of the family was by implication being handed to her.

'She's so cool,' whispered Fenella, their model for the day. 'What a lovely, lovely story. Want me to help pass the samples round?'

'Please.'

Bianca had sat down again; it seemed the only thing to do. She was clearly not going to be invited on to the platform to share Athina Farrell's glory.

'Now, most wonderfully,' Athina was talking again through the hum of appreciative noises as people sniffed at the tiny phials, 'I have the formula for this fragrance, so we can create it in large quantities, although it will not be easy. It is handwritten in the old apothecaries' measures, which are more or less indecipherable, written as they are by hand. But more wonderfully still, I have managed to find Monsieur Chagard's son, also a perfumier, working in Paris, and he can convert it for us. It won't be an easy task, for of course synthetics have replaced many of the animal products used then and the original ones will be, of course, very much more expensive. Some adjustments will need to be made. But I am sure we can re-create the original to a very great extent – and then think of the story we will have to tell. A fragrance that has, like the Sleeping Beauty, slept for many, many years and is only now being awoken, as lovely as ever for women – and men, of course – to enjoy.

'Thank you so much for listening to me,' she said. 'I so enjoyed telling you my little story And I shall enjoy seeing our *Passion* brought to life for the second time.'

She gave a modest bow and the applause broke. Everyone was smiling, clapping furiously, several people on their feet. It was an extraordinary moment, and in spite of her rage and sense of betrayal, Bianca was impressed, half swept along with it herself. And not a note had Athina needed, not the scrappiest piece of paper.

She looked at her, as she stood there on the platform, revelling in this, her triumph, her moment of infinite revenge, the bad fairy, the wicked godmother, the ice queen. But only to her, Bianca thought, only to the very few who knew. To everyone else she was the star of the day, spinning a tale of beauty and wonder for them that they could now turn, each and every one of them, to huge and unarguable success. For who could resist that story, Lara thought, and Susie too, and actually Jonathan Tucker as well; who could not wish to read about it and then to wear it. It was tough, almost unbearably so, on Bianca, and Athina had known exactly what she was doing, but actually . . .

So it was now open warfare; but her own tactics must be most carefully judged.

Chapter 37

More lies, more and more, how could she tell them so blandly, so successfully? She should have told the truth. And had it been rage confronting her, had it been the violence, she could and she would have done. But it wasn't. It was bewilderment, hurt, tears even.

So how could she have said, 'I'm sorry, Henk, but this time it's really over, there's someone else.'

It would have been a cruelty she wasn't capable of. She must bide her time, pick her moment. That was the right way, the only way. Given what had happened, given that he had to know.

Not all of it, of course. Not that she had driven back to London, her heart feeling as if it was almost singing, as fast as she could that lovely sunny frosty morning, looking incredulously, whenever the road was straight enough to risk it, at her phone on the seat beside her, at his text that said *I really want to cu, come whenever u cn* and then rolling round in her head, his voice, listening over and over again to it: 'I've really missed you, Susie. I've got the day off, any way you could possibly come to my place?'

And most wonderfully, she could. It was Friday, the conference over, proclaimed a triumph, and a group email had come from Bianca saying thank you and well done and take a day off, you've earned it. And if that wasn't fate, wasn't meant, wasn't written in the stars, all those corny things – what was?

She'd got lost, of course, driving into Canary Wharf. The satellite connection died in the underpasses and she drove round and round, tearful with frustration, and finally saw a car park, not the right one, but at least she could use it, and came out and hired a cab which dropped her at one of the great towers and she walked in and into the lift and pressed the button for the twentieth floor, and when she got out, he was standing waiting for her, his eyes soft with pleasure, and he reached out and took her hand and kissed her quite formally on the cheek and said, 'It's lovely to see you, come on in.'

It was, quite simply, amazing up there; she stood in his living room, his huge, white, light, vast-windowed living room, with its white sofas and its bleached wood floor, looking out and around at the glittering, shimmering expanse of sky and glass and water that lay before and below her and then turned to him, and smiled, and he smiled back and that was it really.

The sex was staggering. A sweet, safe, dizzy discovery of one another, a swift, slow journey into pleasure so intense, so right, so sure, so gentle. There was no inhibition, no uncertainty, no concern, no thought of anything but pleasure and the pursuit of it and it was as if they had anticipated this all their lives, as if every other experience they had ever known had brought them to it.

He came with a great groan, she with a high, bright cry of joy, and 'My God,' he said, 'Oh my God!' and pulled her to him, his mouth in her tangled hair. And after a while she eased away from him, just a little, settled with a sigh of absolute contentment against him, her body eased, her head and her heart in a perfect, disorderly happiness.

It was still early, long before lunchtime, and the day assumed an endless quality: excellent coffee was drunk and they sat on one of his sofas and held hands and looked at one another, smiling slightly foolishly, and after a while, felt bound to return to the bed and the pleasure; a while after that they ate lunch, one that he had produced from an absurdly vast fridge, crusty bread and an Époisses cheese that threatened to crawl across the table away from them, and sparkling water and a bottle of perfectly chilled white wine, and most amazing of all, tomatoes that actually tasted of tomatoes. They listened to some music and she found, idly looking through his CDs, that she owned many of the same, and the same with his DVDs, film after film they had both loved. Another return to the bed and then he suggested a little fresh air perhaps, as the blue and beautiful winter dusk began to drift in, and she said that would be nice, but could she have a shower first, and they stood in his twin-showered wet room together, the hot water beating down, laughing and beginning to sing foolish songs like 'Singing in the Rain', and then somehow it was actually dark and too late and clearly too cold to go out.

They settled down then, to a movie, *The Artist*, for which they both declared a passion, and which he had a copy of because a friend was on the BAFTA panel. There was a little more of the wine and holding hands, twisting, caressing, stroking hands, sexual desire and contentment intertwined, laughing at the absolute happiness of the day.

'Like a present it's been, a gift-wrapped present,' she said smiling at him delightedly, and he kissed her and said how very poetic she was and he supposed she needed to be, doing her job, and she said there wasn't much poetry involved in PR.

And then finally it was evening, proper evening, and he said, 'Dinner?' and she said that would be lovely, and he stood up and said, 'I'll go and put some clothes on.' And she said, 'Me too,' thinking happily she could wear the black, slinky, slithery dress she had worn the first night at the conference, and went into what he had described to her as the guest room, and while she was there she got her phone out of her bag, for the first time in what seemed like many days, and was pulled with a lurch of shock back into real life. And she sat staring at five missed calls and six texts, all from Henk, who was waiting, she remembered now, in the wine bar, where they had agreed he would be when she got home from work that evening, before taking her out to dinner.

Panicked, she looked at her watch: already seven and they were to have met at six. *Sorry sorry sorry!* she texted. *Got held up, can't make it, huge meetings, going on forever*, and tried to believe that would work, would set her apart from it, from him, from reality. But it didn't, it couldn't; the day was spoiled, damaged, and whatever she did, however hard she tried, she could never regain it, return it to its pristine perfection.

Bianca walked very slowly up the steps of the house. It was early afternoon; she had actually gone in to the office that morning, to take stock not only of what had happened but her reaction to it, because she still felt physically shocked, as if someone had punched her hard, over and over again, completely unexpectedly.

Lunch, after that morning session, had been a nightmare. She sat at her table, chatting animatedly to anyone who approached her, watching Athina at hers, the star of the day, smiling, laughing, receiving kisses, compliments. Occasionally her eyes would meet Bianca's across the room and she would smile graciously, incline her head just a little: 'I'm winning now,' that look said. 'Don't even think about trying to regain what you've lost.' And then someone else would come up to her and she would turn to them, take their hand and say something and Bianca would be left feeling more alone than she could ever have imagined.

At one point Florence came up to her, her dark eyes concerned. She smiled and said simply, 'I'm so sorry,' and patted Bianca's hand and there was no need for any more, and Bianca felt at once comforted and astonished that Florence, sweet, kind, gentle Florence, could have withstood over fifty years of such treatment and survived. She was truly the most remarkable woman.

The afternoon session was actually rather good; the conference was fired up, loved the idea of The Shop and its heritage, its counterparts in other cities. It did, of course, blend perfectly with the perfume story.

Bianca spoke well, she knew, adrenalin driving her on, reclaiming some of the territory she had lost; talking about the shops, painting a picture for them of these precious ambassadresses for the brand, in London and Paris, telling their story, their heritage, their Englishness, at a time when the eyes of every country in the world would be fixed on London, admiring and envying them; it was a perfect pitch. Athina spoke again, of course, of the glory days of Farrell's, of its birth in coronation year, of royalty visiting the arcade

– funny how suddenly she was happy to speak about that, Bianca thought, when she had been so emphatically opposed to it before – but not for long, as if she was aware that she must not overdraw on her success. She was truly the most masterly tactician.

There was only one question, posed by one of the new salesmen, that clearly threw Bianca – how many more of the little shops would there be, would two really be enough to tell their story?

'Let me put it this way,' she said, smiling at him. 'One in the centre of London is invaluable to us. We already know that. As will be the one in Paris. Especially from a PR point of view. And in time, of course I envisage many more of them. The journey of a thousand miles and all that sort of thing.'

But it wasn't quite enough – and she knew it.

'Great conference,' said Hugh, raising his glass to her as they sat in the bar after dinner and the dancing began. 'You've done a fantastic job. Bringing Old Mother Farrell on was brilliant – made all your stuff about heritage and so on sound a million times more interesting. Everyone seems really fired up. Seriously, Bianca, it's been terrific. Well done. Oh, now look, that young designer of yours is having a good time!'

Tamsin was up on the stage with the DJ. She'd wrested the microphone from him and was dancing with it, only it wasn't embarrassing, it was very funny. It was obviously an act she'd rehearsed many times.

'Always a good sign when the hair gets let down,' said Mike, who had joined them. 'I'm just debating whether I should ask Lady Farrell for a dance. She'll need a slow number I suppose.'

'Don't kid yourself,' said Bianca. 'Apparently, she does a mean rock and roll. Lucy, her granddaughter, told me.'

'How terrifying. Think I'll steer well clear.'

'I would,' said Bianca.

'But she was superb, Bianca. Clever of you to give her such a star role.'

'Well – if you can't beat them, join them,' said Bianca modestly. This was clearly the line she was going to have to take. Somehow, in the most extraordinary way, Athina's hijacking the conference had made it a great success. Or at least a greater one. Except for those few who knew it shouldn't have happened. And even they seemed quite happy about it.

'I know she's a wicked old witch,' Susie had whispered, squeezing her arm after lunch, 'but it was magic, that story of hers. And I know the rest of the presentation will go really well. Don't worry, Bianca. Just go for it.'

'She's an evil old hag,' Lara had said, 'but a very clever one. And at least we have a perfume – for now, anyway. A very beautiful one. Let's make the most of it. And if we can get it manufactured – well, it's a terrific story. Wonder why she didn't mention it before?'

'Oh, I can't imagine,' said Bianca.

Jonathan Tucker was beside himself with excitement, and so was Felix Bradbury, the new sales manager. As for the advertising boys: 'Sensational,' Jack Flynn had said, embracing her. 'Marvellous story! And it's going to fit in with our campaign perfectly.'

Bianca wondered briefly what they'd all be saying if it had been her and Ralph Goodwin on the platform. She decided it would be rather less effusive.

The thought had made her more miserable still . . .

She had given everyone the day off, largely for her own sake. She needed time to recoup her energy. Nothing had been as hard as this, ever. She had had, in her other companies, to gamble, to bluff, and at times to lie; she had spent weeks on end in a state of ongoing exhaustion and dread. She had been hated, feared, reviled even, but she had gone calmly, icily on, knowing exactly what she was doing and how it must be done. She had never felt as she did now – out of control.

She looked at her watch: only three. Too early for the children, so she would maybe call Patrick. He was in New York and it was morning there, the ideal time. He had sent her a couple of texts while the conference was on, wishing her well and telling her how much he was enjoying the project. She sat staring at those texts, resentful that he wasn't at home, angry that he wasn't safely there for her, the supportive, loving force in her life that he had always been. Now his entire energy-force, his every concern, seemed to be directed at bloody Saul Finlayson. Who had called her that morning to wish her well.

She was putting her large leather Gladstone bag, duly emptied, into the suitcase cupboard when she heard the front door, and ran down the stairs, calling, 'Hi!' It was Milly, standing alone in the hall, dropping her bag, pulling out her phone, pushing back her waterfall of dark hair all in one seamless movement.

'Oh, hello.'

Her voice was flat, dull and she looked at her mother as if she hardly knew who she was, and cared less.

'Good week? Sorry not to have called more.'

A shrug.

'But – I'm back now, out of school like you. Want to do something, go shopping, maybe do a movie?'

'No thanks. I'm going out.'

'With?'

'Friends.'

'Anyone I know?'

Another shrug. 'Don't think so. Scuse me. I need to change.' As she picked up her schoolbag, it flipped over and a stash of books and magazines fell out on to the floor; she looked at the mess as if it had nothing to do with her, turned away from it, and moved towards the stairs

'Milly, darling, pick those up, would you?'

'Not now,' she said. 'I'll do it when I get back.'

'Milly!'

'Yeah, what?' The dark eyes met her mother's, absolutely hostile.

Bianca shrugged. 'Nothing.'

'OK.'

And she continued on her journey up the stairs and slammed the door of her room.

The door opened again: Fergie.

'Hi.'

'Hi, Mum.'

'You OK?'

'Yeah, thanks. Ollie asked me back to his house and to stay, that OK?'

'Yes, of course. Where's Sonia?'

'Parking. Just got to get my stuff.'

'Right. Well, don't let me keep you.' She smiled, a bright, affectionate smile.

'OK.'

And he too was gone.

She went into the kitchen, made herself a cup of tea. Sonia came in.

'Hello, Bianca. You're early.' She didn't like Bianca entering her time: her time and her territory. 'How did it go?'

'The conference? Very well, thank you. Er – Karen? And Ruby? They about?'

'Ruby's got a playdate, won't be home till bedtime and Karen's gone to see her sister's new baby.'

'I see. Well – well fine.'

A new baby! These absent people who didn't seem interested in her or to need her had been new babies once; defenceless, needy, trailing their own overpowering love.

Milly left; Fergie left; Sonia left.

Bianca picked up her phone and texted Patrick: after five or ten minutes, he texted back: *Sorry on a conference call, will ring later. Hope you're OK.*

'No, Patrick!' she shouted at the phone. 'I'm not OK. I'm really really not.' For the second time that week Bianca started to cry: helpless, hopeless tears. And realised she had never been properly unhappy before.

Lara felt disappointed. She knew it was absurd, but she had set great store by that conference. And it had been wonderful professionally, and she was excited, inspired by its success. But she had hoped, while trying not to admit it even to herself, that with the strange potency of the whole conference thing, she and Bertie might move forward, and acknowledge that there was something between them and – well, who knew after that? Conferences were

401

safe houses, freeing confidences, holding secrets. In the heady, highly charged atmosphere they ran on, you were released, however briefly, into a new and more reckless persona; you looked your best, you talked your best, you enjoyed your best. Other things helped, of course, ongoing proximity, alcohol, adrenalin, sex. Sex was just everywhere. She had seen funny old Hattie being chatted up by one of the salesmen, his eyes tipping into her straining cleavage, Jemima, saintly Jemima, dancing very closely indeed with Jonathan Tucker, Susie falling tipsily into the lap of Mark Rawlins and staying there, her lovely tousled head resting on his shoulder, and Tamsin, wonderful Tamsin, doing her dance with the microphone. None of it mattered, none of it meant anything – unless you wanted it to.

And she had thought that she would ask Bertie to dance, and he would say first no and then yes, and she would be able to hold him, and be with him, and talk to him and tell him how wonderful she thought he was and how she enjoyed being with him.

And what had happened? None of it. Defeated, demoralised, first by his wife and then his mother, he seemed hardly to be there. He had scarcely looked at her, certainly not spoken to her; he had kept apart from everyone.

Lara had tried, had brought him drinks, cracked jokes, praised his presentation, admired his dinner jacket – and for all the good it had done her she might as well have, in one of her own favourite phrases, farted into the wind. In the end she had lost her temper with him – not visibly, of course – and started flirting outrageously with one of the conference organisers, who was flattered by her attentions. They had drunk a lot of champagne, laughed and joked rather loudly through dinner, and then taken to the dance floor. And if there was one thing Lara could do well, apart from her job, it was dance. And she did the even more difficult thing, of making her partner able to dance well too. She danced every dance that night, with every man in the room.

And the only man who didn't ask her to dance, who sat miserably trying not to look at her, was Bertram Farrell, the only man she really wanted to dance with.

* * *

God, what a dreadful experience it had been; Bertie, reliving the conference through the weekend, found it difficult to set it behind him. He had had such hopes of it, too; and of course, to an outsider, it had been a success. Sitting in the bar of the hotel before dinner he was relieved and amazed to hear all the appreciative comments, about the wonderful new products, the concept of the relaunch, but it had all faded into insignificance compared with the perfume and its story. And the telling of that story.

He had never been so shocked in his life, as when his mother had stood up, completely unannounced, and just taken the whole thing over. Or so sorry for anyone as he had been for Bianca. Who had been just as shocked, but had had the added ignominy of her own starring role being hijacked. It had been the rudest, most aggressive piece of behaviour he had ever witnessed. God, his mother was a nightmare, a brilliant, unscrupulous nightmare.

And he had had to sit by and watch as his boss, the woman he was really very fond of, and who had invested in him at considerable risk, was publicly humiliated by his own mother. It was almost unbearably painful.

The other near-unbearable thing had been Priscilla. She could hardly have humiliated him more. There, where his whole new future, his first tentative successes, were on display, where he was doing something well, for the first time in his life – to diminish him there, that was beyond forgiveness.

And Lara. Lara, who he had been foolish enough to believe liked him, spending the night flirting and dancing with that dreadful organiser fellow. Well, it served him right for being so foolish. She showed him her usual friendly warmth at the beginning of the evening, giving him a kiss in the bar, telling him how good she had thought his presentation had been, but he had been feeling too depressed, too numb to respond and watched morosely as she gave up and started working the room and felt like bursting into tears.

But mostly he felt ashamed and he knew now, without a shadow of a doubt, what he must do. And as he lay awake a second night, his resolve hardened, clarified. He had no place any longer with the

403

House of Farrell or indeed the family; he must find somewhere else to go.

Afterwards, over and over again, she wondered what would have happened if Milly hadn't dropped that pile of magazines on the floor and then refused to pick them up; and if she hadn't been so depressed and lonely and frozen into the kind of torpor that makes you sit and read a catalogue about thermal underwear, or an article about ten new ways to get rid of limescale, simply because you cannot be bothered to so much as lift an arm and reach for something else to read. But anyway, as she slumped on to the battered sofa in the corner of the kitchen it had caught her eye, lying on the top of the heap, and she'd reached for it, and its content was, actually, much more interesting than thermal underwear or limescale. Or rather *he* was: Jay-Z, clever bloke, most successful rap artist of all time, worth countless millions, and married to one of the most beautiful and successful female musical artists in the world. She sat there reading it, drinking tonic water without gin because she couldn't face getting drunk alone like so many saddo failures – and there it was. The idea. *His* idea. There for the taking. How he'd published a book he'd written on the rock industry and his own life within it, and on its launch had put every single page separately on billboards and truck sides and buildings every day for a month, so that his devoted fans could find each one, online, with the help of something like Bing, and download them, and . . .

'Shit,' said Bianca. 'Fuck. Oh my God. Oh my God!'

Chapter 38

Tod Marchant was having a well-earned rest and, halfway through a second beer, was more than half inclined to let Bianca's call go straight to voicemail. But she was a pretty major client, so, 'Hi,' he said and then, clocking that her voice sounded quite – odd, put down the beer and sat up a bit straighter and then: 'Yes, of course I know about Jay-Z.' And then, 'Yes I do remember something like that, yes, but what . . .' And then finally, 'Holy fuck! Sorry, Bianca, but – Jesus wept, that is quite something of an idea! Can I come round? Like – now? Great. Yeah, I'll just – Christ. Yes. See you in about forty-five.'

It was something of a miracle that he didn't crash the car on the way from Fulham to Hampstead. Not because of the beer, but because his brain seemed to have been caught up in some kind of whirlpool, surging and crashing inside his head, and Bianca looked like someone he hardly knew when she opened the door to him: not her usual cool self, she was fiery, agitated, her grey eyes brilliant, her voice quick, the words falling over one another as she explained her idea over and over again, what she thought they could do.

And it was genius, that idea; there was no doubt. One in a million, stunning, gorgeous in its potential and breadth.

They talked for hours, drinking first coffee, then Coke, then finally wine. A girl child arrived home, complete with minder of some kind: she was greeted, hugged, kissed, listened to. He was impressed by Bianca's ability to do this, while so clearly in entirely another place, another time. He supposed that was what women –

or rather mothers – could do; he would have found it impossible.

The child went upstairs, with the minder, or rather the nanny, and was told Bianca would come up when she was in bed and have a cuddle; another, half-adult, half-child came in, unaccompanied, a beautiful hostile creature who managed a half smile at her mother and at him and then disappeared also. Bianca's phone rang; she looked at it, and then at him, and said, 'It's my husband, ought to take it, sorry.' 'Fine,' he said, 'shall I . . . ?' And she said, laughing, 'Of course not, don't be silly!' And had a short, rather cool conversation. And every time she came back to him and the idea it was as if it excited her all over again, pushing her hair back, grinning, her eyes shining.

For the first time, seeing her like this, what she was about, what made her who she was, he found her sexy.

'I tell you what though,' he said, another hour later, washing down some of the pizza she had cooked for them both with yet more red wine, 'we can't do this with two or three piddling little shops, Bianca. This needs to go global. Dubai, Hong Kong, Tokyo, as well as New York and LA. Othewise, we'll just be pissing in the wind.'

'I know it,' she said. 'I know. And yes, it will. It'll take me way over budget, but I'll get some more money somehow . . .'

'Great,' he said. And he had no doubt that she would do so.

'Bianca, no. I'm not even going to say I'm sorry. No. That's it.'

'But—'

'Bianca, you heard what the man said.' Hugh's face was less stern than Mike's but the solidarity was clear. 'There is no more money. You're overspent already, the cash flow looks bad – you've a very long way to go before you can claim any extra expenditure is justifiable.'

'Yes, I know, but – this is. It's totally, utterly justifiable. It's going to save Farrell's, I know it is. Can I just run through it again – so you totally understand.'

'Bianca, we *do* understand. And it's a very clever idea. But it's not quantifiable. You're not promising to spend an extra two million and make another three. It's all airy-fairy stuff. Promises, dreams, nonsense! Unlike you, if you will forgive the observation.'

She sensed she was at the end of the road with them and gave in. She could see that she was exasperating them. She could see she was being not like her. But then – the situation was not like her either.

Susie sat staring at Bianca; she, too, felt slightly dizzy with the excitement, the brilliance of the idea. Despite the considerable personal trouble she was in, she still found herself totally caught up in it, aware that this was the most amazing, most exciting thing her professional life had ever offered her.

'My God,' she said, 'my God, Bianca, that is just – just amazing. However did you think of it?'

'I'm not sure. It just sort of slithered into my head. You know how ideas do. Now, first thing: obviously, absolute and utter secrecy. This is really, really original. If any of the other houses got hold of it we'd be done for. And as for Lady Farrell, she mustn't get even the faintest whiff of it.'

'Of course. I understand.'

'Tod says we have to work with the bloggers, first off. And only then at the last minute. And perhaps one, maybe two at the most, very key, very big journalists.'

'He's right. I need time to think, but it's brilliant. *You're* brilliant. But there is one thing, Bianca.'

'What's that?'

'We can't do this with just three shops. We have to go global.'

'I know it,' said Bianca with a sigh. 'That's exactly what Tod said.'

Susie went back to her office; she felt shaky and overanxious. Partly because of the brilliance of Bianca's idea – it was genius – and how much of its successful execution would rest with her, but also because her mind was at least fifty per cent focused on her own problems. Which were considerable.

She and Jonjo had met again on the Saturday evening and it had been really very lovely, but there was a slight shadow drifting over everything, like the wispy clouds that start drifting across a previously cloudless sky, announcing an approaching storm.

They had gone to the cinema and then out to dinner, and talked until the waiters stopped smiling at them and began looking baleful.

'I really love being with you,' he had said, over pudding (Eton Mess), taking her hand and kissing it. 'It's just – well, lovely.'

She smiled at him foolishly, wishing she could think of something clever and witty to say and failing.

'I only wish I'd met you before,' he said. 'I can't wait to tell Patrick and Bianca. They'll be so pleased.'

'Really? Why?'

She had been rather daunted by the prospect of her entry into this small charmed triangle, one member of which was her boss.

'Oh, that we're having fun together. They're very generous friends. And Patrick and I go back a long way.'

'I'm sure. Did you enjoy school, boarding, all that stuff?'

'Yes, I did. Even prep school. I was really good at games, you see, and that makes such a difference. You don't get bullied and once my dad got married again, I was just so glad to be away from home.'

'Was it that bad?'

'Yup. She's a horrible person. Worked quite hard at coming be-tween us – my sister and me – and my dad. She was – still is, actually – very good at being what he wanted, a flashy, flirty bit of stuff.'

'Yes, I see.'

He grinned at her. 'You couldn't, quite, not till you'd met her.' He hesitated then said, 'Will you come back to my place tonight?'

'I – well, maybe not tonight.'

'Oh – OK.'

That had been the first bit of wispy cloud; she could see it had hurt. Funny, how sensitive he was. She'd always thought those City boys must be tough, sexist shits; so wrong.

'Any particular reason?' he said now.

'Well . . .' What could she say? That she'd promised to spend the next day with Henk and she was going to tell him she didn't want to see him any more? There was no way she could explain that to

Jonjo. Not now, not when she'd already said there wasn't anyone else.

'I have a ton of work to do. I really need to start early on it, get it done.'

'What, on a Sunday? That sounds suspiciously like you've got to wash your hair to me.'

'It truly isn't. Well, I might wash it, I suppose, when I've finished my work.' Her voice sounded not quite right even to her. 'It's all about the conference. Bianca is having a huge debriefing on Monday morning.'

'Oh, OK.' He smiled at her, but she could feel him withdrawing from her. 'You've got to do what you've got to do, I suppose. Bianca is clearly a bit of a slave driver.'

'Maybe I could come round in the evening?'

He looked immediately more cheerful; the sky cleared again.

'Maybe. As long as your hair's clean.'

'It will be. Promise.'

He smiled, then said, 'Susie, there's something I should tell you. I've – well, I've finished with Guinevere.'

She felt, absurdly, a rush of panic.

'Not just because of you, of course. But she was really getting to me. She is one spoilt cow. I told her I didn't think it was working any more and I wanted out. So, result is I'm a free man!'

Susie smiled at him, as confidently as she could.

She had decided to talk to Henk in the flat; it was bound to become emotional, and it seemed unfair to expose him to the world as he wept, or raged, or both. She slept badly; a tender farewell from Jonjo had left her more strung up, not less. What was she doing, risking this lovely, potentially perfect thing, for a man who had abused her emotionally and physically. Was she quite mad?

Henk came as arranged, at ten, bearing flowers, and some perfect croissants.

She made coffee, squeezed orange juice, sat down at the table with him; her hand shook as she picked up her croissant, dipped it in the coffee; he noticed.

'Hey, babe. What's with the nerves?'

'Oh – nothing. I . . .'

Go on, Susie, say it now, start, begin to get it over. But he was already munching on his croissant; better wait till he had finished. She managed a couple of bites, drained her glass of orange.

Her phone rang; she looked at it. Jonjo.

Best ignored. She could tell him she'd been in the shower.

'Who was that?'

'Oh – Mum.'

'I have some news,' he said. 'I got a commission to do some pictures for the *Sketch*.'

'Henk! That's amazing. I'm so pleased.' She was; it would help if he had something going right for him.

'Yeah. Anyway, how about another coffee? Then we might go out for a walk? It's a lovely day. And we might see a film later. What's on?'

'I have no idea.'

He fished out his phone and she went over to the coffee machine. After this coffee she'd start. A shudder of fear rose in her throat, so strong she physically had to swallow it down again.

'We could do – something else,' Henk said.

She knew what he meant; another shudder. They hadn't done it since he had left, having smacked her around and, oddly, he had accepted that. It was all part of the monumental effort he was making to please her, to show how much he had changed.

'Let's see,' was all she said. 'Look, Henk, I need to talk to you.'

'Yeah? What about? Look. I'm not rushing you into me moving back in. You don't need to get all stressed about that.'

'No, I know. No, it's not that.'

'OK. So – what?'

'I'll tell you. I – I just want to have a pee.'

She went into the bathroom, sat on the loo, texted Jonjo. She felt a sudden need to be in contact with him, to gain the courage. *Sorry was in the shower. I'll call you vv soon.*

No reply.

She went back into the sitting room; Henk was lounging on the sofa. He patted the seat beside him and she joined him reluctantly, took a deep breath, counted to five, then said, 'Henk, we have – *I* have to finish with this. With us. I want it to be over, Henk. It isn't – isn't working.'

There was a long, throbbing silence. He stared at her, his expression puzzled.

Then, 'Oh no,' he said. 'No, sorry. That just won't do.'

'What won't do, Henk?'

'That. That's fucking nonsense. We're just getting it together again. You can't stop it now.' He was looking at her very oddly, like a puzzled child, told something it didn't understand.

'I can, Henk.' Why didn't she feel stronger, more certain?

'No, Susie, you can't. Because I'm doing everything you want. Having life counselling, leaving you alone.'

'Henk, I know that. And yes, you've been wonderful, and I really, really appreciate it. But – it's still not right, the whole thing just doesn't work any more and I just don't feel right with you.'

'Well, that's ridiculous.'

'It may be, but it's true. I just feel frightened of you . . . can't trust you.'

'But the whole point of this counselling I'm having is so I won't do that any more. Of course you can trust me. That is just fucking insulting. I don't understand!'

He was getting angry now; she felt afraid.

'I can't believe this. Can't believe you're doing this to me.'

'I'm not doing anything to you,' she said slowly, 'I'm just trying to explain. It's not your fault, Henk. I – just can't go on with it. With you.'

'Oh shit,' he said, and he sat down again, and buried his head in his hands. When he looked at her again, there were tears in his eyes. One was rolling slowly down his cheek. He took a deep breath and it was more like a sob.

She felt terrible; of all the reactions she had feared, tears were the worst.

'Susie – *please*. Please don't do this. Not yet. I love you so much. Give me another chance. I'll think of something, prove it to you somehow. You've got to let me try.'

'Henk, I can't. I'm sorry.'

He looked at her then, more tears trickling down his face, his eyes almost frightened.

'I can't bear it,' he said. 'You've no idea what you're doing to me. I just don't understand. I've done everything you asked. And I love you, I told you that. I keep telling you. I don't see why you can't accept that.'

'I do accept it, Henk, of course I do. But – it's not enough.'

'So you don't love me?'

An agonising silence; he reached out for her hand. Reluctantly, very reluctantly she gave it to him.

'I – I don't love you, Henk, no. I'm sorry.'

And then he really started to sob, wracking sobs, wiping his nose on his arm, staring at her, clearly horribly hurt. Finally he said, 'Is there – is there anyone else? Please tell me, Susie. I need to know.'

And she said, and this was her fatal, dreadful mistake, struggling to save him further pain, and afterwards she could hardly believe she had said something so stupid, so dangerous, 'There could be . . .'

He had left soon after that, saying he needed to think, and she kissed him briefly on the cheek, said she was sorry, that she hoped he would be all right, that she would never forget him, that he had been very special to her.

She went very slowly into the bedroom and lay down on the bed; she felt completely exhausted. She looked at her watch: only eleven. How had she lived a lifetime, several lifetimes, and the morning only half over?

She must have fallen asleep, for when she looked again, it was after one. Incredible, amidst all that turmoil. Just escaping, she supposed. She looked at her phone: nothing from Jonjo. That was bad. She took a deep breath and texted him, desperate for some proper contact. *Things going well. Might be able to come earlier. OK with you?*

Surely that would get a response. It didn't.

◇ ◇ ◇

412

Jonjo had gone for a walk. The streets and quaysides of Canary Wharf were busy, people enjoying the frosty sunshine. He felt a bit disorientated. There she was, this gorgeous, sexy, funny, warm, perfect girl, who had been dropped into his life by some kindly fate or other, at a moment that would have seemed ideal for both of them and something wasn't quite right. More than that, something was wrong. He had no idea what, but whatever it was, she wasn't being entirely truthful with him. And if there was one thing Jonjo couldn't cope with it was dishonesty. He needed, more than anything, more than the sexiness and the gorgeousness and the warmth, absolute honesty, for knowing where he was. One minute Susie had seemed honest, the next there was a sliver of deceit in the way she looked at him, the things she was doing. Better to end it, quickly, to turn away, however much it hurt, than trail after her, hoping for the best. He'd called her this morning first thing, and she hadn't answered. That was odd, he thought, for a girl who was supposed to be glued to her laptop. Her later text, that she was in the shower, didn't quite ring true. He'd steeled himself not to answer it. He'd gone for the walk to try and clear his head, tell himself he could be making a mistake on the slenderest of evidence; he'd taken his phone, but failed to notice it was almost out of juice – a clue to the emotional turmoil he was in; normally it was part of him, required to function perfectly.

He stopped for a coffee and croissant and to pick up a paper, and when he got back and realised, and plugged it in to return her call, his heart suddenly wonderfully lighter, there was no reply.

Susie was sitting, trying genuinely to work, to distract herself from what was a long failure to reply to her text, when there was a hammering on her door. Her heart sank; she was afraid she was actually going to be sick.

'Susie!' It was Henk. 'Susie, it's me. Let me in, I have to see you.'

She got up, double-locked the door, hoping Henk wouldn't hear, and sat on the sofa, staring at it; if she waited long enough, surely he would assume she was out, would go away. Even so . . .

'Susie, we need to talk. I know you're there. Let me in.'

She sat, silent, motionless; time passed. The hammering, the shouting went on. She had never been so frightened, never felt so trapped.

Her phone rang; she looked at it. Damn, damn, damn! Jonjo, and she daren't answer it – Henk might hear her. She went into the bathroom, shut the door, thinking she could text him, then realised there was nothing she could say that made any kind of sense.

She started to cry and heard other voices, her neighbours from downstairs, a nice middle-aged couple, telling Henk to stop making such a noise, that they had no idea where Susie was.

The hammering stopped, and the shouting. She waited, her heart thudding, for fifteen minutes. She was far too frightened to open the door.

Inspiration struck her and she called the couple downstairs – they'd insisted on her having their number, in case she ever had a problem or locked herself out. She was very sorry about the noise, Henk was upset, they'd had a row, but could they possibly just look and see if he was there, she was frightened to come out.

They were up in thirty seconds, kind and reassuring: he had gone, they'd seen him go. She should have called before, would she like a cup of tea, should they call the police?

She thanked them, said she was fine for now, and that if he came back she would call the police; thinking she could at least threaten Henk with that.

All of which took over half an hour; and when they had gone, then of course she called Jonjo back, and actually managed to have a half-reasonable conversation with him and he said he was sorry, he hadn't got her text and of course she should come over sooner, or should he come to her? Which was tempting, because then she wouldn't have to go out, but then suppose Henk came back while Jonjo was there? So she said no, she'd come over, maybe about four? Which would give her time, she thought, to have a bath and recover her equilibrium; and she could order a cab to Waterloo and just shoot out into it – that would give her some protection; Henk wouldn't dare attack her in the street.

Four would be just great, Jonjo said, and she ran a bath and lay in it for a long time, and then did her hair and dressed very, very carefully casual – jeans and a sweater and a Kate Moss-style parka – and ordered a cab and when it rang to say it was outside, shot out, double locking the door and down the stairs and into it, and was so frightened still that she kept looking out of the back window all the way to Waterloo, and as she ran down the escalator to the Jubilee line she still half expected him to be behind her, and at each station they came to she stared at the people coming in, as if Henk could possibly know where she was going, and when she finally reached Canary Wharf, she ran up the impossibly long escalator into what was now darkness and Jonjo was there, waiting for her as he had said he would be, and she collapsed into his arms crying, and said she'd had a horrible experience with a neighbour, and he said she should have told him, and she must go to the police and tried to make her do it there and then, but she got out of it somehow, and promised to do it first thing in the morning, and he said come on then, I have crumpets and a boiling kettle, and everything was magically and wonderfully all right again. And she felt she could have flown with happiness and relief and later he tried to make her stay, and she said she couldn't, she had nothing with her and it was Monday in a few hours; so he said he'd send her home in a cab and not too late either, because he had to be at work at six, and after a takeaway they settled down to some more snogging, and finally, reluctantly, she said she should go.

She got home safely, peering fearfully out of the cab as she reached her flat, shooting inside, the kindly neighbours' number ready on her phone; but it was all right. He wasn't there. He must have accepted it, after all. The worst was over; she could move on.

And then the texts began.

Chapter 39

He'd asked her to marry him. Properly, down on one knee, smiling at his own foolishness as he did so, ring in pocket, eyes anxious.

She was seriously tempted. She didn't love him, of course, but she was very fond of him and they had much in common: music, books, a love of walking. Sex had not entered the equation – he was too much of a gentleman even to propose it, but he was tactile and warm, liked her to take his arm, often reached for her hand in the cinema, or in concerts, kissed her tenderly when he left her. She was sure it would be – well, fine. And how important was it, after all, at her age?

She asked for time to think about it. She would want to continue with her career, she said. Would that be acceptable to him? He was retired, he might want her constant company. But he said that was fine, it was one of the things he most admired about her, her professional expertise; he had his golf and a lot of committees, and he had no wish to deprive her of something so important in her life. And he loved to hear the gossipy stories about the industry; about how Elizabeth Arden had her racehorses massaged with her Eight Hour Cream to improve their coats, how Helena Rubinstein loathed Charles Revson, creator of Revlon, but also admired him to the extent of buying Revlon stock, and how she witheringly referred to him as 'that man'; and how, when he launched his male line, Revson christened it 'That Man' by way of a rejoinder.

Timothy Benning was a widower; his wife had died five years earlier.

'It was a happy marriage,' he told her, 'and I know she would have wished me to find happiness again if I could.'

He had been a solicitor, and was tall and quite good-looking, sixty-five years old, with two delightful grown-up children who clearly loved him and welcomed Florence into the family. Such straightforwardness, such overall pleasantness seemed almost incredible to her, after the tortuous ramifications of the Farrells.

She had met Timothy at a supper party and afterwards he asked for her telephone number and said he would like to take her to a concert – there was a programme at the Wigmore Hall that she would clearly enjoy.

The Wigmore, being permanently linked in Florence's mind with her first serious encounter with Cornelius, didn't seem to her ideal and she gently suggested an alternative at the Festival Hall.

'I hope you won't mind, but I do prefer orchestral music to chamber.' And Timothy said actually, so did he, and a great and happy friendship was born.

If it could only have remained so, Florence thought. But romance managed, most wonderfully and sweetly, to find its way, and after three months of concerts and walks and art galleries, Timothy took her one night to a restaurant – a small, unpretentious one in Victoria, for he lacked both the income and the style preferred by the Farrells and their set, and took her hand rather awkwardly as they waited for dessert and said that she surely must have realised he had grown very fond of her, and was feeling emotions stronger than friendship for her. Flattered and charmed, Florence had leaned forward and kissed him gently on the cheek, and thanked him, but asked if they might take things a little slowly, whereupon he acceded very happily. But after another few weeks, the proposal came, and she lay awake most of the night, confronting what was temptation of a considerable kind.

For yes, she did love Cornelius, deeply and passionately, and knew she always would; but she was tired of being a mistress, tired of always being the good guy, against Athina's bad, always being sweet-tempered, sympathetic, fun, sexy. Tired of lonely weekends, holidays, Christmases, birthdays often: although they had a little ritual for those, dinner at some new, and surprising place – his challenge to find it – and then, dangerously but determinedly, back to her house, where they went straight up to her bed with the bottle of champagne he had had delivered days before, and then a wonderful present, usually jewellery, not necessarily of the precious variety: she had developed a taste for Butler and Wilson's witty brooches – she had a leopard, a Scotty dog, and a petrifying, Tarantula-size spider – but occasionally Chanel jewellery, or one of her long pearl chains.

He was less lavish with his gifts these days because there was less money; Farrell's were no longer shooting stars: they trailed in the wake of other, newer, names; even Revlon trailed behind Lauder and L'Oréal and Clinique, as did many other great names.

Lauder reigned, brilliantly confident, inventive, with vast resources; Mrs Lauder was a living legend, dazzling, charming, gracious – and a saleswoman to the last drop of her blood.

Athina could not stand her, seeing her as the embodiment of what she might have been herself; she denounced her as vulgar, while admiring her tactics, and as greedy, while envying her ability to buy up what seemed half the cosmetic universe.

The great brands now were all skincare-based, houses like Clarins, with its seemingly untouchable image of quality and purity, and there was much talk of a holistic approach, where health and fitness were far more important than the colour of eyeshadow – everyone was going to the gym and to Jane Fonda-style exercise classes. Skin and hair care led the research field and L'Oréal were said to employ over a thousand chemists in the early eighties.

Perfumes were no longer about smell, but that mysterious thing called lifestyle, pioneered a decade earlier by Charles Revson launching the lovely Shelley Hack from *Charlie's Angels* as his sexy, trouser-suited Charlie, and followed by the entire market. The actual scents were all intriguing, chemically based, very potent and long-lasting and their one virtue for Athina, at least, was that they made Lauder's *Youth Dew* seem old-fashioned. Florence's favourite was Rive Gauche, with its glorious message *'Ce n'est pas un parfum pour les femmes effacées'* – 'it is not a perfume for women without personality'.

It was the era of Princess Diana, and her lovely face with its over-glossed lips and over-mascara'ed eyelashes smiled radiantly, or sometimes a little sadly, from every cover of every magazine, every front page of every newspaper, every country in every continent. She was a phenomenon, her looks as much as her emotional life analysed, wondered at, and copied.

There were still colour houses that mattered; Mary Quant led the field, and a few of the teenage brands, Boots Seventeen, Rimmel, Maybelline, but with the exception of Quant, they were despised by Athina Farrell. Indeed as the years went by, she despised more and more and admired less: a dangerous condition for a creative mind.

'I fear we are floundering,' Cornelius admitted to Florence more than once. 'We need a new direction and we are not going to find it with Athina in this mood.'

'Perhaps you could find it yourself?' Florence volunteered.

'My darling, creativity was never my forte. I just know it when I see it. And I don't see it. At this rate we're going to have to sell the Hove flat, which will be utterly dreadful. Weekends in London, so depressing.'

'I'm sure you'll survive,' said Florence briskly.

'Well, of course we'll survive, darling, it just won't be so much fun.'

He was sometimes extraordinarily thick-skinned but she supposed he needed to be, to endure life with Athina, and in the event, Athina did come up with something: clever, rather than brilliant, but catching the mood of the moment. She designed the Skin Breathing collection: 'Every product so light your skin breathes night and day!'

Wildly inaccurate scientifically – 'For what product could possibly stop the air getting to your skin?' Francine said rather witheringly to Florence. They nevertheless got away with it because the beauty editors were having a lean season, so the consultants had something to talk about and the public went for it. The advertising campaign, shot by the brilliant Terence Donovan, showed a girl riding a bicycle down a country lane, her long hair streaming behind her. Cornelius had a field day, talking it up and selling it in, and the Hove flat was able to remain unsold. For some reason, this made Florence more rather than less keen on the idea of marriage to Timothy.

She had been rather hurt by Cornelius's open admiration for, and flirtation with, the model for the Skin Breathing range, a lovely dark-eyed, dark-haired girl called Gilly Gould; he had insisted on being present at the photoshoot, and at the launch party paid the most inordinately extravagant tribute to her and her beauty, presenting her with a huge bouquet of red roses, and bore her off to dinner at The Ritz with Athina – who was equally irritated, but was at least permitted to show it. Florence had to pretend it was nothing to her; but when, a week later, after a promotion at Selfridges where Gilly Gould modelled the range, Cornelius seemed able to talk of little else, she told him she was finding his conversation a little limited and was leaving.

'But darling, I thought we were all going to drinks at the Connaught?'

'You all are. I have better things to do.'

'That might look a little rude.'

'To whom?'

'To Gilly, to Athina. And to me.'

'Cornelius, Athina never minds if I am present at a function or not. To Miss Gould I am the hired help. I don't think she has ever uttered more than two consecutive words to me. And I think I have earned the right, just occasionally, to be rude to you.'

He understood at once. 'I'm sorry, my darling, I've been tactless. May I come round later? Athina is dining with Caro and Martin and I've pleaded overwork.'

'I . . . suppose so.'

'Not very enthusiastic. Miss Hamilton, do be kind enough to allow me to call.'

'All right.'

He arrived with a vast bouquet of white roses, and said he was sorry.

'I'm just an old man, besotted with a young beauty. Pathetic. But it happens, my darling. We can't help it, we old chaps.'

'Of course.' And she smiled at him, drank two glasses of champagne, said that of course she understood and then made it very plain she had no desire to go upstairs.

'I'm tired, Cornelius, it's been a long day. And we old ladies, we need a little more rest than we used to.'

Normally she would not have dreamed of saying such a thing, of implying that she was no longer as passionately attracted to him as she had been in the heady early days, but today she felt she had a right to. That was all the difference, she thought: he could claim attraction to a young beauty and a need to boost his flagging sexual prowess and she must accept that as his right. Which was all right if a man was your husband, but a long-term lover . . .

She decided, sitting there, contemplating Cornelius with more irritation than she had ever experienced, that she would accept Timothy's proposal. Cornelius would rage and rant and quite possibly cry, but then, at the end, he would have to accept it. It was finally time for her to be selfish.

'Right,' he said, easing himself up from the sofa, 'I must go. Now, I hope you don't mind, but I'm taking the Trentham with me.'

'You're what?'

'Only borrowing it,' he said, smiling at her. 'I didn't think you'd mind and Leonard needs it.'

'Well, he can't have it!' she said, panic rising. Cornelius had never spotted the fake, but Leonard would.

'Sweetheart, it's only for a few weeks.'

'Even so. And what for?'

'Well, he's a bit on his uppers, poor old boy, and he's going to hold an exhibition and needs as much of his work as possible to hang. It won't be sold, you'll get it back. Well, I suppose someone might make an offer he can't refuse . . .'

'Don't be ridiculous,' she said, fear making her irritable. 'That painting's priceless to me, you know it is!'

'Well, that's nice to hear. But like I say, you'll get it back.'

'Cornelius, I really don't want to let him have it.'

'Now you're being silly,' he said, taking the picture down. It wasn't very big: only about eighteen inches by twelve in its frame. She looked at him in horror.

'Cornelius . . .'

'Is there a problem?'

'No. Well – yes. You're being rather high-handed.'

'And you're being a bit dog in the manger, if you don't mind my saying so. He's an old friend, Florence, he needs my help.'

'It seems to be *me* that's giving the help,' she said, but she didn't argue any more. There was no point. She would just have to sit it out.

Timothy phoned later; would she like to spend Saturday with him? They could go for a walk on the Downs, he said, and then he would cook dinner for them and introduce her to a new rather sophisticated hi-fi system he had just bought. 'And then, of course, you must stay the night, and we can savour the joys of the village pub next morning. I have to go to church, I am, for my sins, churchwarden, but after that I am a free man.'

It all sounded wonderfully pleasant and undemanding and she accepted with pleasure. But as she packed on Saturday morning, lots of soft jersey casual separates and her stout brogues for their walk, she felt the opposite of relaxed, fearing every moment for a call from Cornelius about the picture.

It did not come, and she left for Waterloo and the Guildford train feeling calmer and more optimistic. Perhaps if he didn't want to sell it, Leonard Trentham would simply hang the picture – in its original frame – without paying it too much attention.

The weekend passed happily and easily. Timothy was so – so uncomplicated. He spoke fondly, smiling even, about his wife, Barbara.

'She was such a lovely person, you would have liked her. So kind and so generous. And so brave. We were very happy. And for a long time I didn't think I could bear life without her. It seemed so utterly pointless. But – things have proved otherwise. And you know,

Florence, they say people who have known one happy, stable relationship are able more easily to form another. Do you agree with that?'

'I – don't know,' she said carefully. Could her relationship with Cornelius, with all its attendant complications and deceits, its wild highs and its sorry, lonely lows, be described as either happy or stable?

'I suppose not. Your marriage was so very short you could never really have known real fulfilment. I feel so sad for you, over that.'

She wondered what on earth he would say if he knew about Cornelius; he would be shocked, undoubtedly, but would he be able to accept it, understand? She would never tell him anyway, so it wouldn't matter. Only . . . it would. So large a part of her, that second, hidden life of hers, there for the discovering. It was a big risk, on more than one level. Could she, *should* she do this, yield to this sweet, uncomplicated temptation?

The walk on the Downs, dusted with winter sunshine, slowly awakening to spring, was wonderful. He took her hand at one point, helping her up a steep slope, then continued to hold it. 'You don't mind do you?' he asked, half serious, and she leaned up and kissed his cheek and said, 'No, of course not, it's lovely.'

Dinner was delicious, eaten at his kitchen table: an excellent cottage pie followed by rhubarb crumble. 'Nursery food,' he said, 'so good after a long walk.'

And then they sat by the fire listening to Handel on the hi-fi and she started worrying again, wondering what might be happening in London, what furious, or indignant messages might be left on her answering machine, whether Cornelius or Lawrence Trentham or both might be looking for her, outraged and avenging, or speculating on where she was.

The concert ended. 'Nightcap?' Timothy said.

'I'd love a cocoa,' she said.

'I meant something more exotic. But cocoa you shall have.'

He brought two mugs back, set them on the low table between them.

Then he looked at her.

'I am so very fond of you, Florence,' he said, 'I am so hoping you will give me the answer I want.'

'Timothy—'

'But I am not going to press you. I understand you need time. There are many things for you to come to terms with, not least sharing your life full-time. Something you have never done.'

She smiled at him.

'I appreciate your understanding so much, Timothy,' she said.

'I just think – *know* indeed – that we can be very happy together. And I know my children feel the same. They like you enormously.'

'As I do them.'

'Laura told me a secret today. She is going to have a baby.'

'Oh, Timothy, that's so lovely.'

'I know. I am very excited. Sad, of course, that was something Barbara most grieved over, never having a grandchild. But very wonderful for me.'

Goodness, Florence thought, I would be a step-grandmother. How amazing, after a lifetime of spinsterhood. Would that ease the pain of her own, never-forgotten baby? Or make it worse?

'Things like that, you see,' he said, smiling at her, 'are best shared. And I think you would be a very delightful grandmother by marriage. But – wrong of me to put even that pressure on you, dear Florence. I am resolved not to do it. Now – bed. Goodnight, my dear. I'll see you in the morning.'

She got up, kissed his cheek; as she reached the door, he said, 'I don't want you to think I am not longing to take you to bed, Florence, but again, it would be wrong before you have made up your mind. It's not the blessing of the church I am looking for, but your own.'

'Of course,' she said quietly.

'And besides,' he said, with an odd, slightly embarrassed smile, 'I feel rather nervous, just contemplating the whole thing. I have no idea, of course, whether you have had relationships, I'm sure you have. And I don't want you to tell me unless you choose to. But it will be a challenge, in any case. I have only ever made love to one

424

woman and I might prove very unsatisfactory to you; I really have no idea.'

'Oh, Timothy,' said Florence, walking back to him, kissing him again, 'I'm sure you will prove extremely satisfactory. But I think you are right; we should wait a little longer. Although, like you, I like the idea of it very much.'

'Really?' he said and his smile was brilliant suddenly. 'How very good that is to hear. Goodnight, my dear. Sleep well.'

Oh, he was so incredibly nice. What had she done to deserve him? What? Nothing, she told herself, as she lay wide awake, far in to the small hours, you don't deserve him in the very least.

In the morning she accompanied him to church. Raised to attend morning service, she found herself jerked back into childhood and the singular pleasure of singing hymns, the words of all of which she remembered. They then went to the pub and had a drink in the bar, and were inveigled into eating a rather bad lunch. And after a short walk, she finally, and reluctantly, returned to London.

Sitting on the train, she felt bathed in ease and happiness, wondering that such things were hers for the taking. She compared it with what she knew: disorder, unease and much emotional discomfort. Where was the problem, why did she even hesitate? Was she quite mad?

Deciding that she was, she took a taxi from Waterloo. And immediately tumbled back into discord.

There were eight calls on her answering machine: three from Lawrence Trentham, sounding distressed, asking her to call him, then five from Cornelius, making the same request.

She phoned neither of them. She called Timothy to say she was safely home, as he had requested, and then settled down to watch TV, some foolish Sunday serial.

She slept badly, dreamed feverishly. The morning dragged next day and shortly after two Cornelius arrived at The Shop.

'Anyone here?'

She shook her head.

'Good.' His voice was cold, his face hostile. He locked the door, put the notice on it.

'What's going on, Florence?'

'I – don't know what you mean.'

'Of course you do. Leonard says that picture's a fake.'

She didn't tell him, of course, the real reason. She couldn't. But she did tell him she had needed some money urgently.

'But why? And why didn't you ask me for it?'

'Cornelius, there's a limit even to my lack of pride. It's humiliating, to be dependent on you. I – had some financial problems and I really needed money.'

'Why?'

'I don't think that is any of your business.'

'Of course it is. Since you decided on this major deception, using a gift of mine.'

She was amazed at the way the lies flowed.

'Well, I'd taken on Duncan's mother's nursing home fees – oh, not all of them, just filling in a gap for the family.'

'Florence! When you have so little? Kind, generous, but – rash.'

'I know. Anyway, I did it. So I had to honour it. She's very old and frail. So I – I decided to – to sell the picture.'

'Our picture.'

'No, Cornelius, *the* picture. Mine, if we are to be precise. You gave it to me.'

'And only the other day you had the gall to tell me it was priceless to you.'

'I know. I'm sorry. But – well, I thought I might get it back one day.'

'Who bought it?'

'The Stuart gallery.'

'That little shit! Do you know where it went?'

'Overseas, I'm afraid. Cornelius, it's no use. We'll never get it back. I'm so, so sorry.'

'Well, what's done's done. I'm very disappointed in you, Florence. But I suppose I understand your motives. Do you want that other painting back?'

'Of course I do! It's very precious to me. Real or fake.'

426

'I do find that hard to understand.' His expression was close to dislike.

'Cornelius,' she said, hurt making her desperate, 'please, please try to understand what it's like to be me. Always, always, I'm the underdog. Playing second fiddle to Athina—'

'That's absurd!'

'It's true. She is your wife, has the status, the security, I have nothing . . .'

'You have me. And my love.'

'No, Cornelius, I don't have you. I've been hidden away now, notionally at least, for nearly thirty years. It's been lovely and I entered into it with my eyes completely open but sometimes, just sometimes, I long for security, normality. I have to manage on my own, most of the time.' She was pale now, not tearful, but desperately sincere. 'And I have to be alone, most of the time. It isn't easy, while enduring Athina's high-handed attitude. I have no security—'

'Yes you do,' he said. 'You have great security, as you know. When you need to claim it.'

'Yes, of course. And I'm grateful for that. Although I find it hard to imagine I'll ever use it.'

'Florence, you must. If you need to. That's why I did it.'

'I know. And I'm grateful. But – anyway, I do have to manage everything, deal with the world, on my own. And I need you to understand how difficult that is.'

There was a long silence; then he said, 'Come here, Little Flo.' He drew her towards him and said, 'I love you. I love you so much. I am so very lucky to have you in my life. I don't deserve you.'

'No,' she said, smiling suddenly, 'you really don't. But—'

'I know. I cannot imagine life without you. How I would bear it all. And I do realise that it could happen, that someone, some decent chap, will come along and ask you to marry him. And you would have every right to leave me for him. Every right.'

And suddenly she knew that Timothy Benning was not for her. He was far too good for her. She had not lived the life of a good person. She had been an adulteress, had deceived the woman to whom she owed everything, deceived her ruthlessly and without remorse. Would remorse have made it better? Perhaps a little; but she had not felt it. Had even found succour in the thought, as Athina snubbed and belittled her, that she had her husband's heart. And his body, quite frequently.

A person such as that had no business moving into the life of a person such as Timothy Benning. Moreover, there were new deceptions now, layered one upon another. She had lied, with hideous ease, to her lover, had concealed from him that she had aborted his child, had found a spurious reason for doing what she had done. And that alone, Timothy would have found unforgivable. That she could have aborted a baby without considering other, more virtuous options – and while concealing its very existence from its father.

And she could not have kept it all from him: not always. Marriage, certainly to someone as good and transparent as Timothy, was about truth, about trust; it could not be built upon lies and suspicion. And, gradually, she would have wrecked what Timothy Benning was about; besmirching his goodness. He would have looked at her with those smiling, affectionate eyes, and gradually, inevitably, they would have seen what was really there: a capacity for, and indeed a history of, infinite deceit. She could not do that to him, could not destroy him and his happy, easeful life. It would be the final act of wickedness, worse, far worse than deceiving Athina. Who, after all, was fairly wicked herself.

And so, with many tears, she wrote to Timothy. She knew that no emotional reason would persuade him; she said simply that she felt that their lives were too different, too difficult to blend, that she was unable to fit into his life, charming and pleasant as she found it, and that she feared they would make each other unhappy, being the inherently different creatures they were.

Indeed, I think we should not meet again, for I have made up my mind and seeing you might make it waver. Thank you for the happiest three months of my life and, most recently, the happiest two days of those very months. I long to accept, long to join you. You are very special, very good and very, very

428

dear to me; I am so fond of you. For that very reason, I know I cannot hurt you as I know I would.

Thank you for everything and please forgive me. And try in due course, to remember me lovingly as I do you.

Florence

She addressed the envelope, read the letter three more times, weeping as she did so, then walked to the postbox and pushed the letter in by sheer force of will, holding on to it with the tips of her fingers and then finally letting go and, crying quite openly now, walked back through the dark, cold streets to her little house, and to her lonely, difficult, sometimes dark life that she had thought briefly she could escape from, into warmth and light and happiness, and now knew she never could.

Chapter 40

This was so terrible. It took the whole thing and her unhappiness up to a new level. She'd walked into the classroom after lunch one day – she'd taken to hiding in the loos during lunch – and there on her desk had been an envelope. Fearing the worst, she'd not picked it up or opened it for a while. *Milly* it said, and a little kiss underneath. Probably someone feeling sorry for her, wanting to let her know. One of the less popular people, perhaps – no, they'd be too afraid of reprisals themselves. It wasn't in handwriting so she couldn't begin to guess, but in rather elaborate capitals, with decorations on each one, flowers on the 'M', twining up it a little figure forming the 'I', then the two 'L's turned into swans' necks, and finally the 'Y' forming a kite, with a long tail trailing down. Surely no one would do that if they were being mean? Feeling a bit as if she was jumping into an ice-cold pool she suddenly ripped it open; and it wasn't mean, it was a note from Carey:

Hi Mills,
    I've missed you. We all have. Time to make up. Come for a hot chocolate after school. Friends reunited, huh? Sorry if we've been a bit mean.

Of course what she should have done was rip it up, look coldly at Carey, say no, sorry she was busy; but it was like – well, getting out of that dreadful cold pool and walking into a gorgeously warm one, with the sun shining down on her after months of dark skies, and she sat there, smiling foolishly at the note, and when Carey came in and smiled at her, and then all the others, she smiled back and it was as if none of the misery and loneliness had ever happened.

'Starbucks after school, yeah?' said Carey. 'We've got to do something first, so not till four thirty. We'll all be there.'

'Cool,' said Milly.

The afternoon dragged; she had fixed to see Jayce, but cancelled her. She knew it was mean, but she could make it up to her . . .

She hung around in the library and then arrived, carefully not even a minute early, at Starbucks in the Fulham Road, her heart thumping, wondering what she would say to them all, because it was actually a little bit difficult – she had no idea what had brought about this sudden change, but something had, and all she felt was gratitude. No doubt they would tell her in due course.

Starbucks was almost empty at half past four; she frowned, went in and walked all round, in case they were hiding under a table or behind a pillar, ready to say 'surprise, surprise!'. But there was nobody else there, apart from a couple of mothers with small children and a man working at his laptop. Milly walked out again; waited for a very long ten minutes and still nobody came. Finally, thinking Carey must have been held up, and having checked her phone for the umpteenth time, she went in again and sat down at one of the tables. Whereupon one of the Starbucks' staff came out from behind the coffee machine, walked over to her and said, 'Are you Milly?'

Milly nodded.

'Your friends asked me to give you this. Said they'd had to go.'

She ripped open the envelope.

Hi Mills,

Can't believe you fell for that. Did you really think we'd be seen dead in Starbucks with you? You might have brought your fat friend and how gross would that have been? Best go home now and get on with your homework like a good little girl.

It was so absolutely brutal, like getting a slap across the face when you were looking the other way, that Milly burst into tears and sat there for quite a long time crying, her head on her arms, until the girl who had given her the note came over to her and said awkwardly, 'You OK? Sorry if it was bad news. Can I get you a hot chocolate or something?'

And Milly, unable to bear even such detached kindness, shook her head and ran out and down the road, all the way to the tube station, while dreading that one of them would be waiting for her in a doorway, to do some other horrible thing.

Only they weren't, and she finally arrived home so white-faced and exhausted that Sonia decided she must be ill, and sent her up to bed, and then called Bianca to say exactly that and that if Bianca could come home early, that would be nice, but if not she could hold on until Patrick arrived.

But Bianca's phone was on message and Sonia rang the office number and got Jemima, who said she wasn't expecting Bianca back, that she'd gone out to a meeting; and then added awkwardly that Patrick wasn't coming back for another two days, he'd been held up in New York.

Sonia said icily, which she knew was unfair because it was hardly Jemima's fault, that no one had told her and that she couldn't stay indefinitely and if Jemima heard from Bianca could she please tell her to call her immediately and that Milly really wasn't well.

Bianca had been looking forward to seeing Patrick; he'd been away for over a week now and it had been uncomfortable and stressful. She'd missed him on a personal level too, but so swiftly was he changing from the old Patrick, from the loving, attentive person she thought she knew, into this strange, distracted, remote creature, that this hardly entered the emotional equation when he called to say that Saul wanted him to stay on and dig a bit deeper into an engineering company. 'He's fired up over this one, Bianca, I really have to stay on.'

Asked to list them in order of importance, those emotions, she would have put rage, indignation and frustration well below a hostility towards Saul Finlayson so strong, that if he had walked into her office now she would have thrown the rather large and heavy flower arrangement that resided on her desk at him and hoped it would deal a fatal blow.

As she slammed down the phone, her mobile rang; it was Saul Finlayson.

'I'm sorry about Patrick,' he said, walking into her office five minutes later. 'Very sorry. I can see how annoying it must be for you . . .'

'It's more than annoying,' she said, eyeing the flowers, wondering if she was strong enough to throw them, and deciding, regretfully, she was not. 'It's quite serious. I was totally relying on him this evening, I have a meeting with the VCs, Sonia can't stay on to look after the children, he's already two days late and—'

She stopped, realising this was not perhaps quite the message that she should be sending to Patrick's boss: that her main reliance on him was as childminder.

'I'm sorry,' he said again.

'So why are you here?'

'To say I'm sorry. You did sound quite – cross. And I was nearby, so it was easy to come in, not as if I had to make a special journey of it.'

'I'm so pleased about that,' she said.

'Well, I wouldn't have come otherwise, obviously. But this thing he's investigating for me could mean millions, and all the difference between losing them and winning them. I thought I should explain that.'

'Well, I can see how important it is, but he had promised to be back—' Stop it, Bianca, stop sounding like a whingeing wife, it's not clever.

'Bianca – I did warn you about this sort of thing. Maybe it's time you stopped relying on Patrick for domestic backup. He's not working for the family firm any more.'

'Well, thank you,' she said. 'You must give me your views on other aspects of my personal life some time.'

'Oh, I wouldn't presume to do that,' he said, so seriously that she

433

started to laugh. 'I'm sorry, that wasn't meant to be funny.'

'I know, but it was.'

'Look,' he said, 'do you really have to cancel your meeting with the VCs?'

'Yes, I do. Of course it isn't really very important. Just about a few millions, actually. Not as important as yours of course.'

'Would it have taken very long?'

'Probably all evening, and now I only have about half an hour.'

'I see. Well, would that leave you enough time to have a coffee with me? Before you go home?'

'No,' she said, anger rising again. 'No it wouldn't.'

'Well, that's a pity. I wanted to know how your plans were coming along. And about how the conference went.'

'I'm surprised you should remember something so unimportant as my sales conference,' she said, adding briskly, 'Patrick always comes to my conferences, for the dinner and so on. He had to miss it, for the first time ever.'

'I know. And I'm sorry about that too.'

'Did Patrick tell you?'

'No, of course not. He never mentions his personal arrangements. But I remembered your talking about it at Christmas.'

'Oh,' she said. She felt stunned, as if he had said he remembered her birthday.

'I wondered if you managed to get round the perfume problem?'

'Not exactly perfectly,' she said, and she felt as if she might lose control now, being hideously near tears. She managed a bright, tight smile.

'What happened?'

'I – oh, you don't want to know.'

'I do. I've told you before, I find you, and what you do, very interesting. Look, are you sure you don't have time for a coffee? Before you go home and after you've cancelled your meeting?'

'Oh God,' she said, smiling at him suddenly, 'you really are not like anyone else, Saul.'

'So I am told,' he said. 'But I don't see what that has to do with it.'

Sitting with him in Starbucks – Starbucks, of all places, not some cool lounge of some cool hotel – drinking coffee, her meeting cancelled, Mike and Hugh audibly annoyed, texting Sonia to say she would be home in an hour and to give Milly some paracetamol, she sipped her double espresso and found herself telling Saul not only about the conference and Lady Farrell's intervention, but her own brilliant idea. She was surprised to hear herself telling him this, but suddenly it seemed oddly comforting and reassuring. And there was no way he would talk about it to anyone.

'That is extremely clever,' he said, staring at her. 'I'm impressed. You really do have a very good brain, you know.'

'Thank you. Just lately, it hasn't felt like that.'

'No, probably not.'

There was a silence, then he said, 'I do hope you're not even thinking about squandering that on just one or two outlets?'

'I might have to.'

'Well, that's pure stupidity.'

'Thanks. The alternative is finding a few more millions. Oddly, they're not always entirely easy to find.'

'Well, of course they're not,' he said, slightly impatiently, 'I thought you'd realise that.'

She sighed. 'You don't have a great sense of humour do you, Saul?'

'No, everyone says that,' he said. And then, after a pause, 'Was that what your meeting was about?'

'Yes. And of course you're right. Everyone who knows about this, which is about three people—'

'That's good,' he said.

'Yes. Anyway, everyone says the same thing. I have to go global. Unfortunately that means more money. A lot more.'

'And the VCs say no?'

'They do.'

'Fools,' he said. And then, looking at his watch, 'Look, I'm sorry. I'd love to stay but I do really have to go. And you have to get that money. You really do.'

'Thanks for the advice,' she said.

'That's all right,' he said, 'any time, just call.'

And then something quite extraordinary happened as they waited outside looking for cabs; he suddenly moved towards her and gave her a hug. A slightly tentative, brief hug, but a hug just the same; his arms went round her and pulled her close and instead of resisting him, as she would have expected herself to do, she moved into him, closer still, and turned her head and rested it on his chest, and felt a thud of emotional, rather than sexual, excitement and a sense that something important had happened, without having any clear idea why.

And then, while she waited for some tender, or even affectionate words, she felt him release her and his arm go up and his voice shouting, 'Cab!' And she started to laugh, because it was the only thing to do.

'Why are you laughing?' he said, and his face was quite hurt. 'I thought you were in a hurry.'

'I am,' she said, 'and thank you.'

And then she reached up and kissed him, just very lightly, on the mouth and before he could begin to react in any way, climbed into the cab and waved him goodbye.

A minute later she got a text from him: *Try not to worry. It'll be all right. Call me if you want to*.

She would have liked to think there was some romantic, or even sexual double entendre to this but she knew there was not. Just the same, as the cab made its way to Hampstead, she sat back and looked out of the window, smiling. And wished, she realised rather unsuitably, that there was.

It had to be said, had to be done. He would never respect himself again if he didn't. It was hard. For over half a century he had kept silent, not arguing, accepting criticism, turning the other cheek when ridiculed, turning a blind eye to her excesses, her rudeness to everybody when she chose to give it, wishing his father would do it, speak up, confront her. But he never had and Bertie had decided, after considering other options, that his father was a coward. A charming, handsome, rather lazy coward. He did what he had to do, what Athina required him to do, in order to ensure Farrell's success, and to keep her from haranguing him constantly; and where there was an option, an easy option, he took it. It was quite ugly sometimes, watching Cornelius not stand up to her, allowing her to insult people, belittle them, ignore their feelings.

It had always been thus. He could remember disagreements over buying the flat in Hove, a new nanny who he and Caro hated, his being sent away to school at eight, all things he knew his father was against but never opposed. He had tried himself to get his support over school, had gone to him in tears, said he was very unhappy, that he was homesick, wetting the bed, being beaten. He didn't mention the worst thing, because he couldn't even find the words, but anyway: 'Oh, don't be silly, old chap,' Cornelius said, 'I didn't like my prep school much either at first, but I got used to it. Didn't do me any harm, I can tell you that.'

'But will you think about it, Daddy, please? And talk to Mummy?'

His father had said he would, and clearly had, for it was Athina who came to talk to him: what was this nonsense, she said, about leaving St Peter's? It was such a fine school, the headmaster was a charming man, and Bertie's housemaster absolutely sweet. 'He's not sweet, he's horrible!' Bertie shouted at her and burst into tears, and she'd looked at him witheringly and said that if he was a cry baby at school it was no wonder he did so badly, nobody would respect him or have time for him; and so he'd just given up, didn't say a word about the housemaster and the horrible things he did. For how would she understand anyway?

No one had ever stood up to Athina and she'd just got worse and worse, saying and doing whatever she chose, and even humiliating Cornelius in the boardroom, delivering some withering criticism of him. Bertie, forced to watch and listen, would find himself most vividly back in Mr Keith's study, knowing he was entirely helpless to do anything to stop it.

Only now suddenly he felt he could.

He phoned her to make an arrangement to go round to the flat one night when he was sure she would be on her own and concentrated, in the meantime, on looking for another job and a solicitor who might be able to handle his divorce.

Apart from that, he kept his head down and his office door shut, working extremely hard and avoiding everyone, particularly Lara. He knew that one word of kindly curiosity from her as to whether he was all right would render him unable to maintain his silence. And after a while, rebuffed several times over offers of lunch, drinks, and even coffees, Lara withdrew. There was no way she was going to expose herself, especially within the company where she had her position to consider, to either ridicule or pity, as a divorcee of a certain age chasing after an openly disinterested man. She'd seen it happen several times herself and it was not a pretty sight.

He didn't mean it, of course he didn't. Everyone knew that. Of course he wouldn't kill himself, the people who said they were going to never actually did. It was just a cry for help. And designed to frighten her, to get a response. He was mad. Or at least unhinged.

It had started the very next day: after she'd got back to her office after talking to Bianca about her idea.

A text: *If you shut me out now, I'll kill myself. I mean it.*

She stared it, bile rising in her throat; she ran to the loo, threw up. This was hideous, terrifying. She heard another text arrive, flinched. But it was from Jonjo.

Hi. You free tonight?

She texted back, *Sorry no. Tomorrow?*

She just couldn't do it tonight, not with this nightmare going on. Only it would still be going on tomorrow, wouldn't it?

Back in her office she stared fearfully at the screen as an email arrived.

She suddenly felt she knew how it felt to be stalked . . .

They had had something of an altercation that morning, following Milly's refusal even to allow her into her room the night before.

Milly had come down to the kitchen this morning and she looked dreadful. She was clearly exhausted; white-faced, heavy

438

rings under her dark eyes. And she was very thin. She hadn't properly noticed that Milly's blazer practically hung off her. What sort of a mother did that make her? God, don't say she was developing anorexia. She was exactly the age . . . Milly smiled at her now, almost imperceptibly, said goodbye, made for the door.

'Darling, have some breakfast.'

'I don't want any breakfast.'

'Sweetheart, you must eat something. How about a waffle with maple syrup?'

'I said I didn't want anything. Didn't you hear me? Let me say it again.' She raised her voice: 'I don't want anything! OK? I'm going now. Bye.'

As the front door slammed, Bianca jumped up to call her back, then realised it would be pointless. She looked out of the window, and her heart turned over; Milly was trudging along the street, in the slightly pigeon-toed walk of girls her age, her head drooping. She must do something to help her, Bianca thought, stabbed with fresh remorse. But how was she going to even begin?

If she was being subjected to a bullying campaign, then the school would surely know about it – they made such a performance about it all, assuring parents that they were absolutely on the alert for it, and had a zero tolerance policy. Maybe she should have made her own inquiries, but she'd been so busy. Later today she'd email Mrs Blackman, demand a meeting, but right now, she had to get into work . . .

Milly walked dutifully to the bus stop and waited. But as the bus arrived she saw the smirking faces, the fake waves of two of her tormentors, and simply turned and walked away. She couldn't face another day, another hour, even another minute at St Catherine's. They had broken her; they had won.

She walked down Haverstock Hill and then along Adelaide Road to Swiss Cottage and into the shopping mall where she and Jayce had spent so many hours, and settled herself into the coffee shop.

* * *

'These are – lovely, Lady Farrell. Really beautiful.'

Only God would ever know what that had cost her to admire the prototypes for the perfume packaging Athina had had mocked up. It was truly beautiful: dark, dark red lettering on white, the word *Passion* scrawled recklessly across the box.

'I'm so pleased you like it. The bottle is one *you* found, reminiscent of the Arpège design. Of course we really should do something original. It's a crime to cheapen the whole thing with stock packaging.'

'Unfortunately, that would treble the cost.'

'In our day, that would have been seen as an investment. However . . . Now, you must excuse me, I have a meeting in the lab.'

Which you shouldn't be having, Bianca thought, as I've made so plain so many times. But might as well tell lightning not to strike. She smiled feebly at Athina and went back to her office. Susie had asked to see her, and Mike and Hugh were due in fifteen minutes.

'Hello.'

Milly jumped and looked up from her phone. A policewoman stood in front of her. A second one stood a few yards away.

'Hello,' she said carefully.

'No school today?' said the woman.

'Um – yes. Yes, of course. But I've been to the dentist.'

'Right. Where do you go to school?'

'St Catherine's, Chelsea.'

'That's a long way from here, isn't it?'

'Well – yes,' said Milly, 'but girls go there from all over London.'

'So, if you've been to the dentist, shouldn't you be getting along there now?'

It was beginning to dawn on Milly why she was being questioned. The policewomen thought she was playing truant.

'I'm – I'm waiting for my mother,' she said, inspiration striking. 'She's driving me to school.'

'And where is she now? Didn't she go to the dentist with you?'

'Well . . . no. She's busy.'

'I see. Right. Well, what time are you meeting her?'

Milly looked at her watch. It was half past eleven.

'Midday,' she said.

'So where do you live?'

'Oh, P-Primrose Hill,' said Milly.

She was beginning to feel a bit sick. Inspiration struck her.

'I need to go to the toilet,' she said. 'I won't be long.' She could give her the slip surely, then head off to school.

'I'll come with you,' said the woman, 'if you don't mind.'

'Lucy! Hello. What are you doing, loitering in the corridor? Looking for your dad?'

Bianca really liked Lucy; she had met her for the first time at the sales conference and thought she had a real talent as a make-up artist. She was also touched by her clear devotion and loyalty to her father, and OK, so she clearly also adored her grandmother, but nobody was perfect.

'Oh, good morning, Mrs Bailey.'

'Please, call me Bianca. Mrs Bailey is a very old person. Which is what I daresay you think I am.'

'Of course not! I hope you don't mind me being here. I'm looking for Dad, but I'm also killing a bit of time, waiting for Grandy. She's in a meeting, apparently, and her office is locked. She's taking me out to lunch. To – to celebrate something.'

'Which is? Oh, sorry, maybe I shouldn't ask.'

'Oh, no, of course you should. I've just got two days' work doing make-up at London Fashion Week in April. And I can't believe it! It came through a big charity show I did – I've managed to get on that circuit – and word's got round, I suppose.'

'Lucy, that's fantastic! People would kill for that gig! Very well done. Lovely to talk to you, and enjoy your lunch. Your dad's definitely around because I just left him. If you can't find him, come and sit in Jemima's office and have a coffee.'

'Oh, cool. Thank you. Lovely to talk to you, Mrs – er – Bianca. And I did enjoy the conference. I thought it was really cool.'

Bianca went into her office, smiling; if Milly turned out that charming and easy she would be very pleased.

'I've been thinking some more about your idea,' said Susie. 'In fact, I can't stop. And thinking about the launch – it's going to be amazing. I've got so many ideas already. I do have one question, though.'

'Yes?'

'How many shops are we talking about?'

'Ah,' said Bianca, 'we're not sure yet. But – quite a few.'

'So what's a few?'

'At least four, maybe more.'

She smiled at Susie; but she didn't smile back. She looked embarrassed.

'Bianca, that – well, that won't be enough. This'll only work if you have loads of them.'

'And how would you define loads?' Bianca's voice had developed a cool edge.

'Well – well at least a dozen. All over the world. Sydney, New York, Dubai, all the big shopping places. Otherwise, time-wise alone, it won't be exciting enough. I'm sorry if it sounds rude, but I just don't think you'll get the interest otherwise. Get the story going.'

'Well, I'm obviously still investigating that side of things,' said Bianca. 'I'll keep you posted about that as well. Meanwhile – oh, hello Mike, Hugh, come on in. Didn't Jemima—'

'She's not there,' said Mike. 'She's downstairs in reception and sent us on up.'

'Oh – OK. Well, I'm just finished, so . . .'

Jemima, most unusually flushed, looked round the door. 'Excuse me, Bianca, but there's someone – well, that is, maybe you could – should – come outside. It's quite important.'

'Jemima, whatever is it? Has Lady Farrell come back?'

'No, no, it's nothing like that. Although Lucy is waiting to speak to you when you're done with Hugh and Mike. And – and she's got Bertie with her. But this – well, it's personal.'

'Jemima, please tell me what's going on.'

'Bianca—'

'Oh, for heaven's sake! All right, I'll come out. Would you excuse me?' she said to Hugh and Mike.

She walked into the outer office – and felt the ground heave. Milly stood there, tear-stained and defiant, a policewoman beside her. She stalked into the office, the policewoman following her.

How had this happened? Bianca wondered. How had she raised a daughter who not only played truant and had to be brought into the office by a policewoman, who was even now telling her, in distinctly disapproving tones, that children under sixteen should not be roaming shopping centres unsupervised, but who was now screaming at her dementedly.

Telling her she was a stupid, bloody, selfish cow who didn't care about her, that if she did she'd have noticed something was wrong, gone to the school, tried to sort things out, but she'd been too busy with her stupid bloody job, hadn't noticed what she was going through.

'I *did* notice,' Bianca kept saying helplessly. 'I asked and asked you to tell me, but you wouldn't—'

'Oh, so you couldn't notice for yourself that I never saw my friends any more, never got asked anywhere, never went out?'

She was crying so hard she was shaking violently. 'And Daddy, he's as bad these days, never talks to me. He's obsessed with that stupid, stupid man, and his own stupid job. Ruby noticed, and Fergie's been really worried, and I know he said something to you and what did you do? *Nothing!* I hate you, I hate you both, with your darling this and your darling that! You don't deserve to have children! Jayce's mother, with all the boyfriends and everything, she's a better mother than you!'

'Who's Jayce?'

'My friend. My only friend.'

'Oh, is she the girl you were with when you met Ruby on Primrose Hill—'

'Yes. The fat, spotty girl, who you wouldn't approve of, who's kind and generous and really cares about me, who you'd never have in the house because what would your friends say, and the other mothers, Carey's mother and Sarajane's and Annabel's, all those dear little girls, who speak so nicely and say "thank you for having me, Mrs Bailey" so beautifully and who've made me wish I was dead, and – God, your values are just so disgusting!'

Somewhere, interspersed with this monologue, the policewoman asked questions, filled in a form, asked her to sign it and left.

Milly stopped screaming.

Jemima reappeared.

'I'm so sorry, Bianca, but Mike needs a quick word, very quick he says, then they'll be off, but a contract needs signing and apparently it can't wait . . .'

'Oh God!' Go on, Bianca, just say you can't see him now, ask him to come back later . . . but she couldn't. The contract was completely vital.

'Milly, could you just give me five minutes? I have to see this person, very briefly.'

Milly shrugged. 'Makes no difference to me,' she said, sullen once more.

'Milly, if you want to come into my office, I've got loads of magazines.' This from a tall pretty blonde woman, standing just behind Jemima, who had been with her mother when she arrived.

'I'd rather stay here, thanks.'

'Milly . . .' It was another girl, much younger. 'Milly, I have to wait for about half an hour too, for my grandmother. Would you like to come and have a hot chocolate with me? Would that be all right, Mrs Bailey?'

'Oh, Lucy, how kind, I'm sure she'd like that, wouldn't you darling?'

Milly shrugged again.

'OK.'

She followed Lucy out of the office, feeling, for some reason, vaguely better. She supposed it was because she had now seriously embarrassed her mother. It wasn't the sort of thing that would be good for her precious image, having a policewoman arrive in her office, with her own daughter practically handcuffed to her. She might have gone now, the policewoman, but enough people had seen her to realise why she'd been there. Well, good. It was revenge of sorts. She was beginning to wish she'd been smoking. Or had been found with a spliff on her . . .

'I won't ask what that was all about,' said Lucy with a grin, as they settled at their table in Starbucks, 'but I can imagine. How horrible for you.'

Milly shrugged. 'Not really.'

'I was always doing it. Playing truant, I mean. But I never got caught. Want a muffin?'

'No thanks.'

'Still, she's pretty cool, your mum. I'm sure she won't be too bad.'

'Is she? Cool?'

'God, yes. I met her at the conference and she was fantastic. My mother is *so* not cool,' she added. 'My Dad's OK. He works at Farrell's; he was in the office when you arrived.'

'He works there too?'

'Yup. Oh, we're all Farrells. My grandmother, well, with my grandfather, they started it.'

'Wow!' Milly forgot to be cool and miserable. 'So your grandmother is Lady Farrell? I've heard my mother talking about her.'

'That's right. Now she's cool, even though she's eighty-something.'

'So do you work for them too?'

'Yes. Not full-time, just doing make-up, creating looks. I did some for the sales conference. I'm a make-up artist. And I got a really cool assignment this morning, doing the make-up for something called London Fashion Week.'

'Oh, I know,' said Milly. She felt much better suddenly. 'What a cool thing to do.' Make-up artist: that was the sort of job that would make sense. That would be good. Rather than a lawyer which her father was so keen on.

'Yes, it is. Hard work but I really do enjoy it. I was at uni, and I left to go to make-up school.' She grinned at Milly. 'My parents acted like I'd gone on the streets.'

'Oh what?' said Milly. 'That is just so pathetic.'

'I know. But they can only think one way, parents.'

'Tell me about it.'

'You sure you don't want a muffin?'

'Well . . .'

'Go on. So . . .' She looked at Milly casually. 'School? How's that?'

'Crap,' said Milly. 'Totally crap.' And burst into tears.

Lucy delivered her back to Bianca's office just before one.

A woman was there who looked rather glamorous, or would have if she wasn't so old. She had snow-white hair and a red dress and was wearing a lot of jewellery and she looked Milly up and down as if she was something in a shop window.

'Good morning,' she said finally. 'And who are you?'

'I'm Emily Bailey,' said Milly, meeting her eyes, refusing to be cowed. 'Bianca Bailey's daughter.'

'Oh, really? Shouldn't you be at school?'

'Grandy!' said Lucy, shooting an embarrassed look at Milly.

'I should, yes,' said Milly firmly, refusing to elaborate.

'Sorry,' said Lucy, clearly feeling an introduction might help. 'Milly, this is my grandmother, Lady Farrell.'

'How do you do?' said Milly politely.

'OK, Grandy, I'm all set. She's taking me out to lunch, Milly, to celebrate London Fashion Week. It's been so nice to meet you. Don't forget what I said. Oh, Daddy, hello again. You joining us for lunch?'

'Absolutely not,' the old lady said, glaring at a man who was also rather old, although not as much as her, who had put his head round the door. 'This is an exclusive occasion, Lucy. Come along. We'll lose our table.'

Jemima emerged from Bianca's office.

'Milly, hi. Your mum says to tell you she won't be much longer.'

'There really is no hurry,' said Milly. It was true; once her mother was free, she would probably take her home and really get going on her. She pulled out her phone and started texting Jayce.

Chapter 41

It was hard to imagine anything worse. More humiliating, more confusing, more totally dispiriting. Everything else: the personal disaster of the conference, the relentless downward spiral of the Farrell brand, the subversive politicking of Lady Farrell, even her relationship with Patrick, her own once-happy marriage, changing so astonishingly, but unarguably, before her eyes: what were any of these things set against failing her child, her beloved firstborn, subjecting her to a cruelty of such sophistication, such savage competence on a daily basis – and yet failing to see any of it. Sending her off every morning into that arena, where there was no hiding place, no comfort to be had of any kind, with nothing but a brief kiss, a fatuous phrase and an immediate redirection of her attention to her own affairs. Her so-important, professional affairs.

How could she have done that, been that blind, that self-obsessed? And how could it have been left to another child who she would, she knew, have dismissed as of little worth, to supply what she should have done, kindness, support, and understanding; and how ultimately shaming that it must be a professional, not a friend, who would bring to her attention Milly's wretchedess and the danger it had led her to.

It had been a long and dreadful day, that one; and the horror of it being conducted, not only before many other people, but other people who worked for her, and who had held her in at least some esteem, had multiplied the horror. At home, no longer angry, and with her father there as well, Milly had told them everything, in a long session full of heartbreaking details, in tones that were almost matter-of-fact, her face expressionless. They were both appalled, not only at the depth of cruelty she had endured, but that she had felt there was literally nowhere to turn. When it was over, and Milly had said she would like to go to her room, they had been unable to look at each other for a while, so filled with remorse did they feel.

Patrick was as shocked and appalled as Bianca and, as she had known he would be, as ready to shoulder the blame. They sat up long after Milly had gone finally exhausted to bed, talking, discussing, proposing.

They had agreed that arrangements would have to change, had tried to work out a basis for it, but so potentially explosive had that become, so dangerous in terms of blame and guilt and personal ambition, that they had been afraid to continue.

And again, and yet again, Bianca wondered what had gone wrong, how they could have moved so far and so fast from where they had been a year ago. How easy and straightforward life had been then, how clear the delineation of parental and even marital duties. She wondered too if there was any escape from any of it, short of Patrick returning to a career he hated, or she renouncing one she loved. Not that she was exactly loving this one right at the moment, but abandoning it would be at best irresponsible and, at worst, legally impossible.

'Well,' Patrick said, refilling his whisky glass for the third time since dinner, 'at the very least we must go to the school, talk to Mrs Blackman, and tell her exactly what vile things are going on under her complacent nose. I can hardly wait to show her how zero tolerance of bullying is conducted in her school.'

'I agree,' said Bianca. 'I'll call her first thing. And tell her Milly will be staying at home for a while.'

'And – will you stay with her?' His voice was dangerously innocent; she met his eyes.

'As – as much as I can.'

The discussion was not completed.

* * *

Mrs Blackman was full of charm and understanding; of course she would like to see them and as soon as possible; her policy was one of complete openness and dialogue over problems.

'Well, that's excellent,' Bianca said. 'When can we begin?'

A meeting was set for the following Monday; in the meantime, work was sent for Milly to do at home. She stayed quietly in her room, for the most part, venturing out only to meet Jayce on Saturday. Bianca suggested she asked Jayce to the house.

'No, Mummy,' said Milly, the new steely Milly, 'the front door alone would petrify her. Just think about it. I'm not having our friendship wrecked now. It's hard enough for her knowing where I live and go to school and all the other rubbish.'

Bianca thought about it and didn't argue; but she was fairly sure that if Jayce had coped with Milly's situation thus far, she would cope perfectly well with the rest.

And then on the Sunday, after tea, Milly said she didn't want them to go and see Mrs Blackman.

'But why not?' Patrick said.

'I've been thinking about it,' Milly said. 'I don't want you to. It's just not a good idea. Because there's no point. They'll still win. Carey and the others.'

'I doubt that, Milly. They should be expelled.'

'They won't be. They can't expel a whole class. And every single one of them was doing it, don't forget. Even the real losers. Even poor Tamsin.'

'Who?'

'You know, with the spots and the BO? I had her to a sleepover once. I thought it would be kind. She was obviously really grateful.'

'Well, they can expel the ringleaders. Carey for a start.'

'Carey is so clever, Daddy. And a brilliant actress. She'll lie and lie and it's her word against mine. And – well, the real point is, with bullying these days, it'll go on anyway. You can't stop it. Facebook, texts, Ask.fm. There's no hiding place. Even if you move schools. And no one could make Carey feel ashamed. She's a truly horrible person. I just don't see the point. I've been thinking and thinking about it, and I just don't want you to go.'

'Milly, something has to be done. We can't just let it go unpunished. And what do you propose to do? You have to go to school, and surely you, brave as you are, can't consider going back?'

'I might. In a week or two.'

'What?'

'I know, I know. But what I want to do is win. And if I leave, *they* have.'

'But my darling, look at the state they've got you into. Look what's happened to your life. You can't handle this on your own. I hate to say it, but you need grown-up help.'

Milly looked at him.

'I know. But it's got to be the right sort.'

Her face wore its new steely expression; Bianca and Patrick were learning not to argue with it.

'You are just so so special . . .' Jonjo looked at Susie across the bed. They'd gone out to dinner and then, halfway through, they'd looked at each other rather intently, and that had been that really. Without saying a word, they'd known they were wasting their time, talking however happily, amusing each other however genuinely.

'Shall we go?' Jonjo had said and 'Yes, I'd like to,' Susie had said, and they'd had to explain to the waiter that there was nothing wrong with Susie's fish or Jonjo's steak, they were really very nice indeed, and they hadn't been suddenly taken ill, and nor had they had some bad news, they simply had to go, and they were very sorry and Jonjo paid for the whole meal and left a huge tip and they found a taxi quite quickly, which was as well, since they were both so impatient to be together, mouth on mouth, skin on skin, eyes fixed on one another, learning each other still, yet beginning to grow familiar, to know what was good, what worked, what was tender, what would excite, and that in itself was lovely, to have even that much knowledge of one another, and finding it so very very good, while knowing there was so much more to come, to discover, to learn. And knowing that whatever more there was, was bound to be as good, if not better, than what they had already, so perfectly suited, so utterly attuned to one another they seemed to be.

This must be love, Susie thought confusedly, pulling Jonjo to her, kissing him again and again, as if she had not been doing so for some time already; and she almost said it then, but then she didn't, and neither did he: pulling back from her, pushing her hair away from her face, smiling delightedly at her, almost in surprise, as if he had just discovered some glorious treasure, rich and precious – as indeed he supposed he had.

'So – what do you think?' he said, by way of compromise; and she said, 'Think about what?' And 'Us, each other,' he said. 'Do you think we're important, do you think *this* is important?' And 'Of course it is,' she said, 'terribly important. And terribly lovely.'

That was when he said she was special.

Later they sat in bed watching some terrible movie, for it was still early, not even eleven, and she said, 'I suppose I should go.' He smiled at her and said, 'Do you have to?' She smiled back and said, 'No, I don't.' And revealed that she had in her rather large bag, which he had noticed before but not remarked upon, feeling it might sound ungallant, a gorgeously new Joseph sweater and some clean underwear, and what she called her face stuff and he laughed and said she was a hussy, and she said nonsense, she was simply practical and he said yes, OK a practical hussy then; and then he said, 'I'm so pleased, I love practical girls and let's stop watching this.' And they'd snuggled down and gone to sleep easily, and rather surprisingly, and she woke to hear his phone going off and him saying, 'Oh fuck!' and shooting out of bed saying, 'That's my second alarm call! Bloody hell, first one didn't go off. I'll get you some coffee when I've had my shower.'

And then, then it happened. Feeling safe for five minutes, hating what she was doing, but knowing she must, for it had been nagging somewhere deep down in her subconscious, she reached for her bag and pulled her phone out of it, and God, oh God, there were about a dozen texts, all from Henk, all saying the same thing, that he meant it, he was going to do it, he was going to kill himself, and unless he heard from her that day, that would be it, it wasn't a game, he meant it, he couldn't face life without her, that he loved her and knew she loved him; and while she was sitting there, her stomach churning, her face clearly showing what she was feeling, the terror and the guilt, she frantically called his number and she was just saying, 'Henk, Henk, are you there, it's Susie, are you all right?' when she heard Jonjo say, 'What is it? What the fuck is it? What's happened?'

'I can't tell you,' she said, stupid with misery and shock. 'I – I can't.' She looked at him. 'I'm sorry. I must – must finish this call.'

'Well, go ahead,' he said, his voice harsh and angry suddenly, 'don't mind me. I'm out of here anyway, in five minutes. Or maybe it wouldn't be too much to ask you to wait till I've gone.'

'Yes – no – yes, of course I will,' she said and more than anything in the world she wanted to explain, but how could she, now, and what would he think of her if she did? That she was, to a degree, two-timing him, that there was still a man, another man in her life, that she had lied about, denied; a man who was threatening to kill himself if she did not go back to him.

It would all sound so flimsy and so ugly, set against what they had been sharing for the last glorious hours, the closeness, the happiness, the edge of love. What explanation could she possibly give that would satisfy him, make him understand? The truth perhaps? But what would that do to him, to them, now?

In the scruffy flat he was now sharing with some friends, Henk brewed up a strong coffee while he waited patiently for her next call. He had lots of time and not a lot to do. And he could see he had her seriously rattled now.

'No. I don't know how many more times we have to spell this out to you, Bianca. *There is no more money.* I know it's the most brilliant idea since the wheel, but if it costs two or three million then it ain't going to happen. Sorry.

'And if your success, and indeed Farrell's success, depends on this in the way you say it does, maybe you should rethink your whole strategy. It might seem a little fragile. Now, we have another meeting, so if you could . . .'

Bianca stood up, reached for her coat. It was a measure of their exasperation with her that neither Mike nor Hugh helped her on with it.

She walked out into the cold, dark February evening, feeling she simply didn't know what to do. It was becoming a rather familiar sensation.

She decided to go home. It was early, only five, but she was making a huge effort to be home for Milly and she could do most – if not all – of what she had to do later, when things were quiet.

She called Patrick, who was working at home, and told him what she proposed: 'And I'd love to talk to you about something else, nothing to do with Milly, a problem I've got here . . .'

She used to do that a lot: talk her problems through with him. He never did much more than listen, occasionally throwing in the odd observation, but time and again she found it helped. Since Saul – well, Saul was taking a back seat for a few days at least.

'Sounds nice,' he said, 'but actually, you'll have to count me out. I was just going to call you. I've got to go into the office, only for a few hours, but Saul just emailed me, wants to go through some stuff with me and—'

'Patrick, not tonight! Surely tomorrow will do?'

'Of course it won't,' he said, his voice patient, as if he was talking to a child. 'Tomorrow I have to go down to Exeter.'

'Exeter! You didn't say, why?'

'Well, I didn't know. Bianca, I've been around a lot the past few days, and Saul's been very good about it—'

'Is that right? I must call and thank him.'

'Bianca, please, don't even think of—'

'Patrick, for Christ's sake. Your sense of humour is becoming as non-existent as his. But I do actually fail to see why you shouldn't work at home from time to time, when he told us both specifically that could be part of the deal.'

'Yes, I know, but it doesn't work like that in practice. As I'm sure you know. And at least I've been here a lot more than you have, in spite of all your fine words.'

'Oh, just shut up!' said Bianca. 'It would have been impossible for me, I've got a complete nightmare on my hands.'

454

'How very unusual. Well look, it would be helpful if you did get here fairly soon, because I'd promised Ruby I'd help her with her project so maybe you could take over. And Fergie has a lot of test papers to go through, and—'

'Yes, all right, all right, I'll come. I can see my problems can't begin to compete with Saul's!'

'Oh for God's sake, do we have to have this, every time, even now. It's so childish, Bianca. I never, ever complained about any of your bosses, or backers, and the hours you need to keep. But I'm not the automatic go-to for domestic backup any more, we have to share it, more than ever now with the Milly situation.'

'Oh, all right,' said Bianca wearily. She could feel Patrick slipping back very fast from his position on the Milly day, as she thought of it. He really wasn't the Patrick she had been married to even six months earlier. She wasn't sure what her predominant emotion was, but there was certainly some fear within it somewhere. And she felt horribly alone.

Susie had agreed to meet Henk in a wine bar, her local, just a few doors down the street. It was dangerous in one way, but she'd feel safer in another, knowing that she could get home quickly if he turned nasty.

She had googled suicide and read various websites, and the only thing she properly took in was that there was a rise in suicides among the young, and that there was a suicide helpline. God, she needed some help through this.

She was even more frightened of losing Jonjo – and he had been scarily silent all day, no texts, no emails, except one cancelling an arrangement for the following evening with no explanation. God, it was all so horrible. So unfair.

She felt worse as the afternoon went on; half wishing she'd not made the arrangement with Henk at all, wondering if she could cancel, knowing it was impossible.

She'd agreed to meet him at half past six and at half past five she went to the ladies' to get ready. She wanted to look the opposite of sexy so she wiped off most of her make-up and tied her hair back.

A wave of terror hit her, as she looked at herself in the mirror; terror and nausea. How had she ended up like this? How?

The door opened and Jemima came in; she smiled at Susie in the mirror.

'You look tired. Been burning the candle at both ends?'

'A – a bit.'

'Lucky you. Wish I had.'

'No you don't,' said Susie, and overwhelmed by a new flood of fear, she suddenly started to cry.

'Susie, Susie, whatever is it? You've been so much happier lately – you haven't gone back to the boyfriend, have you? The one who beat you up?'

Susie stared at her. 'I – well, not exactly. But how . . . ?'

'Oh honestly!' said Jemima, putting her arm round Susie's shoulders. 'I'm not a complete moron. I was so worried about you. So glad when it all seemed to have stopped.'

'Oh, Jemima . . .' Susie looked at her helplessly. 'Jemima, I've made such a hash of things. A total, utter hash.'

'But why, how? Look, everyone's gone home including Bianca. Let's go into my office and I'll get us a coffee or something.'

'No, no,' said Susie. 'I've got to – got to meet someone at half past six.'

'Well, text and say you'll be half an hour late. Go on. You can't go out in that state. Who're you meeting, anyway, new boyfriend?'

'No,' said Susie and started crying again. 'There isn't a new one. There might have been if I wasn't so stupid. Oh, Jemima, it's all such a filthy mess.'

'Look,' Jemima gave her a gentle shove in the direction of her office, 'go and sit down, I'll get the coffee.'

Jonjo, having spent a wretched day grieving over what had promised such happiness and had become such misery, hurt and shocked beyond anything, almost more than when he had discovered his wife was being unfaithful to him, was waiting for Patrick in his office.

He hadn't seen Patrick since the night of the private view, when he had met Susie for the first time and the sight of him brought it back rather vividly.

'Hi,' he said rather listlessly.

'Hello,' said Patrick. 'How's it going?'

Jonjo was too miserable to lie. 'Badly. Since you ask.'

'I'm sorry,' said Patrick without inquiring what.

'Thanks. You?'

'Er, fine. Yes.'

How would it ever be otherwise, Jonjo thought, for Patrick with his perfect wife, his perfect family, how could he know about rejection and deception and pain?

'You coming or going?' he said.

'I was waiting for Saul. But he's been held up, got to cool my heels for a couple of hours.'

'You haven't got time for a drink I s'pose?'

Patrick looked at his watch, hesitated, then said, 'Oh, why not? Otherwise it's research on Georgian architecture.'

'Doesn't sound too much like Saul.'

'No, no, it's for Ruby. She's working on a project.'

Jonjo managed half a smile. 'I thought Saul had liberated you from projects. Come on, quick one won't hurt.'

In the bar, halfway through his beer, Patrick said, 'So everything OK, then?'

'Yeah, sure.'

'Really? Come on, Jonjo, you haven't asked me down here to discuss the weather.'

'No, I know. But I don't want to talk about it.'

'Well, start, see how you get on. We can always switch to the weather.'

'That is just so appalling,' said Jemima. 'You poor, poor thing. Oh, Susie, no wonder you're in a state. And you're going to meet him? That's awfully brave.'

'I know. But I thought it might help. I don't see what else I can do. I can't get any advice from any of the professionals, they all say

457

they don't give second-hand advice. And I can't just ignore it. I know everyone says people who threaten it never do it, but I don't know that, I certainly can't be sure.'

'No,' said Jemima, 'you absolutely can't. He already feels abandoned, it would simply be making it worse.'

'That's what I thought.'

'You thought right. How ghastly. How totally unfair.'

'I know. But Jemima, what can I do?'

'What I would suggest,' said Jemima slowly, 'is try and persuade him to see a psychiatrist, or a therapist, not just the counsellor he says he's seeing. I know it won't be easy but that's the best thing you could do. And maybe offer to go with him, if he'll let you. It would show him you were properly concerned. Although it might encourage him to think you still cared about him.' She stopped, looked at Susie, then said, slightly hesitantly, 'You know, Susie, suicide is the most aggressive act possible. It forces everyone to think about that person for the rest of their lives. What they're saying is: I can't bear this any longer, you're going to have to bear it now. He's massively envious that you've got your life together, as he sees it, and he's turning his aggression on whatever has attacked him – in this case you.'

Susie stared at her. 'You seem to know an awful lot about it.'

'I should do,' said Jemima with a sigh. 'I've been training as a psychotherapist for years. Keep failing my exams,' she added.

'No!' Susie was jolted out of her misery. 'Jemima, that's amazing. Why didn't you mention it before?'

'I didn't want everyone to know. Specially Bianca – she'd have thought I wasn't going to be properly committed to the job. So I'm trusting you not to say anything.'

'Of course I won't. God, you'd be a wonderful psychotherapist. Wish you were mine!'

'Well, I shouldn't even be playing at it,' said Jemima, 'because I'm not qualified. But I have learned a lot. And I do know quite a lot about suicide – one of my case studies was one.'

'Well – well, I'm glad you think I'm at least on the right lines, doing what I am.'

'I do. But I also think the whole thing is a bit dangerous. Walking on a field of landmines, doddle by comparison. Would you like me to come with you this evening?'

'No, he'd just freak out.'

'Well, ring me, the minute you feel you can't cope. I mean, he's violent, Susie.'

'Well, he says he's having counselling for that. And ever since the last time he's shown no signs of it at all. Except for almost knocking my door in,' she added, 'when I told him there was someone else.'

'What! You should have gone to the police.'

'I know, I know. But somehow . . .' She trailed to a stop. 'Anyway, the neighbours underneath me, lovely people, they've kept an eye on me ever since, told him to go away and he just did.'

'Interesting,' said Jemima, 'that he should be so easily dissuaded.'

'Is it? I wouldn't know.'

'I think so. So who's this someone else?'

'No one,' said Susie, 'any more.' And burst into tears again.

'I thought – well, I almost thought I'd found Miss Right,' said Jonjo. 'Bloody gorgeous Patrick, she is – well, you've met her – she was at Guinevere's party.'

'Well, she seems very sweet,' said Patrick cautiously.

'And I thought she was pretty damn perfect. We were doing so well . . .'

'For how long?'

'Oh, well, not that long. Actually. Only a few dates. But you can tell, can't you?'

'Sometimes,' said Patrick.

'Well, anyway, I was wrong. She's bloody cheating on me. Got someone else.'

'How do you know?'

'I heard her talking to him. She was sitting in my bed, for Christ's sake. I was in the shower, came in, there she was. Saying she was so relieved to hear his voice. I mean, you don't imagine that sort of thing, do you?'

'Not usually,' said Patrick. 'But you don't know the background. Did you ask her?'

'Course I didn't bloody ask her! I didn't want to hear any pathetic excuses. I just went to work. She left a little note, saying she'd like to explain, but – well, pretty hard to explain that sort of thing. Oh shit! Another of those? Or do you want to move on to something stronger?'

'No, I've got to work later. In fact, I think I'll go for Saul's tipple. Tonic and tonic. It's a really good drink.'

'Don't be ridiculous! Have a beer. You're a bit obsessed with Saul, you know that?'

'That's what Bianca says,' said Patrick, trying to sound light-hearted. 'Anyway, I think you should have it out with her,' he added, as Jonjo waved at the waiter, 'ask her what's going on. You never know, might be different from what you think.'

'How?' said Jonjo.

'Well, might have been her dad or something. I just think you should presume innocence till proven guilty, that's all. I admit it sounds a bit dodgy. But you don't know. I'd go and see her if I were you. Talk to her.'

'Patrick, I just couldn't. I'd feel like the total loser I seem to be, listening to some half-arsed explanation. Look, let's talk of happier things. How is Bianca?'

'She's fine,' said Patrick, 'but – excuse me.' He looked at his phone. 'Jonjo, I have to go. Saul's back, waiting for me in his office.'

'You know what, Patrick?' said Jonjo. 'You shouldn't be quite so in awe of Saul. Drink up, he'll wait ten minutes, he doesn't own you.'

'Yes he does,' said Patrick, grinning. 'Anyway, my advice still is, go and see her, try and sort it out. I must go, Jonjo. Cheers.'

'Cheers,' said Jonjo. 'And ask Saul to call me.'

He watched Patrick leave the bar and then downed his gin and tonic in a very few gulps. It made him feel better. He decided to have another before going home to his apartment. His extremely empty apartment. Where Susie had sat, in his bed, staring at him with huge frightened eyes, breaking his heart. Bloody women. Always causing trouble. Much better without them really . . .

'Hello, Henk.'

He didn't look too bad; in fact, he looked rather well, not gaunt and hollow-eyed as she might have expected.

'Hi.' He stood up, kissed her cheek, indicated for her to sit down.

'Sorry I'm late. Hope you got my text.'

'Yeah, yeah, I did.'

'It was just that I had to—'

'Work late.' He grinned. 'You know, that used to be the excuse of the errant male. Those were the days – when men had it all. What would you like to drink?'

'Oh, white wine spritzer please.'

She could sip at that for a long time without getting drunk, and it didn't look like she wasn't drinking at all, which might seem a bit headmistressy.

'So – how's it going?'

'Oh, fine, thanks. Yes. Work's good. You?'

'Oh fine. Yes. I've got a job as an assistant to a studio photographer.'

'You have? That's great!'

'Yes. Doing some work of my own too.'

'Good. How did the shoot for the *Sketch* go?'

'You remembered! Fine. Yes. Cool. And they want me to do another one.'

'Henk, I'm so pleased for you.'

'Thanks.'

There was a silence. Susie sipped her drink.

'Henk . . .'

'Yeah?'

'Henk, we need to talk properly.'

'What about?'

'You know what about. Your – your texts. It's terrible for me, getting them, Henk, terrible.'

'Yeah?'

'Yes. Look, I've been thinking and—'

'You'll finish with this bloke?'

'That's not what I was going to say! I – I think you need help, Henk. Proper, professional help, not just a life counsellor.'

'No I don't. I keep telling you. I just need you back. I'll be fine then.'

God, thought Susie, he really is a bit mad. She must be very careful.

'Henk,' she said, as gently as she could, 'I really am so, so sorry I've caused you such distress.'

'It was all so good,' he said, his voice almost plaintive. 'We were so good together. I just don't – don't understand where it went wrong.'

Susie saw a possible strategy here. God, how she longed for Jemima. 'Yes, well we were once,' she said carefully, 'but things have changed.'

'But why? How? I don't understand.'

'Well, that's why I think you need help. Because you *don't* understand. And—'

'Look, Susie, I feel how I do because you want to leave me. Nothing else. No shrink can change that.'

'Henk, I know that, but I do think we should go and see someone, to talk about it. Together maybe. So you can understand. And – well, I can understand a bit better too.'

'Do you think so, babe? Do you think that would really help?'

'Yes, yes I do. Would you like me to try and find someone?'

A long silence. Then, 'Yes,' he said, 'yes, possibly.'

Jonjo looked round the bar. It was almost empty. No one to talk to. And he needed to talk. Not about Susie, Patrick was the only person for those sorts of conversation and even that was a struggle. But he felt really lonely suddenly. God, if only he had Susie to talk to, she'd understand. Only – no, she wouldn't, because it was down to her that he was so miserable and had no one to talk to. Which was terrible. Because, God, she was fantastic. In every way. So loving and fun and sexy and utterly gorgeous. Only she had someone else. But did she? He didn't actually know for sure. It looked like it, but maybe Patrick was right. Clever old sod, Patrick. Always had been a good friend too. Maybe he should do what Patrick said, give Susie a chance. To explain things at least. He wouldn't be any worse off, even if he was right and she was cheating on him. At least he'd know. Yes, he'd do that. He'd just have one more drink, and then he'd get in a cab and go over and see her. And talk to her. But he wouldn't tell her he was coming, or she'd have a chance to cover her tracks if she was – well, if she really was carrying on with this other bloke . . .

Susie looked at Henk. They had been chatting fairly easily for about half an hour. She had persuaded him to tell her about his work, what he had to do. It was a bit menial, she could see that, but it was impressive he was doing it, and he said he was actually learning things, about lighting, reworking his portfolio. It all sounded rather sensible – and he seemed rather sensible too. If he would now agree to see a therapist, even if she did have to go with him, maybe he would make real progress. Into what she wasn't sure.

'And this flat you're in now, how's that?'

'Oh, bit of a tip but they're all being very supportive.'

'Of you?'

'Yes. Of course. What did you think I meant?'

The aggression resurfaced suddenly and she shivered mentally. She looked at her watch.

'Henk, I have to go. I'm sorry.'

'I thought you'd – we'd have longer.'

'No, I broke off what I was doing, haven't nearly finished.'

'Oh, OK. So I have to be satisfied with my ration?'

'Henk, please. Don't spoil everything. It's been so nice, hearing you talk about your work and everything, seeing you looking better than I expected – I was so worried about you, Henk.'

'Well, I suppose that's something. That you cared whether I lived or died.'

'Henk, of course I care about that, don't be ridiculous!'

'Good,' he said, 'that's all right then. So – what do we do now?'

Suddenly she was frightened, out of her depth again. She didn't know what to do or how she was supposed to do it; but she needed to get rid of him.

'Well,' she said and it took all her willpower to sound normal, 'well, right now I have to go home. Sorry.'

'OK,' he said sounding genuinely regretful. 'Fine. But we can talk again?'

'Of course.'

'Good. Well, thank you for coming. I'll walk you home.'

'Henk, no, there's no need.'

'No, but I want to. See you safely to your door, like a gentleman. Don't worry, I won't try to force an entry.' He smiled at her, a genuine, rueful smile. He stood up, held out his hand to her. She took it reluctantly.

It was very cold outside; she pulled her coat round her, tied her scarf.

'Right, let's go,' he said. He took her arm and she let him. It seemed harmless. They walked along together.

'What – what are you doing tomorrow?' she said.

'Oh, big fashion shoot. Very humble role for yours truly. But it'll be interesting. It's for *Now* magazine.'

'Really! I'm impressed. Wish I could come along.'

'Well, you play your cards right and I'll see what I can do,' he said. He smiled at her and she couldn't help smiling back.

'Thanks for coming, Susie.'

'It was fine. Honestly. And you will think about what I said. About – about seeing someone?'

'I will. As long as you promise to come with me.'

'I – I said I would.'

'Thanks, babe.' They'd reached her front door. She stopped, terrified he'd try to come in, but he didn't. He smiled at her, let go of her arm, and bent and kissed her, very gently on the mouth. She tensed, tried to relax, and after a few moments pulled away.

'Night, Henk,' she said, 'take care of yourself.'

And let herself into the front door, ran upstairs, and into her flat and double-locked the door, leant against it, her eyes closed in relief. She had done it; and it hadn't been too bad. It might even have done some good.

Jonjo, whose cab had been travelling very slowly along the street while he tried to establish which house number 82 was, had suddenly seen Susie, leaving a wine bar with a man. He had told the cab to stop and then sat there, watching the man take her arm, watched them as they walked along, chatting and smiling at one another: and then watched as the man bent and kissed Susie on the mouth, and then unable to bear it any longer had half shouted at the driver to take him straight back to Canary Wharf.

'Cost you a bit, guv. That's all the way back where we been and more. Looking at, like, eighty, hundred quid. Want to give me something on account?'

Jonjo hurled a couple of twenty pound notes at him and sank back into the corner of the cab.

Henk walked down the street, smiling to himself. Silly bitch. Silly, silly bitch.

This could run and run.

Chapter 42

They were having the most terrible rows. Day after day, saying cruel, horrible things to one another, that neither of them deserved, things that could not and would not ever be forgotten; Cornelius felt more wretched than he could ever remember, abused, discarded, misjudged.

He knew why it was, of course; it was because the House of Farrell was failing. From being admired and copied, they were almost sneered at. Their counter space had been cut everywhere, there was less money for promotion, the staff were demoralised and Athina was in a permanent state of outrage.

Florence was the only good thing in his life, and he wondered frequently what he would have done without her. At the same time it was harder even than usual to find times when he could see her; but when he did, she was always happy, encouraging, and loving. She was an extraordinary person – so generous with herself, so undemanding, so supportive. He often thought that if he had not had her, he would have long left Athina; and would then reflect rather wryly on how that fact went against every theory, every philosophy of a successful marriage.

She was also extremely clever: one of the few successful promotions Farrell's had done in that miserable decade, a double-textured lipstick, a firmer outer shell encasing a softer glossy one, had been her idea. She had ventured it in a product development meeting, and Athina had pooh-poohed it, later re-presenting it as her own. When Cornelius had rather boldly said he thought the idea had been Florence's, Athina said of course it hadn't and, most unusually, Florence had stood up for herself and said she distinctly remembered proposing the lipstick – by then named Soft-Hearted lipstick – whereupon even the sales manager supported her.

Athina was reduced to saying that it might have been something Florence said that inspired her, but it certainly had been her idea, as had been the name, adding witheringly, and illogically, that she was surprised that anyone should care whose idea it was, as long as it was successful. Cornelius managed to remain silent, knowing he would be lighting the blue touch paper for a very big rocket indeed if he defended Florence; but he managed to invent a store manager who needed taking out to dinner that evening and arrived at the little house in Pimlico with a huge bunch of red roses, and a declaration of love for Florence so clearly genuine that she told him, he hoped truthfully, that the whole miserable business had been worthwhile.

'Beloved Little Flo,' he said, kissing her tenderly. 'You are so good a person, so true, so brave, I don't know what I have done to deserve you.'

There was a general downturn in the Farrells' personal fortunes as well: the Hove flat had finally been sold, as had some of the paintings that had hung on its walls and the extremely good furniture it had contained, Athina's new clothes were no longer couture, but bought off the peg.

It was not a happy time; and into it came the threat of greater unhappiness still.

Athina, lying in the bath one night, discovered a lump in her breast. Wretched months of treatment followed, radiotherapy to shrink the tumour, followed by a partial mastectomy, followed by brutal chemotherapy. She was brave, of course, but her behaviour was otherwise impossible, for she regarded it as an outrage, meeting it and everyone near her with anger and vindictiveness. Cornelius, being the nearest of them all, fared the worst.

She shouted, she ranted, she abused him; and when he did see Florence, soothed and eased by her quiet, comforting presence,

467

guilt consumed him to such an extent there was little pleasure in it for either of them. Florence was, for the most part, patient and understanding, but one particularly dreadful evening she told him that if all he was going to talk about was Athina and how brave and how impossible she was, she would like him to leave and not to come back.

'I can see how hard it is for you, Cornelius, and we are all concerned for Athina, but I do not wish to hear, on the very few occasions when we manage to be together, exactly how many things she has thrown at you in the past seven days, both literally and metaphorically. Nor indeed, does it give me any pleasure to hear how your admiration for her courage is beyond description.'

He did his best to placate her, saying he was under a great deal of strain and begged her forgiveness, but she said she was under considerable strain herself, and was getting nothing from him to make her feel it was worth enduring.

A row followed and he left in a state of rage and despair, pacing the streets for hours, unable to face either going home or back to Florence to ask her forgiveness. It was weeks before a truce was declared between them, and that because he not only begged for her forgiveness but told a journalist that the idea for Soft-Hearted lipsticks had not been Athina's idea, or indeed his, but Florence's. This found its way into the beauty pages – mercifully at a time when Athina was so weakened by her chemotherapy she was hardly reading or indeed taking anything in, but it assuaged Florence's wrath as perhaps nothing else could have done. It also served to make her realise, with some surprise, that she was more competitive than she would ever have believed; she sought Cornelius out in his office, and not only thanked him, but apologised for her own recent hostility.

He left Athina's hospital room earlier than usual and spent the rest of the evening with Florence; it was not only an emotional reunion but a physical one, and quite wonderful. They both admitted afterwards that not only had they not thought of Athina, they had felt no guilt whatsoever the entire evening.

◦ ◦ ◦

There were other problems created by Athina's absence; products had to be approved, copy written, showcards produced; Cornelius was doing his best, but struggling with much of it. Finally, but with considerable anxiety as to the ultimate outcome when Athina came to hear of it, he asked Florence if she would mind taking on some of the work. Florence accepted and, tentatively at first, then with growing enthusiasm, embarked on her new role.

She found a dreadful loss of morale; the decline of the company combined with a total lack of leadership was not only depressing but disturbing the staff.

Florence, initially only required to approve or reject, found herself increasingly looked to for decisions and inspiration, especially from the lab: Maurice Foulds, the chief chemist, took briefs and comment from her with relief, rather than resentment as she had feared, as did the design studio. The result was a more ordered and straightforward chain of command than anyone had known for years; Florence was instinctively communicative, partly as a result of her years in the shop, dealing with the public, and a meeting with her was not the complex, and frequently humiliating affair conducted by Athina Farrell. She spent an increasing amount of time in the Farrell offices, working at the temporary desk a rather tight-lipped Christine Weston had had set up for her in the boardroom; this gave her a status and authority greater than she had ever looked for and made Cornelius even more nervous, while thankful at the same time that his own job was considerably eased.

Everyone remarked upon the greatly increased simplicity of their daily lives and work, and how much more they were enjoying both; and indeed, when Cornelius ended one meeting with the announcement that Athina would shortly be returning to Farrell's, albeit only for half-days initially, there was a lack of enthusiasm so distinct that it was hard to imagine how Athina might ever recapture her authority. Indeed, it was only a day later, when Florence heard two of the younger members of the company chatting over their lunchtime sandwiches about how much more pleasant life had become and they wished Miss Hamilton could carry on running things, that she realised just how much she was, albeit unwittingly, playing with fire.

There were further repercussions from the Soft-Hearted lipstick affair, too; the women's editor of the *Sketch*, Thea Grantly, a sharply intuitive journalist, decided there might be more to the story than lipstick formulation and telephoned Florence and asked her if she might interview her about her work at Farrell's.

'I know your primary role is running that lovely shop,' she said, never having visited it, but having been carefully briefed by her assistant, 'but clearly you do a lot more, and it would make such a nice piece for our readers to hear about how you have become involved in other, perhaps more crucial, issues in the company.'

Florence's first instinct was to say no, recognising the huge potential for trouble if she said yes, but Soft-Hearted lipstick was doing rather well, better than any other product launch for years, she was hugely proud of it, and in spite of Cornelius's lavish remorse, she was still smarting from Athina's original denial of her involvement.

And so she invited Thea Grantly to The Shop, took her upstairs to her parlour, where she plied her with pastries from Fortnum's and Earl Grey tea and, as lunchtime approached, a glass of champagne, and talked lucidly and amusingly for over an hour about the brand and her work, mainly in the past, but touching more than once on her present involvement in Athina's absence. Thea Grantly, who had interviewed Athina a couple of years earlier and disliked her intensely, was charmed by Florence and asked if she might send a photographer down to The Shop; Florence, faced with a temptation beyond endurance, said of course she might but that the next day might be better.

She spent the rest of the afternoon at Leonard of Mayfair, having her hair carved into a thirties-style bob, and the evening sorting through her wardrobe. She was aware that, under the circumstances, a Chanel suit seemed a little dangerous, not something an employee could possibly afford, but having tried it on three times, alternating with more modest labels, more in tune with her supposed situation, she decided a black-trimmed white bouclé jacket, adorned with a gardenia brooch, and a simple swinging jersey skirt of exactly the right length to show her still-perfect legs, were unbeatably flattering and wore them. The resulting photographs of her, smiling at the door of The Shop, captioned *The stylish new face at the House of Farrell*, occupied, together with Thea Grantly's interview, a double-page spread in the *Sketch* and caused a great stir in the industry, leading among other things to conjecture that in the light of Athina Farrell's illness, Florence might be taking her place.

Cornelius, now quite literally shaking with terror that a copy of the *Sketch* might find its way into Athina's sick room, went to see Florence and begged her not to give any more interviews. Florence, enjoying her brief sojourn in the sun, smiled at him sweetly and said she was sorry, but she had imagined it would be helpful to keep the House of Farrell in the public awareness, in Athina's absence. 'And don't forget, Cornelius, we all agreed that there was a danger that the trade might regard her illness as a serious threat to the brand itself.'

'Of course, of course, but I need hardly tell you how important it is that her own profile remains unchanged. I fear she might regard this as something of a – a takeover bid.'

'Oh Cornelius, don't be so ridiculous,' said Florence, her smile sweetly innocent. 'How could one article in one newspaper possibly change the public's perception of Athina and her place at Farrell's? And besides, I did mention her many times and how she had given me my job all those years ago and therefore how much I owed her and indeed what a legend she was in the industry.'

'Yes, yes,' he said distractedly, 'it's just that she is particularly vulnerable at the moment.'

'Of course. And I should have thought to ask you before agreeing. I'm sorry. But it's all wonderful extra publicity for Soft-Hearted lipstick and sales are reflecting that. So it's not entirely bad, surely?'

'Of course not,' said Cornelius.

But this was not the end of it either; Thea Grantly was not the only journalist to recognise Florence's extraordinary grasp of the industry, and indeed her overview of several decades of it, and this, combined with her charm and undoubted style, led to requests for further interviews; Florence sweetly but firmly turned them down, but was to be persuaded – without too much difficulty, it must be said – into giving quotes over the telephone on such disparate matters as Princess Diana's make-up and the change in women's attitude towards their own bodies since the fifties: thoughtful, to the point, and often amusing – usually accompanied by the picture from the *Sketch*. Cornelius was beside himself, and when the final crunch came, in the form of an invitation to be interviewed on *Woman's Hour*, he went to see Florence again and, visibly angry, told her the whole thing must stop.

'I'm sorry, Cornelius, that is all very well for you to say, but they all have this number and I will not be rude to them. And short of sending me on a six-month holiday, I cannot imagine how I am to obey you.'

Cornelius glared at her. 'I would not have believed this of you, Florence.'

'Oh really? You mean after thirty years of absolute discretion, of obedience to your rules, of unswerving loyalty, not only to you, but to Athina, and really, if we were to be honest, very little benefit accruing to me, I am expected to step back once again into the invisibility that suits you both so well?'

'That is grotesquely unfair,' he said, 'and you know it. You have always said you loved me, as I love you; you have always known I could never leave Athina or acknowledge our relationship; I've been fair and honest, and done everything I could for you that was within my powers.'

'Is that really so, Cornelius? Did you never stop to think of what I might have liked, beyond the usual baubles handed to the mistress?'

'Be careful,' he said, 'be very careful.'

'Cornelius, the truth is not always a careful commodity. Yes, of course I love you, and I do not resent devoting my entire life to that, hard as it has often been. But there are other things that might have consoled me in my loneliness, in Athina's arrogance, in your complacency that I would always be there when required . . . and it hurts me very much that this has never occurred to you. You should really be able to see how sweet these last weeks have been to me, to be valued, listened to, even admired. And I find I do not want to give that up. Not entirely. And I also find I don't intend to.'

'This is outrageous of you,' said Cornelius, 'and I would not have believed it.'

'Actually,' said Florence, 'I think it is your attitude that is outrageous. Outrageously blind, outrageously arrogant. And suddenly I don't like that. I think I am worthy of more. And I want you to give it to me.'

'And what do you mean by that, for Christ's sake?'

'I mean I want some kind of increased status at Farrell. I want people to know I am more than the wonderful middle-aged lady who runs The Shop. If I can't have more of you – and I accept that I can't – I want more of a career. It's a little late in my life, but I'm sure you can think of something.'

'And if I don't?'

'Then the articles will start again with a vengeance. I'm sorry.'

'This is blackmail!' he said.

Florence looked at him, seeing him suddenly rather clearly, almost as if for the first time, a handsome and charming, but undoubtedly weak man, and smiled at him very sweetly.

'Yes,' she said, 'you're right. I'm sorry, but it is.'

Two weeks later an internal memo went round the company, announcing the promotion of Florence Hamilton to the board of the company, with particular responsibility for retail outlets.

Bianca was sitting at her desk one early evening, the offices empty around her – and even that seemed to symbolise her overall situation, the phones silent, the emails stopped, desperately trying to summon the energy even to stand up and walk out of it, when her mobile rang. It was Saul. She didn't answer it, left it to tell him that she was unavailable; almost at once a text came through saying *Bianca, please call me. I've had an idea.*

She waited for a moment or two then, unable to resist, called him; he sounded most unusually animated.

'Hi, I'd like to talk to you. About your project. What are you doing right now?'

'I'm about to go home to my fatherless children,' she said briskly.

'I'm sorry? Oh, you mean without Patrick.'

'He is generally accepted as their father, yes.'

'Sorry. And sorrier about Hong Kong. If it's any comfort to you, he was keener about going than I was. He could perfectly well have done it from here.'

'Not a great comfort, no,' said Bianca. 'Rather the reverse.'

There was a silence; then, 'Well, anyway, what's important now is this project of yours. It's too clever an idea to waste, Bianca, you have to do it.'

'That's all very well, Saul, but there's no more money in the pot, the VCs have closed the lid, and everyone, including you, has told me it won't work without a full complement of outlets, in the most expensive pieces of real estate in the world.'

'There's another way. I just thought of it this afternoon.'

'And?' Bianca said, torn between irritation and intense gratitude that anyone, and Saul of all people, should be thinking about her problem.

'Franchises.'

'I'm sorry?'

'Franchises. Look, we should meet. Do you have even half an hour? It's so important. And I'm very pleased with my idea. You still in the office? I could come there.'

'Yes, I am. But—'

'I'll be with you in fifteen minutes.'

He walked in, in his impatient, swift way, said hello, sat down in the chair opposite her desk.

'Now, this is what you do—'

She laughed, in spite of herself. He looked at her, clearly mildly hurt.

'What did I say?'

'Nothing, Saul. I'm sorry. Very rude of me after you've been so kind. Go on, I really want to hear.'

'OK. You go to your VCs and you tell them you're going to open shops in every shopping capital of the world and if they won't give you the money, you're going to franchise them.'

She felt a stirring of excitement so strong it was almost sexual. 'God. That is – well, it's clever.'

'I know,' he said, looking like a small child who had just been praised for a piece of good behaviour.

'But can I do that? Under my contract with them?'

'I should think so. I'll have a look at it for you. But the point is, you tell them what's in it for them.'

'Which is?'

'Money,' said Saul, 'only thing they'll care about.'

Mike and Hugh looked at Bianca. Their faces wore identical expressions: irritation.

'Bianca, we've told you too many times. There is no more money. The rent on half a dozen or so shops, in the top shopping cities of the world, would run into millions. Let alone fitting them out, stocking and staffing them. It's too much of a risk. Sorry.'

'OK,' said Bianca, 'but I have an alternative plan.'

'Which is?'

'Franchises.'

'What?'

'I think we should turn the shops into franchises. So they will hardly cost us anything. The franchisees will provide the cash. I know it's feasible. And provided you agree, I'll give you twenty-five per cent of their profits. Over and above what you'll get when we sell Farrell's, obviously.'

There was a very long silence: then Mike looked at Hugh and Hugh looked at Mike and Mike said, 'Will you excuse us for a moment?'

She sat waiting for them to return, looking alternately out of the window and at her phone. A text arrived from Saul.

How's it going?

Not sure.

Let me know.

Of course.

She just had time to press send. Hugh and Mike sat down and looked at her in silence for a long moment. Then, 'It's another brilliant idea,' said Hugh, 'but we don't think it can work.'

She stared at them, struggling against the absolute defeat she felt. Don't give up yet, Bianca, don't . . .

'Why not?'

'Because so much is against you. Time for a start. Do you really think you can find six locations, to match your brief, in the time? And then fit them out, equip them, hire staff? Do you think you can find people with that sort of money, to do what you want?'

'Yes,' said Bianca firmly, 'I absolutely do. Look: let me try. None of us will be any the worse off if I can't find anyone. But at least we'll know for sure instead of endless conjecturing. In which case I'll never, ever again mention the most brilliant idea in the history of advertising – until someone else does it. Which they will. What do you say?'

'I suppose,' said Hugh, 'that can't do any harm. Mike?'

'I suppose . . . we could think about it,' said Mike.

Thinking about it was good. Better than – well, not thinking about it. But . . .

'For how long?' said Bianca. 'You just said yourself, time is against us. So if you're prepared to think about it, then you can't think it's an entirely bad idea.'

'It's not a bad idea,' said Hugh, 'but it can't work in the time. And you cannot delay the launch. It has to coincide with the Jubilee; we're all agreed on that. And that certainly isn't going to be delayed.'

'But if I could guarantee that, then you'd be prepared to go ahead?'

'Possibly,' said Hugh, after a long pause, 'but you can't. So—'

'Hugh! Please! Please think about it. Just a bit longer.'

Mike sighed.

'OK. We'll think about that. But if it's no—'

'Then I still won't give up,' she said.

'Jesus, Bianca,' said Mike. 'Look, just get out of here for a few minutes, will you?'

She left the room, pulled out her phone and texted Saul.
They're thinking about it.
They'll do it.
Not sure.
They will.

She knocked on the boardroom door before going in, found herself
confronted by their backs. They were looking out of the window.
How well they must know that view, she thought, every roof, every
brick practically, of every building.

'Hi,' she said.

'Hi,' said Mike, turning round. She smiled at him; he didn't
smile back. Hugh turned too, looking equally serious. It was not a
good moment.

'Bianca,' said Hugh, 'we've considered it.'

'And,' said Mike, 'we wondered if you have contacts in any of
these cities?'

'Some, of course,' she said, determined to sound upbeat. 'New
York, Milan. Possibly LA.'

'Sydney? Tokyo?'

'No.'

'Dubai?'

She shook her head.

'That's exactly what we thought,' said Hugh.

'But I'll find them.'

'Not easy. I mean how do you think you're even going to begin,
for God's sake? Your name means nothing in those places, and
Farrell's certainly doesn't, and you are going to need to generate
one hell of a lot of interest if you've any hope at all of pushing this
through. You're living in a dreamworld.'

Suddenly she felt angry. 'I don't think so. And even if I am, I
would like to remind you that cosmetics are a dream world in
themselves. You have to think differently, you—'

'Bianca,' said Mike, 'that's crap. Money is still money. Whichever
world it's spent in.'

She was silent; looked down at her file, her notes, some stuff

477

Saul had said would be sure to persuade them. He'd been wrong about them, about the whole thing. She felt angry with him suddenly, as well as Mike and Hugh. He clearly wasn't quite the genius Patrick seemed to think.

'Bianca?' said Mike.

She looked at him, forced herself to smile.

'I'll find them,' she said determinedly. 'You can't stop me doing that.'

'We wouldn't dream of it,' said Hugh. 'But you really can't manage on your own. Believe us. Anyway, that's precisely why we thought we'd help.'

'Oh,' she said rather dully. She felt at once too overwrought, too exhausted to take this in.

'Well, you could sound a little more enthusiastic.'

'Sorry. I—' And then it hit her and she stared at each of them in turn.

'You'll help?'

'Yup. Not too surprisingly, we have contacts in many of those places. To be quite honest, we don't expect much of a response, but we're up for sending out a few emails, see what happens. How would that be?'

'Oh my God! That would be amazing! Oh, thank you. Thank you so much!'

'There probably isn't much to thank us for,' said Mike. 'I'm afraid we remain somewhat sceptical. Meanwhile, so we can act fast, which is essential, we'll get the lawyers on to drawing up a few agreements, both between you and us, and the company and the franchisees. I'll send over a draft of our emails to our contacts later, so you can make sure we haven't missed anything crucial. A photograph of the shop in the Berkeley Arcade would probably help. I'd say you might add its annual turnover, but I don't think that's going to tempt anyone to part from their capital. OK?'

'OK,' said Bianca. She found herself rather alarmingly near to tears. 'I'll – I'll look forward to receiving those. And of course I'll send over some shots of The Shop. Do you want a brand policy statement, strategy, anything like that?'

478

'Nah,' said Mike, 'much too soon. Now look, we've got another meeting we're already late for, so . . .'

'Yes, yes of course. I'm off.' And suddenly she did something she had never done before, in her entire working life. She went over to them and hugged first one and then the other, wiping her hand impatiently across her eyes at the tears that were so determinedly making themselves felt, sniffing and laughing at the same time.

'Sorry,' she said, standing back, seeing their almost shocked expressions. 'I'm so sorry, very unprofessional of me . . .'

'Bianca,' said Hugh, and he was smiling now, and so was Mike, 'don't worry about it. This is actually not a very professional decision!'

Come on, come on, answer, answer, please, *please*.

But the answerphone wasn't having any of it.

Well she could try.

'Hi Jonjo, this is Susie. Look, I really need to talk to you. Whatever you heard yesterday morning wasn't what you think. Give me a call, and let me explain properly. I'm so sorry if you're feeling bad, which I guess you are. I – well, just call please and let's arrange something. I . . .' She hesitated. She couldn't say 'I love you' although she longed to; but she wanted to let him know how badly she felt, how much she cared. 'Miss you,' she finished, hoping it wouldn't sound too pathetic.

She clicked off her phone; that was all she could do for now. If he called, if she could just speak to him, maybe she could talk him round. But if he didn't . . . She sighed, and decided all she could do now was wait. And distract herself with work.

She had told Jemima about her meeting with Henk, in as much detail as she could. It had assumed surreal qualities, especially the walk along the street, his taking her arm, his kissing her. Henk doing those things, when it should have been Jonjo. God, what a mess.

Jemima was sympathetic, clearly intrigued on a professional level. She'd said it was good that Henk hadn't been totally opposed to seeing someone, asked how he'd seemed, calm, hostile?

479

'Quite calm, actually. And very sure of himself, in control. Is that a good sign, do you think?'

'I'm sorry, Susie, I don't know what to think. It's all so complicated. Everyone's different, so there aren't any rules. Was he hostile to you, in any way?'

'Only a bit. He just seemed – normal. Nicer than normal, even.' She managed a smile. 'So – what do I do now?'

'Wait, I'm afraid. The hardest thing of all. See what he does next. I'm afraid he's not going to just go away.'

'No,' said Susie, with a rather feeble smile, 'no, I'm afraid so too.'

There was no reply from Jonjo all day. No call, no message, no text. Just silence. And it was horrible. She did all the things everyone did; checked her phone constantly, phoned it from the landline on her desk to make sure it was working, charged it just in case, checked her texts over and over again, and began to hate everyone who called because they weren't Jonjo. And at the end of the day, she left early – Bianca was tied up with the VCs and there was no one else to notice – and hared home to check her landline. The answering machine had three messages: two were from her mother, one from an old friend. Well, had she really thought he would phone her on that?

Was it possible that he hadn't got the message? Possible, yes of course. Maybe she could text him, just say *Hope you got my call. Let me know if you didn't.* It sounded a bit desperate, but she was feeling desperate. And things could hardly be worse. Before she could debate it any further, she sent the text. She had hardly pressed send, when the phone rang. This was amazing. He hadn't got it! Thank God she'd sent the text! Shaking, weak with relief, smiling, she picked up her phone. 'Hi,' she said, struggling to hold her voice steady. 'Hi, lovely to hear from—' And then, too late, far too late, looked at the screen.

It was Henk.

Chapter 43

'You can sell the house,' said Bertie. His eyes, hard and cold as they so seldom were, met Priscilla's across the sitting room. She was sitting on the sofa, surrounded by papers, working on her next big charity event; she stared at him.

'You agree?'

'I do agree, yes.'

'Well that's – that's very good news. I thought you'd come to see it was best in the end.'

'Indeed.'

'I think, if we can act quickly, those Americans are still around. I'll tell the agent in the morning. In fact I'll send an email now. Well, this is excellent.'

'I'm glad you think so. And they were offering – what?'

'Three million. So that should get us a nice flat in town and then we shall have a fair bit over to put in our pension fund.'

'I'm afraid you have to think in terms of half that, Priscilla,' said Bertie.

'I'm sorry?' She looked at him and then half laughed. He hated that half-laugh. She did it a lot. 'Agents' fees and stamp duty aren't that high, Bertie. No, we should clear at least two eight.'

'*We* won't be clearing anything, Priscilla.'

'What on earth do you mean?'

He found, with a slight sense of shock, that he was enjoying himself. Good. He'd had very little pleasure recently.

'I mean you'll clear half of whatever we make, and I the rest.'

'Bertie, I hope you haven't got some crazy notion about separate finances, to save tax or something.'

'No, not at all.'

'Then what do you mean?'

'I mean I'm leaving you.'

She was silent, staring at him for a moment; then, 'What did you say?'

'I said I was leaving you. It's quite simple. I want a divorce, Priscilla. I've got a new job, a very nice job actually, nothing to do with Farrell's.'

She gave another of the half-laughs.

'Don't be absurd, Bertie. You can't leave Farrell's.'

'I can leave Farrell's, and I'm looking forward to it. My contract holds me for three months, but I daresay Bianca will let me go as soon as she finds a replacement for me. And then I'm off.'

'Off where?' For the first time she was looking uncertain; even a little pale.

'Physically, the Midlands. I've always rather liked the Midlands, they're much maligned in my view. Some of the country is lovely and of course I shall be able to buy an extremely nice house.'

'And – what does this company do?'

'It runs garden centres. Big growth area, garden centres, if you'll forgive the pun. MD's a very nice chap, we hit it off rather well. Quite a big chain, twenty or so. There's one near Basingstoke, you might even have been there.'

'What a ridiculous idea!' She was moving back into her default position of superiority, of belittling him. 'And what are you going to do for them? You don't know anything about garden centres.'

'I spend quite a lot of time in them, Priscilla. If you'd ever taken any notice of what I did in my spare time, you'd have realised that. I love gardens – especially this one, of course. I shall be sorry to leave it – I've put twenty years or so of care into it – but it will be good to start again. And I certainly know a lot about gardens, and why people love gardening. It's the Englishman and his home being his castle, or rather, the castle grounds. Anyway, my job will be in personnel, which I do seem to have a talent for, recognised by Bianca, of course. I shall miss Bianca.'

'Bertie . . .' Priscilla was looking less sure of herself. 'Look, I don't think you can have thought this through properly.'

'I've thought it through very properly, I assure you.'

'But you can't move up there alone. You'll have to look after yourself, for the first time in your life.'

'On the contrary, Priscilla, no one has ever looked after me. Certainly not you, if that's your implication.'

'Oh, don't talk such nonsense,' said Priscilla. 'Of course I've looked after you. Who do you think prepared your meals, washed your clothes, cleaned your house?'

'You did do those things, of course,' said Bertie, 'but you never seemed to think your duties encompassed things like encouragement, thoughtfulness, consideration, support – the more basic qualities one would look for in a marriage. The nearest I came to being looked after in that sense came from Lucy, who seems to have a clearer understanding of my needs than you ever did. Anyway, none of it matters any more. Our marriage is over.'

'Bertie . . .' She was beginning to look mildly anxious now. 'Bertie, we should talk about this properly. It's not right for you to leave Farrell's, you're part of it and—'

'I'm not really part of it,' said Bertie. 'My mother and my sister have always made it plain I was only there on sufferance. I have enjoyed my new role there, and I shall always be grateful to Bianca for realising my potential. But the three of you have continued to belittle and criticise me relentlessly. I want to get away from the whole thing, make my own way. It's as simple as that. As for our marriage, that is beyond redemption. I've been very aware of its shortcomings for a long time, but it was the sales conference, and your incredible rudeness both to and about me, and to the people I work with—'

'I suppose you mean that rather tarty woman. I could see she'd got her talons into you!' She stopped, her expression suddenly rather sharp. 'She put you up to this, didn't she? You probably seemed a rather good catch to her. Part of the set-up that employs her, on the board, clearly well off – what will she have to say about this new job of yours, I wonder? Rather less glamorous, and certainly less secure.'

'Priscilla,' said Bertie, his face white now, 'never, ever talk about Lara Clements in those terms again. She has been a very good friend to me, and has helped to give me confidence in myself, which God knows wasn't easy. She knows nothing about my future plans, but she was deeply shocked by what happened at the sales conference, my mother's behaviour in particular, and unfortunately, that has affected her attitude to me.

'I'm going to my study now, to start sorting out my affairs; I suggest we find a solicitor about a divorce, I think we need someone specialised. I will break the news to Lucy and Rob if you like.'

'You will not,' said Priscilla. 'I don't want Lucy getting some garbled version about all this and your extremely distorted view of our marriage. And besides, I haven't agreed to anything whatsoever. We have a great deal of talking to do before we make any kind of decision.'

'There is really nothing to talk about,' said Bertie, 'except financial arrangements and we can do that with a solicitor. Of course, if you want to oppose a divorce, then it will all take much longer and become rather more unpleasant, for you in particular. I would advise you to take the line of least resistance and you can then present things however you wish to your friends. But that is your decision. I am very anxious, naturally, for you to have exactly what is due to you. Now, if you will excuse me . . .'

'Bertie, this is madness! We've been married for almost twenty-five years, perfectly happily.'

'I grant you the twenty-five years,' said Bertie. 'But any happiness enjoyed together, even of a most imperfect kind, is a figment entirely of your imagination.'

She was great. Dead sexy; and clearly gagging for it. And fancied him. A much better proposition than that neurotic cow.

She'd come in for a casting, had clearly thought he carried a lot more weight than he actually did, and it had been a pushover, the whole thing. He'd asked her for a drink and the very first evening they ended up in bed. She was amazing, did everything he wanted and more. He lay watching her in the morning as she got dressed and rushed off to another casting, thinking that for the first time in his life he really was having it all. He could enjoy her; and continue torturing Susie. It was a very happy prospect indeed . . .

'Bianca? This is Lucy Farrell.'

'Oh, hello Lucy, what can I do for you?'

'It's about Milly.'

'Oh really?' She could hear her own voice sounding wary. 'And what about Milly?'

'Well, I don't know if you realised, but we talked quite a lot that day. When I took her off to Starbucks. She told me about school and bullying and stuff and it sounded so dreadful. And – well, *I* was bullied at school. It was the worst thing that's ever happened to me and I really would like to do something for Milly. She's so sweet, and so brave. So forgive me if I seem to be interfering, but I had an idea. Which just might help.'

'Really?'

'Yes. You see, the only thing with bullies is to beat them at their own game. And all this pretending you don't care really doesn't help at all.'

'Lucy, we know all this. We're not ignoring the problem. Not now we know about it . . .'

She felt ashamed of herself for being so hostile and defensive. But the conversation was irritating her profoundly.

'No, of course not. I realise that. But what Milly needs is something of her own, that she can talk about at school, that the others would envy her for.'

'Well, I daresay it is. But I don't see—'

'Bianca, Susie's asked me to work on your idea of some different looks for the launch, that we can use in promotions and so on. And that's very difficult, without a model. And most people don't want to spend their evenings and weekends having make-up piled on to their faces endlessly. But I know Milly would. She kept saying what a wonderful job I had, how she'd like to do something like that. And she has a friend too, Jayce—'

'Lucy, I don't know if you've met Jayce, but she doesn't sound to me an ideal model.'

'You know what, it really doesn't matter. It's a face I need, not a model's face. Think of a blank canvas—'

'I believe Jayce has spots,' said Bianca coldly. You cow, she thought, why are you being like this?

'Even that doesn't matter. It really doesn't. The point is it all sounds rather glamorous. Something Milly could just mention casually at school. And I may be wrong, but I think it would get those girls regarding her rather differently. It would change her into something a little bit special. You know how all these girls want to be models . . .'

'Well, of course they do. But – and I don't want you to think I'm not grateful, of course I am – but Milly is, as far as I can make out, completely friendless. Nobody talks to her. There's no one to mention anything to.'

'Well, they look at her Facebook page, we know that. If only to put horrible things on it. She could just mention it on that. I could even photograph her and she could put that on.'

'Oh, I don't think so,' said Bianca quickly. 'I think that could be asking for more trouble.'

'Really?'

'Yes. They could criticise her, and how she looked.'

'Well, they could. But it's unlikely in my view.'

'Lucy, I really appreciate this, of course,' said Bianca, 'but I think it's a rather risky plan. And Milly is very busy, she has a lot of homework and you want to do this at the weekends.'

'Ye-es . . .'

She could hear Lucy withdrawing, sounding embarrassed even.

'Well, I'm sorry. I just thought it would be something we could do together. Even if it didn't help at school, I do genuinely need a model and it would be a bit of fun for her, cheer her up. But if you think it might actually do more harm than good—'

'I do, I'm afraid. But thank you anyway. Now if you'll excuse me, Lucy, I'm already late for a meeting.'

'Of course. I quite understand. Goodbye, Bianca.'

You, thought Bianca, looking at the phone after ringing off, you are a complete cow. Here is this extremely nice girl, caring about Milly, wanting to help Milly and what do you do? Tell her to piss off. And it *could* help; it was an ingenious idea. And even if it didn't work at school, it would be very good for Milly, give her something else to think about. So why?

She knew perfectly well why. It was all part of the guilt. And her sense of failure as a mother. She should be able to help Milly, solve her problems. That was the only thing that was going to make her feel better. She didn't want some stranger doing it. Especially – and she knew this was at the heart of it – not a stranger called Farrell, the granddaughter of her enemy, the person who had already humiliated her beyond endurance. She could imagine Lucy talking about it all to Athina, and Athina pouncing on this new faultline in her, imagine them laughing about it.

'Not only is she failing with the company,' Athina would say, 'she can't even run her own family.' And she would quite likely use it, bring it up, in her brilliantly barbed way, ask after Milly, say how upset and sorry Lucy had felt about it. It would be awful. Terrible.

And how much does that matter, Bianca Bailey? she asked herself. And answered: not in the very least. The only person who matters here is Milly; Milly who still cries in her room at night, Milly whose once sparkling little face is haunted and heavy, Milly who has no power whatsoever to put things right by herself, Milly who needs, as Patrick said, grown-up help.

And here some grown-up help was, and what did she do? Turn it away. It had been an appalling piece of behaviour. She had failed Milly a second time; only this had been worse than the first, because she had done it knowingly. And how could she possibly climb down now? Did she say, oh, sorry, Lucy, I think it's a great idea after all, I was wrong, why don't you come round to supper one evening so we can all discuss it? Yes, that's what she ought to do. But Lucy would no doubt find that rather pathetic, would probably tell her grandmother that too . . .

And anyway, she was probably already lining up some other models . . .

'Bianca, that meeting starts in five minutes. Have you got everything you need?'

'Yes, Jemima. Yes, I think so. I'll be up in the boardroom in five minutes.'

'Right. Harriet's just brought up some of the new colours for the paintboxes. They're gorgeous. I thought once you'd approved them, we should let Lucy have them so she can start working on her new looks. She is really good, Bianca, I think she's going to be one of the great make-up artists one day, up there with Gucci Westman. One of the magazines is doing a piece about her and Susie's over the moon.'

'Really? Really that good?'

'Really that good.'

'I see. Well . . .' Go on, Bianca, just do it: now before you lose your nerve. Go on. Milly is who matters here, not you, not your stupid pride. You really don't have any right to that of all things. Go on . . . go on . . .

'Jemima, could you get Lucy on the phone for me, please? Right away? And send a message to the boardroom I'll be five minutes late. Yes. Thank you . . . Oh, Lucy. Hello. It's Bianca. Look, I've been thinking and I – well, I owe you an apology. That could be a very clever idea of yours for Milly and I'm sorry I wasn't more enthusiastic. Would you like to come for supper one evening this week, so we can discuss it and with Milly? And the looks you're thinking about, of course. I might ask Susie to come as well. I think Milly will be over the moon. In fact why don't I get her to call you? Would that be all right?'

Nothing from Henk today – nothing for three days. Maybe he was going to accept what she'd said, maybe she could begin to relax.

◦ ◦ ◦

'Lara, have you got five minutes?'

'I could have,' said Lara with a grin. 'You're the boss.'

'You could have fooled me. Anyway, let's not get into that. It's about Bertie. Did you know he was leaving?'

'Leaving! No!' She felt cold and a bit sick. 'Where's he going, what's happened?'

'It's all rather odd, really. He's going to a company that runs garden centres.'

'That's not odd – he loves gardens and gardening.'

'Yes, I know. But – what I mean is, leaving Farrell's, leaving the family, leaving the industry, striking out on his own – that's huge, when you think about it.'

Lara shrugged. 'Is it?'

'Lara, of course it is. Don't be silly. He didn't give me a real reason, was a bit cagey about it all. Apart from being really sweet about how much I'd done for him, given him the confidence to think for himself, as he put it, he was very brief and businesslike. Said it was partly for personal reasons which he'd rather not discuss, but also this was a field he was rather more comfortable with than cosmetics. He was so sweet, so anxious about causing me problems, and at such a time, as he put it, altogether at his most Bertie-like, that I couldn't be cross with him. Oh, and he's moving up to the Midlands. I presumed that was the personal bit, so I didn't press him on it. Anyway, keep it quiet, I promised him I wouldn't tell anyone, but I don't count you—'

'Thanks,' said Lara.

'You know what I mean. You're family. Speaking of which, what's that I hear out there – could it be – it is – good afternoon, Lady Farrell.' In what was now a rather familiar scenario, Jemima appeared in the doorway looking apologetic and embarrassed, with Lady Farrell inserting herself in front of her.

'Mrs Bailey, we must talk.'

'About?' Bianca's voice was sweetly courteous as always. Anything else was counterproductive.

'The perfume launch. And in private, if you please.'

'Lady Farrell, Mrs Clements and I are in the middle of a

489

meeting. If she is agreeable, we can certainly interrupt it, but only for a short time. You and I can perhaps talk later, if necessary. But do please tell me what is concerning you. Lara, is that all right with you?'

'Of course,' said Lara.

'Very well.' Just occasionally Athina would accept defeat. 'It's about the advertising campaign for the perfume.'

'Ah, yes.'

'I have seen nothing as yet, no visuals, no copy. It's already late, and we need to be in the July issues for June, perhaps you didn't realise that?'

'I did, yes,' Bianca said, hanging on to her patient smile with difficulty.

'And that in turn means final copy, and indeed artwork, to the magazines by early April at the latest. And here we are, mid-February and nothing even presented. I have to say that Langland Dennis and Colborne would have had a great deal to show us by now – unless of course your people, those rather casual young men, have done some work already and you haven't seen fit to show it to me? I'm sure you would agree that the perfume is my project. It wouldn't exist without me. Perhaps you have forgotten that.'

'Lady Farrell I . . .' Bianca paused. 'You're quite right, they are being a little slow. And I should have chased them before this. I'm – I'm most grateful to you for bringing it to my attention, and I'll see they have something to show us by next week. And I'll make sure the date is convenient to you.'

Athina appeared to accept all this. Just as well, Bianca thought. If she'd felt miffed enough, she'd have been quite capable of going to another agency altogether and briefing them herself . . .

'Well, I'm pleased to hear it,' she said, 'and I have to say that if they don't come up with something very impressive, I would consider going to another agency altogether . . .'

When Athina had gone, Lara said, 'She's right. I was thinking it was getting on a bit.'

'I know. But the thing is, everything's up in the air now. Rethink all round. Including budgets.'

'Oh, I see. Because of your idea?'

'Because of my idea. It's got a lot to answer for, my idea has!'

Right. She was probably beginning to relax, to think he was out of her life. Or at least calming down.

So, what should he say this time? It would have to be a bit different, scary still, but maybe lulling her into a sense of false security. Then it would be more of a shock when he pulled her out of it. God, he was enjoying this. It really was eye-for-an-eye, tooth-for-a-tooth time. Serve her right for thinking she could just dump him. Anyway, he hadn't that long, he was meeting Zoe straight after work. There'd been another one in this afternoon, giving him the eye, almost as gorgeous; he really should have seen what an opportunity this job was, when it came to pulling. Worth the odd bit of sweeping up and being ordered about. For a bit anyway. He pulled his phone out of the pocket of his jeans and moved into creative mode.

And then thought of how he could make it different.

As she passed Bertie's office, Lara saw him engaged in a clearly rather intense conversation on the phone. He gave her a half-hearted smile and then got up and closed his door. It hurt Lara more than anything, that gesture. Bertie, who she thought was her friend, to whom she had felt at one point so close, fancied even, making this huge decision without even hinting at it. And moving away, for personal reasons. What did that mean? Only one thing, in Lara's experience: he had met someone and he wanted to move to be nearer to her. God, it hurt. All those lunchtimes, those jokes, the growing closeness – all misread . . .

Well, the one good thing was that it would be one in the eye for that cow of a wife of his. But she felt such a fool. Thinking Bertie fancied her when clearly that had been the wildest fantasy, when obviously she wasn't his equal intellectually, socially or indeed any other way.

In her office, she switched on her computer and started scrolling through the morning's emails. She was trying to make sense of a report on stockholdings when Bertie appeared in the doorway. He smiled at her nervously.

'Sorry about that. Did you want to discuss something?'

Lara shook her head. No way was she going to appear to be chasing him, when his sights were set so firmly elsewhere, and besides, he had asked Bianca to keep his news confidential so she certainly wasn't going to so much as hint she knew or cared about it.

'No,' she said, briskly, 'no, I didn't.'

'OK.' He looked at her rather sadly and disappeared again.

Back at his own desk, Bertie looked at the piece of paper covered with notes from his conversation with the rather sharp solicitor he had briefed to handle the divorce, and sighed. It would have been so nice to talk to Lara about it, not just because she had been through it, but because he needed her friendship and warmth more than ever. He would have liked to talk about the new job too, and see what she thought about it, and even explain why he was going; but she had been so odd since the conference, so distant, so that was clearly out of the question too. He missed her; she had made every day funny and interesting, with her ability to see things differently and positively, her can-do attitude, her swift, pragmatic judgment. He wondered if she'd met someone at the conference: there'd been enough men there and one of the conference organisers had clearly rather fancied her, the one she'd been dancing with so much. He'd seen them laughing together, and dancing at the disco, which would explain a lot. He had thought at one point their relationship was rather special; had even – well, clearly he had been completely wrong. Poor, silly Bertie had got it wrong again.

Susie was asleep when her phone rang. She grabbed it, stared at it stupidly.

'Hello?'

'Susie, it's Henk. I feel so bad, so terribly bad. I just can't go on. Susie, you've got to help me!'

492

'Henk, Henk, please!' Her brain was still blurred. 'It's two in the morning – what do you want?'

'You know what I want. *You.* I've got to see you tomorrow, OK?'

'Yes, yes, OK, OK. Where and when, just say.'

Then he rang again, just after four, saying he wanted to make sure she was coming.

She was still wide awake, of course, terrified. But it was a dreadful shock, just the same. As it was when he called at five. What was she going to do, what?

Chapter 44

He knew he should be going back to London: the whole trip had come out of nowhere and he'd promised Bianca it was only for two days. Now he was running into the fourth, but it was the most intriguing – and potentially most important – case yet. It could make billions for Saul. Or prevent him from losing them.

Of course Saul had said there had been no need to go out there in the first place, but he'd been wrong. The chap Patrick had talked to on the first morning had set him on a trail he'd never have found just from trawling through documents. More and more it seemed necessary to be personally involved. And Saul was so appreciative of his efforts, kept saying he'd never known anything like Patrick's dog-at-a-bone approach so it really did seem he was bringing more to the job than Saul had expected. Which was a great feeling. Heading up a family business, seeing it go smoothly along, keeping its clients happy – how could that compare with the almost physical excitement of following a twisting, convoluted trail, leading he knew not where, knowing he was doing something very very few other people could?

All of which was making him feel differently about life: about Bianca, about his role in their marriage, their marriage itself. Once, they were his main priorities, central to his life; now what she demanded of him, what had seemed right, looked increasingly questionable. His own career, his own progress, were growing in importance day by day; and thus his own needs and requirements. It was subliminal, much of this, and he was most aware of it in a deterioration in their relationship and an interesting reluctance, a refusal indeed, in him to face what was clearly necessary to restore it to what it was. Had he been asked if he loved her still, he would have said unhesitatingly yes; but increasingly he saw her as selfish as much as ambitious, demanding as much as driven, and her success dependent on him to an extent he had never properly realised. The price had been his own fulfilment – and was beginning to seem most unfairly high.

So – he was going to stay on. Bianca would have to cope. Which was exactly what he had been doing for the last thirteen or so years.

Patrick settled down at the desk in his room on the fifteenth floor of his absurdly luxurious hotel and abandoned himself, not to the delights of room service, or the excellent TV and media channels, or even the complimentary bottle of champagne that had been waiting for him on arrival, but the notes he had been making throughout the day and the slightly mysterious rise in construction costs over the past six months in the electronics company he was investigating and which had declared, as its policy, a five per cent reduction each year . . .

Jemima was increasingly intrigued by the stories she heard of Henk. She would not have dreamed of saying anything to Susie, but her description of his behaviour bore no resemblance to any case involving suicidal tendencies she had ever heard of or studied and something just didn't ring quite true. Henk's calmness, his openness to Susie's suggestion to seek professional help, the fact everything was going well with his new job – a humble job, moreover, that seemed unsuited to someone of his arrogance and aggression – and above all the cosy walk back to the flat with Susie; it just . . . niggled.

She had spoken to her tutor about it in theoretical, not actual, terms and he was dismissive.

'You cannot leap to conclusions, Jemima, or generalise in any way the behaviour of the person you describe. This theoretical creature you've pieced together as an exercise – who I suspect is as factual as you and I, but we won't go into that – is clearly complex in the extreme and he's a nasty piece of work by any standard. That does not, however, mean he is an unlikely candidate for suicide. I would only beg of you not to express your views to anyone concerned with the case.'

'Of course I won't,' said Jemima. 'I wouldn't dream of it!'

'Good. Now, if we could turn our attention to last week's case study . . .'

Nevertheless, she continued to fret and next day she found Susie white-faced, and heard about the night calls.

'So, will you meet him tonight?'

'I have to. From everything you said, everything I've read even, it would be dangerous not to. It's so scary, Jemima, you've no idea.'

'I think I have – totally awful. But let's see what he says, shall we? And what will you do if he tries to come home with you, or won't let you go?'

'Oh, Jemima, I don't know!' Susie's voice cracked.

'Look, I've got a lecture this evening,' said Jemima, 'and the Institute's not that far from here. I'll be away about nine, so fix it somewhere near-ish and if you're in trouble, text me and I'll come right over.'

'You're such a good friend,' said Susie. 'I couldn't cope with any of this without you. I feel so totally terrified.'

'Of course you do, anyone would. But we'll get it sorted, Susie, promise. No news from Jonjo?'

'Of course not,' said Susie, her voice brisk suddenly, 'that's obviously so over. I'm OK about it, actually.' She managed a quick smile. 'I'm much more worried about Henk now than about Jonjo.'

Which, Jemima reflected, was exactly what Henk wanted.

Lara sat listening to Tod, who had brought what he called his technical team – a team of one, called Jules – for a briefing meeting on Bianca's idea. Her own head was still reeling at it. It was so original, so absolutely fit for purpose, so totally of today in concept. It was at such times that she realised how it was that Bianca had reached the pinnacle of her profession; she might make mistakes, she might take wrong turnings, but she had a brilliantly innovative mind and a capacity for lateral thought that made Lara's head spin.

'So let's recap,' said Tod. 'There's going to be all these little Berkeley Arcade lookalikes in the shopping capitals of the world, OK? And, of course, there will be virtual shops online, with a facility for internet shopping. People can wander in, select things from the shelves, that sort of thing.'

'Ye-es.' So far, the technical person seemed underwhelmed. 'OK. Now, this is where it gets clever. Every shop – every *real* shop – will open at the same time, I mean literally the same time, ten a.m. UK time, because Farrell's is an English company, and that's what we're making so much of as you know, the heritage thing, anyway. So eleven a.m. in Paris and Milan, six a.m. in New York, nine p.m. in Sydney or whatever – you get the idea?'

'Sorry, you've got me there. Are people *really* going to go shopping at six in the morning in New York?'

'Possibly not. But they'll want to see it happening online. We're talking a global launch here. How it will work is that when the punter logs on, the site will recognise the country she's in and automatically divert her to the correct shop. Like here, it would be London obviously. And if there's more than one shop in your country, like New York and LA, you'll be able to go to your local, so to speak. And of course go to other countries, if you want to check out Tokyo, say. Anyway, you, dear customer, will be there in real time, outside the London shop and as soon as it's open, you can start shopping. Be first in line at a global cosmetic launch, see the doors of each shop open for the first time. And it will be the real thing, filmed using a webcam and downloaded on to your computer. You'll be able to watch people going in, wandering round, outside in the street, outside Farrell shops all over the world. So how amazing is that? And then you can start shopping. That'll be virtual, obviously. And if you fancy nipping over to New York, you can. It's going to be *huge*, the buzz we can get going. Nothing's ever been done like it: we're personalising internet shopping in a way that's never been done and the PR will be incredible. The most hardened editors and bloggers will love it.'

The technical team turned to Bianca and grinned.

'And this was your idea?'

'It was.'

'It's fu— bloody brilliant.'

'Well, thank you. I thought so too. Excuse my modesty. It wasn't actually entirely my idea. Well, it sort of was, but Jay-Z, you know, the rock star—'

'Yeah, I know, course I do!'

'Sorry. Anyway, he did something a bit similar, you might even know about it?'

The technical team shook its head.

'Well, he published every single page of his autobiography separately, but simultaneously, somewhere in the world, sides of trucks, posters, subways, so in theory people could download the whole book and read it. And I thought: how amazing to have all these people sitting by their computers, waiting for whatever time it is where they are, to be first in line, as all the little virtual shops open—'

'Oh my God,' said Lara interrupting, 'are we doing lots of shops now?'

'Yes, we absolutely are. We'll have the shops because we're going to do a franchise operation. How clever is that? Not my idea, that one. Had a bit of a time getting Mike and Hugh on side, and I'm not sure they believe in it even now, but they're doing their bit, putting feelers out to their contacts where I don't have any. No joy yet, but – well, it's going to work, it's got to.'

'And – sorry to be negative – can we do it in the time?'

'Oh yes,' said Bianca airily. 'Same reason, because we've got to. There is simply no room for failure And there won't be.'

She smiled round the room. 'So what do you think?'

'I still think it's amazing,' said Tod. 'Amazing.' He smiled back at Bianca.

She was changed, Lara thought, from the humiliated, half-defeated woman of the conference and the following week; she had her confidence back, her sheen, her sure touch; she knew absolutely what she was doing.

'Well, the first thing we have to do is build a microsite,' Tod said, 'with a link to the main Farrell one. Built-in HTML5, I would say. Agree, Jules?'

'Yeah, probably. There'd be animation in it obviously, movement within the site, interactive techniques – all kinds of fun.'

'And timing?' said Bianca. 'I imagine it won't be exactly easy.'

'No, it won't. But Bianca, it can be done,' said Tod. 'Trust us.'

'OK. I have to, don't I?'

'You do,' said Tod with a grin.

'And the other thing I thought was: suppose it broke down under all the hits – millions, hopefully – how totally awful that would be?'

'Totally,' said Jules, 'so the next thing we do is run a beta version of the site on a server which is not accessible to the public, and basically try to break the site. Throw as much as we can at it. So we know it'll be all right.'

'So there we are,' said Tod, 'lots of pretty little shops, fantastic website, excited public – how do we tell them about it in the first place?'

'Well,' said Susie, 'press is too slow, really, although I've got some ideas for them. But in the immediate build-up, bloggers, the dailies, TV. I have a feeling that we need an event too. On launch day. Something simple, like totally stopping London's traffic? No, seriously, I'll think of something. And of course online, banners, that sort of thing. And a teaser campaign, that's a must.'

'Yeah, and we've got a line for you,' said Tod. 'See if you like it. It's "Something beautiful is going to happen". It will appear wherever the Farrell logo is. Just that, to begin with, nothing more.'

'I like it very much,' said Bianca.

'Good. Then after a month or so we'll add "June 1st" and anything else that we think necessary. It's intriguing, and wherever they go, they'll find it, in magazines, online, possibly even radio, on the website and the Farrell Facebook page and Twitter, of course. Those eight little words. No more.'

'Great,' said Susie. 'Really really great.'

'Good. Oh, and we think you should have a Face of Farrell,' said

Tod, 'a supermodel or, better still, an actress, plugging Farrell's with their every breath.'

'Now that we can't afford,' said Bianca. 'Totally impossible.'

'Bianca,' said Susie slowly, 'I like that idea. Can I have a go at finding someone?'

'Yes, if you really think you can. But it absolutely mustn't cost anything. Well, hardly anything.'

'OK,' said Jules. 'Now, do you want to be involved in building the site?'

'Only on the visual side – I wouldn't understand most of it.'

'Of course. But that would come a bit later. Let's get the technicalities out of the way, and you say there'll be a dozen shops minimum?'

'Maximum,' said Bianca. 'Minimum two. But there will be. Don't look at me like that, Tod! It's just that I really am dependent on finding people to put their money into us, and until they do . . .'

'Of course.'

'The minute there's one, they'll all come tumbling in. It's that first in the bag that does it.'

'I had to sell ad space once,' said Lara, 'for a new magazine. Total nightmare, no one would risk it. Then, finally, Revlon took a page and bingo! They were fighting each other off.'

'I bet. So all we need is a Revlon. Notionally speaking. But – I'll keep you posted.' For the first time that morning she looked less confident, less positive even.

'Right,' said Tod, 'one more thing. We wondered about having a countdown device, ticking away on the site, like a digital clock, marking every second till June 1st. I know it's a bit corny, but it's very intriguing, just the same. But we need to make it different, memorable – we don't want it to look like the Olympic clock.'

'How about,' said Lara slowly, 'some sort of device that starts as the tiniest dot in the corner of the page – I mean screen – getting bigger and bigger and then more and more recognisable as a face by June 1st. Just think of her, coming into focus, starting with a fleck of eye colour or a scrap of eyelash.'

500

'That's *genius*,' said Tod, staring at her. 'I love it! It could be part of the teaser campaign. She could be our supermodel. How about that?'

'Yes, yes, yes!' said Bianca. 'Goodness, this has turned into some brainstorm. Fantastic work, everybody. Thank you so much. Now—'

Jemima appeared looking as near to flustered as she was capable of.

'I'm so sorry, Bianca, but it's – well, it's Saul Finlayson. He says he has to talk to you right now, that it's really, really urgent. I'm so sorry.'

'Oh, all right,' said Bianca. She was struggling to look cool, Lara thought: interesting. 'I'll – I'll take it in there.'

Jemima followed her out of the room, closing the door with an apologetic smile to everyone. They all tried to appear not to be listening but it was difficult, because Bianca's voice was getting increasingly loud, saying, 'What? Oh what? I don't – you can't – Oh. My. God! That is just so incredibly amazing! Yes. Yes, of course. Yes. Fantastic! Just – just hold on a minute, would you?'

And she appeared back in her own office, flushed and brilliant-eyed and clearly near to tears.

'We've found our Revlon,' she said, her voice shaking slightly, 'resident in Singapore. Wants to open a Farrell shop like yesterday – well, on June 1st of course. Just try and stop us now!'

Susie was horribly aware of not having been very impressive at the meeting; she was so terrified about the imminent meeting with Henk and what she was going to do about it, not just this evening but longer term, that she could hardly have told Bianca her name, never mind come up with some brilliant idea. She simply couldn't go on with this; it was too much for her to handle and she found it difficult to think of anything else. More than once she'd seen Bianca looking at her with a particular expression of hers, a kind of watchful impatience that everyone was afraid of, far more than open criticism. She knew she already wasn't performing up to standard, and it could only get worse as time went on.

She had suggested a wine bar midway between Farrell's and Jemima's college to Henk, which he agreed to, and Jemima had promised to be there within ten minutes of getting an SOS. Just the same, she got ready in a state approaching terror, and when Bianca's face appeared behind her in the mirror of the ladies', she started shaking and had to make an excuse to rush out of the room.

Henk was late; over half an hour, and she was just about to give up on him when he finally appeared, looking rather sheepish, saying he was sorry, he'd been held up.

'You could have called me,' she said almost crossly, and then remembered she wasn't dealing with someone in a normal state of mind, and apologised.

'It's OK. You got a drink?'

'Yes thank you.'

He looked at her spritzer, then said, 'Shall I get a bottle of the house white?'

God, Susie thought, he was clearly envisaging a long evening.

'I – that sounds rather a lot. I'm not supposed to be drinking at all, I'm on antibiotics.'

He shrugged. 'OK. I'll just get a beer.'

When he sat down next to her he said, 'Good day?'

'Yes, thanks. Yours?'

'Lousy. Susie, let's not play games, it's too important. I told you how bad I was feeling.'

'Yes. Yes, I'm sorry. Henk, did you think about what I suggested, you know, about – about seeing someone? Someone professional who could—'

'Not really. I just don't see the point. Only one thing's going to make me feel better and that's being with you again. I *told* you.'

'Yes, but Henk, you've just got to – got to—' Go on Susie, say it, 'Got to understand that – well, that isn't going to – to happen.'

'No,' he said. 'No, I don't understand. It *has* to happen, Susie, we were so good together and I don't see the problem. You're not with anyone else now and . . .'

Susie suddenly felt she was going to scream. This was *Groundhog Day*, playing for real, the conversation going round and round

502

in the same setting, even to the half-drunk white wine spritzer on the table in front of them. Was she ever going to get away? Was she going to have to spend the rest of her life in a wine bar with Henk?

'Excuse me,' she said, hoping her voice wasn't shaking, 'I just need to go to the loo.' And sat there, crying frantically, texting Jemima: *Please please come, please as soon as you can.*

Poor Jemima, she thought, trying to clean off the streams of mascara – how come tears made it dissolve so easily and tap water didn't? – she was probably in the middle of a lecture. But she had promised . . .

It took her quite a long time to calm down, to get back in control, and when she finally got back to Henk he was staring moodily across the room.

'You took your time,' he said. 'Trying to get away from me, are you?'

'No, Henk, of course not. I'm sorry.'

'OK. So, what are we going to do? Stay here, find something to eat?'

'I – well, I can't be—'

'Can't be what? Don't tell me you've got some important meeting to go to, Susie, it's getting a bit monotonous. We need time together, to sort things out, to get to know each other again. Come on!'

The panic was rising again; she felt sick, shaky, sat staring at him, trying desperately to think of what to say.

'Babe! Hello? I'm here. Come on, what shall it be, stay here a bit longer, maybe they do food.'

'I – I'm not—' Not hungry she was going to say, while hopelessly aware that it was no excuse at all, certainly wouldn't satisfy him. Then . . .

'Susie! Oh my God, it's so great to see you. How are you?'

Jemima! Lovely, lovely Jemima, standing in front of them, smiling at them. She could have hugged her – and actually did. Picking up on Jemima's script, she stood up, hurled her arms round her, said, 'What a coincidence! You look amazing! How are you?'

503

'I'm good, thanks. Working at the same old thing, medical secretary.'

That was clever, Susie thought, giving her background.

'And you? How's the PR business going? Bit more interesting than hearing about people's bones – was I working for the orthopaedic surgeon last time we met?'

'No, I think whoever it was then was in stomachs,' said Susie, and then giggled, partly with relief, partly at her own turn of phrase.

Jemima smiled back, then said to Henk, 'I'm so sorry, you must think I'm terribly rude, but I just had to say hello to Susie, we haven't met for yonks – must be three years, Susie, yes?'

'At least. Henk, this is Jemima, Jemima Pendleton. Jemima, Henk Martin.'

'Hi, Henk. I do hope I'm not ruining your nice quiet evening – I know how annoying that could be.'

'No, it's fine,' he said, managing to smile, clearly with a great effort. 'You go ahead. Can I get you a drink?'

'No, thank you, I've probably had one too many already. Husband's away on business and I'm out on the razz with another girlfriend – well you know – actually just going home.'

'Well, we're about to go and have a meal,' said Henk, 'so—'

'A meal!' said Jemima, smiling at him ecstatically. 'Oh my goodness, now that does sound tempting. Soak up some of this alcohol. But are you sure? I don't want to gatecrash?'

God, she was a good actresss, Lucy thought. She had got it to perfection, her role, and how clever to choose the thick-skinned friend, misunderstanding, imposing herself where she was so clearly not welcome.

'No, that wasn't what—' But Henk stopped, floored by the impossibility of not sounding rude, and looking at Susie for a possible escape.

And she, aware that she must tread carefully, not overplay the situation, said 'Well, the thing is, Jemima, we've got a lot to talk about, me and Henk, and—'

'Well, look, why don't I just have a starter or something and then leave you to it. But it would be so nice to have just half an hour catch-up, Susie. Gosh, what a bit of luck spotting you! So, Henk, what do you do? It must be something creative if you know Susie. Let me guess, something creative – you have such a creative aura! I know, advertising. I can just see you dreaming up some wonderful campaign!'

'No,' said Henk, scowling at her. He was getting really pissed off, Susie could see.

'OK. So what?'

'I'm a photographer,' he said.

'A photographer! Oh, how exciting! What, fashion photos for *Vogue* and *Tatler*, that sort of thing? Or do you do celebrity pictures, people like George Clooney and David Beckham? Anyway, you can tell me about it over our meal. Where should we go? Do you fancy Greek or Italian or Indian, maybe?'

'Look,' said Henk, 'count me out.' He was looking really angry now, glaring at Jemima, avoiding Susie's eyes. 'You two go off and enjoy yourselves. I've got work to do.'

'Oh, now I feel really terrible. Look, you two go off. Maybe you could both come round to mine one evening later in the week? That'd be fun and I could get to know you, Henk. In fact, how about tomorrow?'

'No, no, much better this way. I'll see you tomorrow, Susie. Call me first thing to fix something, OK? Without fail.' It was a menacing phrase. 'Nice to have met you,' he said to Jemima, pulling on his coat, 'enjoy your meal.'

And he was gone, without even kissing Susie goodbye. She looked after him, panic-stricken. 'Jemima, that was a bit much. Poor Henk! He's in such a state! Maybe I should follow him?'

'Susie,' said Jemima, 'Henk is *not* in a state. He's fine, sane as you and me.'

'How do you know, how can you tell?'

'Because I've been watching him. I got here before you texted, just in time to see you go to the loo. I stood in the doorway, watching him. Honestly Susie, the minute you'd turned your back, he looked round, then got out his phone, called someone up, started laughing

505

and chatting, totally OK. I couldn't hear anything he said, of course, except I could see at one stage he was kissing into the phone. You were ages and he went on and on, chatting away, nodding, looked at his watch, nodded again – he was having a really nice time. Then as the loo door opened he said something very brief, switched off his phone, pushed it into his pocket, slumped down in his seat, and went all moody-looking. He's a bastard, Susie, a good old-fashioned bastard. He's playing games with you, and I think you should have a really serious check on him. Like go to the studio where he works, something like that—'

'Jemima, I couldn't!'

'But I actually don't think it's necessary. I'm one hundred per cent convinced he's just leading you on, and it's just outrageous and so cruel. Do you have the numbers of any of his friends?'

'Well – yes.'

'OK, call one of them up and say you're really worried about him, he seems so miserable or something like that.'

'I – I don't know,' said Susie. 'I'd feel dreadful if they said yes, that they were worried too . . .'

'Well, I will then,' said Jemima impatiently. 'If I hadn't seen him with my own eyes, switching from fun guy to depressive in the course of a nanosecond, I wouldn't be so confident. But I am, totally. He's a very good actor, Susie, that's all – well, apart from being devious and sadistic and all kinds of other nice things.'

'You're not so bad at acting yourself,' said Susie. She was beginning to believe Jemima, to feel a relief so intense she felt almost physically lighter, rather silly even. She giggled. 'I was beginning to find you quite irritating myself!'

'Yes, well, I was quite good at acting at school,' said Jemima modestly. 'Even played Juliet. OK, so how are you feeling now? Still want to go after him?'

'No way!' said Susie. 'Tell you what, I think we should actually go off and have a meal and lots to drink, and talk about your creative aura. How about that?'

'Sounds good to me,' said Jemima. 'God, Susie, you look so different already.'

'I feel it,' said Susie, smiling at her. 'Totally different. Although a bit scared still. I hope to God you're not wrong.'

'I'm not wrong,' said Jemima, 'and I don't often say that. Come on, let's go. I'm starving.'

'You know what?' said Susie. 'So am I. For the first time in weeks.'

Chapter 45

'I wondered if I could buy you a drink this evening. If you're free . . .'

'What for?'

It was not the most enthusiastic response to an invitation. Clearly she'd read more into that hug than she should have done. She'd thought he was – well, becoming human. Not making a pass, obviously, as if, and how awful that would be – well, it would . . .

'Well, to say thank you,' she said. 'And I'd like to hear a bit more about this person you've found. It is so kind of you.'

'It really wasn't at all kind. I just mentioned you to someone. He thought it was a good proposition. He wouldn't have offered otherwise. I certainly didn't go looking for him. Or indeed anyone else.'

'Yes, I see . . . well, I'm very grateful, however it happened. Whether it was kind or not. So I'd like to – and tell you where we've got. With the campaign and so on.'

'That would be interesting. But it would have to be another time. I'm busy this evening.'

'Oh.' She really hadn't expected that, had somehow thought he was always free, on his own, apart from his phone and its demands. 'I see. Right. And – are you doing something nice?'

'Not particularly.'

She gave up.

'OK. Well, another evening then.'

'Yes. When your husband is back, perhaps the three of us. I think that would be best.'

Talk about a put-down! Did he really think she was trying to make a move on him?

'I'm sorry,' he said, into the silence. 'That sounded rude. I didn't mean it to.'

'That's OK.'

'Anyway, I don't drink.'

This was so ridiculous she laughed aloud.

'Why is that so funny?'

'Well, because – because it's such a stupid excuse. Buying someone a drink has nothing to do with alcohol. It's a social gesture.'

'I don't really go along with social gestures,' he said, 'as you know.'

She sighed. 'Yes, I do. OK, I won't make any more. Not to you anyway. Have a nice evening, whatever it involves.'

'It won't be nice,' he said. 'I have to go and see my ex-wife. She wants to talk to me. I have no idea why. It might be about Dickon.'

'I see. Well, it might be nicer than you think. I hope so. Meanwhile I have to go home and get on with my project.'

'What, the campaign?'

'No. Georgian architecture. It's for Ruby,' she added, into the silence.

'Ah. A school project?'

'That's right.'

'I quite like those,' he said, 'I'd like to do more. But my wife does most of them. Although she did allow me to get involved in one recently. It was about astronomy. I'm quite interested in that. It puts us in our place, I always think.'

'Indeed. Well, goodbye. Hope it's OK.'

'Thank you.'

And so she went home, had a brief chat with Sonia, waved at Fergie who was in position in front of the games console and acknowledged her with a vague nod, tapped nervously on Milly's door, then put her head round it.

'Hi, darling.'

'Hi, Mum.'

She was usually Mum now, not Mummy. Milly was cool, no longer actually hostile, but not the Milly she knew. She seemed to have grown five years older and made her feel awkward, nervous even. Which was ridiculous. Wasn't it?

'Lucy Farrell called me today,' she said. 'Have you spoken to her?'

'Not – not really.'

'Ah. Well, she's had an idea, Milly. Do you want to hear about it? It concerns you, partly.'

'Me!'

'Yes. Although actually I think it would be better if she explained it. Why don't you call her? She's expecting to hear from you.'

'Really? I do like her, you know. She's so nice.'

'She's extraordinarily nice,' said Bianca. 'Do you have her number?'

'Yes. She put it in my phone that day.' It wasn't necessary to spell out which day.

'Well, give her a call. Or text her. I'll be interested to hear what you think about her idea. You don't have to tell me, of course,' she added hastily.

'OK. I'll text her.'

'Well, I'm off to get to work on Ruby's project.'

'Oh, yes, Georgian architecture, isn't it? Good luck!'

She retreated, went down to the kitchen where Ruby was having her supper with Karen.

'Ready when you are, Ruby.'

'OK. Mummy, when can I have a mobile? Lots of my friends are getting them.'

'Are they? Well—'

'Don't say you'll see. That just means no. I'd rather you said not for a year. Or five years. Or ten.'

God. Even Ruby was getting stroppy now! And later, when she was ensconced with John Wood the Younger in Bath, Ruby read the latest Jacqueline Wilson, and occasionally looked up at what was on the computer screen and said in a kindly tone, 'That's great, Mummy.' Bianca didn't remonstrate with her; it didn't seem worth it because the project was getting done and, right now, that was what mattered.

After an hour Ruby went up to have her bath and Bianca sat on the edge of the bath, laughed at a couple of Ruby's jokes – she loved jokes, said she wanted to be a stand-up – and then offered to read her a story.

'No, it's all right, Mummy.' She waved the Tracy Beaker book. 'This doesn't really go with being read aloud. But thank you,' she added, dutifully polite.

Bianca felt very thoroughly dismissed. And there had been no sign of Milly. Well, Lucy was probably out. Or working.

'OK. Well, I'll be up in half an hour to say goodnight.'

She went back downstairs, poured a very large glass of wine, cut herself a slab of cheese, and went to her computer. Somehow, Georgian architecture wasn't quite distracting enough and almost against her will she went back to the rough visuals Tod had shown her and immediately felt better. That was the thing about work: it didn't fail you and it more or less progressed, if not predictably, controllably. Not like relationships with men or children.

She and Florence were going to Milan in two days' time to look at areas that might be suitable for shops and she was just embarking on finding them on screen when there was a ring on the bell. She frowned. Too late for Milly's friends, and it wouldn't be anyone from work . . .

It was Saul. He stood and looked at her, his face shocked and tense.

'Hi,' she said struggling to sound unsurprised and normal. 'Everything all right?'

'No,' he said. 'Nothing's all right. My wife's moving to Australia. Getting married again. And she wants to take Dickon with her. Can I – can I come in?'

Florence was packing for the trip with Bianca – which she was looking forward to enormously – when she realised she wasn't feeling very well. Her throat was sore, and the cough, which at supper had been irritating and tickly, seemed to be sinking into her lungs, causing a rough, rasping pain. She frowned. How terrible if she was about to be ill; she had only been to Milan once and that only for an uneasy twenty-four hours with Cornelius during the period of Athina's illness. Bianca's company, she now knew, was fun, curious and generous.

Well, she had forty-eight hours. She could go to the doctor in the morning and get some antibiotics and knock whatever bug she had on the head; meanwhile, it was probably sensible to go to bed instead of folding up underwear in tissue paper and checking on the contents of her sponge bag. She got ready for bed, made herself a hot toddy – Cornelius had sworn by the medical virtues of the hot toddy, and passed his enthusiasm on to her – and took herself and the *Telegraph* crossword to bed.

She fell asleep with the light on and two hours later woke, feeling worse, feverish, and disoriented; scarcely aware of what she was doing, she pulled from her bedside table drawer, where she normally kept it, safe from prying eyes, the framed snapshot of herself and Cornelius, arm in arm in front of their courtyard, smiling at the obliging stranger who had taken it, and lay looking at it, reliving that magical, most wonderful of all the days that over the years they had shared.

'I – don't know what to say. I'm so sorry.' Bianca was genuinely shocked by the raw grief Saul was displaying. It was as if Dickon had been diagnosed with some terrible illness rather than moving to somewhere which, distant as it might be, was hardly inaccessible, especially to someone of Saul's huge wealth. And then immediately chided herself for thinking in so simplistic a way: how would she feel if Patrick moved to Australia, taking the children with him, away from her, changing month by month into people she would have to struggle to know and understand, leading and learning a way of life she had no concept of?

'It's just totally wrong,' he said, not for the first time. 'She has no right to do it. To take him away from me. He's mine. He's all I have. She can't think she has any right to do this. She'll have a new husband, other children possibly – how can she expose Dickon to that? To having to share her with some half-sister or -brother, who will take all her time and attention?'

'Saul, most children have to learn that. It – well, it can be quite good for them.'

He turned on her, half angry. 'You don't understand. Dickon has always had our entire attention, all his life. That's what gives him his security, makes up, as I see it, for the other losses in his life. And these will not be his siblings, they will be children of another man, who is not me, not his father.'

'Yes, but—'

'And that's another thing. He's old enough, or about to be, to be able to think, to understand what's going on between his mother and this – this person.' His tone implied Dickon's putative stepfather was some kind of inferior being. 'Nine is a delicate age, on the cusp of puberty.'

She felt, even in her sympathy, astonished. Not so much at what he was saying, as that he was saying it at all: Saul, so conversationally dysfunctional, so emotionally stilted.

'I won't let her. I have to stop her. I've spoken to my lawyer, of course. I have to call him back shortly. In ten minutes.'

Bianca looked at her watch: at nine thirty? Yes. Of course at nine thirty – at two in the morning if he so wished. That was what powerful people could do. Did. But could the most astute, the most skilful legal strategist in the world stop Janey Finlayson – who after all had joint custody – from taking her son away to live with her, in what could well seem to the judge a more satisfactory household, a family with the possibility of more children? While the alternative was not a family, but a lone father, famously solitary – and an opposing lawyer would make much of this – working impossible hours, often out of the country? It would be at best a hideously bitter battle, at worst one that Saul would lose.

She felt a savage wave of sympathy, not for Saul but for Dickon, so gentle a child, so devoted to his father. 'My dad says . . .' prefaced many of his utterances, interspersed with, 'I can't wait to tell my dad!'

Of course his dad was the treat person, with offerings from some

513

magical kingdom: horses, private aeroplanes, fast cars, an obsession with making and keeping Dickon happy. It was a dangerous mix. And yet Dickon was not a greedy child and Saul did not over-endow him. He and Dickon enjoyed the most ordinary of pleasures, went fishing, dinghy sailing, watched the school cricket team, all of which he loved; yes, Saul took him skiing, and deep-sea fishing and to Disneyland, but so did a thousand, a million fathers, and he was strict about manners and obedience and even modesty. Bianca had never heard Dickon say, as he could and with truth, that his dad had a dozen racehorses or a Maserati or that they'd been to New York for the weekend. Clearly, that was partly his mother's influence but she knew, had seen for herself, it was Saul's too.

'What do you think?' he was saying now, looking at her with his intense green eyes. 'Do you think she has a right to do this, do you think she can?'

'Saul, I don't know. I'd love to come out with lots of comforting platitudes, but it would be terribly wrong of me. What I do know is that I feel desperately sorry and sad for you. I really do.'

'He's all I've got, you see,' he said again, 'the only thing I've ever really loved.'

That was interesting, that word: 'thing'. A lawyer would make much of it, implying that Dickon was merely another of Saul's possessions, but she knew what he meant. Which was that Dickon was the centre of his world, his universe, of an infinite concern, object of a passionate, desperate love. And she found herself saying, yes she knew that (without actually knowing it at all, for what knowledge did she have of Saul's private life, of his feelings, of his women, his friends?). Presumably he had loved Janey once, had desired her, had decided he should share his life with her. And others too: had he really never had anyone else? Was his life really bounded by Dickon and his work? Patrick thought so; and so, she knew, did Jonjo; but did they really know, did they understand him, and his ferociously complex psyche? But nor did she, she reminded herself slightly nervously; don't fall into that trap, Bianca, of thinking you're close to him, this is dangerous territory you're in.

'What did you say to Janey?'

He stared at her. 'I told her it was out of the question, of course. That she had no right to do it and that she would be stopped. And that she would be hearing from my lawyers.'

Guaranteed to gain Janey's cooperation and sympathy, then.

'What would you expect me to say? That we should discuss it, try to find some way round it?'

'I – I don't know,' said Bianca.

'I wonder if you grasp this at all,' he said, glaring at her. 'I thought you'd understand, realise that kind of attitude was totally pointless. Anyway, it's nine thirty, I have to phone my lawyer, if you'll excuse me. But perhaps I should leave now.'

'Saul, don't be ridiculous. Call him from here, it's fine. I'll go and make some coffee, I'll be in the kitchen.'

'Yes, all right,' he said, not looking at her as he dialled the number.

She put the coffee on, had another small glass of wine – she longed for more, but if ever there was an occasion requiring a clear head it was this one, and for want of anything better to do, returned to Georgian Bath. Her own phone rang; it was Patrick.

'Darling, hello. Everything all right?'

'Yes, fine thanks.'

'Anything happening?'

'No, no, just doing my Georgian architecture project.'

There was no way she was going to tell him Saul was there. Either he would want to speak to him, or he would fret in that ridiculous way that she wasn't doing enough for him. She shied away from the third reason. Which was that she just didn't want Patrick to know, for reasons that were hardly formulated, even in her subconscious. She just felt it was . . . wiser that he didn't.

'Good girl. Glad to hear it. Well, I'm awake early, as you can tell—'

'No, not really. What is the time there?'

'Five thirty. It's a very nice morning and I'm just going up to the pool – it's on the roof, rather nice, then I've a meeting at eight.'

'Marvellous,' she said briskly; and then thought she was being a lot less than generous, and said, 'How's it going?'

'Oh, pretty well, I think. Definitely home tomorrow. In fact, I've booked my flight.'

'Again,' she said.

'Yes, again.' He was clearly irritated by this. As he should not have been, she thought. 'Anyway, I just wanted to make sure you were OK.'

'I'm fine, thank you. We're all fine.'

'Good. Children? Milly?'

'Patrick, I said we were all fine.'

'Good. Well, see you tomorrow. No, what am I saying, the day after tomorrow, keep forgetting the extra seven hours.'

'Great. Look forward to it. Bye, Patrick.'

'Bye, darling.'

Putting down her phone, Bianca thought remorsefully that she really was a bitch; twice in one day she'd been vile. First Lucy, then Patrick. Patrick, who'd always been so loyal, so long-suffering about her absences; she really owed him a little tolerance. She sighed.

'Bianca!' Saul, calling her from the hall.

'I'm in here, got the coffee. Go back into the snug and I'll bring it.'

When she went in he was sitting on the sofa, his head flung back, his eyes closed.

She sat down beside him, set the tray down.

'OK. So what did your lawyer say?'

'He said,' and his voice seemed to be dredging some depth of misery she had no concept of, 'he said we *could* try to stop her. Not that we *would*. That it might not be easy. I mean, how could it not be easy? She has no right!'

'Saul . . .'

And then he turned to her and there were tears in his eyes, and his voice was breaking and he said, 'Bianca, I cannot bear this, I really cannot bear it.'

And then he started to sob, loudly and hoarsely: and then he reached for her, and took her in his arms, and held her against him so hard, so desperately that she could scarcely breathe, and she pulled his head down on to her shoulder, finding herself profoundly

516

moved by his awful, dreadful grief, murmuring platitudes, soothing nonsense about how it would be all right, and she was sure he would find a way, stroking his hair, kissing his forehead. And then suddenly he was kissing her on the mouth, hard, almost angrily, and she tried to resist and found herself quite unable to, and all the strange, struggling, intense emotion that had existed between them ever since that first odd evening in the restaurant was released, a huge violent bolt of it, and she kissed him back, her desire for him so powerful she was shocked at it herself.

It went on for a long time, that kiss; finally, he pulled away from her and sat back, his green eyes boring into hers, and after an oddly long silence, he said, 'I shouldn't have done that. I really shouldn't.'

As always, his behaviour was totally unexpected. No heady spiel about him being carried away, or how lovely she was. She sat, still physically shocked, half amused, half intrigued to hear what he might say next.

'I do find you so attractive, you see. And I do enjoy being with you.'

'Well – that's nice to hear.' It was a fatuous response she knew; but anything not fatuous would have been dangerous.

'It's why I didn't want to have a drink with you this evening.'

'What do you mean?'

'Well. Patrick being away. I thought it would be a bit – unwise. Especially after the other evening.'

She stared at him.

'What other evening?'

'Outside that bar. When I – well, when I put my arms round you. I wanted you so much, it was terrifying me. That's why I pushed you into the taxi. I didn't dare stay with you a moment longer.'

He was truly extraordinary. He talked, behaved indeed, like a virginal adolescent. What was it Patrick had said about him? Something about people like him, doing the job he did, being a bit unhinged and not caring about people, only the money. She supposed it must create a lack of balance.

'Oh Saul,' she said, wary of hurting him, still feeling her way, 'but it was such a nice surprise.'

'What was?'

'Well – what you did. Put your arms round me. As you put it.'

Could that, perhaps, she thought, make him do it again? Just sitting looking at him made her want to tear her clothes off; she had always found him sexually disturbing, she realised, just denied it, crushed the awareness through sheer force of will. Now she felt weak, almost sick with it; the will defeated, she was floundering, helpless, longing for more.

But he didn't do it again; he frowned at her, drew further away.

'So how would you have put it?' he said. He sounded slightly belligerent.

'Saul, it doesn't matter.'

'No, no, I want to know.'

'I – I thought of it as a hug.'

'That doesn't sound very sexy.'

'Sorry.'

'No, no, don't apologise. I'm just trying to work all this out.'

Now what did that mean? 'Anyway,' she said, 'I was – well, I was a bit surprised. And especially by the taxi bit. But I suppose I'm getting used to you.'

'What do you mean, getting used to me?'

'Your not being too much like other people.'

'No,' he said, and sighed heavily, 'no, I know I'm not. I wish I was. In some ways.'

'Well I don't,' she said, smiling at him. 'I like you how you are. There are plenty of people to be like each other.' This was becoming very convoluted.

'So you do like me?' he said, his tone at once anxious and defensive.

'Yes, I do, Saul,' she said, abandoning caution. 'I like you very much.'

'And do you – well, find me attractive? Sexy, I suppose I mean?'

'Of course I do! Can't you tell?'

'Oh God,' he said, and he looked quite distraught.

'What does God have to do with it?'

'It's just that it's more – more complicated in that case.'

'Saul, there's nothing to be complicated. At the moment,' she added.

'Of course there is,' he said, 'if I find you sexy and you find me sexy, that has to be complicated. Given our situations.'

'Well, in that case,' she said, smiling again, 'if you're worried about that, why come round here, to my house, knowing my husband is on the other side of the world. Especially as you turned down having a drink with me earlier.'

'That was different,' he said, his voice almost indignant, smiling back at her, a quick, awkward smile.

'Oh really? In what way?'

'I needed you,' he said, as if explaining that night followed day. 'You were the only person who would do.'

To say he was unlike anyone she had ever met was an under-statement of enormous proportions.

And now what was going to happen?

Chapter 46

She could never remember feeling such a mishmash of emotions. Angry. Stupid. Outraged. And, of course, relieved.

So relieved. It was like all the clichés rolled into one, a huge burden lifted, coming out of a long dark tunnel, able to breathe again – wonderful. But – he was evil. There was no other word to describe him. It had been an inspired plan of his, that was for sure, but what sort of warped, sadistic mind would conceive it.

'Hi!' It was Jemima, smiling at her in the doorway. Susie got up from behind her desk and hugged her.

'Oh, Jemima, I love you!'

'Hey, steady on. What's happened?'

'I called the studio just now, from a payphone, seemed a bit more subtle than ringing the flat, asked for him, and some girl said he wasn't in today, he was doing a shoot of his own, could she give him a message. So I said yes, could she say his girlfriend had called and could he ring me back, and she said, sounding a tiny bit cautious, "Zoe?" and I said yes, and she said, "Oh hi, didn't recognise your voice, thought you were working together today. Yeah sure." Easy as that.'

'Oh my God!' said Jemima. 'The bastard. The total bastard.'

'I know. Incredible, isn't it? I don't know whether to laugh or cry. My immediate reaction was to call him on his mobile, but then I thought no, revenge is a dish best eaten cold and all that, so I'll just wait for his next call. And say – well, I haven't quite worked out what I'll say. But I'm looking forward to it already.

Jemima, I don't know how to thank you. I really really don't.'

'You don't have to. Honestly. It's so lovely to see you looking so – so normal. And it was fun last night, I enjoyed it.'

'Good. Oh – morning, Bianca.'

'Good morning, Susie. Jemima, I need you in my office right now, please. Complications with the trip to Milan.'

She looked at her most harassed, Susie thought. Which was hardly harassed at all, because she was so good at appearing cool, but they were all learning to read the signs.

'Of course. Sorry, Bianca.'

'It's Florence,' Bianca said, 'she's ill. She sounded terrible – confused, upset, nearly in tears, says she can hardly breathe, she's called the doctor and was of course told to go to the surgery, and she's clearly not remotely up to that, so I'm going to go round there, see what I can do.'

'Well, that's marvellous of you,' said Jemima. 'But Bianca, does it have to be you? I could go – you must have a thousand things to do, you're off to Milan first thing tomorrow—'

'No, I feel I should go myself,' said Bianca firmly. 'I've actually got a clear two hours and I'm very fond of Florence. Meanwhile cancel her flight – I'll have to go to Milan on my own. Well it's not the end of the world, it was a bit of a self-indulgence, taking her . . . Pity, though.'

She smiled at Jemima; there was something . . . odd about her this morning, Jemima thought. No, maybe not exactly odd, but . . . different.

'OK. Shall I call you a cab?'

'Yes please. I've told her I'm coming – she protested of course, but then said the neighbour had a key. I mean, if she can't even get to her own front door – poor Florence. Right, I'm on my way, I'll be back for my meeting with Hattie at eleven thirty of course.'

'Good morning, Francine. This is Lady Farrell. I would like to speak to Miss Hamilton please.'

'I'm afraid she's not here, Lady Farrell.'

'Not there! Well, where is she?'

'I'm afraid she's ill. That's why I'm here; she called and asked me to come in.'

'Ill? In what way ill?'

'I'm not sure, Lady Farrell. But she sounded dreadful. She had the most terrible cough, and quite a high temperature, she said.'

'Well, she must call the doctor.'

'I believe she has, Lady Farrell, and was told she must go to the surgery.'

'How absurd! She shouldn't accept that sort of treatment. Anyway, I need to discuss something urgently with her, I'd better go round and see her I suppose.'

'Yes, Lady Farrell.'

'Florence . . .'

Bianca knocked gently on the bedroom door and went in; Florence was lying on a pile of pillows, coughing incessantly, her colour high, her eyes brilliant. She looked at Bianca as if she scarcely knew who she was.

'You poor poor thing. How are you feeling? Oh, don't even think about answering that stupid question. Look, I'll call your doctor, do you have his number?'

'Yes, yes, it's here . . .' Florence held out a battered leather address book. 'Dr Roberts. But he won't come.'

'I'm sure he will.' Bianca smiled at her. 'I'll explain how bad you are. Now, what can I get you? Cup of tea, warm milk?'

'Some hot lemon and honey would be so nice,' said Florence. 'You'll find the wherewithal to make it in the kitchen. Bianca, you shouldn't be here, you've got far more important things to do, I'm so sorry . . .'

She struggled to go on and couldn't.

'So kind,' she finally managed.

'You deserve it. Now, let me just tidy up a bit here . . .' she scooped up several tissues, a glass of water, another glass that smelled, rather surprisingly, of whisky, and went to find the kitchen.

It was the prettiest little house, one of a short terrace of Victorian cottages still possessed of all its cornices and stair rails, and even a fireplace in the small sitting room. It was carefully furnished, in period for the most part, with draped curtains, button-backed chairs, a chaise longue, a round dining table with four chairs in the window, and a shabby but clearly once-valuable Indian rug on the floor. There was a very pretty watercolour over the fireplace of a small Parisian courtyard, viewed through a half open door, and a photograph in a silver frame on a low round table, of a young couple, she in a white dress, holding a bouquet of flowers, he in uniform, Florence and her bridegroom, clearly, on their wartime wedding day.

Bianca peered at it, fascinated; they were both smiling at the camera with a joy that shone down the sixty-odd years, Florence so lovely, a flower-trimmed straw hat on her wonderful curls, he both handsome and rather dashing, a flower tucked rakishly into the officer's cap that was tucked under his arm. Clearly a sense of humour, then: he looked fun, Bianca thought. How sad it was; such happiness and such love doomed to extinction, like so many such wartime marriages. And all part of Florence's sad, lonely story, Bianca thought, and left the room swiftly, feeling suddenly as if she was prying; she was supposed to be looking after Florence, not poking into her past. The kitchen was traditional, distressed pine cupboards, Italian tiled floor, all clearly high quality and expensive – how did Florence afford these things? Bianca wondered for the hundredth time. The tiny garden was full of shrubs, admittedly rather February-bare, but still pretty, with a stone seat at the rear, and a female figure, also in stone, clearly Victorian, in the furthermost corner, gripping a harp with one hand, and some rather cleverly trained ivy with the other. That wouldn't have come cheap either . . .

Bianca called Florence's doctor, told a sullen-sounding receptionist that if a doctor didn't call to see Miss Hamilton soon, she wouldn't like to answer for the consequences, and made the hot lemon and honey drink.

Florence was lying with her eyes closed; she managed a smile and indicated the bedside table.

'If you could just put it there – so kind, Bianca, so very kind . . .'

'I hope it helps. The doctor will be here soon. Just let me make room for the cup. I'll move your book and this—'

'This photograph' she was about to say, and then didn't. For the photograph, little more than an enlarged snapshot really – no, actually a snapshot, she thought, only half-looking at it, nicely framed, but clearly very old, faded black and white, showing a rather glamorous young couple. And here she focused on it with shocked and total attention, felt her heart thud, her mind blur. The man's arm was around her shoulders as they smiled in front of a courtyard, clearly a Parisian courtyard, and it was – yes, it was surely the one in the painting she had just seen downstairs. And the woman, so beautiful, with wild curling hair, and huge eyes, so young, no more than thirty, wearing a tightly waisted, swirly skirted dress, the height of late fifties fashion, was unmistakably Florence, and the man, dashingly handsome, was also instantly recognisable, for a portrait of him hung in the boardroom at Farrell House. The man was Cornelius Farrell.

And suddenly everything became very clear.

'Yes, that's right, pull over here, please.'

Athina looked up at Florence's little house wondering, as she always did, how anyone could endure to live in something so cramped. She had often suggested Florence sold it and moved into a modern flat with a few more conveniences – 'So much more suitable at your age,' she would say, as if Florence was a decade at least older than she was, instead of five years younger, and Florence always said that she loved her home and she had no intention of leaving it for a soulless modern flat.

The fare was nine pounds ninety; Athina gave the cabbie a ten-pound note, told him graciously he could keep the change, marched up to Florence's front door, and rapped sharply on the brass knocker several times.

And was more than a little disconcerted to find it opened by Bianca Bailey; who seemed slightly less cool and even more disconcerted herself.

'Oh,' she said, 'oh, Lady Farrell. How – how nice to see you. Do please come in.'

Bianca could think of only one thing at first, as she confronted Lady Farrell: of the photograph she had placed back on the bedside table, where Florence clearly liked to keep it. After which she thought several more things, that Lady Farrell must be prevented from seeing it at all costs, that it would be fairly difficult to prevent her as she was already halfway up the stairs after giving Bianca a gracious nod; and that Florence was far too feverishly confused to think to remove the photograph and place it out of Lady Farrell's sight.

'Lady Farrell,' she called, rather hopelessly, at the imperious back now almost at the top of the stairs, 'do let me make you a coffee or something. Florence is asleep, and the doctor is about to arrive.'

Lady Farrell paused and half turned.

'No thank you; she'll be pleased to see me, and I would like to speak with the doctor myself anyway.'

'Right . . .'

What should she do? What *could* she do?

Bianca looked wildly round the hall and half ran into the kitchen; a water jug stood on the draining board. She grabbed it, empty as it was, and ran up the stairs after Athina to see her disappearing into Florence's bedroom.

She followed her in, glancing at the bedside table as she went; the photograph was still there. An oblivious Florence lay coughing, her eyes closed; she seemed unaware of Athina's presence.

Athina was standing at the foot of the bed, staring down at her, pulling off her gloves, unwinding her scarf. 'Florence!' she said, and then, as that brought no response, 'Florence, you look dreadful. How are you feeling?'

There was no reply, although Florence's eyes flickered open.

'I really do think,' Bianca said, 'she should be left to rest until the doctor arrives. Do come down and—'

'Mrs Bailey, I don't want to come down. I shall wait here for the doctor to arrive.' She looked at Bianca. 'What on earth are you doing, carrying that empty jug?'

'Oh, is it? Goodness. Florence had just asked for water when you arrived and I suppose I must have picked up the jug and forgotten to fill it. Very stupid. Look – she clearly isn't awake; wouldn't you be more comfortable waiting downstairs?'

'Mrs Bailey, I am not infirm. I don't need to be comfortable, as you call it. I shall wait up here, as I said.'

She took her coat off and slung it over the brass bedrail, then went over to Florence and peered down at her. Any moment, thought Bianca, any moment now she's going to look at the bedside table . . . please, Florence, move, scream, throw up, do something! But Florence lay lifeless apart from the dreadful coughing spasms.

There was the sound of a car in the street below; Athina straightened, turned and said, 'Is that the doctor?'

'I have no idea,' said Bianca.

The doorbell rang. Athina walked over to the window and peered out.

'Yes, it is. He's coming over to the house. Doctors are so scruffy these days; look at him, dreadful sort of anorak he's wearing instead of a decent coat. Well, hadn't you better go and let him in?'

'Yes, yes, of course. I'll just . . .' and as she went past Florence's bed, she deposited the empty jug on the bedside table, picked up the book that was lying there and the photograph with it.

'Oh – hello.' Lara smiled uncertainly at Bertie; he could hardly ignore her, standing in the same lift.

'Hello.' He smiled back, clearly equally embarrassed. 'How – how are you?'

'I'm fine, thank you. Yes. Er – Bertie, I'm sorry to hear you're leaving.'

'That's kind of you. Yes, well I'm sorry in some ways, but it's for the best.'

'Well, if that's the case – and the job sounds interesting. Bianca told me a bit about it,' she added hastily.

'I hope it will be. More my line of country, anyway. Literally. Did you know I was moving out of London?'

'Yes, I had heard that.'

'To the Midlands. Very underrated, the Midlands, in my view. I can get an extremely nice house with a big garden for less than half I'd be paying here.'

They had reached the ground floor; he stood aside to let her out.

'Thank you. I'm on my way to the West End. Maybe we could share a cab, where are you going?'

'Oh, not in that direction at all,' he said, looking embarrassed, and adding rather belatedly, 'Thank you.'

'Oh, OK. Well, nice to talk to you, Bertie. You're around for a little while, I hope. You won't disappear up the M1 in a puff of smoke while we're not looking?' She smiled, an over-bright smile.

'No, no. I'll come and say goodbye, of course. When – when the time comes. Well, good to talk to you, Lara. Bye now.'

'Bye Bertie.'

She stood looking after him as he strode out into the street and walked briskly away. She felt silly and absurdly near to tears. She had had some brush-offs in her time, but that had been quite severe. Well, she wouldn't try again. Being an embarrassment was not her style.

Bertie hoped he hadn't seemed rude but he was rather afraid he had. He would have loved to talk to Lara about the new job, but she had so clearly been avoiding him for weeks, it hadn't seemed appropriate. As for where he was going – how could he have shared a cab with her and asked to be let out at Lincoln's Inn which was so clearly legal territory. She was bound to have heard the rumours about his divorce, but there was no way he was going to confirm them so unmistakably.

He was dreading the afternoon: meeting the solicitor with Priscilla, going through the legal and financial essentials, and it would have been wonderful to talk to someone who had been through it themselves and could encourage him, even prepare him a little for what might happen. Perhaps in the old days their relationship would have withstood such complex and uncomfortable matters; but as things were, it would be asking far too much. More and more he felt sure she was in a new relationship; she was looking wonderful, whole lot of new clothes, she seldom worked late, always rushing off somewhere or other – no, it would be out of the question to ask for her advice and even guidance.

He was having a dreadful time; his mother had taken to giving him regular lectures on the folly of what he was doing, both personally and professionally, reminding him constantly that he had never worked outside the House of Farrell, that he had never been successful within it. 'Oh, I know you've made a fist of this new job, but really, Bertie, hardly a difficult field. Personnel!' And she continually told him, with considerable force, that divorce was a rough and expensive business and that he had no idea what he was embarking upon.

'Your father and I had our differences, everyone does, but no marriage is perfect and there is a great deal to be gained from staying within it and seeing it through. It's a miserable business being on your own – I should know. And I hope you're not harbouring any ideas about finding someone else or starting again, because you're far too old, and not exactly a catch, especially without the House of Farrell behind you . . .'

On and on it went, day after day; he was beginning to work with his door shut and leave promptly on the dot of six, but she managed to corner him just the same. And he was forced to continue to live in the Esher house, as did Priscilla, who alternated between outright hostility or, less frequently, a rather uncomfortable display of conciliatory behaviour. He wasn't sure which was worse.

The nice girl at Cathay Pacific Airlines had managed to change Patrick's flight to one twelve hours earlier and so he reached Heathrow in the early evening rather than the following morning. He called Bianca, but her phone was on message; he rang the house and was told that Bianca and Patrick Bailey were unable to take the incoming call, but if he would leave his name and number they would call him back as soon as possible.

He left no message on either phone, preferring to go home – it would be at least nine, possibly half past before he retrieved his luggage, left the airport and reached Hampstead. The traffic was dreadful, the cabbie told him, and there was nothing more irritating than having to call repeatedly and say he was going to be later and later still. Or indeed receiving such calls.

It was actually almost ten when he reached the house; it looked extremely dark and still. Damn. He had been sure, foolishly perhaps, that Bianca would be at home; she certainly hadn't mentioned any possibility that she might go out, rather that she would be very much at home, working either on the franchise aspect of the launch, something that Patrick was most intrigued by, or the Georgian architecture project which was now overdue.

He called out from the hall, disappointed in spite of himself; Karen appeared from the snug.

'Oh, hello, Mr Bailey, I wasn't expecting you.'

Patrick said, trying not to sound sarcastic, that he was sorry and where was everybody? The children were all asleep, she said, even Milly who had come home very tired after spending the evening with Lucy Farrell at Lady Farrell's flat. 'Bianca knew about this of course, was very happy about it.'

'I'm sure. And Bianca?'

'Well, Bianca's also out. Having a meeting and then dinner with the advertising people. She said she might be quite late, so she asked me to stay. But now you're home . . .'

'Yes, yes of course. You go, Karen, that's fine.'

He made himself a sandwich, feeling foolish as well as rather sad, and after watching TV for a while decided to go to bed. Jet lag was beginning to hit. He looked at his watch – twelve thirty, for God's sake. Bianca didn't do late nights in the week, and she was going to Milan in the morning.

He rang her mobile; still on message. And he had no idea of the advertising boys' numbers. He couldn't even remember their names. There was nothing he could do about any of it.

Patrick left a note in the hall that he was home, took a sleeping pill and went to bed; in spite of the pill he woke up at half past two, and was amazed to find Bianca still not home, or not in the bed; maybe she had gone into the spare room, so as not to disturb him.

He padded cautiously along the corridor, peered into an empty guest room, before going, angry and worried in equal measures, down to the snug to wait for her, then going back to bed, still sleepless, and calling her number repeatedly. She did not reply.

He finally went back to sleep, but his awareness of his own unhappiness and the deterioration in their marriage had deepened sharply and another fear, also subliminal, that he could never have even imagined a few months before, struggled nearer to the surface.

She was enjoying it so much. If only she'd had something like this to do, when she'd been so desperate. It wasn't just that it was fascinating watching Lucy work, transforming her from this personality to that, sweet to cool, classic to wild, it was entering this new grown-up world, and such a wonderful one too. The evening they had gone to Lucy's grandmother's flat really had been like going back in time: it was clearly exactly as it had been when she first lived there, full of wonderful furniture and ornaments, which Lucy explained to her was deco – all mirrors and bronze figures and fringed lamps. 'It's the period she loves best, she says house style has never been so glamorous.' And then Lady Farrell herself was incredible, very, very stylish, with the most amazing white hair and wearing sort of loose silky pyjamas which Lucy explained were called palazzo pyjamas, and by a very famous designer called Pucci. She'd stood watching Lucy as she worked – apparently she was still so involved with the company that she had to approve every single little thing, which of course included the looks Lucy was creating. Milly hadn't realised that; she'd thought her mother was in charge of everything.

Lady Farrell had produced some smoked salmon sandwiches halfway through the session and offered Lucy some of the champagne she was drinking, but Lucy said she really couldn't because then she'd make a mess of the make-up. She didn't exactly talk to Milly; in fact she treated her a bit like a specimen in a laboratory, studying her intently and in silence for long periods of time and addressing all her comments on the looks to Lucy, not even asking Milly what she thought of them. As Milly would have been petrified to pass any comments at all, this was actually a rather good thing. They were there for about three hours, and when they left Lady Farrell said they could come and work at the flat any time they liked. Milly hoped they'd be able to go there again, but Lucy said it was actually easier working in the make-up room at Farrell House, which was kept stocked with every product in every shade they produced and a lot of the competitors' products; it had a mirror with lights all round it, like actresses had in their dressing rooms, and Milly felt like a film star when she sat there.

One day next week, Jayce was coming in to have some of the looks done on her, and some new ones created as well; she was so excited, she told Milly, she couldn't sleep or eat. As this was over a Big Mac and a large strawberry shake, Milly didn't take too much notice. But she thought it was a good thing Jayce hadn't got to face Lady Farrell.

And then there was something else really amazing: Lucy had a friend who did a beauty blog and she might be going to write about the new looks when the launch happened and Lucy said she might do some pictures of how to do it and that was just impossibly exciting.

It was even helping with the thought of going back to school, which she had decided she must do the following week; it was a bit like falling off a horse, the longer you left it, the more frightened you felt about getting back on.

Carey and Co had been weirdly silent the first few days she was away, no horrible messages on Ask.fm or sneaky texts – she supposed they must have thought they were about to be in huge trouble – but as the days went by and nothing happened, it started again, slowly at first, with texts saying, in the awful code they used that could never get them caught, things like *We do miss you, darling Milly, can't wait for you to be back* and then some quite nasty things on

Ask.fm, like was she really actually ill or just pretending and was the medicine working and if not maybe she should try taking the whole bottle at once.

Anyway, that had been two days ago and here she was, in her father's car – her mother was away – being driven to school because somehow sitting on the bus just seemed too scary, and he was very sweet and kept asking her if she was sure about this, and she had only to say and he'd come in with her. And when they got to school, and she saw everyone walking in, she really thought she might throw up, and she grabbed her father's hand and said actually, yes, could he just walk in with her. He said of course he would and pulled over, but it was a double yellow and as he started to get out a very large lady traffic warden waddled over to them and said did he realise he was illegally parked and she would have to give him a ticket if he stayed there for more than three minutes or something and he said that was fine by him, and she got out her warden's camera and her book of tickets, and suddenly it didn't seem worth it and Milly took a deep breath and said, 'It's all right Daddy, I'll be fine.' And feeling exactly as she had when she had first dived from the middle board at the swimming pool, not the lower one, she got out by herself and walked very quickly into school.

Going into the classroom was the worst thing; a complete silence fell, everyone turned to look at her, and then Carey said, 'Mills! How lovely. We do all hope you're feeling better!' And everyone started giggling and Milly sat down at her desk and started unloading her schoolbag, and thought if their plan, hers and Lucy's, didn't work, she really would have to give in and find another school somewhere, maybe in the wilds of Scotland. Or outer Mongolia . . .

Her parents, unbeknown to her, had gone to the school, and confronted the headmistress with what had happened; initially she expressed disbelief, and then some slightly reluctant remorse.

'Of course it must have been dreadful for her, and we should have spotted what was going on . . .'

'As should we,' Patrick had said. 'None of us can afford to be complacent.'

'Indeed not,' said Mrs Blackman, mistakenly imagining she was being let off the hook. 'And this sort of thing has gone on since time immemorial, as we all know, merely the methods have changed.'

'Nevertheless,' said Bianca, 'one would not condone the torture inflicted on innocent people.'

'Well, of course not. But I hardly think this amounted to torture.'

'Oh, but it did,' said Patrick. 'The blind eye is a dangerous object, Mrs Blackman. Vigilance is essential, wherever there is so much as a suspicion of wrongdoing. I find it a little hard, for instance, to believe that Milly's form mistress could not have noticed she was the only child in her form to have no Christmas cards delivered by the school post.'

'Oh now, Mr Bailey, I think that is asking rather a lot of our staff. They are very busy, especially at Christmas, and—'

'Mrs Blackman, you cannot tell me in one breath that we all know that bullying has always existed and, in the next, that you are too busy to look out for it.

'Milly has decided to return to school, showing remarkable courage and determination, and she is absolutely determined that nothing should be said to the girls. We actually promised her we wouldn't come, but we felt you and your staff should learn something from this whole wretched business. I would personally like to confront the girls and their parents, but Milly insists that would merely expose her to further misery when all the fuss had died down and the girls punished. And I fear, having heard what she was going through, that she is right.'

'I can't believe that!' said Mrs Blackman.

'Unfortunately for Milly, we can,' said Bianca.

Bianca walked into the house, exhausted after her trip to Milan. Fergie was sitting at the breakfast bar when she walked in, his face dark and moody. God, he was going to be an adolescent soon; could she stand two of them?

'Fergie, what's the matter?'

'I'm being picked on, that's what's the matter.'

Not another one, not another of her children being bullied. She struggled to sound cheerful and matter of fact.

'Who's picking on you, Fergie?'

'Mr Thomas,' he said.

It was almost a relief that it wasn't other boys.

'Really. Why?'

'He says he's taking me out of the scholarship class if I don't put more work in. He says I haven't been working – and I *have*. He's sent you an email, he says, but he probably hasn't. He lies about *everything*!'

'Well, let's see, shall we . . .' She pulled her iPad out of her briefcase. And there it was, an email from Mr Thomas, Fergie's form master, headed 'Fergie's progress'.

She skimmed through it.

'Dear Mr and Mrs Bailey, Regret to inform you . . . very little effort going in . . . have to withdraw him from the scholarship class unless sustained improvement . . . would welcome a meeting with you both . . .'

Guilt hit her; she knew she hadn't taken enough interest in Fergie and his scholastic progress recently. What with trying to sort out Milly and working on Ruby's Georgian architecture project there had been very little of her 'quality time', as it was so enragingly known, left. She had assumed that Fergie had less need of her at the moment; he was always so cheerful and successful and it wasn't this academic year that he would sit his Common Entrance for God's sake, and yes, she should have done more, but then Patrick hadn't been much cop either, thanks to Saul . . . bloody Saul . . . who she hadn't heard from since— No, don't start thinking about Saul, Bianca, don't . . .

Her mobile rang; it was Patrick.

'Hi. I just got Mr Thomas's email. Very disappointing. I think we should discuss it. When will you be home?'

'I'm home already,' said Bianca. It was the only moment of the day she had enjoyed.

'Ah. Right. Well – see you in an hour or so.'

'OK.'

She put down her phone and gave Fergie a hug; for once he didn't resist.

'Don't worry, Fergie, we'll sort it out.'

He managed a grin.

'Thanks, Mum, and I will work harder. Promise! Um – all right if I go into the snug?'

'What? And start playing one of your wretched games? No, it is not all right. I just suddenly feel on Mr Thomas's side. You go up to your room and get on with your homework and we'll see you later.'

'Dad home tonight?'

'Yes, he'll be home in an hour.'

Ruby arrived back from a playdate; 'With my new best friend. She's called Hannah. She's coming here tomorrow. Karen said that would be all right, didn't you, Karen?'

Usually, Ruby would have asked her if she could have a new friend round, Bianca thought. Another sign of the times . . .

Patrick arrived ten minutes later.

'So – how was the trip?' he asked.

'Fine. Successful, I think. But I'm very tired,' she said, desperate not to have the conversation about Fergie now.

'Of course.' His tone was only a little loaded.

'And – yours? Your trip?'

'Oh, it was very good. I'd really like to talk to you about it. Got a bit of a problem. Maybe over supper?'

'I'd – I'd like that, of course. But I've got a load of papers to go through – got a very early meeting with the VCs and the lawyers. It's really important.'

'Of course.'

'Maybe tomorrow? Or the weekend?'

'Maybe.'

He said nothing for a while, poured himself a beer, then sat down looking at her.

'Bianca . . .'

'Yes?'

'We need to have a conversation.'

'Really? About your trip? I said I'd like to, but not now, not tonight.'

'No, not about my trip. Or yours. About Fergie.'

As she could have predicted, the conversation about Fergie and his problems was familiar and dispiriting, the blame knocked backwards and forwards between them: not enough attention was being given to the children and their work . . . Fergie and Milly were at crucial stages . . . Bianca hadn't put in the extra time she had promised . . . and had Patrick put in any time at all? . . . well he was owed a little latitude on that one surely . . . he'd done it all for years and years . . . on and on it went. Finally she told him that she had talked seriously with Fergie, that he'd promised to work harder, and they composed an email to Mr Thomas agreeing they should have a meeting and asking him to suggest some dates – *mornings, the earlier the better, are best for both of us* – and said they had had a very serious talk with Fergie, who fully understood the importance of what had happened.

'Right,' said Patrick, 'now I want—'

'Mum, Dad!' The door had opened; it was Fergie.

'Jesus,' said Patrick under his breath.

'Yes, Fergie?' said Bianca with exaggerated patience.

'You going to be long in here? I've finished *all* my homework and I've got this really cool new game that Dan lent me, I want to try—'

'Fergie! I cannot believe you have the nerve to even *think* of asking that,' said Patrick. 'The answer's no. Now get out of here and up to your room and—'

'Yeah, OK, OK, Dad. Hang cool.' He was totally unfazed by his father's wrath. 'See you later.'

'That is *your* fault,' said Patrick, when the door closed.

'What is my fault?'

'Obviously you were far too lenient with him. Otherwise he would never have dared come in here, asking if he could play on the Wii. He's got to understand what's happened is very serious. Otherwise we're on an extremely slippery slope.'

'Oh, Patrick, do stop it,' said Bianca, wearily. 'I'm sorry if that's the case. I'll go and buy a cane tomorrow . . .'

'I don't think this is cause for flippancy.'

Bianca looked at him; the cold, raw distance between them was growing by the day. It was terrifying what had happened to him, to the good-natured, gentle, funny man she had lived with until a year ago. Who had been the sweetest, most successful of fathers, the most understanding and generous of husbands. Who she had loved so much and been married to so happily. Where had he gone? Where had the marriage gone? And what had driven him away? Was it really her? Her and her job? But she had *always* had a job. A big job. This had never happened before. The odd tiff, perhaps, the occasional complaint. But then, none of the jobs had consumed her as Farrell's did, had taken over her entire life, her heart, her very self.

'Let's just get on, shall we?' she said, attempting to smile, to be pleasant. 'What is this very important thing you want to talk about?'

'I'd be grateful if you didn't trivialise it.'

'I am *not* trivialising it. If it's important to you, then it's important to me.'

'I did think that once,' he said, 'now I'm not so sure. You've changed so much, Bianca, I hardly recognise you. Our relationship has ceased to exist, as far as I can see, and I can't take much more of it. We never talk, even on the phone, you're never at home—'

'Oh, is that so? Patrick, I seem to recall you've been away, and worked late far more often than I over the last few months. At least I come home from trips when I say, not three days later, and I'm with the family every weekend.'

'That's unfair. I don't go away at the weekend.'

'You spend at least half of them locked into conversations with Saul Finlayson. I can't remember when we had a meal at which he wasn't present. Notionally, at any rate. You've become as rude and as work-obsessed as he is.'

'I think you're exaggerating. OK, it might have happened rather a lot recently, but perhaps you've chosen to forget that I spent at least seventeen bloody years of the eighteen of our marriage at your beck and call – or rather, your family's beck and call – allowing you to devote yourself entirely to your fucking, self-aggrandising career.'

'That is *so* bloody unfair! I do not devote myself to it – you know that. I've always put the children first!'

'Oh really? I must have been out of the room when that happened. Is that why Milly is so happy and well-balanced and Fergie is working so hard, and—'

'Shut up! Just shut the fuck up.'

'I won't. And if you put them first, how about cancelling your morning meeting and being here for Milly, taking her to school, it really helps her at the moment.'

She should, she really really should. She knew. But the morning meeting was with the VCs and the lawyers, signing the new contracts relating to the franchises; they were already late, in danger of their losing some of the leases and . . .

'I can't,' she said, 'I really can't. I've got to sign these papers, see the VCs—'

'I don't care who you've got to fucking see. Your place is here, at home, caring for your daughter.'

Guilt tore at her; he was right, it was. But then . . .

'It's you that's changed,' she said. 'Ever since you've been working for Saul.'

It was rash of her to bring him into it, she knew. But suddenly the truth seemed more important than anything.

'Ever since I've been enjoying my work, actually,' he said, 'and how you resent that. It seems to me it suited you far better for me to be bored and miserable.'

'That's a filthy thing to say!'

'It's true. Your life was so much easier when I was running about at your beck and call, and the children's.'

'And I suppose you're not running about at Saul's?'

'Oh, stop it,' he said wearily. 'This is not what I wanted to talk about.'

'Which is what? Exactly.'

'OK . . .' He took a deep breath – and her mobile rang.

'Oh Christ!' he said.

'I'm sorry, I'll just ignore it. It'll go to message.'

'Just switch the fucking thing off,' said Patrick quite quietly. Adding, 'Please.'

The please made his request more sane.

'I will.' But as she reached for it, she saw it was from Tod. 'I'm sorry, Patrick, I just have to take this. Very quickly. Hello, Tod. Oh, no. Oh, God! Can they fix it? God, they have to, they absolutely do. Look, I'm sorry, I can't talk now. No! I can't. Tomorrow. I've got a very early meeting, can we talk after that? About nine? Yes, fine.'

'I'm so sorry,' she said, putting her phone down. 'It was Tod, about the site, the test one's crashed, and—'

'I don't really want to know,' said Patrick, 'and will you now please switch that fucking thing off.'

She did.

'Thank you, Bianca.' He stopped, then visibly took a deep breath and said, 'I've had enough.'

'I'm sorry. I could say the same.'

He ignored this.

'On and on it goes, the VCs, the budgets, the franchises, the fucking advertising campaign and how brilliant it is. When did you have time for me, my job? When did you listen to *my* problems, *my* concerns, never mind the children's? Bianca, please listen very carefully to what I have to say.'

She sat silent, frightened suddenly. He looked as she had never quite seen him, utterly determined, utterly still, his eyes fixed on her almost sadly.

'I'm listening,' she said.

'Good. Because I want this to be very clear. Either you leave that company or I leave you. And, to be quite honest, I really don't care which. But I've had enough.' He stood up. 'I'm going upstairs to my study. Let me know what you decide because I'd like to start making some plans.'

He walked towards the door and when he got there he turned. 'Oh, and I want your decision very soon. Within – what shall we say? – a week. Is that long enough for you? And I want you to leave the job pretty well immediately, by the end of the month. Not at some point in the future which never quite comes.'

'But – that means – it means before the launch!'

'Oh dear, the launch. The all-important launch. I'd forgotten that, just for a moment. How could I have? But you know what, Bianca, it doesn't change a thing. This really shouldn't be something you need to mull over. I hope that's clear.'

And he walked out of the room, shutting the door very gently behind him.

Chapter 47

'Susie? Babe, where have you been? I've been texting you all day.'

Henk's voice was plaintive. She could exactly visualise his face. OK. She was going to enjoy this. One of the more satisfactory phone calls of her life.

One of the others had been at two this morning when he'd called and she'd told him to get lost. She could feel his outrage down the line, smiled with pleasure, went back to sleep, her phone switched off.

'I'm sorry, Henk. I was very busy. So – what can I do for you?'

'Babe! You know what you can do. Meet me. I need to talk to you badly. I've been pretty low. I'd have thought you'd realise that from my texts. And last night – I don't know how you could have done that, cut me off . . .'

'Sorry. I was very tired.'

'I can't take another night, Susie, not like last night. I kept looking at the sleeping pills, wondering if I should take them all—'

'I thought you said you'd stopped taking them?'

'That was the anti-depressants. Look, what's going on? You don't seem to understand how desperate I am.'

'Oh, I think I do.'

'You're not acting that way. Well, we can talk tonight.'

'Henk, I'm sorry, I can't see you tonight. I'm going out with a girlfriend.'

'Not that cow from the other night? I could have killed her, why didn't you tell her to fuck off?'

'I don't often speak to my friends like that. Oddly.'

'Susie, I swear to God, if you don't meet me tonight, I'll take all those sleeping pills. I can't go on like this, I feel like I'm going mad! Cancel that friend of yours, for Christ's sake.'

'I can't, I'm afraid.'

'Jesus!' She could hear his voice change, anger taking over. 'So you don't give a fuck about me, what I'm going to do . . .'

Right. Go on, Susie. Move in for the kill.

'I've got one suggestion, Henk.'

'I don't want any fucking suggestions.'

'Well, here it comes anyway. I think you should go out with Zoe instead. See how sympathetic she can be.'

There was a complete silence. A very long one; she could almost hear him breathing. Her own heart was thumping and she felt frightened suddenly. Suppose she was wrong, suppose Jemima had been wrong, suppose Zoe was just a friend? She pictured the bottle of sleeping pills, saw them in Henk's hand, being poured out, heard the call from the police the next day . . .

'You bitch,' he said. 'You filthy, fucking bitch. Playing along with me, risking my life . . .'

'I don't think so, Henk.' But she was still frightened.

'Zoe's just a friend. She's helped me – more than you have.'

'Well, that's good. I'm glad. Tell her to keep it up.'

Another silence: then it came, a tirade of filth. She felt sick, listened, stricken, for a minute or two, then said, 'I'm sorry, I'm going to ring off. I can't stand this any longer. And I'm busy.'

'So you put your work above my life? Or rather my death?'

'Henk, we both know this whole thing of you killing yourself is a farce. What you've been doing to me has been utterly cruel. I was desperate with worry, couldn't think about anything else. Until I saw it for what it was. Not content with beating me up physically, you decided to attack me mentally. And it was very successful for a while. You're a very good actor, Henk. And a good photographer. You're just a lousy person. I'm sorry I ever met you.'

And she switched off her phone. She was shaking violently and she felt very sick. And she was crying she realised, shocked, frightened tears. It had been the most hideous and terrifying thing she had ever had to deal with. Far worse than being beaten up. She would never forget it. But, she thought, blowing her nose, forcing herself to calm down, to control her tears, she could put it behind her now. It was over. Really and truly and properly over.

The charter company that controlled the leases of all the shops in the Berkeley Arcade was a venerable one. Formed in 1820, when the arcade was built, it had remained impressive. It employed a firm of respected City lawyers, and another of rigorous accountants. Rents were reviewed regularly, regulations updated – although it was still possible for tenants to tether their horses to the posts at either end of the arcade, and to use candlelight rather than electricity, should they so wish. Planning laws were adhered to strictly.

Farrell's had always been exemplary tenants; they had paid their rent and the charges on the lease promptly, invariably grateful that they were not nearly as high as they might be, given the arcade's situation.

One morning in early March 2012, Mark Rawlins, the financial director of Farrell's, received a letter from the directors of the charter company, informing him that the present lease was about to expire and had been reviewed. They suggested that he might like to come in and discuss the terms with them, as both the lease and the rent were to increase considerably and that they would require a sum of – and here Mark Rawlins had to blink, rub his eyes, and take a sip of coffee before realising that he had read correctly the size of the sum required – or alternatively let them have his company's cheque for the full amount, which included a year's rent in advance.

He read the letter several more times, phoned to make an appointment with the charter company, and then returned to a slightly panic-stricken review of the financial state of the House of Farrell. Things were looking rather bad . . .

Bianca was sitting at her desk, trying to deal with not just one, but a series of panics, when a text came through from Saul.

I keep thinking about you and I'd like to see you but I can't, it said.

As lover-like notes went it would have won no prizes; but it made her smile and, albeit briefly, feel just a little better . . .

Bianca sat on the plane and thought about marriage. About her marriage, mostly, but in general too, its nature, its requirements, its strengths.

The one she and Patrick had created had, over almost two decades, always seemed to her successful. It had contained all the necessary ingredients: love, tolerance, good sex, mutual respect, and then children and a shared, passionate concern for them, a similar, if not identical view of the world, shared pleasures, and an agreement that those that were not shared should be partaken of singly. It was not, after eighteen years, constantly exciting – how could it be? – but it had a sturdy happiness to it that she had always assumed would survive in the face of no-matter-what assaults.

But she had, she thought, been wrong. It had had a frailty, after all, the assaults made on it recently too much for it to withstand, and she should have recognised it, instead of blundering blindly on, pushing their joint tolerance to the limit. She had, she knew, taken it for granted, that happiness, that support for what she wanted to do; it had been a warm, comforting thing to return to after the storms and the difficulties of her days, an absolute, unquestioning security.

It was an impossible thing that Patrick had asked of her; it was a denial of her very self, of what she was. Did he really think that she could turn her back on that self, or that great part of herself, did he honestly believe that so much of what he had fallen in love with, desired, possessed, promised himself to, could be removed from her and that he would love her still? Clearly he did. His ultimatum had not been a swift, impulsive thought, born out of a flare of rage, a flash of resentment; he had meant it, absolutely and totally, and the small, sad statement that he didn't really mind what her decision was told more than anything.

Of course she should have said, yes, of course our marriage, our family, are far more important than my job, my career; but she knew, even as she stared at his face, that new, hard, hostile face, that she couldn't do that. And what did that make her? Some kind of self-seeking, hard-souled monster? Was that what she had become? Was that why he didn't mind, didn't care any more?

That was a particularly hard thing to face; but she forced herself to, sitting there on that long night, staring out into the darkness as the plane roared on. For the worst, the very worst thing of all, was being forced to face herself and what really, genuinely, truthfully mattered to her. It was very painful that, very painful indeed.

And Saul, this extraordinary interloper into her life, was he in any way responsible? She decided not, in so far as their relationship was concerned. It had been a strange, sad evening, immensely revealing. She felt deeply sorry for him, intrigued by him, and sexually disturbed, but there it ended; whatever was or might be between them had nothing to do with the breakdown of her marriage. He had a great deal to do with it as it related to Patrick, however: his ruthless intrusion on Patrick's time and attention, and the intense pleasure and happiness he offered Patrick on a professional basis, had changed Patrick almost out of recognition and with terrifying speed. And the domestic support she had always had from Patrick was gone; and that had changed both of them.

Nothing had happened after that last text; she waited, teenager-like, watching her phone hawk-like for another, but it had been followed by a complete silence.

When finally she texted him, because she was worried about him, saying simply *Are you all right?* he had texted back saying yes, he was fine, very worried about Dickon, and then as she read it, *I am thinking about you. Thank you for your help.*

Which from Saul Finlayson was virtually a sonnet.

She had at least won a little time. Twenty-four hours, not seven days, after Patrick's ultimatum she told him that their marriage deserved surely more than a hasty review and an ill-considered decision. If he had to take that as a no, then so be it. She had to go away, she said, it was essential, and that would give them both time to think further, and to her immense surprise he had agreed.

'But I do want a decision,' he said, 'and I have to tell you I am already disappointed.'

Which was probably the most chilling thing he had ever said to her.

She was on an insane, eight-day trip, taking in Sydney, Tokyo, Singapore, Dubai and New York. She was not to be dissuaded, she said firmly, and with increasing irritation, to everyone else who could not see the necessity of it either. How could she trust these people, these franchise holders, to realise her vision, her precious duplicates of the House of Farrell? How could she know, without seeing for herself, what they had chosen, the right buildings in the right streets, with the right décor and the right staff, and even having done all that, create the right ambience. Her entire life, her whole reputation was at stake; how could she not give a week to ensure things were all as good, as close to perfect, as they could possibly be.

She was travelling alone, she said to Mike, so the cost would not be too prohibitive, and she was prepared to pay her own fare if he didn't agree. They were in the eye of the storm, she said to Lara and Susie and Jonathan Tucker, the brand was created, the products formulated, the packaging designed. The website was being built, the faults overcome, the advertising campaign well under control, the PR exciting. There were no immediate crises, and if one arose there were phones, emails, texts, and a great many brains other than hers to deal with them. The owners of the other brains, aware they would not be allowed to deal with very much, nodded with faux enthusiasm when she pointed this out.

And she would ask nothing of Patrick, she said, speaking to him across the icy wasteland where they were presently residing. Sonia and Karen were both moving in full-time, fully primed of possible problems, and neither Patrick, nor consequentially Saul, need fear that they might suddenly find themselves possessed of a less than one hundred per cent capability to handle any global crisis that might present itself. And she would, at the end of this endeavour, this stupendously heroic odyssey she was embarking on, be fully possessed of all the knowledge required to bring about the small miracle that would be unleashed upon the world on June 1st 2012.

Florence lay awake, night after night, her stomach churning, her head throbbing, alternating between panic and terror and disbelief at her own stupidity, until it was morning – when the day followed a similar emotional pattern. She felt sick, she couldn't eat, she couldn't concentrate on anything. It was dreadful.

And she simply didn't know what to do. There was no one to ask, nowhere to turn.

Every time the phone or the doorbell rang she jumped. She wasn't sure what she expected, but Athina in an avenging fury was certainly one, and Bianca shocked and hostile another.

She was still frail physically; the cycle set up by the sleeplessness and inability to eat was vicious indeed. And as day followed day she felt worse. She had a few visitors – Francine came, of course, concerned and anxious to help, and the lovely Jemima, bearing flowers and grapes and the offer to go food-shopping for her, but while she was initially pleased to see them, she found them tiring and irritating, and not the distraction she would have hoped. From Athina there came not a word, apart from a few solicitous calls from Christine who said she hoped she was feeling better and that Lady Farrell had asked her to let her know when she felt ready to see her. That, she felt, was horrifically coded . . . And the worst thing was the mystery of it all; how had the photograph made its way from her bedside table to the drawer of her small desk downstairs, carefully covered by her blotting pad? She had only found it on the third day of her illness, after searching its usual resting places in an increasing panic. Who had put it there and why? It seemed unlikely it had been Athina, she was not given to discretion, but then she might be feeling too shocked and humiliated to do more than retire and brood upon what she had discovered. Florence, aware of Athina's emotional unpredictability, feared it was infinitely possible.

She spent a lot of time reviewing the events of that dreadful morning, as she lay feverish and scarcely conscious; she did know the photograph had been on her bedside table, she could remember looking at it from time to time, like some kind of talisman, but the sequence of when each of them had arrived, Bianca, Athina, and the doctor, eluded her. She berated herself constantly: how could she have behaved in so incredibly stupid a manner, that an infinitely dangerous secret, that had been kept with such infinite care and discretion for over fifty years, was tossed into full and glaring view, and with the potentially most terrifying and painful consequences? And all for want of a little sentimental comfort? Florence Hamilton, you are the most incredible fool.

'Where are you?'

'Dubai.'

'I need to talk to you.'

'Well, I'm here for about an hour.'

'No, no, talk properly. Where are you staying?'

'At the Mirage. Or as they call it The One and Only Royal Mirage. And it is *gorgeous*. Only hotel in Dubai which isn't fifty storeys high.'

'I might fly out and join you.'

'Saul, you can't,' she said, suppressing with an intense effort a rush of sexual excitement. 'Don't be ridiculous. Anyway, I'm leaving tomorrow. Off to Singapore.'

'I could meet you there. I suppose you're staying at Raffles?'

'I am. Is it wonderful?'

'I have no idea. I always stay at one of the airport hotels.'

'Well, why not talk now? What's happened?'

'She's fighting back.'

She should have known better than to think he wanted to talk about anything to do with them.

'This man she's talking about marrying, he's a complete asshole. I put a private investigator on to him. I couldn't allow Dickon anywhere near him.'

Saul never used bad language. She imagined a wife beater, a drug addict, a bigamist.

'What does he do?'

'He's an adman. You know what that means.'

548

'Er – not necessarily. What sort of adman?'

'He's what they call a creative director. Well, they're the worst. Called Bernard French. Bernard! What a name. Divorced, of course. And he's been offered this job in Sydney. I mean, who would want to live there – probably the only job he could get, he's probably been fired.'

If it wasn't so tragic, it would be funny. 'Saul, he doesn't sound too bad.'

'Of course he's bad. Anyone proposing to take another man's child out of the country, away from everything familiar to him, is bad.'

'Have you spoken to Janey?'

'Of course not. We're communicating through our lawyers.'

'Saul, it might help. Lawyers are awfully good at muddying the waters. And the more mud, the more's in it for them.'

'It's pretty muddy without them. Where else are you going on this trip?'

'Singapore,' she said carefully omitting Sydney, 'Tokyo, New York.'

'I could come to New York. Talk to you properly. This really isn't very satisfactory.'

'I won't be there for six more days. Everything could have changed by then. And anyway, then I'll be back in London in eight days. It's—' Crazy she was going to say, then stopped. Saul was in a dangerous mood; calling him crazy wasn't wise.

'It would be nice to be in New York with you,' he said, sounding rather wistful.

It would, oh God it would. 'Yes, maybe, but Patrick has my itinerary. What is he going to think if he knows you're in one of these places at the same time?'

There was a long silence; then, 'No, you're right. And I'd hate to upset him. He's such a good analyst . . .'

'So, has anything actually happened?' she said carefully,

'Well, my lawyers say I can take out an injunction and stop her taking Dickon out of the country immediately.'

'But is she going to take him immediately? The very fact that she talked to you about it in the first place, in what sounded fairly reasonable terms—'

'You weren't there. How do you know they were reasonable?'

'I'm merely playing back to you what you told me. That evening. I honestly think that if you want to drive Janey and Dickon to go to the nearest airport at high speed, then talking about injunctions is the way to do it.'

'They couldn't go if I took out an injunction.'

'Saul, I'm speaking figuratively. Look, suppose the worst came to the worst and you did that, how do you think it would make Dickon feel? He's too little to cope with something so drastic—'

'He's too little to cope with going to Australia.'

'That's a matter of opinion.'

'It's not, Bianca. He's nine years old.'

'It's a matter of opinion.'

'You just don't understand,' he said after a long silence. 'I thought you did. I'm disappointed in you, Bianca.'

And the phone went dead.

'Florence? This is Athina. How are you? Good. Look, I need to talk to you. It's very important. I shall come tomorrow afternoon. I presume you'll be in.'

Florence was too frightened to hedge and say she wouldn't be. In any case she wanted it to be over, to know the worst. Clearly Athina *did* know, had seen the photograph and had been wondering what to do and say to Florence ever since, although why she had put the photograph in the drawer . . . Maybe she had been too upset, or too shocked, to replace it where it had been. If only Bianca was still here; but she was on some world-wide tour and she really didn't feel it was a subject she could broach on the phone. What would she say? Did you see a photograph on my bedside table of me and Cornelius and did you then hide it in my desk?

'Very well, Athina,' she said, her voice still husky and rather feeble. 'I shall look forward to that.' No point in anticipating the form the interview would take. 'I've got rather tired of my own company as you can imagine.'

'Oh, I'm not coming for a cosy chat,' said Athina, 'rather the reverse. And don't go getting some elaborate tea ready for me. I won't have time for that.'

Jess Cochrane was seriously fed up. It was all very well being hailed as one of the most promising actresses of 2011, and one of the faces of the year in 2010, but when you'd only done one proper film you needed to reinforce that, keep yourself in the public eye. And one film did not a film star make.

She was one of the leads in a film that started shooting in September, a costume drama, based on a Georgette Heyer novel, but it wouldn't hit the cinemas until autumn 2014 and between then and now was a yawning gap. Her agent had got her a TV series, which would have been perfect, but it had been cancelled; and there had been a stage production of an Alan Ayckbourn, which would have been perfect, very prestigious, but it clashed with filming and her agent, Freddie Alexander, had advised her to take the film. Which she knew was good advice and financially it was a no-brainer, but still left the gap. And when Freddie put her up for interviews in the glossies, most of them were already turning her down. 'Let us know when she's got something new to talk about,' they'd all (more or less) said.

What she needed was some kind of a story that would get her in the headlines now; but short of cycling on a high wire across the Thames or parachuting out of an aeroplane and landing in the courtyard of Buckingham Palace, every single column inch and nanosecond of airtime being devoted to the Diamond Jubilee, she couldn't think how on earth she was going to do it.

'Oh, Athina. Do come in.'

'Yes, thank you. You look perfectly all right to me. I suppose you've had a lot of rest. Which is more than I have. I'm exhausted.'

'I'm sorry. Let me put the kettle on . . .'

'Well, just a cup, perhaps. Nothing else. There's quite a lot to talk about, and I don't have long.'

Florence filled the kettle and reached for the teapot; she noticed her hand was shaking. Athina was wandering round her small drawing room, picking things up and putting them down again. Looking for further incriminating evidence, perhaps. She paused now, in front of the Lawrence Trentham.

'Terribly overrated I always think, as an artist. Of course Cornelius always liked his work. Did he give you this?'

Florence felt she might be sick.

'Well . . .'

'I suppose you'll be telling me it's an original, next. Or that he told you it was.'

'Well—'

'Of course it's not, they're worth a fortune. Do get the tea, Florence, we need to get down to business. No sugar for me, remember.'

'Yes, I do remember, Athina.' She went out to the kitchen, poured the tea, filled a jug with milk, put it all on a tray, stood gazing out of the window, delaying her return . . .

'Florence! What on earth are you doing out there? Are you trying to postpone this conversation or something?'

It was too much for Florence. She took the tray into the sitting room, set it down and said, 'I'm sorry, Athina, I suddenly feel – feel—' And fled into the small downstairs cloakroom where she was extremely sick.

Jemima was tidying the cupboard that Bianca used as a wardrobe when she saw the Post-it note. It had fallen on the floor and was clearly, she realised, intended for her.

URGENT it said in capital letters and then: *Please call Florence and tell her not to worry about the photograph. And that I'll call her the minute I'm back.*

Jemima stared at it in horror; it had clearly been there for at least two days, must have fallen out of Bianca's pocket as she changed jackets. But if it was urgent, then two days was a long time. So should she still deliver it? A lot might have changed since then, and the photograph might now need worrying about. Or it might be too late. She decided she would have to call Bianca and ask her what she would like her to do. It might be a rather delicate matter, because Bianca didn't often leave cryptic messages.

Slightly nervously, she called Bianca's mobile; which told her Bianca couldn't come to the phone right now.

She left a message asking Bianca to call her as soon as possible and returned to her task.

'I'm so sorry, Athina.' Florence emerged from the cloakroom, white-faced and shaking. Athina looked at her rather coldly.

'I thought you were supposed to be better?' she said. 'I do hope what you've got isn't infectious. Now, if we could begin . . .'

'I'll just – just pour myself a fresh tea, if you don't mind.'

'Jemima, it's Bianca.'

'Hi! How's Dubai?'

'It's like landing on the moon – quite extraordinary, Now, I can't be long, I've come out of a meeting, what is it?'

'I just found a note which I think was for me. A Post-it, saying to ring Florence and tell her not to worry about the photograph.'

'What? And you haven't done that?'

'Well no. How could I have?' said Jemima, mildly indignant at this slur on her efficiency. 'I only saw it because I was tidying your wardrobe. It was on the floor.'

'The floor? Oh God! I was in a fearful rush and I must have just dropped it when I was looking for some gloves. Oh, dear, and it was so important!'

Jemima said, 'Shall I call her now?'

'No, no,' said Bianca, 'I'll do it myself. It will sound odd coming from you now. I'll do it right away. If I can't get through to her I'll call you and ask you to do it.'

'OK. Now do you want me to run through some messages?'

'No, no, I absolutely don't, I must do this and then I'm going to meet the woman who's taken the franchise here and see the site she's suggesting. It sounds most unsuitable, in something called the World's Biggest Shopping Mall, but there certainly aren't any tiny streets here. Well, there are, but they're full of tatty jewellery stalls. Right Jemima, I must go; call me tomorrow first thing. Around seven, Dubai time.'

This would mean Jemima rising at four, but she didn't argue; Bianca was, after all, on a particularly exhausting mission and no doubt missing a great deal of sleep herself.

'Fine,' she said.

'Right, I must go. I really have to speak to Florence. I don't have to tell you that this is highly confidential, do I?'

'No,' said Jemima, allowing a touch of irritation to creep into her voice, 'of course you don't.'

Florence had returned to the sitting room and sat down in one of the button-back chairs; Athina was sitting on the chaise longue which was considerably higher than the chair and therefore left Florence looking up at her in what was, under the circumstances, a rather unfortunate way.

'Right,' Athina said, 'I think you can imagine what I've come to talk about.'

'Athina, I would like to say before anything else that I – we – never meant to – to . . .'

To what? Hurt her? Deceive her? When they had been doing that for the best part of forty years, in the full knowledge it would be painful beyond all imagining.

'I simply cannot understand it.'

And then, blessedly, the phone rang; a stay of execution, Florence thought.

'Don't take that, please,' Athina said. 'I presume your answering machine is operating.'

'Actually,' said Florence, with perfect truth, 'it isn't. And I had asked Francine to call me, so it's probably her and I think at the very least I should answer her and tell her I will ring her back. I'm sorry, Athina.'

She picked up the phone, which seemed rather heavy suddenly, and said, 'Francine?'

'No,' said Bianca's voice. 'It's not Francine, it's me, Bianca. I should have called you long before this, Florence, and I'm so sorry, but – well, better late than never. I'll explain another time. I can't talk now, but it's really important you should hear what I'm about to say.'

'Yes?' Florence felt she might throw up again. Maybe they had already discussed things, Bianca and Athina.

'It's just that you're not to worry about the photograph. The one on your bedside table. I put it away. No one else saw it. Now I must go – I have to meet the woman who's bought the franchise out here. I do wish you were with me, Florence, but speak soon and I'm so sorry if you were worried.'

'Oh, no,' said Florence, and it was astonishingly easy to sound careless and light-hearted, because she felt suddenly more careless and light-hearted than she had ever been in her entire life and had just time to admire the way the sun was shining through her window and dancing off the large vase of flowers that stood on one of the side tables in the most appropriate way, before adding, 'Not worried at all. Well, maybe just a little, and thank you so much, Bianca, for calling. I wish I was with you too. Goodbye.'

And she turned, with a radiant smile, to Athina.

'I'm so sorry. That was Bianca Bailey.'

'I did gather that,' said Athina, glaring at her. 'What on earth was she calling you for?'

'Oh, something to do with the shop out there. Nothing very important.'

'Well, I really would like to get on. I'm appalled at the way this whole thing of the launch is being handled, absolutely appalled, without reference to me. It suddenly seems to have become top secret, with those irritating young men holding meetings with Miss Harding and that Clements woman. I am going to have to insist on being involved, and I need your help in achieving that. Florence, are you listening to me? You really don't seem to be quite here this afternoon.'

'Sorry, Athina. I suppose I am still a little tired.'

'Yes, well I suppose that's understandable. But you've been away for over a week now and I would have thought that was enough.

You really can't expect to be away indefinitely and other people to do your work.'

'No, no of course not, and we should be involved of course. But I certainly haven't attended any advertising meetings, I can assure you of that . . .'

Chapter 48

'So – how was your trip. Satisfactory, I hope?'

'Yes, very. Thank you so much for coming to meet me.'

'You must be exhausted,' he said and his voice was detached, as if he was talking to some distant acquaintance. 'And it was worth it?'

'Yes, we've made huge strides. Dubai wasn't ideal, in that we have to be in a shopping mall, and not only a shopping mall, but one that's billed the World's Biggest Shopping Mall, but with temperatures hitting fifty, you can sort of understand. Although mostly I was cold there, the air conditioning is so vicious.'

'How uncomfortable.'

His voice was as cold as the air conditioning. She was aware she was babbling, but couldn't stop.

'Yes, it was rather. God, it's a weird place. So shiny and flashy, and then the second afternoon there was a sandstorm, just a mass of it blowing in from the desert; you couldn't go out, and when it was over all the cars were covered in sand and the whole place looked like a disaster movie.'

'And Sydney?'

'Sydney was great. God, it's beautiful. It's like a piece of music, sort of ebbs and flows – anyway, yes, we've got a shop in a gorgeous mall, called the Strand Arcade. Really perfect, and a very nice woman, I liked her so much, she just totally got the whole thing.'

She felt his disinterest and it made her worse. 'Singapore is great. The shop, I mean, in a lovely street called Ann Siang Hill, and a very good chap there, name of Mr Yang, believe it or not. He took me out to dinner in an amazing place called Lao Pa Sat, near the shop, which is like a vast open air market, only it's not, it's sort of a vast open air restaurant. Tokyo, fantastic, well, you know that, we've been there together, and the woman there, God, was she high-powered, wonderful though, she'd found a real little gem in the—'

'Bianca, this is all very fascinating, but I really don't have all day. You can tell me about the others later.'

'Oh – yes, of course. Sorry. It's just so exciting that it's all really happening, all these little treasures of shops, in all these wonderful cities.'

'Yes, it must be. And New York?'

'Yes.' She looked at him sharply but his expression was still coolly blank. 'Yes, we've got something there, bit more of a struggle. Shop in SoHo . . .'

'And did you hear from Saul? He seemed to think he could help.'

Oh God – but his voice was completely neutral, without any edge to it.

'Yes, yes, I did and he was really helpful. In fact it was he who suggested SoHo. He actually—'

'Bianca, I'm sorry, I really do have to go. I am interested, of course, but I'm also very busy.'

'Of course. Will you – will you be in tonight?'

'I will. Well, here we are. I'll just put your bags in the hall and then I'll go and find a taxi. I've got to meet someone in the West End. See you tonight, then. We can talk further about my – what shall we say? Proposition.'

'Yes, of course. That would be . . . good. Thank you again for meeting me.'

She stood looking after him as he loped down the road; she felt seriously unnerved. He was so cold, so remote. He had obviously moved further down the road he had set them on than she had. Maybe it was already too late.

Or did he suspect anything? He couldn't, surely? Just the same, what did she do? Pre-empt any conversation about it? Say – well what should she say? She remembered the words of a serially adulterous friend of hers: 'If he catches you in bed together just say you were very cold, and he was trying to keep you warm.'

It was probably, she decided, extremely sound advice.

She had enjoyed New York hugely; she always did. She did have friends there, but had kept her trip from them; it was too short – less than forty-eight hours – and she couldn't spare one of her precious two evenings.

She arrived late at night and it was past midnight when she got into a cab. She was not staying at the Carlyle, which had become so absurdly expensive it was just irritating, and had settled, on a whim, on the Algonquin. She had stayed there many times when she was younger. It was probably one of the most central hotels in Manhattan, and while the rooms were small, it still had a certain magic and she loved it. The Round Table restaurant was still there, haunted by the acerbic ghosts of Dorothy Parker and her friends, Matilda the cat was still there – well, one of her descendants, or so you were urged to believe – and the lobby was still a theatrical set of a place, with its palms and black marble pillars, and huge, leather, wing back chairs.

New York was behaving as it always did whether it was midday or midnight; heavy traffic pouring into the city, all the shops downtown open, and the pavements crowded with people walking, shouting, greeting. She was exhausted from LA and, half asleep, checked in, stroked the cat, booked a 7 a.m. wake-up, and fell asleep in the bath.

She had invited Lou Clarke, who was taking the New York franchise, for breakfast. It was partly a test: if she insisted on the Four Seasons, she would know she had a lot of work to do. Lou Clarke didn't. A diminutive forty year old, part Chinese, with jet black hair and huge almond-shaped dark eyes, she said she adored the Algonquin and as she settled her size zero frame on to a chair that looked too big for her in the restaurant, said she would have trouble not ordering a martini with her breakfast. 'It's not that I'm an alcoholic,' she said. 'They just make the best in New York.'

She said she had two properties to show Bianca, one in the Meatpacking district, another in the Village. 'You'll love both areas, I know, and they are just so totally where it's all happening.'

She toyed with a brioche and sipped a black coffee and Bianca, suddenly hungry, ordered what the Algonquin called a 'Cage Free and Loving It' omelette, with hash browns on the side and a large white coffee to which she added a great deal of sugar. Lou Clarke watched her with the sort of frozen fascination that might have indicated Bianca was preparing a line of cocaine.

She was in the fashion business, or so it had said in the biography she had emailed through, 'wholesale, accessories, shoes, jewellery, bags'. Anxious that it might prove rather tacky, Bianca discovered that while half her empire did indeed supply the flashy downtown shops, the other half made seriously gorgeous scarves, gloves, bags and hats. She was wearing a small sequinned beret which Bianca admired.

'I'm so glad you like it. It's been one of our bestsellers over Christmas, so darling – $650 dollars – it would look just wonderful on you.'

She said they should start in the Meatpacking district; Bianca, who had not been to New York for three years, was astonished at the changes in it. Cool, expensive boutiques in small covered arcades, but, she felt, not right for a Farrell shop, smart cafés, cobbled streets. And the Standard Hotel, standing on two vast struts, so cool it had its name hung upside down on its façade, and how ridiculous was that? Lou took her up to the Boom Boom Room bar on the eighteenth floor with its panoramic view of Manhattan, through infinity windows, even in the restrooms. There was to be the new Whitney museum, said Lou, at the end of the new High Line walk, once the West Side Freight Line; and a magnificent new Apple store.

'So you see, it is seriously cool.'

Bianca said she could see that; and that she did like it, and liked the little shop Lou had found, but over lunch at an ultra chic café with every item on the menu calorie counted as well as priced, she said apologetically she really didn't see a House of Farrell there.

'It's too cool, we're looking for tradition and charm, rather than hyper chic.'

Lou smiled at her, as if this was exactly what she wanted to hear, and said fine, she realised that, and that the Village was far more suitable. Which of course it was. Both tree-lined and glossy, Bleecker Street was absurdly fashionable now, studded with the smartest names, Ralph Lauren, Marc Jacobs. 'And your Burberry, of course,' said Lou with huge satisfaction, as if she had set it up there herself, 'and Jo Malone. That must say something to you.'

It said to Bianca that Jo Malone would not be there if she was still an independent – as Farrell's was – rather than owned by Estée Lauder, and a site anywhere near it would be impossibly expensive. Lou, and an incredibly pushy agent, showed her the minute place Lou had found, in a tiny street just off Bleecker, that was exquisite and perfect in every way but way outside budget. Lou said she could almost certainly do a deal, whereupon the agent said Chanel was after it at the full price, and ready to offer more. Lou, thunder-faced, took her outside and conducted an intense whispering conversation with her; Bianca, looking out at them and the rich, pretty people wandering past, crossed her fingers and didn't feel very hopeful. Lou came back inside and said everything seemed fine, and the agent was ringing her later to confirm. Bianca didn't believe her. Back on Bleecker, she looked at *Sex and the City*'s Magnolia Bakery, absurdly pretty, with people standing outside drinking hot chocolate and eating cupcakes. Bianca, who was suddenly very tired, decided a shot of sugar might help, bought a piece of Red Velvet cheesecake for herself and a cappuccino; Lou declined anything either to eat or drink, and said, her almond eyes almost round with shock, 'How you keep your wonderful figure, Bianca, I cannot imagine.'

'So,' Lou said, as they climbed into a cab and directed it uptown, 'what do you think? Wasn't that perfect?'

Bianca said yes it was, absolutely perfect; and right on cue a call came in from the agent to say a new shoe designer had just outbid Chanel and was prepared to do the same until the shop was hers.

For some reason Bianca couldn't define, she wasn't as disappointed as she should have been.

'But there are others,' said Lou, putting her phone away, 'and you saw for yourself how perfect the area was. If I can find another shop, and I just know I can, would you be happy with that?'

'Very happy,' said Bianca, as the cab stopped outside the Algonquin, 'and it's been a wonderful day and thank you for all your hard work. And now you must excuse me, Lou, I'm absolutely dead on my feet, or rather my backside, and I need a nap.'

'I would love to buy you dinner,' said Lou, but Bianca was able to say gracefully and truthfully that she was taking a cosmetic buyer to dinner.

'Where are you going?' Lou asked. 'Because if you want, I can certainly direct you to the perfect place. These people are terribly picky.'

Bianca said that was very kind but they were going to the Gordon Ramsay at The London, which silenced Lou for just long enough for Bianca to get out of the cab and blow Lou a kiss from the doorway of the hotel.

In her room, she fell asleep at once, having booked a wake-up call for two hours' time and was woken from a fog-thick sleep to a call from the concierge to say there was a gentleman to see her. Presuming that this must be the cosmetic buyer, come to the wrong place, she asked to speak to him.

'I am so so sorry,' she said, 'I got hopelessly held up. Do please order yourself a drink, and I'll be down in ten.' And wondered, even as she said it, why everyone started talking American in this ridiculous place, and adding that she couldn't recommend the martinis highly enough.

There was a silence, and then, 'Bianca, are you never going to remember? I don't drink?'

It was Saul.

She went down to see him, confused and disoriented.

'What are you doing here?' she said.

'I said it would be nice to be in New York with you,' he said. And leaned forward and kissed her on the cheek. She smiled back at him rather foolishly.

'It's very nice to see you,' she said, and then sat back in her chair.

'It's nice you think it's nice,' he said.

She asked him how he knew where she was, and he said he'd had trouble with her mobile, and remembered Patrick mentioning she was staying at the Algonquin.

She hauled her mobile out of her bag to check it; it would indeed be giving trouble, it was completely out of charge. So unlike her and a measure of her exhaustion, she supposed.

'But does Patrick know you're here?' she said, sipping her (extremely good) martini, and feeling, for the first time that day, a flash of genuine gratitude to Lou Clarke.

'As in here at your hotel, no. As in here in New York, yes. I wasn't going to lie about it. I don't tell lies,' he added.

'You never say enough to lie,' she said irritably.

He looked at her blankly for a moment and then gave her one of his swiftly disappearing smiles. 'I suppose that's true. Anyway, he won't mind. I told him I might have a location for you. Haven't you spoken to him?'

'Not spoken, no. He's emailing me every day though,' she added, hoping she didn't sound defensive. 'He didn't say anything about it this morning.'

'Well, never mind. What are you doing this evening?'

'Having dinner with a cosmetic buyer. Then going to bed.'

'Not with the cosmetic buyer, I hope?'

'Not with the cosmetic buyer.'

'I'm glad.'

'Why?' A bit of flirtatious chat now?

'It would mean your business was in very poor shape. That you should have to do such a thing.'

Serve you right, Bianca.

'And tomorrow?'

'I was going to do the stores tomorrow. Then see yet another property with my New York franchisee.'

'Any good?'

'Not so far.'

'Well, cancel that,' he said, 'I have exactly the right place for you. I'll show you. It's in SoHo. Do you have to do the stores? I can see you have to look at them, but I'm leaving at five.'

'I could do it later. When you've gone. Where are you staying?'

'It's actually rather smart. Not my style. But near where this shop is. Place called the Mercer. They claim to offer their guests authentic loft living. Whatever that might mean. I've stayed there twice and I still don't know. Anyway, it's very nice.'

'I'll come there in the morning then,' she said, 'if that's OK.'

'Of course. There's a café adjacent to the foyer. Meet me there. Nine o'clock. Well, if you're not free tonight, I might as well go. I've got a lot of work to do.'

She laughed. She couldn't help it.

'Do you ever send ladies flowers?' she said. 'Or buy them champagne?'

'No of course not,' he said. 'Why would I do that?'

She gave up. 'I'll see you in the morning.'

'OK.' He leaned forward and kissed her very briefly on the lips. 'I'm sorry we can't spend the evening together.'

'Me too,' she said carefully.

'But I do have an awful lot to do.'

She slept well that night and felt much better and arrived at the Mercer to find Saul drinking coffee and talking on the phone. He waved at her, called the waiter over, while continuing to talk. She sighed and ordered a croissant and a cappuccino, studying him. He was dressed, as usual, in jeans, with a red cashmere sweater over a pink and white striped shirt and under a grey tweed jacket and as a fashion statement it didn't work. But then he had no interest in clothes – his own at any rate. She could imagine him grabbing things from the tops of piles in the morning, with no thought as to what he might look like; she rather liked that; it was a welcome change from men who looked as if *Men In Vogue* was compulsory reading.

There had been an email from Patrick when she got in from her dinner.

'All well here, more or less. Hope trip continues to be a success. You might hear from Saul, he said he might have a location for you. Patrick.'

The cosmetic buyer – from Parkes, one of the great Fifth Avenue stores, which had stocked Farrell's quite successfully in the glory days, and had dropped it in the late nineties – seemed mildly interested in the relaunch, rather more so in the shop.

'That's a cute idea. It certainly gives you something to talk about. You should be on Fifth, though. You won't get much volume any place else. I'll visit the shop when it's open and probably not decide on an order until then. See what sort of volume we were talking. And I can tell you now, we won't take the perfume. It's a sweet story but you're not spending nigh on enough. Now, how about a brandy? And then I should let you go to bed. You look all done in.'

She arrived back at the Algonquin feeling depressed, looked at the table she had sat at with Saul, half expecting him to be still there. And how ridiculous was that? She'd be hallucinating in a minute.

'Right,' said Saul now, finally switching off his phone. 'How was the buyer?'

'Useless.'

'I could have told you that. Bianca, this town runs entirely on money. Not cute little ideas.'

'I know, I know – but we have legend on our side.'

'Legend doesn't pay the bills. Right, you done? I'll show you this place. It's very near.'

The shop was in a small street just off Wooster; it was charming: cobbled, tree-lined, chic, but not as cool as the Meatpacking district, nor would it get swallowed up as it would in the Village. She could see that now, recognised the reason for her reservations.

It was presently a book shop, with small windows and a stout wooden door, raised from the street by a couple of steps. It looked vaguely Dickensian, certainly could be English.

'Contact of mine tells me they're about to go bust,' Saul said. 'You'd get it pretty cheaply, I reckon, if you jumped in with an offer now. You'd better get your colleague down here smartish.'

She went in, wandered round; it was divided into two, one area leading to the other through an arch. It even had a tiny upper floor reached by a spiral staircase. Shades of Florence and her parlour, she thought, and smiled.

'It's perfect, Saul, I love it! How did you find it?'

'I know the guy who owns that lot. Global chain, I expect you know them.' He indicated the shop next door, a huge-windowed fashion emporium; she smiled.

'Yes, I do. I've contributed to his profits Well – it's wonderful. Let me call Lou.'

She made the call; Lou said she'd always thought SoHo would be the perfect place, and she could be with Bianca by four.

'Great. I'll meet you there.' She turned to Saul. 'I can't thank you enough.'

'That's OK. What are you doing now?'

She looked at her watch. It was, astonishingly, only just after eleven. 'Would you believe nothing? You?'

'Nothing. Just waiting on a couple of calls. And I'd budgeted some time for you.'

'Well, I'm honoured,' she said.

'Don't you do that?'

And she realised that of course she did it all the time. Even for the children. Certainly for Patrick. 'Yes, I do.'

'Want to look around the neighbourhood a bit? That's important to you, I imagine.'

'It is. I specially want to go to Balthazar's; everyone says it's the most wonderful place, not to be missed.'

He sighed. 'I hate places that are not to be missed.'

'Well, I'll go on my own then.'

'No, I can cope with it with you.'

They walked through the sunlit streets; Balthazar was on Spring Street, a big, buzzy restaurant and bar in a converted leather warehouse, a vast open space, absurdly Parisian-looking, all brass rails, wooden bench seats, hanging lights and the waiters' uniforms unmistakably French. They sat at the Oyster Bar on high chairs and Bianca smiled at him slightly nervously. He gave her one of his brief smiles back.

'It's very nice to be with you,' he said.

'I'm glad you think so.'

'You know I do.'

'I suppose so. Um – drink?'

'I'll have a glass of champagne,' he said, 'I imagine that's what you're having.'

'Yes, of course but . . .'

'I do drink very very occasionally. If the occasion demands it.'

'And this does?'

Don't flirt, Bianca, it doesn't work. But, 'Yes, I think it does,' he said, looking at first her and then the bar contemplatively.

He sipped the champagne in silence while checking his phone; clearly the flirtation was over.

Then he suddenly looked at her and smiled again. 'You look very nice,' he said. 'I like that jacket with the red scarf. Red suits you, you should wear it more often.'

'Thank you.' She was astonished that he should notice.

That really did seem to be it; he returned to his phone and she looked at the menu – very French, *huîtres, frites, frisée au lardons* – and at the rows of wine racks high, high above her, laden with dust-covered bottles that had clearly not been disturbed for years or even decades.

'It's wonderful,' she said. 'Perfect. My customers are here, look at them!' He looked obediently and briefly at them, all chattering and laughing and kissing, in between studying their iPhones and their iPads, New York's successful young.

They walked some more and he kept away from her, never so much as brushing against her. When they got stuck trying to cross the road, he grabbed her hand and made her run and she wondered if this was a prelude to further intimacy, but he dropped her hand again as soon as they were safely on the pavement. Had she dreamed the other night? she wondered. Had it ever happened at all? It seemed rather hard to believe.

He showed her a bar called 89, so cool it carried a sign that said 'no tourists after 10 p.m.'.

'How ridiculous!' she said.

'I wouldn't go there on principle,' he said. 'Mind you, I won't go to most bars on principle. That one today, all right, but—'

'You should open one,' she said laughing, 'and put a sign on the door that says: "No customers".'

He grinned at her, delighted with the thought. 'I might just do that. What a good idea. Right. So, shall we go back to the Mercer, have some lunch? It's still only twelve. That café there is a legend round here, you can't book, but they will keep you a table if you say you're only going to be ten minutes. Of course you can be as long as you like.'

'Perfect,' she said.

He chose a small table in the middle of the room, and sat opposite her; clearly there was to be no intimacy here, not a hint of it.

'Saul, I can't thank you enough,' she said.

'You already did,' he said.

Over lunch, which he wolfed down and she pushed around her plate, remorseful that she had failed him last time, she asked him about Dickon.

'He's extremely upset, of course. But there's nothing I can do for the time being. I really don't want to talk about it.'

'Fine. What shall we talk about then?'

He looked at her very seriously, clearly about to say something; then his phone rang.

'Sorry,' he said, 'must take this. Then I want to discuss something with you.'

'Can't the call wait? Just this once?'

'Of course not,' he said, as if she had suggested he took all his clothes off, or overturned the table. 'It shouldn't take long.'

She sipped at her mineral water. The champagne had gone to her head and she couldn't afford to be even mildly drunk.

Important deals had to be done, and possibly important things had to be said.

The call ended and Saul put his phone in his pocket. 'Sorry,' he said, 'I promise I won't answer the next one.'

'I don't believe you. Go and give your phone to the maître d'.'

Of course he wouldn't. It was only a joke. But he hesitated, and then said, 'All right; I will.'

He stood up, walked over to the desk, said a few words to the maître d' and handed his phone over.

Then he came back and said, 'How was that?'

'I'm very, very impressed,' she said.

'Good. You should be. I've never done that for anyone. Except Dickon, of course.'

'Now I'm really flattered.'

'It wasn't meant to be flattering. It was a fact. I don't like flattery.'

'I had kind of noticed.'

'Now, I'd like to have a completely truthful conversation with you,' he said, ignoring this. 'Is that all right? I don't want to upset you, of course.'

'No . . .' she said. Now what?

'The thing is,' he said, sitting back in his chair and putting his hands in his pockets, 'I've been thinking about you a lot. I enjoy your company. I find you extremely attractive. I really like being with you. And I suspect we would have a very good time in bed. No, that's not true. I'm *sure* we would have a very good time in bed. Don't you agree?'

'I – well, yes. Possibly we would,' she said finally, struggling to stay calm, not to laugh or alternatively walk out of the restaurant. What was he *like*?

'I'd like to know how you feel about being with me,' he said.

'Well – it's – you know – I . . .'

What did she feel? Disturbed? Distracted? Irritated?

'I can see you're not sure,' he said. 'I know I'm not the most socially accomplished person.'

'That's true.'

He looked hurt.

'Saul,' she said, putting her hand over his. He looked down at it, as if wondering how it had got there, and then at her, and his expression was so intense, so unmistakable in its intent, that she felt quite dizzy.

There was a long silence; he went on looking at her. She felt absurdly unsure of herself, had no idea what to say or do. For want of anything more inspired she struggled to answer his question.

'I really, really enjoy your company. I'm very sure about that. But – well, it's a little bit hard to say; I haven't had much of it, you must admit.'

'No, that's true,' he said and smiled suddenly, releasing her hand. 'Well, as long as it's not unpleasant.'

'It's not unpleasant at all.'

'Good. Well, the thing I wanted to say was that I would really like to have an affair with you. Really like it.'

The shock was so intense that she sat back in her chair, feeling totally disoriented, looking round the room, almost wondering where she was, seeking normality, and then back to him. He was looking at her quite calmly, didn't even seem particularly concerned. He gave her one of his smiles.

'Bianca?'

'Oh!' she said. It seemed to be the only response.

'How would you feel about that? Given what you said about us having a good time in bed and so on? Would you consider it?'

She sat staring at him. What should she say? What *could* she say? He really was a bit mad. He was sexy and intriguing and brilliant, and actually extraordinarily nice. He had been the greatest help to her. She owed him a lot. But he wasn't quite . . . normal. And there was no normal reaction to him.

So she just smiled at him. He smiled back at her, and this time it was not fleeting, it went on and on, sitting back in his chair, still not touching her, not even reaching for her hand. The smile clearly had to do. This was extraordinary. She remembered a piece of advice Patrick had once given her when she was in a particularly difficult situation. 'Just breathe in and out,' he said. 'Keep breathing

570

in and out.' It seemed rather appropriate to this occasion too. At least it stopped her wanting to laugh, which was one of her predominant emotions. She waited for the next words, his next move. They came rather swiftly.

'Have you ever had an affair?'

'No,' she said, too surprised to prevaricate. 'No, I never have. I've never really wanted to.'

'I thought you hadn't. Have you thought about it even?'

'No. Patrick – well, Patrick's always been everything I wanted.'

'I see. Well, I've given it a lot of thought. Having one with you.'

'Really?'

'Really. Have you ever thought about it? With me, I mean?'

Oh, God she had. A hundred times since that night, when she had longed more than anything to take him up to bed, or even there, on the floor, when desire had flooded her in a way she had thought never to feel again, violent, desperate, careless of consequence.

'Actually, yes,' she said finally, 'yes, I have.'

'Well that's very good,' he said, 'very good for me to hear, I mean. I'm pleased.'

And he smiled at her again, a joyful, satisfied smile; he looked rather like a small boy who had just accomplished something difficult for the first time.

Then, 'But I don't think we can. Can we?'

Any minute now the Red Queen would come rushing through the restaurant shouting 'Off with her head!'.

'Well – no,' she said. It was clearly the only answer; but she could hear her own hesitation in it, her disappointment.

'Bianca, of course we can't. For so many reasons. The first being your husband. I like him more than almost anyone I've ever known. And he likes me.'

'He's obsessed with you!' she said, trying not to sound bitter.

'I – well, perhaps. A little.'

'Saul! You dominate our lives.'

'Now I'm sure that's not true. It's the work that does that. It's a requirement, really.'

'OK. But I think there's a little more to it than that.'

'Let's agree to differ. Anyway, you're very good together. I can't move in on that. I see you and him and I feel such envy. Of what you've got, your family, your shared life, your—'

'It's not shared,' she said miserably, 'not at the moment. And we're not good together. Not communicating. Quarrelling. We've never done that before. It's mostly my fault, I'm sure. And my job. He's very jealous of the job.'

She longed to explain, to tell him Patrick's ultimatum, knew she couldn't.

'I'm surprised.'

A long silence; then, 'Well I'm sure you will be again. Good together, I mean.'

'I hope so,' she said, and there was a great passion in her voice, 'I do so hope so.'

'You will. It's such a vicious circle, that sort of thing. Misunderstanding breeding misunderstanding. I should know.'

'I know. But it's such a mire, you get in deeper and deeper. And so fast. It's terrifying how fast.'

'You'll get out of it. You have to. You're too clever not to. You are very clever,' he said, studying her. 'I find that so attractive. I could never find a stupid woman attractive. That Guinevere woman, if she came after me with that sexually explicit mouth of hers, those magnificent breasts bared, and offered to do whatever I asked, I'd become completely impotent.'

'Good God!'

'What?'

'Well, I suppose I'm amazed that you should even have noticed her – her assets.'

'Bianca! What do you take me for? Of course I noticed them. I'm not made of stone.'

'But,' she said, curiosity getting the better of discretion and even pride, 'if you find me so attractive, how come you never even touched me until the other night? And then you said it was only because you were upset.'

'Well it was. As I said, I wasn't myself. But I've wanted to – to kiss you, of course I have. And go to bed with you, for that matter,

572

ever since I've known you, that night in Paris, that time in the woods, I just knew I mustn't.'

'Oh!' she said.

'It would have been very destructive. But I did so want it. You. It was only how I felt that night, so wretched, so afraid, somehow I couldn't fight it any longer. It – *you* – became irresistible.'

'Oh,' she said.

'But of course, and it's rather ironic when you think about it, with all this dreadful business with Dickon, of course I can't. I can't risk anything. If Janey found out – well, that would be it. I'd lose him. And the most amazing time in bed with you wouldn't be worth that.'

'Oh,' she said for a third time, wishing she could think of something more intelligent to say.

'Don't get me wrong,' he said, 'it isn't easy, telling you all this. When what I really want is to take you up to my room and screw you stupid.'

She was mildly shocked by this; by the sudden sexually explicit language, his lurch into comparative normality.

'Of course we might not be found out. But I think it's likely. People usually do. And of course I'm so incapable of lying, I'd be hopeless at the whole subterfuge thing. And then think of the damage we would have done. And I mean, I'd have to stop working with Patrick. Which would be a tragedy. He's such a brilliant researcher.'

'Is he?' It seemed the only thing to say.

'And then, and this is the most important thing of all, neither of us really has the time. I mean, that's an important consideration.'

Bianca finally started to laugh. It was really rather funny. Especially the thought that they were both too busy for even some occasional sex. And then she felt ashamed again, thinking she was so often too busy for Patrick, not just for sex, but talking to him, and poor little Milly, and Fergie and Ruby – all of far more importance to her than Saul Finlayson.

'You're right of course,' she said, finally composing herself, 'much too busy.'

'And I mean, how could we deceive a man who is so nice he trusts me and you to be together in New York, encourages it in fact – and Paris come to that. We couldn't, Bianca, could we?'

'No,' she said, 'no we couldn't.'

'Right,' he said, looking rather satisfied, 'that's settled. I just didn't want you to feel I didn't want you. Which I thought – after the other night – you might find a bit – odd.'

'Um, maybe a bit.'

'Well, I'm glad I've explained. And you agree. But it is a terrible shame.'

He glanced at his watch. And then he sat up very straight and said the one thing she would not have expected, not in a hundred thousand years.

'But, you know what? God, I hate that expression – I caught it from Dickon. It's still only one o'clock. We have a whole afternoon ahead of us.'

'Ye-es?' Now what was coming?

'And we've talked this through, and we know how impossible an affair would be.'

'Ye-es.'

He was smiling now, and he reached across the table and took her hand. 'Don't look so alarmed, I'm trying to be romantic.'

'But we've just agreed there is no room in our life for romance. With each other anyway.'

'There isn't. Not really. But suddenly there is. Three hours until you meet your agent, and until my car arrives to take me to the airport . . .'

'Ye-es?'

'We could have a first and last time, a hello and goodbye. That could be . . . nice.'

'Well it could,' she said, carefully, 'and then again it couldn't. And that would be a shame. And all the things you just said are still true. About the risk and hurting people who trust us. With which I totally agree.'

'Yes, I suppose so. But, just this once – and God, I'd like it so much – in fact, I would say we deserved it.'

'Deserved it?'

'Well, yes. For behaving so well.'

'We deserve to behave badly for behaving well? Oh God, this is so ridiculous!'

'No it's not. It's rather reasonable. I—'

'Mr Finlayson . . .' It was the maître d'. He was holding out Saul's phone as if it was a bomb about to go off. 'Mr Finlayson, it's your PA. She said it's desperately important.'

'Desperately?'

'Desperately.'

'Good God,' said Saul, 'she hardly ever says that. It must be the Hong Kong – well, anyway. That is amazing. Excuse me, Bianca, I won't be long . . .'

And he left the restaurant and went into the lobby.

And Bianca stood up, before she could even think any further, and picked up her coat and bag and wound her red scarf round her neck, and half ran out of the restaurant and down the street. And then she heard her name called and she turned, and he was standing on the steps waving her back and she stood there, feeling literally unable to move and with absolutely no idea of what she was going to do.

Chapter 49

'I simply cannot imagine you can feel pleased with this. In fact, I rather hope you don't.' Athina's face was disdainful as Tod finished his presentation of the perfume campaign. 'This perfume is called *Passion*. Well, it was. Somehow it has become *Passionate* which I find far less compelling. I am aware Elizabeth Taylor has one called *Passion*, but I can't believe you can have put up much of a fight to use it now. People are far more familiar with her diamonds.'

'I assure you we did, Lady Farrell. Put up a fight, I mean. But it was no good. And *Passionate* is a very good substitute. In my opinion.'

Tod smiled at her. She looked back at him, her expression stony.

'If you really think that, then you shouldn't be in advertising. But we can discuss the name further later on. The point is, the perfume has a superb story behind it, a beautiful bottle which I found in our archives, a marvellous name – well, we did have a marvellous name – altogether an opportunity for some really superb advertising, and all we have here is a few photographs of a girl with her hair blowing about.'

That was true: Tod had to admit it. And he wasn't that gone on the blowing about himself. What was it with photographers and wind machines?

'Very pretty, I daresay, but conveying nothing whatsoever. Where is so much as a hint of a wonderful, romantic story? Where are the clues that this is something special? Where is the passion indeed? Nowhere. I'm extremely disappointed.'

They were all at the agency; Bianca looking exhausted, Lara, her usual vitality somewhat depleted, and a wan, pale Florence whom Athina had insisted on being present. The only person who appeared to have any energy at all was Athina, and she had it in spades. Dressed in a scarlet shift dress, higher heels even than Lara's, and her green eyes sparkling dangerously, she looked – and arguably was – in charge of the meeting.

It was a politically complex affair. And the important thing, as Bianca had stressed to Tod, was that the online scheme was not even mentioned. 'We cannot afford for her to get even a hint of it.'

Nevertheless, she did feel Athina had a point. Clearly, all the creative endeavour the agency possessed had gone into what was codenamed 'global' and their ideas for the perfume ad were very lacklustre. And lustre was the essential ingredient in every aspect of the new brand, Bianca was fond of saying.

'We need a man in this for a start,' Athina was saying, 'and I don't want to hear that's unfashionable, and we need a sense of time and place. When I presented that perfume at the sales conference, people were on their feet, they were so inspired by it, as you saw for yourselves. I am simply not prepared to present them with this; they'd feel horribly let down.'

Ignoring the 'I' Bianca looked at Tod. 'I do feel Lady Farrell has a point,' she said, and her voice was very firm. 'This ad doesn't say passion or even romance. And while I'm not sure that just putting a man into the mix would particularly improve it, I do think we want a real idea. You saw the reaction to Lady Farrell's presentation at the conference so that's what we want to evoke with this ad. It's got to go on counter cards, as well as in the press and online of course. It needs to be very hard-hitting.'

'Now, I have something to show you,' said Athina, and she produced a large envelope from the Asprey briefcase that had attended half a century of board meetings. 'I would suggest you look at it very carefully.'

Oh, God no, Bianca thought; and, This is asking too much of us, thought Tod; and, God, she can't be doing this, thought Lara – but she was.

'It is only rough, of course but it does at least contain an idea. As does the copyline. Here, you can each have one, I've made several copies . . . Florence, perhaps you would distribute them.'

They all took them obediently, sat looking down at them.

And, Lord, this is really good, thought Bianca; and, Maybe she does have something we can work on, thought Tod; and, God, she understands this business, thought Lara.

And Florence sat watching them, their carefully controlled, polite expressions changing slowly as they studied them and was reminded why, in spite of everything, she admired Athina so intensely, and had continued to work with her for what sometimes seemed an unbearably long time.

She had admired the ad the evening before, of course, when Athina brought them to her house to show her 'and just in case you have any comments or indeed possible input. I would not imagine so, but of course I will consider them.'

Florence had no input to make – her creative talents lay in different areas; but sitting now, observing the switch in the room's mood from tight-lipped tolerance to grudging admiration and indeed, in Lara Clements' case, clear excitement, she felt proud herself to be associated with it.

The visual was crude but compelling: a rough sketch by Athina in black and white, showing a couple standing and staring at one another on either side of a very grand fireplace. The copyline beneath it read *Passion: on and on.* (or *Passion Lasts. Passion Endures.*)

Bianca spoke first, looking almost dazed. 'Lady Farrell,' she said, 'I have to say this is a very good copyline. Very good indeed. Don't you think so, Tod?'

'I – yes, I do.' Tod was looking almost shocked. 'Er – what about you, Jack?'

'Yes,' Jack's voice was almost amused. 'I think it's great.'

'I'm glad you like it. Mrs Clements, you haven't said anything yet. Do you wish to comment?'

'Lady Farrell,' said Lara simply, 'I think it's one of the best copylines for perfume I can ever remember.'

Athina smiled at her graciously. 'How kind. I presume you've all recognised the double entendre. That the perfume itself is exceptionally long-lasting, as of course is the passion conveyed in the photograph. I struggled a little with the visual, wondering how we would best convey the heritage element we are looking for; the fireplace would evoke grandeur and style, of course, but I think what we really want is something unmistakably English, which would mean ideally it would be shot outside. Perhaps a formal Capability Brown garden, or a small classical bridge – I would hope you could manage some suggestions along those lines?'

'I'm sure we could,' said Tod weakly.

'I like the fireplace,' said Lara, 'I think it says it all.'

Lady Farrell looked at her as if she was seeing her for the first time.

'Indeed?' she said, and her voice was almost friendly. 'Well, I'm delighted.'

She addressed the room. 'Mrs Clements, of course, is at the sharp end of marketing cosmetics. She knows there has to be a hard-selling message. She can't afford the luxury of hoping a pretty picture is all that is needed. I could see this making a very good counter card, and I imagine you recognise that, Mrs Clements?'

'I do. And can I just say one thing?'

'Of course.' Athina inclined her head graciously.

'I think it would be marvellous if the ads were shot in black and white. As in your visual. It looks so much more – classy. And moody.'

'Well, I would obviously prefer that myself. How perceptive of you. Mrs Bailey, what do you feel about colour versus black and white?'

'I love black and white,' said Bianca, 'the Eternity ads were shot that way and it didn't do them any harm. Jack, Tod, what do you think?'

'We should shoot it both ways,' said Jack in a clear bid for regaining at least some control. 'You never quite know what you're going to get until you've got it. We can decide when we're looking at the ads themselves.'

'Very well,' said Athina. She was now totally in charge of the meeting. 'So shall we meet again in a week, and see what you have for us? Oh, and do try to find a male model with a little class. Most of them look so extremely common.'

'Of course,' said Tod, 'and this *is* only a starting point, wonderful as it is. I think you can rely on us to produce something very interesting now.'

'I would have hoped so,' said Athina.

'Is that Freddie Alexander?'

'Yes. Yes it is.'

'Hello. My name's Susie Harding. I'm the publicity director of the cosmetic company, the House of Farrell.'

'Oh yes?'

God, she was sick of making this call. She forced herself to do five a day; it had been all right at first, quite exciting just *talking* to people who represented people like Keira Knightley and Carey Mulligan – not that she'd get anyone that famous obviously, whatever she was offering – making her pitch, believing them when they said they'd get back to her. Now, after ten days of it, she could hardly bear to pick up the phone to yet another on her list, and start all over again. But it had to be done, she had to find someone; she'd told Bianca she would and she was going to, or die in the attempt.

Which it was beginning to look as if she would.

'We are relaunching in a really big exciting way this June – timed to coincide with the Jubilee, and we're looking for a young actress to front it. Or some of it. To be our face so to speak. We've got an incredibly exciting campaign planned—'

'I'm sorry, Susie. I think it's unlikely. None of our clients usually does that sort of thing, I will put it to a couple of course, but we find it almost always diminishes them as actors. Of course, I don't know what sort of fee you're looking at.'

'I'm afraid the fee wouldn't be very high at all,' said Susie. She knew she should have said actors, that they all felt being called actresses was demeaning, but it was difficult, because she then had to explain it was a female they were looking for. 'But the publicity would be amazing.'

'I'm sure, but as I said, our clients are actors, not models.' She made the word model akin to prostitute.

'So are Keira Knightley and Kate Winslet,' said Susie. She knew that was silly, but she couldn't help it. This girl was so rude.

'I daresay, but representing Chanel and Lancôme – rather different from – who did you say? Oh yes, Farrell. Certainly not in the same league. But I'll get back to you. Perhaps you could give me a few more details about this campaign. You say it's very exciting. I would need to know in what way . . .'

'I'm afraid I can't give you many details unless you have someone seriously interested,' said Susie. 'It is extremely original and therefore highly confidential.'

'Then I doubt if I shall be able even to interest anyone. You must see that. But I'll do my best.'

Susie thanked her effusively, and put the phone down. She decided she couldn't face another call without a really strong espresso, which meant going out to the coffee shop. Which could be regarded as a waste of time but meant she could carry on addressing her main preoccupation, which was whether or not she should call Jonjo. Or text him, or email him.

That would be less terrifying. A phone put down on you, or worse, not answered, was particularly humiliating. Anyway, she did feel it would be worth risking a bit of humiliation. They might not have been together for more than a few days, she and Jonjo, but it had been so extremely special, unlike anything she had known before, ever. And the sex had been amazing.

Although actually, she did feel his rejection of her had been just a little – harsh, his judgment a trifle swift. He hadn't even allowed her to try to explain. And he hadn't actually seen her with another man, so a lot of it was assumption on his part. Clearly he was seriously damaged both by his own unhappy marriage and that of his parents, and was emotionally very vulnerable – but that made him the special person he was. Very, very special. Worth fighting for.

But somehow, she couldn't quite find the courage to do it. And as time went by, she felt less and less inclined to fight.

So she had been playing the field, going out with anyone who asked her, having fun, going to nice restaurants, bars, clubs – and mostly not enjoying any of it. Occasionally, if someone was really nice, really sexy, she would tell herself she was having a great time, that it was more fun this way, not getting over-involved – but then she would remember those few lovely days, when she and Jonjo had been together, and wonder if she would ever find anyone as special as he was again. It was all so very sad.

Jonjo spent quite a lot of time wondering if he should call Susie. Or text or email her. That would be less scary. Of course she might put the phone down on him, or not answer the emails. But surely she was worth risking quite a lot for? They might not have been together for more than a few days, but it had been so extremely special – exciting, tender, fun. And the sex had been amazing. And perhaps his rejection of her had been a little – harsh. He could have given her the benefit of the doubt, allowed her to try to explain. But the fact remained, she had been on the phone to another bloke, and not just in his apartment, but in his bed for God's sake. If it had been only that, he might have listened to her explanations – but then he had seen her with this bloke, whoever he was, and the very same day as they had woken up together, after a long, wonderful day and night, walking along arm in arm with him, chatting, laughing, kissing him goodnight even.

That would have taken a lot of explaining and he couldn't imagine anything that could have made it acceptable. And as time went by, he felt less and less inclined to fight.

So he didn't call her, didn't text her, just retreated into himself, determined to forget her and the lovely thing he thought they had had. He went out with a few girls, pretty, sexy, good-time girls and occasionally, if one of them was specially pretty and specially sexy, he would tell himself it was much better this way, more fun, not getting involved – but then he would remember that lovely time when he and Susie had been together, just the two of them, exploring, pleasing, enjoying one another, and know that it wasn't better, wasn't anything of the sort, and wonder if he would find someone as special as she was ever again. It was all so very sad.

Mark Rawlins had expected his meeting with the trustees to be short and to the point, possibly unpleasant, but – manageable. In fact it was so shocking in its content, while being perfectly pleasant in its conduct, that he left feeling physically dizzy, and so appalled that he decided the only thing to do was go straight to Mike and Hugh, bypassing Bianca. He could sort out the niceties of breaking the report chain she was so bloody obsessed with later; this was too important, time was not on their side, as it wasn't in any part of this insane venture that he had, against his better judgment, allowed himself to get involved in. And spent quite a lot of time now wishing that he hadn't.

'Look, aren't they nice?'

She showed her mother the pictures on her phone.

'Darling, *really* nice. Beautiful, in fact. You look gorgeous. And so different in each one. Lucy's so clever.'

'She is. She's not quite there yet, she says, and then her grandmother has to approve them.'

'Oh really? Did – did Lucy say anything about me approving them?'

'Yes. She said she thought Lady Farrell would show them to you when she was absolutely satisfied.'

'I shall look forward to that,' said Bianca.

'Anyway, Lucy wants to do some pictures of the make-up being put on, step-by-steps, I think they're called, and possibly a little film as well. And she said – well she's going to ask you herself, of course, but I said I'd talk to you first, about using me as a model. Not for the final pictures, of course, that'll be a proper model, but just about someone trying the looks out. Because she's got this friend who does a beauty blog, quite a famous one, and she said she'd put them in the blog. She said it was a nice story, the relaunch, and she said she knew how important the timing was and everything and what it said about the relaunch.'

'Right.'

'And then she did one on Jayce.'

'And?'

'It was lovely, really lovely. Jayce's face looked much thinner and her eyes much bigger. And of course, Lucy covered up her spots. And, something really exciting: she told Jayce she had an amazing look and if she improved her skin and lost a bit of weight, she could look really great. Jayce was well excited. She said no one had ever taken any notice of what she looked like before, except to tease her, so we're going to work out a diet for her. Lucy chatted to her about what she ate and said if she cut out chips and burgers and doughnuts just for starters, her skin would improve as well as her figure. I mean, I've often thought that, but of course *I* couldn't say it, she'd be upset, but coming from Lucy . . .'

'Of course. And – and how was school today?'

'Not too bad. They just ignore me now, no one speaks to me, but they've stopped sending me horrible texts and stuff.'

'That's a start. Oh, Milly, you've been so brave. Much braver than I could ever be. I really, really admire you.'

'Thanks,' said Milly, and smiled rather uncertainly at her mother.

She'd been a bit odd ever since she'd come back from her world tour, as she called it. Kind of over-excited, and whenever her father was around she talked a lot more than usual. And she was always rushing round the house, doing things, and she'd started doing ridiculous extra classes like kick boxing at the gym. Bit weird, because she had more than enough to do, really. Anyway, it was good she liked Lucy's faces as she called them and seemed happy about the blog. Milly had been afraid she'd say no and start worrying about paedophiles or whatever. Parents were so obsessed with all that stuff . . .

'Lucy, I need to talk to you. Quite urgently. Can you come in tomorrow?'

This had to be serious, Lucy thought, for Bianca Bailey to demand – for that was what it amounted to – to see her at twenty-four hours' notice.

'Of course,' she said. 'I'm free all day. Recovering from London Fashion Week,' she added, lest Bianca might think she was out of work or – worse in Bianca's book she was sure, plain old-fashioned idle. And you did need to recover from it; her two days had left her so shattered, so drained, so over-excited that she hadn't gone to sleep until five in the morning. The sheer effort of keeping calm in all that chaos was utterly exhausting. Her head still ached, almost a week later.

And she had never been so frightened either: the vast backstage area, filled with models – of course – but designers and PRs and other make-up artists, and hairdressers, all milling about, eyeing one another up. There was huge competition between the hairdressers and the make-up artists, and no love lost between them; each considering their job the more important. And they took up so much space with their dryers and curlers and tongs; and quite often an assistant too, and it was enraging when quite often all they seemed to be doing was a scraggy ponytail. Then there were the racks and racks of clothes, with the models' names on them, and carefully stacked shoes – and it was all actually as ordered as a military operation, disguised as chaos. She really felt she had no place there at all, almost bolted.

What she had to do, she knew, was find a model. It was as random as that. Not one of the really big names, that was all done and dusted, but one of the others; some were already stars, or nearly, and had a look that was different, that had caught on; the make-up girls practically fought over them. The models were exhausted, had been hustled around from location to location, show to show; the young ones were bewildered, some of them hardly able to speak English, and Lucy made for a very young one, who was lovely but so far unspoken for; she appeared near to tears.

'Hi,' she said, 'I'm Lucy, and I'm going to do your make-up. That OK?'

The girl nodded feebly.

'Would you like to go to the toilet before I start?'

Another nod, this time a grateful smile as well. Very few people thought of that, apparently, they'd been told at FaceIt. It was almost barbaric. And the end result was tantrums and a lack of cooperation, all for want of a little thoughtfulness.

Sometimes there was a demo by the head make-up artist, of the look that was wanted, but not that morning; there was a face chart, that was all. She would just have to busk it. She studied the chart; it wasn't the natural look, that was for sure, orange eyeshadow, absurd green eyelashes, painted on to the skin, white lipstick – not easy, she thought, praying the girl wouldn't have any make-up on, that her skin would be cool. A hairdresser arrived, his assistant (damn) set down his enormous bag and the girl came back, smiled gratefully again at Lucy, and accepted the bottle of water she gave her. The hairdresser started yanking her head about as he brushed her hair through.

'I can't work while you do that,' said Lucy.

'Has to be done, darling.'

They struck a deal; he could get the rollers in, then Lucy could have the girl to herself.

'But we haven't got long,' he said, 'really up against it.'

He was back in five minutes, claiming it was ten; Lucy struggled with the eyeshadow as he pulled rollers out, then had to order him off when one of the painted eyelashes smudged and he had a tantrum, complained to the dresser.

And then it was done and the dresser claimed the girl, and they disappeared into the throng and Lucy grabbed the next make-up chart and it all started again. No wonder she was exhausted.

'Well, how about twelve thirty?' Bianca was saying now. 'I've got a lunch, but a late one, so that'll give us half an hour. Which is all we need I think.'

Oh God. Was she going to tell her she didn't want her working for Farrell's any more? Or – and this would be as bad in a way – did she want the sessions with Milly to stop?

At twelve thirty precisely, Jemima called her up from reception.

'Go in,' she said. 'Don't look so frightened.'

Lucy went in.

Bianca smiled at her, briefly, then said, 'I'm very worried about this business with Milly, Lucy. It's not the make-up sessions;

Milly loves them and it's clearly making her feel altogether better. No, I'm worried about your friend the blogger and what she might write. I don't need to tell you how powerful these things are. I appreciate it would be marvellous publicity, but Milly is only thirteen, and hardly representative of Farrell's customers; or rather, the Farrell customer we want to attract. Had you considered that?'

'Honestly, no,' Lucy said, 'but I can see your point. Well – we don't have to do the blog. I can just tell her we don't want to.'

'That seems a shame. I hate to seem ungrateful. And of course Milly will be very disappointed. But . . .'

'It's a shame all round,' said Lucy, and she felt very sad suddenly: more for Milly than herself. 'But yes, obviously getting the image of the brand across is vital, I do understand. But I tell you what we could do: turn it into a sort of feature story. Fay Banks will do whatever we want – it's a bit of a scoop for her anyway. We can play the Farrell card, and me being Lady Farrell's granddaughter, and say something along the lines of how I kept running out of models and Milly and Jayce said they'd like to do it if it would help, and even though they are much too young, they've still got faces, something like that. That way we could still plug the Farrell name, get some nice publicity, and not disappoint Milly. What do you think?'

'I think,' said Bianca, smiling at her, 'that's a genius idea, Lucy. Really clever. Thank you. Thank you so much. Now I must go.'

'Me too. I'm having lunch with Grandy – she wants to know about London Fashion Week.'

She was very different from her grandmother, Bianca thought; very very different. Of course, she was also Bertie's daughter . . .

Athina greeted Lucy effusively.

'Lovely to see you, darling. You look marvellous. I like your hair. It makes your face look thinner.'

'Thank you, Grandy. I wasn't aware it was fat.'

'Not fat exactly, darling, just rather plump!'

* * *

Lara had had two dates now with the conference organiser whose name was Chris Williams. There was much to be said for him. He was good-looking, a natty dresser, prided himself on being a man about town and had taken her to the rather smart One Aldwych and on the next date Sheekeys, which she had told him she had always wanted to go to; his remembering this had made it even better. He was very generous, was fun and funny and always admired what she was wearing and told her it suited her. And although he had kissed her on the second date there had been no suggestion that he might be asking anything more significant any time soon.

He was forty-five, divorced, but amicably so, and had two teenage children with whom he seemed to get along very well. He was altogether, as she remarked to Susie, too good to be true. But he had one great failing, which she didn't remark upon to anyone: he wasn't Bertie. Who might as well have decamped to Birmingham already for all the contact between them, and she missed him dreadfully; his fondness for chatting, his self-effacement. She still felt proud of giving him just a little more self-confidence, of improving his sartorial taste, and encouraging him on his diet. His resemblance to his absurdly handsome father was increasingly remarked upon. She was actually almost looking forward to his leaving; once he had gone, she could cut any remaining emotional ties easily. Or so she told herself as she stood at the mirror in the ladies', putting on fresh make-up, smoothing her newly highlighted hair, checking her manicured nails, in readiness for her third date with Chris Williams. And wishing she felt more excited about it.

'Mrs Clements, good evening.' It was Athina. She smiled at Lara, a rather distant smile to be sure, but still an improvement on the frozen expression with which she usually greeted her.

'Good evening, Lady Farrell.'

Athina's eyes swept across the array of make-up on the shelf in front of Lara.

'I hope you will forgive me, but I wonder why you are using that perfume, when it should be *Passionate*. We should all wear it at all times and get people's reaction to it. Not that I would dream of altering so much as a note, but it would still be interesting.'

'Indeed, Lady Farrell, and I was wearing it regularly but my supply has run out and the lab won't let me have any more.'

'Really? How odd. I shall speak to them. Mrs Bailey's officious systems are to blame, no doubt. One seems to have to fill in a form in triplicate to get so much as a packet of envelopes from the stationery cupboard these days.'

This was grotesquely unfair, as Bianca kept any kind of regulation to a minimum, but Lara knew better than to argue with Athina.

'Now, when you did wear it, did people admire it?'

'Oh yes. Very much so.'

'Men?'

'I'm sorry?'

'Did men admire it? That's what we want. Given its name.'

'Oh – yes. Yes, I think so.'

'I would hope. Now, do you have a date this evening? With a man? You rather look as if you do.'

'Well – yes.' God, she was outrageous.

'And what does he do? We really aren't interested in the wrong sort of opinion. Is he a professional person?'

'I think you could say that,' said Lara, taking a deep breath. 'He runs conferences. He ran ours, as a matter of fact.'

'Oh, really? They were a slightly motley bunch I thought, but they did the job very efficiently. Clearly he knows what he's doing. Now I shall go and get one of my bottles of *Passionate*, so that you can wear it. I was very pleased, incidentally, at that disgraceful presentation from the advertising people the other day, that you admired my own advertisement. Thank you. We should liaise regularly on that. I welcome your input and they are already late with any further kind of presentation. Do feel free to telephone or, indeed, visit my office at any time. It's so agreeable to find a modern young woman with a modicum of taste.'

Lara thought she might faint.

'Clever woman, Mrs Clements,' said Athina, putting her head round Bertie's office after delivering a small phial of *Passionate* to Lara. 'A little tarty of course and that accent is not attractive, but she certainly knows her job and rather surprisingly has taste.'

'I'm glad you think so,' said Bertie wearily, 'and I'm sure she'd be very pleased to hear that. Although perhaps not the bit about her accent.'

'Well, she can't help that, I suppose. Although elocution lessons might be a good idea. Perhaps you could suggest them.'

'I shall do no such thing,' said Bertie, 'and I would advise you not to either.'

'Oh, nonsense. I would express my views very tactfully. Now, I hear from Christine that they have found a replacement for you. That didn't take long. Well, it's hardly a difficult post to fill. When – when might you be leaving?' A sharp ear might have discerned a tremor in her voice.

'Oh, in four weeks' time. The new chap can join almost immediately.'

'Really? Not really an accolade that, I would say. That his firm are so happy to release him.'

Bertie said nothing, There seemed little point.

'And have you found somewhere to live up there?'

'A very nice house with a big garden. That's the attraction, of course. The house is really too big for me but I hope Lucy and Rob will be visiting frequently.'

'I hope so too, but it's a long way to travel.'

'Not really. It's two hours on the train.'

'Yes, but rail fares are exorbitant these days. I wouldn't bank on that, Bertie. Anyway, Mrs Clements is going out on a date, with the young man who organised our conference. I've given her some *Passionate* to test on him.'

'Really?'

'Yes. She's clearly out to impress him, rather too much make-up to my mind, but there it is.'

Bertie felt as if he was having his teeth pulled, one by one. It was agonising.

'Mother, you must excuse me,' he said, standing up. 'I too have a date. With my daughter. She's taking me out to supper.'

'How very kind. Well, do give her my love and enjoy your

evening, Bertie. You won't be seeing nearly so much of her in future.'

Bertie said he was sure he would, and left, trying not to think about Lara and how her wretched boyfriend would react to *Passionate*. Badly, he hoped.

'Oh my God, that is incredible. So exciting. God. It's amazing!'

'It's not quite done, of course. But glad you like it.'

'I do. I really really do. Well, I more than like it. I love it! It's the site to end all sites. Or it's about to be. It looks totally wonderful!' She looked back at the screen and smiled joyfully. 'It's so alive and so inviting and it makes you feel good, just looking at it.'

'Well, this bit was Jack's idea.'

'Where is he?'

'Refused to come in to see you, the bastard.'

'Why?'

'Oh, something totally unimportant. His wife's having a baby.'

'What – now?'

'Yes. This morning, I hope, so he'll at least be here this afternoon. She insists on him being there, apparently, and he's agreed. Now how unprofessional is that?'

'I hope you're joking!'

'No.' His expression was innocently puzzled. 'Of course not. I said to him where's your sense of proportion, Bianca's coming in and he said – well I won't even tell you what he said. No, of course I'm joking, don't look at me like that! Anyway, this is his idea, and I love it. For launch moment, we thought why not have a little shot of each of the managers actually opening their doors. I mean in real time, not recorded. And saying welcome to the House of Farrell in whatever language it was.'

'Can we do that?'

'Bianca, I keep telling you, what you can do with technology now is only limited by your own imagination. Almost anything is possible. This is easy. I've checked it out with the geeks. We can film it beforehand anyway, that'd be easiest. And then, at the moment when God says "Let there be shops", there they'll be.'

'You mean Florence could be in the arcade, opening the door?'

'She could and she will. And so will whoever is in New York, and Sydney and—'

'Oh my God,' she said, staring at him, 'you two are such geniuses.'

'Nah . . .'

'You are, you are.'

'Well – all right, maybe we are. But it was your idea first off, don't forget.'

Bianca laughed. 'I won't, don't worry. But I do think that's wonderful. Now I must dash, I've got to go and see Mike and Hugh. You wait till I tell them about this! And let me know about the baby and give Jack my love.'

'Oh, is that Susie Harding? Susie, this is Freddie Alexander. We talked the other day about your relaunch campaign. Well, we do represent a young actor who wants to meet you and discuss it.'

'Oh!' said Susie. She was so astonished that was all she could manage.

'Her name is Jess Cochrane. You'll know her, of course. She starred in *A Little Bit Married*. Very successful. She got an *Evening Standard* nomination for it.'

'Yes,' said Susie. 'Yes it was amazing. *She* was amazing.' This couldn't be true. Jess Cochrane who had been *the* young actress of 2011, her lovely face everywhere: and who had since then hardly been seen.

'Yes, indeed. She starts shooting a new film in the autumn, but as it happens, just at the moment she had a window.'

'Yes. Yes, I see.' Resting in other words.

'Of course she would need to be persuaded that the campaign would be right for her. You were reluctant to tell me anything about it last time we talked.'

'Yes, well it's very confidential,' said Susie.

'So you said. Anyway, I suggest you meet and you can do a presentation, so to speak. Would lunch tomorrow be any good? Obviously I shall come too.'

Susie would have cancelled lunch with the Duchess of Cambridge to meet Jess Cochrane.

'Absolutely. Yes.'

'Good. Jess likes Le Caprice. Shall we say twelve thirty?'

'Certainly. I look forward to meeting you both. And the small fee? That's not a problem?'

Freddie Alexander, clearly deeply uncomfortable with what she had been told to say, said, 'Providing Jess is happy with the concept, and the exposure, then she is not too concerned about the size of the fee.'

'I'm really sorry, Mark.'

Why did lawyers always say they were sorry when they so patently weren't? And with that faint, slightly condescending smile. It must be a compulsory part of their training.

'I've had the team go through this over and over again. There is nothing you can do. Except cough up. Or clear out. Which is it to be?'

'Not up to me, thank God. I'll see what the VCs say and get back to you.'

'OK. Don't leave it too long though. Every day makes it worse.'

Chapter 50

So he was dying. And she was not able, of course, to be with him. He had had a heart attack, suddenly, swiftly, without warning. It could have come any time, the doctors said; a lifetime of smoking and drinking had weakened the heart and clogged up the arteries, so that when the attack did come, it was brutal.

And how merciful, they said, that he had been at home, rather than driving, or on a train, had been sitting at the dining table, extolling the virtues of the Époisses cheese he was eating, opening the second bottle of red wine he said it deserved. And that Athina had been with him, and could summon the ambulance, get him to hospital without delay.

And how merciful, Florence thought, that he had not been with her, in her home or, God forbid, in her bed; that it had not been her who had had to summon the ambulance, get him to hospital without delay: and then had to call Athina, explain why and where she had been with him.

She hadn't even known about the heart attack for thirty-six hours; Athina had seen no need to inform her until the diagnosis had been made and active treatment declared pointless. She was not, after all, a relative, not entitled, as were his children and grand-children, clustering round his bed; a mere friend and colleague, whose presence would have been superfluous.

Not for her the consolation of being there for the last hours, the comfort of the last words, of the last I love you, the relief of seeing the suffering ended. Not for her the last embrace, the last kiss, the last look. That was not her territory, not where she had any right to be.

It had been Bertie, kind, gentle Bertie who had rung her at home and told her what had happened, who asked her if she was all right for, try to disguise it as she might, she was audibly shocked and distressed.

'Yes, yes,' she said, 'I'm all right. Don't worry about me, Bertie, really. It is a shock of course, we have been close for so many years –' adding hastily 'all of us', aware even in her stunned grief that she must watch every word, every reaction.

'Of course.'

'I'm so sorry, Bertie. How is – how is your mother?'

'She's fine,' he said. 'She has told the doctors that she wants him home; they said it was unwise, the care would be better where he was, but she faced them down. Unless he has a second attack before then, which would anyway be . . . be fatal, he'll go home tomorrow morning.'

'Good, I'm glad. He'll feel happier there. Which is important.'

'My mother said,' he added, humour briefly in his voice, 'that no husband of hers was going to die in a hospital bed and certainly not a hospital gown.'

She had had a brief conversation with Athina when she herself phoned with the news, and had said she would like to come and see Cornelius if he was well enough.

'But you must be the judge of that.'

'I will be, Florence. He is extremely ill; there is no question of his recovering. He is scarcely lucid much of the time and I cannot imagine any purpose could be served by your seeing him.'

'I would like to – to say goodbye,' said Florence staunchly. 'We have been friends for a long time.'

'Yes, yes, I can see that, but as I say, he is hardly conscious. And if all his life-long friends came to see him, there would be a queue round the block. He finds any visitors very tiring, even the children. And I have always considered these lingering farewells so sentimental, and really rather unnecessary.'

'Yes, I see.' Desperation drove her on. 'Even so—'

'Florence, please! When and if Cornelius asks to see you, then I will let you know. He wanted to see Lawrence Trentham, I can't imagine why – I had a lot of trouble getting hold of him.'

Jealousy hit Florence with appalling violence. Lawrence Trentham! How could Cornelius have asked for him, wasting his failing strength, his dwindling hours, when he could have seen her? She felt sick and dizzy; it was hard to speak.

'Well – he, like me, is a very old friend,' she managed, in a last feeble bid.

'I suppose so. I must go, Florence, I have a great deal to do. The nurse I've hired treats me rather like a skivvy, demanding this, that and the other non-stop.'

Good for the nurse, Florence thought, putting the phone down. No one else had ever accomplished such a thing.

All she could do was think about him. Was he thinking about her? Probably not. He was too ill. She felt disconnected from reality, could think only of Cornelius and the lifetime of joy and sorrow they had shared, saw the love she had shared with him slipping away from her exactly as he was, its ending unmarked, unacknowledged.

She was dozing in front of the television when the call came; it was six in the evening. Athina's voice was peremptory.

'You'd better come. He's asking for you.'

She arrived at the Knightsbridge flat oddly calm. She had talked herself into this state of mind on the journey, knowing that an excess of emotion, any emotion, would enrage Athina, who opened the door looking tired and drawn but immaculate in a white dress and jacket, her hair freshly done, her make-up flawless.

'Do come in,' she said. 'I will take you in to him. He is very tired and so you mustn't stay long.'

'No, no of course not.'

She felt frightened suddenly, of what she might see, of a Cornelius so changed it would have been better to have left him safe in her memory, handsome, laughing, charming.

'Miss Hamilton has come to visit my husband,' said Athina to the nurse, opening the door into the marital bedroom, with its overlarge bed and heavy furniture, transformed horribly into a sickroom by its accessories lying on a table by the bed, a stethoscope, thermometer, blood pressure gauge, oxygen cylinder and mask, and, Florence noticed, quickly averting her gaze, something that looked horribly like a bedpan.

The nurse, fully uniformed and starch-faced, looked suspiciously at Florence.

'He is very ill,' she said severely, 'please don't tire him.'

Florence wondered wildly what she expected she might do: demand he tell jokes, or dance, perhaps?

'I have already explained that to Miss Hamilton,' said Athina. 'She is a very old friend of ours.'

'Very well. But his pulse is very weak. I—'

'Nurse Billings,' said Athina, 'please leave us.'

The nurse left the room. And Florence turned her gaze on Cornelius, on her love, the love of her life, about to leave her for ever.

In some ways he did not look so very different. He had not been ill for long enough to have lost much weight; he was still a large, solid shape in the bed, full-faced, his white hair thick and strong. But in others he had changed; his skin had a sallow, almost dingy look, his eyes were dull, the hands that lay outside the bed covers veined and limp. His breathing was laboured and loud, his voice soft and hoarse. But he still managed to smile, to reach for her hand, to take it briefly, to turn his head to her.

'Florence,' he said. 'How kind of you to come.'

'Not – not at all,' she said, and then, in an effort to lighten the conversation, 'How kind of you to invite me.'

He smiled; slowly, almost, as if it hurt him.

'Do sit down,' he said, indicating a chair at the side of the bed. Florence sat. 'How are you?'

'Oh – very well. Yes, thank you. And you – how do you feel?'

'Tired,' he said, 'that's all. Can't sleep very well.'

'That's nonsense, Cornelius,' said Athina, 'you slept for twelve hours last night.'

'Did I? I don't remember.'

'I assure you, you did,' said Athina. 'I envied you. I am finding it very hard to sleep.' She said this almost reproachfully, as if it was Cornelius's fault. 'I have had to move to the guest room,' she said to Florence, 'for the time being.' This seemed tactless, even coming from her. 'The bed in there is far less comfortable.'

'I'm so sorry,' said Cornelius, with a flash of his old mischief, 'perhaps we should swap.'

'Oh, don't be ridiculous!' said Athina. She had taken up a position on the other side of the bed from Florence and sat ramrod straight, her eyes fixed on Cornelius. It was oddly touching, Florence thought, the first sign of the grief that she must be experiencing.

There was a silence; Cornelius's eyes closed. Then with a great effort he said, 'Athina, could I have a cup of tea? And I'm sure Florence would like one.'

'Yes, of course. I'll ask the nurse.'

'Oh, please don't. I don't want her and her peevish face back in here. And she makes disgusting tea. Could you possibly make it yourself?'

'Oh, all right,' Athina said, getting up reluctantly. As she reached the door, a phone started to ring.

'Bloody thing, never stops,' said Cornelius, 'and she will insist on answering it. Never mind, gives us a bit more time. Shut the door, Florence, for goodness' sake.'

Florence looked at him, startled; and saw a sparkle in the faded blue eyes, a half smile on the pale lips.

'It's so good to see you,' he said, 'you look lovely. I always liked that dress.'

'I know,' Florence said, 'that's why I wore it.' And she smiled back at him, and leaned over and kissed him on the cheek.

'That's my girl. Now listen, we don't have very long. Athina's a bit suspicious, I think. I asked Leonard Trentham as a sort of false trail. So it wasn't just you I wanted to see. But there are a few things I need to say. Hold my hand, would you? I'm a bit scared, to be honest. Unlike Peter Pan, I don't see dying as an awfully big adventure. I'd rather go on doing some dull living.'

'Hardly dull, Cornelius.'

'Well, maybe not. Anyway, first of all, you are to make sure you use my gift to you. I don't want any sacrifices with you living in penury.'

'That's all very well, Cornelius, but it would cause such problems. Such trouble. Hurt Athina so much.'

'Oh, nonsense. Think of all the lies we've both told, and so successfully. This is just one more.'

'Bit more complex than the others.'

'You'll manage. Oh – oh God!'

He winced and held his chest. She looked at him, frightened suddenly.

'Does it hurt?'

'Not so much now.' The husky voice was strained, weaker. 'It did. Christ, it was like being kicked in the chest by a very large horse. They're giving me something for it now. So – you promise? You know what to do? Those lawyers I found – they'll sort it out for you.'

'Yes,' she said, afraid of his becoming agitated. 'Yes, I promise.'

'Good. Now – a few more things.'

'Yes?'

'Well, the most important of all is this. I love you, Florence. I've loved you all these years and I always will. I shall sit down there, up there if I'm lucky, loving you.' He smiled at her, raised her hand to his lips. 'My beloved. My beloved Little Flo . . .'

Florence closed her eyes briefly; it was all she could do not to cry out, so intense, so violent was her pain. But then she heard her voice, level and gentle, and she smiled at him and said, 'Thank you for all those years, Cornelius. I love you too. So much. So very much. It's been lovely. Happy and lovely. Enough to keep me happy even now, even without you.'

That, at least, she could give him, she thought. Not just her love, but courage and a sense of joy. Nothing else would be appropriate; nothing else would do.

'Good. I'm glad.' He smiled at her, lay back on his pillows. 'You look so – so beautiful, Florence. What a picture to take with me to eternity. How lucky I am. How lucky I have been . . . Oh, Jesus!'

His face distorted again. 'This isn't – isn't too good. I feel awfully cold suddenly. And a bit sick . . . maybe you'd better get that chilly creature in. Oh Christ!'

She stood up, alarmed and he reached for her hand, pulled her near to him again.

'If – if this is it – goodbye, dearest Little Flo. Thank you . . .' The husky voice was growing more laboured. 'Jesus . . .'

She looked at him, terrified, then ran to the door.

'Athina! Nurse! Come quickly!'

He died two hours later; again, Bertie called her to tell her.

'I heard you were here, when he had the second one, and I knew you'd want to know. It was – it was very peaceful in the end.'

'Good. I'm glad.'

And she was. And she had, almost, been there.

She sat for hours that evening, completely unaware of time passing, not even grieving yet, but thinking, remembering, reliving. Fifty years had separated the first kiss, in the taxi, after the heady flirtation in the bar at The Ritz, and what she now knew had been the last that day, and the time between, the lovely, loving times came swiftly back to her, making her smile, keeping faith with him. Their first night together in Paris, in the small, charming *pension* and the dinner at Brasserie Lipp that had made it so inevitable; their apartment, on the edge of Passy, and whole weekends spent there in bed; shopping at Chanel, Cornelius lavishly generous, the glorious days in Grasse, dining at the Colombe d'Or, and Cornelius's promise to her; long, gloriously dangerous afternoons in her parlour in the Berkeley Arcade. She set aside the other, less happy memories, the lonely days and weeks without him, the baby, her romance with Timothy Benning, allowed herself the great, albeit guilty, savouring of her raised profile at the company, her elevation to the board, while Athina fumed; reliving all the fun, the excitement, the sheer delight in so many ways that he had brought her: Cornelius, her love, her great, true love.

She remembered every Cornelius that night, not just the charming, brilliant, generous Cornelius, risking everything so that they might spend an evening or a day together, sitting smiling at her across a room or a table, or a bed, telling her how lovely she was and how much he loved her, but the frequently irritable, sometimes pompous, occasionally morose Cornelius, railing against business, marital and even extra-marital problems, managing at the most extreme of these moods to blame her for many of them.

And through them all, all the memories, she knew she had been more lucky than many many women, who had been married to men they did not really love, or even like, mean men, dull men, impotent men. The man she had shared her life with, and certainly the very best of her life, had made it richer, more exciting, more full of joy. She had felt loved and valued and enjoyed; that had been his gift to her, and no one could take it away; and now, even as grief began to move in on her, cold and dreadful, she knew she would not have changed a moment of any of it.

Chapter 51

It turned out to be a match made in heaven, Jess Cochrane and Farrell's. Susie could see it would be from the moment she was shown to their table, just from the clothes she was wearing, not some flashy dress, but jeans, a pale pink crêpe shirt with huge sleeves, and high-heeled boots. She had a mass of blond hair, falling straight over her shoulders, what had once been called a rosebud mouth, that curved into large dimples when she smiled, and enormous green eyes, with extraordinarily long eyelashes which were, astonishingly, real.

She must have been aware, Susie thought, that the entire restaurant was staring at her, pointing her out, but the first thing she said, in the most unluvvie-like way, was, 'Hi Susie. I'm Jess,' as if Susie might not have known. And then, as she sat down, she said, 'I am just so, so excited to meet you and hear about this.'

So as well as being seriously beautiful, she was nice. That was probably the most important thing after the beauty. Freddie Alexander, on the other hand, overglossed, dressed almost entirely in black, with only a massive gold necklace dangling into her cleavage, was clearly not nice. And then Jess was hugely intelligent, and up for anything and full of ideas. Maybe that was *the* most important thing.

In fact, without her idea, Susie had to admit, the whole campaign would have been a lot less exciting.

Talking her into the campaign had been a breeze; she jumped at it.

'I love it,' she said, to Freddie Alexander's clear disapproval, before they had even ordered, 'love, love, love it. It's perfect. I'd adore to do it.'

'Jess,' said Freddie Alexander, with a venomous glance at Susie, 'surely we need to discuss it, you need to think about it a bit more—'

'I don't want to discuss it and I don't need to think about it. I love it.'

Susie felt she was falling in love with her herself.

Two days later, she came into the office to meet Bianca.

'Hi,' she said, 'lovely to meet you. I hope Susie's told you how thrilled I am about this?'

'She certainly has,' said Bianca, 'and I can tell you I'm as thrilled.'

'It's going to be really, really fun. And I just love the thought of being projected on to the front of your building, it's so cool. But . . .' She looked at them and smiled her ravishing dimpled smile, 'I had an idea. I think it would be even more wonderful.'

'Yes?'

'Well, I wondered about a competition? Guessing whose face it was, building up, day by day. And then revealing it at your launch. How about that? Of course if you don't like it . . .'

Susie and Bianca looked at each other and spoke in unison: 'We like it.'

'And then I thought, but it would have to be shot in profile, and maybe a bit of the rest of me as well, so it wasn't immediately obvious, and I don't know how you'd feel about that?'

Susie and Bianca felt pretty good.

It was all too good to be true.

And so it was all beginning to happen. Fragments of Jess's lovely face, shot in profile, as she had suggested, her back turned to camera, dressed in a long, sequinned sheath dress, her hair draped simply over her shoulder, the fragments slowly forming the image as the clock ticked away the seconds; the message on the website and in the press and innumerable tweets that something beautiful was going to happen at the House of Farrell; and telling them also, that if they cared to go along to the House of Farrell and look at its frontage, they would see it slowly come alive; a press release and leaflets on all the Farrell counters (and, of course, the website) announced the competition and that the lucky winner would be invited to the launch of the new Farrell's and meet the owner of the face; and Susie called all her favourite journos and bloggers, telling them they should go along and look at the clock. 'And this is only the first part of our incredibly exciting launch, for Farrell's is being reborn, so don't write it off as a brand of the past' and tweeted endlessly day after day saying 'Have you seen the Farrell clock yet?' or 'Are you entering our amazing competition?'

Dozens of builders and shopfitters were working on the shops all over the world; The Collection itself, large numbers of it, was formulated and packaged and looking wonderfully classy, waiting in the warehouse; space was booked in the July issues of the major glossies . . . God it was amazing, Bianca thought, as she walked briskly down Holborn to her meeting that sunny March morning, all that agonising and misery, all that stress and exhaustion, all so so worth it. It was going to be all right, she knew, it was, it was . . .

'Hi,' she said, grinning happily at Mike and Hugh, who were waiting for her in Mike's office, 'I can't tell you how well it's all . . . is something the matter?' she asked, the joy and confidence draining out of her, slowly taking in that Mike's face was extremely grim and so was Hugh's.

'Sorry, Bianca,' Mike said, 'but I'm afraid it is. We've just had some rather bad news . . .'

Two million, the landlords had said. Upfront, if they wanted to renew the lease. The lawyers had been through it all with them and were unable to help.

'Well – well that's terrible. They've got us over a barrel, I can see that. But what choice do we have?'

'Er – not to pay?'

'But we have to, surely. Otherwise they'll sue.' She looked from one to the other of them, smiled uncertainly. They didn't return the smile.

'Yes, of course they will,' said Mike.

'Absolutely right,' said Hugh.

'So – look, I don't understand. Where's the dilemma? We have to find the money.'

'Well perhaps you'd like to do that,' said Hugh, and his voice was very hard, 'because it's not coming from us.'

'What? But – I don't understand. Is there an alternative?'

'There is, I'm afraid, and it's the one we have to go for,' said Mike. 'We have to get out of the arcade fast. There's no question of finding another two million, Bianca, I'm sorry.'

'But we can't stop now! It's unthinkable. It's crazy. What about the global campaign, what about the ticking clock, that's already started? People are talking about it!'

'It will have to stop or change. We cannot find another two million pounds, Bianca. *That's* what's unthinkable.'

She stared at them. 'I just don't believe this. You can't do this, not now.'

'I'm afraid we have to. Look, we've already put in two extra million. Over and above the original money. We've listened to you and been persuaded by you many times. But we can't do any more. The brand is haemorrhaging money. Every day it costs more and sales are down to virtually nothing.'

'But we've hardly begun. The campaign is only just starting. You know how revolutionary the idea is, you know the excitement it will create . . .'

'And it will cost us two million pounds. That's two million off any potential profits, don't forget. It's not going to be cancelled out just because the launch is successful. It's money gone for ever. I'm sorry, Bianca, but that's our last word. No more money.'

There was only one person she wanted to talk to, who might be able to help; and he was the only person totally out of reach. Contact between them was ended: absolutely and unarguably. It would be dangerous beyond anything. They had made a pledge, that day in New York, that extraordinary afternoon, and it could never be broken.

For of course, she had gone back down the street to Saul, and followed him into the hotel – there was no question of doing otherwise. Had she not turned, had she not seen him calling to her, then perhaps there might have been; but she had and a bright, brilliant certainty possessed her and she knew not just what she would, but what she must do. He had not taken her hand, lover-like, or even kissed her, as she reached him, and she didn't even expect it; she was getting to know him a little at least.

And as she had known it would be, it was quite extraordinary; not merely sex, not merely a fusing of her body with his, of his mouth on hers, her skin with his, a fervent concentration within her, seeking, asking, and then finding, not merely a progression, a mounting of pleasure, not merely an explosion of violent release, but of absolute physical joy and at the end of it, perfect peace and a sweet tangled confusion.

And there were other things too: a sense of timelessness, of removal from reality, a freedom from time and place. And astonishingly, she felt no guilt. And even more astonishingly she didn't cry . . .

But she did cry then, that dreadful morning, in the taxi travelling back to Farrell House; and could never remember feeling so alone: and so helpless.

And Patrick Bailey, at the same time, hurt and angry beyond anything, and with insidious demons whispering of infidelity and circumvention ever louder in his ear, looked back in wonder at the happiness that he had known less than a year ago and wondered if it was even remotely possible that he could return to it.

Lucy too could never remember ever being so miserable. And this was miserable misery. Hopeless, aching, unsolvable misery.

Her father had called to invite her to dinner; she had actually had something else on, but she cancelled it. He wasn't going to be around to take her to dinner much longer.

He told her about the house he'd found in Birmingham, and how it was big enough for her to visit and he hoped she would often and bring her friends.

She said she would, of course, and thanked him, but she knew it wouldn't be very often, it couldn't possibly be, and hated to think of him all alone in a clearly much too big house.

'I'll miss you so much,' she said.

'Oh, nonsense. That career of yours is taking off, you won't have time to miss your old dad.'

'You don't need time to miss people,' she said rather sadly and was surprised when he went quiet and looked out of the window and said he knew that.

'So – when are you leaving Farrell's?' she said, more to break the silence than because she wanted to know.

She had actually tried not to think about it. Always, all her life, he had been at Farrell's; every single thing in her life was changing, along with his. The Esher house had been sold; her mother had bought a flat, not in the Barbican, which she couldn't afford, but a house in Fulham which she almost couldn't either. Lucy was to live with her for a few weeks, while she found somewhere of her own. She couldn't even contemplate living with her permanently; she had become increasingly unpleasant, angry with Bertie, at odds with everyone else in the family, furious with Lucy for not wanting to share her new, tiny house. As if, Lucy thought, looking at her sour face. She had also quarrelled with Athina who seemed now to blame her for the break-up, and therefore for Bertie having to leave Farrell's, and with Caro, who seemed to hold the same view.

'And the job?' she asked him. 'That still looking good?'

'Yes, pretty good. They are extraordinarily nice people. It might seem rather quiet after Farrell's, but that could be considered a positive.'

'And how do you feel about moving somewhere so totally different?'

'Oh, fine. I'm not exactly a social animal, as you know. I'll be fine hunkering down on my own in the evenings, me and the telly, and I'll have the garden, of course. That'll be very exciting.'

'Yes.'

It didn't sound very exciting to her; but then he wasn't twenty.

'I'm leaving on Friday fortnight,' he said, answering her original question.

'Having a leaving party, I hope?'

'Oh good Lord, no. Why should I do that?'

'Dad, you must! People will feel very hurt if you don't; you're part of Farrell's, literally, it will look like you don't care. I'll help you organise it, if you like. Jemima and I could get together on the catering and so on. Go on, be brave. It doesn't have to be a rave, you could just have a drinks do in the boardroom. I really think you should.'

'Do you?' He looked seriously alarmed. 'God, how terrifying.'

'Don't be silly. You know how everyone there loves you.'

'Hardly,' he said and his voice was very sad again.

Lucy leaned over and kissed him on the cheek.

'Yes, they do. I know they do.'

The country, that spring, was gripped with Jubilee and Olympiad fever; indeed, the extremely funny television series 2012 with its constant references to the Jubolympics did not overstate it. Plans were everywhere for street parties, pageants, on both river and village green, concerts both grand (at Buckingham Palace) and modest (in village halls), the lighting of beacons, the composition of songs and symphonies. Companies managed to extend their wares, however unlikely, to formulate Diamond Jubilee or Olympic products (although this was officiously stopped for no reason and to no benefit that anyone was able to see), the extra bank holidays were in place and the royal family was seen to be enjoying a period of public affection unsurpassed since the marriage of the Prince of Wales and Lady Diana Spencer. Republicans muttered and wrote letters and were awarded airtime on the *Today* programme and even occasionally *Newsnight* and found themselves almost ruthlessly silenced by what appeared to be a tsunami of royalism. Every magazine, every newspaper, produced Jubilee supplements, every publisher produced books on the Queen's sixty glorious years. William and Kate became the most popular double act since Morecambe and Wise, Harry's stature changed from Playboy Prince to National Treasure-in-Waiting and even the Duke of Edinburgh was forgiven for decades of tactlessness and gaffes and became the beloved patriarch.

And against this background of patriotism and heritage and world interest in all things British, Bianca Bailey should have been finalising her plans for relaunching the House of Farrell. Building to a large degree on the incomparable bonus of its having been founded in the year that the now elderly and beloved matriarch had been a young and beautiful girl at her coronation.

Only she wasn't; she couldn't. Due to the absence, within company funds, of two million pounds.

It was agony: one day she had had everything going for her, the next nothing. Hugh and Mike had given her one more week; after that, they said, they were pulling the plug. 'We can't risk it, Bianca. We're getting deeper and deeper in and that's exactly what we said we wouldn't do.'

She had tried to get a bank loan, secured by her shares. They had checked with the venture capitalists, who had, not too surprisingly, said no. Her contract forbade her going to another set of VCs. Mark Rawlins suggested that she should cause the business to crash, and put it into administration.

'That way you could buy it back with some new VCs who would fund this lease crisis.'

'Really?'

'No, Bianca, not really.'

Every time she thought about the company going under, she felt like screaming. She thought of all the incredibly hard work that had gone into getting where they were; and not just hard work, but loyalty and, in many cases, a genuine love for the House of Farrell.

People like Susie, who was working eighteen-hour days, releasing information slowly and tantalisingly to a chosen few journalists, promising exclusives in return for absolute discretion. She simply said, when Bianca thanked her, that she was enjoying every moment: 'It's all so dangerous, and so exciting.'

And Lara, raring to go with countrywide mini conferences, the week of the launch, and Jonathan Tucker, winding up his sales force, promising them they'd be wetting themselves if they knew what was coming, and with a whirlwind tour of his own planned for the Thursday and Friday before launch. People like Hattie Richards and Tamsin Brownley (who had casually remarked one day that her father was Lord Brownley, which had interested no one particularly except Athina, who had known Tamsin's grandmother when they were debs) came to see her together – an odd pair, they were to be sure – to tell her how excited and proud they were about the launch and how grateful to her for enabling them to be part of it. Tears in her eyes, she told them it was she who should be grateful and that they didn't know the half of it yet, and would be a lot more excited when they did.

And Tod and Jack of course, who were living the project 24/7 now, Jack's baby taking second place to it most of the time – indeed, his wife had said crossly perhaps he would like the baby to be called Farrell; and dear Lucy, creating dazzling look after dazzling look.

And of course Athina, who still had no idea about the global launch but was desperately excited about the rest of it, deny it as she might, particularly her perfume and the advertising campaign, which did indeed bear a very close resemblance to her own. Her rage and humiliation if that did not survive would be savage; as would the scorn which she would pour upon Bianca, having been entrusted with her beloved House of Farrell and allowing it to fail. And all the other people, the secretaries, the marketing assistants, the girls in reception – they had all been caught up in it, the excitement, knowing that something wonderful was going to happen, and that they had, in however small a way, been part of it too. The thought of telling them all, disappointing them, letting them down was almost impossible to contemplate and she felt not only sad but ashamed of herself, that she had presided over something that would not be, after all, a triumph, but, at very best, a modest success and at worst nothing very much at all.

With two days to go, she decided to go and see Florence at The Shop. She would need to know before anyone.

Florence, almost fully recovered although still rather pale, promptly put the 'closed' sign on the door and took her up to her parlour.

'We have things to talk about,' she said firmly, 'and we must not be interrupted. Tea, Bianca?'

'Oh please, that would be very nice. But, Florence, there is really no need for you to – to talk about anything.'

'I think there is,' said Florence, 'and I would feel happier if we did. I know I can rely on your discretion and I owe you a great deal for what you did that day, cannot thank you enough.'

'Florence, it was nothing.'

'It was not nothing. It was everything to me. And it was kind and – and enormously generous of you. I really want to acknowledge that.'

Bianca said nothing.

'I don't intend to go into great detail,' said Florence. 'That would be both unnecessary and embarrassing. But I wouldn't want you to think it was some sleazy, one-night stand.'

'I would never think anything you did could possibly be sleazy, Florence,' said Bianca. 'The word associations with Florence Hamilton are things like style and class.' She looked at Florence and smiled at her suddenly. 'And besides, how could any union that was blessed by Chanel jackets be anything else?'

'Well indeed,' said Florence, blushing slightly, 'and it was blessed by other things too. Like love. True love. I have to stress that, it's terribly important you should understand. And happiness. And faithfulness,' she added. 'An odd thing to say about an adulterous affair but it was. We kept faith with one another for over fifty years.'

'And she never knew?'

'She never knew. She never must. It would destroy her.'

'You're very loyal to her, Florence. When she's not very nice to you, a great deal of the time.'

'Oh, I know. But she doesn't mean that, it's just her way.'

'A difficult way,' said Bianca, 'I would say.'

'To you, of course. But you see, we've been friends for a very long time. She is actually extremely fond of me. Ironic, isn't it, when I was having an affair with her husband for half a century, but there it is. She is actually,' she added, looking at Bianca, 'quite fond of *you*.'

'Me! Don't be so ridiculous, she loathes me.'

'Oh no, she doesn't. She respects you, she admires your courage, and the other day she said you had a certain style.'

'Goodness me!'

'Of course it's very hard for her; you came in, picked up her most precious possession and ran away with it, doing what she saw as dreadful things to it as you went.'

'Of course. I can see that. But most of the time she's extremely rude to me.'

'She's rude to everyone,' said Florence. 'You should have heard her with Cornelius.'

Bianca digested this; then she said, 'What was he like?'

'Oh – charming. Clever. Generous. Extremely courteous. All the good things. And some bad ones too. A tremendous egotist. Stubborn. Very quick tempered.'

'Really?'

'Yes. And, of course, absurdly good-looking. Well, you've seen his portrait and the photographs – so, a little vain. The clashes between him and Athina were frightful at times. She liked to diminish him, you see.'

'But their marriage survived?' said Bianca.

'It did. And I think I helped do that. I know that sounds very conceited and it's a very unfashionable view, but – well, I'm not going to try and justify it, of course I can't. But for us, the three of us, it was a wonderfully successful – what shall I say – scenario. They needed one another in many ways. He would never have left her and I would never have allowed him to. It would have broken her entirely.'

'It must have been so hard for you,' said Bianca, staring at her in a kind of awe.

'It was, but think of my life without him. Very, very bleak.'

'Was – forgive me for asking this – was your first marriage happy?'

'So happy. We were absolutely suited, in every way. I suppose that led me to the relationship with Cornelius. Who wasn't in the least like Duncan, but he provided me with the same complete fulfilment.'

'And, forgive me again, but this is so – so fascinating. Didn't you ever meet anyone else? All the time you were with Cornelius?'

'Only once, and that was a temptation, I have to say. He was so extremely nice. I was older by then, well into middle age, and beginning to worry about the future. He wanted to marry me. But he wasn't quite . . . enough. Enough to make me give up Cornelius. That's the only way I can express it.'

'Oh Florence,' said Bianca, 'what an amazing story.' Her voice shook slightly, and her eyes filled with tears. She brushed them impatiently away. 'Sorry. I – I thought I too had the perfect marriage. Until quite recently. But now I don't know. Everything's changed.'

'Because of someone else?'

'No,' said Bianca, a little too quickly she feared. 'It's the job. Well, both our jobs, I suppose. But right now it feels mostly about Farrell's, that's our biggest problem. And it's a huge one at the moment. I mean really huge.'

'I'm so sorry,' said Florence gently. 'And if you ever want to discuss it further, then I'm here. But I suspect you'll sort it out for yourself. You have a lot on your plate, Bianca. You'll feel so much better when the launch is over and you can relax a bit.'

'No,' said Bianca, 'no, I won't. I've got something else to tell you, Florence. In fact, it's actually why I'm here, there's something dreadful which almost nobody else knows about – yet.' And she burst into tears.

And Florence indicated to her to join her on the chaise longue and put her arms round her and Bianca, between sobs, told her the whole dreadful story of the lease and the needed two million, and that the launch, the wonderfully brilliant launch would have to be cancelled; and then, when finally Bianca had finished and was wiping her eyes and blowing her nose and saying how sorry she was, Florence said very quietly, 'I think I might be able to help.'

* * *

'Oh – hello!' God, she was gorgeous. He'd almost forgotten . . .

'Hello. Nice to see you.' God, he was amazing. She'd almost
forgotten . . . 'Um – what are you doing here?' Could he possibly,
by the remotest chance, be looking for her?

'I'm waiting for Bianca.' So – no. Not. 'She and Patrick are taking
me to dinner,' he said.

'Oh really? How nice.'

'Yes, well it's my birthday.'

'Oh goodness. Happy birthday, Jonjo.'

And was it perhaps a good sign he was spending it with Bianca
and Patrick and not some hot blonde?

'Thanks. Yes. Forty today. I was going to have a party but then,
well, decided not to.'

Because he wasn't feeling terribly sociable? Because he didn't
have anyone to throw a party with?

He smiled at her rather awkwardly. 'And they felt sorry for me
and said I must do something. So, yes, they're taking me out.'

'That is so nice. They are so nice.'

'They are indeed. And—'

The revolving doors opened and a very pretty girl – blonde, big-
eyed, very good legs, quite a short skirt, came in, flung her arms
round his neck and said, 'Jonjo, sorry I'm late! Happy birthday!'

'Thanks. You look great. So pleased you could come. Susie, this
is—'

But Jonjo never completed his introduction; he was interrupted
midway as the main doors opened again and an incredibly cool-
looking bloke – tall, dark, and pretty bloody handsome really, came
in.

'Hi, darling,' he said, kissing Susie. 'How are you?'

'I'm fine. Look, shall we go to the wine bar down the street? I
really need a drink!'

'Sure. God, I'm pretty wrecked, after last night – amazing, wasn't
it?'

'Amazing. Excuse us, Jonjo, nice to see you again.'

And Susie and the cool bloke were gone, into the street, leaving

614

Jonjo feeling faintly sick, shocked to find how upset he felt, and wanting more than anything to run after them and punch the bloke quite hard in the solar plexus.

And Susie hurried away from the building, feeling intensely relieved that at least she didn't have to smile at the girl and shake her hand when she wanted to draw her nails slowly down her face and possibly kick her shins as well.

'Sorry about that.' Jonjo looked faintly embarrassed.

'Who was she? Very pretty. Bit odd, though.'

'Yes, well, she was my girlfriend for a short time. We parted a bit badly and I suppose she felt awkward.'

'Oh, I see. You and your exes, Jonjo. Time you found Ms Right.'

'I wish. I thought I had.'

'Her?'

'Yup.'

'Oh, dear. Well – oh, hi Bianca, so lovely to see you. Thank you so much for asking me along.'

'Not at all. I always love our foursomes. You're looking great, Pippa. Isn't she, Jonjo?'

'Yes – and she's got a new job at just about the smartest lawyers in town.'

'You must be very proud of your little sister.'

'I am. Um . . . I just saw Susie.'

'Oh yes?'

'Yes. With a rather flashy character, dark leather jacket. Is he the new boyfriend?'

'No, no, that must have been Tod Marchant. He looks after our advertising. Nice chap. Very good at his job. He is a bit flashy, but really, really nice. We were all out last night at an advertising bash, and he and his partner, Jack, picked up three awards.'

'I see.' Jonjo felt a little better. 'So who is her new bloke?'

'She hasn't got a new bloke. Or even an old one. I keep her much too busy here. Now come on, Patrick's booked the table for eight, so we can have a quick drink somewhere here and then go

615

over to meet him. We thought the Orrery in Marylebone High Street. That OK for you?'

'Yes, great,' said Jonjo. He was feeling slightly bemused, scarcely hearing what Bianca was saying.

'Sounds wonderful to me,' said Pippa. 'Jonjo! Where are you going?'

Jonjo knew about timing. His instincts about it were very finely honed; a lot of his job was about it, and how crucial it was. A second's delay on a deal could literally cost billions.

He ran out into the street looking wildly right and left; no sign. Fuck! If he went the wrong way, minutes, not seconds, would be lost.

'Scuse me mate,' he said to a passer-by, 'where's the nearest wine bar?'

The man looked at him and grinned. 'You must be desperate. One that way, but it's crap. There's one the other way, bit further, about four or five minutes' walk, but worth it. You could always run I s'pose.'

'Thanks.'

He ran. Praying it would be right. Surely Susie wouldn't go to a crap wine bar?

'I'll have a white wine, please, Tod. Bit hungover.'

'Me too. Hair of the dog's what you need, always works. I hit the vodka with my morning coffee. Felt great. Hey, don't want to be critical, Suze, but this is hardly my idea of a wine bar.'

'I know. But I just wanted to get away from that bloke. The one in reception.'

'He looked quite cool to me. Don't tell me he's some kind of perve?'

'No, but we had a – a bit of a fling and it all ended not very well.'

'Oh, OK. Well, we'll have one drink here and then go back to your office. Where I thought we were meeting anyway.'

'Yes, we were. Sorry.'

* * *

They weren't in the nice wine bar. However hard he looked, even venturing into the toilets, waiting for someone to come out of the ladies', they weren't there. Or rather *she* wasn't there. Fuck fuck fuck! He'd lost her. Maybe the other wine bar was where they'd gone. He ran out into the street again, past Farrell House and on. Susie, Susie, I can't lose you now . . .

The wine bar was empty. Shit. This was awful. Of course he could phone her, but he knew, he totally knew, that the time was now. Now would work, now contained her, in all her sexy, gorgeous rightness; later he'd have time to think, she'd have time to think. Minds might be changed, courage might fail, common sense prevail . . .

'Jonjo, what the fuck are you doing?' Pippa was on the pavement looking for him, pink with anger. 'How could you be so rude? Bianca's waiting and they've gone to a lot of trouble to give you a nice birthday, and you just run away. Without a word.'

'Sorry.' He raised his hands. 'Sorry, sorry, sorry. I just – well, doesn't matter.'

'You being filthy fucking rude matters. I'm so ashamed of you. Now will you please come back, apologise to Bianca and let's try to have a nice evening. You're very lucky Bianca hasn't just gone home.'

'Yes, I know. I'm sorry. Come on then.'

They walked back into Farrell House; Bianca was looking amused.

'It's OK, Jonjo. Honestly. These things happen. But let's cut the drink and go straight to the Orrery, shall we?'

'Sure. That sounds great.' It sounded awful.

There was a pause; then Bianca said, her face not entirely innocent, 'Susie came back, by the way. If it was her you were looking for?'

'She came back?'

'Yes. About two minutes ago. They'll be in her office. You could—'

'Jonjo! I can't believe this. Where are you going?'

Bianca put her hand on Pippa's arm. 'It's OK. It's very, very important.'

Susie and Tod had their back to the door when Jonjo reached the office, looking at some roughs she had tacked on to her board.

Jonjo stood there, staring at her, at the fall of streaky blond hair, the slender figure that still managed to contain a very sexy bum, the seriously excellent legs, the superbly sexy high heels, and didn't say anything, just stood there, drinking her in. Then he said, 'Susie?'

And she spun round, her eyes huge and round and shocked, and said 'What?' really not very warmly at all. Jonjo took a deep breath, and spoke across the vast distance that seemed to separate them. Saying what had to be said, quickly, before it was too late. Before he lost her again. This was no time for small talk.

'Susie, listen to me. Please, please listen to me. I – well, I've missed you. *Really* missed you. In fact I – well, I think I might love you. Something like that anyway. Oh, and the girl downstairs is my sister; her husband's babysitting which is why she's coming out with us. Ask Bianca if you don't believe me. Please, Susie, can we just – just be together again? Please?'

And it was indeed the right time, the right moment, and he knew he had judged it perfectly, and he had caught it, and made a lot more than a billion. Deal done. For Susie stood very still just for a moment and then took one step forward and then another, and then half ran across the room and hurled herself at him and put her arms round his neck, and kissed his face over and over again, laughing and crying at the same time and not saying anything at all.

And Tod Marchant looked at them and then grinned and picked up his things and walked out, patting Jonjo lightly on the arm as he went.

'I'll leave you to it, mate. Never liked playing gooseberry. I'll call you tomorrow, Suze.'

And Jonjo said, 'Thanks, mate, cheers.' And then returned to the rather more important task of kissing Susie, and then suddenly pulled away from her and pulled out his phone and said, 'Sorry,

Susie, but I have to do this, I've been quite rude enough already. How would you like to make up a fivesome for the evening? I'm sure Bianca would agree.'

'I'd love to,' said Susie. 'It sounds wonderful.'

Chapter 52

Bianca faced Mike and Hugh across the boardroom table.

'Listen. Both of you. Could I please have just a few extra days? Something – well, something extraordinary's come up and I might have found a solution.'

'What sort of solution?'

'I can't tell you. I'm sorry.'

'Bianca,' said Mike and his face was grimmer than Bianca had ever seen it, 'if you think we're going to risk hundreds of thousands of pounds, which is what it costs to keep that company going for a few days, without your giving us a sound economic reason, rather than some secretive twaddle that is frankly unworthy of you, we'll know for sure what we've suspected for quite a long time. Which is that you have no idea what you're doing any more.'

'Oh *what*?'

'I agree,' said Hugh. 'This is a business endeavour with an enormous amount of money at stake, not a soap opera. The answer's no. Saturday midnight is your deadline.'

'But I may not be able to deliver by Saturday midnight!'

'Well, that is your misfortune. Either you explain what on earth you're talking about, or we pull the plug.'

'But I can't do that. It would be betraying an enormous confidence if I explained. I simply can't. I promised. You have to trust me. Just for a few more days.'

'Bianca, no.'

'Well, all I can say is, you could be very sorry.'

'And then again, we could not. We're not prepared to risk it. Let's meet again on Friday and see where we – *you* – are.'

She pulled out her phone in the taxi and called Florence.

'Is there any way we can speed things up?'

'Well, I don't think so, no. The solicitor is away until Sunday and I don't have a mobile number for him. And nobody else knows about it. Literally. I'm so sorry, Bianca. So very sorry.'

'Oh, it's not your fault. They . . .' she hesitated, '. . . they said if I could tell them what it was all about, they might consider a few extra days. I said I wouldn't. And I won't. Unless you say so. But you don't think . . . ?'

'No, Bianca, I don't. I'm sorry. Too much is at stake. In human terms, that is. I gave you this information because I trust you totally. You cannot, indeed you must not, betray that.' Her voice filled with anxiety suddenly.

'Florence, I won't. Of course I won't! But – it's so hard. We could – we will lose Farrell's.'

'My dearest girl,' said Florence, 'there are things in this life even more important than Farrell's.'

She arrived home early; she hadn't the heart to stay at the office and for the first time in her entire working life, she used illness as an excuse, told Jemima she thought she was developing flu.

'Which I can't afford to do, so I'm going to try and ward it off.'

Jemima looked at her sympathetically. 'Good idea,' she said, 'and there's nothing in the diary, so why not? And you need to be on form tomorrow, for Bertie's leaving party.'

God, she was dreading that now. All the jolly speeches, the references to how much they would miss him, when everyone would soon be missing everyone. And of course she would know, as she made her own speech, that he was doing exactly the right thing, getting out while he was ahead. HR directors of bankrupt companies didn't usually find it very easy to get new jobs. He had chosen, for some reason, a Thursday rather than a Friday to leave and in a way she was glad: the party wouldn't turn into a Friday booze-up, and last half the night.

'Anyway,' Jemima said, looking at her watch, 'it's nearly five and most people wouldn't consider that particularly early anyway!'

If only, Bianca thought, if only she was most people. Most people didn't have a multi-million-pound company to rescue. Most people wouldn't have run up an extra two million pounds on the investment in that company; and if they did they probably wouldn't even care. Most people weren't about to let an entire workforce down; most people weren't about to look totally foolish and incompetent; most people weren't about to lose an exceptionally high-profile, professional reputation for ever. And most people hadn't been given an ultimatum that was impossibly awful by their husband and have to give him an answer within the next twenty-four hours.

She wished passionately she could become most people.

Patrick came in looking in a very black mood.

'You look jolly,' she said. 'Drink?'

'No, thank you. I think we should retain clear heads. You seem to have started,' he added, with a nod at her glass of wine.

'I – need it. I've had a hideous day.'

'How unusual.'

She ignored this. 'How about yours?'

'It was fine. I'll just go and change. You could make me a strong coffee perhaps.'

She made the coffee while checking her emails and texts. Hoping against absurd hope that there would be something from Florence. Or the VCs. Or . . . anyone, really.

There was one text, but it was from Jack. They were desperate to show her the site; it was finished. It looked sensational. Could they come over in an hour or so?

Bianca texted back, grateful that she didn't actually have to speak to them, lest they pick up something from her voice, and said she was sorry, but she was at home and really couldn't be disturbed.

She added briefly, trying to sound light-hearted, *Trouble with schools. Just you wait till it's your turn for that.*

Jack wrote back: *OK. Tomorrow morning then? No time to lose, we've got to get going with the test site asap.*

Yes, hopefully. I'll let you know.

Thanks.

She could tell she'd disappointed him. 'It's going to get a lot worse than that, boyo,' she said aloud to her iPad and closed it.

Her phoned pinged; an email from Florence. Could they have a talk? She was very worried about the way things were going and was beginning to regret saying anything about 'the possible solution'.

'Oh God,' said Bianca, staring distractedly at the screen and reaching for her phone at the same time. She was scrolling through it for Florence's number when Patrick said, his voice icy with courtesy, 'I would be grateful if you would put your phone away. I would like to have a conversation.'

'Oh Patrick, for Christ's sake don't be so pompous,' said Bianca. 'I have to call Florence, it's terribly important.'

'Please don't,' said Patrick. 'We have something else I want to discuss. I realise it's nothing to do with Farrell's but I would like to think it mattered a little.'

'Patrick, please let me at least make this call.'

'Will it take long?'

'It – could.'

'Well, let it wait.'

'But why, you're home for God's sake, we've got all evening.'

'I have to call Saul later.'

'Fucking Saul!' she said. 'Always fucking Saul and his fucking phone calls.' While thinking how grotesquely unfair of her it was to blame Patrick for Saul's behaviour when . . . 'All right. Well, let me at least email Florence, tell her I'll call her later.'

'Yes, all right. Would you like another of those?' Nodding at her glass.

'Yes please. That is . . .' better have her wits about her '. . . no, I'll have a coffee please.'

He disappeared, she emailed Florence; sat back on the sofa, smiled nervously at him when he came back in.

'Right. Do I have your attention?'

'Yes, you do.'

The door opened; Milly looked in.

'Hi, Mum. Hi, Dad. Could you just look at these? I'm so excited. And they're going to go on this girl's blog next week. Oh, and this is Jayce. Doesn't she look amazing?'

'Yes, she does!' said Bianca. She had been expecting something very different from this smouldering-eyed creature, with high cheekbones and slicked-back, short blond hair.

'She had sort of long hair before, just bundled up in a messy ponytail. Lucy suggested she had it cut and she's lost loads of weight already, about four kilos, and Lucy says it always shows on your face first. And look, here are the step-by-steps – it's so clever – and then I'll show you the little film, well actually it's the stills speeded up, that was the photographer's idea, she was really cool.'

Bianca and Patrick looked at them together, at the dozens of photographs, united briefly by seeing their daughter slowly transformed, little by little, from the near-child they knew so well into someone almost unrecognisable.

'They're lovely, Milly,' said Bianca.

'Absolutely agree,' said Patrick.

'You really think so?'

'We really think so. And your friend – Jayce – looks great too.'

'I think so. Cool. Um – I was just wondering if, well, if I could ask her here sometime. Maybe for a sleepover? I think she could cope with it now. Now she looks so much better.'

'Of course. Of course you can. Or we could all have supper together maybe?'

'Mum,' said Milly, giving her a withering look, 'we're not children.'

'No. No, of course not,' said Bianca humbly.

'I'll ask her,' said Milly. 'We're not going to the country this weekend?'

'No,' said Patrick and 'We're not,' said Bianca, their voices equally adamant.

'Cool,' said Milly. 'We haven't been for ages. Not that I mind,' she added hastily, 'but – any reason?'

'It's complicated,' said Bianca, 'but—'

'No, no, it's OK,' said Milly. 'You don't have to explain.' Her voice was slightly ironic and she grinned at them. She really was more herself, thought Bianca. At least something – a very important something – was going in the right direction.

Milly disappeared and Patrick looked at Bianca.

'Right. It's to do with—'

Bianca's phone vibrated. She looked at it.

Florence.

'Patrick, I have to answer this. I'm sorry.'

He sighed. 'All right. But I do want to talk to you about our future and I have to say a message seems to be coming over rather loud and clear that it is of little interest to you, without your having to actually spell it out.'

'I'm sorry. Truly. I won't be long.'

Florence sounded excited, slightly breathless. 'I can talk to the solicitor first thing tomorrow. He got my message, some secretary had taken pity on me and managed to contact him. He told her to ring me and . . .'

'Oh my God, Florence, that is – that is amazing! Look, hold on a moment.'

She looked at Patrick. He was looking oddly resigned, almost patient.

'Patrick, I do have to take this and it will take time. I'm sorry, and I'll explain when – when I've talked to her. It really is desperately important. You'll understand I promise when I explain . . . Florence, hello, don't go away—'

'She doesn't need to,' said Patrick, getting up. 'I really have better things to do than sit here, listening to your phone calls. I think I probably have my answer, Bianca. There seems very little more to be said. If you have anything to add, I shall be interested to hear it, of course, but I find it hard to imagine it will be of much interest to me. Meanwhile, don't let me keep you any longer from your extremely important work.'

Bertie woke up feeling absolutely terrified: that he was finally leaving Farrell's, which meant the family, as much as the job. No point pretending he could have it both ways, work for someone else and still be part of this extraordinary, difficult, brilliant, demanding, and quite often unpleasant thing that was not just his family, not merely (merely?) his mother and his sister but a creative and commercial force, the thing their parents had created. And having created it, had forced all of them to live within its confines.

And there he had been judged and found wanting, not just by his parents, but by the company itself; he was not clever enough, not creative enough, not even efficient enough to contribute to it and its success. Never mind that his talents lay in quite different areas from the ones that the House of Farrell demanded; to pursue those talents was deemed not even worthy of consideration. He knew he would have enjoyed being, and done well as, a teacher, say, or an architect, but as a member of the Farrell family that would have been of no account: he would not have been one of them, and in the future that would also be the case. He would be an outsider, dismissed, of no real consequence; dear old Bertie, poor old Bertie, and in the case of his mother, disloyal and unfilial Bertie.

It seemed a disproportionately large step, therefore, that he was taking; and although he was still sure it was the right one, increasingly terrifying.

Lara woke up feeling depressed. As she woke up at five, she had a great deal of time to feel it; she opened her curtains and lay staring into the slowly lightening sky, thinking about Bertie and how dreadfully she was going to miss him, wondering, for what must have been the hundredth time, what had gone wrong between them, and also how she was going to get through the party without crying and making a complete fool of herself. So many people had noticed their friendship over the months since she had joined Farrell's; their sandwich lunches, their shared jokes, their rapport in meetings, and she knew were speculating upon its cooling. For this reason alone she was glad to have Chris Williams in her life to talk about, at least, and had arranged a date with him that evening: partly to distract her from her misery but also to have an excuse for leaving the party before it got too late. Otherwise, she knew, she would never have been able to tear herself away.

Bianca woke up feeling sick. And for the second time in her life, the first having occurred two days earlier, completely helpless. The point being there was no clear answer to the dilemma Patrick had put her in; however passionately she might love him and value their marriage, there could be no excuse in human terms, never mind professionally, for walking out of a company in the week it was quite possibly declared at worst, bankrupt, and at best, impossible to save. What did she say to them all, to her loyal, incredibly hard-working team? Sorry guys, but I'm leaving today, giving up work to spend time with my family and oh, by the way, there's no more money, so there'll be no global launch, no advertising campaign, and the company will probably go down, hope you're OK with that.

And even if by some miracle – and it would be one – it didn't go down, and the relaunch actually happened, she was the cornerstone of it, the face of it, to a large extent, directing it, driving it through. So either way she would fail them all utterly.

She had tried to put this to Patrick, begged for a bit more time – she seemed to spend her life doing that at the moment – but he had just looked at her in his new, distant way and said since she was still hesitating, then he felt he had his answer. She had said he had nothing of the sort, and she was simply not prepared to let him think so; he said he was sorry, but it was all very simple to him.

She felt extraordinarily confused; at the same time shocked at herself for not seeing her marriage as of prime importance in her life while wondering if, indeed, it was any more, angry with Patrick for what she saw as the ultimate emotional blackmail, desperately sad that they should have come to this, and, of course, anxious about the children, who had already endured enough at her hands and those of both Farrell's and Saul.

There was no one she could talk to who was not already involved with one situation or another; it was, as Patrick had so forcefully pointed out, *her* decision. His small, sad statement when he first delivered the ultimatum, that he really didn't mind very much which way that decision went had made her heart ache and her sense of guilt soar.

And given what had happened in New York, did she deserve Patrick? The new one perhaps, the cold distant, harsh one: but she had no right to the old one, the loyal, patient, supportive Patrick, who had been at the centre of her life for sixteen years or more and who had loved her and she had loved so very much. What had happened to them? she wondered again and again as she moved through those horrendous days, with not an hour of any of them happy. Where had they lost one another so totally, as it seemed, and how? Even facing all her wrongdoings – and she was merciless towards herself – she still couldn't quite believe it had happened.

Athina woke up feeling, most unusually, nervous. This being Bertie's leaving day, and this ridiculous party planned, she wasn't at all sure how she was going to cope with it. Clearly she must attend; it would be seen as the most extraordinary breach of family as well as professional etiquette if she did not, but she longed to be able to stay away. She still felt that Bertie's move from the firm was an appalling display of disloyalty and, in her opinion, arrogance as well, that he could think he was going to achieve success in a firm where he had no history, no reassuring inbuilt support. For the whole of his working life he had been sheltered from the consequences of his inadequacies; first Cornelius and then she had tolerated him as he bumbled his way along, first in sales, then admin and finally as financial director of Farrell's, a job he would certainly not have been employed to do with any other company.

'We've got excellent accountants,' Cornelius said once, when she was complaining bitterly about Bertie's most recent lapse, failing to put the rising rate of VAT into his financial forecast. 'They'll save us from really serious problems. And we have to give the boy a job. I for one don't want to see him in another firm, doing something second-rate and failing even at that. He's not over-bright, I know, but people seem to like him and that's important.'

Athina said people liking Bertie wasn't going to help the company if he continued to place them in financial difficulties, but Cornelius said she was exaggerating and that he was not prepared to move Bertie into another inferior position, and indeed it was one of his last requests in the days following his first heart attack, that she should remember Bertie was their son and doing his best, and she should never even consider that someone else take over his job.

Well, Bianca Bailey had done that very swiftly, and moved Bertie into that foolish position which anyone with even half his brain could have done; and what was the result? An inflated opinion of himself, and a distressingly public break from the family. She could never forgive him for that; and now she had to go along this evening and pretend with everyone else that he had done wonderfully at Farrell's and he was a great loss. Well, hopefully it would soon be over. She had been approached for a contribution to his leaving present, but had declined, telling Christine that it would be inappropriate for her, as his mother, to do such a thing.

'Whatever would people think?' she said. 'You might as well suggest I contributed to my own present when I leave.'

She failed to notice that Christine, usually so swift to agree with her every utterance, remained silent.

Bianca Bailey had asked her if she would like to say a few words, but she had looked at her in astonishment.

'What on earth could I say that was remotely positive, when I feel so very strongly he is making an appalling mistake, and displaying considerable disloyalty to me and indeed to the memory of his father at the same time. I'm sure you'll be able to find a few meaningless words suited to the occasion.'

But now that the day had come, she found herself surprisingly saddened at the prospect of her only son leaving the family as well as the firm, deny it as she might, and she rather dreaded showing this in public. Eyes would undoubtedly be on her and she didn't want to make a fool of herself.

Well, no doubt it would all be over quite quickly. She decided she would arrive at the party early, since attendance was bound to be low and thus be able to leave after a very short time. She was keenly looking forward to that at least.

'Good morning, Miss Hamilton. Simon Smythe here, Smythe Tarrant Solicitors.'

'Good morning, Mr Smythe. It's extremely kind of you to interrupt your holiday in this way.'

'Oh, not at all. In any case, it was less of a holiday, more of a break, if you follow me. And besides, this is an important matter we need to discuss. Certain things have changed since I set up the deed of gift for Sir Cornelius, with which I need to acquaint you. I was debating as to whether I should contact you, but Sir Cornelius was always emphatic that the first approach should come from you, and naturally I took my instructions from him. We spoke a day or two before he died, and he stressed that once again.'

'Yes, and that was my wish also,' said Florence.

'Indeed?' said Simon Smythe, audibly brushing aside any wishes she might have had in the matter as of little importance.

'Yes. Very much so.'

'I see. Well, as I say, I am merely following Sir Cornelius's instructions. Now when can we meet?'

'As – as soon as possible, please,' said Florence. 'The situation that has driven me to contact you is quite pressing.'

'I see. Well, today is out of the question, I fear. I could see you tomorrow at our offices, which are in Guildford. Could you make your way there?'

'Yes indeed.'

'Excellent. Well, shall we say ten o'clock? And I would be grateful if you were not late. I have a very heavy schedule, first day back in the office . . .'

'Ten would be splendid,' said Florence, 'and I do assure you I am not in the habit of being late.'

'That's what all the ladies say,' said Mr Smythe and there was no hint of humour in his voice. 'My experience is a little different.'

'Mr Smythe, I will not be late. I am a working woman, I value time, my own and other people's, very highly. So. If you could just give me the address?'

'Perhaps you could ask my secretary for that,' said Mr Smythe. 'She can give you directions as well, you'll obviously need them . . .'

He clearly saw imparting such information as the work of minions. Preferably female ones. Florence said she would ring his secretary.

'He is the most irritating man,' she said to Bianca on the phone, 'incredibly patronising. He sounded quite old. Entrenched opinions, no doubt.' Florence always made it clear that she did not consider herself in the least old. It was one of the few things she had in common with Athina. 'But he does seem to have something to tell me. Something important I mean.'

'God, I wish I could come too. But I have to see Hugh and Mike. Which I can't duck; they're going to spell out the new terms, I'll have to sign things, oh, God!'

'I would have liked that,' said Florence. 'You could have asked all the clever questions I'll forget. But I'll do my best.'

'I'm sure that'll be quite enough,' said Bianca. 'And anyway, Mr Smythe might not have liked it. What he has to say is probably highly confidential.'

'Bianca, I am the client,' said Florence firmly. 'As such I can decide who to bring with me – although Mr Smythe clearly has difficulty with that.'

'Oh really? Who does he think is the client then?'

'Cornelius, clearly,' said Florence, 'even from beyond the grave!'

'Good morning, Bertie. Big day today!' Lara's voice was carefully upbeat. There was no way she was going to allow Bertie to see she was even remotely cast down by his imminent departure.

'Yes, indeed.' He carefully avoided meeting her eye.

'I'm looking forward to the party. I may not be able to stay too terribly long, I—'

'Oh, it won't be going on long,' said Bertie, looking alarmed. 'Just a few drinks and—'

'A few speeches?'

'Speeches? Oh, good lord no!'

'Bertie, you must make a speech,' said Lara, genuinely shocked, 'I know Bianca's going to.'

'Oh, heavens!'

'And everyone's coming, absolutely everyone. They'll expect it.'

'What do you mean *everyone*? I thought just a small gathering was what was agreed . . . ?'

'Everyone, Bertie.'

He looked at her, desperation in his eyes.

'But what on earth am I going to say?'

'Oh Bertie it doesn't have to be a massive speech,' said Lara, 'just say goodbye and how you'll miss everyone. And suppose there's a presentation, which a little bird tells me there will be, you'll have to at least say thank you for that.'

'Oh no! Oh, dear . . .' He looked so terrified she forgot about being cool and distant. 'Poor Bertie, you mustn't worry about it. D'you want me to help you think of what to say?'

'Would you? I'd be so grateful.' He smiled at her and suddenly it was the old Bertie sitting there. 'Lara to the rescue once again. Well, it'll be the last time, Lara. I'll be out of your hair after today.'

'I don't—' She stopped herself just in time from saying that the last thing she wanted was for him to be out of her hair. 'I don't mind at all, honestly. Now, let's see. If I sit next to you, we can do it together and it'll sound much more like you.' She pulled a chair next to his, sat beside him. 'Now then. The main thing is to say thank you for the – the present. Whatever it is. How much you appreciate it. And how much you're going to miss everyone. That sort of thing. Right . . .'

Jemima, looking in to check a few details about the catering for the evening, saw them sitting there, heads together, looking at the screen, smiling, and thought how nice it was to see them how they used to be. What a terrible shame it had all gone wrong. She felt sure Bertie wouldn't be leaving if it hadn't.

632

It was a long day; Bianca felt utterly defeated, unable to do anything. There didn't seem any point; she fielded phone calls, replied to a few emails, composed the few words she was going to say at Bertie's party. That made her feel more emotional than ever; she sat thinking over the past months, and how happy much of it had been, how she had done good things as well as bad, discovering Bertie and his talents very much one of them. She decided that indeed might be the theme of her speech; and then wondered if it would offend Athina and Caro, both of whom were coming. And then thought that they were hardly very considerate of her feelings and decided to do it anyway. It would please Bertie and he was the main person to worry about.

The boardroom was extremely full. Just seeing everyone come in amazed Bertie and gave him a lump in his throat. Not just the major players, he had expected those, but right down to the most junior IT people, and marketing assistants, dear Mrs Foster who did all the catering and had put on the buffet for this evening, several of the salesmen, Marjorie, Francine – the flow through the door was endless. His mother was there, looking rather terrifying in red, Caro, Lucy, of course, looking particularly sparkly, the reception girls – it was all too much. All telling him how much they were going to miss him, and how pleased they were to have been invited to his party.

By seven, people could hardly move: Bianca stood up and tapped a spoon against her glass. He couldn't help noticing that she looked tired and rather pale. She really did work much too hard. She indicated for him to stand near her.

'Bertie,' she said, 'I was going to say a lot of things, but actually I think this party, and the people who have come to it, say most of them for me. All of us, Bertie, who admire you and are fond of you, of course wish you well, but we would also so wish you weren't leaving us. And we are very very jealous of your new company in having you: they are extremely fortunate.

'I think everyone in this room owes you something; obviously, particularly the people you brought into the company, but also the many others, who just wanted to say goodbye. What you have, you see and it's why we shall all miss you, is the rare gift of making people feel comfortable and less worried about their situation. And you're also extremely approachable; I've often dropped into your office, wanting to discuss something with you and finally given up, so often were we interrupted by people coming to discuss one thing or another with you. This is not a criticism, Bertie, I see it as very much part of your job to be available in this way. It might have been a little annoying, but I came to see I couldn't have everything . . .'

Everyone laughed.

'Of course you have your faults. Everyone does.' A pause, then, 'Your desk is legendary for its untidiness.' Laughter. 'You spend much too much time at the aforementioned desk, working late, working early, eating your lunch there. You really should make an effort to go out to lunch at least once a year, you know. HR people are supposed to like big lunches and gossip. Why don't you?' More laughter. 'And – no, I can't think of any more faults. But to be serious, just for a moment, and to end on a personal note. I have so enjoyed my time here, it's been so – so happy. And one of the things I have most enjoyed was bringing in new people, the sort of people who I knew would add to the team, fit in, be fun to work with, understand what was needed, and give their all. I consider bringing you in to this new job you've done so superbly, working with you, having fun with you, joining with you in building up that team, as one of the things that has given me considerable personal pleasure.

'I shall miss you, we all will. But we do wish you so very well, and we hope you will come and see us from time to time – I believe you still have connections here?' Even more laughter. She took a rather smart-looking carrier bag from Jemima. 'Bertie, I would like you to accept this small token of our esteem and affection, and you are to place it upon your desk when you arrive at your new job on the very first day. Lest you forget us. And as you will see, it's portable; it can move with you from office to office, firm to firm.'

And as he took it she leaned forward and gave him a kiss on the cheek.

Bertie, scarlet-faced and clearly extremely emotional, took the bag and produced from it a box, and from that a very fine silver carriage clock, with *Bertram Farrell works here* engraved on its base.

It was the perfect present, Lara thought, blinking away some rather determined tears – God, the one thing she had sworn not to do, cry – generous, classy, and yet given considerable humour by the text.

Bertie was now trying to speak. He had the notes of what they had written in his hand. He looked down at them. He looked up and round the room. He looked at his notes again. He cleared his throat. There was a rather painful silence. Then he said, 'Thank you, thank you so much, Bianca, for those very kind words. Too kind, I fear.' Shouts of 'no, no,' and 'nonsense' rang from all round the room. 'And thank you, all of you for the present. It's – well it's lovely. And all of you for coming. That's lovely too. I've so enjoyed my new job, Bianca. Thank you for that. It was very clever of you to realise I'd be able to do it. I certainly wasn't doing the one I had before with any great skill.'

'That's true,' called out Mark Rawlins. It could have sounded harsh but such was the affection and humour in the room that everyone laughed.

Bertie grinned at him and went on, 'I've enjoyed working with all of you, you've all been very kind to me, and thank you for that too.'

It wasn't quite what they'd worked out that morning, Lara thought, it was a bit awkward and stumbly, but it was very touching and very sweet. Like him. Stop it, Lara! You'll start crying again.

'A few people have been extra kind. I won't name you, you know who you are, but I want everyone, everyone in this room, to know that I shall miss you . . . very much. Thank you and – yes, thank you. All of you.'

That was clever, Bianca thought; she had been wondering how he could say anything much without either excluding or offending his mother. He was, of course, much cleverer than he let on. She felt very sad suddenly; she was going to miss him even more than she had suspected. If indeed she was here to miss him at all.

She suddenly felt a great wrench of misery; not just about Bertie but her whole situation; she decided she couldn't stay here with all these chattering cheerful people any longer. But she didn't want to sneak off . . .

She tapped her glass again. The room was silent.

'I have to go now,' she said, 'forgive me, please, all of you, but especially you, Bertie. I hope that's all right.' She kissed him again. 'Bye Bertie. Have fun.'

And she was gone.

They each of them, Lara and Athina, realised it simultaneously: that the other was crying. They were both fighting it, but there was no mistaking the fact. Their eyes, their tear-filled eyes, met, acknowledged the other's sadness, and each managed a watery apology of a smile. And then Athina left the room, very quickly and suddenly, and Lara very soon after her.

And Bertie observed it too.

He felt very odd suddenly. He excused himself from a conversation with Jemima and Lucy and went into the corridor; no sign of either of them. His mother's office was the nearer; he walked towards it to find the door was firmly shut.

He knocked; no reply. He tried the door. It opened.

He looked round the large office, where he had spent so many miserable hours, and she was sitting, almost concealed, in the large swivel chair that had been his father's, her back to the room, looking out over the rooftops.

'Mother?' he said tentatively.

'Yes? What is it?'

'I just came to see if you were all right.'

'Of course I'm all right. Why shouldn't I be?'

'You looked a little – upset, I thought.'

'Upset? Of course I wasn't upset. The atmosphere in there was very stifling. I needed some fresh air.'

'Yes, I see. Good. So – you didn't enjoy the party?'

'Oh – it was all right. That was a very generous speech Mrs Bailey made.'

'I thought so too. Very kind.'

'Indeed. And – well, I have to admit, Bertie, she does seem to have unearthed talents in you that I – perhaps I had missed. And it was very – very touching to see that many of those people were fond of you.'

She looked up at him; the green eyes were very bright, suspiciously bright. A tear rolled down her face. She brushed it impatiently away.

'It was indeed,' he said, ignoring the tears, pretending he hadn't noticed them. 'I was surprised too.'

'Of course these affairs are always over-emotional,' she said. 'People sentimentalise, imagine their feelings are stronger than they really are.'

'Of course.'

'But – I would like to add my regrets to theirs,' she said. 'I too am sorry you are going, Bertie.'

It was, he knew, the nearest he would ever get to an apology about anything from her, an admission that she had been wrong about him, her judgments harsh, her view distorted.

But, 'Thank you,' he said. 'That's – kind of you to say.'

'I would like to add my own wish that you would return to visit us – the company that is,' she said, and then, after a long pause, 'And – and perhaps me personally.'

'Of course I will,' he said. 'Did you really think I might not?'

'Good. Now Bertie, there is something else. Something important. Mrs Clements.'

'Mrs Clements?' He was so astonished he felt physically shaky. 'What about her?'

'I think I have been mistaken about her. Oh, I still think her style of dress is rather unfortunate, but I think she has a good heart.'

'That's very kind of you, Mother,' said Bertie, wondering if she would pick up the edge to his voice.

She didn't. 'I think she is genuinely fond of you, Bertie. Not merely after your money and your position, as I had presumed.'

'Oh. Oh, I see.' This was seriously astonishing. Not only what she was saying – Lara? Fond of him? – but that his mother should admit to making two mistakes, in the same five minutes.

'And I have been aware for some time that you find her . . . attractive. And that you enjoy one another's company. Although less of late.'

'That's very perceptive of you,' said Bertie.

'Well, don't sound so surprised. I am an extremely perceptive woman.'

'Yes. Yes of course you are.' It was clearly the only thing to say.

'Anyway, she was very upset at the party. After the speeches. I think you should go and find her. She's in her office. Or she was. I saw her going into it, shutting the door. You'd better hurry though, she may well decide to go home.'

'But – but she—'

'Oh Bertie!' Athina got out of the chair, turned him round to face the door, and gave him a gentle push. 'We don't get many chances in life to put things right, or at least to try. Go on. Go and find her.'

Lara, sitting at her desk, her head buried in her arms, was not merely weeping that Bertie was going and she would not see him again. It was because she felt more than ever aware of what she had lost. A man such as she had not known before, gentle, patient and loyal, with a set of immaculate values. He was a rare creature, was Bertram Farrell; how the family genes had thrown him up, was hard to see. Of course, she hadn't known Cornelius, but he had clearly not been too much like Bertie; and as for his mother . . .

Well, it was over now. Whatever there might have been, whatever she might have had, or been within a breath of having. Bertie was leaving, was going to live hundreds of miles away, and there was nothing she could do to stop him. And perhaps there never had been. The best thing she could do was try to forget him, get on with her life, pursue her relationship with Chris, a far more suitable partner for her. And her career of course. That at least was good; that at least she had.

There was a knock at the door and before she had time to so much as wipe the snot off her face, it opened and Bertie stood there.

'Hello,' he said.

Chapter 53

'Miss Hamilton, good morning. So sorry to have kept you waiting.'

Which he had, for almost an hour. Florence had finished reading all the five-year-old copies of *Country Life* that the reception area of Smythe Tarrant Solicitors offered by way of amusement and was turning her attention to the *Law Society Gazette*.

'I won't say it doesn't matter,' she said, setting down the magazine on the table. 'As I explained to you, when you asked me not to be late, I am very busy today also.'

Mr Smythe was clearly not used to criticism; he cleared his throat, said he was sorry again and asked her if she would like a coffee.

She looked at him; he was not as old as she had expected, probably a mere seventy, she thought. He was quite tall and extremely thin, with wispy grey hair, and rather piercing blue eyes. She tried to imagine him forty years younger, when Cornelius had first gone to see him, and realised he could have been rather handsome. And very young, of course; no doubt Cornelius had chosen him partly on that basis, given that he quite possibly needed to be around for a long time.

He was also rather smartly dressed, in a well-cut suit and extremely nice shoes; the only sartorial mistake – in Florence's opinion – being a blue shirt with a white collar, required dressing for young men about town in the seventies. It was a look that had not stood the test of time especially as this particular white collar sat just below a very prominent Adam's Apple.

'I would like a coffee very much please,' she said. She had expected that at least during her long wait; it had not come. 'With milk,' she added.

'I will organise that. Do please come into my office.'

The office was predictably chaotic; papers piled on every surface, box files stacked up against the wall, filing cabinets, many of them half-open, on every available piece of floor space. Mr Smythe's desk was wooden, with a leather inlay just visible beneath further piles of paper. There was also, rather endearingly she thought, a leather blotter. Not many of those left in working offices. There were no pictures, no photographs, the only decoration being several framed certificates, informing the world that Mr Smythe was a Member of the Law Society, and that Smythe Tarrant were an incorporated firm of solicitors.

Of Mr Tarrant there had been no sign, merely a distinctly unfriendly receptionist who clearly saw no need to supply waiting clients with coffee or, indeed, the occasional apology that they had been kept waiting so long.

'Do sit down, Miss Hamilton. Coffee has been ordered. Now, since we are both such busy people and cannot afford to waste time, let us get straight down to business.'

And what else might they do, Florence wondered, play a quick game of bridge, or even discuss the weather?

'I had expected to see you sooner,' Mr Smythe said. 'It is some years since Sir Cornelius died.'

'Indeed. But I have had no need of any help until now.'

'I see. Well now, the first thing I have to do is explain to you exactly what you have been left. Which is a little more complex than you might perhaps have understood. Or indeed even than Sir Cornelius might have understood, or his father before him. Sir Cornelius was a highly intelligent man but not greatly concerned with detail. Not that it was required that he should have been, in this matter at least. That is my job.'

'Indeed,' said Florence, who was well aware of Cornelius's lack of concern with detail.

'So I must explain the exact nature of the deed of gift,' said Mr Smythe.

'Well, as I understand it, the freehold of The Shop,' said Florence.

'Ah. As I thought, things are *not* clear.'

At this point the sullen-looking receptionist appeared and glared at Florence.

'Sugar?' she said.

'Oh, yes please.'

She disappeared again and Mr Smythe smiled apologetically.

'I think we might wait until the coffee has arrived. Otherwise we shall be interrupted again.'

Florence thought of Christine and Jemima and how they managed to serve coffee charmingly and graciously without appearing to interrupt the most delicate procedures in any way.

'I think that would take a little too long,' she said. 'Do please go on, Mr Smythe.'

'Very well. Now, the whole point about the Berkeley Arcade is that it was set up as a tontine. Do you know what a tontine is?'

Florence shook her head.

'Ah, I thought as much. A tontine is, in essence, something subscribed to by a group, the shares owned by the original founders. It can be a public building, a house, a racing stables, even. It is named after Lorenzo de Tonti, a Neapolitan banker.

'Now the Berkeley Arcade tontine was set up by a hundred young men in 1820. They each put in thirty guineas to buy the land. One can visualise them, can one not, sitting in a coffee house, or perhaps a club, agreeing that it might be rather fun and make them a bit of money?'

'Ye-es.'

'The whole point about a tontine is that, as each subscriber dies, his shares pass back to the original founders. I could list for you, if you so wish, the names of all the members of the Arcade tontine.'

'I don't think that will be necessary, thank you,' said Florence, 'not at this stage at least. But what does that exactly mean? I mean, what happens to the shares?'

'Well, the last remaining member of the tontine inherits all the shares.'

'Oh,' she said. 'I see.'

She didn't, quite, but she needed him to go on; things might become clearer.

'Very well. Also – and this is important – this tontine was set up and administered by a charter company, which means that any profits must be invested back into the company.'

Florence was feeling increasingly bewildered.

'Well now – ah, our coffee. Thank you so much, Mrs Graves.'

Florence had been expecting, given the difficulty with which it had been obtained, that the coffee would be served in fine bone china, on a tray complete with sugar basin and milk jug. She was wrong. Mrs Graves – and how did such an unattractive person manage to become Mrs anything, she wondered – slammed down on the low table beside her a polystyrene cup of what she presumed to be coffee; a cup of water complete with teabag was offered to Mr Smythe with the same graciousness.

'Thank you,' said Florence, 'most kind.'

'Thank you, Mrs Graves,' said Mr Smythe again. 'Most welcome.'

Mrs Graves left, slamming the door behind her.

'Now, if we might continue . . .' said Mr Smythe.

'OK,' said Hugh, 'we need to get this over, Bianca. I would stress that, at this stage, the original investment still stands. We are not pulling out of the deal; rather holding to it, as it was originally set up. I do hope that's clear.'

'It is,' said Bianca, 'but, you see . . .'

She looked at them; they looked back, their faces more than usually blank. Was it something venture capitalists developed, she wondered, that expression and the ability to switch it on at will, or was it there in the first place, a requirement of the job?

'. . . you see, it just isn't going to work without the global launch idea, the franchises, the—'

'Really?' Mike's expression was now one of intense surprise. 'But until a very few weeks ago, you assured us it would. Has something changed?'

'In a way, yes. The franchises have been taken, and replicas of our shop are being created all over the world. With your help, of course. I don't discount that for a moment. The entire advertising budget, perfume apart, has been appropriated to that. It's far too late to develop another one. The heritage idea, the link with the Jubilee, the whole platform we've now built the relaunch on, needs the global launch.'

'But why? We genuinely don't understand. Admittedly your latest idea was far more ambitious, and it must be said, exciting, but the original had much to commend it. At far lower cost . . .'

'No,' said Bianca staunchly, 'the advertising budget hasn't changed. Merely the way we are spending it. Far, far more efficiently, as I see it. We've said all along that we couldn't possibly compete with the Lauders and the L'Oréals.'

'I don't recall your exactly saying that,' said Hugh. 'You assured us the campaign would be so clever, with such a strong premise, that it would stand up very well.'

'I know, but . . .'

'But . . . ?'

'That was before I had this idea. This brilliant idea which hangs on our having the shops. We can't do it without it. In fact, that could be said for the original idea,' she added, 'given the heritage angle. It's given it all so much credence.'

'Well, it's going to have to manage without it,' said Mike. 'We cannot conjure another two million out of the air, Bianca. I'm sorry.'

She was silent.

'And,' Hugh said, 'we have to move out of that shop, pronto. Every day there is costing us mega bucks. Which will have to be found out of the budget,' he added.

'Oh what?'

'Well, of course. I do begin to wonder what's happened to your commercial sense, Bianca. Perhaps you might take a little time to read through the contract again.'

She said nothing.

'So – what suggestions do you have?'

'I – I don't know. None, really. Everything is linked to everything else. The new range, the packaging, the concept, the PR, the advertising – it's all tied up in The Shop. And the other shops. I can't see how we can do it without.'

'Well, you'll have to try. Unless you want to pull out altogether, of course, and we can call in the receivers, call it a day. That way we at least won't lose any more—'

'You can't do that!' Panic flooded her. 'You can't.'

'From what you say, we might as well. Your other way isn't going to work, or so you seem to have suddenly discovered.'

'That's not fair. The other way still needs The Shop.'

'Sadly, that cannot be. The Shop has to go. Look, why don't you go and have a think. Come back in an hour. Ask Mark Rawlins, if you like. He's the only person who knows about this and he's very discreet and very sound.'

'I – might,' she said, but she knew she wouldn't. What did Mark know about interactive advertising campaigns and creative concepts and PR build-up and consumer awareness? She suddenly felt very tired and unbearably sad. She needed to get out of here before she actually started crying. That really would spell the end for her, as well as the House of Farrell.

'I'll be back in an hour,' she said. 'Thank you.'

'Now then,' said Mr Smythe, 'what Sir Cornelius himself failed to recognise, and his father before him – I don't suppose you ever met his father?' He had a way of interrupting himself, and going off into what seemed to Florence, in her agony of impatience, time-wasting tangents. She shook her head.

'Ah. Well, he was very unlike Cornelius, it must be said; he seems to have been a rather unworldly character, an academic, whose needs were simple and his interests scholastic. He lived alone, after his wife, Cornelius's mother, ran off, and was writing a book about medieval map-making which, between the two of us, I consider would have been unpublishable.'

'I certainly won't tell anyone,' said Florence carefully, 'but what was it that he – Cornelius's father – didn't realise?'

'I thought I had explained that,' said Mr Smythe.

'Not – not quite.'

'Dear me. Well, that his father was the last surviving member of the tontine.'

Florence was experiencing a rather odd sensation; her skin felt very cold, almost clammy and she was finding breathing a little difficult.

Surely, surely, this didn't mean – it couldn't mean – no, of course it couldn't. It *couldn't*. She took another sip of her disgusting coffee and said, mostly by way of avoiding the huge, the terrifying, the incredible conclusion, 'But how could he not have done?'

'Oh, very easily. If he wasn't giving it proper attention.' He looked at Florence rather irritably; he clearly felt she could also do better in this department. 'His father, Cornelius's grandfather, died rather suddenly and his will simply stated that he left all his worldly possessions to his only son. There was no time for deathbed conversations, or anything like that. And in turn, Cornelius's father left all his worldly possessions to Cornelius, the will identically worded. Neither of them took any interest in the Berkeley Arcade, especially as it didn't yield any income as such, the profits having to be ploughed back into the arcade – indeed, just recently the charter company have increased the rents of all the shops there to a properly commercial level to take care of some necessary refurbishment on the fabric of the entire arcade. That is one of the things I felt you should be aware of, but as it contradicted Sir Cornelius's instruction . . .'

'But – I still don't quite understand what all this means.'

Mr Smythe sighed once again.

'Dear me. What it means is that Cornelius did not merely inherit the freehold of Number 62. He inherited the freehold of the entire arcade. And that is what he has gifted to you.'

'Oh,' said Florence. 'Oh, I see. I – I wonder if I could have a glass of water . . .'

Bianca took far less than an hour to think about what should be done. As far as she could see, there was nothing really to think about. The House of Farrell was doomed and might as well be closed with as much dignity as possible, rather than scrabbling about struggling to keep its head above the water for another six months or so. Unless she could produce two million pounds, The Shop would have to go and if The Shop was gone, so was her campaign. Even the more modest version, as she had pointed out to Mike and Hugh. She did wonder wildly if they could build it on the global line-up of shops without the one in the arcade but as it was the cornerstone of everything they were doing – The Shop opening on almost the very day the Queen was crowned, the society ladies and famous models of their day all shopping there and Susie had some wonderful interviews with a few of them – it would all ring horribly false. She felt very angry suddenly; it was all so unfair. And there had been nothing from Florence; obviously her legacy wasn't going to help any. She wondered what on earth Cornelius could have been thinking of, bequeathing his mistress, in this flamboyantly romantic gesture, something that was clearly going to cost her, rather than provide her with, a great deal of money. The more she knew of him, the more she found Cornelius irritating.

Mike and Hugh were in their respective offices when she walked back into Porter Bingham. They suggested the boardroom, but she said what she had to say wouldn't take long and she would then leave it to them to tell the landlords that they were not renewing the lease.

'I don't suppose that will take very long either.'

'Probably not,' said Mike.

He looked at her; she could see he read defeat, knew what her answer would be.

'You want out? Or rather out for Farrell's?'

'I don't want it, but yes. I think that's what we should do. It's the only thing to do. Exactly how is clearly your decision.'

'Of course. But I would like to say I do think that's the right decision.'

'I think so. Might you sell it on? To some huge company? I wonder which. I don't see a large queue of bidders. The Lauders certainly won't want it.'

'They might.'

'Oh, come on, Hugh. A failing brand, with no image, haemorrhaging money, as you are so fond of putting it. What's in that for them?'

'They might like the Englishness,' said Mike, 'just as you do.'

'They might. But I very much doubt it.'

'With your campaign . . .'

'Oh please! That's mine. Not for sale.'

'Really? No copyright on ideas, Bianca.'

'Is that so? I think you might find a really hot IP lawyer and check that out. I cannot believe you could even consider flogging my campaign. Anyway, this isn't getting us anywhere. Let's get on with it, shall we? Do you need me to sign anything? I will if you do. Then I'd like to go home – it's been a pig of a day.'

'Possibly.' Hugh was looking uncomfortable. 'But there's no rush, Bianca. Next week will do to start the winding-up process. As long as we can get shot of that lease. We can't afford to mess about with that for more than a day. Literally. I'll get on to that immediately, and yes, I will need a signature for that. Oh Bianca, this is very sad. The end of this particular affair. Well, we've had fun. And hopefully there'll be another.'

'Will there?' she said, meeting his eyes steadily. She could see there wouldn't. She had let them down, as they would see it. Such behaviour was not easily forgiven.

She'd let everyone down, she reflected wretchedly, professionally and personally. Her colleagues, her investors, her children – and her husband.

Her phone rang and she pulled it out of her bag.

'Excuse me,' she said, 'I'll just kill this—' And then saw who the call was from. Florence. Ringing, no doubt, to say the whole thing had been a great fuss over nothing and she couldn't help after all. She almost decided to ignore it, ring her back later, but then she thought that would be unkind. Florence had been so excited about the prospect of – possibly – saving Farrell's. The least she could do was show her a little courtesy.

'Hello, Florence,' she said.

'Hello, Bianca. Look, this is incredible. I—'

'Just hang on a moment while I go out into the corridor. Right, go ahead. What news, what's incredible?'

'Where are you?'

'At Porter Bingham, with Mike and Hugh.'

'And how do things look?'

'Pretty bad.'

'Well, I think I can make them look quite a lot better!'

'Really? Are you sure?'

'Absolutely sure.' Her voice had a self-satisfied note to it. 'Completely, absolutely sure.'

'But – how? I don't understand. Cornelius didn't leave you two million pounds, did he? Because that's the only thing I can think of—'

'Almost as good. Now listen, Bianca. Are you sitting down?'

'No, but I'm leaning against a wall.'

'That will do. Now listen . . .'

Less than five minutes later she walked back into Mike's office. They looked at her awkwardly. They clearly did feel a little bad at least.

She smiled at them; she could tell from their reaction that they could see she was in a different mood altogether. Their body language was interesting; they had instinctively moved closer together.

'Right,' she said, 'I have some news.'

'Ye-es?' said Mike warily.

'Mike, don't look so scared. It's good news. Commercially sound news. Listen. You – *we* – have the facility to borrow that two million pounds.'

'Oh Bianca, please! Not again. On what security?'

'Oh, well, I don't know quite how you might view this, but it seems pretty good to me. Against the freehold of the whole of the Berkeley Arcade. How does that sound to you? And I'm here to tell you, if you won't do it, I will.'

Chapter 54

'It's awfully nice here.'

'Here as in my flat or here as in my bed?'

'Both. Obviously the bed has a certain *je ne sais quoi*, but . . .'

'I still can't believe it.'

'*You* can't believe it! How about me, all those months, thinking how much too glamorous and sophisticated you were and wanting the bright lights and all the time—'

'All the time I was after your money and your position.' Lara leaned over and kissed him.

'What money, you might well ask?' he said with a sigh. 'What position? As it is, you've got yourself an impoverished divorcee with a two-bit job in Birmingham. What a disappointment.'

'Not a disappointment at all,' said Lara, 'in any way.'

'Not even . . . ?'

'Certainly not that.'

'God, I was absolutely petrified. Are you sure?'

'So sure. It was . . . lovely.'

'Hmm. Sounds bit dull, "lovely".'

'No, Bertie, not dull. Not in the very least dull.'

And it hadn't been, she thought, smiling at him across the pillows. Warm and sweet and gentle, it had been, and a little bit surprising (and a little bit anxious), and caring and thoughtful and actually, in the end, really rather good. Lovely.

Of course it had been . . . difficult. He had indeed been petrified, she could see that even at the time, and she felt deeply sympathetic,

651

but she wanted him so much and he quite clearly wanted her, so the only thing was to hurry things on a bit, persuade him she couldn't wait for another time, as he kept suggesting, as that lovely long, absurdly happy evening wore on, and they had been saying – 'I thought you were just incredible' and 'I wanted you to like me so much' and 'I felt so happy with you just straight away' and 'I couldn't believe you could ever want to spend time with me' and 'They were some of the loveliest times I can ever remember' – interspersed with kissing on Lara's sofa in what was indeed a very nice flat she owned near Parsons Green, and drinking a bottle of champagne she had produced from the fridge.

'I always keep one there just in case,' she said.

'Just in case of what?'

'Of something to celebrate. We could do with about six of them tonight.'

From the moment he had come in and stood there, taking in her tear-drenched face, the pile of tissues flung across the desk, her dishevelled hair, her mascara-smudged eyes, she hadn't stopped smiling. And he had shut the door very firmly behind him, and then he said, 'My mother tells me you aren't actually after my money and my position, but that you are genuinely fond of me.'

And she said, 'How does she know?'

And he said, 'Well, she assures me she is a very perceptive woman.'

And she said, 'Well, I have to say I think she is.'

And he said, 'Well I never,' and stood there smiling his wonderful, lovely smile, and she had stood up and walked round the desk and up to him and put her arms round his neck, and said, 'Very, very fond, how about you?'

'Spectacularly fond.'

And that was it really.

She sent him back to his party for an hour or so because she said he really couldn't just leave it the minute he got the present, whatever would everyone think? And he had looked stricken and said did she really believe that and she said well, a bit, and gave him the address of her flat where he should meet her in a couple

652

of hours and he scuttled off back to the boardroom and she called Chris and said she wasn't very well – she couldn't face anything more difficult for the time being at least – and then she went to the ladies' and repaired her face, which was seriously in need of it, and then she too went back to the party which was beginning to run down, and she wandered round the room in a haze of happiness, pausing to chat to people like Lucy and Tamsin, who was chatting up a young salesman she had taken a huge shine to at the conference – she liked a party, did Tamsin – and Marge and Trina and Hattie – all her favourites, really, and noticed that they were the people Bertie seemed to be spending most of his time with too.

And then he stood up on a chair and announced he really had to leave, which was a little uncharacteristic, and thanked everyone again for coming and, after a decent interval, she left too, having first called a cab and all the way home she kept doing whatever the emotional equivalent of pinching herself was, and when she got there he was waiting on the doorstep, because she hadn't thought to give him a key, looking bemused and anxious and happy all at the same time.

And after that things just got better and better . . .

'Oh my God,' said Bianca, staring at the site; 'that is just amazing.'

'Isn't it?' Tod struggled to look modest. 'We are seriously pleased with it. But now look, here's the final refinement, pick your shop – here's the list, look, under outlets – scroll down . . . that's . . . right, Paris, New York, Milan – OK, now click and there you are. Isn't that great? God, they've worked fast, those franchise people of yours.' It was indeed great, a replica of The Shop, in that lovely cobbled street in SoHo, with the tall trees, with the two steps leading up to the glass-paned front door . . . She lingered on that for rather too long, smiling, remembering that street, that day, then moved on, clicked on Sydney.

'And then you see, we go down here, and then here it is, the inside, and then the invitation to go shop – you like?'

'Oh, Tod, I *do* like. It's amazing. I totally love it. It really is as good as I ever dared hope, no, much much better. Singapore? Oh, my God, that is lovely! Look, that street is just perfect, we were so lucky to get it, and the little shop too – this is just so exciting, Tod.'

'I know. And so when we do the global switch on—'

'The global switch on . . .' Bianca looked at him, thinking over the past few days and how nearly there had been no global switch on, no relaunch, no shops, no House of Farrell even, and how devastated he would have been, they all would have been, and sent up a small prayer of gratitude for Florence and the fact that Cornelius Farrell had been so in love with her he had bequeathed this incredible legacy. More incredible than he realised, of course, but that was fine, it meant they could all share it.

Florence's generosity was boundless. She had told Bianca she must regard the money, or rather the facility to borrow the money, as the company's own. She said life would hold very little for her without the House of Farrell, and there was very little she wanted that would require a large – or even a small – loan.

'Except perhaps a couple of Chanel jackets . . .' And she smiled.

'Well, tell you what,' said Bianca, 'two things: I shall personally ensure you have a large salary hike, if the global launch is the success it deserves to be—'

'Not if, will be,' said Florence firmly.

'And then you and I will go to Paris together and to Chanel, and I will help you, if I may, choose the two most beautiful jackets in the collection.'

'You may indeed,' Florence said. 'I can't think of anything I'd like more – unless, of course, it was Cornelius himself. But I would still like you to be there, Bianca. My word, he would have liked and admired you.'

'Really?'

'Well, of course. He always said working was what made women three dimensional. The other sort were only two.'

'That's really nice,' said Bianca. 'I like that. I don't know that Patrick would agree with him – at the moment, anyway. He'd like me very much two-dimensional, I'm afraid.'

'Oh, nonsense,' said Florence, 'a few weeks and he'd be bored to tears.'

'Hmm. Well, dearest, most generous Florence, I must go. I have so much to do.'

'Of course. But there is one thing: we still have to be sure that Athina doesn't have the first idea about any of this. That is the one condition of my doing this. Presumably we can spin some cock-and-bull story about where the money's come from?'

'Florence,' said Bianca gently, 'remember only four of us – five, if we count your Mr Smythe and he's bound by his professional code not to reveal it – anyway, only five of us ever knew there was a problem. Athina certainly didn't. No explanations therefore need to be given, all right?'

'Of course,' said Florence and the smile she gave Bianca was beatific in its happiness and relief. 'That had not occurred to me. How wonderful! Thank you, Bianca. I was still a little worried. No, *very* worried.'

Bianca kissed her and saw her into a taxi, taking her home to Pimlico – 'you've had such a traumatic day, even if the ending was so happy' – and then made her own way in the direction of Cavendish Street.

And thought how extraordinarily sweet a person Florence must be, that she remained so completely determined that no breath of her relationship with Cornelius should ever be suspected by anyone, least of all Athina. Athina, who spent most of her life both belittling Florence and aggrandising herself at Florence's expense.

And then had the slightly cynical thought that everyone loved Florence and considered her wonderful and that view might well change if it was known that she had been conducting an adulterous affair with Cornelius, directly under Athina's nose, for over half a century.

And that made her love Florence even more.

Bianca felt completely exalted; she felt that if she opened the window she could have flown home. As it was, she sat smiling rather foolishly at everyone who came in and she confined herself to rather mundane tasks, aware that if anyone asked her for a rise, or an increase in budget, or even suggested a change in the packaging, she would agree to whatever it was. Only when everyone had gone home did she allow herself the luxury of relishing the joy and the triumph and the sweet, sure knowledge that it was all going to happen, that Farrell's would be safe, that the campaign would happen, and looked back on to the terror of the last week, worse than the worst of bad dreams, and consigned it to history.

She realised something else too; something that she had always known, if she was truthful, how much her work in general, but with Farrell's in particular, meant to her; that it was indeed so intrinsic a part of her that to ask her to part with it would be like asking her to part with a limb, or indeed her voice. She didn't know quite what that made her, clearly a dreadful mother, and quite possibly an appalling wife as well, and she could see also that once Farrell's was safe, she should perhaps leave and do something less consuming. But for now, it was her responsibility, as much as her own children were, and she had to see it through, and to fail it and everyone who worked for it would be dreadfully irresponsible and even wrong. She should not, perhaps, have taken it on in the first place, should have seen the dangers of what it might do to her life; but she had not known then that Patrick would be no longer absolutely behind her, and caring for the family when she could not. Such assumptions were wrong; she should have considered him more. But they were where they were, as Patrick so frequently said, and, under the present circumstances, immovable.

And she would have to tell him that, and she quailed from it. Until now, until today with all its extraordinary happenings, she had still not seen things with quite the necessary clarity. But she had told him now that she had made a proper decision and they had agreed they would talk that evening . . .

To distract herself just a little she returned to the happiness, the new happiness that was the House of Farrell. She logged on to the site, the magical site that had so nearly been wasted and made a tour of her beautiful shops, her own private global tour. Saving until last the one, set two steps up from a cobbled street, in SoHo New York, the one that would always be her favourite, and lingered there for a long time, staring at it, and remembering the time that had followed, that long, astonishing afternoon and knowing with absolute certainty that it had had no bearing on her decision whatsoever.

Afterwards, on that very special day in New York when finally it was done, when they were done, she had looked at him, and he smiled and spoke for the first time since they had entered the room.

'I knew it would be like that,' he said.

She had felt little guilt later; it had been so absolute an experience, removed from reality, snatched out of time, and acknowledged by both of them as such, never to be repeated, never referred to. She remembered it, of course, and she always would, but it had nothing to do with the stuff of her marriage, it trailed no responsibilities, no promises, no love, merely carnal pleasure of the most extraordinary kind. There could be no comparison with the lifelong affair between Florence and Cornelius, for example, so filled with love and loyalty, which was a marriage in its own way. No comparison either, with some careless one-night stand, devoid of humour, charm, and any kind of emotional intimacy. It had come and it had gone again, never to return, a meteor hurtling through their lives, leaving only a brilliant memory. Indeed the only guilt she felt, and was amused by the observation, was that she felt none.

Milly sat gazing at the blog that Lucy's friend Fay delivered to her thousands of followers every day and literally had to dig her nails into the palms of her hands to make sure she wasn't dreaming. For those eyes, those wide, heavily lashed eyes, were hers, and so were those lips, glossy and peachy, and the dark smouldery eyes and dark lips were Jayce's, and what made the pictures fun, and interesting, and had persuaded Fay to use them, and Bianca to agree that they didn't break any embargoes, was that they weren't serious step-by-step pictures; Lucy's friend Fenella had snapped away as she and Jayce and Lucy all worked on each other, laughing and clearly enjoying themselves hugely and Fay had written about her friend Lucy, make-up artist for the House of Farrell, and granddaughter of its founder, working with some young friends who'd volunteered as models on some of the new looks she was creating for the brand's relaunch in June. 'Such a cool story,' the blog went on. 'The brand was launched in the Queen's coronation year, and is relaunching almost sixty years later, as the Queen celebrates her Diamond Jubilee. I'm not giving away any more now, but believe me, you're going to want to wear these looks. And watch this space – there's an *amazing* story to come.'

Tomorrow the blog would be published online and possibly, probably, well certainly, Lucy said, someone from school, probably via their big sisters or mothers, would see it. 'And then let's see what happens, shall we?'

She heard her mother come in; heard her running upstairs. There was a knock at her door.

'Hi, darling. Can I come in?'

'Yes, sure. Mum, look at these. It's amazing.'

'Isn't it?' She looked at the blog and smiled. 'And you and Jayce look so lovely. How exciting. Nice publicity for Farrell's too.'

'Yes, it is. Well, when the launch is a great success, I'll expect a big rise in my allowance.'

'*If* it's a great success.'

'Mum, don't be silly. It's bound to be. With you doing it. That's what Lucy said anyway.'

'I'm flattered,' said Bianca, reaching out and touching Milly's cheek.

'Lucy says you're a complete star.'

'She does?'

'Yes. And she says her grandmother really admires you. And she says that doesn't often happen.'

'Good heavens,' said Bianca. 'Well, she has a funny way of showing it, that's all I can say.'

'Well, she is very grand,' said Milly, 'and terribly important. Anyway, I felt really proud of you. Oh, listen, there's Dad just come in. Do you think he'd like to see this?'

'Of course he will. But possibly not just now, if you don't mind. We have stuff to discuss, very important.'

Bianca gave Milly a kiss and went downstairs to have what she knew would be one of the most important conversations of her life.

Chapter 55

'Mrs Bailey?'

'Yes.'

'This is Athina Farrell. I wonder if I could have a word with you.'

Terror and guilt in equal measures struck Bianca. Had she heard something about the online campaign? Had she confronted Florence? Had she been on to the VCs?

And how, on a completely different tack, had she known that this was the worst possible moment for her to call, with Patrick having just left the house in a mood of such black rage and misery that Bianca feared for his safety. She had only answered her phone because she thought it might have been him, despite the fact he was most unlikely to have called at all and even less likely that he should do it on the landline. But, she thought, snatching it up, it could be the police or a hospital or—

'Oh. Well, I don't know. It's not the most convenient time.'

'It's not very convenient for me either, Mrs Bailey. But I have been very busy and I have also tried several times and found you out of your office.'

'You could have called my mobile.'

'Mrs Bailey, I detest mobile phones. Nobody ever concentrates on what anyone is saying, and they intrude on the most important situations.'

Not like you are doing now, thought Bianca, and on my landline. And why should you think I am going to concentrate on anything you say now, with my husband leaving me and my marriage over?

'Yes, I see. Well, perhaps if it could be quite brief. I've got various problems with the children and—'

'Can't your husband deal with them? I thought that was what men did these days. Unnatural, in my view, but it seems to be considered quite normal.'

A very large lump seemed to be rising in Bianca's chest, making speech difficult; she crushed it as best she could.

'He – he isn't here just now.'

'I see. Well, I will keep it brief. I just wanted to say how much I appreciated your speech at Bertie's leaving party yesterday. It was very – generous.'

Short of Patrick walking back into the room and begging her forgiveness, nothing could have astonished Bianca more. She said nothing.

'He – well, he was always a disappointment to us. But I think perhaps that was partly our own fault. We didn't always recognise where his talents lay. You seem to have done rather better.'

'Yes. Yes, I see. Well, I – *we* – are all very fond of Bertie. And sorry to see him go.'

'That is why I am calling you. I wondered if you had tried to persuade him to stay?'

'Well – of course. But he was quite clear. He didn't want to. For many reasons.'

'I think he might want to now,' said Athina. 'I think you should ask him again.'

'Lady Farrell, I really don't think that would be the right thing to do. Bertie has accepted a new job, he's bought a house, he is – forgive me for mentioning it – getting divorced. For all those reasons I think it better for him to go and for us to respect his decision. Oh dear – excuse me, Lady Farrell . . .'

For the lump had now risen too high for her to deal with it any longer because Patrick's last words to her had been that he respected her decision even if it did mean their marriage was over . . .

'Mrs Bailey, are you still there?'

'Yes, of course.' She swallowed hard. 'Sorry.'

'You sound rather – odd.'

'Yes, I'm sorry. I – well, perhaps I'd better go.'

'You're crying, aren't you?' said Athina, her tone more accusatory than sympathetic.

'No. Not really. I mean, well – I—'

'Is something wrong?'

Of course not, you silly old witch. I often cry when nothing's wrong. And then she remembered how she always cried when she and Patrick had just had sex, and they hadn't had sex for so long she couldn't remember when, and then, to her utmost astonishment, she heard herself saying, 'A bit wrong, yes. My husband and I – we – well, we just had rather a bad row.'

'I'm sorry to hear that,' Athina said, in tones that were not in the least sympathetic. 'But it must be a regular occurrence, surely?'

'Not very, no.'

'How extraordinary. Cornelius and I rowed all the time.'

'Really?' Bianca said politely, while thinking the Farrell marriage was hardly an ideal parallel.

'Oh yes. It's a good sign, I always think, means at least you care enough to bother. Although it is an appalling waste of time and energy. I used to resent that.'

She was right, of course, Bianca thought: all she felt fit for now was going to bed, when she had all manner of things to do, emails to write (and read, that was the downside of the franchised shops), a final media schedule to study and sign off . . . And then wondered what on earth she was doing discussing her marriage with someone who had gone out of her way for over a year to make her life as near to impossible as made no difference. She'd be telling her Patrick had left next.

'You're right about that certainly,' she said. 'I do feel exhausted. And I can't afford that. With the launch and everything.'

'Well, of course you can't. You concentrate on your work, that's my advice. You can't afford not to, not at the moment. I presume he hasn't actually walked out?'

Was this possible, this conversation? No. It couldn't be. She—

'Well, even if he has,' said Athina, reading her silence correctly, 'he'll be back. He'll get over it, they always do. It's hard for them, I do see that—'

'For who?'

'Men, taking second billing. With wives more successful than they are. It's pathetic, of course, but I suppose it's natural.'

'Patrick is – very successful,' said Bianca firmly.

'Well, he may be in his own world. But you're the star. I mean no offence of course.'

'Er – no. Of course not.'

There was clearly little point in discussing this one.

'But surely,' Bianca said, fascinated against her will by this insight into the Farrell marriage, 'but surely you and your husband had – well – equal billing?'

'We did in a way, but he knew I was the driving force, the person everyone respected, no getting away from it. And I fronted the company, of course. Well, I'm sorry you don't feel you can approach Bertie about staying on.'

'I – I really don't, I'm afraid. And I don't think he would, for anyone.'

'I must say you were rather my only hope. I suppose I have to accept it. He is an adult, after all.'

'He is indeed,' said Bianca. 'And now, Lady Farrell, if you'll excuse me, I have to take your advice and do some work.'

'Yes, of course. Well, don't worry about your husband, Mrs Bailey. He'll be back, one way or another. Goodnight.'

Bianca sat and thought very hard for a while about Patrick's real reason for leaving. It had been hard to establish. Very hard. He hadn't exactly accused her of anything, except of putting her work before him. Which had happened many times before. It was baffling.

'We wouldn't be even having this conversation,' he kept saying, 'if you really loved me. You wouldn't be talking about when you'd give up that job. You'd just do it.'

'But Patrick, that's not true. I wouldn't. I can't. I simply can't. Not now. I have *huge* responsibilities. I'm happy, more than happy, to think about leaving, once the launch is over—'

'Yes, I've heard that one before,' he said, and his voice was very bitter. 'There's always a "when this is over" rider. And then, somehow, always another time, another job, another company.'

'But you've always said you didn't want a stay-at-home wife. Always. You have, Patrick, don't deny it.'

'There's a difference between your working, however intensively, and what's been happening recently.'

'You keep saying that. But what?'

'I don't want even to discuss it,' he said. 'If you really loved me you'd know what I meant.'

'But I don't know what you mean. And I do really love you.'

'The two things are mutually exclusive,' he said, 'unfortunately. Anyway, it's your decision and I must respect it.'

'But I haven't made a decision!'

'Oh, but Bianca, you have.' He looked at her, his face almost unbearably sad. 'And I'm going.'

'OK. Susie, what I want is an updated update. We've got – what? – four weeks to go. I want to know exactly how it's all coming together.'

Susie studied her surreptitiously as she pulled out her iPad. She knew this wasn't really necessary; she had been through it with Bianca countless times, and apart from a few very minor details nothing had changed. Of course she was horribly worried and stressed about the launch, who wouldn't be, but she was also behaving out of character quite a lot of the time, not delegating properly, which was normally one of her greatest talents, fretting over tiny details, calling meetings over absolutely nothing at all. And she looked exhausted every day. Poor Bianca. And – not very happy.

There had been rumours of course, and Jonjo had actually confirmed some of them: Patrick, depressed and non-communicative, even with Jonjo, his oldest friend, had told him that he and Bianca weren't getting along very well and agreed they needed a bit of a break from each other, especially while she was so busy with the launch. He was shortly going to join Saul in Sydney for a few days; Patrick was checking out a company there and Saul was checking out Sydney property just in case Janey Finlayson did up sticks and settle there, taking Dickon with her. Although, Jonjo had added, she would be a very brave woman if she did.

Anyway, Patrick was spending weekends at the country house and, during the week, was staying at some grotty hotel – of course, grotty by Jonjo's standards wasn't most people's and probably meant it wasn't five star. Jonjo had said – of course – that Patrick could come and stay at his apartment whenever he liked, but apparently Patrick had looked appalled, and said he really wanted to be on his own.

The whole thing was upsetting Jonjo, who had always regarded Patrick's and Bianca's as the perfect marriage and living proof that such a thing existed; Susie, so in love and so happy that she felt as if she was permanently walking a few inches above the ground, and encased moreover in a shiny, impermeable bubble, tried to reassure him.

'I'm sure it'll be fine. They both live in such total stress it's bound to affect them, especially at the moment. Bianca is just exhausted, and so worried she doesn't seem to know what day it is half the time, there's so much riding on this launch. Once it's over, and they have time for each other again, it'll all be sorted out. Try not to worry.'

'No,' said Jonjo, 'it's more than that, I know it is. I'm going to take him out to dinner, before he goes off to Sydney, try and get him to talk.'

'But Jonjo – maybe he doesn't want to talk.'

'Well, I have to try. I owe him a lot. You, for one thing. Not just meeting you, but he told me to persevere, finding out what had gone wrong with you.'

'Really? Well, you didn't exactly do what he said,' said Susie, kissing him. 'For two months you never came near me.'

'I tried that first night, you know, when I saw you and Henk? How was I meant to carry on after that? Anyway, the point is that Patrick really cared about me and the state I was in. If you don't mind I'll try and nobble him early next week.'

'Of course I don't mind. Anyway, I'm going to be pretty stressed and over-occupied myself. God, I hope it doesn't affect us in the same way.'

'It won't,' said Jonjo. 'Nothing could. I love you, Susie Harding. I really really do. I want you to marry me, I want you to have my babies, I—'

'And I want to marry you and have your babies,' said Susie automatically. And then she stopped abruptly and stared at him and said, 'What did you say?'

'I said I loved you and I wanted you to marry me and have my babies.'

'Oh my God!' said Susie. 'But – but – Jonjo, for heaven's sake, oh my God, why didn't you say so?'

'I just did, you lunatic.'

'I know, but properly down on one knee!'

'Yeah, yeah, and up the top of the Empire State or the Shard, or on a remote Caribbean island with a hundred violins going on in the background. I don't go for all that stuff. Tell it like it is, that's my motto. At the right moment. Which just came.'

'How could you think that was the right moment? Early in the morning, when we're supposed to be going to the gym?'

'Well, it obviously was. You accepted me, didn't you?'

'I did?'

'Well – yes. So we're all good. Now we can go to the gym.'

'Jonjo Bartlett,' said Susie, her eyes wide with wonder, 'I just totally can't believe that you just asked me to marry you.'

'Well, I did. And of course you can believe it because you just said – oh, this is getting too complicated. Come here and give me a kiss. And maybe a bit more. And . . .'

Later, she said from within an even shinier, more impermeable bubble, 'So – do you have the other ingredient necessary to become engaged? Other than two people who agree they want to be?'

'Er – what would that be?'

'The ring, of course. Has to be a ring.'

'Well, I have, as a matter of fact. I've had it a while now.'

'What! Where?'

'In my sock drawer.'

'Jonjo, that's ridiculous!'

'No, it isn't. It's safe in there; it doesn't let the rain in, you weren't going to find it—'

'I might have done.'

'Susie, when did you ever go into my sock drawer? You have been a grave disappointment in one way, I have to tell you. I thought girls got blokes' socks and shirts and underpants and stuff all washed and ironed and sorted. All you do is unsort my underpants.'

'Well, I'm sorry, but I'm a professional woman, I don't have time for laundry work. Can I see the ring?'

'No.'

'Oh, Jonjo. Please!'

'Why does it matter?'

'It just does.'

'You're just like all the others, aren't you? You'll be saying you hope it's a great big rock of a diamond in a minute.'

'No I won't.'

'Well, it is.'

'Oh what? Please, *please* Jonjo, let me see it. *Please* . . .'

'Not till you sort out my sock drawer. Now where are you going?'

'To the laundry basket.' She reappeared, her arms full of dirty clothes.

'It's not in the laundry basket. It's in my sock drawer.'

'I know but you've made me feel so guilty I'm going to put a sock wash on, then you might give it to me.'

'That is seriously mercenary. I don't know that I want to marry you after all. Oh, come here. No don't, go and have a rummage in the drawer instead. See if you like it. It should fit. I took one of yours to have it sized.'

'Oh, Jonjo,' said Susie, standing suddenly very still, staring at him, 'I do love you and I don't need some wanky ring. Just you. What are you laughing at?'

'You. Standing there stark naked apart from an armful of dirty socks clasped to your bosom. Bit of a shame, can't see your bosom, but the intention's excellent. Now let me see if I can find this wanky ring you say you don't want . . .'

'My God,' said Jemima the next day, 'that is some ring. Your actual rock. Where'd you get it from, Ms Harding?'

'I found it at the bottom of a sock drawer,' said Susie offhandedly.

She went over the launch arrangements with Bianca carefully, being as reassuring as she could. It had been by far the toughest assignment she had ever had; the combination of an absolute need for secrecy until the last minute and a carefully planned build-up of excitement at the same time – a PR's nightmare.

And then there was the horrendous balancing act between the bloggers and the beauty editors, so jealous and so wary of one another – in the fashion world now the top bloggers sat beside the fashion editors in the front row. The fashion editors were not overkeen on this . . .

And while it was an invaluable weapon, Twitter had made publicity doubly difficult – some big brand had famously put one of the important beauty directors on the Eurostar to Paris for a sneak preview of some product or other and she had started tweeting about it; the bloggers had got on to it, and been raging for days.

There was also the impossibility of relying on anyone's discretion. Oh, for the days of exclusives and embargoes: now the slightest leak of anything that might be newsworthy was tweeted across the globe in seconds. Mac had had a policy, for a while, of making the bloggers sign an embargo form, but they had to give it up because it simply didn't work.

So releasing details of any new product was unbelievably complex: there had always been the problem of the weeklies versus the monthlies, but now there were the weekly glossies with their six-week lead times, and the bloggers as well. It really was incredibly complicated. She had had to do releases and presentations of The Collection, of course, in the standard way, but that was all; and she was aware that although they liked it, and loved the perfume and its story, it didn't exactly set the Thames on fire.

Of course it would when it was the global online launch – and the Seine, and the Hudson as well, and she yearned to be able to break that story, but she couldn't risk even a hint about that, although she did of course talk up The Shop and its history and the link between the accession and the Jubilee, but again she couldn't see any of the press going wild about it. It was sooo frustrating.

It was frightening, too, the tweeting thing: you couldn't afford the slightest mistake or bit of misjudgment. Nothing got them all on their phones faster than a venue that was less than ice-cool, or canapés that weren't cutting edge. Or anything less than a faultless service; it was not unknown for plaintive tweets to go out about press office phones not being answered.

But so far all was as well as it could possibly be, and there was, without doubt, a slow, steady build-up of excitement.

After a great many anguished meetings and brainstormings and an acceleration of stress, they had moved the entire launch forward a week. Bianca had come in one morning, white-faced and taut, and said she was very worried about timing; Susie, imagining she was simply concerned about the almost impossibly tight schedule, assured her as calmly as she could that everything was going to be fine, the invitations were printed, the venues booked, she was checking them every few days. Whereupon Bianca looked at her, her eyes dark with exhaustion and said that wasn't what she meant; she had woken up at four that morning with the deep conviction that the week after the Jubilee Weekend was a mistake. 'Everyone will be Jubileed out, it'll be all Olympics, whereas the week before we can ride in on the coat-tails of all the Jubilee stuff which will be reaching a climax and capitalise on it far more effectively. In fact, afterwards there'll be nothing to capitalise on anyway. We'll be the carthorse after the Lord Mayor's show.'

Susie, who had had anxieties of her own along the same lines and crushed them ruthlessly, reckoning Bianca and the advertising boys must know what they were doing and envisaging now the impossibility of changing dates and venues, said helplessly, 'But

Bianca!' and Bianca had said, 'Susie, please don't argue, I spoke to Tod about it earlier and he totally agrees with me, says a lot of people will take the whole week off after the four day weekend anyway and I've also talked to Lara and Jonathan and they all agree. So we'll just have to do it somehow.'

Susie, feeling that if Tod and Lara and Jonathan Tucker were all publicly hung, drawn and quartered outside Farrell House that would be far too good for them, said nothing; there was clearly no point and she was going to need every nanosecond left to her to reorganise her campaign. She merely nodded, said she would do what she could, and went back to her office, pausing only to put her head round Lara's door and say, 'Thanks a bunch for that!'

But – somehow she had done it. It had nearly killed her but she had. Well, actually they all had. The reprinting of the invitations was the least of her worries, it was the venue that was the problem; there was no way the ballroom of the South Bank Palace Hotel was going to be available a week earlier. The manager was not going to smile and say yes of course, Miss Harding, no problem at all. What he said was so deeply (albeit understandably) unpleasant, so filled with threats of legal action and massive cancellation fees that Susie found herself weeping into a double brandy that evening, brought to her in her office by Lara, who attempted to comfort her and told her she would go round to the Palace and personally attack the manager in the goolies.

'It's not just that,' Susie said, wiping her eyes, 'it's where we're going to have it. I mean, who will have an even half suitable space available at this sort of notice? I've tried everywhere . . .'

'Well,' Lara said, 'no hotel, that's for sure, or public space. We have to think laterally, Susie. I am so sorry. But it *is* the right decision. If only we'd all spoken up before – but Bianca wouldn't have listened anyway – oh Tamsin, not now dear.'

An hour later she bumped into Tamsin in the loo; Tamsin said she was sorry if she'd arrived at a bad moment, but she couldn't help overhearing what Susie had been saying and she didn't know if it would be any good, but her parents' house in Knightsbridge had a massive reception room – 'They call it the ballroom and my cousin had her coming out dance there. I could ask them if you could borrow it – my dad would love it, I should think, and Mum would go completely mental, she loves anything like that. As long as she was invited,' she added.

Lara said she was sure Tamsin's mum would be invited.

And indeed she was; and not only invited, but she and Lord Brownley appeared (at their express wish) on the invitation as co-hosts with Farrell; how much better, Susie thought, looking lovingly at the proofed invitation, for the launch to be held 'at the home of Lord and Lady Brownley, 1 Sloane Lane SW3' than in the ballroom of some overblown hotel – and how much more inviting and intriguing for the press. And in fact, when she went with Tamsin to meet them and thank them personally, and see the room – which was lovely, high, arched windows and gorgeous wooden floor – she was made to feel she had done them an enormous favour, rather than the other way round. Lord Brownley was a techno buff and deeply intrigued by the notion of a global online event taking place in his house (it was felt he had to be acquainted with some of the details). 'Don't worry, he won't tell anyone,' Tamsin said. 'He's so not a gossip.' And Lady Brownley, who had once been a model she told Susie ('Once is the operative word,' Tamsin said later) was enchanted by the notion of involvement in what was clearly to be an occasion of some glamour.

'I am just thrilled,' she said to Susie. 'It's going to be so exciting. Will Athina be there? She and my mother once had a huge fight, they were both godmothers to the same baby, can't remember who because I wasn't even born, and apparently Athina was determined to trump Mummy's present to the baby, and was frightfully withering about Mummy's at the actual christening. I mean, can you imagine?'

Susie could imagine only too well.

Since then, so far, things had gone brilliantly. Launch Day had now been set for Wednesday May 30th.

'If it could be June, that'd be better, bandwagon-wise, but the lst is a Friday and London will be emptying fast,' Bianca explained to

Mike and Hugh, 'and it's twelve noon for the big Switch On as it's known in the company. It's a compromise of course, but for most of the shops it won't at least be the middle of the night. New York will be awake, at least, it's perfect for Europe and even in Sydney it'll be eleven p.m., Singapore eight – not bad.'

The invitations were for eleven, with champagne and canapés and at eleven thirty Bianca would take the stage; the ticking clock would be beside her, projected on to a screen, and at the appropriate moment, she would press a button, the screen would revolve and there would be Jess, in her sequinned dress.

'It should bring the house down,' Susie said.

After which, pause for brief press conference with Jess, and then the screens would go on; and 'Music lights action,' said Susie, and the Switch On would begin.

They had had a virtually one hundred per cent acceptance rate to the launch. 'But that doesn't mean a lot,' Susie warned Bianca. 'If it's a wet morning, or someone gets Sienna Miller or Cara Delevingne to be at *their* thing, we'll be dumped, just like that.' And her fingers snapped.

Bianca said slightly crisply she didn't need warning – she wasn't entirely unfamiliar with the vagaries of the press.

The 'something beautiful' campaign was working – well, beautifully. Susie got endless calls as to what the launch was exactly about, and how it was global, but refused to give more than the mildest hint, telling them they'd just have to wait and see.

And the ticking clock countdown and the competition was an incredible success. People were coming for the day, it was announced, to stare at it, and they had already a handful of suggestions for the model's identity. As only Jess's hair, an eye and eyebrow and her neck (apart from the dress) were so far revealed, they were inevitably fairly wide of the mark, including one valiant effort of, 'I think it's Marilyn Monroe.'

Susie was pestered endlessly about that too: exactly who was this new face of Farrell, was she a model, an actress, some other kind of A-lister, and how did she fit in with the global launch? She fielded the questions only by saying they must be there, and it was an incredibly exciting event, like nothing that had ever been done before. 'You'll be sorry if you don't come, that's all I can say!'

A week before the event, a handful of the news crews were to be invited to attend, with the two-pronged promise not only of an A-list presence, but a launch that was an online breakthrough. Susie knew the response would be very non-committal; nevertheless she was fairly confident, barring an announcement that Kate Cambridge was giving a press conference, previewing her clothes for the entire weekend, or some comparably impossible event. 'Again it's so marvellous we've got the Brownleys' home as a venue – soooo much more intriguing.'

They had a great stroke of luck as May proceeded; the producers of Jess's new film had found their male lead. Dan Fleming was not only one of the current new heart-throbs and absurdly good-looking, he was also a very good actor and had been nominated the year before for a Golden Globe. His agent was keen to announce the whole package, the film, the stars, the location (Regency London) and, given the excitement about everything that was happening in twenty-first century London, it seemed ridiculous not to. There was a press conference at the Savoy and Dan's and Jess's faces were in every paper next day and on several news programmes that evening.

'Brilliant!' said Bianca. 'Our guardian angels are working overtime for us at last.'

The whole thing should get tweeted immediately, Susie thought (notionally crossing her fingers), make the later editions of the *Standard* and the major blogs and online press by evening and the printed papers the following day. If it all caused enough of a stir, they should make the weeklies, but there was considerable competition that week for column inches.

The only thing they still hadn't cracked was exactly how Athina, arguably one of their greatest treasures, was going to be brought into it all. As she didn't know anything about it still (Bianca was going to take her out to dinner the week before and do a complete presentation), this was not an easy one. Florence was not alone in fearing that, plan as they might, Athina's reaction was utterly unpredictable and could be dangerous. Very dangerous.

It was definitely, definitely getting better. Milly could feel it in the air, almost literally; walking into the classroom no longer felt like braving an icy wind, more of a mild, gentle breeze. A few girls even smiled at her rather uncertainly; she stared them out: she wasn't falling for that. But the day when she knew it had got round, that someone had seen the blog and the pictures, was when Carey passed her a note in registration. She longed not to look at it, to tear it up very obviously, but somehow she couldn't. She was fairly sure she knew what it said; and if it did, that would be the moment she had dreamed of through all the torturous, endless months, her revenge, come at last. And so she opened it, and yes, it did, she was right, wonderfully, incredibly right.

> Hi Mills,
> Think it's time we made up. Hot chocolate after school?
> For real, this time, promise.
> Carey xxxxxxxxxxxxxxxxxxx

And she had felt her eyes fill with tears and blinked them furiously back. There was no way Carey was going to see them. And she met Carey's simpering smile very coolly, refusing to return it, and then she tore a piece of paper from her file.

And wrote on it:

> Thanks, but I'm really really busy.

And pushed it back to Carey. Who looked first startled, and then oddly nervous. Maybe she was afraid of recrimination at last. Well, it didn't matter.

For many years after that, when people were discussing what their most wonderful memory was, debating it endlessly, Milly would smile and say she knew *exactly* what hers was, and then, always, refused to reveal it. Everyone would then imagine all kinds of exotic and romantic things; but she knew there had never been a more wonderful moment than that morning in the classroom, with

Carey looking totally disconcerted, and Milly knowing she had finally won.

Patrick looked rather uncertainly at Jonjo. Who had invited him for a drink at the self-same bar where his new career had started over a year ago. It was all exactly the same, the black and white décor, the sexy music, the huge sofas, the designer drinks. Only *he* felt rather different. Not excited, not anxious even, just – depressed. Deep down, wearily, monotonely depressed. Too depressed to pretend. Well, certainly to Jonjo. He looked at him bleakly as his friend raised his glass.

'Cheers,' Jonjo said. A bit too brightly. And smiled.

'Cheers,' Patrick managed. And didn't smile.

'You OK?'

'Look, Jonjo, you know I'm not OK. So let's cut that particular crap for a start, can we?'

'Oh! All – all right.'

'And if you want a long heart to heart, you're not going to get one. It's not my style.'

'You don't want to talk about it at all?'

'About what?'

'Well – you and Bianca?'

'No, I don't. Nothing to do with you and nothing to say. Only one person can help and that's Bianca. And she isn't going to. So . . . I appreciate your kindness, asking me out, but you should find a more deserving recipient.'

'Yeah, OK. Well, I just thought I might – you know—'

'You might what?'

'Be able to help. If only listen. You were pretty good to me when I – well, when things went wrong with Susie.'

'Jonjo, with respect, you'd known Susie for a week or so at that time. I've been married to Bianca for sixteen years and we have three children; it's just slightly more complex.'

'Yes, of course. Sorry. I just – well, you know, I think you're such a great couple. I've always admired you both, the way you're such – such a team. The way you share the admin and the children and everything. It's really, really great. I only hope I can do it as well one day.'

'Yes, well . . . Well, it isn't easy,' said Patrick heavily. 'I can assure you of that.'

'I'm sure it's not. But – well, anyway, seems I can't help. But I certainly didn't want you to think I don't care.'

'I'd never think that, and I'm grateful. But really, there's nothing anyone can do. Except Bianca, as I said. And she's decided not to. So I think we should have this drink and then I'll go home, if that's all right with you.'

'Yes, of course. Er – where's home right now?'

'Oh, for God's sake!' said Patrick. 'I was afraid you were going to ask me that. It's the same hotel I was in the last time we spoke, very near Tower Bridge. A Travelodge. It's clean and it's functional and it has nice river views. And before you tell me I should be staying at some fancy joint or other, let me tell you I don't want to. I'm very happy where I am. Well, I'm not very happy, but it has nothing to do with what hotel I might be staying at.'

'You don't want to stay with me? For a bit? I do have a spare bedroom—'

'Jonjo, again I appreciate your concern, but no, actually, I don't. And I believe you have another – occupant at the moment. To whom you have just become engaged. Congratulations. She's a sweetheart. And I'm sure it's all very nice but not what I need, I'm sure you can see that. Anyway, I think I told you that I'm about to go on a trip to Sydney for at least a week. Meeting Saul there. So it's not for long, the Travelodge lifestyle. Which, as a matter of fact, I quite like. It has an anonymity I find rather charming. And at the weekend I go to the country. I really am fine.'

'That's . . . good. Splendid,' said Jonjo.

Chapter 56

Athina was reading one of her favourite Sherlock Holmes stories, 'Silver Blaze', when it hit her. She was very fond of Sherlock Holmes generally, as had been Cornelius, but this, which contained the famous reference to the dog in the night-time, was her favourite. She had been feeling uneasy for a week or so now, without having the faintest idea why; everything seemed all right, the new HR director was duly deferential (having been most carefully briefed by Bianca), she was getting on better with Bianca herself – who had clearly taken her advice and was working feverishly, all the hours God sent, the perfume campaign was beautiful, and . . .

And it was the coincidence of this thought about the ads and Holmes remarking to the Scotland Yard Detective, Gregory, that what was curious about the incident of the dog in the night-time was that the dog had done nothing, that made her realise something rather curious about the campaign for the relaunch generally. There wasn't one.

This continued to cause her increasing unease as she tried to return to Dartmoor and the missing horse; why on earth was there not? With Farrell's about to relaunch as a brand, with the maximum marketing excitement, the highest profile it could reach, how could there not be? Why had not that rather scruffy-looking, albeit handsome young man – in her day, no decent advertising executive would have dreamed of attending board level meetings without a tie – why had he not been in and out of Farrell House constantly, with creative presentations, media proposals, proofs to be signed off, for the past two months? All she had seen were her perfume ads; surely they weren't trying to rush the rest of the campaign through without her approval? If they were, they had some explanations to give. If they weren't, then what were they all thinking of: did they really think they could launch – or relaunch – a cosmetic brand without extensive promotion? Clearly this needed her attention! She put aside 'Silver Blaze' and started combing through her diary. When – apart from the *Passionate* ads – had she seen anything at all? Her diary confirmed her suspicions: she hadn't. She must investigate this without delay . . .

To say the weeks following the conversation with Bianca were the most dreadful of Patrick's life was an understatement of dramatic proportion. He felt, indeed, that he was standing at the very portals of hell; lonely, angry, bewildered, with no hope of an escape in any direction. He went to the country that first weekend to try to take in what had happened to him, and begin to think what to do. He felt destroyed and betrayed, sixteen years of happiness and love and family wiped out in one dreadful, shocking hour. How could she do this? Be this selfish, this cruel, this blind to what really mattered?

It couldn't just be the job; he was increasingly certain of that. She had done other jobs, just as big, just as demanding. It seemed to him increasingly and horribly clear – he had been right in his early suspicions, his analysis of the change not only in her but her attitude to him, to the family, to everything.

She was having an affair.

The more he thought about it, the more it made sense. She'd always been a free agent, they both had, they'd always trusted one another – but suddenly it felt different.

And it had clearly been going on for some time. Increasing overnight absences, minutely detailed explanations for them, which never seemed strictly necessary, long, mysterious phone calls in the evening, always taken in another room – what else could it all mean? And that absurd world tour – so unnecessary, strictly speaking, in these days of computers and googling and Skype and conference calls – and that first time she'd been out almost all night, with the rather feeble explanation of being with the advertising boys.

But then – how much did it matter? In absolute terms. When the marriage was so hopelessly over anyway, when she had refused to do what he really wanted, give up her job for him? Although she was still insisting she hadn't refused, that she still needed time. Time to decide, time to be able to leave Farrell's without causing too much disruption. Which was nonsense. She didn't need it. Or she shouldn't. There should be no struggle between a marriage and a job, as he had pointed out to her repeatedly. They simply could not be equated; it was as simple as that. And the more she delayed, the more surely he knew what her answer was: which was why he had pre-empted it.

On the other hand, their marriage had survived the savage demands of her career before. They had rallied, recovered, their wounds had healed; she had had a few months off, devoting herself to him and the children, and they had learned to be together again. This time, it was an affair: her infidelity, her being in love with someone else, having time for someone else, for sex with someone else, even when she had none for him – that had dealt the truly fatal blow.

He became swiftly obsessed with who it was; he suspected that smooth, handsome bugger at the advertising agency, or the new financial director – she spent an inordinate amount of time with him; or one of the VCs even – or was it someone else entirely? Someone he didn't know, or even know of, stealing into their lives unrecognised, unsuspected, seducing, persuading his wife, his beloved wife – for he did love her so very much – away from him.

Patrick was a mild man, patient, trusting, equable; but he knew that if he should ever meet this man, this man stealing his wife, his children, his whole existence, he would be able to kill him, quite easily, with nothing but his empty hands as weapons.

Bianca, equally wretched, consumed with guilt, did what she always did in times of crisis: worked. With three weeks to go, terrified by the imminent launch and the ever-present possibility of failure, she stalked the Farrell offices, demanding, arguing, complaining. She was haunted by the global launch going unmarked, envisaging the vast room at Lord Brownley's devoid of journalists, bloggers, TV cameras, while the representatives of the House of Farrell and of Flynn Marchant stared at screens offering only pictures of empty streets and arcades around the world, and the doors of the Berkeley Arcade replicas that stood in them hopelessly unattended. The whole relaunch followed by a few desultory articles in the press over the next few days about the imminent bankruptcy of House of Farrell and the entirely misplaced faith that had been placed in its chief executive, Bianca Bailey.

At night, when she went home, and after the childen were in bed, she became more wretched still, unable to eat or sleep, worrying desperately about Patrick, missing him dreadfully, and she would sit at her desk into the small hours, trying to work and checking her phone constantly, hoping against all odds he would finally have replied to her endless texts and calls and emails. He never had. His hostility towards her was clearly absolute; he didn't, he couldn't, love her at all.

She was even beginning to wonder if she did still love him.

Saul was in his room at the Langham Hotel, Sydney – formerly known by the rather more romantic name of the Observatory, charmingly low-storeyed and a wonderful contrast to the great glass monsters that were its neighbours – when Bianca's text came through. He was drinking tea and looking out of his window at the view which was truly glorious. The only hotel he could think of that offered a view as stunning was the Crillon in Paris, and its gift of the Place de la Concorde in all its absurd, breathtaking grandeur. This was not exactly grandeur, but it was equally beautiful in its own way: both the Opera House and the Sydney Harbour Bridge, one so brilliantly white, the other so dark, both so absolutely familiar, carved out of the intense blue sky, and beyond it the wider water, teeming with ferryboats and water taxis and of course the endless sailing boats, white wings flying before the wind.

He had been there before, of course, but inevitably, for fleeting, rushed visits, so he had never paused to take it in. If Dickon were to come to live here, and it seemed increasingly, terrifyingly, likely – then he needed to learn the place, every aspect of it, what it might have to offer. Not just basic things like where the best neighbourhoods were, where Dickon might live, what kind of school he might go to, what the price of property was, not merely what it looked like, even, but the feel of the place, its people, its pleasures – in short, its very soul.

The text distracted him from Sydney's soul; he had not expected to see her name on his phone again. Since that day in New York, he had thought of her often, and in many different ways: she was a woman such as he had seldom known. And certainly seldom spent time with. Saul's view of women was for the most part misogynistic; he had little faith in their brains, their skills, their ambitions, however impressive they might be, for they were tempered and affected in his experience, as well as his opinion, by their biology. You would not have persuaded Saul Finlayson to deny the existence of the glass ceiling; it was not a figment of women's imagination, that ceiling, he knew. It was there for a good reason, which was the male distrust of the female and her ability to put the job first.

Most women put the job second to their children: entirely right and proper, he would say, children should be put first because they were the future, and must be nurtured at all costs. And for women, almost all women, that nurturing could not – and indeed should not – be set aside, delegated to an inevitably less satisfactory substitute, a nanny, say, or even a grandmother, so that the job, the firm, the deal, the patient, might take prime position in all circumstances. And however much he was assured by prospective employees that this was the case, he knew that the illness of her child, the unhappiness of her child, the sudden absence of the carer of her child, would mean the prime position was re-allotted to that child. Mothers were never, could not ever, be totally reliable in the workplace, and total reliablity was what he required, demanded, indeed and he would not hear to the contrary; nor would he employ them, or consider their right to be employed by him.

He had been told repeatedly that he could face legal action as a result of this; he merely shrugged and said he would take the law on, or this particular aspect of it, and fight it – if necessary, to the death. So far he had not been required to step up to that particular plate; he had avoided it carefully. He interviewed potential employees rarely, and potential female employees of childbearing age never. His HR director was brilliant at making any senior position sound impossible, stressing regretfully the inevitability of domestic disruption, impossible hours, and an inhospitable workplace environment. Any woman prepared to take such horrors on were generally extremely young and childless. Bianca, however, had fascinated him in her ability to crash through the ceiling, encumbered as she was by her three young children; but she had had the unarguable and immense asset of the one person capable of satisfactorily replacing those children's mother: their father. And Saul had deprived her of that asset by removing him – and turned her world upside down. For which he had felt some degree of remorse; although, of course, Patrick had *chosen* to work for him of his own free will. And he knew, moreover, he had rather underplayed the demands the job might make on Patrick's time; for which guilt was added to the remorse.

He read the text twice, *Hello. I hope your visit is successful, in whatever way you wish. I collected Dickon last night from judo and he seemed very cheerful. Patrick is coming to Sydney as of course you know. He's left me, which you may not. He wants a divorce. Please be kind to him, please listen to him carefully. And keep me posted. xx*

Saul had booked Patrick into the Langham as well. There was a company in their sights, a burgeoning tin-mining complex in Darwin, its value soaring on the stock exchange by the day; its boss, with the absurd cliché of a name of Doug Douglas – how could he entrust the future of his child to a people who coined such names? – was coming to Sydney to meet Patrick and then fly with him up to Darwin to show him exactly what he would be missing if he advised Saul against investment.

But not for twenty-four hours; in the meantime Patrick could brief Saul with what information he had already garnered and his consequent instincts, which were almost entirely positive.

Patrick would arrive at Kingsford Smith airport late that night; Saul had arranged a car to meet him and intended to be, theoretically at any rate, asleep when Patrick arrived, leaving a note in his room inviting him to brunch with Doug Douglas, rather than breakfast in his suite. Patrick would then be as clear-headed as possible for any discussions that might take place, not only with Doug Douglas about the tin mines, but with Saul about his marriage.

It was against his inclination and out of character and he dreaded it; but the acknowledged sense of responsibility he felt towards the Baileys had just been increased considerably. Something had to be done; he must try to do it.

'So,' said Patrick to Saul as they settled down to talk, the fairly dreadful Mr Douglas dispatched to his own hotel, mercifully on the other side of the harbour, 'how much longer are you staying here?'

What he was asking in a code that he knew Saul would crack at once was the situation *vis à vis* Dickon; he was aware not only that Saul might want to talk about it – and would remain silent if he didn't – but that for some reason he had become one of the few, the very few, people that Saul appeared to be willing to talk to at all.

He had no idea why this should be; he was the opposite of the touchy feely male who normally prompted such confidences, but perhaps that was the reason. Perhaps Saul found his public-school reticence reassuring.

'Couple more days,' Saul said. He looked at Patrick's scarcely touched plate; his own was already inevitably empty. 'I want to look at the school Janey and this Bernard French have suggested. And I'm checking out the area where he proposes they live. That's crucial.'

'You sound – well,' Patrick corrected himself, 'does that mean it's looking more – more likely?'

'It's a possibility I have to face,' said Saul. 'I'm still intending to fight it, obviously. But the more knowledge I have the better equipped I am to do that. And if the neighbourhood is bad, it will provide me with increased ammunition.'

Patrick felt this was unlikely; the man in question was a rich successful advertising executive, scarcely likely to be moving to some dodgy area of Sydney.

'Any idea where it is?'

'Mossman.'

'Mossman's extremely nice,' said Patrick, 'big houses, very expensive, lovely beaches.'

'Really? Well, I still need to check it out. How do you know Sydney so well?'

'We had an extended family holiday here about four years ago. Bianca had an aunt here, and we stayed with her. It was – it was a very nice trip,' he said, and the memory of this visit was surprisingly vivid, endless days on sunny beaches, body boarding with the children, cooking fish on the barbecues so thoughtfully provided on almost every beach, exploring the Blue Mountains in a campervan, watching the surfers at Bondi flying in on the huge waves, going to a rock concert at the Olympic stadium, and a children's concert at the Opera House, climbing the Harbour Bridge with Bianca – that had been amazing – catching sight of the whales far out at sea off the Northern Beaches . . . it seemed, in retrospect, a time of infinite, sunbleached happiness, entirely devoid of care. He remembered thinking he had never been happier and when Fergie, just seven years old then, had begged that they move out there to live, he was, momentarily, tempted to at least consider it. Bianca, driven partly by several glasses of wonderful oaky, Ozzie chardonnay, had even said why not, they could give it two years, enjoy it while the children were young enough.

But common sense had prevailed; and they had returned home to jobs and schools and duty, to Bianca's career and his own guaranteed, gilt-edged future – and he cursed common sense now, for having brought them to the wretched present.

He looked at Saul, aware he had been silent for a long time. 'Sorry,' he said.

'That's OK. That's fine.'

Another silence; then Patrick said and was astonished to hear himself say it, 'How bad is divorce?'

'Pretty bad,' said Saul.

'I – I'm considering it.'

'Because?'

He was so – so calming to talk to. No commiseration, no surprise. It was why working for him was good. He just – what was the expression? – cut to the chase. Anything else was dismissed as irrelevant. And of course there was his famous inability to tell a lie . . .

'Because it doesn't work any more. The marriage.'

'Yes, well, that's the only reason that's ever valid, I suppose. I'm sorry. Bit surprised. You seemed good together.'

'We were,' said Patrick, 'very good. But – she's changed.'

A silence while Saul considered this.

'Is it her job? It's pretty full-on. I don't know that I could cope with it.'

'Yes, that's got a – a lot to do with it.'

'But she's always been like that, surely.'

'She has. But this time is different. It's hard to explain. I feel she's, well, put it first. In a big way. Instead of giving it equal billing, so to speak.'

'The job's different maybe?'

'A job's a job,' said Patrick.

'Really? Do you feel that about working for me?'

Patrick panicked. Had he offended Saul, would he feel his job dismissed?

'No! Of course not.'

'Good,' said Saul.

A long silence, while Patrick gulped down several mouthfuls of the excellent Shiraz that Saul had ordered.

'Anything else?'

'I think she might be – no, *is* – having an affair,' said Patrick abruptly. And he heard his own voice, almost unrecognisable, very flat, very hard, as he said it.

'I see,' said Saul, his voice still entirely calm. 'Well, one does always know.'

'Does one? It's never happened to me before.'

'Yes, I see. You're lucky. And do you know who with?'

'No. No I don't. Although I've got my suspicions.'

'Ah,' said Saul. 'Well, the thing is, Patrick – God, this is difficult – the thing is, I know she's not . . .'

Up in his room, Saul called Bianca.

'Hello,' he said.

'Hello. You all right?'

'I'm fine. I can't be long, I'm talking with Patrick.'

'I can't be either. Is – is Patrick all right? What happened?'

'Quite a lot,' said Saul. 'Now listen. And we do need to talk some more when I get back to London because it's quite – complicated.'

If it hadn't been Saul who had told him, Patrick wouldn't have believed it. He would have thought either it was a fruitless attempt to make him feel better or a rather clumsy piece of covering up, of something he knew about that Patrick did not. But everyone knew that Saul never lied. He was incapable of it. There were too many stories about it, this legendary inability, of would-be clients put off at the first meeting, of affronted flirting women, of angry exchanges with employees, of instantly curtailed interviews with journalists, all confronted by the same abrupt, stark response to what others might have considered perfectly reasonable questions or approaches or even obligatory social exchange.

And Jonjo had told Patrick of it, and Patrick had observed it for himself, time and again.

So if Saul said Bianca wasn't having an affair, had told him she never had, indeed, then she wasn't. Of course, Bianca might have been lying to Saul, but given the rather intimate nature of the conversation, that was extremely unlikely. Her rather odd observation that she would not have had the time, apart from never wanting to, gave the whole story great authenticity. It was so peculiarly typical of her attitude to life, so much the sort of thing she would say; and although perhaps mildly insulting, Patrick thought wryly, it was reassuring for more than one reason.

It was an admittedly odd conversation she and Saul had clearly had; he would not have expected her to have talked about the state of their marriage, and nor would he have thought that Saul would ask her if she was having an affair – it seemed to imply an intimacy between them that in itself was disturbing. But be that as it might, Bianca was *not* having an affair; she might be guilty of all the other things he had accused her of, but not that. And now he didn't know how he felt about her, or whether indeed he loved her still: and nor did he know what to do.

He sat on the plane on his way back to England, his laptop open on his table, his files spread around him on the floor, apologising endlessly to people who walked over them or kicked them into disorder, patiently sorting them out again, returning to the figures Doug Douglas had supplied him with, struggling to find distraction from his misery. But he didn't; the files and the laptop and the figures failed him, and all he could think about was what he was going to say to Bianca when he saw her, and what she might then say to him.

That very morning, Tod Marchant was taking a rare day away from the increasingly frenetic global launch of the Farrell empire. He was already totally overspent time-wise on this ad, but he knew the shock and awe, so to speak, that it created would do the agency infinitely more good than a careful adherence to budgets and time sheets and devotion to other clients. However, one of the other clients, a chain of small supermarkets, was growing increasingly dissatisfied with the media schedule in particular, and Flynn Marchant in general, and the boss of the chain, one Neil Fullerton, had told Tod that if he didn't get his arse in gear and thence up to Leicester where its head office was, then he might find that he was minus one client.

Tod agreed to travel to Leicester two days later, and instructed his PA, a highly efficient girl called Paddy Logan, to mind the shop in his absence and if anything cropped up that seemed even remotely important, to confer with Jack Flynn.

However, all things great being bound up, as is frequently

observed, with all things small, not only did Jack's new baby decide to start teething that night, but his mother developed an extremely unpleasant stomach bug and told Jack there was no way she could take care of the baby for at least twenty-four hours and just for once he'd have to put his family first, rather than as a very bad second to the agency, and stay home and face up to his responsibilities. Jack, who was exhausted by a bad night, and imagining this was the easier option, agreed.

Since they were the only two people in the agency with any knowledge of the complexities of the Farrell global launch, and who knew what and to whom that could be told, it was not surprising that Paddy Logan did exactly what she was told when Lady Farrell, who sounded very grand and rather terrifying and was clearly in a position of immense authority at the House of Farrell, called her and asked her for details of the advertising campaign.

'And I don't want it sent over down the line or anything ridiculous like that; I want it to be on a piece of paper, several pieces of paper, I imagine, and sent over to me by messenger without delay. Is that clear?'

Paddy Logan said it was quite clear.

The messenger arrived at Farrell House just before eleven. Christine picked the package up from reception and handed it to Athina.

'Oh, yes, thank you, Christine. Perhaps this will clear everything up . . . but I do feel confused, I must say . . . Heavens above, what is this? What *is* this?'

For what it was made no sense to her at all and seemed to imply that the entire media schedule for the Farrell relaunch – perfume excepted – consisted of an online presence starting at noon on Wednesday May 30th, and continuing indefinitely . . .

Some of it could no doubt be explained, she thought, by the ticking clock countdown which of course she knew about and understood, but the rest? Totally inexplicable.

What did it mean? And why had no one taken the trouble to make it explicable or even to discuss it with her? And what it might mean in advertising terms? Pain and outrage swept over Athina in equal measures; she felt belittled, discarded and, above all, underestimated.

She called Susie Harding on the internal line but Susie was not there. The publicity assistant, Vicki Philips, said she'd be back in an hour. Vicki was an English graduate who regarded the job as just a little beneath her.

'I'll get her to call you, Lady Farrell.'

'Please tell her to come up to my office. But no later than eleven, please, I'm going out to lunch with Lord Fearon. He's a very important and influential newsaper owner, as I'm sure you know.'

'Of course,' said Vicki, who knew no such thing. 'But I'm not sure if she will be back by then.'

'Well, I would advise you to get her back by then. If she wants to keep her job. Meanwhile, do you have any kind of detailed rundown of the PR launch? In my day, it would have been widely circulated and comment invited long before this.'

'Of course, but you see, because this is so different from any other launch—'

'Different? In precisely what way?'

'Well, with the very tight window, time-wise, and the blogging aspect being so crucial—' Vicki stopped suddenly. She knew the bare minimum about the launch campaign herself, except that it was to run entirely online, was hugely confidential, and wasn't to begin for another week. It irritated her profoundly that Susie clearly didn't consider her of sufficient importance within the team to entrust her with its details, and she had been told repeatedly that the little she did know was of the strictest confidentiality and not to be shared with anyone within the company.

But surely Lady Farrell herself must know everything there was to be known? She was, after all, still the head of the company, whatever people like Jemima might say. Vicki was one of the few people in the company who was not in awe of Jemima and indeed considered herself as her intellectual superior. Jemima's degree in psychology from Nottingham could hardly compare with her own in English from Oxford. And her claims that Bianca was the overall *numero uno* at the House of Farrell, and not Lady Farrell, its founder – and living legend within the industry – seemed to her more than a little arrogant.

'If you will just excuse me a moment, Lady Farrell, I know Jemima has the full details of the PR campaign. I'll ask her if she can join us and put you completely in the picture. I'm sure it's merely an oversight that you haven't already had the information you want.'

'Miss Philips,' said Athina, using the iciest of tones, 'I do assure you that I am not accustomed to being overlooked. Nor will I tolerate it. And nor will I be put in the picture, as you call it, by a pair of secretaries. I will wait for Miss Harding to return. Please send her immediately – absolutely immediately – up to my office. Thank you.'

Journeying to Farrell House that same morning, Lara reflected on her extreme happiness. Like Bertie, she was not too familiar with proper, five star, grade A happiness; and it was just – just lovely, that happiness. It accompanied her, wherever she went. She woke up with it and went to work with it and attended meetings with it and went shopping with it, and went home again with it and cooked supper for herself and Bertie with it, and went to sleep with it, and it was like carrying around a piece of treasure, of infinite worth, and nothing else seemed nearly as important. She was still a little surprised by it.

Of course they had a long way to go yet; his divorce was in the early stages and Priscilla was being as difficult as possible. And for the time being they were to be separated during the week. She had tried, and failed, to persuade Bertie to stay in London; he said it was the first time he had got a job on his own merits, rather than because he was a member of his family, and that it was therefore hugely important to him. And Lara had to concede this.

And, of course, it could be that they might not continue to find one another as perfect, as ideal, as they did at the moment. Honeymoon periods they were called. But she didn't actually believe that.

Honeymoons, the genuine articles, were not something she

allowed her thoughts to stray any way near. There was no way Bertie Farrell was going to marry her. That really was unthinkable. How would Lady Farrell, for a start, react to that? She'd be horrified, try to forbid it. Caro wouldn't be exactly delighted either. Or that rather distant, superior husband of hers. But God, the wedding would be fun.

Lara pulled herself together firmly. It wasn't going to happen. She didn't even *want* it to happen. It was unnecessary, unimaginable; she'd been there, done that, got the T-shirt.

She walked into Farrell House, went up to her office, switched on her computer – and Susie rushed in white-faced and wild-eyed.

'Thank God, Lara, thank God you're here. Something dreadful's happened, really, really dreadful, and I just don't know what to do.'

Lara's mind raced over the range of possibilities: the factory going up in smoke taking the new range with it, the global website crashing beyond repair, a mass boycott by the beauty editors of the entire Farrell range . . . But what Susie told her seemed as bad as any of those. And as impossible to deal with.

'She's just so – so *angry*,' Susie said, so distressed that she was having trouble breathing. 'I just don't know what to *do*. What can I do? As if anyone could do anything. She's so totally impossible.'

'Susie,' said Lara as gently as she could, for she was finding her distinctly irritating, 'Susie, are you surprised?'

'What – that she's being impossible? No, of course not. But that doesn't make it any easier to deal with.'

'What does Bianca say?'

'She doesn't know. She's gone walkabout and I can't get hold of her. She's just not picking up – it is quite weird and so unlike her. Jemima can't even get a response with their emergency signal.'

'What's that, for heaven's sake?' said Lara.

'Oh, it's something crazy like: I saw a really good film last night. No one could guess that, you see, and it protects her from outsiders getting hold of her. And we're having lunch with Lord and Lady Brownley today, and Jess Cochrane and Tamsin at The Ritz. So you'd think . . . Anyway, it gets worse: Lady Farrell is having lunch with Lord Fearon, also at The Ritz! I mean, you couldn't make it up.'

'Oh my God,' said Lara, 'but why? Why is she having lunch with him?'

'Well, they're old friends. But you can bet your bottom dollar she'll tell him all about it, not just the campaign, but how she's been spurned, how she gets treated like a second-class citizen here, how nobody respects her opinion any more . . . you can see what a story it would make. With us as the villains, of course.'

'Shit!' said Lara. 'So how did she find out?'

'She stormed the citadel: first the agency and then here, frightening assistants and secretaries out of their wits. I was out, but by the time I got back, it was clear I'd have to come totally clean.'

'And what did she say?'

'Nothing. Just stalked out. Oh, Lara this is a nightmare. If only, if only we could get hold of Bianca! Short of her being in a car accident I can't imagine what she can be doing.'

'Oh, don't!' said Lara.

'Jemima says it has to be something to do with the children.'

Jemima was, as usual, right.

Bianca had, on that volcanic morning, decided to drive Milly to school, where her form was responsible for school assembly.

'I know how busy you are, the week before your launch and everything,' Milly had said, 'but it would be lovely if you could come.'

'Darling, of course I'll come. Nothing can go wrong at this stage and if it does, there's nothing I can do about it. And I want to see your assembly. Are you doing anything on your own?'

'Well, the theme's the Diamond Jubilee, obviously, and we're doing some songs and stuff. And I'm reading something, yes. It's that piece from Shakespeare – you know, about the sceptred isle? It's lovely, but I didn't really want to because I'm still lying low, however, everyone voted for me. Funny that,' she added, her voice suddenly sharper.

Bianca looked at her. She wasn't the innocent, happy child of a year ago. She had grown tougher, cynical even, and her natural expression was slightly wary. She would never get over it and it had been a hideous experience for her; and Bianca knew she too would never be free of the guilt of not probing and pressing and trying to help. But on the other hand, Milly had learned a great deal, not least how to protect herself; her courage, everyone agreed, was remarkable. That much good, at least, had come out of it.

She dropped Milly outside the school gates, parked, and then walked in herself, switching off her phone altogether, not even putting it on mute; Milly was to have her full concentration this morning.

As she reached the front door, she heard someone behind her, calling her name: it was Nicky Mapleton.

'Bianca! How nice to see you.'

'Nice to see you too,' said Bianca, her voice so cold that it would have permeated a skin even thicker than Nicky's.

'I'm sorry the girls haven't socialised so much recently,' Nicky said, 'but of course this shy phase Milly's going through is very common.'

'Shy stage?'

'Yes. Carey tells me she's become paralytically shy, won't go anywhere with anybody.'

'Is *that* what Carey told you?' said Bianca. 'How fascinating. No, Milly's fine, thank you. Not in the least shy.'

'Oh – good,' said Nicky Mapleton, looking rather less sure of herself. 'And I hear she's been doing some modelling, how exciting.'

'Oh, only for a friend of the family,' said Bianca, 'and for a bit of fun. I certainly wouldn't want her to take it any further. Such a horrible world that, I always think,' she added, smiling sweetly at Nicky Mapleton, the one-time supermodel. 'So many dreadful people.'

'Perhaps a few. As there are in your world, I'm sure. Well, I must just go and say hello to a few people, if you'll excuse me . . . I'll catch up with you later. Milly must come round, if she's really feeling better. We were so disappointed she couldn't come to Paris for Carey's birthday.'

'Yes, it was a shame,' said Bianca, 'it sounded very exciting, but there was something else she wanted to do that weekend . . .'

* * *

Milly read very sweetly and Bianca developed, as always, a very large lump in her throat. There were the usual songs, tableaux, prayers (briefly) and then the girls filed out. Looking at them, pretty, sweet-faced, smiling little things, it was hard to believe that every single one of them had been involved in the conspiracy to make Milly's life hell. Carey, extra pretty, extra confident, spotted her and blew her a kiss. Bianca looked extremely coolly back at her.

It was almost eleven by the time she had driven away, after ducking repeated invitations for Milly; for some reason she didn't want to go into the office quite yet. If she did go in there would be some piffling panic that she couldn't face. Her stress levels had been so high for so long that, having been pulled into a slightly more peaceful state, the thought of staying there a little longer was suddenly irresistible. So she *would* stay there for a little longer.

Moreover, she had a lot to think about – not least Patrick and the extraordinary thing that Saul had done – was it really only twenty-four hours earlier? She left her phone switched off; and, astonishing herself, made a detour to Peter Jones to look at curtain fabric and astonished herself still more by finding the process quite engaging, and was sitting in the café, sipping a fruit juice, when she finally felt she must switch on her phone and was hit by a mass of messages and voicemails, the most alarming being from Jemima, telling her she had seen a fantastic film last night, and another from Susie, sounding extremely agitated, and saying she really really must speak to her.

'God, it's been the most ghastly morning,' said Jemima when she finally got through.

Florence had been putting the final touches to the Jubilee window of The Shop when Athina rang.

'Florence, I need to speak to you about something. It's very important. I'm terribly upset and I'm sure you will be too when you hear about it. I'm coming down there immediately. I would get you to come up here but I'm having lunch with Lord Fearon at The Ritz, so it's more convenient this way.'

The lifelong fear that had stalked Florence, ever since Cornelius had first kissed her in the taxi, so many many years ago, struck her with its usual intensity. Someone had told Athina that Cornelius and she had been having an affair; or they suspected this had been the case, and Athina should question Florence about it; or even that Athina had been told about the lease on the Berkeley Arcade and that Florence now owned it . . .

'Very well, Athina,' she said, 'we can talk in the parlour.'

Florence was waiting upstairs when Athina arrived. She did look extremely upset.

'Do sit down, Athina. Tea?'

'What? No. Oh – well, perhaps. Thank you,' she added in a clear attempt at sounding gracious as Florence handed her a cup. Florence was beginning to feel less terrified about the subject about to be discussed.

'So – what is it, Athina? What has upset you?'

'I can hardly bear to talk about it! Oh, Florence you've put sugar in this, you know I don't like it.'

'I'm sorry. Here, have mine.'

'Yes, that's a little better. Too weak, though. Now listen. I've just discovered that there is a major advertising campaign planned for the relaunch and that it will take place entirely on the net or whatever that ridiculous thing is called. An enormous amount of money is being invested in it, and – and this is the most shocking thing – I have been told absolutely nothing about it nor been consulted in any way.'

'Oh,' said Florence, 'oh, I see.'

'Yes, well I don't think you do. You've always had trouble with the business side of things. This is very serious, Florence. What they're saying is that my opinion is of no consequence. I've had to endure a great deal at the hands of these people, but nothing approaching this. Don't they realise, don't they understand that if it wasn't for me there would be no House of Farrell? I don't know when I've been treated with such contempt. Of course they tried to explain it away, said it had been kept from everyone except a few key people. Key people! Who could be more key than I am? What Cornelius would have to say, I cannot imagine . . .'

'Well, I can see that it is rather upsetting for you, Athina. But I'm sure they know what they're doing and the need to keep it confidential—'

'Oh really, Florence!' said Athina, putting down her cup. 'Don't tell me they know what they're doing. Look at the shambles of the whole perfume business, just for a start. What would have come of that, and indeed the entire sales conference, without me? And who named The Collection, and who conceived the idea of the palettes? Oh, I can see I'm just wasting my time talking to you. Sometimes, Florence, I wonder if you understand *anything* about this business apart from stock levels in The Shop and how the windows look.'

'Athina, that's unfair. I understand a great deal about this business. I've worked for Farrell's almost from the very beginning, and it is as much a part of me as it is of you.'

'Oh, for heaven's sake,' said Athina, 'you seem to have a very inflated opinion of yourself and your role at Farrell's. You'll be telling me you know all about this ridiculous campaign, in a minute.'

'Actually,' said Florence, 'I do.'

And fifty years of slights and insults and jealousy were eased and soothed away just a little, at the utterance of those three apparently innocuous little words.

Chapter 57

'Florence, is she still with you?' Bianca's voice on the phone was unusually peremptory.

'No. She's headed off to The Ritz, Bianca, I'm so sorry—'

'Florence, it's not your fault; I underestimated her, as usual.'

'Yes, but I think I made things worse. I should have pretended I didn't know either. She was so angry.'

'Well – maybe. But hindsight is a wonderful thing, and all those other clichés. But you're sure she's going to tell him?'

'About the campaign? I'm pretty sure. The only thing that might save us is that she doesn't quite understand it.'

'Now *you're* underestimating her.'

'Maybe. But what she's certainly going to talk about is how badly she's been treated by you, accusing you of ignoring her, and the fact the company is her creation, that there would be no House of Farrell without her and – well, I don't need to go on.'

'Yes, I can see we won't come out smelling of roses. It's a wonderful story for one of Lord Fearon's columnists. And she'll wring every ounce of drama out of it. Oh God. Well – I'll have to try and speak to her. As luck would have it, or rather *un*-luck, I'm having lunch there too, with the Brownleys. She'll probably make great capital of that too.'

'I think she'll probably be there early,' said Florence. 'She left here in a huge bait, and stormed off down the arcade in that direction. She said she was going to walk there – it's only about three minutes away – and she's hardly likely to go shopping or have a coffee in Starbucks. I'd put my money on the Palm Court, or the ladies'. She'll be skulking away there, working out exactly what she's going to say.'

'Now that, Florence, is really helpful. And don't worry about telling her you knew about it. You'd have had to be a saint of mega proportions not to. It must have been a wonderful moment,' she added.

Florence, who knew she would have total recall of Athina's face at that moment for as long as she lived, said that of course it had been no such thing.

'Liar,' said Bianca.

There was a small flurry of photographers at the side door of The Ritz; presumably, Bianca thought, they had heard Jess would be there. Her profile had become very high since the announcement of the new film. God. Athina would probably see them too. Better find her fast . . .

She was not in the Palm Court; nor was she in the dining room. That meant the ladies'. Bianca took a deep breath and went down the small flight of stairs leading to it and opened the door cautiously. And there Athina sat at one of the dressing tables, applying a fresh coat of make-up. She had obviously been crying . . .

'Oh,' Bianca said, 'Lady Farrell. How are you?'

'I have nothing to say to you,' Athina said.

'Oh, I'm sorry—'

'I shall, however, have a great deal to say to Lord Fearon.'

'About?'

'Oh, for heaven's sake! About how appallingly I have been treated. About your arrogance. About how totally dismissed you have made me feel. About how you have chosen to ignore all my knowledge and experience, to oust me from my position, to make me look foolish—'

'Lady Farrell, that was the last thing I intended.'

'I find that hard to believe. You've made a very big mistake, Mrs Bailey, trying to capitalise on the past and Farrell's heritage and ignoring the one person responsible for that. And, of course this ridiculous advertising campaign – I'm sure Lord Fearon will be *very* interested in that. And I want his readers to be the first to hear about it. Not that I consider it to be remotely suitable to a cosmetic launch but I can see it's very innovatory.'

'Lady Farrell,' said Bianca, and never had she chosen her words with such discretion and care, 'I am so very sorry you should feel like that, I really am.'

'Well, what do you expect me to feel? When I think how my husband would have felt, how angry on my behalf – to see me reduced to . . .' She hesitated, obviously not sure what she had been reduced to. 'To this. He would not have tolerated such treatment, I assure you. And when Lord Fearon hears of it – and he was a great friend to both of us – I know he will be equally shocked. And please don't think you can talk me out of this.'

She turned to the mirror, started applying blusher. She looked so marvellous, Bianca thought, dressed in white, her silver hair sleek, her diamonds flashing, not in the least like a grieving, wronged woman – and thought that when *she* was old, she would like to look exactly like her, chic, beautiful, confident. It was a much better role than – and at that very moment Bianca realised what she could do.

'Lady Farrell, forgive me, but—'

At this point the cloakroom attendant appeared from the room beyond, which housed the row of cubicles; she cleared her throat, smiled at them and cleared the saucer of the few pound coins that had been in it.

'What a lovely day, ladies,' she said.

'Isn't it?' said Bianca, smiling back while Athina gave the woman a look which would have brought silence to the Last Night of the Proms, and turned back to the mirror. Bianca looked at her watch. Twenty to one; she didn't have long.

Two women came in, leather-coated and lacquer-haired, looked at them, and passed through to the cubicles.

'Well, I wouldn't stand for it,' one called to the other.

'I know,' said the other, 'but I do need him. He's fairly essential, really.'

Now who could *he* be, Bianca wondered. A cook? A chauffeur? A husband? Anyway, no time to waste . . .

'Lady Farrell,' she said, 'I really do wish you could see things my way. How much I have tried to work with you, how grateful I am for *Passionate* and your – well, your creation of the advertising campaign for it. And how I have longed to have you as a friend.'

Athina looked at her witheringly. 'A friend?' she said, in best Lady Bracknell tones. 'A friend? Of *yours*?'

'Well, yes. Because, you see, I admire you so much. Your style, your talent, your – well, you are a legend. When I first realised I was going to work with you, I was so excited I couldn't wait to meet you. And I shall never forget the first time I saw you, looking so fantastic in your red jacket . . .' God, she hoped it had been red; she really couldn't remember. 'And I thought I would like to be you, in your position, one day.'

'I think that is highly unlikely,' said Athina.

'I expect it is. But you must be pleased about that, that you are such a figurehead.'

The two women came back, looked pointedly at the stools Bianca and Athina were sitting on, and, realising neither of them were going to move, were forced into sharing the remaining basin and leaning over one another to re-apply their lipstick. They left, depositing two fifty pence coins in the dish; the attendant whisked them away. Clearly she felt they would be an encouragement to others to leave so minimal a tip.

She sat down again, and pulled out some knitting.

'For my granddaughter,' she said, 'my first, she—'

Athina looked at her. 'Please leave us,' she said.

The woman didn't move. It was very hard not to laugh; Bianca studied her nails, her shoes, wondered what on earth she could do.

'I asked you to leave,' said Athina. 'My colleague and I have things to discuss.'

'But madam—'

'Oh, for heaven's sake. Do I have to call the housekeeper or whoever you report to? I merely ask for five minutes' peace and quiet.'

The woman stared at her and then obediently left the room. Athina looked after her and then at Bianca. 'You were saying . . . ?'

So she had her attention: that was something. It was a lot, actually.

'Well, and if I were you, I wouldn't want people seeing me as someone whose day had passed. Someone out of touch and not keeping up with the times.'

'I beg your pardon?'

'No, Lady Farrell, don't misunderstand me. Of course you are none of those things. Look how you had everyone hanging on your words at the conference, how totally amazing they all thought you were. But just supposing this article by Lord Fearon, or one of his editors, the one you're talking about, was misconstrued. People might get the wrong idea, think yes, that you had been treated badly, but perhaps with good reason? It is possible, you know. And instead of being regarded as a great power in the company and indeed the entire cosmetic world, someone wonderfully au fait with everything, one of the great forces – no, *the* force – behind the House of Farrell, someone people envy and are impressed by, imagine if they felt sympathetic and sorry for you – I know which I'd prefer.'

There was a long silence; Athina met her eyes, and there was the expression there that Bianca remembered from the very first meeting at Farrell House, an acknowledgement between two power-ful women who each needed the other. There was a long silence.

Then, 'Oh, what nonsense!' Athina said.

It wasn't until Athina came over to her table at half past two, with Lord Fearon in her wake, turning every head in the restaurant as she did so, and said, 'Lord Fearon, this is Bianca Bailey, our managing director. We have worked together very closely on the campaign I have been telling you about . . .' that Bianca knew she had won.

Patrick had gone home. He was missing the children, he was sick of hotels, and in the end, a five-star job overlooking Sydney

Harbour and a Travelodge near Tower Bridge seemed much of a muchness.

They both were totally impersonal; the blandness with which they were furnished, whether luxurious or basic, was not what you would have chosen; you couldn't open the windows to get some fresh air; and servility on any scale, however welcome initially, became irritating and wearing.

He was also tired of being on his own. Apart from the time with Saul, which had had its shortcomings to put it mildly, and Doug Douglas, he had been entirely alone for over a week. The first night of room service, so self-indulgent and pleasant (what could be nicer than a club sandwich, a half bottle of claret and all the episodes of *Mad Men* or *Borgen* you could wish for?) became sickeningly tedious by the fourth, only serving to emphasise your solitary state; and then what was air travel if not room service in another guise? More films, more claret, more servility – and more windows you were not allowed to open.

For the first time, Patrick was finding the solitude of his job a problem . . .

He arrived home just before midday; Sonia was politely unsurprised to see him, and offered to make him an omelette. The children were all at school, she said, then Milly and Ruby were both going to sleepovers, Fergie was going to the cinema with a friend and Bianca was going to be very late. So much for company.

Patrick refused the omelette, made himself a cup of coffee, and then went up to his study, flung the windows open as wide as they would go, and lay down on the bed. It was absolutely the wrong thing to do, he knew, after coming off a long-haul flight; he should be setting out on a brisk walk but there didn't seem to be much to stay awake for. And anyway, he could read and . . . watch TV and . . . He was asleep in five minutes.

'The thing is, I can't go on employing him,' Saul was saying, folding up the empty box that had held a Marks & Spencer BLT less than a minute before and turning his attention to a can of cola. They were sitting on a bench on the South Bank, the National Theatre's great bulk looming over them; he had told her he needed to talk to her and they had agreed it was probably the most anonymous meeting place they could find.

'Although why we need anonymity I really don't know,' said Bianca crossly. 'It's not as if we were having an affair.'

'True. Sometimes I do wish we were though,' said Saul.

'Saul!'

'Well, don't you?'

'Honestly? No.'

'Well, that's flattering.'

'It was truthful. And anyway, we don't have the time.'

'That was my line,' he said, and grinned at her.

'Well, it's a good one.'

'I agree.'

'And true. But I don't see why you can't work with him. He loves working for you, you say he's the best research analyst you've ever had—'

'Yes, and I've also slept with his wife and then lied about it.'

'True. Yes of course.'

And she had slept with Patrick's boss. And it really hardly troubled her at all. Which had to make her a bad person – cold, faithless, duplicitous. A seriously bad person. Somehow, maybe because it had happened in New York, maybe because she had had so much to do – reinforcing Saul's original argument on the matter – it had remained for her utterly distanced from life. An hour or so of complete unreality, like watching an enthralling film, reading a fascinating book, and as emotionally unimportant as either, it had been frighteningly easy to do as they had agreed, just to draw a line and walk away. It wasn't that Saul meant nothing to her; he did. He had become a valued friend and ally, almost a colleague, in her working life; she was fond of him, extremely so, enjoyed his company, admired his brilliant mind. But a lover he was not; for that one dizzy afternoon he had been, and then the book had been closed, the screen had gone blank and she had walked away, both literally and emotionally.

She never saw Saul, and she and Patrick had hardly spoken over the past few weeks. And Patrick had learned finally not to mention Saul unless it was absolutely necessary. The line had been easy to draw. But Saul saw him most days. Certainly talked to him every day.

'I just didn't think it through,' Saul said fretfully. 'It's not like me.'

Bianca waited, without any hope whatsoever, for him to say she had been irresistible, that her attraction had been overwhelming, that he didn't regret any of it . . .

'It was an appalling mistake,' he said.

'Well thanks!' said Bianca.

'But I can't fire him. And I can't tell him I'm getting someone else in to help . . .'

'Why?'

'Because I couldn't stand having someone else there. Anyway, I'd feel such a brute, he'd be so hurt.'

Not like he'd feel if you told him you'd slept with his wife, Bianca thought.

'Anyway, something's got to be done.'

'Unless Patrick does actually leave me.'

'Yes, I hadn't thought of that. Yes, that would solve it. Look, if you think of anything, just let me know, will you?'

'Of course, Saul,' she said briskly. 'Perhaps you'd like me to hurry it along a bit. A divorce, I mean.'

'Oh, no, that would be unfair,' he said, missing the irony as always. 'It would have to be of his own volition.'

'Yes, of course. Look, I must go. Unless you've got anything else to talk about. Oh, is there any news about Dickon?'

'No. She's playing a waiting game.'

'Does Dickon talk about it?'

'Sometimes.' His voice was abrupt. 'How are you feeling about the launch now?'

'Petrified. Totally petrified. Can't sleep, can't eat, feel sick all the time. I know, I absolutely know, it's going to flop.'

'No it's not. It's going to be a huge, wonderful success. The earth

704

will move for you. You and the House of Farrell. Almost literally, I suppose. And how are things with Patrick?'

'Oh, I don't know,' said Bianca with a sigh. 'I don't know what to do or what to think. I don't even know how I feel about him any more.'

'Oh, I do,' said Saul, and he was looking at her in a way she hadn't seen before. There was affection in that look – and something close to regret. 'You love him.'

'Saul, I don't think so.'

'Oh yes you do. No doubt at all. Take that from your one-time lover. Now, I must go.'

Patrick woke up with a splitting headache and looked at his watch. Seven o'clock. God, he felt terrible. He went downstairs to the kitchen; the house was silent and there was a note from Sonia.

'Tried to wake you, failed. Fergie will also be out till tomorrow. He's going back to stay with Giles after the cinema. Then they're both going to football training in the morning and Giles' dad will bring Fergie home. See you on Monday.'

Patrick sighed and fixed himself a bowl of soup. He had a beer, and then, because it semed like a good idea, another one. His head was no better.

He decided to go for a walk, and then realised he felt really weird and went back to the house where he sank down on the sofa in the snug, determined not to go to bed, and watched some absurd movie for an hour. He considered calling Bianca, but rejected the idea; he couldn't face the excuses as to why she couldn't come home.

The movie had made his head worse. It was now appalling. He'd have to take something for it; and then he might be able to stay awake . . . or even go to sleep.

He went upstairs, rummaged in his flight bag. Right. Paracetamol. What he really needed was codeine, but he tried not to take them, they were so strong and supposed to be addictive. He didn't believe it for a moment, but Bianca was strict about that sort of thing, and scolded him if she found he'd taken any. Not that she was here to scold him now, probably never would again. He took two paracetamol and then, ten minutes later, as the pain intensified – more like a migraine, this – he took two more. They couldn't do him any harm. That was all he had left anyway. The little brown bottle – he always decanted pills into them for travelling because they took up so much less room than those enraging blister packs inside cartons (getting at their contents was like playing pass the parcel) – was empty. He was beginning to feel very weird. Maybe he'd lie down again for a bit. He walked very unsteadily out of the bathroom and into their bedroom. He wondered if he should go into the spare room, but then that would feel more like a hotel again. And the room was a bit swimmy and he wasn't sure he'd make it. He flung himself down on the bed, still clutching the paracetamol bottle, and thought maybe he would ring Bianca after all. If only to warn her that he was home and in their bed. Their bed? Not really. *Her* bed. God, it was all so sad. *He* felt so sad.

'Hi, this is Bianca Bailey. Please leave a message after the tone.'

Patrick cleared his throat. 'Bianca, it's me. I'm at home. Just to let you—'

And then his eyes closed, as if he'd been given anaesthetic, and he dropped down into a huge, black, sleepy hole . . .

Bianca was with Tod and Jack, working on the presentation for the launch. It had been decided that she would talk about the overall concept, the little shops all over the world, the tiny jewels in the Farrell crown, and then they would take over, first Tod and then Jack, explaining what everyone (everyone? One, maybe two, journalists . . .) was about to see, that it was a first, a unique experience, and then, back to Bianca, to do the final few sentences and then – then most probably the site would crash; or there would be a power cut, or the two journalists would say they had to go, or . . .

She didn't hear her phone.

After three attempts, when she had fluffed her lines continually, said she didn't like the music she had chosen and decided the

Singapore shop was rubbish – 'Look, it doesn't look remotely like the arcade!' – Tod told her she should go home.

'You're exhausted and we're not getting anywhere. We'll do it again in the morning. But Bianca, you can't change the shops now, or the music, OK? Bianca – are you all right?'

She was listening to a phone message, a look of dismay on her face.

'No. No, I'm not. It's – it's Patrick. Listen to this – he sounds terrible. I must go home straight away.'

Tod listened. 'He does sound a bit – odd but it's probably just jet lag. Yes, you go, of course. Do you want a cab?'

'No, I've got my car thanks. I didn't even know he was home, I—'

'Should one of us come with you?'

'No, no of course not. I'll – I'll let you know if – well, if I do need you. What's the time? Oh God! He left this two hours ago. *Shit*. OK, I'm off. Bye, thanks.'

'Sure you'll be all right driving?'

'Yes, fine.'

She sped through the streets, driving hideously fast, she knew. The needle shot up to eighty, ninety, a hundred and bloody hell, what was that flashing light behind her? Shit, it was the police, shit, shit, shit!

She pulled over and a cop who looked just a little older than Fergie peered into her window, another one standing on the other side of the car.

'Good evening, madam. Do you realise the speed you were doing just then?'

'Yes, yes I do.'

'And would you like to tell me what it was?'

Sadist.

'A – a hundred.'

'And did you realise this was a built-up area?'

'Yes. Yes I did, but—'

'Have you been drinking, madam?'

'No, I haven't. Unless you count coffee. Look, I really need to

707

get home. It's urgent. My husband is – is . . .' What was he? What could she say he was, that wouldn't delay her still further? 'Just back from a business trip,' she finished.

'You're obviously very keen to see him,' said the other cop. He exchanged a look with the first one. She knew what that meant. They thought she'd been with a boyfriend . . .

'Look,' she said, 'can I please go now? I'm sorry about the speeding, and I'll give you all my details of course, but—'

'I'm afraid we have to breathalyse you,' said the first cop.

'But I've only been drinking coffee.'

'We are still obliged to, madam. I'm sorry. If you could just step out of your car.'

She complied and stepped; it was easier.

She finally got home at two thirty; let herself in, calling his name, running from room to room. There was an empty beer glass in the snug, a soup carton on the sideboard in the kitchen. He did that, when he thought she wasn't looking, heated it in the microwave, spooned it straight out of the carton.

She ran upstairs; along the corridor, looking first in the spare room and then into their bedroom. And there he lay, sprawled across the bed, apparently unconscious.

She went over to him, shook him, trying to wake him, totally failed; he was, and she shuddered at the cliché, dead to the world . . .

'Patrick, Patrick, please wake up, please!'

And then she saw he was holding something in his hand; a small bottle, with – oh, God, no, no – 'Sleeping pills' written on it, on a small white label, in Patrick's handwriting. It was empty. Quite, quite empty . . .

Questions roared through her head. Why? Was he really that desperately unhappy? Why on their bed? Why fully clothed? How many had he taken? The bottle was hideously, unarguably empty. What did she do, ring 999, the doctor? She tried again, shaking him furiously, slapping his face, shouting his name.

Remorse flowed into her. Remorse and panic. Had she really made him so unhappy he had wanted to die? Had her refusal to give up Farrell's for him broken his heart? Had he seen it as the rejection it undoubtedly was, a rejection of him and their marriage? And how could she not have seen it too, the coldness of it, the arrogance? Putting herself and her career and some bloody stupid company before him and their happiness and the happiness of their children? What kind of cold, calculating creature would do such a thing? Her kind, she thought, the Bianca Bailey kind, the self-centred bitch kind, and looked through her tears at him lying there on their bed, the bed that had seen so much happiness, so much closeness, so much laughter and so many ridiculous, laughing, clinging, shaking after-sex tears. She had driven him from that bed, as she had driven him from their marriage, and, indeed, from wanting to live any longer.

Crying openly now, she reached for her phone to dial 999. Berating herself was a self-indulgence, moments were crucial, it might already be too late . . . But even as she pressed nine the second time, miraculously it seemed, he did stir, open his eyes, stare blankly at her, half smile and say 'Hello' before lolling back again, and beginning to snore. She hurled her phone down, heaved him up on the pillows, grabbed the glass of water on the bedside table, tried to force it into his mouth.

'Patrick, Patrick, don't go back to sleep! Don't, please! Here, drink this, come on, come *on*.'

'Leave me . . . alone,' he said, his voice heavily slurred. 'Let me go – go to sleep . . .'

'Patrick, how many did you take?'

'Huh?'

'How many sleeping pills did you take? You must tell me, it's terribly important. How many?'

'Not . . . not . . .' his eyes opened again, tried to focus, then he managed, 'not sleeping pills.'

'What? What then? Patrick, don't go back to sleep, what did you take?'

'Para . . . para . . .'

She sat back, looked at him lying on the pillows. Paracetamol? Was that what he had taken? And was that better or worse? She knew paracetamol caused fearful liver damage if it was left in the system. He could die of that as easily as the sleeping pills . . .

'Patrick, are you sure? Sure it was paracetamol?'

'Paracetamol. Yes. I said. In the bottle. Bianca . . .' And then he was lost again.

'And – how many?'

'Four. Very very bad – bad headache.'

Suddenly she realised what might have happened. He travelled with his various medications in those little brown bottles pills used to come in, labelled by himself. Had he taken the wrong one out of his bag, thinking it was paracetamol? He'd had two beers, he was jet-lagged, he always drank a lot on the plane, he'd have been exhausted and possibly confused. She looked round; his flight bag was on their bathroom floor. She rummaged in it furiously, hurling things out of it. Nothing. She checked his toilet bag, nothing in that, then tried the pockets of the bag, and, yes, here it was! Another little brown bottle, labelled – yes, thank God, thank God, 'paracetamol'. She was right. He had mixed them up. She sat down on the bed next to him, shook him again; this time he surfaced just a little more easily.

'Patrick. Are you sure, quite sure, you only took four of those pills? It's important, Patrick, it's so important.'

'Four, yes. Head terrible. Sorry. Knew you'd be cross.'

'Oh Patrick, darling, darling Patrick!' She put her arms round him, laying him back on the pillow, crying and laughing at the same time. 'Oh Patrick, I'm not cross, I love you, I love you so, so much.'

'I . . .' But he was gone again, lost to her, and she sat looking at him, stroking his hair back, kissing his face, his hair, his hands, her tears falling on to him, so weak with relief she could scarcely sit up.

Her phone rang; not the police, please, please not the police. It was Tod.

'Bianca, you all right? Patrick all right?'

'Oh Tod, yes, yes, thank you, we're both fine,' she said, her voice shaking. 'Just a silly mistake.' And then a thought struck her. 'Tod, do you know if four sleeping pills would be all right? I mean, taken all at once, would it do you any – any real harm?'

Tod's father was a doctor so Tod was a mine of useful medical information.

'Four? Nah, shouldn't think so. But I could ask my dad if you like. Sounds like it could be important.'

'Your dad? But Tod, it's nearly four in the morning!'

'Oh, he's used to being woken up in the night. Old school GP, you see. He'll be round in his PJs under his overcoat, doctor's bag in hand, if you're not careful.'

'But—'

'I'll call you back.'

He rang within five minutes.

'No, four's absolutely fine. He said Patrick would have a nasty head in the morning, but nothing worse. Get him to drink lots of water. As long as you're sure it is only four?'

'I am. I'll ask him again, just to make sure, but I am pretty sure. Thank you, Tod so, so much. You're the best advertising man in the world.'

'Yes, I'd agree with you there,' he said. 'Night, Bianca.'

'Night, Tod.'

She shook Patrick again, asked him again, was he sure it was four?

'Yes, I'm sure,' he said and there was a touch of irritation in his voice now. 'Took two, then two more. Now can I go back to sleep?'

'You can sleep, my darling, darling Patrick,' she said. And went downstairs and filled a jug of water and then lay down, very carefully, beside him; looking at him, hardly daring to take her eyes off him, restored to her in all his dear self, Patrick, who she loved so very much and had so very nearly lost, and reliving all the memories, the most joyful, most important memories – the first time they had made love – and she had cried – the night he had asked her to marry him, nothing specially romantic, just turning to her as they were walking together along the Embankment one Sunday afternoon, 'Because you are so dear to me that I can't imagine living without you.' Then the wedding, when he had told a vast marquee full of guests how much he loved her, and her father, afterwards, more quietly, how he would always take care of her and see it as a privilege; the birth of Milly, their first child, their immortality – all the brilliant, shining moments, interwoven into the stuff of real life, the more mundane stuff, the stuff that mattered just as much, given total importance by the rest.

And she thought two things: that he would probably be very bad-tempered and miserable in the morning, and that she must be very patient and understanding, and that she must have been insane to think that Farrell's was more important to her than he was and that she must convince him of it and resign the very next day.

Well, the very next day after the launch, anyway . . .

Chapter 58

It was today. Launch Day. And she still didn't know how to play it. She hadn't decided. It had given – was still giving – her enormous pleasure, holding back, keeping her counsel, seeing them trying not to ask her, desperate to know. She wondered if she would have told them if she knew herself. Probably not. This way was much more fun.

What Bianca Bailey wanted was for her to join her onstage as she made her first presentation, and for her to say a few words. She didn't entirely like that idea; she knew what the words should be, because Bianca had outlined them, carefully casual: 'You know, something like how much you've enjoyed working with the new team, and how pleased you are with the relaunch, And perhaps a little bit about the birth of the company in coronation year, your memories of that.'

Of course she was obviously hoping for something more fulsome, describing her delight at the whole thing, and how much she had enjoyed working with Bianca, and her confidence in the future of the House of Farrell. Well, she wasn't going to get that.

She had kept faith with Bianca, after the lunch with Lord Fearon (who had assured Bianca of his absolute discretion and certain support from his papers in due course), and had not spoken about the online launch to anyone, even Caro or Florence. Certainly not Florence. She was still so angry with Florence; not only for keeping the information from her, but for being considered as more trustworthy than she was. She'd been toadying up to Bianca ever since she arrived and it really hadn't been the prettiest sight. Well, she'd got her reward of sorts. She had been made part of the Bailey inner circle. And lost a lifelong friendship along with it. Probably the best, certainly the most important friendship she had ever had. Poor Florence. Well, Bianca Bailey would be moving on, and Florence would be left very high and dry indeed, Athina thought; she would see to that.

Anyway, in the meanwhile, what should she do today? She'd attended the run-through the day before, at the Brownleys' house and there didn't seem a great deal of scope for her. Make the insipid little speech Bianca Bailey was hoping for? Bianca, who had three speeches herself, written into the procedure. It was a fairly unappealing proposition. Make a more fulsome one, claiming credit for the global launch itself? She liked that better, but she was still not entirely confident about the technical details; she could get asked awkward questions.

What she really wanted to do was a sort of rerun of her performance at the conference, seizing the limelight, becoming centre stage . . . that would be fun, she might do something like that, but she couldn't quite work out precisely what. But she would, she most certainly would. A small, barbed speech at the right moment would do, but she would prefer something more dramatic. Well, she had a few hours yet; the moment and the method would both present themselves.

She was wearing red. It was so good on television, a brilliant, dangerous red crêpe dress by Valentino that she had had for two decades at least, all her diamonds, even clips in her hair, which her hairdresser was coming in to fix shortly. She looked at the clock; she only had an hour. Bertie, who had, of course, been invited, had said with his usual perfect manners that he would like to escort her to the reception, and was picking her up at ten thirty. So if she was to think of something, she didn't have long.

And then she did. The answer, the perfect answer. That would do it: that would turn the event on its head, throw a perfectly manicured spanner into the works. That would take the edge off Bianca Bailey's triumph beautifully.

She sat down at her dressing table with a pencil and sheet of paper; the speech would have to be impromptu, but a few significant notes now would help . . .

Florence was intensely nervous about her role in the launch; there she would be, online globally, standing at the door of The Shop as she had been, notionally at any rate, for sixty years. It was terrifying. Suppose she tripped, or sneezed, or was sick? She felt the last was the most likely, she'd been feeling dreadful for days. She'd asked Bianca what she should wear, and Bianca had said firmly, 'Chanel. The navy one. And the white camellia. It'll present exactly the right image, even if people don't recognise it as such, classic style and all that sort of thing. God knows what Athina will wear,' she added and sighed. 'A crown, probably.'

'I wouldn't put it past her,' said Florence. 'Has she agreed with you what she's going to do or say?'

'No, not yet. Hopefully not much. Now Florence, do try not to worry. And you know you've only got to stay for five minutes after all; then we move on to the virtual shopping thing, and I want you over here to enjoy the party and my wind-up speech. There'll be a car waiting for you at the end of the arcade and it's only a five-minute drive, ten at the most.'

'May I say, I cannot wait to be in that car,' said Florence.

Susie arrived at the Brownleys' home at nine and went into the ballroom; the boys were already there, putting up their huge screens and setting up a sound system; another man and a girl – 'Techies,' said Tod with a grin – were working with them. The walls of the ballroom were studded with pictures of The Shop taken every decade or so; beginning with a life-size one of Athina and Cornelius cutting the ribbon at its formal opening, Cornelius incredibly handsome, Athina dazzling, both of them laughing into the camera. A podium had been erected at the far end, complete with lectern, and the revolving stand which would bear the image of the clock on one side, Jess on the other.

The caterers were setting up in a side room; florists were filling vases . . . it all looked horribly imminent. Susie stood there, taking deep breaths, wondering what she would do if it all bombed. Kill herself, she supposed: it would be the only thing to do.

'Jolly exciting, isn't it?' said Lord Brownley, who had come in behind her. She smiled at him bravely. He was a dear, she thought, and rather small – Lady Brownley stood at least a head taller than him – and handsome, with piercing blue eyes and a nose that used to be described as patrician.

'Excuse the scruffy gear,' he added. 'I'll change later, of course, don't want to let you down.'

'As if you could,' said Susie, smiling at him, noting the scruffy gear which was an immaculate blazer and perfectly pressed grey flannels. 'And anyway, Lord Brownley, if it wasn't for you we'd be doing this out on the pavement, I should think.'

'Oh, nonsense, my dear. It's the greatest pleasure for me, fascinating all this. Janet's at the hairdresser, but I can't tell you how thrilled she is. She's been fussing over what to wear, threatened her tiara, but I said I thought that was a bit OTT.'

'Goodness,' said Susie, 'perhaps a bit . . .'

She half hoped Lady Brownley *would* wear her tiara; it would certainly trump Lady Farrell's diamonds.

She had hardly slept for several nights, sharing Bianca's night-mares over blank screens, empty shop fronts, no-show journalists – although the omens on that were good, her ring-round yesterday had been very promising, almost everyone saying they were coming, and even the film crews, promised an A-list actress on the clock face and intrigued by the venue, had been very positive, said they hoped to send someone. And it wasn't raining. Yet.

She'd had a bit of a battle with Bianca about the internal guest list; Bianca felt it should be limited to directors: 'That cuts out any petty squabbling, and I do hate those company functions with more hosts than guests.'

But Susie had said that wasn't entirely practical: 'We have to have Tamsin, obviously, and we can't not have Hattie, the entire range is down to her, Caro and Bertie are coming, neither of them are directors any more—'

716

'Yes, but they're family,' said Bianca.

'OK. And Lady Farrell's said she can't possibly be expected to attend without Christine, God knows why not. And then there's Mike and Hugh—'

'Oh, all right,' said Bianca fretfully. 'I suppose if no one comes, there'll at least be a few people to drink the champagne.'

Jess arrived, sequinned dress under wraps; Lucy was doing her make-up. 'So exciting,' she said, 'looks amazing. Freddie wanted to come, but I said she couldn't.'

'I think I'm in love with Jess Cochrane,' said Susie to Lucy as Jess spotted Lord Brownley and went across the room to greet him. They'd got on amazingly at the Ritz lunch and Jess had agreed to draw the raffle at a charity ball the Brownleys were hosting in a few weeks' time.

'Hello, Mother, you look marvellous,' said Bertie.

'Thank you, Bertie. I don't want to let Bianca down – such an important day for her.'

Bertie looked at her sharply. When had his mother ever wished Bianca well?

'Have we time for a coffee?' he said. 'I'm parched. It's a long drive from Birmingham.'

'Yes we do. Two white coffees,' she said to her Polish cleaner, rather as if she was in a restaurant. 'In fact, Bertie, I'm not absolutely ready – I have my speech to polish a little. You're early, you should have warned me.'

'Sorry,' said Bertie humbly, adding: 'I thought we'd get a taxi there – we'll never park in Knightsbridge.'

'No indeed. And I wouldn't want to be seen arriving there in that car of yours anyway. They'd think we were staff.'

'Yes, of course,' said Bertie. 'Right. Well, I'll book a cab, shall I?'

'Do what you like, all I ask is a few minutes' peace.'

'Right oh,' said Bertie.

Not for the first time in the past few weeks, he thought he was glad to be out of the company. Although . . .

Although he did miss the glamour of it all, he realised, walking into the ballroom just after eleven. The new place was nice and peaceful and he was enjoying it, but every day was very much like the next and the people he worked with lacked a certain colour. And it certainly didn't bring him into contact with people like Susie, or Jemima, or Bianca, or, obviously, Lara. Lara was white-faced and tense; she hugged him briefly, and said she'd chat to him later.

'Bertie! How lovely to see you. We've missed you so,' said Bianca, kissing him. 'Lady Farrell, you look beautiful. That dress is amazing. Can I offer you anything? Some coffee, or a champagne cocktail, even? It's a little early, but I'd have one myself if I hadn't got to spend the next hour sounding coherent.'

'I don't know why you think I do not,' said Athina. 'I'll have – well actually, I think I'll have a glass of water.'

This was unlike her; Bianca looked at her. Beneath the perfect make-up, she was a little pale.

'Do you feel all right, Lady Farrell?'

'Perfectly all right, thank you. Why should I not?'

'Well – I don't know. Sorry. Er, have you decided when you would like to speak? I mean, before we unveil Jess, or after the on-screen launch?'

'Oh, I'm still not sure,' said Athina. 'I'm still working on my little speech. But it won't matter, will it? No one's going to want to listen to me.'

'Lady Farrell, of course they'll want to listen to you. More than ever, I'd say. Well, as long as I know before I get up to speak. Now I must go and get Jess into position, everyone will be arriving soon.'

'All right, my dear?' It was Lord Brownley, now wearing a suit of superlative cut, and his wife, magnificent in emerald silk, a notional tiara at least on her head, so unmistakably aristocratic the pair of them, that Bianca felt quite dazzled.

'Oh – yes, thank you. Fine.'

She certainly didn't feel all right, of course; she felt shaky with terror. She couldn't believe it was finally happening, that it was no longer a brilliant idea, a glorious plan, something wonderful that was going to happen on some distant date, but a reality, an untested reality moreover, that would, within an hour, be a great success or an appalling failure and revealed, moreover, in one of those two guises hideously publicly, in front of quite literally millions, which it was possible not to think about, but also a hundred or so of a hugely critical audience, who would be standing in front of her, witnesses to whatever dreadful – or glorious – outcome there might be, and who she most certainly could not ignore. Not for the first time, she wished profoundly she was someone else, somewhere else, and at some totally other time.

But she smiled and said yes, fine, of course and how lovely to see him and had he got a drink and would he excuse her now? And moved off to supervise the settling of Jess on the stand.

It was resolved none too soon; the early-comers, the second row-ers, as Susie called them, the slightly less starry editors and bloggers (although even they were pretty starry), were already arriving, anxious not to be late, followed by the major glossy editors and beauty editors, all quite happy, if not actually hoping, to be late . . .

'My God,' said Bianca to Susie as they filed relentlessly in, phones at the ready. ('It's called Tweet and Greet,' said Susie irreverently.) 'Well, that's one fear proved groundless, Susie.'

'And two to go,' said Susie. 'And oh my God, it's Sky News and lovely Kay Burley! I must go and greet her . . . OK, Bianca, you're on.'

Athina watched Bianca as she mounted the stage, stood smiling at the audience, the epitome of cool and confidence. She thought of their first meeting, almost two years earlier; she supposed she was slightly more kindly disposed towards her than she had been then, although Bianca's apparent assumption that they were no longer enemies after the Ritz lunch annoyed and amused her in equal measure. She dressed well, that was for sure, always a point in anyone's favour, and today was not an exception; she was wearing a silk print wrap dress almost certainly from von Furstenberg in blue and red, extremely high red Louboutins, her thick dark hair as always falling loose on to her shoulders. She was an attractive woman certainly, but arrogant, Athina thought, over-assured of her own ability; she deserved to be brought down just a little. And, hopefully, she would be able to do exactly that. She had deliberately avoided Bianca's eye as she walked towards the platform, clearly seeking her out; and Susie's tentative 'Lady Farrell, would you like to . . . ?'

She shook her head, clearly dismissing them; she was taking this in her own time.

And talking of time, she hoped this would not take too long; standing at her age was harder work than it had been.

As if reading her thoughts, Jemima urged her to a gilt chair she had brought to her.

God, she was marvellous, Lara thought, staring at Bianca as she talked, first thanking the Brownleys for the use of their home, of course, then of her pleasure at being here. 'I consider it the greatest good fortune that I have been able to work on the new Farrell brand that you will discover today.' She talked of the history of Farrell, the brand that she had found when she joined and the one that she had created and that was being launched today. If she had been making that speech, it would have sounded over-enthusiastic, pushy even, Lara thought; Bianca remained as always restrained and, at the same time, confident in her own judgment. She talked briefly of the history of Farrell's and how her dearest wish was to leave that history in all its wonderful Englishness and style, unspoiled and undisturbed, merely to move forward into the future with a new, equally lovely, but slightly more modern face.

'We are lucky to have with us, not only today, but as we work, day after day, week after week, Lady Farrell, who founded the brand with her husband Sir Cornelius Farrell, in coronation year; she is our primary inspiration, our mentor, setting ever higher guidelines for us. Lady Farrell, would you like to say a few words?'

But in response to her sweet smile and charming invitation, the encouraging clapping of the audience, Lady Farrell rose from her chair, shook her head, said 'No, no, really, not now. I'm the past and you are the future.' And she sat down, just a little wearily, once more.

'Well,' Bianca said, 'today the past *is* the future, Lady Farrell, so our heartfelt thanks. And now we will move on: into the future. You will, some of you, have been aware of our ticking clock, building into a picture of one of today's great beauties and the new face of Farrell; before we discover who she is, I would like to thank Lucy Farrell, Lady Athina's granddaughter, who is carrying on the family tradition, which is so very important to us all and which everyone who works for Farrell is so very proud of. She is the creator of our new look. Lucy, take a bow.'

Looking at her, his beloved daughter, standing on the platform, smiling into the applause, Bertie felt two things: one, a sense of huge pride and satisfaction, and the second, an odd sense of loss and regret that he had turned his back so resolutely on all this, the family and the company, with no representative of his generation, the only family left, indeed, being Lucy. His mother had perhaps been right: it was in his veins, literally, this brilliance, it was his heritage, and as such should not be thrown away. But . . .

Bianca was speaking again. 'So now let us show you who our face, our fragmented face, belongs to. I think you will not be disappointed.'

And she pushed the screen, with the clock still ticking relentlessly on, forming its lovely image, and it swung round – and there was Jess, laughing, looking wonderful, blowing kisses, and the room erupted and everyone clapped and whistled and she moved across and kissed Bianca and then jumped off the platform as best as her heels and long, narrow dress would allow her and started kissing everyone, for she seemed to know them all, and cameras flashed and phones were at work, dozens of influential heads bent over them, fingers working overtime.

And then Bianca moved on to the stage again.

'I'm sorry, but that is not the end of today It is merely the beginning – as you have been promised. For we are about to do something very special, something that you will not have seen before – I think, at least – and ask you to watch. Our shop in the Berkeley Arcade has always been our signature, the jewel in our crown, and now, as part of our relaunch, we have opened many more, lookalike stores, sisters to the arcade shop, in most of the great shopping centres of the world, more little Farrell jewels, representing us all over the globe, and I cannot tell you how terrified I am at this moment, for we really are being hugely innovatory – and I'm just going to hand over to Tod Marchant and Jack Flynn, joint geniuses who run our advertising agency – Tod, Jack, over to you.'

And Tod smiled at her as he took the microphone and then said to the audience, 'And if it does go wrong, then it's her you should blame, not us. It was her idea, and completely original; she's the genius, actually, not us. It's been a *huge* privilege to work with her. So – if you just fix on a screen – that one's London, that Paris, that one New York, then Sydney, and – where's that one, Jack?'

'Milan,' said Jack. 'And now you can watch them open, and you can see it's live and for real, and who in their right mind would open a shop at eleven at night as we are. Although we have it on good authority there are customers waiting outside each and every one of them. OK, so now another countdown . . .' and the theme from *A Space Odyssey* came onto the soundtrack with Jack's voice over it saying 'ten . . . nine . . . eight' and down to 'zero' and he clicked on the controls and there was a long, long blankness on the screens, and Shit, thought Bianca, and Fuck, thought Tod, and Dear God, thought Lara and Bloody bloody bloody hell! thought Susie and even Pity, thought Athina.

The room was completely silent, everyone waiting, everyone willing something to happen. And then, suddenly it did, and the pictures formed and there was Florence, smiling outside Number 62 Berkeley Arcade, and there was the shop in St Germain, and there was, yes, Milan, all with their doors opening and, in most cases, people outside, waiting to be welcomed in.

This is too good to be true, thought Bianca. It can't last.

But it did, for there was SoHo, lovely lovely SoHo – and she allowed her mind to dwell on that for just a moment, smiling at it – and there was the lovely Strand Arcade in Sydney, and Ann Siang Hill in Singapore, and now the sound level in the room rose and rose, as people actually cheered, all those cool, seen-it-all, been-there people, cheered and clapped, and suddenly it was too much for her and she started to cry. She had done it. It had all been worth it. And Susie, crying too, was hugging her, and then Lara, and Jess and Tamsin were both literally jumping up and down, and Lord Brownley was shouting and punching the air.

Even Athina was unable not to smile. And then found she really did need to go to the lavatory. She did feel a little odd, slightly confused even; she supposed it was the pressure that she now felt mounting in her, for her own moment had almost come, and besides, she needed to look at her notes, remind herself of the most salient points of what she had to say. She moved through the crowd, attracting, inevitably, attention, people smiling at her, shaking her hand, saying 'well done' and 'what a triumph' and just for a moment or two she faltered in her resolve, wondered if she should do what she had planned . . . but then yes, of course she should. It was absolutely the right thing to do – Cornelius would have thought so too, and after a few moments of sitting quietly, running over her notes, she felt better, emerged and made her way back. Bianca had just started to speak again, and when she saw her, she smiled and said,

'Lady Farrell, do please come and join me, this is your day too.'

And Susie helped her on to the platform and she walked to join Bianca in the centre of the stage and Jess said, quite audibly from the front row of the crowd, 'Oh my God, she is so amazing!' And she stood there, displaying her usual immaculate timing, waiting for the complete silence she needed, very calm, very in control once more, wishing only that the room was less hot and . . . and . . .

And Bertie, watching her, saw it in the split second before anyone else, knowing her as he did so very, very well; one moment she stood there, erect and beautiful, in her red dress, her diamonds flashing, holding up her hand for silence, and the next the tiniest of movements, more a non-movement perhaps, a softening of her straightness, an easing of her pose: and the next she seemed to melt into herself, collapsed absolutely, her legs folding under her, and she fell on to the stage, and lay there helpless, motionless, and her heart, the great lioness's heart that had fought so bravely and determinedly for what she wanted and believed in all her life, had fought off all comers, that had loved and hated in equal measures, and never troubled to disguise which, was first slowed and then stilled.

The indefatigable Athina Farrell was defeated, and the heart beat no more, and she died as she would have wished, in the full limelight, dressed in red, which did indeed prove to be very good on television, her diamonds still flashing in the lights. And it was Bertie, the son she had despised and diminished all his life, who climbed on to the platform and covered her tenderly with his jacket and closed her eyes, and whose tears fell on her as he did so.

Epilogue

It was what she would have wished. Everyone said so.

It was an appalling cliché (everyone also said) but it was undoubtedly true.

And had she planned it herself, it could not have been better. No long, final debilitating illness, no decline into old age, but a last public appearance, lauded, admired – as Susie Harding said, her voice awed, even as she wiped away tears of genuine sadness, 'How did she manage that?'

It had been a massive stroke, followed by a heart attack, over in seconds, no apparent suffering: an ambulance was summoned and she was taken to hospital, but it was merely a formality.

And she did achieve her own ambition for the day: she stole the limelight from Bianca.

She had had her own plans for doing that: and Florence, entrusted with her handbag and jewellery while Bertie and Caro went to the hospital, discovered what they had been. She found notes for a speech, announcing her retirement from the House of Farrell – a small, mean gesture, given the occasion, Florence thought, and unworthy of her, but nonetheless it would have achieved a certain success; people would have said how sad it was that she was going, and how the cosmetic world would be the poorer for it, the last of the great grande dames, perhaps wonder if she had been driven to it by her new masters, concerned above all with finance, not image, and with stock exchange ratings rather than perfumes and products and advertising campaigns.

Florence tore the notes into minuscule pieces and put them into her recycling bin; it seemed rather appropriate. And then she sat down and wept for quite a long time, tears not of grief exactly, but of sadness and loss of a life companion.

She most assuredly did not love Athina – she had endured too much at her hands for too long – but she had admired her and she supposed been as fond of her as was possible, given her personality, and she certainly couldn't imagine life without her. For Farrell's and she were indistinguishable to Florence, even though she had become a little out of touch (although her performance at the sales conference belied even that); she had created it, breathed life into it, and driven it through the decades with a steely determination. Its personality might have become dated, but it had retained a certain quality, a reputation, even though it belonged in the past. And Bianca had recognised that, and undoubtedly restored it, but that had only been possible because of its heritage, Athina's heritage. And Florence knew she would have to face a life alone within a company that would cease in time to value her; once this rebirth was accomplished – and she had already told her stories of the early days to endless journalists – she would become, slowly at first, increasingly unimportant, an old lady, Athina Farrell's protégé, part of the old days which were over, however successful the new.

She must find an exit line of her own.

'I suppose she'll have a state funeral,' said Lara, as she and Bianca sat among the debris of the Brownleys' ballroom, not sure whether to laugh or cry.

Bianca smiled. 'Of course. Oh, Lara, how incredible was that? Talk about perfect timing! Clever, clever old thing. And I do feel very sad, very upset in a way. Talk about the end of an era. They really don't make them like that any more. It was ghastly really, when you think about it. I suppose we're still in shock, it hasn't hit me yet. It won't be the same without her, that's for sure.'

'Certainly won't,' said Lara briskly.

'Poor little Lucy was in floods. How's Bertie, have you heard from him?'

'Just briefly. He's terribly upset. How baffling is that? When all she did was make his life a misery. Poor Bertie.'

'Poor Bertie. Indeed. Such a tender heart.'

'So tender,' said Lara, and her own eyes filled with tears. 'And—'

She was interrupted by Susie, who was walking towards them, phone clamped to her ear. 'Yes, yes sure. Now? Well, give her an hour. In her office, yes. Four o'clock, Farrell House. OK, that was the *News*,' she said to Bianca. 'They want to do an interview – well, you heard. And then *Woman's Hour*, and—'

'OK,' said Bianca, standing up. 'I'll come. I hope they don't all just want to talk about Lady Farrell.'

'I don't think they will,' said Susie, 'they seem to love the global launch thing.'

'I'll just go and thank Lord and Lady Brownley and then I'd better tidy myself up. I must look like complete shit.'

'Of course you don't,' said Lara, and 'You look wonderful,' said Susie.

And it was true; despite the horrific strain of the morning, far greater than they could ever have suspected, Bianca was looking very good again: happy, confident, almost – given the circumstances – relaxed.

Susie knew, and Lara hoped she knew, the reason.

Bianca's phone rang; she looked at it, smiled, said, 'Hello. Yes, it was wonderful, thank you. Well, most of it was wonderful. It worked brilliantly. Every single one. What? How do you know? Oh of course, you were watching online. With Saul? Goodness. But something else happened, very dramatic, very sad as well, I'll tell you later. Or you could watch the six o'clock news. I'll be on it, by the way. Well, yes, all right, I'll tell you now . . .'

The entire country appeared to be red, white and blue. Patriotism and royalism had become intertwined. Every street, every tree, every hanging basket, was festooned with flags and ribbons and bunting and balloons; every window, of every shop, from the largest department store to the smallest boutique, from the grandest food store to the most humble corner shop, was adorned with more ribbons, more flowers, and expressions of loyalty and delight over the rather small, white-haired, sometimes stern-faced elderly lady who was Queen Elizabeth the Second, who had sat on her throne and reigned over her country for sixty years and been held in deeper and deeper affection with every one of those that passed.

And the four-day weekend, bestowed upon the country in which to celebrate, each day with its own schedule, had begun early and on the Friday, the capital, along with the shires, was in holiday mood. Tourists were arriving in droves; lunches were long; the afternoon short; nobody could talk about anything except the celebrations and how they were going to share in them.

Saul Finlayson was spending the Saturday at the Derby; he had no horse running and it wasn't, on account of the razzmatazz as he called it, one of his favourite meetings, but this year was obviously going to be special and Dickon was desperate to go and to take Fergie with them. 'The Red Arrows are going to be there, Dad, they're going to parachute on to the course!' And forcing himself to recognise the fact that this could be the last time Dickon would be around for the Derby, he agreed that they should not only go, but, most unusually, he took a box.

When he'd picked up Dickon the night before, Janey had looked at him slightly awkwardly and said, 'Saul, we need to talk.'

He knew what that meant. Or he thought he did. But he didn't want his day spoiled. 'Tomorrow evening, you here?'

'Yes. But I don't want Dickon involved.'

'He doesn't have to be. He's having Fergie to stay the night. They'll be perfectly happy, playing on the Wii. Come around eight. We're going to McDonald's for tea.'

'After a box at the Derby? Honestly, Saul!'

'What? It's what they want to do, not go to some poofy restaurant. I agree with them.'

Janey said she'd be there at eight and rang off.

The Derby was wonderful fun; even Saul had to admit it. It was cold, but it became obligingly sunny just as the Queen arrived. God, or whatever superior power was in charge of such things, clearly wished that the Diamond Jubilee should have the sun shining upon it. The 150,000 strong crowd was in celebratory mood, the band of the Royal Marines played splendidly, the Red Arrows duly dropped in on their parachutes, trailing red, white and blue smoke, and deposited a vast Union Jack on the course, near the finishing post. Katherine Jenkins, the Welsh mezzo soprano and national treasure, dressed rather inappropriately for the occasion, Saul thought, in a long, skin-tight, strapless number, sang the National Anthem as the Queen arrived (dressed rather more appropriately in a warm blue coat), driving down the course with Prince Philip in the state Bentley.

Horses ran, races were won (and lost), a great deal of money was won (and lost) and when nineteen-year-old Joseph O'Brien won the rather cumbersomely rechristened Diamond Jubilee Cup, presented to him by the Queen, Dickon and Fergie vowed that one day they would race against each other in the Derby.

'Well, I'll be there I hope,' said Saul, and Dickon said of course he would, they'd need his horses to ride.

'Yeah, and anyway, you'll have to drive the horse box,' added Fergie.

'Great,' said Saul, 'I'm glad my role is to be so major.'

They both smiled at him tolerantly.

Tea at McDonald's proved unnecessary; protesting, Saul was dragged to the funfair, where the boys ate copiously from every burger and hot dog stall, in between taking hair-raising rides; Saul refused to go on any of them until Fergie finally persuaded him on to the old-fashioned carousel and, sitting on a red and gold horse, its nostrils flaring, the honky-tonk music playing, and looking at the sun shining on the course and the crowds below him, and grinning back at Fergie and Dickon riding behind him, he felt a flash of pure happiness.

He was unused to emotion of any sort, particularly of a positive nature – the last time he had experienced it was when he had been in New York with Bianca – and he tried to savour this one, make it last. Perhaps it was a good omen for the future. And Janey's visit.

Only it wasn't.

She arrived, looking flustered, first refused, then accepted his offer of a glass of wine. He poured himself a beer.

'So? This is about Australia, I would hazard a guess.'

'It is, Saul, yes.'

'And, guessing again, you've absolutely decided to go?'

'I – I have, Saul, yes. If – well, if you agree.'

'Well, of course I don't agree,' he said. 'Why would I? It'll be terribly disruptive to Dickon, ghastly for me. I'll fight it every step of the way . . .'

'My solicitor says you can't possibly win.'

'Oh really? Funny that, mine says *you* can't.'

This wasn't quite true, but he wanted to rattle her.

'And I think it would be nicer for Dickon if we went with your blessing. Rather than had a sordid court battle.'

'Well, that's a view.'

'Yes, it is. A very valid one.'

She waited, looking at him; he didn't respond for a while. Then he said, 'Well, Janey, I have a plan of my own.'

'Yes?'

'If you go – and I agree about the court battle, very bad for Dickon, and I don't propose to initiate one – if you go, I have a plan of my own.'

'Oh?' She looked at him suspiciously, then saw he was entirely serious.

'Which is?'

'I shall open an office in Sydney.'

'What? You'll *what*?' She was staring at him, clearly horrified.

'I'm glad you like the idea. Yes, I like the place, and I like what Australians I've met. With one exception. And no doubt your new husband will make two – I gather he's an Australian heading for home again.'

'But Saul, your entire working life is based in London. All your contacts, your staff – surely, surely you need to be here?'

'Not all the time, no I don't. I've thought about it a lot. The terrible flight that people make such a fuss about doesn't bother me – I find the plane a perfect place to work, and I have no idea what this thing called jet lag is about. I actually think it's been invented by a load of hypochondriacs. Of course I'll keep the office here and spend a great deal of time here, but I want a base near Dickon. I shall miss him . . .' His voice shook and he stopped talking for a moment, took a gulp of his beer, then said, 'I really don't know how you can do this, Janey, take him away from his friends, his school, me . . .'

She was silent.

'Anyway, you're not taking him away from me entirely, this way. We can still spend plenty of time together: all the school holidays, of course – I know the Australian schools have four terms a year – and plenty of weekends, and it's wonderful sailing out of Sydney harbour . . . No, no, my mind is made up . . .'

She left soon afterwards, visibly shaken. Saul went to join the boys and found them playing what seemed to him a most unsuitable game. He switched the console off.

'Oh Da-ad!'

'No, no, it'll give you nightmares. How about a game of snooker?'

Then, when they had gone to bed, he went downstairs and poured himself another beer. It had been amusing, seeing Janey's reaction. God, she must hate him. Well, he'd given her a very hard time; and she would no doubt see his remaining in her life as a continuation of it. He wondered if her decision to move to Australia had been a bid for freedom from him; if so, she'd failed.

He was aware that when the lawyers heard of his new plan it would weaken his case, strengthen hers, but he didn't care. As long as he remained in Dickon's life, he had discovered, he didn't care about anything much. Besides it wouldn't be such a hardship because it was true, he had liked what he had seen of Australia – liked it a lot. And – of course – it would solve another problem he had. Very neatly.

Susie and Jonjo were to watch the river pageant from an apartment on the Thames, just upriver from Waterloo Bridge. It belonged to a friend of Jonjo's, and the great sheets of window opened on to a balcony; it was, like the rest of her life Susie thought happily as she tried to decide what to wear, too good to be true. Would red, white and blue be corny – she had a new white sweater from Joseph, a pair of very narrow red jeans, and a blue jacket, just for instance, or just the white sweater and blue jeans, and possibly a red decoration in her hair? Or should she play it cool and wear – well, green, or a new cream dress she'd bought from Reiss – very Mrs Cambridge. She settled on that, thinking she could put a red cardigan into her bag. The friend's wife, Hester, was lovely, but a bit of an airhead, and very much a fashion plate, and she didn't want to let Jonjo down. There were to be about twenty of them, most of whom Susie didn't know, and she was a little intimidated by them, they were all so bloody rich – they'd been to a wedding the week before with over three hundred guests in some massive country pile which she honestly hadn't enjoyed very much; it was so impersonal, and she never even got to speak to the bride and groom. She was a bit afraid Jonjo would want something similar. In fact, she was almost certain he would. He had clearly been impressed by the wedding, and had said at least twice that it would give them lots of ideas for their own. It was her one anxiety at the moment. A perfect wedding to her was a party, with family and friends, not a blatant display of extravagance. But if that was what Jonjo wanted . . .

'What are you thinking about?' said Jonjo, coming over to her and giving her a hug as she stood at the window, staring out at the cold grey day. The Greater Power seemed to have lost interest in the Queen of England's Jubilee and left the weather to its own devices . . .

'How much I love you,' she said truthfully.

'And I was thinking how much I loved you. So there's a thing. Now buck up, we can't be long; they're closing the roads at midday.'

'And what time do they get to us?'

'About three thirty, I think. I thought we'd go to the Savoy and have a drink on the river terrace before we go to the party. And then walk across the bridge, get a bit of atmosphere. How's that?'

'Lovely idea. Oh my God, I'm so excited. Do you know there's a thousand boats in the procession. I know I'm going to cry.'

'Cry! Whatever for?'

'I always cry at occasions like this. They're such emotional occasions – everyone joining in together, everyone wishing the Queen well, and loving her – oh dear, I've started already!'

She blinked her tears away, gave him a watery smile.

'Heavens,' said Jonjo. 'I seem to be in love with a lunatic.'

It was amazing on Waterloo Bridge; a sea of flags and people smiling and a huge wave of affection and pride that was tangible. Nobody seemed to mind being jostled or held up, nobody seemed to mind anything. They had been standing there for hours and many of them had camped out in the freezing cold; the fact that there were hours still to go seemed not to bother anybody. Susie half wished they could stay there and watch it. Leaning over the parapet, just a few feet above the water, she felt part of it, part of this huge, loyal crowd, so many nationalities, all proud of the Queen and her day, wishing her well. It was a bit like the small, friendly wedding as opposed to the flashy one . . .

'Come on,' said Jonjo, 'it's bloody freezing – you'll get pneumonia and then what will I do?'

'Marry someone else, maybe?' said Susie, reaching up to kiss him.

'No,' he said, 'never, ever, not in a million years. Oh, for heaven's sake, Susie, don't start crying. It's much too early.'

The party was fun: and warm. And dry – it was beginning to rain. They watched the start of the pageant from Chelsea Pier, saw the royal guests go on board, ferried out in the launch from the royal yacht *Britannia*, the Queen at her best in white, the Duke still handsome in his full naval uniform, the princes in theirs (although

Harry's blue beret was generally felt to be less than flattering). The girls all admired Kate's red dress, the men all admired Kate. Hester's mother who was there admired Prince Charles, and they all gasped at the incredible royal barge, all red and gold, as she set sail and led the procession of a thousand boats, large and small, down what had become, for a few amazing hours, a royal highway. And as it passed beneath each bridge the church bells in the surrounding area all rang out and mingled with the cheers. Susie, watching the television, surreptitiously mopped her eyes and saw the uber-cool Hester doing the same thing.

'I'm so glad you cry too,' she said.

'I can't stop today,' said Susie.

'Me neither. And – tell me, you work for Farrell's cosmetics, don't you?'

'Yes. Yes I do.'

'Were you anything to do with that amazing event the other day? I logged on because I follow them on Facebook a bit and I've bought a few things from them occasionally. Anyway, I watched that global launch thing. So clever . . .'

Susie said modestly she had been a bit to do with it. 'But only the PR, that's what I do.'

'Oh, really? What fun. Anyway, I'm going to go to the shop in the Berkeley Arcade next week, and then we're off to Paris at the weekend, so I thought I'd go and see the one there. Such a good idea.'

There was no doubt it had made its mark. Susie felt a pang of intense pride and then Jonjo sat down beside her.

'All right?'

'Yes, I'm fine thank you.'

'Good. Budge up, I want to talk to you.'

'I'll leave you,' said Hester. 'Susie and I have been crying together.'

'No, no need.'

But she went anyway.

'I've been thinking . . .' He picked up her hand and studied her ring. 'You still pleased with that?'

'Oh, no,' she said, 'I'm thinking of giving it back. Of course I am, you idiot! I adore it.'

'Good. Well, all this pageantry has got me thinking. About weddings and so forth.'

'Oh?'

'Yes. I'd like it to be quite soon, Susie, I don't want to hang about – I thought maybe early autumn.'

'But, Jonjo, that's only three months off!'

'I know. Does it matter?'

'Well – there's a lot to organise.'

'Really?'

'Well yes. I mean, think of that one we went to the other day.'

'Yes, I imagined that was the sort of thing you'd want. It was rather splendid. Would that take so much organisation?'

''Fraid so. Look, I know about functions, they're a big part of my job. Venues, dates, catering, flowers . . .'

'OK. Well, it can be a bit later on. Just as long as it takes.'

She took a deep breath. Even if he was disappointed, it seemed very important suddenly.

'Honestly,' she said, 'I'd rather it wasn't like that.'

He stared at her.

'Really? But it's your big day, you want something to remember, so—'

'It'll be my big day,' she said, 'because I'm marrying you. Even if there was no one there, I wouldn't care.'

'Oh,' he said, 'oh, I see. Are you – are you sure?'

'Yes,' she said, smiling, 'I'm absolutely sure.'

'Good God! I thought – I mean – well, in that case maybe I should tell you something.'

'What?'

'Patrick and Bianca have offered their house for our wedding, the one in the country. But I turned it down.'

'Why?' said Susie. 'I've seen pictures of it, it's lovely.'

'Well, it's not really very big. Or grand or anything.'

'So?'

'Well – well . . .' He seemed to be waking up after a big sleep. 'I see. Well, it *is* terribly pretty. And we could have a marquee in their paddock, Patrick said.'

'It sounds wonderful to me,' said Susie.

'Really? Well, it did to me too.'

'So why didn't you at least consult me about it?'

'Well, because of all the things I just said. I thought you'd want a big number.'

'Do *you*?'

'No. No. I don't. Not really. I hated that thing the other day to be honest. I'd like family – well, I'd like some of them, my sister and her husband and her children and my mum—'

'You have to have your dad too.'

'I do?'

'Yes, you do.'

'And my stepmother?'

''Fraid so.'

'If you say so.'

'I do.'

'Well, all right, family. And then just a few special friends. Say about – I don't know – fifty each. Altogether I mean. That's my idea of a wedding. I just didn't want you disappointed.'

'Jonjo,' said Susie, putting her arms round him and kissing him, 'I will not be disappointed. And,' she added severely, 'this is not a good omen for our marriage.'

'Why?' He looked alarmed.

'You mustn't go assuming things about what I want.'

'You were assuming them too.'

'That's true. OK. Sorry. Is it too late to have it at their house?'

'Of course not. They'll be well chuffed.'

'Wonderful. Then let's.'

He kissed her, then sat back, studying her face. 'Oh God,' he said.

'What? Do I look awful? Has my mascara run?'

'A bit. But that's not what I was thinking. I love you so much, Susie Harding. So very much.'

'And I love you, Jonjo Bartlett. So very, very much.'

At which point the procession reached them. They went over to the window holding hands. Teeming rain had set in.

'So mean of it,' said Susie – and insisted on going out into it, out on to the balcony, and waving and shouting and getting completely soaked; the others all teased her and then most of them joined her. Including Jonjo. And it was truly incredible: big boats, small boats, tugs, barges, small row-boats (they made her cry the most), the armada of sea cadets, with their guttering flags, the Maori canoes and a group of what looked like old fishing trawlers.

'They were the ones who went across to Dunkirk and rescued our troops,' Hester's mother said, wiping her own eyes, 'some even smaller than those.'

And then: 'Oh my God, look at them,' said Susie as a final barge went past carrying the Royal Philharmonic Orchestra or some of it, and singers from the Royal College of Music, voices uplifted, undaunted by the rain. And she looked up at Jonjo and saw that his face was wet.

'You're crying!' she said.

'No I'm not,' he said, 'it's the rain.'

But Susie knew differently. And whether it was the singers, the occasion or simply on account of their recent conversation, she absolutely didn't care.

Bertie and Lara watched the pageant for a while on television, and then went out to a party that was being held in the street. Flags were in practically every window, red, white and blue baskets of flowers hung from every lamp post, sat on every table, and tables and benches lined the entire length of the street for the children to sit at, and some enterprising person had found canopies to shelter them from the rain. Lara, who seemed to know almost everybody there, had made dozens of sausage rolls and a cake as her contribution to the party, and wandered up and down, chatting to everyone, including the children, occasionally leaning over to take a handful of crisps or one of her sausage rolls; most of the adults were doing the same, while drinking a great deal of what was on offer. The conversation was almost entirely limited to platitudes:

admiring remarks about the Queen, cheerful moaning about the weather, usually ending in 'well, it makes us what we are, doesn't it?' and saying how wonderful it was to see the country all united in the celebrations.

Someone had hired a small roundabout which was at one end of the street, and someone else a mini-bouncy castle which was at the other; an obliging ice-cream vendor had parked in someone's front garden, and his signature tune mixed with the shrieks and the laughter, and frequent wails as balloons blew away.

Bertie, who had never been even remotely involved in such a thing, both his mother and Priscilla considering themselves far above local affairs, was enchanted; he could have stayed there for ever, downing lager and Lara's sausage rolls, teasing the children that he was going to eat all their food, blowing up balloons to replace the ones that were constantly blowing away, and chatting up the mothers. It was only when one of them, a busty girl wearing a great deal of make-up, invited him to 'come into the warm' that he took fright and fled to Lara's side. She said she'd been watching him and she should have warned him. 'You take Sasha Timpson on at your peril. She sees saying "hello" as an invitation to bed.'

'Blimey. I didn't think I was going to get away alive!'

Lara laughed, then looked at him thoughtfully and said, 'I don't think you should be exposed to the hazard any longer. Come on, Bertie, time to go inside. I'm bloody freezing and they're packing up anyway. I wouldn't mind you coming into the warm with me. If you fancy the idea . . .'

Bertie said he fancied the idea greatly, and, afterwards he made some tea and took it back to her in bed.

'I want to talk to you.'

Lara crushed the ridiculous hope that would keep rising at such moments, and said, her face carefully blank, 'What about?'

'I've been doing a lot of thinking. Since last week.'

'Oh yes? What about?'

'Farrell's.'

The hopes withered into insignificance. 'Oh – yes. Of course. I expect you have.'

'I feel things have changed. A lot.'

'They have indeed.'

'You see, with my mother – well, gone – there's no family left there. Except Lucy, of course. And she's still very young. She can't exactly be a figurehead.'

'No.'

'And, well, I do feel very strongly that the family should remain in place. It's that sort of company. Even more after the relaunch if anything.'

'Yes.'

'Do you really think so? You sound a bit – unsure.'

'Bertie, I do. Yes.'

'But – I don't know how everyone would feel about me coming back. Bianca might tell me to get lost.'

'Everyone would feel so, so happy about you coming back,' said Lara. '*Especially* Bianca. She's really missed you.'

'She has?'

'She has. She's told me so. Several times.'

'Good heavens.' He was silent, drinking his tea. Then, 'But what do you think I could do? HR obviously, but it's not quite . . . quite . . .'

'Quite grand enough? For a figurehead?'

'I didn't say that.'

'No, but you meant it. Didn't you?'

'I – I suppose so. I'm so not a grand person.'

'That's very true. But don't you think your heritage as the family representative in the company makes you one?'

'Well – well I don't know.'

'Oh Bertie, of course it does,' said Lara impatiently. 'You really do yourself down.'

'I've been well-trained in that,' said Bertie rather sadly.

'I know. But – but she can't do it any more, can she?'

'No,' he said and blew his nose rather hard, 'no she can't. God, I'm going to miss her. In spite of everything, I did love her.'

Lara was silent. There was simply nothing she could say.

'And – well, it's a funny thing to say, I know, but I was proud of

739

her. She was so brave. And so magnificent. We've agreed, Caro and I, that we should probably have a big memorial service later in the year. A bit like my father's. That was marvellous. What do you think?'

'I think that sounds excellent,' said Lara.

'Good,' he said. 'Well, I'd better talk to Bianca, then. If you really think she won't mind.'

'Bertie, I've told you. She'll be *thrilled*.'

'How about you?'

'Well of course I will be. I've told you enough times.'

'I know. I love you, Lara, I really do.' He looked at her, then said, 'There's something else I want to talk to you about . . .'

'What's that?' Hopes up. Pulse rate up. Don't even think about it, Lara, don't don't . . .

'I thought we might set up a charitable foundation. The House of Farrell. What do you think about that?'

'I – I think it's a wonderful idea.'

'Oh, good. A lot of big cosmetic companies – certainly the ones with a history – do that. It would raise our profile in a very good way.'

'It would.' She felt like crying. 'Er – what sort of charity would it be?'

'Well, I thought something to do with gardens.'

'Gardens?'

'Yes. Gardens are so good for people. They make them happy. What's a key part of this Jubilee? Flowers. Flowers everywhere. Imagine this street, imagine most of the streets in the country, without their hanging baskets, the Queen's barge without that great bank of flowers. I'd like every school – well, every inner-city school – to have its own garden, for the children to grow things, not just flowers but vegetables; it would be so good for them. And we could have an annual award for the best.'

'You could grow a Farrell rose too,' said Lara, forgetting her disappointment momentarily, 'exhibit it at Chelsea.'

'That's a wonderful idea. Yes. So you like the idea?'

'I do. Very much.'

'I'll talk to Bianca about it then.'

'Yes. Do. I think she'll really like it. It would be the thing you could run as well. As the Farrell family figurehead.'

'I suppose it could. That's an idea. It really is.' He sat contemplating this for a while. Then, 'Right, well, we'd better get up. We can't spend the whole evening here.'

He threw the bedclothes aside and Lara looked at his back miserably.

Then he turned to her again. He looked awkward.

'There is just one other thing,' he said.

This time her hopes didn't even rise; they seemed to have slumped permanently.

'Yes, Bertie. What is it? Can I have the shower first, please?'

'You can. But – but I was thinking . . .'

'Yes, Bertie?'

'I was thinking, well, I was wondering – oh dear, I don't know what you're going to say . . .'

He's found a new marketing manager, she thought.

'I was wondering . . .' Long silence. 'Wondering how you'd feel about – well, changing your name?'

'Changing my name?'

'Yes.'

What was this? 'Why should I?' she managed. 'What's wrong with my name?'

'Oh dear. I was afraid you'd say that. Oh well, never mind. Go on, then, you have your shower. I'll make some more tea.'

'Bertie,' said Lara, 'I'm sorry but I don't know what you're talking about.'

'You don't? Well, I thought – you being so successful and high profile, you might not want to. I mean an awful lot of women don't these days. I—'

'Don't change their names? Bertie, you really have lost me – when don't they change their names?'

'When – well, when they – they get married.'

'Married!' Her hopes recovered themselves, lifted, soared. 'Bertie, are you asking me to marry you?'

741

'Yes. Yes, of course I am. I thought you'd realise—'

'Of course I didn't realise, you ridiculous, absurd, lovely, lovely man. How could I? Of course I'll change my name. To whatever you like. But ideally to Farrell. *And* I'll marry you – if that's what you want. But you've got to ask me properly, Bertie. Come on. Now!'

'All right.' He took a deep breath. 'Lara, I love you. Will you marry me? Please. Just as soon as I'm free? And change your name and yes, Farrell would be best.'

'Oh Bertie,' said Lara, laughing and crying at the same time, 'Bertie Farrell, I'll marry you, of course I will. I'd love to. Absolutely love to. Thank you!' She leaned over and kissed him. Several times. 'Now go and make some tea. And I really don't see why we can't stay here all evening.'

'You know what?' said Bertie. 'Neither do I!'

Timothy Benning had also been to a street party: or rather a village green one. He actually had quite a large part to play, being the Grand Old Man of the village. He had personally paid for the maypole that stood on the green and that the village children, dressed as Elizabethans, had all danced round, chaotically but happily, and when they had finished, they all processed over to Mr B as he was known, and each and every one of them handed him a flower.

'Because a bouquet is made up of single flowers,' the oldest of them explained, bobbing him a curtsey in what the local dancing teacher had informed them was Elizabethan style, 'and we wanted to make one up for you.'

They made up a rather disparate bouquet, ranging from roses to buttercups, but lovely nonetheless, and he smiled as he put them into two different vases. One large, one small, when he got home.

He then decided he should have a rest before the evening's entertainment, which was a concert in the village hall, and lay down on his bed – he was, after all, in his eighties now – with the *Telegraph* and opened it as he always did these days on the births, marriages and deaths column.

And there it was:

742

Farrell, Lady Athina, b. 1927, widow of Sir Cornelius Farrell d. 2006. Lady Farrell who continued to play a major part in the running of the cosmetic company she and her husband founded in 1953 died suddenly from a heart attack on Wednesday May 30th. She is survived by her two children Bertram and Caroline and two grandchildren. Private funeral June 8th, family and close friends only.

It was an odd announcement, and oddly cold; there was no reference to where she had died, or her being surrounded by her family.

He wondered, as he often had over the years, how Florence was. If indeed she was still alive: increasingly, old friends were shuffling off their mortal coils, and it was one of the worst things about old age, one was being left, part of a smaller and smaller band. He still missed her and the happy time they had had; she had been a most special person and he had never even considered sharing his life with anyone since. He had never tried to contact her, her rebuttal of him had been so final – but now suddenly he wondered if he was brave enough. She would be eighty, now; surely now she could not object to his writing to her, as an old friend, offering his sympathy at the loss of her oldest and closest friend? Presumably she wasn't still working; but he wondered if she was still living in that pretty little house of hers. Suddenly he wanted very much to know how she was, and what had become of her . . .

Well, there was no hurry; he would do nothing for a day or two, let the idea simmer. He had great faith in ideas simmering; he found it was an excellent way of making a decision.

The Baileys had stayed in London until the Sunday evening; they too had watched the River Pageant, and gone to a street party, of a sort: a rather grand one, in someone's garden, or rather in a large marquee, but Bianca and Patrick wanted to be in Oxfordshire for the Sunday, where there were to be more celebrations on their village green, and still more in the evening, high in the hills above the village for the lighting of the beacons. Bianca felt this would actually be the most special occasion of all: watching as the flames moved across the country, two thousand of them, from one peak to the next, lit one by one, to a strict timetable, starting at 10.30 p.m. in the Mall. Progress was swift, their local one timed for 11.16; they were advised to be up in the field by 10.

Bianca was deeply happy; the launch behind her, her decision to resign made (and discussed with Patrick), her heart filled with a slightly self-righteous satisfaction. Patrick had been a little startled when she said she was planning on retiring altogether.

'Darling, won't you be bored? Surely you want something to do, less demanding of course, but something?'

And, 'No Patrick,' she said, 'I'm just not like that. I'm an all or nothing person, you should know that by now. Either I work at something totally demanding, or I don't work at all. There's no middle way as far as I'm concerned.'

'Well, I'm not sure it's wise,' he said. 'It'll be lovely, of course, for me and the children, but aren't you a bit young to retire? You're not forty yet, and—'

'No, Patrick, I'm not. It's time I learned to live quite differently; I can't even cook properly, apart from omelettes and stews. I intend to become cordon bleu. And get the house done up. Do you know, I really enjoyed going round Peter Jones the other day, looking at fabrics, and then I'm going to take riding lessons and I'm going to read the entire works of Trollope, and – well, I want to look after you properly, Patrick, won't you like that . . . ?'

Patrick said hastily that he would, in case she changed her mind, and the conversation was cut short anyway by Milly saying that she'd just had a huge, long conversation with Jayce and that she was going to come for a sleepover next weekend in London, and Lucy was going to try some more new looks on them, and Jayce had lost another kilo, and wasn't that really, really good?

They agreed it was, just as they agreed that the celebrations in the village were exceedingly good; it was a much better day, clear and sunny, and the games organised for the children including welly throwing and a relay race round the green hugely well attended, as was the dog show, complete with a prize for the dog that looked most like its owner, and later in the day a cricket match.

'I do wish we could have a dog,' said Ruby longingly, looking at a vast Newfoundland, 'just like that one; isn't he lovely?'

'We can have a dog,' said Bianca, smiling at her, 'of course we can. Not like that one, but maybe a spaniel, or even a lab.'

They all looked at her in astonishment; a dog had always been out of the question, given the complexity of the family's life already.

'Did you say we could have a dog?' said Ruby.

'I did.'

'But you've always said we couldn't, that you and Dad were too busy,' said Fergie.

'Well, now I'm saying we could,' said Bianca.

'But how, why?' said Milly.

'We just can. I'll explain later. Come on, Patrick, they're coming out of the pavilion now, time you joined them. Got your bat?'

'He ought to have a new one,' said Ruby. 'That one's an antique, he had it when he was at school.'

'Well, we can give him one for his birthday, perhaps,' said Bianca.

'That won't help him today.'

Bianca, who knew, given Patrick's skills on the cricket field, no bat on earth could help him today or any day, said the best way of helping Daddy was to go and cheer him on. And so they did.

And the beacon lighting was wonderful: the muddy field was packed, the village band was playing alternately tunes from Rodgers and Hammerstein to 'Land of Hope and Glory' and 'Rule Britannia', there was a bar dispensing very warm beer and watery wine, and a few acrobats leaping rather inexpertly through flaming hoops.

'I bet I could do that,' said Fergie.

'You couldn't,' said Milly.

'I could.'

'Children,' said Patrick, 'let me say once and for all that if I find any of you trying to jump through flaming hoops, every electronic device we have, including your phones, will be confiscated for three months. I mean it.'

'I haven't even got a phone,' said Ruby, 'so I don't care. Mummy, please please please can I have a phone? It's not fair, I'm the only girl in my class who hasn't got one!'

'I slightly doubt that,' said Bianca, 'but I promise we'll think about it very hard for your next birthday.'

'I know what that means,' said Ruby, 'you'll think I can't have one yet.'

'Not necessarily . . .'

'Yes it does!'

'Shut up, Ruby,' said Fergie. 'We're getting a dog and that'll be cancelled if you go on like that!'

'Look,' said Patrick, 'they're getting nearer.'

And they were, the light leaping up from the adjacent hills, high into the darkness: the band switched again to 'Land of Hope and Glory' and then it was their turn, and the chosen person – 'Lucky, lucky him,' said Fergie wistfully – climbed up on to the platform, held the flaming torch aloft and there was a great roar as the beacon took light, the band played the National Anthem, everyone joined in, and Bianca burst into tears.

'Not here,' said Patrick, grinning at her, 'not in front of the children!'

'What do you mean?'

'Darling, I'm afraid you crying has very carnal associations for me.'

'Oh,' she said laughing and wiping her eyes, 'it's just all so lovely. You can give me a kiss, anyway.'

He bent to kiss her. 'OMG,' said Milly and 'Yuk!' said Fergie.

They got home after midnight; drank tomato soup and ate garlic bread; then Bianca said, 'I've got something to tell you. Well, *Daddy* and I have got something to tell you.'

The children looked at them.

'You're not getting divorced, are you?' said Milly anxiously. 'Half my class's parents are.'

'Didn't look like it, up in the field, did it?' said Fergie. 'Don't be a wally.'

'No, we're not getting a divorce,' said Bianca, 'but – well, I'm going to give up work, stay at home. Be a proper mother.'

There was a long silence: then, 'Oh, what?' said Fergie, his voice horrified.

'You can't!' said Milly.

'You really can't,' said Fergie.

'You really, *really* can't,' said Milly.

'Oh,' said Bianca uncertainly, 'I thought you'd be pleased!'

'Don't be horrid to Mummy,' said Ruby.

'Thanks, Ruby.'

'What would you do all day?' said Milly.

'Well – you know. Cook and—'

'You're a rubbish cook,' said Fergie.

'Fergie!' said Patrick.

'Well, sorry but she is. Her cheese sauce is all lumpy and—'

'Thanks,' said Bianca again.

'What else?' said Milly. 'What else would you do?'

'Well – I thought I'd do the house up. Or rather get it done up. It's looking very shabby.'

'That won't take long.'

Bianca looked nervously at Patrick.

'Say something kind to me,' she said.

'Won't it be lovely though, to have Mummy home when you get in from school?'

'Yes, well that would be nice – I think,' said Milly. 'Although all the people I know whose mothers don't work say it's awful, and they have to tell them everything they've done and what marks they got and all that stuff.'

'But Milly, that's exactly what I mean. I *should* be there asking you all that stuff. You might never have been bullied if I'd been at home.'

'It wouldn't have made any difference,' said Milly. 'I know I said it would, but I really don't think it would. I've thought about it a lot. Anyway, it's you I'm thinking of. You *love* your job. You love working.'

'Yeah,' said Fergie. 'You'd be miserable at home.'

'And bored,' said Milly.

'She might not,' said Ruby staunchly.

747

'You're too little to know,' said Fergie.

'I'm not!'

'You are.'

'And anyway,' said Milly, 'we're proud of you. What you do.'

'Yes,' said Fergie, 'we really are.'

Patrick, listening to his children giving voice to his own misgivings, wondered at their wisdom.

'It was better when Dad was working for his old firm,' said Fergie. 'I do think that.'

'Well, he can't go back there,' said Milly.

'He could. Uncle Ian told me the other week, when he and Aunt Babs came for lunch, he'd love to have Dad back, they all miss him, says they've never found anyone everyone likes.'

Patrick felt a sudden pang of nostalgia for the old days. Yes, they'd been boring quite a lot of the time, but it had been sociable. He considered the trade-off: on balance, he thought, working for Saul still definitely had the edge.

And then his phone rang; he looked at it. 'It's Saul,' he said to Bianca.

'Oh, what? What does he want, doesn't he know it's one in the morning? Forget I said that,' she said hastily.

Patrick went out of the kitchen and she shooed the children upstairs. She felt rather shaken by their reaction.

Patrick wasn't very long.

'What was it?'

'Well – well, he more or less just gave me the elbow.'

'He what? But why, how?'

'Well, Janey is definitely going to Australia. So he's going too.'

'He's going too? That poor woman, what she has to endure. But what about the business?'

'Well I'm exaggerating a bit. He's going to open an office in Sydney. And here's the thing, he'd want me to be available to him there as well as here. Whenever it was necessary. I don't know how he thinks I could do that. I mean, it's impossible. Totally impossible.'

'Maybe,' she said carefully, 'maybe it wouldn't be very often.'

748

'Bianca! Of course it would. You *know* what he's like. I'd be permanently on that plane. I can't sign up to that, I really can't.'

'Darling, I'm so sorry. So very sorry. But if I'm at home . . .'

'Bianca, I don't think you should be at home. That was never what I meant. I think the children are quite right, I'm afraid. I think you'd be miserable. And bored.'

'Oh,' she said, 'well clearly everyone values me really highly.'

'Darling, of course they do. But they value what you *are*, not what you think you can be.'

She was silent: contemplating the reality as she had not really before, caught up in her vision of herself cast as domestic goddess: of spending her days doing what she absolutely wasn't good at. It was true, she was a rubbish cook. And even the second trip to Peter Jones had been less enjoyable than the first. And she got very bored reading after a bit. And – well, there was still a lot of work to be done at Farrell's, building its new image, with no Athina ready at every turn with some booby trap or other, and it would be far less frantic, quite peaceful, really. She'd probably get home at quite a reasonable hour most days and . . .

'Well,' she said, 'it does seem fate is trying to tell us something. Along with our children. But I really don't want you to feel you've got to go back to BCB, Patrick. There must be lots of other jobs.'

'Oh no,' he said, 'I'm not grubbing around looking for jobs with other people. I couldn't, not after working for Saul. And I'm not going to work for some other firm of chartered accountants, am I? So—'

'Darling,' said Bianca, 'you're jumping the gun. It's not going to happen just like that, any of it. Let's sleep on it.'

But she couldn't sleep; she was too excited by all the other things she wanted to do at Farrell's, and hadn't allowed herself even to think about. Like what to do with the rest of the range, how and when to phase it out, what new products she could add to the *Passionate* range, meeting the undoubtedly increased orders for The Collection – and marvelling at Saul and how clever he was. How extremely, extremely clever.

* * *

Florence was sitting and listening to her favourite Mozart symphony, the much-lauded Fortieth, wondering how that dreadful thing that was going on at the Palace could possibly be called a concert, and thinking that if bank holidays were bad for single people, double ones were more than doubly so, when her phone rang. She almost didn't answer it, thinking, just for a second or so it would probably be Athina, complaining about something – and then remembered that it would never be Athina again. It was going to take a while for her to absorb that . . .

'Hello?' she said, finally picking it up and wondering who on earth it could be, and 'Florence?' a tentative voice came down the phone. A tentative male voice. A voice she had never thought to hear again.

'Timothy?' she said, after a long silence, thinking first that his voice had not changed at all, and second that it couldn't possibly be him, just someone with a very similar voice. A very, very similar voice.

And, 'Yes,' he said, sounding delighted, 'yes it's me. Do forgive me for telephoning you, I thought of writing, but then I thought a conversation would be better because I saw in the *Telegraph* that Lady Farrell had died, and I wanted to tell you how sorry I was. You must be very sad, a lifetime association over.'

'Indeed,' she said.

'Of course it's – what? – six years since her husband died. I thought of ringing you then, but in the end my courage failed me.'

'Your courage?'

'Well yes. I was afraid you wouldn't remember me, or worse, tell me to get lost.'

'Timothy, I shall always remember you,' said Florence, smiling. 'You gave me such a happy time. And I am far too well mannered to tell anyone to get lost.'

'Yes, of course you are. Well, how are you, my dear?'

'I'm well, thank you, Timothy. The last few days have taken their toll, I have to admit, but yes, very well. And you?'

'Oh, you know. Mustn't grumble.' That had always been one of his expressions, and he never did.

'Good. Well, it was a long time ago, wasn't it, Timothy? That we last met.'

'It was indeed, almost thirty years. You – you never married again?'

'No, no, I never did. You?'

'No, no. The opportunity never presented itself.'

There was a long silence; then Timothy Benning said, very tentatively, 'I don't suppose that we could – should – meet one day? In town, perhaps, or—'

'No,' said Florence and the word came out more sharply than she had intended. But her parting from him had been so painful and so final, and she had recovered from it so totally; and what would be the point of seeing him now? And having a conversation that was merely more of this one: awkward, stilted, peppered with awkward silences. And she remembered him so very fondly, and so vividly, that last weekend, walking with him on the Downs, both of them still so fit and strong, her arm in his, anything now would be a sorry echo of that, two old frail people, struggling to keep up with their memories. 'No, I don't think so, Timothy. But – but thank you so much for ringing. It was wonderful to hear from you. Goodbye.'

Timothy Benning said goodbye and rang off; he felt very sad. Had he been another generation, he might have wept. But men of his age didn't weep. They just got on with things. He had had an almighty struggle, calling up his courage to ring her, had picked up the receiver and put it down several times. And then, reminding himself that she was most unlikely to be there, took a deep breath and dialled her number. Hearing her voice had been the most extraordinary experience: utterly unchanged, still low, musical, and very level. And listening to it, the years had rolled away. It was a terrible cliché that, but it was exactly what they did: like watching a film go backwards and there she had been, smiling at him across his sitting room, raising her glass to him, so pretty and beautifully dressed.

Well, she was probably right: it would only spoil the memories if

751

they were to meet now. She always had been sensible. Far more so than him. He sighed and went over to the sideboard, poured himself a large whisky, and put on his favourite recording of his favourite of Mozart's symphonies, the Fortieth . . .

Florence put the phone down and felt very sad also. Of course it would never have worked, they would just fumble about, trying to relive the past and fail utterly. Far better to leave things as they were. She went into the kitchen and poured herself a large glass of red wine. It had been good to hear his voice. And to know that he still thought about her. Very good. And perhaps if they – no, Florence, don't even think about it, as Bertie and Bianca and indeed all the young people would say. You have your life and your work and – and suddenly then she thought of Athina, saw her disapproving face, heard her voice, dismissive and condescending, feeling her almost in the room: 'For heaven's sake, Florence, see this man if he wants you to, why on earth not? You won't have a job much longer, that's certain, don't think they'll keep you on without me, and there certainly won't be any more men either, so you might as well make the most of this one. Just don't expect too much, that's all I can say.'

And she sat for a moment, then stood up and walked across to the phone.

'You're right, Athina,' she said aloud, 'thank you.' And she picked it up and dialled Timothy's number, carved into her memory as it was.

'Hello?' he said.

And, 'Hello Timothy,' she said, 'it's Florence. Look, I'm sorry, I think I was a little hasty; it might be good to meet. What? Well, as soon as possible, I would suggest. *Carpe diem* and all that. Yes, Thursday would be lovely. Tea at the Savoy? Very nice. Four o'clock, yes. Now, there is just one thing, though. If we are to start seeing one another again, there are a few things I need to tell you. What? Well, about myself. Things that you probably would never have expected . . . but let's see how things work out on Thursday, shall we? Yes, I shall look forward to it very much too. Is – is that

Mozart's Fortieth I hear in the background? I thought so. I have it on too. What a coincidence. A good omen, perhaps.'

'A very good omen,' said Timothy Benning. 'Well, goodbye, my dear, for now. And I can hardly wait to hear these things you are going to tell me. It sounds rather exciting.'

'Oh, I don't know,' said Florence. 'Just a few – what shall we say? – chapters from my own life. Which sometimes, I must admit, actually seems quite a good story now . . .'

Delve deep and discover more **VINTAGE VINCENZI**
with the epic *Spoils of Time* trilogy:

NO ANGEL

In pre-war London, Lady Celia Lytton is the perfect
hostess, throwing glittering parties. But there are tragedies
her family will not escape: the Titanic, the First World War,
the flu epidemic. And beneath their perfect image, the
Lyttons cannot ignore the changing world around them.

'Satisfyingly compulsive' *Mail on Sunday*

ISBN: 978 0 7553 3240 3

SOMETHING DANGEROUS

As the beautiful and glamorous Lytton family escape the shadow of
the First World War and rebuild their publishing house, they
discover fresh dangers – not least those from Nazi Germany.
In London, Lady Celia faces the Blitz, while in New York,
the depression brings new troubles.

'Seductively readable' *The Times*

ISBN: 978 0 7553 3241 0

INTO TEMPTATION

Lady Celia Lytton has led the family for more than five decades,
through two wars, three generations, and countless scandals.
Under her guidance, the Lytton empire has become a publishing
powerhouse. Yet as she nears retirement, the family faces destruction.

'An addictive experience' Elizabeth Buchan

ISBN: 978 0 7553 3242 7

headline
review